D1234402

ORACLE

ORACLE

A *House War* Novel

MICHELLE WEST

DAW BOOKS, INC.

DONALD A. WOLLHEIM, FOUNDER

375 Hudson Street, New York, NY 10014

ELIZABETH R. WOLLHEIM
SHEILA E. GILBERT
PUBLISHERS

www.dawbooks.com

First Printing, May 2015
1   2   3   4   5   6   7   8   9

DAW TRADEMARK REGISTERED
U.S. PAT. AND TM. OFF. AND FOREIGN COUNTRIES
—MARCA REGISTRADA
HECHO EN U.S.A.

PRINTED IN THE U.S.A.

For John David Swain,

A bastion of my life, and a constant—and surprising—friend, no matter where in the world he is.

Acknowledgments

I once believed—as a new writer, and a newly published one—that writing was only hard because I was so inexperienced. Surely, I reasoned, once I gained that missing experience, I would know what I was doing, and things would become much, much easier, and much less stressful.

This has proved largely true when it comes to understanding the publishing process, although that's always a moving target.

It has not, sadly, become true of the writing. In part, this is because with the aforementioned experience comes more awareness, and in particular, more awareness of the mistakes and errors you didn't notice when you were writing earlier books.

This has been a fraught writing year. I have made more—and bigger—mistakes, and have done more extensive revisions than I have since I first started writing in the '90s.

Throughout, Sheila Gilbert has been a godsend.

An editor is the point at which the creative art meets the business—because publishing *is* a business—and she balances between the demands of each side of her desk: the creative endeavor and the publishing. In the ideal world, there's no conflict between these.

This has not been the ideal year.

I want to make clear that delays in publication of my books have been entirely my fault; they are due to my rewrites, my revisions, my delays. Sheila (and Joshua Starr) have done everything they can to get the books to readers *when they have the books in hand*.

But Sheila has let me rewrite and rewrite and rewrite to make those books *work*.

Terry Pearson, alpha reader extraordinaire, has been subject to rather more whining and uncertainty this year than in any other year since he started alpha reading. His is kind of a thankless job—except it isn't really a job, because I don't pay him. He is forced to endure pretty raw first draft (and often a chapter at a time, or less), and he brings a reader's eye to the books; he has read every one of my West novels more often than I have.

I'm particularly grateful because he's constantly being asked to look behind the curtains, but can still believe—while reading—in the Great and Powerful Oz. So to speak.

Prologue

SILVER, GOLD, DIAMOND.

Three trees, in a silent dawn forest.

Shadows cut falling light; the movement of branches in brisk, morning breeze softened the edges of their darkness on the ground. Nothing softened the edges of the woman who stepped across them. Only the chime of metallic leaves broke the silence.

"I saw it *firssssssst.*" That, and the voice of bored cats. In this particular case, it was Night, but Snow's hissing growl of a rejoinder was almost instantaneous.

"It's not *my* fault you are *so slow.*"

There were no servants in the forest; there was no furniture, no carpets that would be instantly rent when the claws came out; there were no statues, no standing vases, no carefully displayed suits of centuries-old armor. Jewel therefore let them fight. Their squabbling was almost a comfort, she heard it so often.

It was one of the few things she would take with her when she left. She looked up; the manse in the distance could not be seen beyond the trunks of the many, many trees. She had said her good-byes. Her den, in kind, had said theirs. It had been beyond awkward; only Jester had dared to whisper, "Find him. Find him. Bring him home."

She had been surprised; had pulled back from a very, very rare hug to catch his expression. What she saw in it burned; she looked away—but not before Jester did. Jester of the many masks. Jester, master of hiding in plain sight.

She had no answer. He expected none. Jewel did not make promises she couldn't keep. She made wishes—they all did that. But she didn't know where she was going; didn't know what was expected of her when she arrived there, if she ever did. She knew that Carver was no part of the Oracle's test.

No. That wasn't true.

She prayed that he was no part of that test.

If she could not take her den with her—and for the sake of the House, she could take only one, and even so she was willing to do so because he would not be left behind—she sought to carry things that would remind her of home, and so, she had come to the forest that stood on the edge of the hidden and wild world. Here, silver, gold, and diamond grew as if each were a living thing. The trees themselves shed no leaves.

She gathered the leaves of the *Ellariannatte* first, because they did fall. They were the bridge between her life in the hundred holdings and her life as The Terafin. Even her Oma had approved of the ancient trees that girded the Common, and Jewel had gathered those leaves, as if they were flowers, to lay in the old woman's lap.

She took three; each perfect, each larger than her hand, each edged in ivory.

She rose slowly and made her way to the trees of silver; she was not surprised when a low branch descended until she could comfortably touch it. Three leaves fell into her hands before that branch rose; they were far heavier than they looked. And smooth. And cold.

Gold was no different, except in weight. The tree offered her three leaves, and she took them, and she found them as heavy, as cold to the touch, although the color was warmer to the eye.

Diamond was different. Harder and sharper, it seemed untouched by something as trivial as morning cold. It was not untouched by sunlight, and when she lifted one leaf to catch the rays of a spoke of light, she winced at the brilliance it produced.

Shadow hissed.

"I told you not to stand behind me," she said, without much sympathy. She lowered the leaf and set it beside the others in a large leather pouch that hung at her waist. That pouch had been a gift from Haval in her early years, and it showed its age.

"We're *bored*. Are we leaving *yet?*"

"Soon," Jewel replied.

"That's what you said *hours* ago."

"It was less than fifteen minutes ago, Shadow."

Cats—at least these ones—weren't particularly fussy about the accuracy of their grievances. Jewel left the great gray one to mutter as she approached what she thought of as the heart of her forest: the tree of fire. It burned, of course. Since it had grown, its flames had never guttered. It was, in all ways, an impossible creation: a tree that was not consumed by the flames it generated. Warmth emanated from fire, as it did in the world Jewel thought of as real. She stood beneath its boughs, lifting her face as heat banished the morning chill.

And when this tree lowered a branch, she raised a hand far more hesitantly. She had not intended to take its leaves; she had some experience with fire and its aftermath. Instinct argued with experience, and because Jewel was seerborn, instinct won. She accepted the leaves that fell into her upturned palm.

They were warm. The fire that lapped at their edges burned nothing, and as Jewel watched, the flames died; the leaves they had fringed—just as ivory fringed the green of the *Ellariannatte*—were a deep, bright red. The color of new blood.

The cats were not fond of this tree, and only Shadow approached it. "Are you *finished?*" he asked, still aggrieved.

She exhaled.

"Adam is *waiting.*"

"Yes. Yes, I'm finished." She slid these leaves into her pouch, praying that they did not consume anything else she carried within it.

Jewel had never been a gardener. She couldn't name any tree but the *Ellariannatte*. It was ironic, then, that these were the contents of her satchel: three leaves from each of her trees. And a lone leaf, something that looked like it should have grown on a tree of iron—and felt it, too. One vial of fountain water. One dagger, as old as the satchel itself, and just as significant. One small, unadorned wooden box.

In that box lay the hope of a race.

And in that box, beside the lone surviving sapling upon which Summer in the ancient, wild world depended, was a large, fragile book which contained the hope of Jewel's den.

"Yes," she said again, when Shadow nudged her with the top of his head. "Let's go meet Adam."

The Terafin was unapologetically dressed for the road, not the court. So, too, her companions. Angel and Adam wore Terafin colors—shades of blue, light and dark—in layers; the jackets favored by the patriciate were absent; the heavier coats and sweaters favored by laborers were not. The boots, as well, had been made to endure mud and snow, even if Averalaan saw snow seldom. They shouldered packs, Adam's lighter than Angel's by necessity; Adam was slender and slight of build.

Terrick carried twice the weight Adam did. He had come in his own clothing, and seemed prepared for Rendish winter. He also wore an ax that the Kings' Swords were only *barely* willing to let him keep.

Kallandras' weapons were daggers—but as a Master Bard of Senniel College, he was considered almost above suspicion. Had the bard carried the ax, there would have been less difficulty.

Avandar was recognized as The Terafin's domicis. He carried no weapons; he shouldered a pack that was equal in weight and bulk to Terrick's. His silence, while cold, was almost deferential, and the Swords were accustomed to making no obvious public note of servants.

Inspections were cursory. The Kings' Swords, while tense, had clearly been given specific instructions. Jewel was surprised—and pleased—to see the way they reacted to her great, winged cats: they acknowledged them as members of the Terafin party. That meant any destructive or unfortunate behavior would be laid at the feet of Terafin, of course. The cats knew it. Jewel knew it. They managed to behave.

They didn't manage to do it silently, but if there were to be miracles today, Jewel didn't want to waste them on the cats.

Only when inspections were complete did the Seneschal appear to guide them to their destination. The halls that the Seneschal led them through were less familiar—and far less grand—than the halls to which Jewel had become accustomed in her tenure in Terafin, but this was not, in the end, a public, a *political* meeting.

Even the pages, so ubiquitous in the palace, were notable by their absence. Were it not for the cats, the procession would have been funereal in its silence, but as it approached the stairs that led into the basement, Jewel saw two men, surrounded by the Exalted.

As she approached them, she stumbled. Avandar caught her before the stumble became anything as awkward as a fall. The slight smile King Cormalyn offered made it clear that he understood what had caused it: he—and King Reymalyn—were not dressed as monarchs. They were, of course, well dressed—but no more so than the average successful merchant of Jewel's acquaintance.

But their eyes were golden. "You yourself are not attired for royalty," the

King said. He offered her his arm, and she almost stumbled again—but that would have been too much embarrassment, even for Jewel. She took the arm, and only realized after how very awkward it would be to offer the Exalted the full obeisance she normally offered them.

She wondered if that was the reason the arm had been extended, and performed the half-bow that her current position allowed with as much grace as she could muster.

The stairs were now well-lit; magestones adorned brass holders meant, at one point, for more economical torches. The arch that led to the basement rooms was likewise well-lit; it looked far more majestic—and forbidding—when seen so clearly. At the base of those stairs was another surprise: Sigurne Mellifas. Sigurne offered Jewel the bow that Jewel had been unable to fully offer the Exalted, which furthered her discomfort.

"So," the mage said as she rose. "You are here."

Jewel nodded. Her mouth was unexpectedly dry; the informality of the meeting somehow made it seem more—and not less—profound. It was a gesture of trust, an exposure of—of humanity. The Kings had never seemed so normal, so human, before. They were an office. They were a law.

And so, she thought, was she. Yet she was here, and the House over which she had claimed rulership was not. She had stripped herself of almost all of the things that defined her as Terafin.

She struggled to find words to express herself, and failed.

"Will you enter, Terafin?" Sigurne said. If the Kings had chosen informality, the mage had not; she wore lined robes, and the medallion of the guildmaster was on full display. She stood between two arches, neither of which contained a door.

"There are two rooms," Jewel said softly.

"Yes. You have seen only one. Did you wish to see the other?"

"Should I?"

"I cannot answer that. You are seer-born." At Jewel's slight wince, she added, "I have seen the room. It is not architecturally as impressive as the one you have already visited."

"Does it also contain statues?"

"No. Your statuary looks, to the untrained eye, like the work of an Artisan at the peak of his powers. Sadly," she continued, although her lips creased in a wry smile, "it also looks that way to the trained eye. Master Gilafas was slightly put out when we could not answer his many, *many* questions."

"Did he examine the other room?"

"He did."

"What did he say of it?"

"Almost nothing, Terafin. We are not certain if the unanswered questions posed in the first room displaced Guildmaster Gilafas' careful consideration of the second; the opinions of the Exalted and the Kings vary."

"Your opinion?"

"The room is not, in any way the magi could discern, magical in nature. It is, however, obviously magical in nature, given its interior dimensions and the exterior dimensions of the room which houses it," she added. "It appears to be a seamless, round room, but there are one or two deviations from that description within the interior." She hesitated again.

The Mother's Daughter was watching in a neutral silence. "Terafin?"

"Yes," she finally said, wondering, as she did, if her desire to remain in the city that had been her home for all of her life was now guiding her decision; she could delay her departure by a few minutes. "If the Stone Deepings disgorged the statuary, and the statuary is significant, the other room must be significant as well."

To her left, facing the arch, was the statuary.

To her right, the unknown. But no, she thought, as she exhaled and forced her shoulders to rest as far down her back as they could, it was *all* unknown. Here, even the familiar was a lie.

If she had intended to inspect this unseen room on her own, her companions quickly disabused her of the notion. Lord Celleriant's glance was cool and autocratic; he offered the Exalted and the Kings no respect as he moved past The Terafin toward the arch that led away from the statuary. He offered no obvious disrespect, and that was probably the most she could hope for.

Kallandras offered the Exalted a very fluid bow, and rose. His grin, as he met Celleriant's rather cool glance, was both wry and amused. He intended to enter the cavern at the side of the Arianni Lord.

Avandar, content to walk behind the august body of rulers, now closed the gap; Shadow hissed. But Angel joined Jewel as well, his fingers dancing in brief, curt sign.

She nodded, and he said something to Terrick in a language that was only vaguely familiar to her; Rendish, unlike Torra, was not a common street tongue.

To Jewel's surprise, the cats were silent. Silent, still, devoid of the usual near-violence that accompanied their territorial squabbles. They looked at the arch, and the shadows that lay beyond it, as if they were momentarily sharing one mind.

Then, more disturbing, they turned that same stare on her. Waiting. Judging.

Celleriant said, "I prefer them this way," as if she'd given voice to the sharp, sudden discomfort they caused.

"Why?" She walked toward the arch.

"It is when they forget themselves, Lady—when they forget you—that they stand revealed."

"As what? Predators? Threats?"

"Both."

She grimaced. "They're *cats*, Celleriant."

"No, Lady, they are not."

Shadow hissed.

She glanced down at him. "I won't order you to accompany me," she told him. "But I swear to all gods living and dead that you will suffer if you cause any injuries while I'm in the room."

He glanced pointedly at Night and Snow.

"They count. I mean it."

Snow sniffed and turned his head to look at anything else.

Night, however, said, "*How* will we suffer?"

"I'm not sure yet," she replied, without pause for anything but breath. "I'll need time to come up with something appropriate."

He hissed.

"I could plant you," she offered.

His eyes rounded and his ears flattened. Celleriant—damn it—drew sword, and the resultant blue light scattered across the flat, smooth surface of stone in its various shapes as if it were water.

"Celleriant," she said, her voice far colder than it had been when she had admonished the cats. "They are never going to try to kill *me*."

His silver eyes narrowed. "Will they not?"

"No." They had already tried once, and Celleriant knew it; the Kings and the Exalted did not.

Arianni lips thinned into a shape that resembled a smile. "A pity."

"They're not *Kialli*."

"No, Terafin, they are not—but you have seen them kill my kin."

And she had.

"They are a challenge. They are a test. They ride the storms with an ease only the adepts can achieve."

"They have wings," she pointed out.

"Wings are not required." He did not sheathe his sword. "Viandaran."

Avandar nodded and preceded Jewel through the arch. Celleriant followed as Angel came to stand by her side. "You don't trust the room," he said quietly.

She really didn't. She had walked once through the arch opposite this one, but on that day, she'd been terrified of the Kings, the Exalted, and the Lord of the Compact; the contents of the room—right up until a statue began to move—had been of lesser concern.

The Kings did not wait in this one. As she stepped beneath the arch, the shadows deepened; her eyes did not adjust quickly to the lack of the harsher magelights that now adorned the outer halls.

Avandar.

Light flared in the darkness directly ahead of her as Avandar responded to her request. A spark of pale gold appeared in his cupped palms, lending an orange-red glow to his hands. He whispered a word and it rose, gaining brightness as it did. The floor beneath his feet—beneath all of their feet—took on visible texture.

Jewel stiffened. Beneath her feet, the floor was stone—but it was not the impressive, worked stone of the palace. It was worn and rough, as if rivers had carved their way, slowly, through dense earth, long before she chose to tread here. It reminded her of the narrow pathways carved through the Stone Deepings.

"Yes," Avandar said, although she hadn't spoken. "They quarried the Deepings, when they built these foundations."

"The palace isn't old enough—" She caught the words and held them. She felt his smile as she approached his back. "The undercity."

"Yes, Jewel. Except in your dreams, I have never seen the ruins of that ancient place—but I know what it looked like at the height of its power."

"It didn't look like this."

"No." He let his arms fall to his sides; the light continued to shine, as if it were a trapped star.

"I don't understand the purpose of this room."

"No. No more do I, or the god-born. Do you understand the purpose of the room you call a statuary?"

She started to say yes, and paused. "I understand the purpose it serves for *me*."

"Yes. But it is not in the Terafin manse; it is housed in its entirety within *Avantari*."

"It's not."

He smiled, and this time, turned to face her. "No, Terafin, it is not. It touches wild and hidden places; it does not travel *to* them, but it is of them. As is this."

"It looks exactly like the Stone Deepings in the mountains."

He glanced, briefly, around the shadowed cavern of a room. "It does not," was his soft reply. "Not to me. But you are seer-born. Lord Celleriant?"

Celleriant's blade shed as much light as Avandar's spell, although it was a colder, harsher illumination. He said nothing.

Jewel turned to Angel. She gestured in the dim light. *What do you see?* The question had once been meant for those rare situations in which Duster or Carver played point while the others remained hidden, but Angel understood what she asked.

"I see a room," he told her. "The ceilings are as tall as the Terafin foyer. The floors are smooth, slab stone—not marble—and they look well traveled." He hesitated. Gestured. *You?*

"I see a cavern. The only light in the room is the one Avandar cast. I can't see the cavern's height; it's too far up. I can't see the walls, either. The floor is rough, rough stone; a groove runs down the middle, like a rock riverbed, and we're in it. I don't see anything up ahead besides shadows and rock formation."

"That's . . . not what I see."

"Celleriant?" she asked the same question that Avandar had asked, and in the same way. The Arianni Lord glanced down at her, as if from a great remove. "I do not see what you see," he finally said. "Nor do I see what your liege does."

She frowned. "When you rode with the Wild Hunt through the Deepings, did they not look like this to you?"

"No. But these were not the roads we traveled, Lady."

"Would you recognize every road you traveled?"

His brows rose. After a long pause, he said, "Yes."

"What do you see?"

He did not answer. Her hands curled into fists.

Do not ask again, Jewel, Avandar told her. *This room is wilder—and therefore more dangerous—than the room you call the statuary. We define, in some ways, what we see.*

She had been walking, and stopped, lifting a hand in swift den-sign to make certain Angel did the same. "It's not safe to walk here."

"Can you not hold the road?" Celleriant asked her softly.

"Hold it how? We don't even see the same thing."

"We did not see the same thing when we first met."

It was true. But she felt the hair on the back of her neck begin to stand on end, and in the darkness, she heard the slow, heavy sound of breathing. "Angel, can you hear that?"

He was silent. She turned to look at his hands; they were still.

"What do you hear?" Celleriant asked, his voice sharper and colder.

"Breathing," she whispered. "Very loud, very deep breathing."

Celleriant turned to Kallandras, who had fallen silent. Bards were, in general, far more talkative than Kallandras, a fact Jewel seldom noticed. She noted it now. He watched her for a long moment. "I cannot hear what you hear."

He was bard-born. The bard-born heard everything that lay beneath the surface of words, if they were skilled enough. And powerful.

Celleriant exhaled. "Viandaran."

"I do not hear what she hears," Avandar replied. "But she hears it. It is not mortal fear of the darkness or the unknown."

"Do you recognize it?" Celleriant asked, acknowledging the bond that Jewel herself did not, on most days.

"I am mortal," was Avandar's evasive reply. "Time is a current that wears the edges off memory."

"You have your suspicions."

"I have some."

Avandar.

Silence. Silence interrupted by breath, by breathing that she felt beneath her feet as the rumbling of earth.

"Matriarch," a soft voice said. She turned so quickly she would have tripped had she been wearing skirts.

Adam was standing beside Terrick; the Northerner carried his ax. He was grim and silent, but his presence suited this vast, stone space.

Jewel swallowed words as she struggled for composure. If there was any person in the palace she did not want in this room, it was Adam—but she was taking him someplace no safer, no better known, in the end. After a significant pause, she said, "Yes," in Torra.

"I see a cave."

This caught Celleriant's attention. Avandar, more accustomed to the random outbursts of the merely mortal controlled any outward expression of the surprise Jewel nonetheless knew he felt.

"And I hear breathing. It is loud and rolling, like distant thunder."

"You see what I see."

"I think so, yes." His voice was very grave. He knelt and placed one palm above the ground, then hesitated, watching her.

She shook her head, deciding. "Not yet," she told him softly. "We have to confront what we see at some point, but not yet."

"Soon?" he asked, withdrawing his hand.

"Soon. Come. You haven't seen the statuary yet." As Jewel turned to leave the room, the almost hypnotic breathing shifted; the rumbling became, for a moment, a voice. Syllables cut the silence like lightning, absent illumination. Jewel froze. Her own breath stopped; she held it, waiting for the foreign words to pass.

All eyes were upon her. What she had heard, her companions had not. All save Adam, whose eyes widened, and whose breath momentarily ceased as well. She realized then that something slept in this chamber, something vast, immortal, ancient. Her steps, her presence, were an intrusion, and if she did not leave, that unknown creature would wake.

She did not expect that waking to be gentle or joyful; she certainly wouldn't be if mice crept into her bedroom and skittered across the surface of her counterpane. She felt very like she suspected the mice would, if they could speak. Without another word, she turned and headed toward the open arch.

Unlike the arch that led from her personal chambers in the Terafin manse, this one seemed to stay put.

The Kings were waiting in the statuary, as were the Exalted. Sigurne Mellifas stood to one side of the Mother's Daughter. The *Astari*, if they were present at all, were dressed as Swords, and the Lord of the Compact failed to appear. It was the one bright spot in an otherwise grim and early morning.

The cats were pacing back and forth in the stretch of hall that contained the arches, but their ears twitched the moment Jewel stepped across the threshold that divided cavern from architectural stone. Shadow immediately shouldered Avandar out of the way; Snow cast a speculative glance at Celleriant.

"The Kings are waiting," Jewel told him.

He sniffed. Night hissed. But they fell in behind Shadow and did not, as far as Jewel could see—or hear, really—attempt to step on his tail. Angel and Terrick, Adam between them, brought up the rear. Angel was not in a particular hurry to see more of the Kings, but Terrick did not appear to find their presence discomforting. He was not, on the other hand, required to speak.

Had he been in House colors, he might have been one of the Chosen; he had the same peculiar ability to be aware of every element of his surroundings while simultaneously appearing to notice none of them.

The statues appeared as they had the first time Jewel had seen them.

This time, she thought she understood what they signified, and turned to the Mother's Daughter, whose slight nod implied that she had expected some questions.

"I recognize at least five of the figures carved here," she said softly.

"We noticed," the Exalted replied.

"I met them in the South, in the Stone Deepings. I don't know all of their history. This," she said, approaching the first, a figure only partially emerged from the wall, "is Calliastra." She glanced at the Mother's Daughter, and was not surprised when the older woman nodded.

"The child of the god we do not name and the god we have oft called Love."

Jewel continued to walk. The rest of her party, except for the cats, remained just beside the Kings; only her domicis shadowed her steps. "This," she said, "Is Corallonne."

"She is the Mother's Daughter."

"And her father?"

"I have never been bold enough to ask," was the wry reply. "The information was never offered me. But Corallonne is sister to all who bear the Mother's blood. You did not fear to touch her likeness, here."

"No," was the soft reply. Jewel did not, however, touch her again.

She walked instead to Ariane. Of the statues here, only Ariane's was not trapped in the wall; she stood—as the statues of the gods in the palace proper—as if the red-brown stone beneath her feet was a pedestal. Jewel swallowed, reached up, and touched the hand of the Queen of the Wild Hunt.

Beneath her fingers, the stone was cool and hard. It did not respond at all.

"Winter Queen," she whispered.

Wind swept into the room, curling around strands of her hair. But the statue itself was silent and still.

"She will not hear you," Celleriant said softly.

She moved on, pausing once to examine the only figure contained in this room that did not take mortal likeness. Frowning, she glanced at Avandar. "The last time we were here, this figure was different."

"Yes."

"Now it looks almost human." And it did. The feathers, the scales, the uneven mismatch of limbs, had receded. Its face no longer looked like a carving of quilted flesh, each piece belonging to a different species. It looked almost like a man.

"You are certain?" the Mother's Daughter asked.

Jewel nodded slowly. "I am."

"And troubled."

"Yes, Exalted." She hesitated for a long moment, and then glanced at Shadow. Shadow was staring at the statue in challenge; the statue, being stone, failed to respond. "Do you know its name?"

"No, child. In any real sense, it has none."

"Do you know its parentage?"

"No. But I know this: it claims no single parent, no duality; all of the gods were some part of its creation. It is not like Moorelas' sword, but it is not like the others depicted here."

Jewel nodded and continued past the figure. She glanced once at the Warden of Dreams; he was almost as discrete as Ariane in appearance. And then, because it could not be put off any longer, she approached the cloaked and hooded figure of the Oracle. Like all of the statues except Ariane, she was part of the wide, curved sweep of wall; like all of those statues, she was chiseled and polished and presented as a gray-white likeness of life.

She was, however, the only statue that moved, and when Jewel whispered "Oracle," her hooded head turned. Her robes rustled—a grinding sound at odds with the visual ripple of cloth—as she stepped forward and out of the relief.

"Jewel." She lifted her hands and cupped them in front of her chest, as Jewel's throat tightened. But no crystal came to grace those palms; the Oracle did not offer a glimpse of the uncertain future.

"Yes," Jewel replied, finding her voice. "We've come."

"You will find the roads much changed," the Oracle replied. Jewel frowned. The statue spoke not to her, but to Celleriant.

"No doubt," was his cool reply. "But more to my liking than mortal streets."

"You serve Jewel Markess ATerafin."

"I do."

"An odd choice of master, for one such as you."

He stiffened, but did not reply; the Oracle's lips turned up in a cold, hard smile—a smile whose texture had nothing to do with the stone of her lips. She turned her attention to the three cats. "And you, are you here at her behest?"

Snow hissed.

"You understand the rules of entry, and your master is mortal; she does not have the time to waste in the games you might otherwise play. Do you serve her?"

The cats exchanged a glance and a few growls. They did not speak.

The Oracle, however, nodded and lifted her head to meet Jewel's gaze. "You do not understand what they are, or how they came to be here."

"Can you tell me?" Jewel asked. Night hissed. Shadow nudged her with the top of his head, and she reached down to place a hand on the back of his neck.

"No. It is one of the things you will either learn to see or never understand. When dealing with the ancient and the wild, Terafin, it is never wise to offer information they themselves guard and hide. Do so only if you are certain you will survive it."

"They can't kill you."

"Can they not?" The smile the Oracle offered as she spoke was markedly different. "Perhaps you are correct. But they can try, and if they are not to be feared, they are oft to be dreaded. They have never been entirely predictable creatures. Not even the wise could have predicted the results of the Winter King's careful planning; what he wrought, we do not fully understand."

Shadow's eyes were golden; they were almost the same hue as the eyes of the god-born. Almost, but not quite. "Tell her," he said to Jewel, voice almost a growl, "that we serve you when we're *with* you."

Jewel, however, frowned. "The Winter King considered the cats his greatest work. Did he not create them?"

Snow howled in outrage. Night was too dumbfounded to find his voice. Shadow, however, hissed.

"They are your responsibility, Terafin. I do not think it would be wise to leave them here. They are not, in my opinion, in danger where you will walk—but you have seen the danger they can be, if I am not mistaken."

Adam stiffened. Jewel lifted a hand in den-sign, and he held his peace. Adam, more than anyone present, understood the danger the cats represented; Shadow had almost killed her at the behest of the Warden of Dreams. Had it not been for Adam's presence, she would have died.

She knew it. She knew that the cats were deadly; she had always understood that. But Duster had been deadly as well, and Duster had been part of her home. "I don't want to leave them behind," she said quietly.

"I judge their presence a risk. You do not know the ways in which that risk might present itself—but such ignorance, even to one seer-born—is part of life. Only the dead are predictable—and even then, they are oft misunderstood.

"Do not seek this path if you seek certainty. A glimpse of the future—even a future of your choosing—will not quell doubt. Doubt exists where there is life and breath to draw it. Only the dead have no doubts."

"I'm not so sure about that," Jewel replied, thinking—for the first time in months—of the Terafin spirit.

"No, daughter, but I am. I will accept the presence of your cats if you will surrender to me some token as surety of their behavior."

"Pardon?"

Terrick now cleared his throat. "Pretend that this is, for the moment, the Merchant Authority. You have asked for leave to route your caravans through passages that are not Imperial in origin. The men who own those passages do not know you; they do not trust you.

"You post a bond as a financial guarantee of your intent. If the merchants in your caravan contravene the accepted codes of behavior in the lands they traverse, the bond is forfeit. If I am not mistaken, this woman is asking you to post such a bond."

Jewel nodded slowly and turned to look down at the cats. They met her gaze with the faux-innocence she found so exasperating—and, in the end, so endearing. "This," she said—for the benefit of an entirely absent Teller, "is why I never wanted cats." Pushing her hair out of her eyes, she exhaled. "Avandar, can you get the gem bag from my pack?"

Avandar nodded, but before he could carry out her request, the Oracle lifted a hand. "If the analogy Terrick has offered is apt, it is inexact."

The Northerner stiffened slightly; in no other way did he betray the surprise his name on the Oracle's tongue had caused.

"There is no monetary component to what you must now do; no exchange of gold awaits you at the end of your journey. If you benefit, it will not be in a way that mortals will easily understand—and if they did, Terafin, you might become the object of sympathy—or its darker cousin, pity.

"I therefore ask that you leave, as surety, an item of value to you. The item might be priceless among your kind; it might be worthless among your kind."

"Everything I value with which I might part, I left at home," Jewel replied. "All of the things I now carry with me, I carry because they might be of practical use." She glanced at her wrist, where three strands of winter hair were twined in a near-invisible bracelet. "If I'm to have any hope of returning to a home that still stands, I can't leave them with you. I brought gems as trade if the road leads us back to mortal lands. We've brought food of the type that is meant for long, sustained travels.

"I have my companions, and I will not leave them behind; nor would I willingly leave them in your lands while I ventured into the wilderness. Even if I was willing to do so, they are not my possessions. I don't own them, and I cannot simply give them away as a gesture of good faith." If the Oracle had been willing to take the gems, Jewel would have left a greater part of their number in her hands; she'd made clear she was not.

What else did she now carry?

She could not part with Ariane's gift. She considered the leaves she had taken from her forest, and even opened her pouch to remove them—but her hand froze before she'd unbuckled it. Not those, then. What else of value did she have? She had the dress Snow made. She had worn it once, and she was not in a hurry to don it again. The problem with the dress—aside from its obvious importance to Snow—was that she did not truly value it.

She wore one necklace. The links, as she drew it up from the confines of her traveling clothes, were warm where they'd lain so long against skin. It was the necklace Snow had given her to wear with the dress he had made. The pendant, in this room, seemed to pulse like an exposed heart; it was not a comforting sight.

"No," the Oracle said, before she had pulled the pendant clear. "Not that. I will not question your effrontery in wearing it, and I will not refuse you passage in spite of its presence—but the danger is now entirely yours to bear. Cats will leave all manner of things in their wake, but in general, the wise do not wear them." As she spoke, she glanced at Snow, who appeared to have lost a few inches of height.

He muttered.

"You are bold," she told him. "But it is left to others to bear the weight of your momentary whims." She fell silent as Snow continued to lose height and bearing.

Jewel glanced, last, at her empty palms. In the oddly muted light of the statuary, the gold of the two rings she wore made her hands look unaccountably white and colorless, as if they had never seen sunlight.

Rings. Two rings.

She turned her hands over, although examination wasn't necessary. The ring on her right had been a gift from Amarais, an inheritance of a kind that could not be laid out in wills and signed testaments. Left in the center of the fount that was the justified pride of the Terafin terrace, it would have remained hidden in perpetuity to any eyes that weren't Jewel's.

Jewel had never completely understood why Amarais had chosen to hide one ring and one sword—a fine sword, but of the kind that the patriciate commonly owned—in the center of that fountain; to do so had required all of the magical skill and subtlety Morretz had accumulated over his life.

But she understood why Amarais had left the two items to her. They had belonged to Ararath. They had belonged to Rath. So proud, so angry, he had, in the end, loved them both as he could. And they had loved—and lost him. The ring itself was a signet ring of heavy gold; a stylized H contained rubies at the end points of the Weston letter's height. One was cracked—it had arrived that way.

Rath was dead. The dead had no need of rings. They had no need of memories, either. Only the living did—but Jewel was still alive. Her right hand closed in a fist as she looked, last, to the ring that adorned her left.

It was the Terafin House ring. Not the ring she had worn for most of her adult life as a Council member, but the House ring itself. There was one, only one, of its kind. She had worn its weight for a scant few months. No, she thought, counting, two months and nineteen days. It was not her possession; it was, in its entirety, the smallest symbol of the office she'd taken. When she died, it would be passed to the woman—or man—who succeeded her.

But she knew, as she studied its heavy gold face, sapphires glowing as if displayed in direct sunlight, that this was what the Oracle was waiting for. She had not removed the ring once since she had been acclaimed Terafin. Her hands shook as she removed it now.

No one spoke. Angel briefly touched her arm and gestured. She wanted to shove the ring back onto her finger. She told herself that she could afford to lose Rath's ring; she couldn't afford to lose the House signet. She could give away the damn leaves—she had an endless number of them. Even the dress, although she'd have a put-out or enraged white cat to deal with for the rest of their journey. Or the rest of her life.

But the ring rested in her open palm, and her hand was steady as she held it out to the Oracle.

The Oracle nodded. She passed a hand over Jewel's upturned palm—and the ring it contained—and the ring vanished. She had not touched it. "Yes," she said softly. "It is always difficult to decide what to leave behind, and often, there are no good choices. I will safeguard your ring to the full extent of my ability to do so. Only if you transgress will it be lost to you forever."

"What are your rules?" Jewel asked stiffly. "By what laws am I to be bound?"

Shadow snorted in obvious disgust.

Night said, "What did you *expect?* She's *stupid.*"

Even Celleriant was smiling. It was a condescending, arrogant smile.

The Oracle, however, did not appear to notice any of this. "It has been many, many years since a daughter of the ancient cities has approached my realm. Not all who reach its heart choose to accept the challenge offered. But if it will comfort you, know this: none of the supplicants had the luxury of time. Many came alone.

"Isolation is safety, of a kind—but it is not, in the end, your safety." She turned. The wall, curved and smooth in her absence, waited. She did not point or gesture; she did not speak. Instead, she placed her hands against her chest; Jewel stiffened as they sank beneath the surface of stone robes and stone flesh.

The air was still, the hush expectant; no one in the room, not even the distant Kings, appeared to breathe as the Oracle withdrew a crystal from the center of her chest. The resultant light from its heart flooded the room, washing out the color that remained.

"The more you see, the more there is to fear—but regardless, the future will come. It will shape you, Jewel, if you allow it. But if you are strong enough to pierce the veils of now, you will be allowed, in some small way, to shape it in turn. It is the only gift I offer, and acceptance is costly: it was not meant for mortals."

"Why," Jewel asked, breaking the hushed silence, "was it given to us at all?"

"That, I cannot answer."

"Because you don't know?"

"Because, daughter, I do not know."

"You're reputed to see everything."

"And so I might, should I so choose—but what is seen is oft misunderstood, as you yourself must know. What is seen at a distance is a glance, no more. Such a glimpse might inspire dread or greed or rage. I see you here, before me, as I saw you when first we met. I understand, in some limited way, what motivates you. But I cannot see the whole of it. I cannot *be* you.

"And there are things about you, Jewel Markess ATerafin, that I do not think I could fully understand unless I lived the life you have lived in near blindness."

The wall from which the Oracle had stepped began to shift, stone moving, slowly, as if it were the surface of melting ice.

"And Evayne?"

"Pardon?"

"Evayne. Evayne a'Nolan. Do you understand her?"

"Better, in many ways, than I understand you. She is not what you are, Jewel. She is god-born and bound by geas and bitter, bitter hope. You will speak with her again; perhaps before you have made your choice. I will say this much: she does not choose the roads she walks. What choice she has—and it is imperfect—is what she sees when she walks them.

"If she comes to you, she might be your age. She might be the age you were when you first crossed Terafin's threshold. She might be your peer, and she might rival Sigurne Mellifas at the height of her many powers. I ask, if she arrives, that you allow her to speak, regardless of age. Where you walk, you take some part of your home with you.

"Where she walks, she is forced to walk in isolation." She turned to Kallandras. "Be kind."

He did not reply.

Nor had he need; the stone that had once housed the back half of the Oracle as she was currently constituted was now a whirlpool in miniature.

"I know what you seek, Kallandras. You will not find it where you travel, but if you survive, you will at last be upon the final leg of your long journey. So, too, Evayne." She held the crystal in her hands aloft, and in its heart, there were roiling clouds and small flashes of light that made them appear a storm in miniature.

That lightning leaped beyond the confines of the crystal to the wall; it struck the heart of vortex. Liquid stone scattered, pushed outward in an oval that solidified to form an arch. It was round, not rectangular; it looked like uneven, melted glass when it ceased motion.

"It is not an easy thing to reach the heart of my lands," the Oracle said softly. "Reaching them is the first part of your test." She turned to the Kings and the Exalted, and tendered them a bow that was almost Weston. She did not speak. Instead, she lowered her arms. The crystal remained in cupped palms, like an offering.

"Go," she told Jewel. "I must remain to close the way."

Chapter One

5th of Morel, 428 A.A.
Terafin Manse, Averalaan Aramarelas

HANNERLE WAS NOT IN a happy mood. Years in the company of his wife made this clear to Haval, although the rest of the people in this impromptu gathering did not know her well enough to realize it.

On the other hand, she wasn't angry with *them*. They had spent the earliest years of their lives—almost half of them—in environments in which anger directed at other people was safety, of a type. Or perhaps they were perceptive enough to realize that the age difference between Hannerle and themselves made it unlikely that they would become targets for her anger.

Looking mildly distressed, Finch stood before Hannerle, her hands enveloped by Haval's wife's. "Are you sure you won't stay?" she asked, squeezing her hands as if Hannerle were a beloved aunt and not a recovered convalescent.

"If I stay much longer," Hannerle replied, "I'll forget how to look after myself."

Finch's brows rose in mock-derision. "That's impossible."

"Trust me, it's not. The Terafin manse is impressive, but in the end it's not mine. And there's very little I can do to make it mine. You let me putter about in the kitchen—but the servants hate it, and can't say as I blame them. It's stressful being a guest."

"Haval, help me." Finch cast an imploring glance at the clothier.

"I have offered my wife every possible entreaty to remain," he replied, his shoulders slumped, his expression one of regret at his failure.

Hannerle frowned. "You're the only reason I would stay," she told him, voice sharp.

Finch cringed. Not even she could pretend that the comment was delivered with any affection.

"It pains me to watch my husband wrap you all around his fingers," Hannerle continued. "I've half a mind to break something over his head—but none of the things here belong to me, and breaking *your* crockery seems like poor thanks for your hospitality." Her hands tightened briefly before she pulled them free. "I understand why he's here. I don't like it, but I understand it.

"So I'll give you advice, and it's worth every penny you pay for it. He's arrogant. He thinks the world of himself. And he hates to lose. He notices everything, so you might as well not bother trying to lie to him. But if you put your life in his hands, he'll keep you safe.

"Don't put more than your life in his hands."

"Hannerle—"

"Jay trusts him? Aye, I know. As do I. But I know him, Finch. If he causes you trouble, kick him out. If he causes you too much trouble, come to me."

Finch nodded. "I will." When Hannerle hesitated, she smiled. "He's not the only older man I have to keep an eye on."

"That," his wife replied, with a significant glance at Haval, "is exactly what I'm afraid of."

"I *like* the girl," Hannerle said, when she was of a mind to speak to Haval. This did not occur until they were almost at the bridge that separated the Isle from the mainland.

"Yes."

"I like Teller as well. Don't involve them in games they can't play."

"Hannerle, I am unlikely to involve *them* in anything. They are—in case it has slipped your mind—the putative regent and the *actual* right-kin of one of the most powerful Houses in the Empire. I realize they are young, but they are not incompetent children; there is no need to coddle them. If they actually require such coddling, there is very little I can do to preserve them."

"You know what I meant."

He did. He considered, and reconsidered, the wisdom of his present position. "Hannerle," he finally said, scrubbing his face of all expression.

"I hate it when you do that."

"I know. But you also hate it when I lie."

"It makes me wonder why I married you in the first place."

He smiled—and that, at least, was genuine. "I have often wondered that myself." He slid a hand over both of hers; they were not so loosely clasped in her lap. She had withered during her convalescence, much of her weight lost to lack of food and near endless sleep.

"Do *not*," she said, as if she could hear his thoughts, "mother *me*." But she did not pull her hands away. Instead, she met his unblinking gaze and held it.

In decades past, there were very, very few who could meet and hold that gaze. Duvari. Jarven. Ararath. Not his godfather, Hectore. Rath's protégée, the young woman who was now The Terafin, could—but only when anger swamped her uncertainties.

"Why have you accepted my involvement in Terafin affairs? I gave you my word that I would cease all my meddling and return to the store if you would but wake on your own."

"I didn't wake on my own," was his wife's stiff reply.

"It is unlike you to quibble trivialities, Hannerle."

She glared. The glare was comfortable and familiar. It was not, however, comforting. His wife was afraid.

Haval understood Hannerle on an instinctive level; he always had. She was no more a mystery than The Terafin or her many allies. But she had a combination of characteristics that he found in very few. She was the sovereign of her domain, but she had always been willing to share the spaces she created. She considered her responsibilities burdens—but in the way that children were, to other couples.

They had never had children.

He wondered, now, how Hannerle might have changed if they had.

And he wondered, as he observed her, his own expression remote and impenetrable, what had occurred while she slept. He felt the edge of anger; it was bracing. He was given to frequent irritation, but anger, seldom.

"What happened?" he asked, after a long moment of silence.

She frowned. "Don't play games with *me*. You were present in the Terafin manse for my entire stay; you probably have a far better idea than I do." She clasped her hands in her lap more tightly, and her knuckles whitened. Her skin was pale, and her cheeks, hollow. Months of forced inactivity had taken their toll.

And that would, of course, affect her. She required her home, her space, the rules of her carefully disordered life. She needed—had needed—her husband to be part of that. He had, of course, fully expected to dance around the implacable ultimatum he expected to be handed the moment she realized she was no longer trapped in sleep.

He had not expected that no ultimatum would be forthcoming.

He knew his wife. There was only one reason she would forgo what was absolutely her right. "Hannerle." He did not touch her again. She had withdrawn in place, and touching Hannerle when she was so barely self-contained had never been wise.

She turned to stare out of the window. It was not, sadly, the window by which Haval now sat. He gentled his voice. "Hannerle."

She knew him. She did not know the details or particulars of his past; she never had. But she knew Haval. Perhaps that was the singular gift she had to give: she *saw* him. Facts were the detritus that, observed, confirmed what she knew—but Hannerle had never required outside confirmation of her knowledge.

As proof, she said, sharply, "Jewel did not *do* anything. You've never felt threatened by her before—don't start on my account." When he failed to reply, she turned to glare at him. "I mean it, Haval. Don't take this out on Jewel. Don't you even *think* of taking it out on poor Finch."

"Hannerle, you misjudge me." One brow rose as her lips thinned. He felt anger recede, but like any sharp-edged object, it left its mark. "You haven't answered my question."

"So? You've never answered all of mine. I don't recall answers being a condition of this marriage."

"Hannerle—"

"I mean it. I don't want to talk about it. I don't want to think about it. I want to go home. I want to go home while I can still believe I have one." She exhaled, her shoulders curling inward, as if to ward off blows from an opponent Haval couldn't see. "Will she survive, Haval?"

"Who?"

"Jewel."

He understood what she wanted from an answer, and it was not information. She wanted comfort. Unfortunately for both of them, she was far too perceptive to take comfort from meaningless phrases. "I do not know. I do not know where she now travels—but my conservative estimate is that the lands she now enters resemble the most startling elements of her personal chambers. She is unlikely to venture into friendly territory, but she numbers men of significant power among her small personal guard. If she is attacked—"

"That's not what I mean."

He held up one placating hand. "It is not always clear what you mean." But it was, now. "Hannerle, I *am* fond of The Terafin. I have always felt a debt of conscience to her."

Hannerle nodded. Jewel was one of the many subjects they discussed with care, skirting around the edges of events that could not be changed, and a sleeping anger that could be wakened.

"I have followed—from a safe distance—her rise to power. It did not surprise me. But at the same time, it did. I could just as easily see her as the woman behind a shop that deals exclusively in fashions for the wealthy."

A grin tugged at the corner of his wife's lips, but faded into grimace before it fell away. "She's a good girl."

"She is mostly that, yes. I do not believe that she has ever done anything of which you'd disapprove—and not merely to avoid the cost of your disapproval, as I have. Hannerle, love, what did she show you? What did you see?"

"She showed me nothing," his wife replied. After a pause, she added, "I will not have you angry at her in my own house."

"We are demonstrably not in our home at the moment." When she failed to reply, he added, "I have given my word that I will not lie to you. I will not, therefore, promise that I will not be angry; I know myself well enough."

"She showed me nothing," Hannerle repeated. Her hands separated and curled into tighter fists. "But as you've guessed, I'm angry."

He had guessed she was afraid, but was wise enough to keep this to himself. "She is no longer the child she once was," he replied, gentling his voice. "Were she, she would not be Terafin. You think of her as young—as young Jewel—because she was, when she first entered our lives. But she's grown. She cannot be counted as a child forever."

"Do you understand what she faces?"

His wife was one of the few people he knew who never failed to surprise him. But he considered her question with the same care he might have considered a question posed to him by the Kings themselves. "No. You have not seen Jewel's personal chambers; I have. They are no longer part of the Terafin manse, although the doors that lead to—and from—them are.

"You have seen her cats. They are the smallest part of the magic that now surrounds her, in my opinion. If Jewel herself understood what all of these things presaged, I *would* understand what she faced. But she does not."

"Do you understand it better than she does?"

He smiled. "I have never been a modest man, Hannerle. I believe that I understand many things better than Jewel does. But in this, I am willing to admit that I am stymied. It does not suit me," he added.

"No. It doesn't." Her smile was weary, but she leaned—at last—into his shoulder. He slid an arm around her then. "She's afraid."

"Yes. And she is wise to be so. I know very little of the dangers she now faces; I did not put much credence in children's stories in my youth. I do not think what she faces will change her beyond all recognition—but yes, Hannerle, that is the heart of her fear. She has defined herself for the whole of her life by the family she's built—and with a single exception, it is not one she can take with her while she travels.

"She does not know what she will face. Nor do the wise. The only thing we can do for her is preserve the House."

"Can you," she replied, putting the responsibility for it upon the correct shoulders, "while also preserving yourself?"

"I have not changed, love. I have grown wiser, perhaps; I have become less competitive. Nothing I do for the House, or within it, will alter the substance of who I am. There is only one thing that could. I will not pursue this if it will threaten you in any way."

She stiffened but did not withdraw. "You'd leave them on their own, then, because I demanded it?"

"They are *not children*, Hannerle. Finch numbers, among her allies, the right-kin of the House. She will have the whole of the Merchant Authority at her disposal. She is no fool."

"She's a—"

"Young woman, yes. But like you, she has a spine of solid iron; she will not bend. She is more graceful in the way she refuses to bend, of course. Your home is the shop we've created between us; her home is House Terafin. She will not do less to protect it than you yourself would do were *Elemental Fashion* to be threatened. I am not certain that I have much to contribute to her success."

"Liar."

He chuckled. "I am attempting to be modest."

"I didn't marry a humble man. If I believed you believe what you say, I'd be seriously worried about *you*."

"You already are."

She exhaled. "Yes. Because I *want* you to play your gods-cursed game. I would never, *ever* have said that would be possible—the wanting, I mean. I didn't believe you'd ever stop the game."

"You know why I did."

"Yes. Because I couldn't handle the cost."

"And now you can't handle the cost of my inactivity?"

"I know you're right. I know they're not children."

He waited.

"But they're like Jewel: they've never played the games you've played. I feel as if they'll be walking blind into a situation which could kill them—and if they die, Haval, I'll feel responsible."

"It will *not* be your fault. I am one man. If they die on my watch, I will not consider myself responsible."

"And you promised you'd never lie to me."

"I am not lying. While I understand the sentiments that The Terafin and her den invoke, I have trained men and women far younger than they to acts far more difficult. I understood the possible consequences before the training started—but I also understood the possible consequences were there no such men and women employed.

"I cannot materially change either Finch or Teller ATerafin. They do not have the time or the resources necessary to learn what I might once have taught."

"Does anyone?"

Haval did not reply. Sadly, Hannerle did not fail to notice.

7th of Morel, 428 A.A.
Terafin Manse, Averalaan Aramarelas

Jester was fifteen minutes late. He spent those fifteen traversing the public galleries with a very junior servant who was new to the Household Staff. Servants were hired for temporary duties; it happened frequently. But they were not given a place on the Household Staff without earning it.

Janni was new to the Staff, but not the manse; she was certainly new to the subtle changes in uniform. Her parents were inordinately proud of her new job, and she was therefore aware that she had much more to lose. Jester, like Carver, was fond of almost every element of the Household Staff. The exceptions, of course, were to be found in the senior echelons, and in the Master of the Household Staff herself.

Jester navigated the world by finding the humor in any situation.

The Master of the Household Staff starched her face, as far as Jester was concerned. She did not in any obvious way respond to Jester's presence; nor would she. He was nominally adviser to a member of the House Council, after all. But she had ways of making the rest of the servants suffer.

The servants themselves were willing to grouse about the Master of the

Household Staff, but they did so reluctantly—and not on short acquaintance. If they despised the woman—Jester did—they also held her in a fascinated awe that approached reverence. Jester couldn't understand why; he found ample fodder for comic relief in her parched, pinched voice, but little else.

"I don't know if you'll be assigned to the West Wing or not," he told Janni. "But I have hopes."

Her smile was genuine and entirely inappropriate, which is probably why Jester liked it so much.

"I, on the other hand, have an appointment which I was told I couldn't afford to miss."

Her dark eyes rounded. "Are you late?"

He smiled. "I'm always late. If I were on time, any number of older patricians would die of shock, and I don't want *that* on my head."

Janni tilted her head to the side. In her strong, soft voice she said, "I'm not sure I believe that."

Jester passed between the two House Guards stationed outside the double doors of the West Wing. They were new additions, and he didn't care for them, but Teller—or Torvan, more likely—insisted on their presence. They weren't Chosen. It had been decided—and by whom, Jester wanted to know—that the reassignment of Chosen only a week after Jay's departure would send the wrong signals.

Jester was not fond of the House Guard. They were the House equivalent of the magisterial guards, and looked every inch of it. He understood, thanks to Arann's careful and oft-repeated explanations, that guards—any guards— did their job best by being intimidating; the whole point of their presence was to discourage illegal or inappropriate behavior.

All of the den's earliest run-ins with the magisterians had involved the thin line of the law: they took what they could, when things were desperate. But never when they weren't. He grimaced as the doors closed at his back. Ellerson failed to emerge from the servants' room.

Ellerson, starched and consistently *proper*, had never been Jester's favorite person. Ironic, then, that his absence could create this hollow, silent space that implied loss. But it was a loss he could face. Carver's absence was in all ways harder. It brought back sharp, hard shadows: it was an echo of the end of their life in the twenty-fifth holding. Lefty, Fisher, and Lander lost; Duster dead on the day the rest of the den had made their narrow escape.

Duster dead because if she weren't, none of them would have made it out.

He couldn't remember Lefty's face. He couldn't remember Lander's or

Fisher's, either. But Duster? She never left him. Every time he looked at Finch, he could see the echo of Duster's face. He'd never talked to Duster much. She was always on edge; a joke could make her laugh one day, and the next, be cause for drawn dagger and spitting, furious threat.

He understood the fury. He understood the pain.

He understood how hard it had been for Duster to make the choice she'd made on the night a fat, self-indulgent patrician had come under her knife: kill cleanly, or walk away from the den.

Jester would have been fine with the messy, lingering death. No one had asked him. Duster had asked Lander—only Lander. But Lander had been the most obviously broken by their shared experiences. In his pain, she saw a reflection of the pain she herself would never acknowledge. In Jester, she saw nothing.

Jester saw nothing himself. Nothing except the family that had been so haphazardly built. It was an awkward, angry family, prone to theft when all other avenues of extending its sputtering existence had vanished—but it was his. He was part of it. Part of it, and separate from it, as well.

He was like Duster; he didn't acknowledge pain. Unlike Duster, he didn't acknowledge anger. Neither made any difference.

Jay was gone. This time—this time she'd had the time to say good-bye. This time, she'd taken Angel with her. Angel with his broken spire, his hair flat against the curve of a skull they'd almost never seen. He looked like a stranger. He talked like Angel. Having him here wouldn't do any good; he'd climbed walls when Jay'd been in the South.

That left Finch and Teller, the two quietest members of the den. Teller had a sense of humor. He liked cats. He hated confrontation, but he'd learned how to diffuse the worst of it. Barston, his starched taskmaster of a secretary had seen to that, over the years. Jester knew that Teller was new to his role, and the role itself was as secure as Jay was. Jay, who wasn't here. He still didn't worry about Teller.

He worried about Finch.

He worried about Finch because he knew Finch intended to take the House in everything but name. She intended to launch herself into the game patricians played—using many of the same tools: the Merchant Authority, the external contacts she'd built there over the years, her position as House Council member—even if it was junior.

No one, after the events of The Terafin's funeral, could take the House from Jay. Not that they hadn't tried, in one way or another, but Jay was just damn hard to kill.

None of the rest of them were. None of the rest of them had *ever* been hard to kill. They'd arrived at House Terafin in Jay's wake, and in that wake, they'd been installed in the West Wing. Because of Jay. Because of her vision.

They were still standing in her wake, in most ways, but they'd bled into the House as well: Arann as Chosen, Finch as merchant, Teller as right-kin. Carver was their unofficial ear behind walls. Daine was their Alowan, and if he had far more edges than Alowan had, he was also sixty years younger. Angel was her liege.

And Jester?

He was Jester, same as before—in better clothing. He talked to the servants in Carver's absence because someone had to, especially now. He knew how to be practically invisible in a crowd—and he did it by demanding attention, rather than hiding from it. But the attention he demanded was jovial, friendly, and entirely noncommittal; no one felt threatened by it.

He opened the doors to the great room and entered.

Haval was standing by the fireplace, his hands behind his back, his clothing unusually austere. He wore no apron. Only when Jester closed the doors in his wake did the clothier turn.

"You asked to speak with me," Jester said, entering the room.

"Demonstrably."

Jester sauntered over to the cabinet. "Are you drinking?"

"It depends."

"On?"

"The drink and the length of the interview. My wife is not particularly pleased with me today, and this is not the only appointment to mar my day's productivity."

"Teller told you I'm seconded as adjutant to Finch on the Council?"

"He did, indeed, make that clear. He feels that your clothing is not appropriate for the position."

Jester shrugged. He lifted a bottle of fortified wine from the cabinet, considering it for a long moment. "If I were there for anyone but Finch, I'd refuse to change."

"Yes. I believe he is also aware of that."

"And you?"

"I am aware that clothing does not make the man. Do you have any particular preferences, or will you trust my sensibilities?" Jester retrieved two glasses. He set them down, poured, and lifted them. He had none of the fluid elegance—or the starch—of the Household Staff, and accepted the lack; he sauntered over to where Haval stood, observing him.

"If it's good enough for Finch, it's good enough for me. I don't care for fussy skirts, though."

"No. I don't believe they would suit. There are certain shades of color it would be best to avoid, as well; most of the blues the House requires will work with your hair."

"You don't appear to be carrying a measure."

"No."

"You know my measurements."

"Yes. The knowledge is inexact; it is based in its entirety on observation."

"And you had me summoned because you wanted exact?"

"No. I wish you to answer a few questions before we proceed to the measurements—or, more precisely, the fittings."

Jester shrugged. Questions didn't bother him, no matter how pointed. They were just words. He could slide out from under them by answering. His answers, however, weren't generally heavy with meaning. "Fire away."

"What, exactly, do you do here?"

"I see you're starting with the easy questions first." Jester smiled. It was bright and lazy. "As little as I can get away with."

Haval didn't smile. He didn't blink. His expression was smooth as stone, and it gave just as much away. "How little is that?"

"These days? Finch expects me to deliver three messages—in person—this afternoon. Without giving offense to their recipients."

"I believe you have it in you to manage that."

Jester handed Haval a glass; the older man accepted it without comment. "In at least one case, yes." He walked to the largest couch in the room and sank into its center as if his spine were melting.

"It has come to my attention that you've been spending some time in the garden, with the groundskeeper."

Jester drank. "And?"

"While I laud your ability to play host to a new employee, you've been spending time with Birgide Viranyi."

"I happen to enjoy her company."

"You are aware of who she is?"

"One of the most famous botanists in the Empire. The Master Gardener has been at great pains to threaten me personally in the hopes of keeping my behavior on the up and up."

"I imagine he has. Have you found her company instructive?"

"I still have dirt under my fingernails, if that helps."

"Let me ask you the question again. What occupies your time in the Terafin manse?"

Jester drank, regarding Haval as if seeing him for the first time. Smiling, he said, "You're not going to let this go, are you?" Without waiting for a reply, he sipped his wine. Jester's lazy smile bounced off Haval's face.

"Birgide?"

"She's *Astari*," Jester replied. Haval did not appear to be surprised by the accusation. He barely appeared to hear it. "For reasons I trust I don't have to explain, I don't trust the *Astari*. If the Kings aren't here, they shouldn't be either."

"You have not asked her about her botany?"

"I've asked her questions she couldn't answer without some research," Jester replied. "Not many, though. Whatever she does for the *Astari*, the botany's real."

"You feel you are now enough of an expert to make that judgment."

"After weeks in Birgide's company? Damn right."

Haval's lips twitched. "It was not one of my more stellar inquiries. What do you think her role in the *Astari* is?"

Jester hated, on point of principle, discussion. This, on the other hand, could barely be considered that—it was an interrogation. He could just get up and leave, but he was curious. Curiosity was not one of Jester's obvious, public failings. It was, however, a weakness. He generally satisfied curiosity by observation. Observing Haval, on the other hand, was like watching rock grow.

Teller had made clear that he considered this appointment significant, and had all but begged Jester not to screw it up. What Jester wanted to know at the moment was why. He therefore chose to answer Haval's questions. He knew it was a bad habit to develop. "Poisons."

"Very good. Does she keep them here?"

"I doubt it." He didn't. "She's been studying the big trees in the back. She tried to take a couple of silver leaves, and the branches moved. They don't apparently like to be studied."

"Interesting. The other trees?"

"Same effect. She's made no attempt to touch the burning tree."

"No. She is not a fool."

"Do you know her?"

"I know of her. My role as clothier to the powerful and well-placed does not often put me in the path of a botanist, however well-regarded." Haval lifted his glass to his lips. "Do you understand what is about to occur in this House?"

Jester nodded. "Is that why you're here?"

"It is."

"And the clothing?"

"A lesser part of my responsibilities. It is not, however, optional. You will attend Finch in the Council hall, and you will do so in a fashion that does not embarrass her."

"I *highly* doubt that."

Haval's lips twitched again, and this time, he surrendered a smile. "Very well. You will embarrass her in ways that do not reflect poorly on *me*. You have managed to answer very few of my questions. Even Finch is more forthcoming."

"If you want a weaker link, try Teller."

"Indeed. How much training have you had with weapons?"

Jester rose and headed back to the cabinet. "About as much as the average orphan from the twenty-fifth holding."

"Truly?"

"No." He poured. Back toward the clothier, he continued. "I know Jay trusts you," he said. "I've never understood why."

"Ah."

"You sent her to Lord Waverly." He turned, glass in hand.

"No, Jester, I did not."

"You had to know what would happen."

Haval met, and held, Jester's gaze. Give the old man credit; he didn't blink. Literally. "Clever," the older man finally said. "And perceptive. You have not talked with Jewel about this."

"No point. Waverly died. Duster came home with us."

"Duster also died."

"She was always going to die. The only surprise was why—she bought us time."

"You don't resent Jewel for her death."

He didn't. He was beginning to resent Haval Arwood. This conversation was circling a space where Jester did not go. "Should I?"

"There is no imperative one way or the other."

"The right-kin made clear that this appointment was somehow important. I've got maybe five more minutes of good behavior left in me. You want to tell me what you want?"

"Tell me about the Master of the Household Staff."

"I'll take that as no."

"As you please. What are your impressions of that woman?"

"She terrifies the crap out of the rest of the Household Staff; she butts heads with the right-kin's secretary—frequently—and she'd support Iain ATerafin in any position he chose to adopt on the House Council. She is not friendly—she considers it a lowering sin—but she's consistent. She's not loved. She *is* respected."

Haval nodded.

"She has a small plot in the grounds, a flower bed. The Master Gardener is fine with this because he's just as terrified as any of the under servants. She grows flowers and one or two plants that might or might not produce something edible."

"Are they poisonous?"

Jester laughed. He drank wine, briefly, as if it were water. "Yes."

"Has she killed many members of the Household Staff?"

"Not that I'm aware of."

"You acknowledge the possibility."

"No, I don't. If she had reason to kill a member of the Household Staff, she would fire them first. It would probably cause the person more pain in the long run. Resigning from a position on staff is one thing; being dismissed in disgrace, quite another. If any member of the House causes difficulties for any member of the Household Staff, she has the pull to have that person removed; she can't do it directly, but she's respected."

"You do not consider the contents of her small garden odd."

"Not as odd as this meeting."

Haval smiled. "How did you come across the garden?"

Jester shook his head. "I'm not answering that one—she hates me enough as it is. If it helps, I don't take tea with her."

"Possibly wise. Do many?"

"I'll let you answer that."

Haval inclined his head. "Three. She will, on occasion, speak at length with three members of the House Council. One of them is Jewel herself; it is not a meeting that I imagine engenders much joy in either woman. The other is, as you've suggested Iain. Iain is a scrupulously careful treasurer; he is also old enough to treat almost everyone with healthy suspicion."

"That's two."

"You will have to unearth the third for yourself, although I believe you know of whom I speak."

"If you don't mind," Jester replied, "I'm about to get drunk. This conversation couldn't possibly make any *less* sense."

"You will have to drink far more than that. You have a naturally high tolerance for alcohol."

It was true.

"You have several scars on your hands, and one long scar on your left wrist. They are not, to my eye, wounds taken in sword practice."

"The twenty-fifth holding was a rough place."

"Oh, indeed. I imagine you bear scars from your years there—but the scars of which I speak were not taken in the hundred holdings."

Jester shrugged. "I don't remember where they came from."

"I highly doubt that. I will assume a familiarity with daggers and throwing knives. If you had some skill with long daggers, it might prove useful, but it is not entirely necessary. If you are required to kill, it is best to do so in a way that necessitates no obvious weapon and leaves no obvious trace."

"I am never required to kill."

"A figure of speech. I have known the current Terafin for over half her life. She would not command any of your den to kill."

"She wouldn't command anyone in House Terafin to kill; she'd accept death as an outcome of their duties—but only then."

"And so we come back to duties. Tell me, Jester, what are yours?"

Jester glanced at the empty glass in his right hand. He rose. "I think we're done here." He walked to the cabinet and set the empty glass down.

A knife flew an inch to the right of his hand and embedded itself in the rounded lip of the narrow shelf. Jester sighed—loudly—and retrieved the bottle. ". . . or not." He filled his glass, cupped its crystal bowl in his left hand, and turned. "As a way to keep a conversation going," he added, grabbing the knife's slender handle and pulling it free, "that's not going to get you invited back into many polite houses."

"Possibly not. I'm seldom concerned about such invitations on my own behalf, and my wife dislikes patrician company. She doesn't dislike it enough to refuse their custom, however." He crossed the room as Jester held the knife out. "Your reaction is interesting."

Jester shrugged. "You can't afford to kill me. Not that way."

"No."

"Which meant you wanted my attention. Now, you have it." He drank.

"Remarkable," Haval said. "I thought you had potential; I didn't realize how much."

"I have, in theory, wasted potential," Jester replied. He was grinning. "I'm considered a bit of a gadfly, and a general social failure of the type people enjoy."

"Meaning you tweak the noses of the powerful in a way that the rest of the Terafin patricians cannot safely do."

Jester nodded. "It's one of the few amusements I have. I'm not fond of patricians. I make exceptions for my friends, and they've obliged me by refusing to become what I detest. It's a delicate balance."

"How familiar are you with the layout of the manse?"

"The only person with a better sense of the labyrinths behind walls is Carver." Jester grimaced. "We don't mention his name much. I don't suggest you bring him up in polite conversation in this wing."

"I had noticed that you've become somewhat less withdrawn, of late."

Jester shrugged. "The cats could cause more of a ruckus—with less consequence—than I could. They're gone. It's on me, now."

"Yes," Haval replied. "It is. As you have failed—several times—to answer a simple question, I will assume, as people will, that you have. And of course, that the answer suits my purpose."

"What is your purpose?"

"I wish to employ you."

Jester laughed. It was hard to sustain laughter, given Haval's utter lack of amusement, but Jester had had a decade of practice. "To *hire* me? I suggest you run that past your intimidating wife. I'm sure she won't approve."

"She will, as you suspect, have a dim view of the prospect; it is, and will remain, immaterial. You will not be an apprentice clothier." Haval frowned. "I don't think you have the patience for it; I do believe you have the eye."

"What do you want me to do?"

"More or less what you have been doing, with a single notable exception."

"You want me to report to you."

"Indeed. I have a few questions to which I require answers. They are not," he added, stepping past Jester and reaching for the wine, "direct questions for you. Even I have a limited supply of both patience and time." He topped up the glass that Jester had given him one abrupt bend in the conversation ago. "Before she left, I spoke with The Terafin. I suggested that you were underemployed in a variety of ways, and she—reluctantly—gave her approval for this interview."

"Did she reluctantly give my consent?"

"No. I don't believe she considered the matter; were she here, I would perhaps take her to task for that failure. Or perhaps not. She is seldom subtle, and this appears to be a subtle maneuver on her part."

"She expected me to say no?"

"In retrospect, I believe that was the case." He drank. He did not have Jester's garrulous energy; all of his movements were economical. "You know how to throw knives."

"Yes. And yes, I've had some practice with long knives. I tried the sword, but I don't have the height for it."

"Height is not an excuse. With the right weapon—"

"I don't have the height for the House Guard. Short of that, there was no point."

"And the knife-work?"

Jester shrugged. "Helps me sleep at night." He swallowed the rest of his wine in one long, acerbic gulp. "I'm not great at it. I'm good enough for my purposes."

"I will not ask for an explanation of those purposes as you seem to find it wearying. I will give you three names."

"Do they have anything in common with the messages I'm to deliver— without offense—this afternoon?"

"Very good."

"You know the names. You clearly didn't pick up on the 'without offense' part. I'm well-known for some of my unfortunate foibles—but even those won't be good enough excuse for accidentally finding myself in possession of information that is not, strictly speaking, public."

"You do not feel you are up to the task."

"I don't even know what the task is, but given your expression, no, I don't. I don't particularly feel bad about it, either." He set the glass down, and glanced at the mark in what was otherwise pristine, well-oiled wood. "Nice arm, by the way. Especially at your age." He headed for the doors.

"You are aware that Finch has already been subject to one assassination attempt."

"I'd be surprised if it's that low," he replied. But he did not reach for the door's handle. "When?"

"If Finch has not discussed this with the den, I am not certain I'm at liberty to do so."

Bastard. Jester turned. "I like playing games as much as the next man, but only when I have a shot at winning. There's no win in any direction here. Are the three involved—in any way—with that attempt?"

"Two are not, in my opinion. The third is a possibility."

"Name the third."

"I decline. You are an observant young man, and you are resourceful. You have taken up the task of being the loud and the obvious in any gathering; it allows you to control the image you present, and allows you, further, to hide behind it. I was capable, in my youth, of doing as you do; it is not an avenue open to me now."

"You'd need to be consistently—"

"Obnoxious, yes. I believe you have twice caused House Terafin embarrassment that was not immediately dismissed. Given the years you have been ATerafin, I consider that significant; you have certainly not spent most of your life behind the shut doors of this wing. I should not keep you further. But if, after the events of the day, you wish to entertain my offer of employment, I will not withdraw it." He then pinched the bridge of his nose. "I will, however, insist that you be properly attired. I want exact measurements, now."

"Of course you do."

The three people to whom Finch had written messages were merchants. Two were ATerafin, but had not been given quarters within the manse. Like Lucille, that veritable dragon of the Merchant Authority, they made their residences elsewhere. Unlike Lucille, in Jester's opinion, they hadn't been offered the option. Lucille was the commander of any building she happened to live, or work, in—and the Terafin manse already had one.

No other merchant was this practical. The Isle was considered important and significant, but it was also expensive; only one of the three boasted a home on the Isle. The others, like Lucille, lived within the hundred holdings.

Jester chose to visit Ludgar ATerafin first, as he was closest. He hadn't exactly lied to Haval; he preferred to get by on as little useful work as possible. He also proposed to be home by the early dinner hour, and therefore took a Terafin carriage. It wasn't necessary, and in the more crowded streets of the holdings, it wasn't *faster*, but in general people were more inclined to be respectful and polite if the carriage was obviously from the manse itself.

Jester was not a member of the House Council, although he could in theory attend as Finch's adjutant should he so choose.

He considered the House Council matter with a grimace. He did *not*, in the usual run of things, choose to sit in the closed, stuffy chambers; he found the politics both irritating and boringly obvious. He knew in advance where each member would choose to offer their support; some were subtle, some like thunderstorms in the rainy season. He knew that they would talk until they were blue in the face, given half a chance, and he knew he would be forced to listen. Finch had made clear he would listen *obviously* and *attentively*, and added a trailing *please* after she'd made this request.

Jay, to her credit, had never tried—but Jay had the smarts she was born with. Like Jester, she didn't put effort into anything pointless; like Jester, she was practical. She was more obvious in her suspicion—but she was also capable of trust. It was a weakness. Jester knew it. Carver had spent his early years with the servants not just because he wanted to bed Merry, but because he knew they were the best source of gossip, and that gossip, if not entirely reliable, would be close enough to give the den warning, if necessary. Not all of the servants considered the West Wing a personal favorite, but many did. They knew where the den had come from; they knew that the den had none of the built-in advantages that birth generally conveys.

They knew that, in part, the West Wing was, and had been, in their hands. They were invested in its success, and in the success of The Terafin—a woman of mean birth and no connections who had risen to prominence by her contributions to the House itself. She was like them, not like the patricians who generally climbed the rungs of House political ladders.

The servants offered Carver quiet warnings, and Carver passed them on, stripped of all identifying marks, to Jay or her kitchen council, most of whom were willing to trust Carver's take on the advice. Carver had, on the sly, checked out some of it himself—he had access to the back halls. Jester strongly suspected that the Master of the Household Staff knew this, but as she treated everyone with stiff disdain, it was hard to be certain. She made it difficult to access those halls on the best of days—but Carver liked the challenge, and the Master of the Household Staff had never taken her suspicions to The Terafin—either Terafin—directly. It was a game to both.

Jester didn't particularly like the Master of the Household Staff; he did, on the other hand, admire her. No rank—not even The Terafin's—was proof against her ire or her suspicion. If she treated the new maids and servants like carpeting that needed to be thoroughly beaten and trod on, she treated anyone that way. She was not particularly fond of the West Wing—but she was not particularly fond of the House Council, either. He knew almost nothing about the Master of the Household Staff, and the servants were incredibly reluctant to talk about her at all—as if she, like ancient creatures of myth, were invoked by the mere mention of her name.

But he knew about her small garden. He knew about what she grew there. He knew that, on three separate occasions, men—always men—had fallen extremely ill shortly after they had overstepped the bounds of their authority. He had not lied to Haval; none of them had been Household Staff. One had died. If The Terafin suspected foul play—and certainly the servants did—she had said, and done, nothing.

But House Terafin harbored men and women of great ambition, as any House did, and she accepted the behavior that did not politically embarrass her House, either externally or internally. She, therefore, had many men of the caliber of Ludgar under her auspices. She had passed them on to Jay.

It wasn't Jay who had deposited Jester in the Council Chambers as Finch's adjutant—it was the previous Terafin. He had spoken no more than a handful of words to the woman whose House Name he bore; he had spoken several thousand *about* her, but not in her hearing. She occupied a central role in his thoughts, which he kept largely to himself.

The only exception to that—and it was a rare exception, and prone to make him uncomfortable after the fact—was Finch. He knew where Jay had found Finch; she had found Jester in the same place. He knew that Finch had been sold to the brothel by her family, that she'd been saved as something "special," and that if she escaped, she had nowhere to go. The only people likely to offer aid were also likely to abuse her in exactly the same fashion, without the need to pay someone else for the privilege.

Speaking to Finch was speaking to someone with a breadth of common experience—and neither of them talked much about that past. Neither of them spoke about Duster. Jester vastly preferred not to speak about unpleasant things; they caused pain, to no one's amusement or benefit.

But he thought, as he mused in the interminable carriage ride to Ludgar's, that Haval had observed what Jester himself rarely thought about for long: Finch was important to him. All of the den was, but Finch occupied a space no one else did—or would. He was not, had never been, in love with her; he frankly doubted the existence of that emotion, at least as it pertained to himself. She was like a sister to him; sometimes an older one, sometimes younger. He really never thought more about it than that.

But it was clearly obvious to Haval, and that irked him. Nobody took Jester seriously enough to search for his weaknesses; Haval, almost unobtrusive, had merely noted them. And he had shown, in one baffling and inexplicable meeting, a willingness to use them.

What did he want?

He had asked Jester to work for him. He hadn't explained in exact terms what he expected, but the specific lack of explanation made clear—to Jester—what that work entailed; subtlety and possible sleight of hand. Jester would not be surprised if it involved more than that and, frankly, of a more dubious legality.

The clothier had waited until Jay left to make his offer of employ. This said something to Jester. He had no doubt that Haval had discussed the possibility with Jay—but every doubt that he had made clear what he wished Jester to achieve. Yet Jay trusted the old man.

Trust was a luxury she could not afford. They were all far too trusting for Jester's liking; all except Finch, and no one considered Finch naturally suspicious. She wasn't. She didn't sort people into trustworthy and untrustworthy; she didn't appear to make judgments at all. She accepted them as people— and she knew full well what people considered respectable by a vast swathe of humanity were capable of.

He adjusted the ring on his finger. It identified him as ATerafin, but frankly, anyone could wear one, if they could find a jeweler willing to create it. Ring on hand, he generally chose not to wear House colors. All official correspondence was delivered by House messengers; as Jester had not been sent in that capacity he had no desire to appear to be one—although he had, a handful of times in the past, chosen that camouflage when it suited his purposes. Finch had not elected to use the official service, for reasons of her own; Jester was the informal option. Informal or no, Ludgar would be well aware that Jester served—occasionally—as her adjutant; any message he carried would therefore be weighed with that knowledge in mind.

It was not the first time he had been sent to both carry and fetch messages. It was unlikely to be the last. In truth, he enjoyed Ludgar's company; the man had a sense of humor, something often absent in the pompous and pretentious. He did have a healthy sense of his own importance—but Jester found that true of most of the Terafin merchants, especially those who spent half of their life at sea, as Ludgar did.

He would not have considered Ludgar a threat, although he was well aware that Ludgar could throw his weight around when it suited him; Ludgar was both ambitious and practical. Practical, smart people were generally predictable if one understand the paradigm in which they worked: they took calculated risks, not stupid ones.

Was Ludgar involved?

He had certainly paid court to Finch—in her role as House Council member—when things appeared to be up in the air; he had kept an otherwise respectful distance since then. Very few people were afraid of Finch; very few were not wary of Lucille, and Lucille had practically posted signs on Finch's forehead warning people off.

Ludgar, however, knew how to charm Lucille. She didn't trust him, but liked him in spite of herself. He was capable of subtlety when he chose it; he didn't choose it all that often.

Then again, he was a giant of a man in almost all ways. It was rumored that he hoped for a position equal to Lucille's or Jarven's, and Jester admitted it was a possibility—but he privately thought the man would go mad within the month trapped as Jarven was. Jarven was canny, competent, and seemed to care less for his personal dignity—or authority—than the much more voluble Lucille.

Jester didn't believe it.

Chapter Two

LUDGAR LIVED ON THE Isle. Had he chosen to forgo the more prestigious address, he might have commanded a large manse with equally impressive grounds; on the Isle, all the money in the world couldn't buy that. Birth might, or marriage—but most of the land was owned by older and wealthier merchant families. Ludgar was not among them, which was perhaps a second reason to admire him. He made no bones about his mean birth; on the contrary, he treated it as a matter of pride.

Pride did not, in any way, make him kinder; it made him more like Haerrad. Were it not for Haerrad's actions against Teller, Jester would have remained largely neutral toward him; he considered Haerrad to be dangerous, but he was a full-frontal danger. He never pretended to be anything other than he was: ruthless, brutal, domineering. Ludgar was not Haerrad, but he had built a reputation among the Terafin merchants that was similar; Haerrad had the birth and breeding to assume a seat on the House Council. Ludgar did not.

Neither did Teller or Finch—yet they, unlike Ludgar, had been granted that status within Terafin.

The thought made him uneasy today. Jester had accepted The Terafin's decision—and command—as the act of desperation it was; The Terafin had not offered either Finch or Teller a choice. She had made clear that she wanted Jay as Terafin, and installing both Finch and Teller on the Council was meant to shore up Jay's claim if The Terafin herself was dead. But he was aware that no other ambitious ATerafin was likely to accept it as easily.

He glanced at the sealed message he carried. Finch seldom chose to correspond with Ludgar, although Ludgar offered her a diffident respect he seldom offered any other member of the House Council. Indeed, he offered the same respect to Lucille and Jarven, and no others that Jester was aware of; he had not been witness to any of the private meetings between The Terafin and Ludgar. Jay hadn't summoned him to an audience since she'd taken the chair—she'd held three formal audiences in all, and Ellerson had been pinched and oh-so-correct for three days on either side of each.

He grimaced, shying away from thoughts of the domicis when he saw where his thoughts were leading him. Ellerson was Jay's problem, if he was now a problem that could be solved.

Ludgar, however, was not.

Jester didn't play politics. He hadn't lied to Haval, although he had no qualms about doing so; he was lazy, and liked to remain free of entanglements. He kept an eye out for the den, inasmuch as he felt it could be done. Carver had taken the lead there; no one knew as much about the inner workings of a great house than its staff of servants. Not all of the servants cared for Carver's presence, but all of them accepted it, even the dour and humorless Master of the Household Staff.

But Carver was gone. The specter of his absence haunted that same staff, although only Merry obliquely begged for any news that might come their way.

In the absence of any responsibility, Jester had taken to the life of a well-to-do idle patris; he spent time drinking with some of the younger Senniel bards because he found them disarming and amusing. But it wasn't their company he craved, although many did; it was the way they could work a room. He watched them.

Jester didn't expect that people would like him; given his birth and his lack of connections, there was no immediate advantage in even the pretense of collegiality. But he did believe that collegiality was a skill like any other; it could be practiced. It could be learned. He wasn't particularly interested in being liked as himself; he wasn't even certain what that meant.

Bards were not considered the apex of political power, but bards could be found gathered wherever the powerful gathered. They offered each other polite, subtle warnings where warnings were necessary; on more than one occasion he had seen them control the flow of liquor, gauging the belligerence of the audience.

Ludgar was, unfortunately, a mean drunk. He was at his most insecure—and therefore least pleasant—when alcohol had been served too freely and the room was too highbrow. It amused Jester to watch; he was not enamored of the people who considered themselves the ruling class, and he took perverse pleasure in their humiliations, large and small.

But Finch was now one of them. He grimaced. Jay was at the head of the class. She hadn't changed in any obvious ways—behind closed doors. But she was The Terafin. It didn't matter where she'd found Jester—or Finch, if it came to that. Rath had taken her by the scruff of the neck, and shaken information about The Ten and the various merchant houses into her. It had been a source of frustration and conflict between Rath and Jay, and Jay had acquiesced only—in Jester's opinion—because she needed a place for the den to live.

She'd found it easier when Teller asked if he could sit in on the lessons, presumably because misery loved company. But Teller found Rath's knowledge fascinating. He didn't join Jay out of any sense of long-suffering obligation.

He didn't join many of the weapons lessons, either. Jester did. Not because he found them fascinating—he had a strong aversion to bruising, which was impossible to avoid—but because he thought it would be practical.

It hadn't proved as practical as the lock picking. That was one of the few lessons in which Jester had instantly excelled. Rath had also taught them how to pick pockets, cut purses, and sneak into a house through the front door. Jester felt no particular qualms about doing any of these things; Jay, however, did. She allowed theft only when the only other option was starvation. She put the den first—but what she'd wanted for the den was not that they live up to the name.

She'd wanted what they had now.

Jester watched the passing streets slow as the carriage approached its destination. She wanted what they had now, but even she could see that absent fancy clothing and larger fortunes, the games the patriciate played were almost identical to the games the dens in the holdings did. They had to be more subtle than street dens, sure. They had to understand the laws in order to not quite break them.

But the spirit beneath all their polished sophistication was the same. They staked a claim to their turf, and they demolished all challengers. If they were prevented from killing those challengers, it wasn't because they had scruples—most didn't, in Jester's opinion—but because they had so much more to lose if they were caught.

They were much better at not being caught than the dens in the holdings; they didn't run. They deflected. They sent letters. They held dinner parties and larger entertainments. If they were hunted, they were hunted with care, and with the tools given the rich: the Merchant Authority, the Port Authority, the weight of guilds.

If you bought into the system—if you could afford to do so—and you played by the nebulous social rules of the patriciate, the system had a percentage in keeping you relatively safe. You just needed to understand the game being played. Sometimes—most times—it was like cards. You played the hand you were dealt. But if you were adroit and you could handle misdirection with aplomb, changes could be made. They weren't without risk, but Jester was insulated by House Terafin. He'd misplayed his hand once or twice in the early years, and he'd been burned—but Jay had protected him from the worst of it: he still had the House Name.

He believed he would always have that, and he learned from his mistakes. He spent more time with the bards. He learned how to give offense in a way that made it difficult for the offended man—or woman—to acknowledge it; he learned the subtleties of the interaction. He learned when power was theoretical, and when it was an act of consensus, a delicate balance of unspoken agreement.

People consented to be ruled. Rath had said that, time and again—but in Jester's youth, no consent had been asked, and none required. He'd had no desire to end up in a brothel, and little choice; he was physically weaker, he had no protectors, and he was therefore at the mercy of those who were stronger. He'd come, with observation and time, to understand that Rath had been right: people with money consented to be both bullied and ruled.

Ludgar's single nod to his seafaring past was the attendant who answered the door. He was not, precisely, a domicis; nor was he by any stretch of imagination a patrician steward. He was first mate to Ludgar's captain, a scarred, windburned man who was missing a tooth. He kept his mouth shut for the most part, and the tooth wasn't prominent, but it was obvious to Jester. As obvious was the fact that he was not comfortable in the clothing these duties on the Isle demanded; nor was his Weston as smooth and polished as Jester's had become.

Jester liked the man better for it. Servants were never addressed directly; Jester offered a casual nod and his most winning smile. "Ivarr."

The man grinned back, relaxing. In repose he looked infinitely more dangerous; he slid out of the confining element of patriciate servant, which suited him poorly. What was left was a man more comfortable with daggers on a heaving deck than cutlery at a dining table.

"Jester. It's been a while since you've been sent to fetch and carry."

"Not nearly long enough," Jester replied.

"You're here for himself?"

"I am. And as recompense for my service as messenger boy, I've taken the liberty of procuring one of The Terafin's finer vintages." He withdrew a bottle from the folds of his cloak and showed it to Ivarr; he didn't, however, hand it off.

Ivarr whistled. "Taken the liberty, have you?"

"Aye."

"They'll notice that one's gone missing, mark my words."

Jester shrugged. "It's early enough in the morning I thought I'd give Ludgar incentive to get out of bed. He was out late last night."

Ivarr frowned. "I don't know where you heard that, but you need a better grade of informant."

"I heard it from Scoville."

"Aye, well. Himself was *invited* to attend Patris Winhaven."

"So was I. His wine cellar's good, and he usually invites men and women of note, but the man is a pompous windbag."

Ivarr laughed. "That's kinder than what Ludgar says."

"I'm a smaller, weaker man," Jester replied, with the same easy grin, "and I have more need to watch my words—at least the words that will travel back to Winhaven."

"I'll tell himself you're here. Head on into the far room."

"The parlor."

"That's the one. I'll be by with glasses."

"Bring three."

Ivarr's frown could have soured milk. "I'm not invited to drink when the guests are of import."

"I'm an errand boy, as you've said, and I've no intention of letting Ludgar polish this off on his own. I suppose you *could* bring just one glass on the off chance Ludgar insists on patrician formality."

Ludgar arrived in the sitting room within the half hour. In that time, Jester conversed with Ivarr and glanced at the shelving upon which very prettily bound books sat. He very much doubted Ludgar had read them, but noted by their titles that many were of recent vintage. The furniture itself had seen a notable upgrade since Jester had last paid a visit; the glasses that Ludgar procured were likewise new.

None of this was suspicious in and of itself, but Haval's bland words had done their work; Jester was alert. Alert, however, meant Jester became far less formal; he chose to shed the subtleties that Ellerson had done his best to instill. The desire to please, to appeal, was at its strongest when danger was present; Jester worked with it, rather than against it. He eased himself into a chair, adopting a seated posture that Ivarr wouldn't notice and Ellerson would have disliked in the extreme.

"Jester," Ludgar said, as he entered the room. He cast a glance at Ivarr; Ivarr shrugged. Ludgar was at home in this house, and Ivarr did not consider Jester to be a threat.

Neither, if it came to that, did Ludgar, who not only took a seat, but dragged it across the carpet to bring it closer to both his visitor and his visitor's theoretically fine vintage.

Jester chuckled. "I'm aware I'm not the star of this show," he said, handing the bottle to Ludgar for the merchant's inspection.

Ludgar did not whistle, as Ivarr had. His eyes rounded slightly, and then narrowed far more noticeably. He set the bottle down on the table between them as if it were now the stakes for which a hand of cards might be played.

Which is why Ludgar was captain to Ivarr's first mate. He did not, on the other hand, demand that Ivarr retreat into invisibility. Jester noted that Ivarr didn't pull up a chair. He was watching both Ludgar and Jester as if he was trying to figure out the game now being played.

"I've been informed that you've been sent with a message?"

"I have." Jester shifted in his chair and removed the scroll case Finch used in moderately important correspondence. It was sealed; the seal had not been broken. Long years of practice had made clear just how tricky breaching such a seal was if one wanted to read a private message without either sender or receiver being aware of the intrusion.

It was not, however, impossible.

Ludgar's frown was a natural part of his face. "You don't know the contents of this message."

"It wasn't verbal, no. In general, Finch doesn't trust me with important verbal messages. She feels I get too distracted."

Ludgar lifted a brow in the direction of the unopened bottle. "Not without cause."

Jester offered an unrepentant smile. "I've never said she's a fool."

"She sent the wine?"

"Let's just say it came with her message."

Ludgar did smile, then. "The steward of the cellar's going to be blue in the face at the loss."

"It wasn't doing anyone any good in the cellars," Jester pointed out. "And The Terafin has never developed an aficionado's sense of wine."

"Meaning you think she won't care, is that it? She will, boy, when she sees the value this bottle has in her steward's books."

"I, however, have had the good sense to develop an appreciation for the finer things. May I?"

Ludgar grinned. "With my permission, yes."

"You've learned grace and the manners of a gentleman," Jester replied. He reached for the bottle and fished a corkscrew, with a suitable lack of elegance, out of a pocket. He did not appear to be watching Ludgar with any concern; he was.

Ludgar rolled the tube in his hands, inspected the seal with unflattering suspicion—of Jester, of course—and finally conceded to open the damn thing. Jester hadn't lied; he had no idea what the message itself contained. He could, with a lot of work, tamper with such cases, but it wasn't guaranteed to work smoothly. He'd considered doing it anyway, and just delivering the message in a more traditional envelope; Ludgar was unlikely to know.

He almost wished he'd taken that risk.

The scroll was compact; the message was not. Jester grimaced. He had his den leader's natural distrust of magic, and the case itself was clearly one of the expensive cases obtained from the Order of Knowledge. These cases were constructed in some nefarious way; they could hold a message of any size. The parchment was not confined to the case's shape. Why Finch had one—or possibly three, as all of the messages were in similarly sized and sealed cases—Jester didn't know. In general, he didn't interfere in the external business of members of the den.

He was not feeling highly charitable toward Haval as Ludgar began to read. Ivarr was studying his master's face with the same concern and the same suspicion that Jester himself felt, but Ivarr was not a man who had learned the finer art of hiding such suspicions. Ivarr, like Ludgar, depended on the fear—or, the kinder word, caution—engendered by his physical presence.

Jester was not, and had never been, large. That had been Arann's job. He'd never been dangerous; that had been Duster's, a role she'd owned in its entirety until her early death. That death had taught them all something, both about danger and the strange effects that loyalty—unexpected, unpredictable loyalty—could have.

He had never intended to have Duster's death. He did not intend to face it now. He poured three glasses, rising to offer one to Ivarr. Ivarr blinked and accepted the glass with a grimace; it was stemmed crystal, which was not Ivarr's ideal drinking cup.

Jester set a glass down to Ludgar's right; Ludgar reached for it without comment. Without, in Jester's opinion, any real thought, either. He was absorbed by whatever it was Finch had written, his eyes bright, narrow, and clear.

Jester felt conflicting things as his eyes grazed Ludgar's expression. Finch was seldom noticed, and when she was, she was treated as a slight or insignificant presence. He understood why, and understood that in part Finch chose how she was seen. So did Jester, but he couldn't choose invisibility; the red-orange shock of his hair had always denied him that. Yes, he could dye it; Rath had made that clear.

And he had, on a few occasions. But his hair and the pale skin that came with it were the two characteristics that people remembered. They implied personality. He had lived up to the expectations people brought to the hair.

Finch had lived down to the expectations with which she was generally regarded. But the Finch that those expectations presented couldn't write a letter to a man like Ludgar that commanded the whole of his undivided attention.

And Finch had clearly written just that letter. He felt something he might once have identified as pride, but with it, a darker thing: fear. If he had had any doubts about Haval's bald assertion, they crumbled. Someone had tried to assassinate Finch—and it was not, as Jester had hoped, the act of a fool. It was not, as the attack on Teller had been, meant as a warning to Jay.

It was Finch. He knew it with as much certainty as he knew anything. He drank as he watched; if Ludgar was a mean drunk, Jester was not. Jester could drink bards under the table, and had on one or two occasions; it was a costly endeavor.

Somewhere between sober and mean, however, was garrulous. Jester did not make the mistake of assuming that drink made Ludgar stupid; it didn't, more's the pity. But it sharpened his perceptions in a particular way. His instincts had been honed on ship decks and unruly streets; they had been refined with care. It was the care that he lost by slow degree. He knew who he could threaten or bully, and knew who to avoid. He recognized the fawning and the sycophantic for exactly what it was, but also knew the men—and women—who did not play the game.

Jester did not play the game. What Ludgar had, he didn't want. He wasn't interested in either fear or acclaim, and if he took center stage—and he did from time to time—he surrendered it with an easy, careless grace. If he chose to express either anger or contempt, he did it with humor, the way the bards did, and with a certain resignation, all of which implied he cared little.

Ludgar cared a great deal, but considered Jester well quit of the games men who jostled for power played. He drank, rereading the letter, with particular attention paid to the final page. When he was done, he handed it to Ivarr.

"Were you aware that your little mouse has assumed position in the Merchant Authority?" He paused and took a much slower sip of the wine that was dwindling in his very fine glass.

"She's had a position in the Merchant Authority for well over a decade," Jester replied.

"Not the position she now occupies," was the acid reply. "Ivarr, give me that."

Reading was not one of Ivarr's more notable abilities. It was not one of Jester's, either, but Ellerson's earliest harangues had guaranteed competence in at least Weston. Jester had picked up other languages as they seemed useful—and to be fair, they had not seemed useful until he had encountered the bards.

Ivarr frowned but complied. Ludgar then made show of reading the document again—or perhaps it wasn't show. "What does this mean to you?" He demanded, handing the papers to Jester.

Jester immediately lifted both hands. "Honestly, Ludgar, it looks too much like work." He didn't need to read the documents to see what so annoyed Ludgar; the final signature was Finch's, but the seal beside it was Jarven's. There was no second signature to indicate that Finch served in the capacity of secretary—a position that was very like babysitter, in Jester's opinion, if the baby in question were a lying, patrician bastard.

"Is this, or is this not, Finch ATerafin's signature?" The papers shook with each syllable Ludgar spit out. Jester carefully refilled his glass.

"It is, as you well know, although Jarven is perfectly capable of forgery."

This gave Ludgar brief pause. In the merchant's opinion, Jarven was capable of far worse than forgery. It was an opinion that aligned fairly well with Jester's own, not that he shared it often; it annoyed Finch. She never disagreed with a word Jester said; she merely questioned his need to say it.

Since he was relatively certain Jarven took no small amount of pride in his notoriety, he felt this unreasonable, but he lived with Finch, not Jarven. Haval had implied that one of the three people to whom Finch had sent these messages had a hand in the assassination attempt. While each of the three might consider Finch an impediment to their future plans of power within

House Terafin—and the Merchant Authority in particular—none of the three would benefit directly from her death. Or rather, none would benefit in the obvious, legal ways.

"I would've bet every coin I had that the girl's a mouse. She's caught between Lucille and Jarven. She hasn't had time—or reason—to develop a backbone; gods know she hasn't developed any character." Ludgar spit. "I should have paid more attention."

"You've not been negligent," Jester pointed out helpfully.

"Aye, I've sent her the odd trinket or bauble—but any idiot could see she's the way to Lucille's heart."

"I've not heard it said Lucille has one."

"You've not been listening, then. She understands debt if you're lucky enough to do her a favor, and there is no greater favor than watching out for her lame duck." He shook his head. "Women understand women. I should've paid heed to Verdian."

Jester whistled.

"Aye, and *there's* a woman."

Jester didn't disagree, but he found Verdian brittle and humorless. Then again, that could be said for most of the patrician women who sought to rule in the Empire, including the former Terafin. Lucille was a bright spot in an otherwise perfect and ultimately lifeless landscape. Jester treated her with deference and respect, but in Lucille's case, that involved high amounts of what she called cheek. She was not particularly shy about correcting misbehavior either.

"Verdian told you to be careful of Finch?" he asked, affecting confusion to perfection.

"She told me," Ludgar said, "that Finch has Jarven wrapped around her finger."

Jester choked on what he was drinking, which was a criminal waste of an expensive vintage—and quite possibly a shirt. "Jarven *ATerafin?*"

Ludgar laughed. It was a sour laugh. "The same."

"Has Verdian ever *met* Jarven?"

"Many, many times, I assure you. And before you laugh again, this," he said, jabbing the air with Finch's written pages, "makes fools of the both of us."

Jester sighed and lowered a hand. "Because I respect you, I'm willing to look at missives from the Merchant Authority. I wouldn't do this for just anyone."

Ivarr snorted as Ludgar handed Jester the letter.

Jester read it. He read it quickly, with an air of mild boredom. "Does this make any sense to you?" he asked, on page two.

"Yes." Ludgar's glass was almost empty. Jester considered refilling it, but decided against; Ludgar was on the edge. "If you're referring to the eastern shipping treaty, it's not official; Jarven's been working on it for months behind his closed doors."

"Finch is taking control of those negotiations."

"Aye, I'd noticed."

Jester's brows rose. He could have controlled his expression, but it suited the moment and he let it go. He'd discovered over the past decade that the best lies were those that only barely strayed from the truth. Lies were a game; they required planning, forethought, and an unerring ability to keep score, to remember which hand he'd showed to which player.

As he was lazy, he seldom bothered.

Ludgar lied frequently, but not with any finesse, and he did so for one of two reasons. The first, and in Jester's opinion the least defensible, involved his sense of his own import; he had an ego that needed to be massaged from time to time. He exaggerated his successes and belittled his failures.

Fair enough; it was the reason most people lied, in the end. They wanted to appear to be something they weren't.

The second, however, was also common. He was a man whose focus was always on the pinnacle, and he had no qualms about pushing you off the mountain if you happened to be a step or two ahead of him. For that reason, he was wary of those who were too close to his back. A smart man trusted nothing that fell out of Ludgar's mouth, especially not his promises.

But a smart man trusted nothing that fell out of anyone's. In Jester's opinion, given Ludgar's particular views, he was fairly certain that the Terafin merchant was not in any way responsible for the attempt on Finch's life. Finch was a mouse. He might step on her, but she would never be his primary target.

Not until and unless someone made it very worth his while.

Finch, he thought, as he finished the letter. *What in the hells are you doing?* There was no way to pass this off as the result of awkwardness or nervousness. She made it clear—politely, to be sure—that as of the moment of receipt of this missive, she was in charge of almost three-quarters of the shipping operations that Ludgar oversaw. She invited him to visit her office in the Merchant Authority in five days, but would of course understand if the date, given short notice, was not convenient.

She expected a convenient date to be arranged within two weeks.

Jester swallowed. Not even Lucille could get away with writing a letter like this. There was only one person who could.

"Finch didn't write this," he said, voice flat.

He looked up; he was not surprised to see that Ludgar, cheeks reddened by alcohol and anger, was watching him closely.

"You don't think so?"

"Ludgar, I live with Finch. I know her. Finch did not write this letter."

"Give it here," the merchant said, and Jester complied. He read it with more care, his expression shifting as he reconsidered what had been written. "She's claimed authority and stature commensurate with Jarven's."

"Yes, I noted that. Commensurate. Not superior. Jarven is still in charge of the Merchant Authority; there's no way Finch would have penned this letter without Jarven standing over her shoulder. And drinking tea," he added with a grimace.

"And how am I to answer the little mouse?"

"Pretend she's Jarven, and answer it the way you would if it were Jarven's signature at the end of the document."

Ludgar sobered, literally. "It's been full-on two decades since Jarven sent a missive like this one," he finally said. "But two decades ago wasn't the first time he'd done it. There are men who walked into his office—rumor has it—that failed to walk out. I'm not sure I wouldn't prefer to deal with your mouse." He swore. "But this is Jarven's style—his old style."

Jester nodded. He had mixed feelings about the proclamation. What he had said to Ludgar made perfect sense. It was, in fact, the only possible explanation in Ludgar's mind. The problem with perfect sense in this case was that Jester couldn't quite make himself believe it.

He was certain that Jarven had had a hand in drafting the letter. There were turns of phrase littered throughout its long and formal paragraphs that were uniquely his. But they were turns of phrase that Finch had absorbed over the years. Jester wanted out of this parlor and out of this house; he wanted to head straight to the Merchant Authority and ask Finch what in the hells she thought she was doing.

Instead, he considered the scrolls that had yet to be delivered, because he knew what she thought she was doing: she was building a base from which she could consolidate a regency that none of them truly wanted. She was doing it because she was the only member of the den who *could*.

But this—this was Jarven's game, not Finch's. She wasn't Jarven, and *Kalliaris* smile, she would never become him. If she'd already survived one assassination attempt, she'd been lucky. Luck was a mug's game. She was—with three letters—putting herself in line for a dozen such attempts, this time with a convenient target above her heart.

Why? Why take this approach?

It had to be Jarven. It couldn't be Lucille. Out loud he said, "What does Jarven want?"

"That's the question," Ludgar replied. He looked uneasy. "He's all but retired. He hasn't played politics with this heavy a hand since—" He shook his head. "If I'd had half an idea what you carried in your hands, I'd've told Ivarr to throw you out. I've half a mind to tell him to throw you out anyway."

Jester rose, laughing. "I know when I've outstayed my welcome. But don't waste the wine. I'm not carrying it back with me."

"Any others you're playing messenger boy for today?"

"Two," Jester told him, as he headed to the door.

"I take it back. The wine's not finished. Come back and tell me who they are."

Jester was more than willing to comply. Ludgar's reactions would give him useful information, and he felt he now needed that information.

The second merchant Jester was to visit that day was Ruby, also ATerafin. Rumor had it that she'd traveled the Southern caravan routes, trading silk, spices, and pearls for the gems in the two Terafin mines. If rumors were true, her days on the open road were well behind her; she left them for the younger and hungrier. She was not Lucille, but she hadn't been poured into Verdian's mold either; she occupied a terrain between the two.

She had a sense of humor, but there was enough anger and bitterness beneath her words that her company wasn't generally considered enjoyable. She was therefore frequently without company, which didn't improve her demeanor. Drinking did not noticeably improve it either, but it certainly sharpened her tongue; if Jester was willing to take the risk of drinking with Ludgar, he was not willing to do so with Ruby.

He didn't dislike the older woman, but like most of the sensible world, didn't enjoy her company. Ruby was in charge of a large portion of Terafin's Southern trade routes. Popularity, however, had little to do with her position; she was tolerated—even appreciated, at a great enough distance—for her competence. She could stand toe-to-toe with Haerrad without blinking or stepping back.

Her routes had dwindled to a trickle during the war that had just concluded, and the roads, while in theory clear, had seen the usual rise in banditry that often followed war; this had diminished her theoretical importance to the economic vitality of the House. On the other hand, no one doubted her nadir would end.

Ludgar's commercial ventures had been likewise constrained, but he had—

in his own words—diversified, and there was no war with the northern province of Arrend. The winters in Arrend, however, were harsh and ships were only now venturing out of port.

"Be wary of Ruby," Ludgar told Jester as he escorted him to the door. "She's got a tongue like a razor, but it's not the only thing about her that's sharp. She's survived things that most of my men wouldn't."

Jester was honestly surprised, and took no trouble to hide it. "Ruby ATerafin? Are we speaking of the same woman?"

"You can laugh, boy. You're young. She's one of the very few woman who can put a scare into Ivarr."

Ivarr did not seem pleased by this observation, but he didn't deny it, a fact Jester found significant.

"I'd pay real gold to get a glimpse of the letter your Finch has written to Ruby," he added, with a half-smile.

"So would I," Jester replied, half in earnest. "But she clearly meant the letters to be read by their recipients first, and it's not worth my position to break those seals." He strongly considered doing so anyway—or one better, failing to deliver the message at all. The visit with Ludgar had not gone to plan—and to be fair, he'd arrived entirely without one, as he did on most visits. Delivering the next two missives seem guaranteed to worsen the stand Finch appeared to be taking.

Jester generally affected boredom when presented with news about House Affairs. He listened with more interest to Carver's gossip than he did to Finch's or Teller's, because Carver spoke about the men and women who actually kept the House running, and Jester had no complaints with those who had chosen a life of service.

The single exception to that was Ellerson. And there it was again: the old domicis' name.

Jester generally lived without hope; hope led to disappointment and almost inevitably to despair. Neither were states Jester particularly enjoyed, and he avoided them by stamping them out at the root.

He'd done this one before. He'd sat, back to wall in the cramped, tiny apartment they'd once called home, listening for the floorboards in the hall beyond the den's closed door. Listening for the familiar creak that belonged to one of the den who'd gone missing. He'd watched Arann practically disintegrate. He'd even watched Duster—Duster who treated Lefty with open contempt when she could be bothered to speak to him at all—tense, waiting in the same hope, and the same dread, as the rest of them.

She couldn't acknowledge it, of course. Because she couldn't, she'd snapped at the den when they spoke openly about Lefty or Fisher. She'd isolated herself as if isolation was her highest goal.

And she'd died.

She'd died for a group of people she kept at arm's length. When he died, if he found her waiting at the bridge, Jester intended to ask her why. He closed his eyes and listened to the rumble of wheels as the carriage rolled across a different bridge. He did not want to be here, where fear of death—or loss—was predominant.

But he knew, now, that Ellerson was den. Because the emptiness and the absence of his oh-so-critical breathing was a shadow that he couldn't quite escape.

Carver was alive, somewhere. Carver, like Ellerson, was Jay's problem. But he knew Jay. If there was any way she could find Carver and bring him safely home, she would do it. She hadn't said a word about Ellerson. She didn't know what had happened to the old man.

She didn't know yet what had happened to Carver.

Ruby seemed like a better topic for thought, and he tried, but he had little success until the carriage pulled up the drive to her manor. Ruby's home was far grander than Ludgar's, and it had actual grounds, the advantage of living in the hundred holdings, albeit the wealthier ones. The grounds were not of the same quality as Terafin's, but Jester thought it was because their master didn't really care about the grounds themselves, just the fact of them.

Jester, disembarking, cast a brief glance at the trees and the flower beds. He had learned, with time, to appreciate the difference in quality without in any way developing a desire to own such land himself. He understood that for Ruby, this existed as a visible symbol of her status within the House—and outside of it, as well. She didn't have Ludgar's size; she didn't have the birth connections of Haerrad.

She didn't need them. But she wasn't fool enough to assume they were irrelevant.

Her servants were a cut above Ludgar's; they did not fraternize with guests—or in this case, elevated messengers. Nor did Jester attempt to draw them out. He understood their role; they understood as much of his as they were willing to. They could—and probably had—serve in other manors of note.

Jester therefore told the man who answered the door that he had been sent by Finch ATerafin to deliver a message of some import to his master; the man immediately led Jester to a sitting room, bowed, and left.

This room was much like the parlor Ivarr disdained; it was heavily decorated with books, although some of them, to Jester's eye, had been read. All but a handful were in Weston; the handful were written in Torra. No Old Weston, no other unintelligible languages, graced the spines of these volumes.

He withdrew the scroll case from his satchel and waited; he touched nothing, moved nothing, and went nowhere. Ruby's sense of humor did not encompass acts of aggression—and snooping was an act of unpardonable aggression unless she happened to be the one doing it, in which case, it was just business and nothing personal.

Ruby never forgot a slight.

It was rumored that she never forgot a favor, either—but Jester had seen precious little evidence of that; people did not, in Ruby's opinion, do favors for her. Any small gift—such as the purloined vintage Jester had offered to Ludgar—was treated as proof that you were sucking up to her. It was suspicious, not gracious.

Jester preferred to be above—or perhaps in this case, beneath—suspicion. He brought nothing but the message.

The message, however, drew Ruby ATerafin to the sitting room alarmingly quickly. She was not a woman who liked to be rushed by anyone who was not obviously superior to her in position; if The Terafin called her, she would of course jump through hoops.

Jester grimaced. The *previous* Terafin. Jay had locked horns with Ruby on one or two occasions during her tenure as a member of the House Council, and Ruby's respect for The Terafin—she made clear—was for the title, not the person who, by luck, currently inhabited it.

She had certainly not lined up behind Jay's banner when Jay had been in the South. She had, on the other hand, made offers of support to three of the four contenders. She wanted the Merchant Authority. She didn't want it enough to personally attempt to depose Jarven.

No one wanted it that much. Jester considered this fact far more significant than Finch did.

"They're all afraid of Lucille," she'd told him, grinning.

"Do you even believe that?" he'd asked.

She laughed, and signed *truce* before they could start an argument in earnest.

Jester rose the moment Ruby had crossed the threshold. He didn't bow; she was not, in theory, his superior, and she considered unnecessary gestures suspect. He did incline his head in the controlled nod that she offered first.

"You've a message for me?"

He handed her the scroll case.

"And she didn't choose to send it through the usual channels."

Demonstrably not. Jester kept the thought to himself.

"Did she send it through the Merchant Authority?"

"I'm not retained by the Merchant Authority," he replied, keeping his voice both respectful and neutral. He chose to slouch slightly, diminishing the advantage of height; Ruby was surprisingly short, an impression lost pretty much the instant she opened her mouth.

"Do you know what she's written?"

"I'm not retained by the Merchant Authority, and I'm not authorized to be part of its dealings. I have no idea what she wrote; I was asked to deliver the message today. You know as much as I do," he added, when she failed to take the scroll from his extended hand. "But you have the opportunity to alleviate your curiosity in a manner that is forbidden me."

She frowned.

"You can take it," he continued, "and open it."

He was honestly surprised at her reluctance; she'd appeared all but instantly, which implied a certain eagerness. Or fear. He almost pointed out that he was handling the case itself, without gloves or any other form of protection, and he had not incidentally dropped dead.

That level of sarcasm with Ruby could produce unfortunate results, but he found it difficult, as the minutes wore on, to hold it in. She finally took the case, handling it with enough care that she justified Jester's silent sarcasm.

As this was exactly the type of social debacle he'd been burned by in his early introduction to patriciate society, he avoided it now. But he watched as she walked to a side table beneath the very generous windows. She set it down in the center of the bare, wooden surface. Jester frowned briefly. The table had escaped his notice; there was nothing about it to call it to his attention.

And that should have been clue enough. Ruby generally chose deliberate ostentation; if she chose to have something so sparse and plain in a room, it was meant to serve a different purpose.

The tabletop began to glow. Interesting.

"The scroll case is magical," he told the Terafin merchant, his tone carefully neutral. "The message is meant to be both private and protected."

She grimaced, still watching the table's surface. After a pause of two silent minutes, she exhaled and lifted the case. Ruby was not generally considered paranoid; she was considered both canny and cautious, although she frequently chose to play a rougher game.

Clearly, she expected one now. From Finch.

His anger at Jarven grew edges; he saw the old man's hand in the letter Finch had penned to Ludgar; he saw the old man's shadow in Ruby's reaction to a letter she had not yet read.

He retreated while Ruby, scroll case gripped so tightly it was a wonder it wasn't crushed, magic notwithstanding, took a chair. She took, by habit, the finest chair in the room; not for Ruby the false modesty of hospitality. If you were on her turf, you acknowledged it, and you played by her rules.

Jester was ATerafin, but he labored under no illusions; his value to the House could not in any way compare to hers. Ruby did not labor under any illusions either; she didn't care whether or not Jester was impressed. He was irrelevant.

The seal cracked cleanly and without visible magical acknowledgment; were it not for the contents—documents too large in dimension to suit un-enchanted containers—the magic would go undetected. Jester glanced at the small, plain table.

"No," Ruby said, as she unfurled the letter. "The table's not new. It's old. I acquired it when its previous owner felt it wise to leave the Empire with very little warning. He needed liquid cash. I underpaid," she added, glaring over the top of a letter she had not apparently started to read. "The best bargains are the unexpected ones that come in the wake of someone else's crises."

Her steward appeared in the door, trailing two parlor maids in smart, stiff uniforms; they carried trays. If Ruby considered most hospitality a trial, her social graces were not so poor that she would take a light meal—for that's what it was—without offering the same to a guest.

Given the extremely suspicious way she handled the scroll case, Jester wasn't certain that he could trust the food. Apparently, neither was Ruby, given that one of the parlor maids appeared to test the food before she ate it. Jester made a mental note to ask Carver about servant rumors between the two houses and froze.

Ruby did not appear to notice; she had settled into the fine art of dropping crumbs on extremely expensive parchment. She wasn't Ludgar; her expression, while reading, was controlled. Either that, or she wasn't surprised by the contents of the missive the way Ludgar had been.

Her lips pursed as she reached the end of the letter, presumably signed and sealed in the same fashion Ludgar's had been. He glanced at the shelf to her right, stifling a yawn.

"You're never going to get anywhere with an attitude like that," Ruby snapped.

"So I've been told by many people. What those same people have failed to tell me is where exactly anywhere is, and why I should want to go there."

"This," Ruby said, lifting the letter, "is your anywhere."

He had no need to feign his distaste, and felt it advantageous not to hide it. "The Merchant Authority? How many years have you known me?"

"Too many," was her curt reply.

"If I had your success without your life, I'd consider it. But caravan travel gives me hives, and I don't particularly look forward to facing bandits, either. That, and my Torra is atrocious. It's true that the Merchant Authority by-passes both the travel and the obvious bandits—but it comes with Jarven, which I'm fairly certain is worse."

Ruby gave a very unladylike snort, but she nodded. "Aye, he's worse. Are you to wait for a reply?"

Jester didn't particularly fancy carrying a reply that Ruby had any time to prepare; not given the obvious precautions she was taking. She learned from experience, and what she learned was not always safe for bystanders and casual civilians. "Not that I'm aware of. If I'm wrong, I'll probably be back."

She didn't ask him what Finch's game was. Ruby was clearly certain that she understood it; she evinced no surprise at anything the letter contained. "You'll want to pass an informal message along to Finch," she said, as she rose.

I really won't, he thought, but waited.

"Tell her that I'm impressed. Not surprised, mind, but impressed. I'd like to know just how much she thinks she's learned from Jarven over the years. He's not what he once was," she added, "but he's always been canny. Haerrad won't like this move of hers."

"I wasn't sent to deliver a message to Haerrad."

"You won't have to. I'll see you out."

Jester was grim and silent in the carriage on the way to his third, and final, recipient. He could be; the carriage was empty. He was not being observed, and he faced no expectations other than his own.

He wanted a drink. Or ten. The visit with Ludgar had left him uneasy. The visit with Ruby had pushed him over the edge into fear. Ruby had expected some move from the Merchant Authority. Given her precautions, she had reasons to believe that move might be deadly.

No, he thought, shifting to look out the window. She had expected a move from Finch. Nothing he could have said or done would minimize the truth. Ludgar didn't particularly want to believe someone as unimpressive as Finch was capable of flexing political muscles; it had not been difficult to convince him that she hadn't.

Ruby couldn't be moved in the same way. Jester regretted having avoided her so assiduously in the past. Had he not, he might have been able to influence her opinion.

Ah well. He was not yet done for the day. James Varson, the third man he had been sent to see was not ATerafin. He worked under the auspices of the Merchants' Guild, which was, in theory, neutral. Jester understood the limits of theory. The Merchants' Guild was ruled by a governing body, and the governing body was of course composed of representatives from those families who were both moneyed and old.

James Varson was not a direct descendant of any of those families. His roots were not as poor or common as Jester's or any other member of the den, but his family's wealth was relatively recent. They did not own land on the Isle; they didn't own a lease there, either. James' uncle owned a storefront in the Common, not the High Market. But the store, like Haval's, was prosperous. Unlike Haval's, it did not cater almost entirely to people who would otherwise shop exclusively in the High Market; James' uncle was a cobbler.

Varson was not a man Jester had much social contact with; although he was younger, he was otherwise as much fun as Barston. The only thing that caused the man to show any genuine enthusiasm was music, which is why Jester knew him at all. The bards tolerated him, and one or two appeared to actually enjoy the man's company, although the conversation in their presence took a turn for the technical.

He did not, to Jester's mind, join in the high-stakes power politics that divided the merchant Houses from the common merchants who, like anyone else in the city, were simply trying to make a living. He was therefore curious about both Finch's message and James' possible reactions to it. Unlike Ruby or Ludgar, Finch had no authority over James; an argument could be made that the inverse was true. Terafin had a House member serving as part of the governing council of the Merchant Authority, but Finch did not fill that role.

Jarven did. He did not, however, do so because he was ATerafin; only three of The Ten had managed to gain such a seat. He had earned his place on the council at about the same time he had been adopted into Terafin; Jester did not think this coincidental. The Merchant Authority could in theory ask Jarven to resign, but as the Merchant Authority was composed of men and women who had had various dealings with Jarven over the years, it was likely that no one could be found who was willing to publicly make that demand; privately wouldn't cut it.

Jester entered the Merchant Authority, passing between the Authority guards, who failed to notice his existence. Failure in this case was good; if they did notice someone, it usually boded ill for their chances of entry. He passed the throng of merchants and businessmen who were lined up at the open wickets, and headed toward the offices located to the right.

The guards who fronted the open doors to the offices were less generous in their appraisal of those who approached than the guards on the exterior of the building. It was in these offices that merchants of note, wealth, or significant power bypassed the wickets and the lines which were mandatory for everyone else. For many of those men and women, entrance into the offices was a distant dream, but the enterprising often tried anyway.

Even the lesser members of The Ten were expected to stop and state their business; Jester therefore appeared to be both diffident and slightly bored. Business as usual. He had no reason to lie.

They demanded some proof that he was, in fact, ATerafin, and when he lifted the ring, demanded to see the item being delivered. This was not business as usual. Jester seldom chose outrage when dealing with guards, and settled on confusion instead, opening up his expression slightly to convey mild hurt.

He did remove the scroll case from his satchel; he showed it to the guards but did not allow it to leave his hands. To his surprise—genuine surprise—they demanded that he open it.

"My apologies to the Merchant Authority," he replied, "but the message is to be delivered, in person, to James Varson. It is not to be opened or read by any save James Varson. If you are concerned about its contents, you may make your concerns clear to Jarven ATerafin."

Silence.

"I will take my leave."

"Wait," the guard on the left said. "You said Jarven?"

"I did. You'll note the seal that binds the case is his." He hesitated, and then slid into a less polished variant of Weston. "Look, it's not worth my job to crack this seal. If you're worried, one of you can accompany both the case—and me—to Varson's office. If you're unwilling to do that much, I'll take it back and tell Jarven to deliver it in person." He had now left the narrow and inconvenient path of truth, but again, didn't stray far. He knew that Finch would be ill-pleased, and that Lucille would be enraged. He doubted that Jarven would be anything but amused.

The guards, however, did not.

They shared a significant glance; it was broken when the older of the two exhaled. "Things have been dicey today," he said, adopting the same tone that Jester had. "It's not you. It's not your delivery. You said you're *Jester* ATerafin?"

"I didn't choose the name."

"And Terafin didn't demand that you change it?"

"No. Can they do that?"

The guard shook his head. "Go in." He paused briefly, and added, "You're probably going to be stopped once more. Varson's office is more or less un-damaged; he doesn't seem to have been one of the targets."

Jester blinked. "Targets? Was there some sort of—"

"Yes."

"I think I'll pass."

"It's your job."

"Yes. But I like my head to be attached to the rest of me; if I lose this job, and I'm still breathing, I can find another one." He made great show of re-luctance; it was only partly feigned. The building was not on fire. Jester had assumed that some difficulty with individual members had occurred, causing a security shutdown while it was sorted.

The fact that Varson's office was "more or less undamaged," however, changed that. "When you say Varson's office—"

"You'll see. Are you going to go in or not?"

Chapter Three

JESTER REALIZED HE KNEW lamentably little about Haval Arwood. He intended to remedy that as swiftly as possible. He felt a grudging admiration for the tailor, and buried it beneath resentment. There was no way that Haval could have known that something untoward was to occur in the Merchant Authority, but Jester had no doubt, as he walked past the guards, that *this* was the reason Haval had chosen to make his approach today.

There were more guards in the hall than there had been on the open floors. They were grim and harried; this was clearly not the job they'd anticipated when they'd rolled out of bed this morning.

Forewarned, he answered questions for every few yards of progress; the questions were curt, but stopped short of the ridiculous demand that Jester himself break the seal of the scroll he now visibly carried by hand. His name appeared to ease the suspicion of the guards on the interior, just as it had done the guards on the exterior. Jester was not a name one chose if one wished to remain invisible. He had once considered a change of name; defiance and a certain resentment of patrician attitude had hardened his desire to hold on to it. It seldom came in useful, but when it did, it was a blessing.

He turned a corner to the left and stopped walking.

Fully two of the offices were no longer functional, at a conservative guess. The doors that had previously indicated their presence had been shattered; splinters and long boards had imbedded themselves into the opposite walls.

He didn't ask what had happened to the occupants of the offices, but better understood the guards' offhand comment. James Varson was not a credible target; his position was relatively minor. Or it had been. At least one of the ruined offices belonged to the man to whom Varson reported.

Jester considered retreating; any reaction Varson had to Finch's letter would pale into insignificance this afternoon. But he'd just talked his way through four sets of guards, and cold feet at this point would arouse entirely unjustified suspicion.

There were two guards at Varson's doors, but the exterior room, in size and accoutrements similar to the Terafin offices in the Authority building, was a vast, empty cavern. The desk the secretary usually sheltered behind was unoccupied; the office looked deserted.

But the door to at least one of the rooms was ajar. Jester cleared his throat loudly; in the current state of the office, this was just shy of shouting.

A familiar man peered out through the open door. The dark circles under his eyes implied hangover or lack of sleep; on closer inspection, it appeared to be dirt or soot. If Varson was surprised to see Jester, it didn't show; he seemed merely weary.

"May I help you?" he asked, as if he had spent years sitting in the secretarial chair. "I'm afraid we're understaffed at the moment." James Varson had never been one to exaggerate.

"I can imagine," Jester replied gravely. "And I wouldn't have the effrontery to be here if I'd had word before I arrived in the Authority building."

"The council made the decision to keep the offices running in a minimal fashion," Varson replied, in as neutral a tone as a disgusted man could muster. He ran hands through his dark hair; Jester could see splinters in its strands. "You don't have an appointment, do you?"

"No. If it were my appointment, I would cancel it now, with groveling apologies all round."

That evoked a smile from Varson, who did not appear to recognize Jester.

"I was sent to deliver a message." Jester held out the case he had taken out of his satchel for the inspection of multiple guards, and at last surrendered it. "It was handed to me before the Merchant Authority opened for business; I'm certain it could have waited, otherwise."

James Varson took the scroll case and turned it around so that the seal faced him directly, and Jester lost that certainty. He was not, as Ludgar had been, suspicious; he was not, as Ruby had been, displeased but expectant. He looked up at the messenger and said, "I'm certain it wouldn't." He didn't open the case. Instead, he handed it back to Jester. "Return this to Finch."

When Jester failed to move, James said, "I know what it contains, and I would like it to be safe, for the moment. Our guards are now working overtime, but some of the protections that are normally functional within the interior offices have been destroyed. We've lost a number of important portfolios, and a number of equally important trade agreements.

"I assume no like tragedy has yet affected the Terafin offices."

"I haven't been back to the Terafin offices," Jester replied. "Were other branches of the building affected in the same way?"

James Varson hesitated, and then said, "Yes. Three. The most notable damage has been in the Authority council's offices, but we are not the only occupants to suffer losses."

Jester hesitated and then said, "Come back to the Terafin offices with me. The guards aren't letting anyone through."

"You're here."

"Yes, but I threatened them with Jarven."

Varson grimaced, a sign that he was indeed under stress. "I fail to see why such a threat would be effective."

"He only plays at being harmless and doddering."

"Yes," James agreed, as if Jester's observation was entirely beside the point. "I understand that. But he's unlikely to come here and rate the guards. He has some dignity."

"He might send Lucille?"

"That would be a more believable threat, but given events today, Lucille's more likely to chew you out for being petty during a crisis."

Jester grinned; James was, of course, completely correct. "Fine. Your guards are gullible. Or perceptive. I did have a message to deliver to you, and it was sent by Finch ATerafin. I think you should come back to the office with me."

"You're not employed by the Terafin arm of the Merchant Authority, that I'm aware of."

"I'm not—but after today's work, I fully intend to have a few words with Finch before I head back to a warm bed and a few drinks."

James hesitated. "I'm not certain it would be wise," he finally said. "But it is almost impossible to have a meeting of any import in the usual offices. Very well. I will return the message to Finch myself, if you'll wait."

The guards looked marginally relieved when James Varson and Jester ATerafin left the offices together; James was clearly considered above suspicion. It was a good bet, in Jester's books; Varson was the kind of man you wanted working for you. He was definitely not the man you wanted as a drinking companion, and as most of Jester's interactions with the moneyed were social, he had rarely given Varson more than an irritable stray thought.

He repented of that. Although Varson, in the clearer light of the Authority's public great room, was covered in fine soot and dusted in splinters, his bearing had not changed. He was perhaps a touch paler, but it was hard to tell, given the gray that had settled on his skin and his clothing.

Word had clearly traveled; there were four guards in Terafin tabards posted at the outer doors. Jester recognized two of them by name, but given his companion, offered only a slight nod. They stopped Varson, as expected, and asked his business, but it was cursory; they didn't give him the same runaround the Authority guards had given Jester.

Lucille was behind her bastion of a desk. Unlike Varson, she was clearly pale and clearly upset, but she rose as the doors opened, and her brow crinkled in open confusion. "James?"

"I'm sorry, Lucille," he said, in a genuinely apologetic tone of voice, "but I don't have an actual appointment. I hoped to have a few words with Finch."

"And Jarven," Jester added.

Lucille frowned. "Is Jester working for you now?"

James looked slightly shocked. "No."

"Then why are you keeping his company?"

"He was sent to deliver a message from Finch, and unfortunately, the office is not in a position to properly deal with it at the moment."

"No, of course it isn't. You're all right?"

"I am, yes. So is Vivi. Charlie wasn't as lucky. He was in the magister's office when the attack occurred."

"And the magister?"

Varson's expression shuttered. "Healers have been summoned."

Given the wreck of the office, Jester would be surprised if there was enough left for a healer to work with. He kept this to himself as Lucille came around the desk, abandoning the ledger of official appointments that otherwise ruled the office. "She's speaking with someone now, but I'm certain she'd like at least a glimpse of you. You'll take tea?"

"Honestly, Lucille, I don't think I have the stomach for refreshments today."

The first, and most obvious, thing that Jester noted was that Lucille did not go to Finch's office; she went directly for Jarven. She knocked at the doors, but not in the usual thunderous way she did when knocking wasn't so much a courtesy as an early warning. She entered the office and returned.

"Finch will see you now," she told James. "Give her a moment to see her visitor out."

Her visitor was a large, round bear of a man with a distinctly Northern style of hair. He didn't looked pleased, but there seemed to be no room for pleasure in the chiseled lines of his face. He did not, however, storm out in a huff, and he offered Finch the Northern equivalent of a bow before he exited the office proper.

Finch, however, had turned to James. She held out both hands, and he placed his, briefly, in them. "I'm so grateful you came," she said, in a voice that would have been at home in the West Wing. "I've been huddled in my office worried sick."

His hands tightened. "Vivi went home, but she's fine."

Finch paled. "Charlie?"

James Varson closed his eyes, and Finch's eyes rounded. She turned to Lucille as Lucille headed into the back room. "I don't think he'll have much appetite," she told the older woman, "not for food, but if you could—"

"Already done, dear." To James she added, "Go in and sit down; it's likely the only peace you'll have for the next week."

Finch released his hands, slid an arm through his, and gently guided him toward Jarven's office. She glanced once at Jester, and nodded emphatically toward those doors; he moved to open them. She lifted a hand in swift densign; he almost missed it. *Follow.*

Since curiosity was a character flaw, he did.

As it was Jarven's office, the old man's presence was no surprise, if no delight; the second desk in the office, however, almost made Jester miss a step. Jarven smiled beatifically.

"It's a good desk," he said, with a fond smile at Finch. "I chose it myself."

"It is," James replied, assuming Jarven spoke to him. Frowning, he added, "It's almost exactly like yours."

"It is exactly like mine," Jarven agreeably said. "Finch is in all ways indispensable, but a word to the wise: she is not to be left in charge of furnishing her own office. She prefers the drab and the mundane, and none of my efforts to change this have borne fruit. Come, James, join us. We meant to celebrate Finch's promotion, but given the events today, are forced to let it pass without fuss."

James nodded and took the chair Finch all but pushed him into. Jester, watching the three, felt like an outsider. He generally did, but this was unwelcome, because at the center of this group was Finch.

"You were right," James said, laying both of his arms against the cushioned rests and sinking into the chair.

"That does happen from time to time," Jarven replied. The door opened; Lucille came in bearing a heavy tray. A teapot sat at its center, which made Jester grimace; a bottle of something entirely more welcome sat by its side. There were both teacups and cut crystal glasses, and Lucille brought the tray to Jarven's desk.

To what Jester assumed was Jarven's desk. He cast a furtive glance at Finch, but she was watching Varson with genuine—and obvious—concern. If Lucille mothered, she was a harsh and disciplinary parent; Finch was softer and more soothing. Jarven watched as well, but spared a glance for Jester; he was amused by Jester's discomfiture.

"When you're wrong, ATerafin," James replied, "one always has to look at the advantage you accrue from *being* wrong."

Jarven's eyes crinkled as his lips folded into their familiar, paternal smile. It was an expression Jester disliked. "I was wrong about you," he offered. "The advantage to me in that?"

James look confused.

"Jarven," Finch said, in a voice that sounded surprisingly similar to Lucille's. "I'm not sure today is the right day for your teasing."

It irked. A day that included Jarven was always difficult; Haval had compounded it. In the presence of these two old men, Jester felt young and incompetent, a sensation he did not enjoy.

Sharing a title with Jarven would have been unthinkable two weeks ago. Sharing power with Jarven remained, to Jester's mind, impossible. Jarven was aware of this; the desk was an extreme way of staking Finch's claim. It was not junior to his; it was not shabbier or less expensive. The office had been rearranged so that the desks were side by side, but tilted slightly toward the window so that they almost faced each other on a slant. The shelving remained flush against the wall; Jester suspected that Jarven's office was the same magical fortress that Teller's was.

There was nothing to mark Finch as junior besides the obvious: her demeanor and her age. Even her clothing, to Jester's eye, was sharper, the colors more saturated. Her hair was drawn up in the netting favored by the fashionable, and he saw a glitter of diamond in it.

Yet she looked like Finch, to Jester. A mouse in wolf's clothing. And he knew, as of today, that she wasn't. That he would have to look more carefully, and see more clearly. No mouse, no matter how precious, could occupy the desk she now occupied. No mouse could survive Jarven, and Finch had done more than that.

Jarven was, as rumor oft suggested, fond of Finch. Finch adored Jarven.

Adoration in either case had not dimmed the clarity of their perception; it had only blinkered Jester's. If he were to be honest, and he seldom bothered, it was this fact that he found most annoying. He *lived* with Finch, and had failed to see in her what Jarven had seen.

But he saw it now. Not in Finch, but in the reactions of those around her. In Ludgar. In Ruby. And yes, in the drab and upright James Varson, whose entrance into an office that was famous for the occupant of its single desk showed no sign of surprise at all. Which, given Varson, meant he wasn't.

Yet Finch showed no signs of the cool poise that defined Verdian, no signs of the militant suspicion that defined Ruby, and no signs at all of the draconian territoriality that defined Lucille. She did not take the seat behind her desk, as Jarven had, but instead, had pulled up a chair so she could sit a comfortable distance from Varson, to whom she was speaking in the softest of tones. She was genuinely concerned for him.

"I am so sorry I sent the documents today," Finch was saying. "I had no idea, when the morning began, that events would play out this way."

"You had no idea that they would play out *today*," Varson corrected her— but gently. "You did try to warn me. The documents in this scroll case are the documents that support your suspicions?"

"They're the most critical ones," Finch replied. "I have a few others, but they're much grayer; they need to be seen in context."

"Will you retain them?"

"Will you not open the case and read them for yourself? I have experience only with Terafin concerns; yours is the broader knowledge and experience."

"I forget sometimes that you've only worked within the Terafin merchant arm." He nodded in Jarven's direction. "But Jarven's formative experiences were much more general. He must have offered you his opinion on your findings."

"I have indeed," Jarven told Varson as he lifted a cup of steaming tea. "But she feels that I am somehow incapable of being entirely objective. Me."

"You are incapable of being disinterested," Varson replied. He took the drink Finch now handed him; it was not tea. "But you are entirely capable of being objective."

"And perhaps young Finch will take your word for it; she seems to trust it more."

Finch made a face at Jarven. That single expression, more than any other, told Jester that Finch was at home in the Authority. As at home as she was in the West Wing.

"You understand that if I agree with your suspicions and the manifests, in my opinion, bear them out, I will have to go to the magisterial guards and the Kings?"

Finch glanced once at Jarven before she exhaled. "We hoped things could be taken care of in a less obvious fashion." Jester realized that Finch was lying. He understood then why Varson had been the recipient of whatever documents the scroll contained. He was so straight and narrow a subtle political solution would be beyond him.

Unlike the dens, Varson assumed safety lay in the magisterial guards, rather than in avoiding them. Nobody in the poorer holdings believed that.

"Were you alive in the Henden of 410?" James asked gently.

"I was not only alive, but working in this office."

"We do not want—we *never* want—another Cordufar."

"May I remind you that none of Cordufar's financial transactions broke the laws?" Jarven asked. He dunked biscuits into his tea.

"It was possibly the only thing he did that didn't."

"A number of prominent merchant families did quite well out of Cordufar before the tragedy. I do not believe they were forced to endure the magistrate's court."

"Jarven, please."

"Do not," James said severely, "develop Jarven's cynicism or his bitter sense of humor. And you are—no doubt deliberately—incorrect."

"That's unnecessarily unkind," Jarven said. "I am older and my memory is not what it used to be."

"The families who had benefited directly from Cordufar's patronage or assistance were subject to investigations; the Crowns ceded supervision of the necessary accounting to the Merchant Authority Council, but they were accompanied at all times by members of the Royal Trade Commission. One of those members was ATerafin, that I recall."

"Devon?" Jester asked, although he had intended to remain on the outside of this particular conversation.

"Yes. It cemented his position in the Royal Trade Commission. He did sharp work, there."

Jester had had nightmares that made more sense than this—at least while he was in them. He felt relatively certain that he was awake, but wished he weren't; going back to bed and restarting the day had a very strong appeal.

"No one objected to his House affiliation at the time?"

"Given what had happened to Cordufar, no one dared. One or two houses approached the Authority Council with this concern; they were told in no uncertain terms that the investigation was to proceed as planned at royal request. The Order of Knowledge was also involved."

"Oh, they'll be involved in this," Jarven pointed out. "I expect you'll be hearing from senior members of the Order sometime today."

James rose, drink in hand. "I had best be getting back, then. The documents you prepared deal with difficulties in five disparate locations?"

Finch nodded.

"And we've seen four hit."

She nodded again.

"You consider the Terafin arm safe?"

"For the moment?" Jarven answered before Finch could. "Yes. If you insist, we'll keep the documents in the office. I do ask that you at least peruse them now, however. If our offices are hit in the same way the Authority Council's were, they are likely to be lost, to no one's benefit."

James exhaled. "Very well. But reading them and having them in hand are not, as you are well aware, the same; I cannot point to them as proof if they cease to exist."

Finch rose. "I'll leave you some privacy while you do. Sit at my desk; no one will disturb you except Jarven."

He hesitated, which Jester considered prudent. Finch, however, had anticipated this; she took his arm and guided him toward the desk Jarven said he'd chosen himself.

James shook his head. "Anyone would think you didn't care for this desk."

"I understand why it was required," she replied, "but I find it a touch ostentatious. I would have preferred to have my old desk moved here. Jarven felt it would lower the tone of the office."

James, however, nodded. "You can't stand in Jarven's shadow for the rest of your life. Especially not now."

"James, I've been standing in his shadow since I was sixteen. I hardly know it from roof, anymore. Everyone assumes that my position here is entirely at Jarven's request; they know that Jarven's is the desk—in this office—that counts." She pushed him gently into a chair that had also, no doubt, been chosen by Jarven, and retreated to the doors.

Jester followed like her shadow, half expecting Jarven to comment; he didn't. He was watching, however, as Jester threw him one backward glance.

Finch went immediately to the office she had occupied for four years, and to the desk she professed to prefer. Jester followed, closing the door behind him.

"I'm sorry," she said, sitting on the outer edge of the desk's surface, rather than the empty chair behind it.

"I won't say an apology isn't due, but I'm curious to know which one I'm receiving."

She exhaled. He was angry, and she knew it. "How many things do I have to apologize for?"

He lifted his hands in den-sign, and she reached out and covered them with hers. "Don't tell me it's nothing." Since that had been more or less what the gesture was meant to convey, he was silent. She knew; it was the catch-all *we're family*.

It was a way of avoiding conflict by offering a rough type of forgiveness. He could no longer remember who'd come up with it—Lefty or Lander. It wasn't one he used often because he'd always had other ways of avoiding conflict.

"Don't ask stupid questions, then."

"Fair enough." She leaned back on her hands, still refusing to put the desk between them. There was, her stance implied, enough between them already. "You delivered my messages?"

"All but the last one; Varson wanted it returned, unopened, to you. He didn't seem surprised to see your desk in Jarven's office."

"Technically it's our joint office," she replied. Her voice was soft, even pensive. "Did anything happen with Ludgar or Ruby?"

"If we're playing games, I don't see why I should answer that question."

"Games?"

"You have a good idea of exactly what happened. You know what you wrote, and it's now my guess that you know the intended audience better than I do."

"I know them differently. I've never gone drinking with Ludgar, and I spend as little time in Ruby's company as it's possible for a member of the House Council to spend."

"Everyone spends as little time in her company as possible," he countered. "Finch—what game are you playing here?"

"The same game that's always been played in the Merchant Authority."

"Random offices in the Merchant Authority don't generally explode."

"There was nothing random about the offices chosen, and I had nothing to do with this particular upheaval."

"The letter you sent to James Varson references it—before the fact."

She straightened her shoulders. "Yes. I offered him warning, based on investigations done within the Merchant Authority. The warning, however, did not come with solid proof of our suspicions, and without such proof, the Authority Council as it's currently constituted would fail to act."

"You counted on that?"

"I dreaded it, Jester. Had Jarven been the head of the Council, action would have been taken. It would have been oblique," she added, "not confrontational; the nature of our proof before the fact was tenuous."

"Proof of *what*, Finch?"

"The usual," she replied. "Demons. Rogue mages. Great merchant Houses and assassinations."

He stared at her.

"We won't keep the House," she told him quietly, "if we can't win at least half of the games now playing out across this city."

"Can you avoid playing them?"

She shook her head. "You've no doubt heard that one assassination attempt has already been made."

He considered acting surprised, and decided against it, because she was laying her cards on the table. That they were cards he had never suspected she had in her hand didn't change that fact—it only made him feel more stupid. "Yes."

"You're not surprised."

"I was, when I first heard of it."

"And now?"

"Early tea with Ruby has made clear to me that I might be the only person who *is* surprised."

"Jester—"

"Jay wouldn't be playing these games."

"Jay wouldn't *have* to play them. There isn't an assassin alive that could take her down. She can't be poisoned; I've seen it tried. She just doesn't eat—or drink—the food. I've seen her ignore it, once. I don't have that option. I have to do things the normal way. You were there when we discussed holding the House for her. You were there."

He had been. He remembered it. But he couldn't get from that discussion to this one following the general rules of conversational logic. "Holding the House—"

"How do you think the previous Terafin held the House?"

"Instilling terror in the ranks."

Finch spread her hands, palm up. "You see? It's not—at the moment—an option I have. It's an option I *need*, and there's only one way to get it. With Jay gone, people are jostling for position, within and outside of the House.

The demons that were sent to kill her were—most likely—sent by external enemies."

"I wouldn't bet on it."

"No." She turned to inspect the surface of her desk. "Neither would I. I'd like to be able to, though. It would help me sleep at night."

"Sleep at night?" He almost laughed. "Finch—you've set a target on your forehead. I can mitigate some of Ludgar's anger, but Ruby considers you a serious threat."

"Yes. But, Jester, I am. To her, I am." When he failed to answer, she continued. "Ruby's merchant concerns are weaker at the moment than they've been in the past decade; they won't stay that way. The war in the South worked to our advantage, but it's over. She won't throw in behind us with Jay gone. I don't think she would have thrown in behind us had Jay stayed.

"Ludgar's in Haerrad's camp, but he's not immoveable. He doesn't see me at all; he sees Jarven. I'm invisible."

"Given Ludgar, that's the best possible outcome."

"It's only best if you're invisible."

"Finch—"

"I can handle Ludgar." She lifted her arms and folded them across her chest. "He won't go all out against me, not yet; it would be a blow to his dignity."

"You'd get farther if you threw yourself on his mercy."

"I'd get farther in the very short term." She exhaled. "How long do you think Jay's going to be gone?"

"Finch—"

"I mean it. She was gone for months the last time she left. And she knew—in theory—what she was facing. This time, she has no idea where she's going. She wasn't even certain there was a way back. Whoever controls the demons wanted her dead. Or gone. And various members of the House feel the same. It's not," she added softly, "personal. No one with any sense thought they could take the House from Jay; not after The Terafin's funeral. But if she's gone . . ." She glanced away. "The House is the only thing she cares about, here."

"She cares about us."

Finch's smile was slight, but it opened up her face, and beneath her calm, soft words he saw the heart of her fear. "I owe her my life," she said. She didn't point out that they all did. Finch wouldn't. "She had no reason to find me. No reason to save me. She had no reason to keep me when things got lean;

my own family didn't. I wasn't muscle, Jester. At best, without Jay, I would have been a moving target, and I couldn't keep moving for long.

"I'm still not muscle. I couldn't be what Duster was. Or Arann."

"Neither could I."

She nodded. Had he been a different person, it might have stung. "She has the Chosen. Torvan's still angry that she left without taking him."

"He expected that."

"I think so, too. Doesn't stop him from being upset. I expected you to be angry at me," she added wryly. "And it's still upsetting. I don't enjoy the games Jarven plays—but I understand them. I can play them, if I have to."

"And you have to?"

She spread her hands. "Don't I? Tell me how to avoid them without ceding the House, and I'll do it. Jarven won't be happy—but I will, and he cares enough about me to tolerate what he calls my peculiarities."

"He calls *you* peculiar?"

"Frequently." She stood. "Lucille's not happy, either."

No, she wouldn't be. "And she can't talk you out of it?"

"She respects and admires Jay. She hasn't tried. I considered letting Teller hold the House."

Jester didn't blanch; he had practice. His eyes narrowed as her expression settled into studied neutrality. "You didn't consider it for long."

"I did."

"Seriously?"

"Teller has Barston. I have Jarven. Barston is like Lucille; he has a healthy respect for rank and authority. His pride in the office is based, in part, on that: Teller has to *be* right-kin. Jarven finds rank useful; he pulls it as often as he can get away with. He didn't always have the rank he has now, though—and lack of rank never stood in his way. I could be Jay, I could sit in his office, and he would think of a hundred subtle ways to undermine me if it amused him.

"He lies. He lies constantly, but never to himself. It's trained me to see the truth for myself, and to see how his lies work to his advantage—or, in the odd case, to mine. He plays on people's kinder nature whenever it serves his purpose. But Jester—that's taught me things as well. He's not inherently malicious. He just privileges his amusement over other people's outrage. I can't control him; the best I can hope to do is be aware of his interests.

"But if he'd been Barston, I couldn't do what I have to do. I wouldn't know how. Teller is like me, in a lot of ways. He's quiet. He wants to do his job, do it well, and avoid causing pain to others."

"This is going to cause a lot of pain to others."

"Yes," she agreed. "You haven't told me how to keep the House without causing it."

"I don't even understand what you're doing."

She raised a brow. Finch had never been stupid. "I am bringing Ruby's concerns to their knees for a short period of time. She'll have to play nice in order to wind her way through the Authority. It's possible someone else will take over the Terafin contracts with the Royal Trade Commission should she balk. Ludgar's economic concerns are healthy, but he's put a great deal of his support—in secret—behind Rymark."

"Rymark offered Jay his support."

"Because he couldn't kill her. I don't care what Jay wants from Rymark. I mean to remove his support within the House. With luck, I mean to damage his support outside of it. I mean to leave him with little means to pursue an agenda which isn't Jay's."

"Is he going to be standing at the end of it?"

She failed to reply.

"And your demons? Your rogue mages?"

"They're aimed at the House in Jay's absence," Finch replied.

"How do you know about them?"

"Hectore, indirectly. Not all of Jay's assassins were human in origin, but much of their support in this city is. They require money, and not small amounts of it; they've left a trail. I can't follow all of it on my own, but I've begun to see certain patterns."

"And the attacks?"

"Terafin isn't the only inconvenient House in the Empire," she replied. It was a neutral reply. "And Jester—I did offer warning, where I could."

"Which makes you suspicious."

"It makes me human. I understand that I'll be under some suspicion—but I'm used to that. Jarven counseled against it."

"The warnings?"

She nodded. "For the same reason you look uneasy now. But where I could, I chose people like James Varson."

"You expect James to go public."

"There were other reasons for choosing James as well, yes. But I like him. I admire him. He reminds me of Teller."

"Teller could never be as boring as Varson."

"I'm not insisting you like him. I feel I have justifications for doing so."

"He can take the investigation to the Kings without facing the same censure Terafin would."

She frowned, an expression seldom on her face. "Yes. He can. Jester—you understand as well as I that there are advantageous friendships. Both the advantage *and* the friendship can be true."

"The friendship wouldn't exist without the advantage."

"Does it matter?"

"You know it does."

"No, Jester, I don't. We meet all kinds of people, for all kinds of reasons. Some of them will never make any sense. Jay meeting me. Finding you. Lack of sense doesn't make it any less right, and it certainly doesn't make it any less true. We help each other. Always have. Why?"

"Family's different."

Finch started to speak. Stopped. "The reason James Varson is an advantage is because he's a decent person. He was born in the seventeenth holding. He's never had to worry where his next meal is coming from, or if there's a meal waiting at all.

"I used to resent people like him."

"I resent them all the time."

"And you have that luxury."

His brows rose; he let them. He was almost certain they'd escape his face. "Luxury?"

"Look at us," she said. "Look at what we're wearing. Look at what we weigh. Look at where we're living. We weren't born to it—and in the end, it doesn't matter."

"It does."

She shook her head. "It matters to *us*. It doesn't matter to most of the people who walk through those doors. It doesn't matter to James. He can't imagine what our early lives were like, it's true—but we remember, and we can certainly imagine what his life was, and is. I think, had James had our lives, he would be like Teller. He's not, but you can see the similarities if you look."

"He's like Barston."

"If that were true, I'd find some way to hire him out from under the Authority's nose, and I'd chain him to a desk for the rest of his natural life. And I didn't come in here to talk about James."

"Why did you bring me here?"

"Because I sent you to deliver those messages deliberately. I couldn't use the messenger service if I wanted some idea of the reception the messages received. Messengers, even liveried, can be ignored outright; they're treated as tradesmen or servants. You're a member of the House, and you've sat—when I can corner you—on the House Council. They can't outright dismiss you, and I doubt Ludgar would, unless you wanted him to."

Jester was silent. He was angry, but shock did that to him. "You've spoken with Haval."

She didn't admit it, but didn't deny it either.

"Finch."

"Jester—" She closed her eyes. "Carver's gone." Opened them. "Angel's gone. Arann is wed to the Chosen. I don't resent that," she added quickly, as if it were necessary. Maybe it was. "I adore Jarven; I don't trust him. Oh, I trust him not to work against me—but I don't trust him to view my concerns the same way I do." She rose, at last, and began to pace. It reminded Jester of Jay. "Teller's here. He has his hands full, but he's here. The Chosen watch him."

"They should be watching you," Jester countered.

"As much as they can, they are. But Teller is right-kin and Teller has Barston. I have Jarven."

"That shouldn't make them feel any safer."

"Maybe not. Torvan told me—"

"You discussed this with Torvan?"

"Some of it. Not all—but enough. Torvan doesn't trust Jarven with much, but he trusts Jarven with my life. I do as well." She folded arms across her chest, but didn't resume her seat. "Torvan trusts Barston with the House—but Teller's safety at the moment depends on all of the magical failsafes built into Gabriel's old office. Teller has spoken with Meralonne, and one other member of the Order, but he doesn't think in terms of survival. He understands the undercurrents that drive the House—but all of his experience has been in the office of a right-kin with an undisputed leader."

"All of your experience in the Merchant Authority has been under the same regime."

"You don't know what Jarven's like when he's bored. The Merchant Authority is a vast game to him, but sometimes he likes to know he's facing a worthy opponent. He understands all the games played out behind the closed doors of the offices here—and Jester, so do I. I think I have a much better chance of surviving this than Teller, without intervention."

He stared at her, and she smiled. It was wan. "Yes, you're right. I've adhered a target to my forehead; it's probably larger than I am. But it will focus the attention of our enemies, both the ones we know and the ones we don't.

Teller might receive some of their attention, but I guarantee he won't receive the brunt of it." Her arms relaxed and she sat again.

"Finch—*you* will."

"Did you think that was accidental? I know I'm not Duster. I'm not Carver. I'm not Arann—but I thought you of all people would understand that I don't have to be in order to protect what's ours."

"Jay would never ask this of you."

"It would kill her to lose Teller," Finch countered.

"Do you not realize it would kill her to lose you, too?"

"Teller is special." She said it without resentment, as if it were incontrovertible fact, like rain or dawn.

He shook his head. "You don't see yourself."

"No, Jester, I do. I can't do anything that Jay couldn't do. She loves me because I'm one of the ones she saved—and I *stayed* saved. I stayed alive. She talks to me, yes—but in a house full of men, you have to expect that. I'm not saying she wouldn't be upset if I died—but she'd be shattered to lose Teller."

Jester fell silent. Finch had never been concerned with power, and he finally understood that she wasn't, now. Ruby wouldn't see it, of course. Jester wasn't certain Jarven did. But Finch would never have chosen this course for her own sake. He felt a knot of tension in his brow unravel, and he grinned.

"She wouldn't be shattered to lose me," he offered.

"She would be shattered to lose any of—"

"—Us. Don't shake your head. Maybe you don't see yourself clearly. Jay does. I understand what you're doing. No, I take that back. I understand why. Did you put Haval up to this?"

She shook her head.

"Did you approach him?"

"No."

"He approached you."

"Yes. Two days ago."

"Were the letters his idea?"

Finch looked confused. "Haval's?"

"He knew who the recipients were."

She frowned. "Did he mention them by name?"

"No. He made it clear that he knew."

"Haval isn't above bluffing, according to Jarven. Jarven respects him."

"That is not a recommendation in my books."

Finch laughed, but sobered quickly. "He wasn't privy to the contents of the letters; no one was."

"Not even Jarven?"

"Unless he has some method of standing over my shoulder in the West Wing, no. I wouldn't put it beyond him, though."

"I would. He doesn't cross our threshold unless he's in your company, and I make certain he leaves when you do."

"Jester."

"Jarven finds it amusing."

"Which is why I don't find it more annoying. Jarven considers physical snooping gauche. I didn't discuss them with him; I couldn't afford to have word passed on before these letters arrived. They would have lost all impact." She looked down at her hands. "You're the only one left, Jester. I know you hate work; I know you hate the responsibility and the very real possibility of failure. But you're the only one who I know will have my back." She looked up, then.

"Do I have to like it?"

"The work? No. I'm not fond of it myself."

"Do you really know what you're doing?"

"I know what I'm trying to do."

"Do you know how big this is going to get?"

"I didn't. But I honestly wasn't expecting the attack on the Merchant Authority today. If I'd known, I'm not sure—" She stopped speaking as the door opened. It was Lucille, and she hadn't bothered to knock.

"Sigurne Mellifas is here," Lucille said quietly. "Jarven is entertaining her in his—in your—office."

"Am I expected?"

"Commanded might be the better word."

Jester headed toward the door. "I'll talk to you at home," he said, on the way out. "Mages give me hives, and I don't trust you not to drag me in to take notes."

Chapter Four

7th of Morel, 428 A.A.
Merchants' Guildhall, Averalaan Aramarelas

HECTORE OF ARAVEN STOOD, for a moment, in a crowd. He chose to be silent, although silence was not his particular strength; waves of conversation—and argument—filled the large room. In general, sound traveled, but in general, meetings of the Merchants' Guild were social affairs. Business was seldom conducted in collegial gatherings, but overtures could be made; although the membership itself was comprised of merchants from all echelons of Imperial society, not all of the members understood the social cues by which the guild was informally governed. This caused the occasional awkwardness.

Day-to-day governance of such a fractious and diverse body had never been Hectore's concern; Araven was powerful enough that it possessed an unofficial rank few shared. He had, therefore, made no moves to head the governing body of the guild, and if he did not regret that decision, he considered a change in direction now. He found the events at the Merchant Authority unsettling.

"Patris Araven."

Silence, of course, was not the same as invisibility, although in the case of the man who approached Hectore, invisibility would no doubt be no guarantee of safety. "ATerafin."

"I'm surprised to see you here."

"You are not."

Jarven chuckled.

"Honestly, Jarven, your ability to find humor in emergencies is almost obscene."

"I find humor in your short temper, Patris Araven. In a man of your stature, it is unexpected."

Hectore raised a brow, and Jarven inclined his head. He did not, however, fall silent. "You seldom choose to grace the guildhall with your presence."

"I dislike pandering obsequiousness, except when it's useful."

"Ah. I trust I am not—"

"You could not pander to save your life." This was not, by rumor, strict truth, but it caused Jarven ATerafin to chuckle again. Hectore admired Jarven, but did not trust him; he was a man around whom one let down one's guard at one's immediate peril. "I had not heard that you considered such attendance mandatory yourself."

"I am an old, unmarried man; I have no children and no grandchildren. Therefore, I find the society in the guildhall of interest."

Hectore glanced around the room; it was thick with bodies, and for the most part they were not interested in the politely social; they were both upset and afraid. Men of Hectore's stature did not openly display such fear, but only a fool could fail to feel it.

A fool or Jarven. The older man's eyes were sharp; they glittered like gemstones—with just as much warmth. The lines around eyes and mouth disguised this; he seemed like a genuinely warm, sympathetic man—a man past his prime, and comfortable to be so.

"Where is Andrei?"

"He finds meetings of this nature wearying."

Jarven's smile stiffened. "He is not unlike his master in that regard?"

"I find them necessary."

"The young are bold or foolish, Hectore. You are no longer young. If I may offer advice—"

"Propriety has never stopped you from offering it before, and if I recall, the advice was disastrous."

"You only pretended to take it."

"True."

"And thus proved a point. It was an expensive point," Jarven added.

"For which you've no doubt forgiven me."

"I seldom hold grudges at my age; they require far too much energy."

Seldom. Not never. "Your advice, old friend?"

"Do not forgo the pleasure of Andrei's company in the near future, where pleasure is of course entirely contextual."

Hectore did not argue. Andrei's absence had already caused one disagreement for the evening; he did not wish to rehash it for Jarven's amusement, and it would pain Andrei to know that Jarven actually agreed with him. "You yourself are without House Guard."

"There is always a risk in deadly games," Jarven replied, with a smile that was almost beatific. "And as I am expected to succumb to old age and expire momentarily, the risks outweigh the possible benefits."

"I imagine, old friend, that there are those who are desperate to reach you before you expire peacefully."

"Yes, well. I feel it important that the young develop ambitions, and I hate to discourage them." He smiled again. It reminded Hectore that Jarven in his youth had been considered a handsome man.

A handsome, ruthless, largely amoral man. The last, in Hectore's estimation, was untrue. He was a minorly amoral man. As long as you did not stand in his way, he was amiable and unpredictably helpful. If you did, and you were not extremely cautious, you would not be standing in his way for long. Sentiment did not bind him; affection did not sway him. Yet in his fashion he could be both sentimental and affectionate.

He was old, yes. But old or no, Hectore had never seen the challenge Jarven was willing to accept that he could not, in the end, rise to face. A wise man did not bet against him; Hectore had not always been wise in his youth.

"Keep Andrei with you," Jarven said again. "If such a man had consented to serve me, I wouldn't let him out of the range of my shadow."

"You have Lucille," Hectore replied, grinning. Lucille was almost everything Jarven was not. She disliked Hectore and the Araven business—if dislike was not too mild a word—but Hectore could find no similar disdain for her. "Andrei is far too wise to cross her."

"Andrei accepts the fact that *you* are master of your domain," Jarven countered, with a similar grin. "Lucille has *expectations*. It is remarkably difficult not to disappoint them; the finesse required is challenging." His smile faded, like sunlight on the edge of twilight. "Andrei was correct."

"I'll trouble you not to repeat that; he will be insufferable."

"He is frequently insufferable; it has not notably harmed either you or your many ventures."

"No. Andrei is not generally given to understatement. I will confess that I did not expect an open attack—during business hours—on the Authority Council."

"And the offices?"

"I would not have been surprised—at all—to hear that Terafin had been likewise destroyed. I am surprised—if gratified—to know that it was not. Was that your doing?"

Jarven shrugged. "I am not, in spite of all gossip to the contrary, mageborn. I have, as I have mentioned, no family. I have no wife, and no offspring of whom I am currently aware. I have, perhaps, more time to devote to precautions that would only be necessary in the most extraordinary circumstances.

"Finch is the closest thing I have to a daughter. Do *not* make that face, Hectore; it will spoil my dinner. If you reference this small conversation at all, I ask that you use the word protégée; it is the one with which I have most experience."

"You generally destroy your protégées," Hectore said, speaking as mildly as one might about under-watered potted plants.

"That is harsh, Hectore."

"You're not disagreeing."

Jarven's smile was pleasant, paternal. It set Hectore's teeth on edge. "I give them the opportunity to destroy themselves. They have learned what Finch has learned, and they have seen what Finch has seen. They merely failed to understand and deploy it. If they are to be associated with me, they will prove themselves worthy of that association; I have given them all of the tools they require, and I will not leave overweening fools as my legacy."

"You will not play these games with the young ATerafin council member."

"As you say."

"Jarven—" Hector fell silent. "Look at me; I'm being baited like a gangly, inexperienced youth."

Jarven's grin deepened; he was genuinely amused. "The information that Andrei provided was subtle, but deep. I am not yet finished with it; I have only just begun."

"Andrei's chief concern at the moment is the timing. It is possible that the disaster in the Authority offices had nothing to do with the investigation—but the timing is suspect."

"It is," was Jarven's quiet reply. If successful baiting amused him, failure of subtlety did not. "It is also a clear indication that extraordinary caution is required. You have not, I note, come back with another round of the almost insulting missives you call contract negotiations. Not even Varson could catch all of the annoying little details."

"As it happens, I have just received the latest draft from my scribe; he considers your amendments to be petty, but feels they fall just short of open insult. He is clearly not familiar enough with your work."

Servants began to circulate through the room, carrying trays with finger foods and wine. Food, in a gathering of this nature, was almost always welcome; Hectore was slightly surprised to see how much of it remained. The wine also surprised him; the guildmaster had clearly opened the wine cellars generally reserved for smaller and more elite patrician gatherings.

"The guildmaster expects difficulty," Jarven observed.

"Yes. I've never considered him a fool."

"Have you considered him an ally?"

"An odd question, ATerafin. We are all merchants here."

"Indeed. But have you not noticed that the currency has changed? The game has grown, Hectore. It has become large enough that it is almost impossible to see the entire board."

"Almost?"

Jarven smiled. "We are endlessly inventive; if we understand the language of power, translation should not be beyond us." He looked past Hectore's shoulder. "I believe the guildmaster has arrived."

Guerrin ADurrance was younger than Hectore, but not by much, and he went to some small pains to disguise what remained of his youth, preferring the gravitas of wisdom. Or at least the appearance of it; Hectore did not know Guerrin well. He was not generally impressed by the younger man's pretensions, although he considered some pretense of vital import in the running of the guild. During times of what could tentatively be called peace—as the trade wars were often bloody, long affairs—Guerrin was an acceptable figurehead.

The events at the Merchant Authority did not fall under the rubric of trade war. Had there been deaths by obvious—and mortal—assassins, there would be disquiet and many blind eyes. But magic had been used, and in outrageous and openly illegal ways. The Order and its body politic was already sniffing around the edges of the guild's governing body; the Kings had been informed, and were no doubt ready to unleash their trained specialists.

It was an unfortunate truth of Hectore's life that those of whom he was naturally most suspicious—Jarven being the prime example, if one considered only the men present—were also those he assumed most competent. He considered Jarven vain, but his vanity was almost entirely superfluous. It added a touch of color to the treacherous twists and turns of Jarven's superficially harmless social dealings, no more. At heart, Jarven was pragmatic. If he knew what he wanted, it was his.

Hectore was not cut from the same cloth. He considered most of his fortune to be the result of both hard work—a necessity, in any trade—and luck, the blessed smile of *Kalliaris*. He had, of course, some experience with her frowns, but they were mercifully brief and, to date, they had not been fatal.

He knew when to accept a loss. Jarven did not. A loss was merely a break in the game, while he considered different strategies. But Jarven was older now, and the drive and passion of a younger man's ambition had all but deserted him.

Or so Hectore would have said, a week ago. Perhaps two. The Jarven who stood unapologetically at his side surveying a crowd of hostile, fearful, and yes, obsequious men, was clear-eyed. No, bright-eyed. Not a detail in the room would escape his notice, and possibly his future manipulation.

As Guerrin ADurrance made his way to the lectern by the highly decorated far wall, Hectore said, "What do you think of young Guerrin?"

To Hectore's profound and lasting surprise, Jarven said, "I think it is time to take our leave. *Now*, Hectore."

One argued with Jarven at one's peril, but in general if one chose peril, there were good reasons for it. Jarven was methodical, if unpredictable; he had a mind like an abacus and a heart like a mage's interior offices. Hectore was a man whose decisions were often made on instinct alone. He could explain that instinct after the fact, prettying it up or making it sound more rational and pragmatic than it actually was, but at base, some of the most significant decisions he had made in his history at the helm of Araven had been made without deliberation.

He did not make a run for the doors; that was beneath them both. But he offered Jarven a genial, controlled nod, rather than argument or question. Nor did he seek to leave by the large public doors that he'd entered by; something in Jarven's tone made the well-lit, well guarded doors seem impractical.

Jarven raised a white brow as Hectore turned and headed toward a section of sparse wall.

"It is stuffy," Hectore said, as if in explanation, "and Guerrin understands the tone of a room and its occupants; the doors to the main hall—" the hall in which they were now walking, "are guarded by impressive men in impressive livery and in larger than usual numbers tonight."

"They are unlikely to stop us," Jarven said, following adroitly and gracefully through the thinnest part of the crowd.

"Thanks to you, old friend, I no longer feel that with appropriate certainty."

Jarven grinned. The old bastard was genuinely enjoying himself, and Hectore somewhat resented it. Not enough, however, to become truculent and insist on remaining; he hadn't been looking forward to Guerrin's speech, and in other circumstances might appreciate a good excuse to miss it.

"I had not realized," Jarven said, when Hectore opened the servants' entrance, "that you had reached such elevated, trusted status that the servants would not look askance at your presence among their number."

"I am a merchant," Hectore replied. "I sell whatever is required. It would not be the first time I've slipped out of the guild through the back halls."

"I am shocked," Jarven said, with obvious amusement.

"You yourself recognize the halls."

"Of course. But I am only ATerafin now; in my youth I was vastly less exalted."

"Jarven," Hectore said, as he paused to hand off a princely sum of money to a loitering older man, "your enjoyment of some things is practically obscene."

"What are the other options? Finding the pleasant in the unpleasant seems the optimal choice, where possible."

"A certain amount of gravitas is considered an asset for men of your stature."

"An asset, surely, to be used against me rather than in my favor."

"I've seldom noticed you to be in possession of such assets." Hectore handed a small purse, prepared for just such emergencies, to a second, older woman. She caught his wrist before she allowed him to pass.

"Marjorie," he began.

She shook her head. He met her gaze and froze.

"Patris," she whispered, "what is happening tonight?"

"The guildmaster is addressing all of the membership who've chosen to be present. It's more serious because of the events in the Merchant Authority."

She glanced at Jarven, but asked him no questions.

"Marjorie, what's happened? What's happened in the back halls?"

She bit her lip and glanced down the hall, in the direction of the first man Hectore had so casually bribed. Her answering smile was ghastly, it was so bright and forced. But her hand, still attached to his wrist, trembled. "Take Helen," she said.

"Helen?" He frowned for a long moment. "Helen, the new girl?"

"Take her, Patris. I can't leave—I'll lose my job, and I need it."

"What is she to you?"

She shook her head. "She's my niece. My sister's daughter."

"Your sister passed away—"

"Two years ago. Deathbed promise that I'd care for her and I'd see her placed."

"She'll lose her job."

"I can cover for her. I can take the blame for sending her off on an errand. I can blame you, and they'll accept it; you're important enough, they'll turn a blind eye." Her voice was low; her hand shook.

At any other time Hectore might have been insulted, although he accepted the truth in her words. Had he demanded the presence of a new servant who was low enough in the back halls hierarchy, no one would raise voice in that servant's defense.

But the servant herself might be out of a job, if her masters were feeling uncharitable. "Where is she now?"

"Hectore," Jarven said, "I sincerely doubt we have the time for this."

He didn't argue; he didn't pause to acknowledge. Instead, he removed a ring and placed it carefully in the servant's hand. "I do not know what you fear; I am uneasy, but cannot give a reason for it. I trust my instincts. I cannot wait, but send her—with my ring—to the Araven manse."

"With what instructions?"

"Tell her merely to return it. They will understand when she arrives that she is to be treated well. You might come with her yourself."

Marjorie shook her head. "If I lose this job, I won't find another that'll keep food on the table. I might as well be dead."

He did not tell her not to speak of death; he did not offer the pretense of a humorous excuse. She did not require it. Nor did he ask her not to speak of his presence here. Given her own request, she would not. But he felt, as he left her, that he stepped into the shadows of a future that would see very little light. He thought of the Henden of 410, and glanced at Jarven.

Jarven's face was a mask. The forced joviality that usually adorned it, at least superficially, was gone. "There may be minor difficulties," he said.

"Before or after we leave?"

"When we leave. I would ask, in this instance, that you trust me. Let me lead."

"And run behind to attract the wolves?"

Jarven's laugh was a brief bark. "It is good to know we understand each other."

"I find it less delightful than you clearly find it," Hectore replied. "I am already missing Andrei."

"Oh?"

"He tends to put a damper on your excesses."

"True. If Lucille were here," Jarven added, "we would not now be leaving. She is characterized first and foremost by her sense of exaggerated responsibility." As he spoke, he drew a letter opener from the tailored folds of his expensive jacket. Or at least Hectore assumed, at first glance, that that was its function; it was far too ornate, far too pretty, to be a weapon. He raised a brow.

Jarven did not appear to notice, which meant nothing. Hectore slid his hand into his own pocket; his fingers grazed one of the three stones he carried there. It was a perfectly legal use of magic, a stone meant to insure the privacy of a conversation should privacy be the desired state. Among merchants, this was not guaranteed. The overheard word often carried a peculiar weight, and many men and women took some pains to place those words with care and ostentation.

He activated the stone now. "What trouble do you expect?"

"Given the servants' reaction? There is now very little trouble I don't expect. I don't mind difficulty; most of my last two decades have been an unsuccessful attempt to stave off boredom." His smile was sharp as a knife's edge, and just as warm. He stepped aside and Hectore passed him.

"You don't often seek to escape through the back halls."

"Not often, no. If someone is foolish enough to attempt to corner me at any one of our many guild meetings, I find it amusing."

"In direct proportion to their frustration?"

"In almost exactly that, yes. Lucille feels it lacks dignity; she seldom accompanies me for that reason."

"Which kills two birds with one stone."

"You know, Hectore, were you a younger man, I would have taken you as a protégé in a heartbeat."

"I will try not to find that insulting."

Jarven chuckled. "This door?"

"The far door, nearer the kitchen. It is oft-traveled, but seldom by fleeing merchants."

"And the trade entrance?"

"The trade entrance, as you call it, is frequently used by the more enterprising young merchants as a method of entrance."

"Indeed," Jarven said, grinning fondly. "I remember making strategic use of it myself in the early, hungry years."

"Spare me," Hectore said. "And follow."

The kitchen was strictly off limits to the membership of the guild for a variety of very good reasons. Hectore both approved of and ignored those reasons, as it suited him; he trusted himself, after all. He didn't entirely trust Jarven, but no one sane did, and at this particular juncture, it didn't matter.

The kitchen wasn't silent; it never was. But Marjorie's fear was evident in the men and women who, aprons stained by years of just such work, gathered here. The servants of any establishment tended to be both respectful and cautious when dealing with men and women of any significant rank or power; Hectore was seldom welcomed with any friendliness or joy. He was merely overlooked.

He was not being overlooked now. The furtive glances usually saved for his back were turned instantly, warily, upon him; he saw evidence of relief. Whoever they expected, it was not Hectore. But they expected someone. He slid hand into pocket and deactivated the stone, frowning. He recognized perhaps a third of the twelve people assembled here.

"Where is Bertold?"

He could have slapped them collectively with better results. The glance that passed around the servants who had heard the question could be charitably called uneasy. "Jarven."

Jarven nodded. He saw what Hectore saw. He probably saw more. The easy smile that had adorned his face in the halls had fallen away, but he had not retreated to the harmless expression of the dotard. Hectore did not approve of what remained; it reminded him inexplicably of Duvari, the much-detested Lord of the *Astari*. "Bertold is the cook?"

"He's in charge of the kitchen, yes," Hectore replied. To the oldest woman present, he repeated his question. "Where is Bertold?"

"He's off—he's off sick," she replied.

The quality of the lie was so poor in other circumstances Hectore would have taken it as an insult to his intelligence, of which there had been enough this eve. "And he took sick, as you call it, only today?"

Silence.

"I feel that this was not perhaps the strategic retreat we had hoped for," Jarven said. He sighed. "Ladies, gentlemen. Hectore of Araven wishes to speak—briefly—with Bertold. If Bertold is indisposed, he is nonetheless on the premises. If one of you will carry a message, we will get out of your way and let you get on with your work."

More silence.

Jarven exhaled. "Or, if you prefer, you may direct us to Bertold, and we will carry the message ourselves."

This was not precisely what Hectore had had in mind. It was fast becoming the opposite.

One of the younger men present cleared his throat. He looked straight ahead—at Jarven—avoiding the stares the sound of his voice invoked in the rest of his coworkers. "Bertold is in the pantry." He hesitated, and then said, "He's taken strange, sir. He's . . ."

"When exactly did he take strange, as you put it?"

"This afternoon. Maybe yesterday. He was off. We thought it was his stomach acting up—he's a bear when it does. But it's—it's worse."

Jarven slid his letter opener back into his jacket. "We'll speak with him. If you prefer, we will not say that you sent us."

Relief underlay the silent exhalations that filled the kitchen.

"This is not a good idea," Hectore said. He did not take the lead he'd surrendered. He did activate the stone a second time, although he considered leaving it; the stones, when active, could be detected if someone was searching for them. In general, one didn't expect such a search in the kitchens.

"No, of course not. This was well-planned; it was not the action of a day or a week. I dislike," Jarven added, as if it were necessary, "being a piece on somebody else's board."

"I don't disagree, but there are some boards and some games it is best to retreat from entirely."

"I did not agree to partake in this game; I am not, therefore, bound by its rules."

"I've seldom seen you bound by any rules; you observe form, of course, as do we all."

"We will not get information in any other way, and I desire information. My curiosity is piqued. If you wish, remain in the kitchen."

"I am considering your previous unsolicited advice in an entirely unwelcome light."

"As you should. If I had realized the severity of the situation, I would have given it before the meeting commenced, and with far less tact. I will offer one warning. Do not interfere." He straightened his shoulders; his eyes, as he glanced briefly at Hectore, were sharp and bright.

Hectore was Jarven's junior, but he felt very much older at the moment; Jarven appeared to have shed age. The avuncular old man who liked to babble about tea in his inner sanctum was gone; the man at his core—the man who had risen with such speed and deadly grace to prominence in the rougher merchant circles—remained unhindered in his wake.

Hectore carried a small knife; everyone did. He had not had to use it for years. He doubted that he could, with any great efficiency—but he did not think, seeing Jarven, that the same was true of the Terafin Authority director.

Nor did he assume the item in the jacket was, in fact, the letter opener it had appeared to be. If Jarven did not understand the rules of the game in which the evening had embroiled them, he understood some part of its shape and form.

And a better gamesman had not been seen in the Empire in their generation; Hectore very much doubted that one had been born since. It cost him nothing to admit this; he had tangled with Jarven in their youths, and he had won more than he had lost, but he was aware of how much he had depended—and still depended—on the whim of luck.

Jarven had chosen to enter the game being played. And, really, that shouldn't have been surprising; Jarven seldom cast himself in the role of strict observer. Hectore did, from time to time; there were games he considered too costly. Jarven could not reliably be counted on to remain an observer.

Nor could Hectore, now. If he characterized himself as a frequently disinterested observer, he had that luxury; becoming a nameless, insignificant victim of another man's game verged on humiliation. He understood, as he walked in Jarven's wake, that by choosing to follow, he was entering the game ill-prepared; that would have to change.

How that would change was both problematic and trifling. The city had been imperiled before by forces beyond Hectore's immediate understanding; were they beyond *anyone's* understanding, the city would not now stand, as it had stood for centuries. Putting the whole of his life on the table was a risk he had taken a handful of times; he accepted it. On occasion—and entirely beyond the hearing of his wife and his children—he relished the opportunity and the challenge.

But putting *their* lives on the table—putting the servants directly in harm's way—he did not. He had always had reasonable limits. The man in front of him had not. Oh, Jarven was not particularly mendacious; he was not a man who enjoyed suffering and pain as an expression of his power to cause it. But he was not bound, as many were, by considerations outside of himself. He had chosen to take no wife; he had raised no children. He had eschewed entirely the fraught joy of grandchildren.

He had very little to lose, in the context of Hectore's life. But in the context of his own? Hectore smiled. It was a sharp smile. Jarven was a spider in the center of a vast and complicated web, and he would not allow the center to be moved without his knowledge. Nothing intimidated him, although he could feign timidity when it suited. Nothing truly frightened him except perhaps irrelevance. His own irrelevance.

Hectore activated a second stone. He seldom did so, and more often than not at Andrei's subtle direction. Although it was considered a legal use of magic, it was not considered a sign of good faith. It captured words, and when properly prepared, images. Any of these could be of use during tricky or tense negotiations. Any of them could be of use in other ways; men of power with less self-control than ideal could utter all manner of threat.

He did not expect that now. He was uncertain what to expect; he was not certain he would catch nuance—if, given the servants' reactions, nuance was even possible—and undercurrents if events moved too quickly. Not the first time. But the second? The third?

If Jarven noticed, he gave no sign. The magic itself was extremely expensive; stones such as these existed in the palace, and in strategic locations dictated by the *Astari*. But they were seldom crafted for the personal use of even the powerful; they could be financially ruinous.

"The pantry," Hectore said quietly.

Jarven nodded. They glanced at each other; there was appraisal in Jarven's glance, resignation in Hectore's. It was Hectore who knocked. He slid into the carriage and bearing of the autocrat. To his surprise, he heard two distinct words.

"Go away."

If Hectore considered himself a modest man, and a man with few pretensions, he clearly retained some of the ego of his younger self. He was not accustomed to being dismissed; he was *certainly* not accustomed to being dismissed by a servant, in *any* building.

He knocked again, the knock louder and stronger.

The door flew open. Had he been standing closer it might have hit him— which would have been beyond social disaster for the unfortunate master cook, although it would also have been slightly embarrassing for Araven.

The man who appeared in the doorframe, face suffused with the pink of fury, was in theory a man Hectore had seen on and off for over a decade. He wore the stained uniform the kitchen required. He was a man of middling years and middling weight, with a tuft of beard that suggested the unkempt; it was never completely shaven, but it was never long enough to interfere with his duties.

And today, it was spattered in blood.

For one long moment, Hectore was silent.

Blood was not unusual in a kitchen. It was not therefore unexpected when one attempted to speak with the cook in charge of kitchens whose duties had more than tripled for the evening. But this was not his first thought, when meeting the man's eyes. It came slowly, in the awkward silence.

"Patris Araven."

"Bertold." Long years of habit and the differences in their stations prevailed.

"Forgive me. The kitchen is in some disarray at the moment, and we are at full capacity—"

"Beyond it."

"—In the main hall. The guildmaster's expectations are quite high, as he's been at pains to make clear." It was Bertold's voice. But the timbre was stronger and more certain. "How may I help you? It is not often that a patris of your import chooses to grace the back halls."

"I have come with a request," Hectore replied smoothly. "You perhaps know Jarven ATerafin?"

Bertold's eyes shot past Hectore's shoulder; they rounded—and narrowed—in a way that suggested a yes. But it was the wrong affirmative.

"Or perhaps not," he continued without pause. He leaned in conspiratorially and lowered his voice, although every instinct screamed against it. "Jarven's peak was before your time. He is an august personage now, dependent on the history of many former glories. But he has been a touch unwell, and his digestion is somewhat delicate."

"I see."

"The food that has appeared in the hall is a touch rich for his stomach. We expect the guildmaster to give a long and extended public speech, given the nature of the current difficulties. Something more simple is in order." He turned to Jarven. "Come, come, old friend. Bertold is one of the best cooks in the city, and easily one of the most accommodating."

Neither of these statements were, strictly speaking, the truth, but Bertold had always been susceptible to that oldest of merchant ploys: flattery. Flattery between classes was not common, but used strategically it often produced the best results, and Hectore was a practical man. A sentimental, practical man.

Jarven stepped forward, stumbling slightly; Hectore caught him by the arm, offering him the support one offered those of advanced years. At any other time, he might have laughed; he was certain both Lucille and Andrei would find the scene unamusing. Neither would be impressed—as Hectore was—by the sudden frailty that seemed to engulf the older Terafin merchant.

"Hectore," Jarven said, in a soft, slightly unsteady voice, "I told you this wasn't necessary."

Hectore grimaced.

"A man of your stature and significance," Bertold said quietly, "is entitled to ask for some consideration from the guild's kitchen, ATerafin. Tell me what your dietary restrictions are, and I will be certain food is prepared. I will see to it personally." He closed the pantry door at his back and entered the hall.

Jarven's smile was watery. "You are all so good to me," he said. "But it is a touch embarrassing to need such kindness. I would rather the guildmaster did not hear of it."

"He will not hear of it from me," Bertold assured him.

"Might we speak in your office?" Jarven continued.

"The pantry is my office," Bertold replied. "But given the day, it is not in a suitable condition for meetings of any import. I've given strict orders that I'm not to be interrupted, and most of the members don't attempt to walk the back halls. There is very little danger of eavesdroppers."

Jarven smiled again. Hectore was impressed. Had he not walked by Jarven's side into the back halls, he would have assumed that the man whose weight he now supported had at last been brought low by age. He seemed smaller and vastly more frail than he had ever seemed when Hectore had entered his impressive office; even the smile implied weakness, resignation, and the hesitance that comes with certain loss of power; it implied the trust offered when one had no other options.

"Very well," Jarven said. His voice was slightly quavering; his expression had gained both lines and care. He spoke softly; so softly that Hectore had to lean in to catch the words.

Bertold, significantly, did not. Hectore nodded encouragingly at Jarven; the gesture was so natural and so automatic it was not pretense. But as Bertold spoke again, the Araven merchant's eyes were drawn not to his face, but the beard. Blood. Bertold was not the tidiest of men—one could not be, in his line of work. But Hectore could not recall blood of that color on his beard before.

"Patris Araven, if you wish, leave Jarven in my care and return to the main hall. I will see him escorted safely back to the dining hall in short order. This may take some time, and your absence will no doubt be noted."

"That won't be necessary," Hectore replied. "If I fail to return with Jarven, someone will accuse me of doing away with him."

Bertold's eyes narrowed.

"It will mostly be said in humor," Hectore added, his uneasiness growing.

"I insist, Patris Araven."

Instinct warred with pride. In general, Hectore allowed instinct to win; he was practical. There were always, however, exceptions. "You insist, Bertold?" He let Jarven's hand fall away from his arm and drew himself up to his full height. Bertold was not a tall man.

"I do. I am responsible for the kitchen. I am responsible for the feeding and care of the guildhall's guests. I appreciate the time you took to bring this to my attention—but I do not require more from you at the moment. Return to the guildhall. I will see that Jarven returns there as well."

Hectore smiled. He slid hands into his generous pockets—a gesture considered declasse among the patriciate—and he found the third of the three stones he carried. He activated it by touch alone. "And will you see that he returns alive?"

Bertold froze. He glanced, once, at Jarven and then turned the full force of his attention on Hectore. Hectore was prepared for it; he did not therefore take a step back. But he understood why the servants were in a state of near-panic. Bertold's eyes had darkened. It could have been a trick of the light; Hectore allowed for the possibility. He did not, however, give it credence.

"Pardon?" Bertold said, his voice softer but more distinct. It traveled the length of Hectore's spine.

"I believe you heard me."

"Hectore," Jarven said, in his pathetic, quavery voice. "I believe I will be in good hands. You needn't raise a fuss on my behalf."

"It is not on your behalf," Hectore replied, automatically shifting into a softer register. Damn Jarven. "But if you wish to wait in the kitchen, I will join you there shortly. Clearly Bertold has more he wishes to say to me, and I do not wish to tax you."

"And you are now aware of the ATerafin's dietary needs?"

"It was my suggestion that we pay you a visit," Hectore replied. "I believe I am capable of answering any questions you may have. I will have a few of my own."

Silence.

"Hectore—"

"A pity," Bertold said. He straightened his shoulders, adjusting his posture and bearing. "But if we must improvise, we must; it will not change the outcome of the evening for either of you in any significant way." He smiled. Without glancing at Jarven, his arm shot out to the right, his hand stiff and straight as it passed through the old man's chest—and into the wall behind him.

Hectore heard the stone crack, which was shocking; it was almost as shocking as the fact that Jarven was no longer between that hand and the wall. Hectore knew—had always known—that Jarven played at age the way a cardsharp played at cards, but he himself barely had time to register Bertold's movement.

The fact that his hand had broken through the wall, had embedded itself in the stone, made it clear that Bertold was not simply a tyrannical, temperamental master cook. Yet he had once been; Hectore was certain of it.

Bertold's eyes widened. They widened and they darkened, becoming larger and larger in the hollows of a face that lengthened and stretched, skin and flesh cracking as his jaws opened. They were wider than the whole of his face had been a moment ago.

The sconces in the back halls were not so impeccably cleaned and presented as those in the public galleries, but they cast shadows, and the shadows beneath Bertold's feet were darker and longer than the shadows beneath Hectore's. What was left of the temperamental and finicky Bertold Hectore had known for years was almost invisible. Even the familiar apron had torn at the seams, and hung on his burgeoning frame like new rags. In any other circumstance it would have been ridiculous.

Now, it was nightmare made flesh. It was an old, old nightmare, birthed in a Henden that the city had only barely survived. *Demon.*

The demon—and it could be nothing else—horrified Hectore; he did not and could not move as Jarven had moved. The arm that had not neatly carved its way into solid stone shot out, claws extending; Hectore grimaced as they struck him mid-chest.

Blue light crackled at the contact point; flesh singed. It was not Hectore's flesh. He was driven back, stumbling at the force of the blow; before he could lose his footing, something caught him, righting him.

He heard a voice that was both familiar and strange. "Run, Hectore." He turned in the direction of the voice and saw nothing. But he also heard, of all incongruous things, a brief chuckle. He backed up as the demon's eyes widened into sockets and darkness across half the length of its inhuman face; its fingers were smoking.

He did not take Jarven's advice, although everything in him screamed to do so. Everything except the small corner of his brain devoted to merchant negotiations. Any advice that Jarven offered that sounded good was *always* suspect.

He had a dagger. A flyswatter would have been just as effective, and only slightly more ridiculous. Jarven had not run. And Hectore would not; not yet. Any distance he covered would negate the magical memory capture he now felt profoundly necessary.

Jarven had walked down this hall by his side with the cool confidence of a man who has a plan. Hectore did not assume that plan encompassed the protection of Hectore's life; that was not Jarven's style. But it must have encompassed

Jarven's survival—and the only way to accomplish that was to destroy the demon.

Rock cracked as the demon withdrew his embedded hand. He never took his gaze off the Araven patris; nor did the Araven patris look away from the demon. He had paid a rather princely sum for the device in his pocket. Clearly the money had not gone entirely to waste. He was not certain how much damage it could absorb; it was meant as a defense of last resort if one were stranded in the center of an angry soon-to-be mob.

This creature was equivalent to that, but that was not the entirety of Hectore's concern; the shadows that now pooled at its feet—its flat, splayed, clawed feet—were. They moved as if they were smoke; they glistened as if liquid, spreading up and down the hall as he watched.

He took a step back.

"I'm afraid I can't let you leave, Patris Araven." The creature spoke with Bertold's accent, but his voice made it bestial. "None of you will be allowed to leave when the guildhall doors have closed."

"I fail to see how you will stop me."

The creature laughed. Its amusement reminded Hectore of the thunder that presages storm. He leaped, the shadows clinging to his limbs like shroud or veil; Hectore could see the shape of the hall through their folds, but the hall was pale and almost colorless. The demon did not attempt to pierce chest as he had done the first time; instead, his arms extended in deadly mockery of an embrace.

Hectore did not struggle; he had that much self-control. Dignity failed him briefly when the creature's jaws opened, because they didn't seem to stop; flesh lengthened to reveal teeth that could not fit the shape and expanse of a roughly man-shaped head.

He drew Hectore toward him; Hectore struggled, briefly, before he mastered himself and his entirely visceral fear. The jaws that had opened did not snap or close, not immediately; they opened wider, until they were longer than Hectore's head.

But closing them on that head—which was immediately and obviously the creature's intent—was easier said than done; blue light flashed inches from Hectore; light washed the hall, and shadows sizzled as demonic tongue burned.

The creature *screamed* in fury. Or at least that was Hectore's assumption; this close to the interior of demonic jaws, he could see very little else. The jaws snapped shut on air, and Hectore was thrown off his feet and toward the end of the hall—away from the pantry and the demon itself.

He could not keep his footing, as he was no longer on his feet. He hit the wall and felt his shoulder burn at the contact. If he was not as old as Jarven, he was by no means a young man; this night's work would be costly, if he survived.

He rose, unsteadily, to his feet and looked down the hall. The demon's screaming had not lessened, but it had changed in pitch; fury was mingled with surprise, and surprise gave way to fear. The shadows at the creature's feet were roiling; steam rose from them in a black, dense cloud.

Did demons bleed? They certainly felt pain, which the merchant felt he could enjoy without guilt. Hectore leaned, for a moment, against the wall he'd hit as he watched the demon begin to burn. He didn't recognize it as burning for a few seconds because the smoke looked so much like the shadow, but as the seconds passed the smoke thinned and he could see a light glowing at the center of the creature's chest.

The light grew as he watched. It wasn't the normal red of flame or fire; it was a gold-limned white, and it reminded Hectore of Summer for no reason he could readily identify. As the demon continued to burn, Hectore began to squint; he could barely make out the attenuated form of the creature's limbs as the light grew stronger, brighter.

He had to close his eyes at the last, they were tearing. But he wanted to watch. To set these screams—dying, even as the light brightened—against the screams of decades past, which haunted the worst of his nightmares. The worst, he thought, of the nightmares that haunted those who had been alive during the Henden of 410.

White fire consumed the creature, and when the light at last faded and Hectore's eyes once again acclimated to the natural, dimmer torches of the back halls, he saw that the demon was gone. In his place, or perhaps directly behind where he had chosen to stand, was a familiar figure, and in his right hand, a weapon that Hectore had considered a fanciful letter opener.

"Well," Jarven said, as he met Hectore's gaze, "that was instructive. Remind me to make more deliberate and respectful offerings at the cathedrals upon the Isle in future. I suggest, in future, you take the opportunity to avoid these conflicts when such opportunity arises."

Hectore grimaced.

"You are unharmed?"

"My shoulder is not."

"May I say that I am impressed with the depths of your . . . caution?"

"Or the depths of my fortune?"

Jarven chuckled. "I have always been impressed by that, Patris Araven.

But in the main, you have not mishandled that fortune. I believe I understand the panic and concern of the servants now."

"Do you think this was the only such creature in the guildhall?"

"If you are going to ask remarkably stupid or naive questions, save them for the credulous. I am not as young as I used to be, and physical maneuvers of the kind the creature necessitated take their toll. We should be away, Hectore."

"If you can handle a creature such as this—"

"It was not fear of the creature," Jarven replied. He was almost annoyingly calm; the demon might have been a garden variety assassin of poor quality and middling capability. "But fear of Andrei."

Hectore snorted.

And from behind him in the hall he heard a very familiar voice. "Justifiable fear, and I'm afraid it is a little too late to give that meaningful consideration."

Andrei had arrived.

Chapter Five

ANDREI WAS NOT DRESSED as a manservant. Nor was he dressed as a merchant of middling—or even significant—means. He wore dark clothing, and at that, fitted in a way that implied the need for fast and unencumbered movement.

Hectore grimaced and turned in the direction of his most significant servant; he momentarily lost the thread of words. Andrei was bleeding. It was not, to Hectore's eye, a particularly significant wound; it was, however, visible—a long slash across his right cheek.

"I am not invulnerable, Hectore," Andrei said stiffly.

"I had not intended to imply that you were."

Andrei, however, was glaring at Jarven. "Do not embroil my master in your games."

"I assure you that was not my intent. Rather the opposite."

Andrei's face fell into studied neutrality, which was not a good sign. Hectore pulled himself from the wall and headed—stiffly—toward his servant. "You are saying that the events here—"

"Of course not. I am saying that our presence in the back halls—and in the kitchens—were Patris Araven's suggestion. I merely followed."

"No doubt playing the dotard."

Jarven's grin was unrepentant; it was also sharp. "I prefer that to the role of the servant."

"And you've played the servant long enough to evaluate the differences?"

Jarven chuckled. "You are clearly out of sorts this evening."

"I have been remarkably busy. The evening is not yet over, and I wish Hectore to be well quit of the guildhall before things become difficult."

Hectore laughed, which soured Andrei's unfriendly expression further. "It has already been, as you have probably guessed, more difficult than any previous guildhall meeting. Prior to this, the only threat to health or sanity has been boredom. We need to return to the kitchen," he added. "Unless you took your wound there."

"No. For some reason, the guards posted outside of the guildhall were overzealous in their attempts to keep the doors closed."

Hectore was surprised, and saw no reason to hide his outrage. "This was caused by *guards?*"

"Let us say it was caused by men in guildhall livery. If you are in the back halls, you deduced that circumstances were not entirely the norm. I assume you were leaving?"

"That was our intent, yes. But the back halls were clearly in a state of near-panic."

"Which is why you are here."

"We came to speak with Bertold, yes."

"And Bertold?"

"Was probably the cause for most of that panic. Come, Andrei. We will depart; first, I would like to give orders to clear the kitchen."

"Those orders are not—"

"Araven can weather the fury of the guildmaster—if indeed the guildmaster remains to vent his spleen. Did you enter the main hall?"

Andrei shook his head. Hectore frowned.

"By which door did you choose to enter?"

"The trade entrance."

"Dressed like *that?* I withdraw my ire at the overzealousness of the guild's guards."

Andrei did not find this as amusing as Jarven did. Hectore grimaced; his arm would be almost useless in the morning; it was not notably flexible at the moment. There was nothing wrong with his feet, and he picked up the pace as he headed back to the kitchen. One of the older women with whom he was familiar met his gaze, her eyes narrowed.

"Stacia," he said, offering her a brief nod. He cleared his throat and raised his voice. "The master of the kitchen has asked me to clear the kitchen entirely."

This caused noise—enough of it that syllables clashed with other syllables in a way that made most of the words they formed unintelligible. Given the difference in their status, most of those words should not have been uttered in his hearing, anyway.

"What do you mean, clear?"

"Clear," he replied, "as in: react as if the kitchen were, in fact, on fire."

The older woman blanched. She glanced at her compatriots, and he saw several different fears cross her face, each one vying for dominance. The choices she faced were difficult, and Hectore understood the various textures of that difficulty. If she deserted the kitchens—if she ordered the rest of the staff to desert—and there was no equivalent of raging fire, they could look forward to starving in the streets in the near future.

Jarven coughed, catching her attention. "If you do not clear the kitchen while it is possible to do so, you will all die. It will not be by our hands, of course," he added, lifting a hand as she drew breath. "But there is a reason that Patris Araven and I chose to brave the back halls during a critically important guild meeting.

"We will not delay our departure further, but if you are concerned about the reaction of the master of the kitchen, it is no longer an issue."

Her shoulders sagged. "He is—"

"He has left the building," Jarven replied. "Nor do I expect him to return."

One of the youngest of the kitchen workers turned toward the hall that led to the pantry. Hectore stopped her before she reached the door. Her face was the color of chalk, her eyes too wide. He understood, in a moment, what she feared, and shook his head. "I'm sorry," he said, voice low.

She tried to throw his arm off; Andrei blocked her.

"You will not find your friend; you might find what remains of him—or her." He looked up; Stacia was watching, her lips thinning. To her, he said, "Henden."

It was a single word; a month. But she understood the whole of his intent, and she came—quickly—to catch the girl by the shoulders. She wasn't gentle—but on a night where most of the guild had gathered beneath the roof, there was very little calm, and good temper was generally the first casualty. She had a piercing voice—and a strong backhand which purportedly saw infrequent use—and she raised the former. "Clear the kitchen."

"But, Stacia—"

"I *mean it*. Vanne, pass word to the serving staff if you can do it without risk: tell them—tell them Jarven ATerafin has found some evidence of poison in the food leaving the kitchen and it is not to be served."

"Should we tell them to leave, too?"

She glanced at Hectore, who grimaced. "Yes." This was not to be the subtle, quiet exit that he had first intended. He turned to Andrei. "We will need to leave. It is possible we will need to leave the way you entered—how much of a scene did your entry cause?"

"We will be able to leave that way if we do not tarry longer."

"An alarm was raised?"

"Yes. But not the traditional alarm. It's my hope that the attention of those who might otherwise prevent escape will be focused on newer, unwanted visitors—but I cannot guarantee it."

"No?"

"No. There is only one person who can; if you choose to pray, pray to your *Kalliaris*."

Leaving the kitchen was not the smooth and untrammeled affair that Hectore had initially envisioned when he had entered the back halls. Nor did he immediately make his way to the doors, although Andrei was practically shrieking—in his perfectly silent way. As he had now overstepped what little authority he had in the guild—all of it indirect and all of it due to the rumors of Araven's considerable wealth—he found Marjorie and told her, curtly, that all of the serving staff was evacuating. He considered telling her that fire had broken out in the kitchen, but decided fire was not compelling enough.

"You had every reason to be afraid," he said instead. "And it is growing with the passage of time. Stacia has now emptied the kitchen of everyone who survived."

Marjorie did not ask him what they had survived; nor did he volunteer that information.

Jarven looked bored and irritable, rather than absentminded and frail. This was not a promising sign. "Marjorie, are there other servants—or officials of the guild—who have been as questionable in their change of temperament or personality as the former master of the kitchen?"

She hesitated.

"We do not have time for hesitance. Yes or no?"

"Yes." Before Jarven could ask, she added, "The under-steward."

"Not the steward?"

"He took sick three days ago; he has not been in the halls since. The under-steward has assumed his duties."

"Where is the under-steward now?"

"He's in charge of the arrangements in the great hall. He's there now."

"Thank you. Leave, if you can safely leave. Your job, after this evening, will not be at risk."

"You can't—"

"I can guarantee it, although it pains me to do so." He turned to Hectore. "Now?"

Hectore nodded. "Given the efficacy of your work here, I am almost tempted to return to the great hall to disrupt the meeting and the speech."

"I am incapable of repeating that minor miracle this evening," was Jarven's curt reply. "And were I not, I would still be wary of the hall; it is no doubt where the focus of planning has gone, and the protections and magic there might outstrip the meager offerings merchants keep up their sleeves. Or in their pockets." He turned to Andrei. "Your opinion?"

"We leave. We should have left the kitchen and the back halls; it is not safe to be in the guildhall at the moment."

Hectore spoke, but his words—the few that managed to escape—were lost to the thunderous roar that permeated two doors. The floor shook beneath his feet.

Marjorie turned white and offered no further resistance; she picked up her skirts and ran.

Screams—and there were screams—were thin and almost inaudible as Hectore, Andrei, and Jarven moved with far greater speed toward the exit.

It was easier approached in theory than in practice; the hall was crowded. Word had traveled from the kitchen; it had clearly been amplified by Marjorie. It had drawn servants of every level to doors that should have been open.

Technically, they were. They were not, however, passable. While Hectore could see the exterior grounds—thin strips of grass and significant, if unseasonal, flower beds—he could not actually reach them. A pane of glass—of something that served as glass—now covered the entire length and breadth of the door's frame.

It was not, of course, glass; that would have been too easy.

The servants were accustomed to the hierarchy of the front halls; they allowed Hectore, Jarven, and Andrei to pass them, although the hall grew crowded as they examined the barrier. And it was a barrier.

"What do you think their aim is?" Hectore asked, as Andrei stepped in front of Jarven and placed his hands against what seemed to be solid, thin air.

"Your guess is, no doubt, almost as good as my own," Jarven replied, watching Hectore's servant. "It is, however, surprising given the attack in the Common during the victory parade." To Hectore's mild disgust, Jarven smiled. His eyes were bright, focused; he had been handed a problem that was not entirely outside of his area of expertise.

"Let us assume I accept the superiority of your knowledge, as we are un-likely to aid Andrei in any practical way."

"Not, in my experience, a safe assumption—for me." Jarven's smile deep-ened, sharpened. "But I will accept it for the moment; it has been an exceptional—and enlightening—evening, and I am feeling somewhat gener-ous. Andrei?"

"Believe," the servant replied—in an entirely uncharacteristic way, given the differences in their stations, "that I am attempting to ascertain any struc-tural weaknesses as quickly as possible. If Hectore is entertained by your opinions, I assure you I am not."

Jarven laughed. It was a bold, strong sound, so at odds with the frailty he often hid behind that it was bracing. Hectore felt an answering smile tug at his lips; it was dampened only by the palpable fear of the servants now trapped in these halls behind them.

"The attack at the Merchant Authority was a skirmish; a feint. In my opinion it was meant to test the limits of the defenses the Authority has al-lowed to be put into place."

"Terafin?"

"You will find, when you next visit the office, that it is materially un-harmed."

"But not intentionally."

Jarven raised a brow, but did not otherwise reply. "It also served as a call to arms. Merchants are not generally considered timid; they are, however, frequently either desperate or foolish. The guildmaster called a meeting; the subject was a matter of fear and curiosity that traveled up and down the ranks of its many members. Even you were moved to attend, and you are not fa-mously noted for your sense of merchant community.

"This was well planned. Well planned. Not all of the Averalaan merchants are in attendance; some are involved in business operations outside of the city. But within the city? Only a handful of significant absences."

"That was my thought."

"Imagine the state of the city and its finances if almost all of the merchants of note perish tonight. The disturbance at the Authority will seem—and be—trivial in comparison. We will face almost immediate chaos, and quite possibly ruin. An enemy army in the tens of thousands could not have such catastrophic effect in so short a time."

"The creature that attacked the Kings during the victory parade could."

"Could it?" Jarven shook his head. "I doubt it. Kill the Kings and there will be chaos, yes—but there is a line of succession in place in the event of such an emergency. Kill The Ten and if the Houses are not entirely foolish, there will be successors in place within the week—regents if politics are too severe. But the Houses will function in predictable ways given the change of rulers. The merchant concerns will continue; the money will enter their usual coffers.

"Trade wars, on the other hand, have consequences that are both more obvious and less profound. You've seen your share of trade wars."

Hectore nodded. The urge to smile had deserted him entirely.

"The city does not function on goodwill or bad; it functions on commerce and trade. Food requires, at base, money and the logistics that money provides. If you die here, Hectore, who succeeds you?"

"That is an uncomfortable question, Jarven; I am not certain I am going to answer it."

"An answer is not necessary. You have brokered a compromise between your ambitions and the ambitions of men and women who are content to serve you as long as they profit from it. But many of those men and women are here tonight. They would not shed many tears if you perished here; they would use the opportunity to expand their own concerns. But even that expansion would serve to stabilize the wheels of commerce. If it is gone, what happens?"

"Your point is taken."

"This is not a tactic that was attempted in 410."

Every servant in the hall stiffened at the date, even those too young to remember it clearly.

"Andrei," Hectore said quietly.

"I am uncertain," his servant replied. "But I believe the barrier can be broken."

"Uncertain?"

"If I break it now, it is likely to draw attention." He did not add, because it was not necessary, that the attention would be magical in nature—or worse.

"They require speed," Jarven said. "If they are wise, they will be gone within the hour; they will not leave the hall itself to attend to those who now seek escape. Those in these halls are not their target." He paused, and then added, "It is my guess that they were to be dealt with by Bertold."

Hectore nodded. "If they meant to be at all subtle, they might have set fire to the guildhall and merely blocked the exits."

"Indeed. I do not think subtlety is necessarily their aim."

Andrei said, quietly, "I ask that you all step back."

The servants struggled to comply; those in the back were pushing toward an exit they did not realize could not be used.

Jarven folded his arms and watched; Hectore took charge of the servants. He did not raise voice or shout; he found, in situations like this, shouting was ineffective. He did, however, have a deep voice, and it carried.

"You might help," he told Jarven, without any expectation of aid.

"I am an old man," Jarven replied, grinning. "To be pitied, rather than obeyed. And I find your servant frightening enough that I feel compelled to watch him work."

"Now is not the time, Jarven."

"But it is. You trust him, of course. If he wanted you dead, you would be dead. You would have been dead decades ago—and I can honestly say I would consider that a loss. An advantage as well, of course."

"Of course."

"Andrei has always been a puzzle, to me. He is clearly almost preternaturally competent—but I can say that of myself. I can say that of a handful of my peers. I have seen him fight once. He is not an amateur. He does not rely—as most guards do—on size and the obvious presence of weapons to act as deterrent to prevent violence. He is exceptionally observant, and he is fast. He is not, however, *Astari*. He is not trained by the Lord of the Compact; I believe the Lord of the Compact considers Araven a threat in part because of your servant."

"You will embarrass him."

"I will do nothing of the sort. He is, in my opinion, skilled enough to serve the *Astari* in any of a number of roles."

"Ah. You intend to insult him instead of embarrassing him."

Jarven chuckled. But he did not look away from Andrei; Hectore glanced at his servant and got a very good view of his black-clad back. His shoulders were stretched, his arms raised, his hands splayed—weaponless—against the barrier. There was some indication that he was attempting to exert physical pressure against it, which Hectore would in other circumstances have considered a waste of effort.

He turned back to Jarven, who had not finished.

"He is not a member of the Order of Knowledge. He has never, to the knowledge of the guildmaster, served in any of its scattered institutions, and he has never been formally trained in any of its many halls. He has sworn no oath of allegiance to the laws that govern the use of magic; he is not, and has never been, admitted into the ranks of the magisterial guards—or its sister organization, the Mysterium.

"Yet he is cognizant of many of the underlying principles that guide the work of the mage-born; he is notably sensitive to the detritus of magical effect."

"He has also never been employed as a chef in any of the great houses, but you will not find a better cook. I fail to see the relevance of any of this."

"Yes. And as you are not a fool, I assume that failure to be deliberate on your part. It is poor sportsmanship, Patris Araven. Given his sterling attributes and his unusual—and suspect—skill set, you might expect him to be treated with some suspicion."

"He has not been, to my knowledge. He is a servant."

"Yes. A servant who is granted entrance into the cathedrals, and granted access to the god-born upon the Isle. Have you never considered this odd?"

Hectore was tight-lipped. The ground was shaking enough that he had to brace himself and bend his knees—which were not notably flexible—in order to maintain his footing.

"I myself have always found it odd," Jarven added.

"What I find unusual—given the circumstance—is the amount of care you have clearly taken to observe my servant. The Terafin enterprises have obviously not been difficult enough to keep you respectably busy."

Jarven chuckled. He had not—and would not—take his eyes off Andrei, and that was unfortunate. Andrei was not in a position to hide behind his role, assuming the mantle of invisibility granted to servants by people who were not in the serving class.

Hectore considered knocking the Terafin merchant over, and decided against it; given the speed with which Jarven had avoided the demonic claws that should have ended his life, Hectore reasoned the odds were higher that he himself would end up on the floor. Andrei would then be offended at the harm to Araven's dignity; he was almost certain to be outraged by Jarven's frank and open appraisal.

Neither of which were of paramount import at the moment.

Andrei lowered his hands; it was not a gesture that spoke of defeat. It was a deliberate, slow tracing of the length of the barrier. Hectore could not see his expression; he was relieved to note that Jarven could not see it, either. It was the only relief he felt.

"Andrei—"

"Yes, Hectore," Andrei replied. He turned to Jarven. "I do not know what tricks you have left up your sleeve, but consider readying them now. The magi have not—apparently—arrived." He added, to Hectore, "You will need to wait; keep the servants here until it is safe to leave."

Hectore did not ask how he would be able to determine safety. "And Jarven?"

"You are not—you will never be—responsible for Jarven ATerafin. I doubt even The Terafin could be." Before he had finished speaking the last few syllables he spun on one heel. His left arm shot out—much as the demon's had done—and he drove it through the barrier. Light blazed in the hall; it was almost blinding.

No, Hectore thought; it *was* blinding. The protective spells activated by the stone in his pocket shielded him from the worst of it. He noted, however, that while the servants cried out in shock, Jarven ATerafin did not; the Terafin director's eyes were closed.

Had he ever underestimated Jarven? Yes. Once or twice. Jarven, in his turn, had underestimated Hectore of Araven. He thought, in future—in whatever future was left them—neither would be capable of making that mistake again.

And the future? It had turned. Hectore had faced assassins. Not often, but not infrequently. In his early years, when he had traveled with his own caravans, he had charted courses through bandit-heavy territory. He had played his deadly games with other merchant houses; he had played less obviously dangerous games at the tables of bankers.

He had not, until now, faced demons. He had never, until his single dinner with Ararath's protégée, seen the high wilderness of myth made real. Andrei's right hand struck the barrier, palm flat, and he spoke three dissonant words that echoed in the back of Hectore's thoughts long after they could no longer be heard.

Hectore was not a man given to fear; even in the Henden of 410 it was not terror the demons had instilled, but a sense of helpless, building rage. He felt apprehension now, as shadow and darkness pooled around Andrei's right hand, spreading outward in ripples.

Light met darkness; Andrei staggered forward, using the momentum as he tucked chin and folded the curve of his upper body into a somersault. When he came to his feet, he was on the move—and he was armed.

Jarven followed. Hectore did not try to stop him. He had a fleeting hope that the Terafin merchant might perish at the hands of whatever Andrei expected to face on the building's exterior, but it was out of his hands. The servants were not.

"Marjorie. Tell the girls to stand by the exterior wall. It is not yet safe to leave. Kevan, do the same with the young men—take the rear and give them instructions. The hall is crowded enough there will be injuries if you cannot contain unnecessary panic."

Marjorie said something under her breath, and Hectore grinned. "Believe that this is not the way I intended to spend my evening. We were to listen to a long-winded and pretentious discussion about an emergency; we were not meant to be embroiled in a far more deadly one." His tone was, he knew, more important than his words, and he spoke more loudly than was his general wont; the tone itself carried.

He was aware that there was a very real possibility they might not survive, and he knew that it was uppermost in the minds of people who were not used to taking command—or the responsibility that came with it. It was not a task Hectore himself did with any relish. He did not feel responsible for the men and women undoubtedly trapped within the guildhall proper. He had expected some ugliness, the possibility of injury or even death—but not like this.

"Boy, do not stand in the doorway—" He didn't finish the sentence.

Fire gouted through that open frame, in shape—and in impact upon the facing wall—a battering ram. One girl screamed; the young man did not. He couldn't.

Kalliaris, he thought. *Smile, Lady.* He knelt, briefly, by what was left of the servant's body; it was largely unrecognizable. He was not certain that he himself would have survived, magical protections notwithstanding; the impact of the magical fire had shattered a large section of the wall.

Around him, the servants fell silent; there were muffled sobs, but no words, no more screams. They understood that they were prey, here, and like rabbits, they hoped stillness and silence would prevent attraction of predatory attention.

It was more than he had hoped for; he was, as they were, silent and watchful. He carried no meaningful weapons; he relied—as he often had—on Andrei. On Andrei, who had entered the back halls bleeding.

He listened; he heard the sound of metal striking metal—or stone; he heard movement; the breaking of branches. He heard the crackle of flame, and he heard a roar that contained syllables almost too guttural to be language. In response, he heard a familiar voice reply, and he shivered: Andrei was laughing. His voice was high and tense, and his reply—his reply was also linguistically impossible—but it was not bestial.

Hectore pushed Marjorie out of the way, breaking his own command: he moved quickly toward the open doorway. He was almost too late.

"*Andrei!*"

Light. There was light. And shadow. And fire. At the heart of it, surrounded by all three, imbued by them, Andrei. It was hard to make out the form of the Araven servant; the heat shed by fire distorted everything.

Ah, lies. He could see the demon. He could see the demon, and the red, red blade in the demon's hand; the red shield. He could see the shadow that rose from his back like wings, and the ebon line that bisected his forehead like a crown. Gods must have looked like this in the deadly glory of their distant youth.

And man, Hectore thought, must have looked as he did: old, tired, and powerless. He left the hall, stepping onto scorched grass. "Andrei."

"I would not interfere, were I you," a familiar voice said.

"You are not, and have never been, me," Hectore snapped.

"His foe is not—"

"*Andrei!*"

The demon's sword traced a red arc—two—through the air where seconds before Andrei had stood. He had not rolled, had not thrown himself to the side, had not parried; he had leaped. The sky contained him. Hectore whispered a single word, a name that was already fast becoming too small, too insignificant to contain him.

"What is this?" the demon said, and he turned to look down upon Hectore. Had he been Hectore's height, he would nonetheless have dwarfed him. He was not; he was larger, wilder; his danger could not be contained by shape.

And yet, it was.

The demon gestured; fire surrounded Hectore in an instant. It did not consume him, although he felt its intense heat. He knew that the stone for which he had paid so much would be useless after this eve; he did not think it would save his life again.

But he smiled through the thin wall of fire as Andrei plummeted groundward, the ruins of his jacket smoking, the daggers in his hands glowing faintly as he plunged them into the demon's back.

The fires that caged Hectore banked sharply as he slid his hands into his pockets. Jarven was not wrong. The creature itself was too much for Andrei. But the Araven merchant had seen what neither Andrei nor the demon had yet noticed: the distant glimmer of blue light and fire, the lightning that had nothing to do with natural storm.

The magi had arrived.

Chapter Six

7th of Morel, 428 A.A.
Order of Knowledge, Averalaan Aramarelas

SLEEP MADE A SOUND when it shattered. Matteos Corvel rose before his eyes were half open; he was dressed before he noticed the chilly, dark environs of his tower room. The door to that room was ajar, although he hadn't yet crossed the floor. Even in emergencies, the magi required clothing. Warm clothing.

Stone floor stung the callused soles of his feet; the fire in the grate was embers and ash. Nor did he light it anew. He hadn't the time; time would come later—or never. The trace of Sigurne's magic hung about the room like a pall. She was not given to idle fancy or idle worry.

He made his way up the stairs to her room and hesitated at the closed door. Matteos was one of two men given permission to enter at any time of day or night, and in any situation. The wards and spells wrapped around the door—the magic that seeped into stone and wood and rug and glass—included him. Inasmuch as he could be, he was some part of Sigurne Mellifas, the Guild-master of the Order of Knowledge.

But even so, he understood that there were spaces into which he must tread with care. His fear was not of Sigurne, but for her. She tolerated it, but took neither comfort nor pleasure from its existence. She did not, on most days, deign to notice it.

Today—tonight—was to be one of those days. Matteos opened the door.

* * *

The room was dark with night but bright with magic.

Sigurne had laid out three robes. Two, she wore when she acknowledged the possibility of "difficulties" or "misunderstandings." Thus did she brush off attempts on her life. But the third? The third she had worn perhaps twice. Its presence stilled all need for questions—or their answers.

"Yes," she said, although she did not turn to look at him. "I have summoned Meralonne."

"Have you summoned the magi?" The greater part of the active body of First and Second Circle mages were occupied by the explosions that had shattered walls—and lives—in the Merchant Authority. Some were actually ensconced within that building, to the chagrin or outrage of the merchants.

"Gavin has summoned them."

Matteos did not blanch.

"If I ask it, will you remain here?"

"If I ask it—if I beg it—will you?" Matteos countered. The first time she had asked this of him, it had stung. He had served her for a handful of years by that point; he had been steady, silent, and supportive. She had chosen to take Member APhaniel on a task for the Kings; she had asked Matteos Corvel to remain behind. And it was clear why: Meralonne APhaniel was a *power*. Matteos Corvel was a Second Circle mage, and at that, only barely. He was not proud of the envy—the jealousy—that he had felt at the time, but had made his peace with it. He had been a younger man. Much younger. And much, much more ignorant.

Sigurne exhaled; it was the whole of her answer.

Matteos lifted the third of the robes and held them out for her; she slid shaking arms into its generous sleeves. He whispered the focal words of a small spell; she lifted her hand to his lips and shook her head. In the darkness of room and the brightness of magic, her eyes were luminescent.

She was afraid. "Husband your power," she told him, in her careworn voice. "We may have need of it."

That, too, told him much. He did as she asked; the spell was merely a way of avoiding some of the night's chill; it was not a necessity.

Matteos cursed Meralonne APhaniel, but had the grace—for the first five minutes—to do so silently. The winds at the tower's height were bitter indeed, and shelter from the worst of their bite had been denied him. He did not mind it for his own sake—although it was close—but for Sigurne's. In the clouded light of moons, she looked ethereal, ephemeral. He knew she played at age when it suited her, but in the past decade, she played at it when it did not; she was not young. She had not been young for years.

Neither had Matteos, although of the two, he was the younger. He felt the wind as a physical presence.

Gavin Ossus had, as Sigurne said, summoned the magi. There were four: Eryk, Alldrich, Engel, and Olivia. Not one of them approached Matteos in age; nor were they like him in any other way except for the talent to which all present had been born. Where Matteos had chosen Sigurne as his master— and perhaps his responsibility—they had chosen power. They had learned to hone their talent, to use it, in matters of war.

If they had a master within the Order, it was not Sigurne, but Meralonne APhaniel; they tendered her the respect they did because APhaniel did so, and they followed his example.

Tonight, however, that example was suspect. Five minutes. Ten.

Throughout, Sigurne remained silent, face to the wind, eyes upon moons and sky. Matteos did not understand the complexities of her relationship with Meralonne APhaniel. He did not understand Meralonne APhaniel at all. But he knew—as they must all know—that Meralonne had also been Sigurne's master, Sigurne's teacher, in her distant youth.

Meralonne who appeared ageless. Meralonne, who *was*.

Matteos had only once asked Sigurne what Meralonne was. She had replied with a single word: *Necessary*. Matteos had never asked her again. Nor had he sought information from the other magi or the other scholars housed beneath the Order's many roofs. He trusted Sigurne. He trusted Sigurne's sense of necessity—and also, her sense of discretion. If she was not willing to speak of Meralonne to Matteos, she did not wish the matter to be spoken of at all.

But something had changed in the past year. An edge of uncertainty, something sharp enough to hint at fear, had crept into Sigurne Mellifas. Sigurne was, by nature, both conservative and cautious; she was considered—by the callow and the superficial, in Matteos' considered opinion—timid. She accepted this designation; she had never, in truth, lived up to it. She did not live up to it now, but some unnamed fear informed her actions and her decisions.

Given the events of the past several months, this was reasonable, and Matteos, had he been any other man, would have accepted it as rational, perhaps even inevitable. Had he been any other man, he would not have been in a position to observe the guildmaster so closely.

He moved when she turned away from Gavin; he was by her side when she levered herself up, to the height of the crenellations. He offered her a hand, but was not surprised when she ignored it; Sigurne did not often accept aid. Nor did he attempt to stop her when she leaped from the crenellations, he had seen it so many times. She moved as if she were half her age, and he knew the expression that gilded her face although at the moment he could not see it.

But he did not breathe again until she had fallen ten feet and the wind itself had caught her in its unseen folds.

Meralonne APhaniel existed without context.

His spill of white hair had not lengthened with the passage of years or decades. The lines around the corners of eyes and lips had not deepened; the skin of his hands had not aged, darkened with sun, or toughened with calluses. Even the armor he wore—and he wore it now, beneath the fall of robes—had not rusted or tarnished.

He was one of a handful of the magi in the Order's history who could instantly travel between two known destinations and still be on his feet. His power had not diminished with age—at least, not with Matteos' age. It had, in Matteos' uneasy estimation, grown. It had grown substantially within the past few months.

Nor was Meralonne the only magi to be so questionably gifted.

Gavin and his cohort had likewise seen a rise in power; they did, however, question it. If they obeyed Sigurne, they were Meralonne's men—and women; they obeyed the guildmaster because Meralonne APhaniel did. She knew it, of course. She rose in the wind that surrounded the mage like a personal army.

He was gentle, with Sigurne.

He was not likewise gentle with Matteos, who was more or less yanked off his feet. A glimmer of something that might be a smile—or steel—graced the mage's cold expression. "Matteos."

Matteos grimaced.

"We must be away."

Matteos almost asked where they were going, but a flash of incandescent red answered before he could. It cut the sky like a beacon, suggesting sunset in the blink of an eye before it once again faded to night.

He could not see stars in its wake. He could see only Sigurne, because it was to Sigurne that he looked.

The city rushed past in a cold, cold blur. The more subtle illuminations of protective magics flared as the warrior-magi prepared, midair, as unruffled as Sigurne herself by their manner of transport. Matteos, however, took his cues from Sigurne. She did not expend her power—any of it.

Meralonne spoke to her; she replied. Both sets of words were lost to the wind. Neither were necessary; fiery plumes once again cut the sky. At the heart of those flames, winged and shadowed, a demon stood before the Merchants' guildhall.

A demon. Of course.

Matteos met the ground with just enough time to bend his knees and establish his footing; it was awkward. Gavin and his warriors timed impact with physical movement; they didn't land on their feet, they rolled to them. Golden light filled their hands—and Matteos suspected their eyes—as they armed themselves.

Only Sigurne settled to her feet as if gently set down.

The wild wind retained only Meralonne, but it was Meralonne the demon noticed; no one else—armed, armored, and ready for combat—was worthy of his notice.

"Illaraphaniel," the creature said, as he spread his massive wings, unfurling them both at once and forcing the magi back a step. His voice was deep, resonant, a force of nature that the wind could not diminish or carry away; Matteos felt it as a blow. He might have been caught by it; Gavin was.

But Sigurne was not. Having found ground once again beneath her feet, she moved—swiftly, belying her age—toward two men who stood by the side of the guildhall, observing.

"This is not your fight, not yet," Meralonne said. Matteos, focused on Sigurne and the idiots to whom she rushed, glanced back briefly. There was a third man here—a third man who was not magi. He was armed, but not armored; he wore black clothing, although it was rent and torn. Something about him was familiar, but Matteos could not immediately place it. "Go back to your master. Your time will come, is coming."

The man stood, arms stiff, for one long beat, and then he turned toward Sigurne. No, Matteos thought; toward the men. And he recognized the stranger, then: Andrei. Servant of Hectore of Araven.

Sigurne did not care for Jarven ATerafin, but admired him. None of that admiration showed. "You dispatched one?" The set of her mouth was a single, thin line; her eyes were narrowed as well.

"In the kitchens. He had taken the form of the chef."

"When?"

"A quarter of an hour ago, perhaps less. I will, of course, make a full report when the situation allows for it."

Sigurne nodded and turned her attention to Hectore of Araven. "This is not the place for you, Patris Araven. Take your servant and leave."

The patris managed a smile. "You do not, I see, offer similar advice to Jarven."

"I am too old to waste breath." She turned to Matteos. She exhaled. "They planned well, when they planned this. The servants?"

"There is apparently a magical shield—"

"I am aware of it."

"The servants could not bypass it. We could, but the gap in the shield drew the demon your magi now fight. The surviving servants shelter in the hall nearest the door, waiting."

She was not concerned about the demon; her expression made that clear. "I will deal with the barrier. ATerafin, when it is down, lead the servants to safety."

Jarven nodded, as if she were The Terafin—the only woman with the right to give him commands.

Nor did Sigurne expect anything but obedience. She turned to Matteos. "I need Meralonne in the guildhall."

Meralonne had engaged the winged demon. Sigurne, proving the truth of the words she had offered Hectore of Araven now called for member Ossus. If Meralonne could not—or would not—hear the guildmaster, Gavin was only human.

"Take your men and engage the demon. I need Meralonne in the guildhall. Now."

Gavin was aware of the strange, fey compulsion that enveloped Meralonne APhaniel when he engaged the demons in combat. He hesitated—which for a man of Gavin's temperament was very significant. Sigurne had already turned away.

Matteos said, "Tell him that he dallies with the least significant power; the greater is within the guildhall."

Sigurne's first use of magic that evening was to bring the containing barrier down. Matteos' first use of magic was to erect a similar barrier that was far less ambitious in size or scope: he shielded the guildmaster while she worked. She was not quick—but what she did in ten minutes, most of the magi could not do in an hour.

Jarven ATerafin did as Sigurne had commanded: he took control of the servants who raced from the building, emptying the back halls in their rush to be free of the guildhall. Sigurne glanced at them as they flowed past, to either side. Were it not for Matteos' barrier, she would have been trampled.

Her expression as she at last gained entry into the guildhall almost implied that death by panicked trampling would be preferable to what she found within. Matteos joined her, crossing the threshold; he staggered as the floor beneath his feet shuddered.

Sigurne exhaled. Her shoulders fell, and her chin; age—true age—settled around and within her. Eyes dark, she turned to Matteos. She had faced demons before; she had certainly faced hostile magic. She had investigated the deaths that occurred in the wake of either. He had never seen this expression on her face.

"Sigurne?"

"It is worse than I feared."

"The demons—"

"There are three. Two are ahead of us, in the guildhall; one, you have already seen." Her lined, pale hands seemed as silver as her hair when they curved in brief fists. "I do not know how, but one of them has called the wild earth—and it is waking."

She stumbled as the floor once again shuddered. Matteos caught her as she lifted one hand—and her chin—and spoke. Her lips were less than twelve inches from his ear, but he could not hear a single syllable.

Meralonne, he thought, *what are you doing? What have you done? What are you becoming?* Sigurne was afraid. Sigurne, who was cautious, but almost fearless, was afraid.

The platinum-haired mage entered the back halls. His eyes were luminescent silver, his hair a straight, undisturbed fall of white. The eyes narrowed.

"Can you bespeak the earth?" Sigurne asked.

"Not easily, and not yet; it is waking—but the waking of the earth was always fraught, and the *Kialli* voices that reach it will engender rage, not service."

"Can you kill the demon who is attempting to wake the earth before he fully succeeds?"

The cool glance he now cast at his theoretical superior was the only answer he offered; silence fell.

It was broken by a roar of bestial fury. The floors shook. The aftershock of roar was scream—several screams. Matteos was surprised; he had thought, had expected, that the merchants would be dead. They weren't. Or rather, not all of them were.

That would galvanize Sigurne. It always had. But he saw no like relief or surprise on her face. And he remembered Henden, then. Henden in the year 410. There had been no quick deaths, no merciful deaths, until the end.

Those weeks had been a living nightmare, and he felt that he had turned a corner into that landscape again.

"Sigurne," Meralonne said. He glanced at Matteos. "You know what you must do."

"You know why I have not."

Meralonne nodded. His sword was so painfully bright, Matteos squinted and looked away. "The time is coming. What do you fear?"

"He will hear."

"The god you do not name?"

"Yes."

"It is not the god you will have to fear if the earth is unleashed. The god, in this action, has surrendered all hope of ruling this city. Those who sleep will not be destroyed by so small a thing as the earth's displeasure—even sleeping, they are not at risk. Not in that way. The risk to you is twofold: the earth can destroy this fragile city in its anger, and it will wake in rage—or the earth can do what none have yet done: it can wake the Sleepers.

"And the rage of the Sleepers guarantees the destruction of all you have built."

"And the rage of a distant god?"

"Distant is the important word, there. Do what you must. Make your decision." He turned away; two strides carried him half the length of a long, empty hall. But he turned back. "Matteos."

Things must be grim indeed if Meralonne addressed him by name. "APhaniel."

"She will listen to voices that none of the magi can hear. They will not, as she fears, hear her. That was never the danger. I leave her safety in your hands."

The reply Matteos should have made died on his tongue. He meant to tell Meralonne that Sigurne needed neither safety nor protection, because that had always been true. But life was not static. Sigurne was alive.

"Meralonne," she said, before he turned again.

"Guildmaster?"

"I want the merchants alive."

"They are dying even now."

"Yes. Do not add to the numbers of the dead where it can at all be prevented."

"Very well. The architectural stability of the building itself?"

"When buildings like this one collapse, people die."

He nodded again, and left them. With him went the harsh, cold light of his blade, and the narrowed edges of his eyes. But Matteos had seen the sharp, upward curve of his lips; the slender edge of smile that adorned them seemed almost predatory.

Sigurne did not follow.

Instead, she sank to her knees, the motion deliberate. Her hands, she set immediately against the flat, stone wall. Her lips moved, and as they did, a demon roared again; the echoes of his voice shook the floor. She did not attempt to repeat her words; she swallowed them, closed her eyes, and leaned all of her weight into her hands.

Matteos felt the ground move again. He heard the roar of a demon shift in tone and timbre as it shouted a single name: *Illaraphaniel*.

He did not hear Meralonne's reply. He heard shouts. He heard screams. But through them all, he saw Sigurne. In the end, he did what she did not: he cast a shield around them both. He concentrated on floor and wall—he trusted neither. Meralonne unleashed could destroy half the building without a second thought. Sigurne had given clear instructions—but combat, for the mage, was its own imperative.

Sigurne, he thought, what are you doing?

"Do not speak," she whispered. Her hands trembled. "I must *listen*."

He was afraid he knew. He had never asked her about her life in the North, although he knew of it. Rumor, gossip, angry whispers about hypocrisy, often filled the halls in the absence of the guildmaster. But the Kings trusted Sigurne. Matteos trusted her.

He quieted his growing unease as he always had: by guarding her exposed back. He understood the significance of the wild earth, here. What he did not understand was how she meant to thwart it. What he did not understand was why Meralonne expected that she *could*.

As one mage-born, Matteos could see magic. He could see it as color, as a pale nimbus. Every school of magic, every discipline, had a telltale color associated with its use. He could sense magic. He could, with effort, detect it, if the magic were subtle or faint.

The magic Sigurne now used was colorless. Had he relied on vision alone, he would have said she used none. But without effort, he felt the surge of it; he felt the sudden shift of *power*. Sigurne huddled against the wall, hands extended and white, as if with strain; she bent, her head falling, her eyes closed.

He wanted to catch her. To carry her. To lift her and remove her from this place. And he wanted, simultaneously, to step back, to step away, to shield himself and protect himself from what must surely follow. He had never followed Sigurne because she was weak; he had never admired her because she required protection from the consequences of her actions. She required only support when the actions required were difficult and fraught—and even then, the support she accepted was minimal.

Sigurne.

The demon's voice filled the hall; he was no longer roaring. Matteos did not understand the words he shouted, but knew them for speech.

Sigurne's eyes snapped open; she pushed herself back from the wall, her hands shaking. "I am done for the moment—let us find what survives of the membership of the Merchants' Guild."

Breeze moved down the hall; tugging at the hem of both of their cloaks. "Meralonne," she said, in a voice too soft to be heard. "I have bought time— but in truth, not much. If you do not finish this fight quickly, it will be for naught."

Matteos glanced at her, and understood, as she headed grimly down the hall toward the assembly room, that whatever she had done required power, and she was spending it. He took no joy in watching the savagery of Meralonne at war; he displayed an almost unholy delight in the act of killing. But just this once, he was grateful.

Or would be, if Meralonne heard Sigurne and understood: she had only the time her power granted her, and her power—unlike Meralonne's—was not limitless, and it was never spent without cost.

"Matteos, husband your power."

Matteos nodded. It was a nod that acknowledged receipt of a command, but did not imply obedience. "I do not trust these floors," he told her. It was explanation for the spell he had cast; if the floors gave way, they—Sigurne and Matteos—would not fall. "There is smoke in the distance."

Demons summoned fire; they both knew it. If much of the building was of stone, parts of it were not, and wood burned swiftly when confronted with magical fire. Stone, on the other hand, did melt.

Her lips pursed; she said nothing else. Her expression was both weary and distant: it was as if most of her thought, most of her attention, was elsewhere. This Sigurne, he had seldom seen. In fact, he had only seen her a handful of times—and each and every one involved Meralonne APhaniel.

There was no longer a door between the great hall and the back halls. There had been; splinters and twisted brass were strewn across the floor on either side of its frame. So, Matteos thought, with some disgust, were large chunks of stone. If this were a bearing wall, he had just shortened the time they had to effect a rescue—and from the screams and the sobs growing in volume in the distance, rescue was not yet impossible.

Sigurne frowned. "Did I not tell him that he was not to destroy the building?"

"Not in so many words, no." Matteos' wards flared to life. "How much time do we have?"

Sigurne stepped around him as he paused at the opening destruction had left. She looked up. Matteos did not; the merchants were not in the air. Meralonne was, of course. Meralonne and chunks of debris. The debris itself would kill if it landed in the wrong place.

Matteos cast. Gray light rolled across the debris-strewn floor like a carpet. Orange light encased them both with a harsh brightness that implied fire.

"How many?" she asked. She did not wait for an answer. Where Matteos' protections were a bright translucent orange, the spell Sigurne now cast was gold; it gilded the former.

"A dozen are dead," Matteos said, frowning. "A dozen are dying."

"The rest?"

"Alive. Injured, but alive." He glanced at her. "You are not surprised."

"No. Demons are not known for granting quick and painless deaths where they have any other option. I do not believe they thought to be disturbed before the earth rose. They do not hunt in the city; if they hunt at all—and they must—they are kept on a very tight leash. This would have been a gift to them.

"We must hurry," she added. "They intended to kill all of the merchants present. Now that they know we are here, any sustenance granted from pain and torture is secondary." She did not need to tell him that the demonic ability to kill the remaining survivors was vastly larger than their ability to protect them.

The great hall in the guildhall was two stories in height, the ceiling that capped it, rounded. The Order of Knowledge boasted only two rooms that approached this one in size.

Matteos braced the crumbling stone of the wall that had once contained the servants' entrance and exit. The entrance through which the merchants had come was not, of course, the one that Matteos and Sigurne had followed—but the doors that they'd entered were closed. They were also standing. From this distance, Matteos could see that they were magically protected. They might also be barred; he hadn't the time to waste ascertaining that.

Most of the merchants—those who survived—were huddled against the walls of the great room, or beneath its tables. Some were huddled protectively over those who had fallen; it was folly, of course.

But folly was part of humanity, and there was, in this reckless and hopeless attempt to come to the aid of friends—or even strangers—something they would spend the rest of their life attempting to preserve.

"Matteos."

He nodded. He knew her. He knew what she wanted of him. The demon was occupied with Meralonne APhaniel; Meralonne could not afford to be distracted. Matteos glanced up; the familiar brilliance of blue sword met the sharp edge of burning red in midair; the impact drove the combatants apart. They did not stop; their trajectories were decided by air, by fire, by power. Driven back, they traveled in an arc, the lowest and highest points the moment at which they pivoted, gaining traction in a way that no one mortal could.

They spoke in a language that sounded familiar; the words, however, were taken by wind and rock and the sharp, harsh crackle of flame.

Fire.

It devoured tables in an instant; the merchants screamed as they realized their slender protections were gone. Gone as well were tablecloths, pitchers. Shards of broken crystal littered the floor; they had already drawn blood.

Sigurne gestured then.

The fires banked. In any other circumstance, Matteos would have turned to stare. The merchants couldn't know that magical fires differed greatly in nature. They couldn't be expected to understand the difference between wild, elemental flame and the fires the magi could produce; death was death, after all.

But Matteos knew. Sigurne knew. What the demons summoned was no simple artifact of power; it had will. It had voice. It had a life of its own. Wild elements were lore, legend; only one mortal voice in recent history could be heard by them at all.

She was gone. The ancient wilds had swallowed her whole; no one—not even the Kings—knew if she would return. And in her absence, the demons had attacked. In her absence, they chose to summon the wild earth.

In her absence, Sigurne had lessened their impact. Sigurne had somehow managed to forestall the waking of the earth. The fires did not vanish. But they burned less wildly.

"It will not last," Sigurne said, as if she could hear what he did not put into words. She cast again—and this time, there was blessed familiarity in the spell. Light—magelight—spread across one section of the floor, in a perfect, glowing line, the width of two men standing—albeit tightly—abreast.

She lifted her chin, and as she did, raised her voice, projecting it into the room. She was loud, clear, and unstoppable; her words cut through sobs and shouts, swamping whimpers and even screams.

"Follow the path that appears on the floor in front of you. Those who can walk, help those too injured. We do not have much time." She extended a shield of protection above the path.

Sigurne could sound calm and harmless at the heart of a storm. Even this one. Her glance grazed the characteristic greatcoat of Loren; the merchant had lost the whole of his left arm, and lay unmoving and wide-eyed in his own blood, one of two dozen such bodies.

Some of the living hovered over the corpses, shouting their names in a series of repetitive, cascading syllables that denied not death, but truth. Sigurne understood, and understood further that too many of these people were bereft of their normal good sense.

The Guildmaster of the Order of Knowledge was considered a polite force to be placated when events became "unpleasant." Were the demon and his fire gone from this room, Sigurne could have led the injured away.

He was not, and his fire posed a very real threat—as did Meralonne's wind. Sigurne looked past the dead, the dying, the injured; past the men and women who stared, unseeing, at nothing. She required help, but could not see the logical choice of designated commander, the guildmaster of the Merchants' Guild, in the hall, either alive or dead. An autocratic and proud man, the cut of his clothing would have given his body away, and he was unlikely to cower.

But he was not present.

She exhaled with otherwise unvoiced relief when her gaze alighted on a familiar woman; she was surprised to see her in the guildhall, as she was not aware that the merchant had returned to the city. Eva Juwal had seen her share of death; she traveled, caravan firmly under her figurative whip, through war zones, in which deserters lurked in wait for merchants and their cargoes. Eva was not without scars; she was perfectly capable of wielding a sword when necessary, although she was practical enough to prefer a crossbow at a distance. She was not small; she was not retiring.

Her scars—the visible ones—were stretched and discolored; she was unnaturally, but not unexpectedly, pale. "Merchant Juwal," Sigurne said, gilding her voice with magic so it might carry. Sigurne's talent was not bardic; she could not pitch her voice so that it was heard only by the individual in question—not without a great deal of preparation.

But Eva recognized Sigurne's voice instantly; she turned. "Guildmaster."

"Your help would be greatly appreciated."

Eva, a woman half Sigurne's age on a bad day, had an arm beneath an older man's; he was bleeding at the left temple, his eyes wide and almost unblinking. He moved because Eva supported his weight; if not for Eva's support, Sigurne doubted he would be walking at all. He did not seem to be fully aware of his surroundings. "I'm a bit busy, Guildmaster."

"Of course you are, dear."

A merchant from the tender age of four if one listened to her stories about her own life, Eva frowned. She was taller than Sigurne, although some of that height was due to Sigurne's posture. "I hate it when you 'dear' me." She had the voice of a military man; she regularly terrified men of rank, wealth, and more delicate sensibilities. But fully a third of her personal income came from the Order of Knowledge—she traveled to and from the West, as far as the mottled collection of small countries known as the Western Kingdoms if one didn't happen to live in one of them.

She could not afford to offend the guildmaster, and they both knew it.

Her language when annoyed was salty. She was clearly annoyed at the moment; enough so that she didn't flinch when fire landed two inches above the top of her head, spreading to either side as it flowed around the protections Sigurne had cast.

Sigurne, however, failed to hear her. Eva was a merchant in almost all of her dealings, but the man she escorted to the jagged remnant of what had once been wall was not one of her subordinates. Left to her own devices, Eva's instinctive reaction was almost always to offer aid when it wasn't too costly.

Cost, in Eva's case meant money. She didn't seem to recognize that death generally prevented earning any more of it, but she had always survived what many considered to be her recklessness. Sigurne had never considered her reckless. She waited while Eva barked at another stunned merchant, handing responsibility—and physical burden—to him. That accomplished, Eva strode quickly toward the magi.

Sigurne did not waste time. "I have three different barriers erected at the moment. I cannot supervise our retreat without losing at least half of the people present."

"Conservative guess?"

"Yes. Take command as you can. There is a narrow strip of ground the fire will not reach."

"The gold one?"

"Yes. The protections are not the only work I have done today; in the context of the city, they are not even the most significant."

"How much time do we have?"

"As much as we absolutely need—but not a minute more. Leave the dead."

"The injured?"

"Use your discretion. What did the demon demand?"

"Death," Eva replied, shrugging. "And fear."

Sigurne nodded. "Fear feeds them, in a fashion. If he meant to kill you all, he was far too self-indulgent—but even thus engaged he is not without power."

"And we are."

"Unless you were prepared for demons and magical attacks, yes."

"You'll owe me for this."

Sigurne expected no less; she wasn't pleased, but she didn't have time to make this clear. Loss of a handful of merchants caused difficulty—but loss of most of the guild would be far, far worse for the city. "Yes. Where is the guildmaster?"

Eva frowned.

"Never mind; now is not the time." A cascading rain of raging fire swept the room, charring flesh; the stench made breathing difficult, and the barrier buckled under its concerted attack. Not all of the merchants had moved to safety. There were men and women she could not save. There had always been men and women she could not save. She concentrated only on those she could.

She bent her head as Eva left. The younger woman kept her wide feet firmly planted across the narrow stretch of illuminated floor that Sigurne had pronounced safe. "Listen up," the merchant snapped, her voice filling all of the space not occupied by wind, fire, or immortals. "Corin, get the hell away from the mantel. *Now.* Bring that idiot friend of yours with you."

The idiot friend appeared to have lost half a hand. It was his left.

"Jill—shut it or *I'll* give you something to scream about."

No less a person than the head of House Montaven's jaws snapped shut. She was younger than Eva; she was not a woman to whom commands were given. But she had undeniably been whimpering. And she had never, in Sigurne's hearing, been called an unvarnished "Jill" before. Sigurne was not certain that that *was* her official given name.

Eva never failed to surprise.

The merchant had already moved on. She understood, as Matteos had, exactly what Sigurne wanted from her; it was likely she would have taken the lead regardless, but where it was possible at this late stage, Sigurne did not wish to leave things to chance.

In the rain of fire, lightning was red and blue; thunder was demonic, a great roar of fury that shook the ground—but did not wake the earth as was intended.

Eva's voice was drowned out, twice, by the clash of two swords. What was almost metallic thunder died before the merchant's voice did; she had a job to do now, and bent a ferocious focus upon only that. Demons were foreign, terrifying nightmares—but the magi were now here; men who fought creatures standing on nothing but air were therefore *not* Eva's problem. The merchants were.

She wasn't gentle; she didn't have the time. She slapped at least two people; Sigurne heard and registered the sound, but didn't see who; nor did she now care. The shadows that had sealed the public doors, so effectively preventing escape began to flow away from them.

Toward the merchants; toward Eva herself.

Those doors now burst open; standing in them were armed and armored men. Men, Sigurne thought, not demons.

But men could be bought; men could be coerced. They could also be killed—but not with any ease, not while the barriers were being maintained. The calculus of magic was always difficult; one borrowed against oneself, and one repaid the debt with interest. Some debts could not be paid; a fourth barrier against men wielding plain steel could be erected; it would halve the duration of the other three.

She raised voice. "*Meralonne.*" She called Eva's name as well, but Eva didn't turn; she stilled. She understood.

Not all of the merchants did, and four died running *to* the open doors. Their deaths answered the brief doubt Sigurne had entertained—and such a doubt was folly. Hope often was.

The wind did what Sigurne could not; it bore down upon the armed men who had entered the hall, driving them back into their comrades. Armor clattered against armor, and at least three swords flew in the wind's folds. Fire answered, but it was an imperfect tool; the men could not breach it without burning.

Sigurne did not look up. She shortened the Summer path. She did not intend to offer any succor to men who had sold their swords to a demon. They had; they evinced no surprise at the aerial combat confined—for the most part—to the ceiling's height; nor did they seem surprised at the fire. The wind, yes—but the wind was no part of their forces.

They regrouped, attempting to navigate the fire that now reached for the wind—as it had, in patches, since they'd breached the shattered door. The demon shouted perfectly clear Weston orders. The merchants were to die. All of them. No exceptions.

Orders were barked—in the same Weston. They were passed back through the open doorway through which more men poured. As fire flared, as blue light flashed, Sigurne recognized the tabards half a dozen men wore: they were Merchants' Guild.

The merchants—those that could move, with or without aid—clung to the path that Sigurne had made, fear of the most mundane of the threats they faced speeding their movements. The golden light on the floor did not seem to the unschooled to offer much in the way of protection—but it led away from the armed men. One or two of the merchants sported daggers that had been drawn only in the face of the new arrivals; many of them had faced bandits, and they had all demonstrably survived.

Because they had, they knew survival was never guaranteed. Yes, she thought, as she heard *Kalliaris'* name raised. Pray if you must, but *move*.

Sigurne did not pray. She had long since discovered there was no efficacy in it. Prayers were offered when all other avenues had failed, because at that point, efficiency signified little. All that was left was the pain of raw hope.

It yawned before her now.

Demons were not careful about their merely human servants; fire rose, sweeping across the guildhall floors; what it touched, it consumed. The flooring fell away in large patches. Wood, blood-soaked carpets and the corpses that lay strewn across them, turned to ash, bone, black rising smoke.

She felt a distant, grim satisfaction as armored men fell through the floor to the basement rooms beneath it. The second layer of Sigurne's cast protections maintained the solidity of her Summer path under the feet of the merchants; she had expected this. It had come later rather than sooner, allowing her to husband some of the power she now spent in earnest.

"Matteos!"

He answered, his voice attenuated.

"Tell Gavin—enter the main hall through the front doors; use whatever force he deems necessary. There will be resistance. Very little of it will be magical in nature.

"Eva."

The merchant was now less than ten feet from where Sigurne stood. She herded—there was no other word for it—the last of the merchants toward the gaping hole in the wall. The floor beneath her feet was solid—but the gaps that opened up to one side of it yawned, waiting for a false step. Waiting, Sigurne thought, for the wind that could not—yet—pass her barriers.

"The fire, Guildmaster—"

Sigurne exhaled. "It will die when the demon does." And let that be soon.

Let it be before the exultance she heard in Meralonne's voice reached the ears of the rest of the merchants. "The halls beyond this room are not yet contested. Matteos will tell you where to go—make sure as many of your cohort follows his instructions as you can."

Eva nodded. She wanted to argue—no doubt to demand more information—but that was just instinct, and a stronger instinct overwhelmed it: survival. If Sigurne did not believe that prayer was beneficial, she would nonetheless offer a benediction to the triumvirate for any who survived this evening's work. She held the path. She held it, although her arms began the involuntary shuddering that indicated that she had pushed past—far past—her reasonable limits.

Now was *not* the time for such weakness. It was, however, the time for such risks. "Meralonne!"

She didn't look up, although she desired a glimpse of the most fractious, disorderly member of her Order. She knew that he was almost unconfined here, unfettered by the trappings of life as a mortal. And yes, it stirred her; the ancient and the wild both elevated and diminished her. She could never be what he was; no amount of study or power could change her essential nature.

Yet she could stand, as she might stand in a storm, in awe of a force that was so much beyond her it might have been tidal wave or earthquake. She could no more command a tidal wave than she could command Meralonne; what authority she had, he ceded her. He tolerated it. But obey or no, he had always heard her voice.

He heard it now.

He replied: the wind roared. Fire had been summoned and fire had scorched floor and charred corpses, adding to their count when the living, too traumatized to comprehend basic commands, failed to stand on the only safe ground marked by three different magics. But the fire that had been called was bound to the voice and the power of a ghost.

The wind was not.

Sigurne retreated to the wall; it was far simpler to sustain protections in the gap there, and the moment they were no longer necessary—and that time was coming—she could allow them to lapse without fear of perishing herself. She did not count the merchants who passed her by; she did not tell them to hurry.

Eva did that, her voice strident and clear. She led—harshly—where leading was necessary, but she returned to the stragglers and the back of the line. She was not gentle; if she had ever been gentle, travel with caravans had cured her. Where her words couldn't reach the last of the merchants, her hands could; the sharp sting of her palm was silenced by the wind's anger and the crackle of fire.

She led, cajoled, and dragged. Each merchant clambered out of the gaping hole that had once contained both doorframe and door, passing Sigurne, until only Eva remained. Her dark eyes narrowed as they met Sigurne's.

"Where the hells are the rest of your magi?"

"On the other side of the far doors," Sigurne replied. "Do not tarry here, Eva."

Eva snorted. "I should throw you out first, myself."

"Go. I will follow."

"You're practically unconscious as it is, Guildmaster."

It was true; Sigurne did not waste breath denying it.

She listened. She listened to what she heard in Meralonne, his voice familiar, even if the words that it uttered were—and would always be—beyond her. He rode the wind, and it carried him in graceful, sudden arcs; his sword left a trail of light in her vision, a ghostly lattice, a map, of sorts.

He was as wild, here, as the wind; as wild as the fire. There was beauty in savagery as compelling as storm and mountain and the vast depth of ocean on a clear day. She could not own it; she could not touch it. But she could bear witness.

"Sigurne, come away." The words were no part of the wild; they contained no magic, no majesty. The voice that spoke them was older, rougher; it dipped and faded as the wind roared. It was not the voice she wanted to hear, now.

But she could.

"Sigurne, Eva has taken the last of the merchants. Meralonne cannot finish this combat while you are here."

"He does not see me," she whispered.

"No. But he knows. Come. I cannot maintain the path for nearly as long as you have, and we must be away before the floor collapses."

She did not have the strength to repeat the words of a distant god. But Meralonne was here; she did not have to try. She could listen. She could listen to things that would never, ever hear her voice in their turn.

"Sigurne."

Matteos gripped her arm, pulling her through the ragged hole. Splinters of wood lodged themselves in the backs of her calves and caught in the hem of her robe. Clumsy, really. Had her spells unraveled so much in so short a time?

"Sigurne."

Ah. Yes. Yes, she thought. They had. But the time was not so small a span; she was not in the Northern Wastes, and the demon was not her master; the only thing the past and the present had in common was the white-haired man with the sky-blue sword and the shining, silver eyes. She had watched him in the Northern Wastes, where the snow was so white it caused the eye to water. She stood, tall, as tall as she had ever stood, her hands by her sides, her eyes dry—and wide. She had known he would come for her.

But not before he killed the Ice Mage.

Not before he killed the *Kialli*. The demon lord did not fear him. She wondered if he understood that the white-haired man was his death—if death had any meaning to a creature who claimed that he had died when the world was young and the gods still walked the earth. She had been sixteen years of age. She had had no expectation, at that moment in time, that she would see seventeen—and she did not care.

So many years between that day and this one. She was old, now, bent with the weight of age.

The only thing she waited for was death, but death—ah, death had not come. Not for her, not yet. Sigurne Mellifas had her pride; if death avoided her, she *would not* walk toward it; she would not beg for mercy. Not then, when death would have been a welcome relief, and not now. Not when she still had work to do.

"Matteos." She did not look at him; she tried. But she spoke his name in a voice that was shorn of all strength.

He spared no glance for Meralonne as he shouldered the greater part of her weight, turning her toward the servants' exit. Toward life. Touch alone confirmed what he was too observant to miss, but he did not coddle or otherwise undermine her.

That would come later, in the privacy of her Tower, when the undamaged halls of the Order of Knowledge once again enfolded them both. "Sigurne."

"I know," she whispered. "We are almost done here."

"You *are* done here." He glanced past her, sliding an arm beneath her arms and taking as much of her weight as she was willing to allow him. Her knees were weak; she locked them. She was accustomed to being treated as if she were old and frail, and it had its uses.

It would not be useful here.

"Meralonne?"

Matteos glanced back. ". . . The damage to the guildhall will be extensive."

"And Gavin?"

"I am not certain there will be anything left for Gavin and his magi to detain."

Sigurne grimaced. "Gavin is not a fool. He understands what the Order—and the Mysterium—now require. We cannot capture or compel demons; we can, however, interrogate mortals. The men in guildhall tabards were no demons."

Matteos nodded; it was a gesture meant to stifle discussion, rather than to indicate agreement. The nimbus of orange that had surrounded them both brightened around only Sigurne. "Let your protections go," he told her.

Her nod was mirror to his, and he did not press her. She watched Eva's back until her vision was too blurred to continue. Her eyes closed almost of their own accord as she listened. She had not stopped listening.

"Sigurne." Matteos' voice was thin and rough.

She did not lie to comfort him. "Yes. I was . . . unwise. I did not realize how much of a drain the first cast spell would be. It was not an act of folly," she added, although her voice shook. "The damage done to the Empire if all of the merchants had perished here would be catastrophic."

Matteos did not argue. And Sigurne, shuddering, let the last of her protections lapse as his enfolded her. He was, she thought, her knight, her liege, her oathguard. He would not argue with her here. He would not ask her what spell she had cast, or how; why was enough of an answer. He would not ask her what Meralonne APhaniel meant when he spoke of danger.

He would not ask her what she heard, when she listened. She was grateful. She knew who their enemy was. She knew what he was. She even understood what he wanted, inasmuch as a mortal could. But she could not relinquish the sound of the god's voice, although he was her enemy. Not until she at last surrendered consciousness—and even this, she fought.

Chapter Seven

8th of Morel, 428 A.A.
Terafin Manse, Averalaan Aramarelas

JESTER AND MORNINGS WERE not the best of friends; had he the luxury of choice, they would have been nothing more than nodding acquaintances. He tended to spend too much of the early morning hours with bards or the less fractious merchants, and he required time to sleep off the worst of his excesses.

On this particular morning, he was stone cold sober. He had returned from the Merchant Authority and retreated immediately to the West Wing for a quiet and isolated meal. His retreat did not go unnoticed. One of the junior pages, a girl or boy of perhaps ten, stumbled on the carpets in the long, public gallery; Jester was there to catch her before the stumble became a fall. She apologized profusely, clearly terrified that such clumsiness had been witnessed. But as he helped her to her feet, she slid something into the palm of his hand.

He failed to notice. He failed to notice it as he entered the West Wing, passing between the Chosen who now stood guard at the doors; he failed to notice as he bypassed the dining room and the great room and headed directly for his personal chambers.

He also failed to notice it when he dropped it in a drawer in the pristine desk which was used for very little else. He disliked the desk on principle. Teller had a new desk that was very similar to it—but Teller had insisted that *all* of their desks be replaced.

Jester understood why and saw no point in arguing; then again, Jester seldom saw much point in arguing. He had his own way of dealing with things, none of which involved an empty stomach. At the moment, none of them involved company, either. He had dinner sent to his rooms, and he hunkered there, eating and thinking about the day's events.

They required thought, but he kept returning to Finch. Someone had tried to assassinate her. Jay had been The Terafin at the time—although technically she was still The Terafin. Jester didn't take notes—not written ones. But he thought about Ruby and Verdian. About Ludgar. About Jarven ATerafin, a man he was never going to trust.

The odd thing was that Finch didn't trust him, either.

When he finished eating, he brooded. He considered heading out for the evening, but the events at the Merchant Authority had unsettled him enough that he wanted to sort through the questions that arose from it. The obvious questions, he discarded. Everyone would ask those. But absent the obvious— who was responsible, and what they could possibly gain—subtle questions remained.

Those, he would have to approach with care, and the first step of care was deciding which questions would yield information. Once he had questions, he would have a clearer idea of who his drinking companions for the next week were likely to be.

Evening had surrendered very few questions of use by the time it gave way to morning; it had also offered very little restful sleep. Jester considered catching Teller in the breakfast nook, but decided against it; Teller was likely to ask about his meeting with Haval, and Haval Arwood was not the man Jester wished to discuss. Not with Teller.

In an attempt to put that discussion off, he lingered in bed until he was fairly certain Teller had finished. He then rose and asked that breakfast be sent to his room. Given the dark circles under his eyes, the servants no doubt assumed he was hungover, which happened with less frequency than they suspected, but probably more frequency than was wise.

He was, therefore, less than well pleased when breakfast arrived with company. He was not terribly surprised at the company itself, and briefly considered attempting to discard that company in the same way he'd discarded the message. "I wasn't really expecting visitors," he said, glancing pointedly at his dressing gown. It was too much to expect that Haval would take the less than graceful hint.

"You should have been."

"Yes, well. Did you bring food for two?"

"No. I breakfasted with my wife. With," he added, sharpening his voice, although his face was almost expressionless, "my extremely worried wife. You perhaps have some inkling of what has caused her latest concerns?"

Jester, like any of the den, could eat on the literal run, if necessary. Eating while an inscrutable bloody *tailor* interrogated him wasn't going to be a problem, even if his appetite was fast approaching zero. He walked over to the trays that had been set on the small table, and lifted their silver lids, glancing at a distorted reflection of Haval as he did. "I got your message."

"You did not reply."

"No; no reply was demanded. I'm not sure I approve of your method of delivery."

Haval said nothing.

"I don't recall that I agreed to work for you," he continued, when the long pause had grown awkward, even for Jester. "If I'm to do so, some discussion about compensation is in order."

Once again, Haval failed to respond. Jester dragged a chair across the rug. It was a battered piece of furniture of purely middling quality; he turned its back toward the table. He then sat in it, draping his arms over the top and folding them. "Did you know that the Merchant Authority would be under attack?"

"I did not. It is my guess that Finch suspected there would be difficulties. I doubt that even she expected the scope of them. It will not, today, be her chief concern. You have heard about the difficulties the Merchants' Guild encountered?"

". . . No." Jester began to eat. The food, although warm, had very little taste at the moment.

"If you manage to leave your rooms today, you will no doubt hear every possible rumor."

"How true are the rumors?"

Haval didn't answer.

Fine, Jester thought. He was not in a mood to play games with the tailor. He was no longer in a mood to eat breakfast, but again, mood was seldom a deterrent. "Ruby ATerafin wasn't surprised—at all—by Finch's message. She wasn't happy, but she expected trouble." He grimaced. "She expected a lot more trouble from Finch than anyone reasonable has a right to expect."

"Ruby ATerafin is known for her cunning, not her dispassionate view of life."

Jester's brows rose as he examined Haval's face for some spark that implied deliberate humor. If it was there, the humor was dry enough to catch fire.

"Ludgar mentioned Verdian."

"As?"

"As someone whose suspicion of Finch was correct."

Haval nodded. "You are not suspicious of Ludgar."

"Oh, I am. Ludgar would have no issues attempting to have Finch removed if he thought it would benefit him. But he can't see Finch as a threat—and he's not fool enough to attempt to kill Jarven, more's the pity."

"Is Verdian playing Ludgar?"

Jester shrugged. "He would be easy for Verdian to play, up to a point. I'd worry more about the possible influence she has on Ruby."

"Ruby is not known to be fond of Verdian."

"No—but Ruby's not fond of anyone. Ludgar is Haerrad's man, at the moment."

"And Ruby?"

"Uncertain. She has feelers in at least three camps."

"Three?"

"If you're playing at ignorance, stop. It's spoiling breakfast."

Haval did smile, then, the bastard. "You are not concerned with either Ruby or Ludgar."

"I am. They're just a fair ways down the list at the moment. James Varson is not, in any way, in the running as a possible suspect in the attempt on Finch's life."

"I have not had the pleasure of making James Varson's direct acquaintance. His name and his position are known to me; he himself is not. You do not consider him a possible antagonist."

"No. I consider him a bit of a dupe, if we're being frank."

Haval raised a brow.

Jester found this more amusing when it was aimed at Jay. "I'm not certain what position Varson holds in the Merchant Authority offices as of yesterday; for the sake of his family, I hope he hasn't been promoted."

"Finch's message to Varson?"

"I believe it was a penned warning of possible danger to the Authority itself, given Varson's reaction."

"From Finch."

"Yes."

"Not Jarven."

"Not apparently, no. Jarven knows, of course. I don't think anything happens in that office without his knowledge." He exhaled. "Are you aware that Finch is now sharing office space with Jarven?"

Haval actually frowned. "I assume you mean, by this, that there is a change in her position."

"There is. She is literally sharing an office with Jarven. She has a desk of her own in the office he's occupied for decades. She takes her appointments in that room. I doubt he even sends her out to fetch and carry tea anymore."

"I don't," was the somewhat more acid reply. "Were the messages she sent meant to convey her change in status?"

"Oh, they were certainly meant to convey *that*. They were not, however, otherwise empty. She's threatening both Ludgar and Ruby."

"You are certain?"

"I don't know what she wrote to Ruby; I do know what she wrote to Ludgar." He dropped his chin to his arms. "But I'm not sure either of the two— or Verdian or Haerrad or Rymark—are the biggest danger at the moment."

"You are, in my opinion, correct, but they are not a danger to be dismissed out of hand. Let me tell you what I have gleaned about the events in the guildhall. I would send you there myself, but you are unlikely to gain access."

"I've been on the inside of the Merchants' guildhall before."

"I am not at all surprised. The building, however—what remains of it—is under heavy Imperial quarantine. The magi and the mages of the Mysterium have closed its doors to even its members. Those members," he added, "who survived. You will find that two very junior members of House Terafin perished last night. Two more escaped; I believe they are expected in the office of the right-kin this morning."

"You believe?"

"They are currently resident within the Order of Knowledge. They will be questioned there, along with any of the other merchants who survived."

Jester rose, frustrated. He considered the possibility that Haval was lying, and discarded it; the old man wasn't fond of wasting his own time. "Tell me what the rumors are."

"They are of strong concern to my wife."

Jester actually liked Hannerle. He understood that she was deeply attached to her husband—and frequently disappointed in him. He was less certain that the attachment in the other direction was as reliable, but Jay believed it was. "Hannerle's always been sensible. *What* rumors concern her?"

"Ah. The most disturbing of the rumors? That a demon—that several demons—attacked the Merchants' guildhall in the middle of an emergency meeting last evening. The meeting itself was extremely well attended because of the attacks that had taken place in the Merchant Authority in the morning.

"Very few merchants of note who have been granted membership in the guild were absent—and of those, most were not resident within Averalaan at the time the call went out."

"You mean all of the merchants who have membership were there."

"To my knowledge—which is not complete—yes."

Jester sat down again. "How accurate is this knowledge?"

"There is some margin for error; it is, in my opinion, small." He paused and then added, "Jarven is a member of the guild in good standing."

Jester frowned. "Have you spoken with Finch?"

"No. I was with my wife. By the time I arrived at the Terafin manse, she had departed for the day; she is no doubt ensconced in the Terafin Merchant Authority offices as we speak."

"Jarven's a member of the Merchants' Guild."

"He is."

"Was Jarven present in the guildhall last night?"

"A very good question." Haval glanced at the half-empty breakfast plates. "I have an appointment—on short notice—with Jarven ATerafin. We have an hour before it is scheduled to start."

"You have an appointment. With Jarven."

"Indeed. Appointment in this case is an inaccurate choice of wording; I have been summoned."

"Jarven summoned you."

"Technically, the summons came from Lucille ATerafin. I chose to ignore the summons; my wife did not feel this was the appropriate course of action."

"She doesn't care for Jarven."

"She is barely aware of his existence. She is, however, aware that Finch is his direct subordinate, and that Finch is valued by Jarven. I am, therefore, to attend Jarven ATerafin."

This made no sense to Jester.

"You are to speak with Teller," Haval continued. "He may have more information about the events at the Merchants' guildhall—but I believe the salient points for our purposes are now known." He turned toward the door, but turned back.

"The Master of the Household Staff is not, perhaps, in the most pleasant of moods."

Jester didn't even ask the clothier how he'd come by this information.

* * *

Teller's office was preternaturally silent when Jester entered. Barston was, as ever, behind his desk; he glanced up and the frown etched into his face by constant use deepened. "ATerafin." He was so starched, he could never quite bring himself to use Jester's name.

"Barston."

"You have an appointment?"

"You already know I don't. I'd like to make one, if the right-kin has the time."

Barston glanced at Teller's doors. To Jester's surprise, he rose. He approached the closed doors, knocked, and waited. At some inaudible signal, he opened the doors and entered the room, closing them behind his back.

Whatever reports had filtered back to House Terafin from the Merchants' Guild were bad, Jester thought. Very bad. He had not thought to ask Haval how many men and women had died in total; his own fault. Haval was not a man given to dramatics that served no purpose; information didn't require it.

But Barston's color, Barston's expression, made clear that the answer was not a small number. And it made clear, as well, that rumors of demonic involvement were almost certainly based in fact. The shadow of the Henden of 410 had fallen over the secretary's face.

The door opened.

The Master of the Household Staff exited the right-kin's office, looking as pleased as she usually did. If there was any sign of fear in the pinched, narrow line of her mouth, displeasure swamped it. She glanced at Jester, her eyes narrowing to edges. She was, on the other hand, a woman composed entirely of edges; if looks could kill, Jester would no doubt be bleeding—but Barston would be dead.

Neither the secretary nor the Master of the Household Staff said a word to each other. Jester remembered that discretion was the better part of valor. If he was occasionally bold enough to tweak the tiger's whiskers, he was smart enough to know that now was not the time.

Only when the Master of the Household Staff had left the office did he turn to face Barston.

"The Terafin did warn us that her absence would not please the Master of the Household Staff."

Barston offered a clipped nod in response. "The right-kin will see you now."

"You have no idea," Teller said, pacing the length of the large area rug in front of his desk, "how glad I am to see you."

"Given the expression on the Master of the Household Staff's face? Believe I do. I don't think I've seen her that angry since—" He stopped. "It's not about Jay and The Terafin's rooms, is it?"

Teller shook his head.

"It's not about demons and the Merchants' Guild, either."

"No. At this point, I'm not sure which terrifies me more."

"I am. Her."

Teller walked over to the bookshelves and fiddled with the books there, rearranging them with deliberate care. Jester folded his arms and waited; Teller wasn't prone to needless, nervous fuss.

"I had breakfast with Haval," Jester told him, glancing around the otherwise empty office. "In a manner of speaking."

"Oh?"

"I was the only one eating, and by the end, food seemed kind of pointless. You spoke to our junior merchants."

"I spoke to Guillarne. Call him junior in his hearing and you'll be picking yourself up at the bottom of a long, steep set of stairs."

"Which might be preferable to having to listen to him. He was one of the merchants at the guildhall last night?"

Teller nodded as he returned, finally, to his desk. To Jester's mild surprise, he sat behind it, planted his elbows on desk surface, and leaned his forehead, briefly, into his hands. Jester understood why.

Jay was gone.

"What did Guillarne say? Don't make me talk to him in person; it'll end badly."

"That kind of squabble would be exactly the right sort of distraction," Teller replied. "Who do you think Guillarne is going to support?"

"I didn't know his support was up for grabs."

"It probably wasn't. It will be, now."

Ah. "Word of Finch's promotion has reached his ears?"

Teller nodded.

"And after the events at the guildhall, *that's* what he's angry about?"

That tugged an answering smile from Teller, although as smiles went it was anemic. "He is not particularly pleased with the events at the Merchants' Guild, if that helps."

"Not really. It does elevate Guillarne in my opinion. I thought he was merely a pretentious, ambitious bore. Now I realize he's also an idiot."

"He is an ambitious, clever, talented bore."

"Did Finch send him a missive similar to the ones she sent me to deliver?"

"This may come as a surprise to you, but Finch and I are not operating in lockstep."

Jester was silent for a long moment. "Actually, it does. Come as a surprise, I mean." He glanced at the closed doors. "I see you're not availing yourself of the Chosen."

"Not for you. Not—in general—for the Master of the Household Staff, either. Torvan's been here. We're currently in discussions about the particulars of his guard detail. Finch is not yet ready to retain the Chosen in her duties at the Authority."

"I bet Torvan was thrilled."

"I would have bet the same. None of the Chosen are happy that Jay's gone; she took none of them with her. I don't want to antagonize them while they're still smarting. I thought there was a chance she'd at least take Torvan."

Jester understood what that meant. "Finch really is worried about you, then."

"So I gathered. Torvan is, however, more willing to see Finch head to the Authority without the Chosen than he is to let me continue my own duties without escort. I'm not certain I understand why."

Jester snorted. "Two words. Jarven ATerafin."

"Jarven's an old man. He's unlikely to be much use in a fight—"

Jester pinched the bridge of his nose in an exact mimicry of Haval at his most condescendingly frustrated. Teller surprised them both by laughing.

"You don't think he's helpless."

"You can't honestly believe that he is?"

"He's an old man, Jester. He's—"

"He's probably the most terrifying thing the Merchant Authority contains—and I'm including explosive magical traps in that. Torvan is less worried about Finch because she's *sitting in Jarven's office*. I'd feel more comfortable if Jarven wasn't sitting in it with her. Do you have any idea how often assassination attempts have been made against him in the past five years?"

"Between three and five."

Jester sat down. He made a show of it, but that didn't take any great effort; he was surprised. "Can I ask exactly how you know this? Because if you're accepting the facts from Jarven—"

"I'm not. Look, I know you don't like him much."

Jester didn't bother to disagree.

"And I know Jay doesn't trust him, either. But at the moment, given the events in both the Authority and the Merchants' Guild, we need him to be where he is. If we'd had any idea beforehand, I don't think Finch would have accepted the promotion—it's too much change.

"We didn't."

"We."

Teller nodded.

"Does Finch know about the attempts on Jarven's life?"

"She may suspect."

"The information came from a source you trust?"

Teller hesitated.

Jester's fingers danced in the air.

"I'm willing to trust him," Teller replied.

Jester picked imaginary lint off his trousers. "It's Devon, isn't it?"

"Well, it wasn't Jarven."

"No, I imagine not. That might actually be helpful."

Teller, ever politic, said nothing. He knew how Jester felt about Devon. "Do you think he's lying?"

Jester shook his head. "Duvari can't be Jarven's biggest fan."

"He's not particularly enamored of Jay, either."

Jester shrugged. "He's Duvari. Duvari's consistent. Humorless, dangerous, and incredibly dull, but consistent." He rose and began to pace, something he only did around his den-kin. "If Jarven wanted Finch dead, she'd *be* dead. She's not. For the moment, she's probably safer than she's ever been." He paused and turned to face Teller. "Take the Chosen."

"I'm not without resources of my own."

"In this office, no."

"I'm not in danger in the West Wing."

"You'll stay in the wing, then?"

Teller inspected his hands. "Yes."

"Barston's not happy about it."

"You noticed?"

"Actually, no. Barston is incapable of looking cheerful about anything. I guessed. He's always had a stick up his—"

Teller coughed. "He does care about proper form and hierarchy, yes. Torvan considers the move inadvisable at this time."

"Really?"

"Finch can't move in with me. She'll be in the West Wing, and when she's in the manse, she is under the protection of the Chosen. But they're far fewer in number than they were when Amarais was alive."

Amarais. Jester couldn't recall Teller ever using The Terafin's given name before.

"Jay hasn't added to their number, and the captains can't without her approval. Arann's combed the list of the House Guard for men we might be able to trust in future—but the House Guards haven't settled into uniform service. Not yet. Things are too unstable."

"Is Jarven taking the seat on the House Council?"

"Yes. Before you argue, I think that's where we want him."

"I don't."

"He's sharing his position at the Merchant Authority with Finch. Everything that enters his office will pass beneath her eyes. Guillarne is on the warpath, and he won't be the only one; I expect Ruby ATerafin to descend on my office sometime in the next three days. Should I expect Ludgar?"

"No. I mean, yes—he'll visit. But Jay's on the road and the House Council knows it. His performance will be pro forma; a matter of appearance. He may try to rid us all of Jarven, but at this point that won't break my heart."

"Would any death—besides ours—upset you?"

"Yes. I can't stand Barston, but it would upset me if he was murdered. If, on the other hand, he chose to expire of apoplexy, I'd consider it his just desserts. I'm fond of three quarters of the serving staff. If the Master of the Household Staff expired of anything but old age, I'd be more shocked than upset. Jay, on the other hand, would be upset."

"Jay's not entirely fond of the Master of the Household Staff, herself."

"No. She's not a woman who inspires affection. She is a woman who inspires confidence. She keeps the House running. She'd reached a kind of armistice with Carver."

Silence. Teller eventually broke it. "Carver's not here."

"And I'm incapable of his particular brand of charm. On most days, I don't regret it."

"Today?"

"I want to know why the Master of the Household Staff was in your office."

"She wanted to speak with The Terafin."

"She knows The Terafin's not here."

Teller nodded.

"And she came, anyway?"

"There was a problem. If Jay's not back within the fortnight, it has to be dealt with. She would prefer it be dealt with by the House Council."

Jester stiffened. "What kind of problem?"

Teller shook his head. "At the moment, I'm not at liberty to say."

"Don't start with me," Jester said, approaching the desk.

"I'm not. It's my problem, not yours." Teller reached for a folder on the corner of the desk. He handed it to Jester; Jester ignored it. "Guillarne's commentary. All of it. Terafin is not implicated in the tragedy at the Merchants' Guild, but the Order is now up in arms."

"Why are you giving this to me?"

"Because while Carver is missing, you're all we've got. I don't know if anything Guillarne said will mean anything to you. But Finch is moving, and when she does, the rest of the House will begin to take up arms. If someone's tried to kill her once, they're not going to stop until and unless The Terafin returns."

Jester took the folder. He took the folder, turned, and headed toward the doors. He was angry. It was a restless, energetic anger. There was very, very little that Teller chose to withhold, and when he did, it had nothing to do with official House bureaucracy; Barston would probably die of the apoplexy Jester had mentioned if he'd ever listened in on some of the kitchen meetings.

It answered the question that Teller had declined to answer. Teller was sensitive enough that he tried to avoid the narrow but very deep pits of rage into which Jester could fall.

"Who?" he asked. "Who was it?"

Teller was silent for a long beat. "Jester, it's my problem."

"Carver would tell me, if he were here."

"Yes."

"Gods *damn* it, Teller—who?"

"Vareena."

"Vareena is *twelve!*"

"She is with Daine, now. In the healerie. She's safe for the moment."

Jester was white with rage. White, shaking, his own life at twelve filling the interior of his thoughts until there was almost no room for anything else. "She needed to be sent to the healerie." He spoke softly. Soft meant nothing to Teller; Teller knew him too well. "Who did the Master of the Household Staff implicate?"

"Let me deal with it." Teller folded his hands across a closed book. Jester understood—dimly—that this had meaning. He did not want to fight with Teller. He did not want to hit him or injure him. And he thought he just might if he stayed.

Had she been any other woman—even Elonne, at this moment—Jester would have marched into the domain of the Master of the Household Staff immediately. As it was, he chose to head back to the West Wing.

8th of Morel, 428 A.A.
Merchant Authority, Averalaan Aramarelas

Haval dressed like a merchant of middling wealth. He chose his jacket and his pants with care, and after a moment's bleak consideration, chose a hat as well as a walking stick with a somewhat ostentatious handle. It was not his favorite; it was far too decorative.

But it was, as all things in Haval's arsenal were, practical.

He adored his wife, and reminded himself of this fact as he made his way to the Merchant Authority. He had chosen dark colors with a splash of obvious white, and presented himself to the guards—the very alert, very crisp guards—with an air of mourning and deference. It cost him very little. The guards were not at their best.

But he understood exactly why. The roads around the Merchants' Guild were all but closed to anything that was not foot traffic. The stalls that often huddled beneath the great trees of the Common were nowhere in sight. The shops that faced the guild's main building had been closed; all except for two, and both of those belonged to jewelers who had the money and the status to ignore all but a direct request from the Royal Trade Commission itself. In Haval's estimation, that would not be long in coming.

The Mysterium, aided and directed by no less a person than the Guildmaster of the Order of Knowledge, continued to sift through the wreckage of the building. Magi had been at work reinforcing the support beams that had not been damaged or destroyed; carpenters and stonemasons from the Makers' Guild were allowed entry, although they were escorted by either the Kings' Swords or select members of the Order. The Merchants' Guild had the funds to effect almost immediate repairs; Haval guessed that most of the building would be operational within a month. Perhaps less; he had recognized two members of the Makers' Guild as he had made his way through the narrow path through which the public was allowed passage.

The Merchant Authority was almost empty when Haval was at last given leave to enter. There were, of course, men and women behind the wickets, but the people who had come to do business at the Merchant Authority only barely outnumbered them. The Kings' Swords, however, outnumbered them all. They were grim and wary. Haval was surprised to see them present in such numbers, and allowed this to show.

Because the Kings' Swords were on the floor, he was not particularly surprised to see two of the senior officials of the Royal Trade Commission when he entered the Terafin offices: Patris Larkasir and Devon ATerafin. They were seated. If the lower floor of the Merchant Authority was almost empty, the Terafin offices were not.

Lucille ATerafin manned her desk like an army of one. She was pale, but the set of her jaw spoke of annoyance, not exhaustion. She glanced up from her desk as Haval paused before it. "Yes?" she asked, in the chilly and suspicious tone she generally adopted for strangers.

"I have an appointment to speak with Jarven ATerafin," he replied. "I am somewhat late, and apologize for my tardiness; I did not realize the extent of the gauntlet the Common has temporarily become."

"Jarven is currently in a meeting," she replied. "If you will take a seat, I will inform him that you have arrived."

He bowed and retreated, glancing at Devon and Patris Larkasir as he headed toward a vacant chair. Given Lucille's obvious displeasure, he was not surprised at the silence of an otherwise industrious office; there were at least four people behind visible desks, each bent over what looked like ledgers. They glanced at him as he passed them, but he failed to merit more of their attention; they were stealing cautious glances at the patris. Even Devon, notable within House Terafin for his many successes within the Royal Trade Commission, appeared to be beneath their attention.

If this was the caliber of young men and women Jarven had chosen to employ, the appearance of intellectual frailty was not entirely an act. Given Jarven, that was unlikely. Lucille was more than capable of overlooking raw cunning for diligence and loyalty—but there was, in the covert gaze of at least two of the junior clerks, a touch too much obvious personal ambition. Not Lucille's, then.

The door to Jarven's room did not open quickly. Haval would not be certain, until it did, that this was not a move in some small game Jarven was playing. It would be very much like Jarven to strand Haval in a full waiting room to see what he did—or did not—observe. It was a trick that Haval had employed himself, when he had been in the business of training the overconfident.

He waited. He noted that Devon was speaking with the patris; the patris had aged a good ten years in the last few months, probably most of them overnight. He spoke, with less care and more concern than he might in a more obvious crowd, about the destruction of the guildhall and the probable source of the resultant deaths.

Devon made no obvious attempt to silence him. The patris' genuine horror reflected the horror most of the Merchant Authority felt; it was a fitting tribute to those who had not survived.

"When the magi have finished, we will know who—or what—was responsible." The ATerafin Trade Commissioner glanced at Haval; Haval nodded in response, the gesture deferential and economical.

"A terrible business all round," the clothier said quietly. "My business here feels almost trivial in comparison. I'm not sure," he continued, "when your appointment is—if schedules even matter this morning. But your business here seems to be far more weighty and far more official than mine. If it will be of any aid at all, I will withdraw for the morning; Jarven ATerafin is a member of the Merchants' Guild and a surviving member of its governing body.

"I am certain my business with him can wait." He rose. To his surprise, Patris Larkasir raised his bearded chin.

"The wheels of commerce must turn, Mr.—"

"Arwood."

"Mr. Arwood. If the whole of our city grinds to a halt now, a blow has been struck that an Empire's army could not land in so short a time. Our business with Jarven is perfunctory; a courtesy, no more."

"Ah. Jarven is of an age and constitution where courtesy matters much."

Patris Larkasir smiled. "He is, indeed. We are both products of an age I fear is passing. While the Merchants' guildhall is under reconstruction, the Royal Trade Commission will house the activities of its governing body. The security in *Avantari* is tighter and more efficient than the security in the Merchant Authority—as we have seen. We have yet to find Guerrin ADurrance, living or deceased."

Haval's expression was one of composed but tangible horror.

"Jarven ATerafin is the senior member of the much-reduced council. It is my hope that he will oversee the temporary transfer of guild functions at this time."

"You mean Jarven to serve as the guildmaster?"

"As the *acting* guildmaster," Devon said, when Patris Larkasir nodded. "He is, of course, an older man and we do not wish to tax him overmuch."

This was preposterous. The Ten would be screaming for blood if Larkasir deposited Jarven directly into the position of guildmaster, acting or no. Jarven was the overseer of all of Terafin's concerns in the Merchant Authority. He was now a member of the Terafin House Council, and although this was not yet general knowledge, it was only a matter of time.

"Given his responsibilities in the Merchant Authority, I am not certain—at his advanced age—that he will be capable of doing as you hope."

"There is not another merchant who might, in such an emergency, cajole the terrified and the enraged to act in unison. I believe Jarven is that man."

Yes, Haval thought, he was. How many of those merchants would survive Jarven's rule? Haval had guesses. None of them favored the merchants.

"Finch ATerafin has been confirmed as Jarven's successor," Larkasir continued.

Haval let his surprise show. He was absolutely certain that everyone else in the room was now doing the same; the pretense of minding one's own business could only be carried so far.

"Jarven sent word to the Trade Commission that her seal was to be treated as if it were his own; that in all things related to the Terafin merchant operations within the Authority, she had responsibility and power commensurate with his own. If that is true—and I cannot doubt it, given the message was sealed by Jarven himself—she is obviously capable of running the Terafin operation on her own. Jarven would be absent from the Merchant Authority for a limited amount of time.

"We have sent a request to The Terafin to allow us to second Jarven during this crisis. We have not yet received a reply, but we cannot afford to wait at this juncture."

"Might I suggest," Haval said quietly, "that you consider Hectore of Araven for the role if Jarven cannot be seconded? He is a man who is respected by the merchants and the governing body of the guild; he has been asked a number of times to take the position of guildmaster, and he has refused.

"I do not think he would refuse were it asked—as a favor—in this crisis. I have never been an ambitious man, and in the early years, I was successful enough to support a small family—but the guild dues were beyond my meager means. It is only recently that I have reached a position where I am relevant to the guild, and where the guild itself is relevant to my interests.

"But I have had some interactions with Patris Araven. Very few who are merchants of any standing in Averalaan have not. He is both respected and feared; if he asks a favor it has the weight of command; if he looks with disfavor upon a merchant or a merchant's activities, their activities cease. I understand that you require a banner around which the merchants themselves might group—but Hectore is at least a decade younger than Jarven and he has not yet begun age's inevitable decline.

"I am under consideration for guild membership; I have not yet been admitted to the ranks of the guild. I understand how little weight my opinion might carry—but you are the head of the Royal Trade Commission; you have access to men in the upper echelons of the patriciate that I do not, and will never have. If my word does not carry weight, theirs will.

"I understand your respect for Jarven ATerafin. But he is not the man he once was." Haval bowed. "Forgive me for being so bold, Patris." He bowed to Devon. "Patris."

"Mr. Arwood," Lucille ATerafin said, in her cold, autocratic voice, "Jarven ATerafin will see you now."

"I have had," Jarven said, as Haval entered the office, "a very trying morning. I do not expect that your morning compares to mine in either difficulty or tedium, and I will not entertain either your complaints or your petty resentments."

"I note you have not mentioned the evening."

Jarven glanced at Finch; she was pale, her lips almost of a color with the rest of her skin. Her hair was drawn back and bound in a tight and glittering net; it was black. She wore more white than Haval considered appropriate for her complexion; she wore flashes of black lace at her wrists and her throat, and a sash of black around her slender waist.

Imperial Mourning.

Jarven was likewise accoutered. In Haval's opinion, it suited the older man; Jarven had been responsible for a great many funerals in his time. If, Haval thought, his time had ever passed.

"The evening was not tedious, as you suspect. It was, however, somewhat tense. I have seldom witnessed Sigurne Mellifas so distraught."

"It is to be hoped that you did not contribute to her distress."

"Given the nature of the things that are currently distressing her, I fear that is impossible," Jarven replied.

Haval turned to Finch. He offered her a perfect and correct bow. "It is my understanding that you are to take control of the Terafin Merchant Authority concerns."

"Haval, that is unsporting," Jarven said.

Finch's lips tightened. She folded her hands on the surface of her desk. "That was not my understanding."

"Ah. Forgive me. I believe, in very short order it will be." He looked across the desk to Jarven, sharp eyes bright behind the gentle folds of a paternal smile. Haval could, of course, offer the same smile—but there would be far less obvious wolf in it.

Finch's smile tightened enough that it could no longer be called a smile. She turned to Jarven. "I would like a few words with you."

"And I, of course, would love to have them—but I fear there will be very, very little chance of that today. Haval?"

Haval shook his head. "I, on the other hand, am a clothier. While I have been less pressed for time, I believe time is now of the essence. I require a series of fittings to be done, and quickly. I cannot produce appropriate mourning dress with the materials I have. Mourning is a gesture of respect," he continued, when her lips opened on possible words. "But if I am not mistaken, you worked in this office during the Henden of 410."

Everything about this slender young woman stilled; her face was already pale.

"Yes. You understand. On some occasions, Finch, the best sign of respect we can offer is to continue to put one foot in front of the other. The Merchant Authority will—no doubt—be both quieter and its activities more intense, in the days that follow. I have seen the damage done to the guildhall. I am not yet aware of the losses."

Jarven smiled and handed Haval a stone. It was smooth, gray, and unremarkable in all ways. "Peruse it at your leisure."

"You cannot possibly think," the clothier said, "that I would take this with me, given its source?"

"Of course not. Finch will take it with *her* when she leaves the office for the day."

"Jarven—this is not the time for games."

"Haval," he replied, mimicking the clothier's intonation and beat perfectly, "it is perhaps the best time for them. You do not wish to play, of course; you have grown so stodgy and dull in your advanced years it would be quite possible to believe there is nothing of interest left in you. Since that is what you want believed, I mistrust it, but that is my nature." To Haval's surprise, he rose. "You now wish to tell me that you were never interested in games."

"I would not waste breath on the attempt."

"No, not breath. You might waste lives to make a point—but not these lives." His smile was pure Jarven. "Come. This is not the first time we have joined forces."

"I believe I made clear that the last time would *be* the final time."

"And did you, at that time, see demons? Did you feel the echoes of gods touch the streets of the city? Did you see ancient trees spring full grown from a tame, tepid garden, or great, winged cats walk the halls of mortal mansions? There will be war. The war has already started." The old merchant made his way to the window, turning his back on Haval, which was rare enough to be notable. "Do you remember the Henden of 410?"

"I am certain we all do."

"Do you remember what it felt like, to be helpless? To be less than a pawn on the board, less than a piece in a greater game over which you had no say and in which you could make no relevant moves? We could barely stand as witnesses while events unfolded beyond us." He clasped hands loosely behind his back.

Haval said nothing.

Jarven was not content to allow this. He turned; the light from the window made of his standing form a silhouette. In it, one could see the straight, tall line of his spine, his unbent shoulders, his unbowed head.

Haval inhaled. Exhaled. "Yes. I remember."

"You were always pragmatic, even in your more idealistic youth. You understood the stakes of the games we chose to play. You understood when to sacrifice a pawn, and when to turn a pawn into a queen." He did not glance at Finch as he spoke, but his meaning was plain.

"These are not decisions that I could now make, given my limited understanding of both the board and the rules that govern it."

Jarven's eyes narrowed. "If this is not the time for games, you have chosen a poor way to demonstrate it."

"Very well. I believe there are rules; those rules bind us. We are not immortal. Unless we are talent-born—and I am not—we do not have access to greater, or even lesser, magics."

Jarven nodded. "We can avail ourselves of the magical skills and talents of others, to a greater or lesser degree; where they are amenable, we can avail ourselves of their knowledge, as well."

"Where there is money and access, yes." Haval glanced at Finch. "But it is clear that a different set of rules bind the demons; they are part of the game, but they have both a broader—and narrower—range of play."

"The magi?"

"Uncertain. The guildmaster believes that demons are summoned; the magi are therefore the weak link between safety and disaster. She is known to be both harsh and unforgiving when members of her Order indulge their curiosity for the forbidden. She is not, however, infallible. It is possible that you might converse with her about this subject. You are not talent-born, and you are therefore not her responsibility."

"You fail to understand Sigurne if you believe that."

"Do I?"

Jarven turned to Finch.

Finch, however, was uninterested in joining this small game on Jarven's terms. "Why do you insist on involving Haval?" she asked. Her voice was mild, as was her expression. She did not, however, blink.

"I have not involved Haval; he has involved himself, in an entirely round-about way. He advises The Terafin."

"She is, as you well know, absent. Absent, she does not require his advice."

"I see I am to be surrounded by the harsh and unforgiving this morning." Jarven's smile implied that harsh and unforgiving were his elements; the implication, in Haval's estimation, contained a truth that Jarven's implications generally lacked. "Haval is correct in his assessment; he is, however, incomplete. There are elements at play that he has failed to mention—and given Haval, I assume the failure a deliberate oversight. I am honestly not certain why he bothers when he is speaking with me; he cannot hope that I will overlook it. And given the information, he cannot hope that you will."

"I am not part of your game."

"You, my dear, are close to the heart of it. If circumstances were less dire, I would be less extreme. But I am an old man. I do not have the time. And the city—the Empire—has perhaps as much time remaining as I do if this game is not played, and played *well*. Haval is part of the game; we are all now part of it. We have little choice in the matter. What choice we have is, as Haval suggested, limited by our nature—but we are not consigned to be victims.

"I am not," he continued, holding the gaze that did not waver, "Rymark."

Finch was not nearly as careful with her expression as either of the two old men in the room. "I would," she said softly, "kill you myself before I let you become him." There was no doubt at all in her words. She did not stoop to plea.

Jarven, however, laughed. The laughter did not change her expression at all. It would have darkened Jewel's—but Jewel had, as she so often pointed out, the advantage of her peculiar talent; she could be lax. It would not kill her.

"You see what I have raised, Haval? The young are unforgiving."

"She means it," Haval replied. "And I would almost like to see how it played out, in the end."

This, on the other hand, did deepen Finch's frown. "Haval, please—do not encourage him."

"You simultaneously understand Jarven and fail to understand him," Haval replied, modulating his tone and softening its edge. "He will never become Rymark. Rymark is inelegant; his self-indulgence is far too obvious. He desires power because he believes it will allow him to live without consequences, and in this particular instance, believes it will allow him to survive what will follow.

"Jarven does not believe his survival rests in anyone else's hands. Or he does not believe that it should. He is not content to serve any purpose but his own. We are fortunate in that his purposes are relatively benign."

"I am almost offended," Jarven said.

"I fail to see why."

"You do not."

Finch's glance slid between them; her expression eased slowly into a more traditional form of disapproval.

"She learned that from Lucille." Jarven's smile was fond. To Haval's eye, the affection was genuine. "I do not have the time to waste," he said again, in the same tone. "But I have confidence, Finch. If I had a decade, I would look forward to crossing wits with you; you might be—at the end of my life—a worthy opponent. So few are."

"If you consider gods and demons worthy opponents," she replied, "you would almost certainly be disappointed."

"They are not worthy opponents in the same way because theirs is not a game in which any great artistry can be involved; we are forced to play on the same board, but it is a crudely drawn, temporary board—a thing forced by circumstance.

"Nor is it ever truly complete. The game itself is too large. I consider my part in it very much like a leg of a relay race. I can handle and carry the baton perfectly on the prescribed path; that path, of necessity, is an overlap of our concerns. I do not see the whole of the game board. But, Finch, *neither do they*. The narrow area through which I can run is an area that they barely perceive; I am certain they consider it beneath them. They do not therefore understand all the subtleties; they do not understand the mastery I have over my chosen sphere of influence.

"If I do not see the whole of the board on which the game is to be played at large, they do not see the whole of the board upon which I am master. There are mistakes to be made on either side, but I am willing to grant them superior knowledge in those spheres they control; I highly doubt they are willing to grant me the same. Well, Haval?"

"I have little to add. I believe your assessment and mine in this case to be similar. I have had little truck with the demonic, but will agree that they are possessed of a certain arrogance—and a certain crudeness, at least when dealing with mortals. I have had more of a chance to observe the hunter. Lord Celleriant."

"And?" Jarven's question was sharp with delight.

"His suggested solution to a small political problem was the assassination of the entire Terafin House Council."

Jarven laughed. Finch, notably, did not.

"Could he?"

"Kill the House Council? Certainly. I think there are one or two who might put up some resistance, but the resistance itself would, in the end, be futile."

"That act would fall within the rules of exemption."

"Yes."

"But clearly it was not an option that The Terafin considered."

Finch's mouth fell open. She shut it without allowing the words that obviously wanted escape their freedom.

"And so we come at last to the heart of the game: the thing that binds the whole—immortal, demonic, godly, and mortal."

Haval's guard was almost never lowered in Jarven's presence; raising it made no effective or visible difference.

"The Terafin."

"She is not," Finch said, "yours. She is not a piece in any game you choose to play."

Jarven returned to his desk. He sat behind it, his position crisp and unbowed. His expression was bright, hard; this was the face he brought to negotiations that had proved immune to the subtler wheedling and sleight of hand he employed when he was lazy or when he considered his opponent so far beneath him respect was not required.

Finch's lips compressed; she saw what Haval saw. "No," she told him, engaging where Haval would not. "This is *not* a negotiation. The Terafin is not an object of simple barter. Or complicated barter," she added, as Jarven opened his mouth.

"It is not The Terafin's disposition that we are now discussing. I understand that you do not speak for The Terafin; no more do I, although in theory I have that authority within a limited capacity. I expect you to speak for yourself. Intelligently."

She was silent.

"What does The Terafin want?"

Finch exhaled. "She wants the safety of the House. She wants," she continued, after a longer pause in which she considered her words, "the safety of the city."

"The House is trifling. Difficult, yes, but not a difficulty that is insurmountable. Is it, in your considered opinion, a necessity for the safety of Averalaan?"

"She wouldn't doom the city because the House fell."

"While clever, that was not an answer, and I do not think I will allow it."
She was silent.

Jarven said, "I will not insult you, Finch. I have Haval for that, should my
frustration demand an outlet. You are hesitant. You have that perfectly understandable desire to trust what you know—and the more admirable hesitation because what you know is me. I will not feign insult, today; it seldom
works where you are concerned, and I will husband my resources. If I play at
age, it is not entirely feigned.

"I am invested in the game that I have been given no alternative but to
play. It is dangerous for me to play such a game without understanding the
consequences—but absent that understanding, I will play it regardless. Arm
me, or arm my opponents, as you wish. I am not a particularly cautious man,
as you have observed; I am not without malice, but at the present time, feel
none toward either you or The Terafin."

"I want more than careless proclamations of lack of malice."

"Yes, I imagine you do. And—as we are wasting time—tell me what form
such solid assurance will take. I cannot think of one I would willingly accept
were our positions reversed. What would I do?"

"If you wanted to reach an agreement? You would bargain; you would
demand; you would, depending on your opponent, threaten."

"Even given your lack of ability to trust any agreement that might be
reached?"

She nodded. "In this scenario, I feel that you are utterly necessary—for the
moment. I have already attained the House Council seat—which is necessary
in my opinion; I would trust that a position on that Council would give me
the balance of power should I be forced to act against . . . me. Your position,
of course, would not be entirely stable; your power in the Merchant Authority is divided—at the will of The Terafin. We do not share authority; we each
possess it.

"You have crossed political swords with every merchant that is close to the
Council; you have annoyed Haerrad—but anyone who breathes and thinks for
themselves does that. But you have also cunningly sidelined some of Elonne's
interests; you have not proven yourself entirely friendly to Marrick. Your
power on the Council is therefore muted until you build necessary alliances.
You will build those by compromise and negotiation; given your past record,
no one will move quickly. You are not, by your own design, much trusted.

"The Terafin is not, however, in her seat. You do not face her—you
couldn't, given the way she came to power."

Haval watched Finch's expression with interest; she had lost, sentence by sentence, the wary frustration that had characterized the earlier part of their conversation; what was left was the puzzle set in front of her by the man who had trained her, honing and sharpening the observation that lay beneath her quiet, hesitant appearance.

Jarven was watching as well. "So. You would not stoop to cajole; you would assume the full weight of your authority. You would begin by relying on the friendship we have built over the better part of almost two decades."

She nodded.

"If you were me, Finch, what would *you* want?"

"If I were in your position?"

"Ah, no. If you were *me*. If you were Jarven ATerafin. We have played these games before, you and I. You have observed me. You have seen me at my strongest, and you have seen me at my weakest; I do not necessarily expect you to identify either state accurately, but I am curious. What, exactly, do you believe I want?"

Finch was not Jewel Markess ATerafin. She saw the world as it was; she did not look ahead, to the world and the life that *might* be; she did not choose to live in the future; she navigated the streets she had lived in by the rules she had learned. She had been abandoned by her family, and perhaps that should have colored and scarred her view of the world, as it did so many, especially given the place to which she had been sold. A brothel, as an unwilling participant, did not afford the best of experiences.

But she had been saved by two young women: Duster and Jewel, two disparate strangers who could not possibly feel any obligation toward her. Between them, they had risked their lives to save hers. She had not doubted their intentions; they were as poor and as helpless as she herself had been.

The weak gathered in numbers; it gave them the illusion of strength. In the case of Finch, it had given more: a family of choice. This, too, she had never doubted. She had seen Jewel Markess clearly. She had seen Duster clearly as well. She accepted that the world housed both darkness and light; that if she lived and breathed, she would encounter both for the rest of her life.

But she did not privilege the glimpses of one over the other, and in her quiet way, she reached, always, for warmth. But she reached for the warmth at hand; she did not force herself to believe, as many could, that her daydreams would one day become her reality.

Yet, he thought, her reality now was the product of daydreams that most, born where she was born, did not have.

She was ATerafin. She served The Terafin, a close personal friend. She no longer feared hunger or winter. She did not steal simply to survive. No, he thought; she had translated those skills into these ones. Theft was more subtle, threats more oblique. Strength was not measured in daggers and the numbers a den could amass; it was measured in wealth, much of it theoretical.

She understood wealth. She understood that it was tentative; she understood that much of it was proclaimed by appearance: the cut of cloth, the expense of fabric. She did not choose jewelry, and that, Haval thought, would have to change.

"I . . . don't know."

"You don't wish to take the risk of insulting me."

"I don't wish," she replied, "to make a mistake that puts others at risk."

"And now, you *are* insulting me." His eyes gleamed. Haval thought he was even telling the truth, which surprised him. "You have made decisions, mere hours ago, that will put many people—who are not you—at risk. You have made decisions which, should they be wrong, have the weight to destroy lives. I have even encouraged you to make them."

"I don't know what The Terafin knows. I would happily let her make any decision that involved you."

"But she cannot."

"No. I have made decisions in this office that reach well beyond House Terafin; I have—as you have pointed out—done so with your encouragement. But I have done so with knowledge and experience. What The Terafin knows, what The Terafin *can* know, I cannot. Any decision I make on her behalf, however tentative, is done at the whim of *Kalliaris*, and only a fool bets on her smile."

"You are not, however, betting on that whim, now. What I want is independent of The Terafin."

"It is not."

"Yes, Finch, it is. She is, like any other piece on the board, some element of the game; she has no value to me beyond that." He did not smile. His face was almost as expressionless as Haval's. Haval glanced at Finch, but found Jarven the more compelling of the two.

Finch, however, did not shrink; her eyes narrowed as she lowered her chin, as if to gaze at her hands. "You want what Meralonne wants."

She had surprised Jarven. "Meralonne APhaniel?"

Finch nodded.

"And what does he want?"

"He wants the battle, Jarven. He wants the challenge. He wants an opponent worthy of his power at its height. For Meralonne, that means demons, and possibly Lord Celleriant. The games we play—or the games I do—are not, and will never be, of interest to him."

"But it is of interest to the demons."

She shook her head. "It has utility for the *mortals* who have aligned themselves with the Lord of the Hells. If the shape of the world changes, mortals still require sustenance; they require shelter; they require offspring. They do not *require* power, although many feel it is as much of, if not more of, a necessity."

"Those who have power value it highly. More highly than either sustenance or shelter."

"They've never lived without the latter," was Finch's quiet reply.

"You make assumptions based on your early life, and fail to add to those assumptions with your current experience. In the eyes of most of this city, *you* have never known hunger or cold. You are ATerafin. You define power, in this city. You are not, in the end, so different from me.

"I know hunger, Finch. I know cold. I know it at least as well as you and your den, but at a greater remove. There are some things that are never forgotten." He rose. "I understood the need for power in the streets of my youth. It was the only thing that stood between me and pain or death.

"Where I did not have power, I bluffed. There was no risk inherent in that—if my bluff was called, I was in the same position I would have otherwise been in had I not made the attempt at all. I was," he added, with a very slight smile, "quite good at it. I was not slight of build. I was not meek; I could not afford to be gentle.

"But I was young. In the way of the young and the naive, I believed myself *better* than my tormentors. A better man, if you will. I believed that were *I* to have power, things would be different." He chuckled.

Haval clasped hands behind his back. He lowered his chin as he studied Jarven's profile. He said nothing.

"Were you foolish enough to believe as I did?" Jarven continued.

"No. I believed that my mother loved me. I did not entirely trust the affection of my brothers. I did not expect to be sold to a brothel." She smiled. It was a cool turn of lip. "The walls were not soundproof. I was not harmed." She met, and held, Jarven's gaze. She did not flinch. "I was to be saved for something bigger, something better. I did not have the ability to lie to myself, even then. It was a matter of time.

"And the time itself was not mine. I was trapped in it. I didn't daydream of power," she continued softly. "Only of escape. My dreams were not kind, but my sleep was repeatedly broken. When given a chance to escape, I took it. I didn't wait. I didn't attempt to rescue anyone else trapped there. I ran.

"Perhaps because I could run, I didn't believe that I would do better, if given power. And perhaps I would have become like you."

"You do not say that with any belief."

"No—but I don't want to believe it, Jarven."

He smiled. There was no kindness in it.

And Finch, Haval realized, did not require Jarven's kindness. Not now. He wondered if she ever had, or if she had sheltered behind Lucille, a woman whose tongue was sharp and whose heart was open.

"But I ran to Jay." She used the unadorned name, now; the name that only the den used. Jarven did not appear to note it—but of course he had. "I ran to freedom in the form of a total stranger, a girl my own age. She wasn't rich. She wasn't powerful—not the way the men who bought me claimed to be. Not the way you must have been. She was almost incapable of lying."

"She is still incapable of lying," Jarven said.

"Yes. You can argue that she never learned because she never had to. I won't disagree. I won't, however, believe it." Her answering smile was serene and impregnable. "And because I can't, I've never had to wonder what the world would be like if I were in charge of it. I've never had to wonder what the House would be like. Jay was our leader. Jay will be our leader while she lives—and I believe that everything she has been until now will guide us if she dies."

"That is almost disappointing."

"But not surprising, surely?"

"No," was the grave reply. "Not surprising. You have not answered my question."

"I told you—you want what Meralonne wants."

"Poorly done, Finch. That is not the question to which I refer. Will the Empire stand if Terafin does not?"

"I am afraid to answer your question." She spoke, however, without a trace of the fear she claimed to feel.

Ah, Haval thought, watching her, and watching, as well, the one man he had once considered his superior. *You will never reach the potential that Jarven sees in you. That I see in you. And perhaps, just perhaps, that is a blessing.*

"But I ran, Jarven. I ran into a city in which I had no friends; I ran because I had no power. I found a home. I found the only home I've ever wanted. If I could, I would be like Jay. I'm not. She would die before she let harm come to any of us—but harm comes, anyway.

"My death would never prevent it. But I will do everything within the power I've been given to protect the House she's built." She closed her eyes. "Yes, Jarven. It's my absolute belief that if the House falls—if *we* fall—the city won't stand against the god."

"The god."

She opened her eyes. She had chosen to gamble, Haval thought. "The god is coming, Jarven. If Jay isn't ready—if she doesn't have something to lose—the city won't stand."

Chapter Eight

THE JOURNEY THROUGH AN arch that was constructed of poorly melted stone was neither swift nor immediate—at least not in a forward direction. A door had been opened, and it had swiftly shut when the last member of Jewel's party stepped through. It had shut, on the other hand, with a bang that echoed in the cold, dark air, almost as if it meant to hit the straggler.

Given that the straggler was Celleriant, Jewel wasn't as concerned as she might otherwise have been; she could not conceive of a door—any door—that could kill the Arianni Lord. Angel walked to her right; Adam walked to her left. She held his hand.

This would have offended her den-kin in the past, when they'd been close to Adam's age; they had been far too old to be publicly treated like children. Adam, however, was not the child Jewel had been. He was certainly not Angel or Carver. In many ways, she thought him closest to Arann—but Adam was good with words; he could speak and he could listen, and generally if he did the latter, he heard what was said. Many people heard what they wanted to hear, or feared to hear.

Terrick, to Jewel's surprise, had chosen to take the lead. Senniel College's most famous bard pulled up the rear, walking to the right of Celleriant. Avandar walked to Adam's left, surrendering the spot he usually occupied. This wasn't an act of grace on his part, in Jewel's opinion; nor was it a desire to protect Adam. They'd brought the cats with them, the possessive, attention-seeking, demanding cats who considered the place of pride to be at Jewel's side. They were happy to shoulder anyone who occupied that space out of the way.

Adam didn't seem to notice them. Then again, the cats usually stayed out of Adam's arm's reach.

This marching order remained in force as they walked beyond the Oracle's door, although they walked through what seemed mist—but mist that had weight, texture, viscosity. It caused no pain, no injury, but the suspicious sense that it was webbing made the walk increasingly uncomfortable. Terrick spoke in brief bursts of almost inaudible Rendish. Angel translated, although it was clear that Kallandras understood the Northern man. He was calling all clear and asking, briefly, for guidance.

When none was forthcoming, he continued to forge ahead. Jewel could see the naked ax in his hand; he was the only man present who carried a readied weapon. It seemed part of him, in keeping with his hair, his taciturn, pragmatic demeanor. She wasn't certain what to make of him, but she trusted him because Angel did.

The stop and start nature of his speech was rhythmic; it was, given the harsher syllables of Rendish, unexpectedly soothing. There was a cadence to his brief report, a cadence to his equally brief questions, that engendered confidence, and she grabbed it and held onto it for all she was worth, because she herself had come with so little.

"How *long* are we going to *stay* here?" Night demanded, for perhaps the dozenth time. The cats had started the journey with a surprising amount of decorum—for cats. Shadow, in particular, had been menacing in his silent, exposed fang, way. He didn't trust the Oracle, and that was fair. Jewel had no doubt at all that there was only one way to pass this test, and none of that relied on the Oracle's capacity for either helpfulness or mercy.

There were traps here. There was death, madness, or both. The Oracle had implied that Jewel carried the seeds of that death and that madness within her—but not in those words. Perhaps not in words that anyone else might hear and understand as the challenge and the threat that they were. No. The Oracle carried the seer's crystal. She carried the heart, exposed. All good and all evil, all joy and all despair, lay within the clouds at its center. They lay, Jewel thought, within the clouds at her own—but hers was hidden, guarded, defended. She exposed it seldom, and only at need.

And oh, that was a lie. It was a lie, or her needs were so large and endless they'd informed the whole of her life. They were, in some measure, the whole of her life.

She knew why she had come. She knew what she hoped to find. And she knew that the Oracle knew the truth. Jewel had not undertaken the journey to the heart of the Oracle's land simply for the sake of obtaining a seer's crystal.

She wouldn't have left home—and Terafin—for the possible advantage of control over the visions that had haunted her, waking and sleeping, since her distant childhood.

No. She had come for the sake of her kin. For Carver. And for Ellerson, although she had no idea if Ellerson had survived, as Carver had. They had disappeared through the door of an unremarkable closet because the closet door had opened onto more than tidy rows of expensive dresses. But Ellerson had gone first. Carver had gone in search of him.

At Jewel's unspoken request.

Where's Ellerson?

Where is Ellerson, indeed.

Not here, she thought, and knew it for truth. Neither of them were here.

The gray of amorphous landscape gave way slowly. It might never have given way at all, except for the cats.

They had been walking long enough that Jewel's shoulders had begun the ache heavy packs sometimes caused. Her thoughts had drifted inward to the empty space left by Carver and Ellerson, but the cats, being cats, interrupted everything with their sniping, their squalling, and their attempts to leave rents in each other's fur. They had also begun the litany of boredom, in three parts.

Boredom was apparently going to kill them.

By the hundredth iteration of *I'm bored* and *it's boring*, Jewel wasn't certain that it wouldn't. Even Celleriant was beginning to look unimpressed with repetitive cat whining, which was a first. While it was true that the cats always whined, it was also true that the rest of the world intervened with its frequent and many crises and distractions.

Here, there was a lot of gray. If a crisis happened, it would come from the nowhere through which they now walked, but it hadn't, yet. And the cats were getting impatient.

When Celleriant opened his mouth and lifted his right hand, Jewel shook her head. She considered the apex of boredom had been reached, and when the cats were bored, they could forget themselves in unfortunate ways. Usually this resulted in scarred baseboards, walls, and furniture. Here, there were only people.

Shadow hissed. *"Yes?"*

Celleriant's jaw tightened. He had too much dignity to call out a cat—but too much ego to retreat. He had never considered the cats a personal danger; he had considered them a threat to Jewel.

Remembering that Shadow had almost killed her—that she would, in fact, be dead if not for Adam—she knew he was right. She just had difficulty remembering it every time the cats opened their mouths. They did more than open their mouths here, though. They extended claws, unhooded fangs, and gained the visual height that rising fur lent them.

Adam said, in hushed Torra, "Are they going to fight?" The last syllable had barely cleared his open lips before Night roared in fury and leaped at Snow. Snow moved before he landed, swiping at his flank on the way past.

The colorful language that accompanied these moves was new, and it implied the cats had spent far too much time in the gutter, which was impossible. The second and more likely explanation involved the occupants of the West Wing.

"You better not have used that language around Ariel!" she shouted. She had, entirely unintentionally, released Adam's hand; both of hers were now balled fists sitting on her hips.

"*What* language? We use *their* words. *He* says it!" Snow hissed, pointing a wing in Angel's direction.

"Ariel can't understand most of what Angel says," she shot back, "so it doesn't matter!"

"If we use *his* words, *she* won't understand *us*."

Shadow hissed laughter. Night was still growling, but his fur had descended. They went on a round of far less violent *stupid, stupid girl*, and while they did, Jewel noticed that the ground and the air into which claws had been inserted, or across which claws had been driven in fury had . . . tear marks.

"You two, stop for a second. Did you . . . tear . . . the ground?"

"It wasn't *me*," Night said. "It was *him*."

"*You* jumped. You're too *heavy*. It's *your* fault!"

Shadow, however, sauntered between them and stomped on both of their feet before either could move their paws, which was impressive; Jewel hadn't seen his feet move. "Say *yes*," he advised them. "It's *good*."

They immediately stopped speaking—for at least five seconds—and reversed the direction in which they were pointing their figurative fingers. It would have been funny—it almost was—but they began to squabble, and words descended into the usual accusations before they were tossed aside, once again, for fur, claw, and feather.

Jewel let them fight, watching their claws; watching the way the sharp and sudden descent of wings ruptured the gray, thick air—as if it were dirt and grime that clung to another surface, shrouding it. She couldn't hear tearing—but if they'd been shredding cloth, she wouldn't have been able to hear that, either, given the rest of the noise they made.

"While this is amusing in small doses," Avandar finally said, "it is repetitive in the extreme." He lifted his left hand, palm flat, fingers straight and extended. Jewel saw light gild it briefly, too faint in the gray to have enough color to give her some warning of what he intended.

Hand became fist between one heartbeat and the next; he drove that fist down, toward the ground on which everyone was standing—except, at the moment, Night. The sound that was too quiet to survive the hissing and growling of giant cats was thunderous in response to that single gesture.

It even managed to silence the cats for a few minutes.

What appeared to be viscous, dimly lit fog lifted. Or, in this case, tore and shriveled. Strands were caught in Avandar's fist before he literally burned them away. Webbing, Jewel thought, or spun silk. She didn't attempt to touch it, because as it burned, the light that had emanated from it guttered.

She had assumed they were walking beneath some sort of clouded sun. They weren't, from the brief glimpse of surroundings before all was plunged into darkness, walking in the open at all. She could see a hint of ceiling above before light faded; it was stories in height.

Snow said, "Oh, *that*." His ability to retain anger was vanishingly small. Night had likewise fallen silent; he snorted and sniffed, but failed to renew his furious acts of aggression.

Shadow snickered.

"Did you know?" Jewel asked him.

"Know *what?*"

"He knows more than *you* know," Night said, for spiteful good measure. "Where *are* we?"

"It's still *boring*," Snow observed, just in case the subject of cat boredom had been forgotten.

No one else had a memory as short and convenient as winged, quarrelsome cats.

Jewel was fumbling in her bag for a magestone when Avandar gestured in silence. Light came to his hand. It illuminated the underside of his face, as if it were lamplight, lending a bronze glow to his exposed throat. His breath came out in thin mist. Jewel's followed when she remembered to breathe. She noticed that Celleriant's breath did not. Here, in the dark that light only barely penetrated, he looked like a Winter creature; silent, cold.

The silence, unlike the darkness, was broken as Jewel exhaled.

"If you didn't *mean* to be *stepped on*, you wouldn't have left your *tail* there."

"If *you* weren't clumsy, it wouldn't *matter* where my tail was. *You've* been living with *mortals* for *too long*."

"And if both of you don't start walking, there's going to be trouble soon," Jewel told them. She dropped a hand on the heads of the white and the black cat, and flattened her palms between their ears. They hissed in unison.

"What *kind* of trouble?" Shadow demanded, nudging her back with his head.

"Something interesting and creative. Maybe I'll feed you to a dragon."

Shadow hissed laughter.

Snow just hissed. For some reason Jewel was afraid to examine too closely, the mere mention of dragons caused his fur to rise six inches and his belly to reach for ground.

"How would *you* feed *us* to dragons? You would need to call them, and they would need to *hear* you. You have a *puny* roar."

"Don't *challenge* her," Snow said, in a sulky voice. He fell quiet for at least five minutes.

Jewel was grateful that she had dressed for Averalaan's Winter. Although there was no wind, the chill was pervasive; she could feel it through layers of clothing.

She glanced, now, at the ceiling. It was worked stone, curving in arches above pillars that were both wide and tall. The cats could, if they chose to do so, fly at the heights with ease. Not, she thought, glaring at Night when he "accidentally" stepped on Angel's foot, that they would do it with any subtlety. If things slept in this great hall, they wouldn't be sleeping for long.

She couldn't see wall for darkness. Exhaling, she turned to Celleriant. "Do you recognize this hall?"

He was silent. It was a stiff, watchful silence—but he had yet to draw either sword or shield. "No, Lord. I recognize the style in which it was built, but I do not believe I have entered it at any other time."

She glanced at Angel. His brow was furrowed, his eyes narrowed, as he looked up at the ceiling.

"Avandar."

"I do not consider it wise, at the moment. Husband light; there is no guarantee that further evidence of our presence will not disturb that which should remain undisturbed."

She glared pointedly at the muttering cats. "Determined gods couldn't sleep through that ruckus."

Avandar failed to reply, but Shadow said *ugly* very, very loudly.

"Your companions," Kallandras said, his voice warm with amusement, "are interesting."

"Yessss," Shadow said, padding toward the bard. "*We're* not *boring.*"

"No," was the grave reply. "You are certainly not that. Tell me, do you recognize this hall?"

"*Maybe.*"

"That generally means no," Jewel cut in. Shadow hissed. "The cats aren't terribly good at admitting there's anything in the world they don't know."

"*We* don't know how to be *stupid,*" Snow informed the bard. He growled at Night, took a running leap, and pushed himself off the cold stone floor, toward the ceiling's height.

"Your point is well taken," the domicis told Jewel. He gestured and light flew toward the ceiling, revealing color as if it were painting over the darkness with wide, swift strokes. She had seen this effect once, half a lifetime ago.

"Why don't you ask *him* if he knows where we *are?*" Shadow asked. He batted Avandar with a wing, but not with any force; the domicis failed to move.

"My apologies, Shadow," was Kallandras' grave reply. "Avandar is mortal, if in unusual circumstances; you and your brethren are not. You are ancient and wild, and if there is wisdom to be found while we walk these unknown byways, I thought it might be yours."

Shadow looked deeply suspicious, but there was nothing at all in Kallandras' tone that implied mockery or dishonesty. Then again, there wouldn't be—he was a bard. His voice implied what he wanted it to imply. For this reason, Jewel knew that bards couldn't be trusted, but it was almost impossible to view them with genuine suspicion.

Shadow tried harder. Even the great winged cat failed, in the end. His ego was his weakness, but it was in its fashion an endearing weakness.

"This," he said, walking in predatory circles around the golden-haired bard, "is an *old* place. It used to be *noisy*, but it is quiet now. It has been quiet for *many, many* years. And *boring.*"

Jewel's brows rose; Kallandras' attention, however, was apparently absorbed by the cat. This annoyed Night and Snow enough that they joined Shadow, with predictable results: one bard, three large, hunting animals.

"What lived here?"

"*They* did."

"Who?"

Shadow had turned his golden eyes on Celleriant. "*Her* people. In their youth."

All eyes turned to Celleriant, some more covertly than others. He couldn't fail to notice, but did; he was staring at the heights of distant ceiling. "Viandaran, do you recognize this?"

"No. If what Shadow says is accurate, it was abandoned before my time. I am surprised that it stands at all."

Jewel frowned. "What do you mean?"

He glanced at Celleriant. Celleriant was statue-still for a long moment, before at last inclining his head. "It should have been destroyed," he whispered, voice soft, face slowly lifting. "Viandaran, can you fly here?"

"I will not take that risk. We are not where we once were, and the elements are freer. If these halls have survived the long passage and the sundering, I do not wish to accidentally destroy them."

"If they have survived," Celleriant countered, as breeze began to lift the strands of his platinum hair, "they cannot be destroyed by so simple a thing as angry breeze. If this is, indeed, the deserted ruins of her ancient home, it is not on the ground that we will find our answers. Come. If we are to find our way to the Oracle, and the path begins here, I would see what I have heard about only in song and story." He rose, pausing to glance down at the bard.

Jewel saw the ring on the bard's thumb come to life; the diamond at its center became a thing of magic and light. He did not ask Jewel's permission, as Celleriant had obliquely done, and she did not attempt to deny him. Terrick's face was carved in frown as he watched the two, bard and Arianni Lord, rise. "I'm not much use," he said, in slow Weston, "when my feet can't touch the ground."

Jewel shrugged. "I'm often not much use when my feet can. I don't know where we're going, Terrick. I know only that we have to arrive. I was given no map, and no instructions. But I had the choice of my companions. Can you ride?"

He nodded; it was just as controlled.

"Night."

Night uttered a long-suffering, heavily put-upon sigh. "Why do *I* have to carry *him*? He's *heavy*."

"And you," Jewel replied, "are strong."

"We don't require mounts," Avandar told her. "Celleriant—and Kallandras, if I am not mistaken—are full capable of asking the wild air to carry us all."

Jewel nodded. "But I will not be in the wild wind's debt here, not yet. Not until it can't be avoided. Snow, I want you to carry Adam."

Snow rolled his expressive eyes. He didn't have Shadow's intense dislike of the young healer.

"Do I have to take the *stupid* one?" Shadow asked, glaring at Angel—who glared back.

"Yes," Jewel replied, as he walked to Angel's side and tried to knock him off his feet.

Avandar rose in folds of air. He was never going to ride a cat when any other option presented itself. Probably for the best; Jewel could imagine the cats dropping him out of spite.

She closed her eyes. Breeze ruffled hair that was, for once, unconfined by the strict demands of patrician fashion; she reached up absently to push it out of her eyes. She could have chosen to ride the cats; they were capable of carrying two.

But she understood that in this place, she had one mount. He had not stepped onto the Oracle's path with the rest of her companions, but he was so much part of the hidden path, it wasn't necessary. He had been felled by the Winter Queen, and he had been remade at her desire. There was no place that he could not walk, no path that he could not find, if it had once been touched by Ariane.

Winter King.

He came out of the darkness of the halls themselves, his hooves silent as he ran toward where she now stood, waiting. They did not touch the stone, and the wind that carried three of her companions—the three with the most obvious power—didn't appear to touch him at all.

Her voice did. He came to a stop a yard in front of where she stood waiting. His eyes were the color of cat eyes in this place, but they were luminescent in a way that the cats' were not.

Jewel.

Do you know this place?

My feet know it, was his soft reply. He knelt, lowering his great tines toward the cold, stone floor.

She climbed up on his back, and he rose. He was proof against the bitter chill of the still air. When she rode him, the cold no longer touched her. She thought she could sit astride him in the frozen Northern Wastes and be as warm.

Yes, was his quiet reply. He did not give her warning when he leaped toward the heights, but he didn't need to. While he was willing to carry her, she could not be dislodged by a simple thing like motion. Not even the wind at play could pull her from his back.

She understood, as they rose, that she was not the rider he wished to bear. She was mortal, and frail, and in his estimation, unacceptably weak; she had survived because the grandeur and beauty of true power had been drained from a world that was now fit only for livestock and insects.

Yes, Terafin. But not for much longer. The world wakes. What the hidden paths contained can no longer remain hidden, and things are waking whose sleep guaranteed the safety of your kind.

You've seen this.

Yes, in my travels. I have seen much.

He had not, she thought, seen the Winter Queen.

No.

She heard the longing in the single word; he made no attempt to hide it.

No, he said again, as they reached the height of a ceiling that had seemed, from the ground, to be solid. *It is not a weakness that can be used against me; it defines all that I now am. The only command she gave was that I serve you.*

But if any mortal—any rider*—can find the solitary, hidden path that leads to her Court, it is you. She is not Winter Queen now; nor is she yet Summer Queen. She exists between these two states, and the world into which you have willingly stepped now holds its breath, waiting.*

There are rules that govern the seasons of the world.

Summer or Winter in the lands in which the Winter King and the Wild Hunt were at home were not the seasons of Jewel's childhood. *I don't understand.*

No. No more did I, when I lived as mortal man in the ancient cities. Ariane *is the child of gods. Before the sundering, she was kin to them; she was a power that rivaled theirs. In some cases, it was the greater power; she was of the land, of the world. It heard her voice. Perhaps, in the time before her birth, the seasons were different.*

But when she spoke, she spoke with the voice of the ancient and the wild; the things that lived at the heart of the elements. She bound herself to them, and the world leaped with joy in reply.

What she desires, is desire. *What she loves* is love. *It is not mortal love; it is not built on fear and the necessity for allegiance; it is not a matter of momentary whim, and it is not subject to time.*

It is subject to her seasons. She is Winter, Terafin. She is Summer.

Which did not lessen Jewel's confusion.

One cannot love Ariane and have room for any other love. Even in my existence, what I want is Ariane. Winter Queen. Summer. Just and only Ariane. When I am in your world, echoes of my earlier life distract me. I watch you play at politics, and I remember when those games were complex enough to devour my life if I was not cautious.

But I am not what I was then. I am hers. And while she commands it, I am yours in equal measure. Because she commanded it, I serve. I play no games with you; I do not stoop to lie. I offer you the advice that will serve your purpose.

But this is no part of that. This place is at the heart of her Winter. If this is where the Oracle meant your test to start, I am not certain that any of you will survive the journey.

He knew where they were.

No. I have not been here before; it is new to me. But listen and you can hear the echoes of her ancient sorrow and her ancient anger. Celleriant does not understand what this presages.

And you do.

I understand that it is a monument to the past. It stands with the force of vow, of blood oath. Bredan's fingers have touched the pillars and the stone; his voice can be heard if you but listen. We live because we hide our weaknesses, and that is true, even of gods. There are things here that should not be touched. Tell them.

But she had seen Celleriant's expression, and she doubted very much that her words would reach him.

She felt the Winter King's frustration. *He is yours. He has vowed to serve you. Command him, and he will obey. And she has accepted this. She has planned for it. You do not understand the significance of either of these facts. The Arianni do not serve any lord but Ariane. And yet, Terafin, this one does.*

I do not understand what it means or what it presages. But the fate that awaits Lord Celleriant is death, if she is on her Summer Throne.

And if she isn't?

He was silent for a long beat. *You have promised Summer, Terafin. If you have come to value Lord Celleriant at all, you will fulfill that promise.*

The ceiling was not, as Jewel had assumed, closed to air and sky. At the farthest reach of the long, long hall, it rose in a series of complicated arches that seemed to rest on the air itself. The pillars were of stone, at least from a distance.

They were of stone on approach. But the stone was carved stone, rendered in likenesses of Ariane herself. There were twelve, in all, in various states of dress; some wore armor that looked familiar; some wore dresses. Some wore nothing at all, but hair trailed down the fronts of their bodies in a way that suggested much but revealed little.

Each of these figures stood in midair; their raised arms formed the height of pillars that ended with delicate stone arches. They stood in pairs, but they weren't carved or positioned to be facing each other; they looked in the same direction: forward.

Jewel asked the Winter King to slow as they approached these graven images, but even if she hadn't, she thought he would have regardless. She could see the hand of Makers in these, and not only because they stood on a firmament of air. So, too, the Winter King.

He moved slowly. He did not speak a word.

Moving slowly or no, he almost collided with Celleriant, for Celleriant had, as he reached the foot of this odd construction of arches, come to a full stop. Wind tugged at his hair; it was the only thing about him that moved. That could, Jewel thought, with growing unease, be moved.

Kallandras had stopped a yard ahead of where Celleriant now stood, and turned; wind also tugged at his hair, golden curl to straight platinum fall, but it pulled at his cape and his tunic, tugging at fabric as if it were an impatient child.

His eyes narrowed as he watched Celleriant; his lips moved. No sound escaped them.

"What is it?" she asked softly. "What is it that you see?"

"Traitors," Celleriant replied. But his voice was soft with wonder, hollow with disbelief. Jewel nudged the Winter King forward, toward the statues that seemed to hold the majority of the Arianni Lord's attention.

"These are not different depictions of the White Lady?" she asked.

He turned to gaze at her. She expected contempt or the arrogant dismissal he generally offered. He gave her neither. For a moment, standing in the eye of the wild wind's storm, he looked young, to Jewel. Young in a way that he had never looked, not even on the day she had found him at the height of nightmare made real, and rescued him.

"They are not, although perhaps you cannot see the truth of this in stone. You might have, had you met them when they yet existed." He turned to Kallandras. "I know where we are. I have never been here; very, very few of my kinsmen have. Illaraphaniel would have known these halls immediately, were he to walk them."

"Would he have cautioned us against it?" the bard asked.

"I . . . cannot say." It sounded like yes. He drifted toward the nearest arch, and stopped in front of one of the more martial statues. "They were as we are, if legend is to be believed. As we are, and yet, more like the White Lady than any one of us could hope to be.

"They had names," he whispered. "But I do not know them; they are not— they are never—spoken of by my kin."

"Then how do you know about them?"

"The trees," he replied, his voice still cloaked in hush. "The trees. The wind. The earth itself. They remember what we do not speak of; they speak of what we cannot."

"I asked Meralonne about them, once," Jewel said, as her eyes were drawn, once again, to the carved figures, but she looked away, to Celleriant. He drew attention, demanded it, in a different way.

His brows rose. "You cannot have asked about the twelve; you are still alive." He spoke with absolute certainty.

"I asked about female Arianni. About the women."

His brows shot up, into strands of loose, flowing hair. He looked incredulous. "And he answered?"

"He said there was only ever Ariane."

"There *is* only Ariane. And for the Princes of the Court, that is the absolute truth. It defined them. It doomed them."

"It doomed three," Jewel said.

Be cautious, Terafin.

"It doomed all," he replied. "Or do you think Illaraphaniel was spared? He did not, and does not, sleep—but in all other ways, he is lost, both to us, and to the White Lady."

"That was her choice, surely?"

"Yes. Did you think her choice a kindness in any way?"

"But . . . he didn't betray her."

"No. No, he did not. He failed her. There is no room for failure in the Winter; there is ice and death. If there is mercy at all to be found, it is found in the Summer Court—and Summer never arrives. To some, Winter is our only truth, and it stretches into the future without end." He reached out to touch the cheek of the statue, and his eyes widened; his hand drew back as if burned, and indeed, Jewel thought she smelled the faint hint of singed flesh.

The Winter King leaped toward Celleriant; he landed between the Arianni Lord and the pillar, lowering his tines and pawing at nothing but air.

"*What* is he *doing?*" Shadow demanded. He had come to stand at the top of the first of the stone arches, looking down at them all.

"Which one?"

"The *stupid* one," the cat hissed. "*What* are you *thinking?*"

Celleriant looked up at the cat; if Jewel was uncertain to whom Shadow spoke, Celleriant was not. "Did you know?" he asked.

Terafin, we must move. We cannot remain here.

I don't understand. What has changed? You said you didn't recognize this hall.

I did not. I do not recognize it now. But I understand what Lord Celleriant believes this place must be, and I understand, now, that these columns are not as they appear.

What are they?

Come, he said, and began to walk. Unless she wished to dismount—and given her position what must be a hundred feet about safe ground, she did not—she was a captive audience. Captive, she thought, to more than the

Winter King and the heights; there was something about the statues that he now approached that she found compelling.

They were beautiful, almost in the way the Winter Queen was, for all that they were stone. She glanced once at Celleriant; he did not nurse his hand, nor did he allow Kallandras to so much as look at it. If he was injured, it was minor, and minor injuries were of little note—or so said his bearing. But his eyes were dark, the curiosity, the muted wonder—which was almost all the wonder he exposed—guttered. He watched the Winter King in a tense silence; he did not move to join him.

Come, Jewel. There is history here lost to all but the gods—and perhaps it is lost to them, as well.

Celleriant doesn't seem to care for it.

You misunderstand. These halls were left standing as a monument and a warning to such as he.

And not to you.

Me? No. I am mortal.

He was a stag that rode at the head of the Wild Hunt. He had lived far, far longer than any mortal of Jewel's acquaintance except Avandar. He was not, by any definition Jewel accepted, mortal.

It is not your definition that marks me, he replied. *It is hers. I can travel any path her feet have touched; it is both her gift and her curse. But I cannot speak as Celleriant can; nor even as you do. If she knew that I walked here, it is not upon me that her wrath would fall. She could not expect that I would be immune to the grandeur and the beauty of the ancient. Not when it is so much kin to hers.*

And it was.

She could not expect, he continued, as he walked, *that you would be, if she conceived of your presence in this place at all.*

She didn't bring mortals here?

Jewel—there were no *mortals in her Spring.* As he spoke, he walked past the four women in their impressive, forbidding armor; he walked between the four who wore dresses that were so fine—even made, as they were, of a single color of stone—that the white dress she'd worn on the first day of The Terafin's funeral seemed almost ordinary and unremarkable in comparison.

Because she did not wish to hear cat complaints for the rest of the voyage, she kept this thought to herself; only the Winter King heard, and only the Winter King chuckled. He was, on the other hand, amused at the idea of outraged Snow. It was the only amusement in him. All else was given to awe with a tinge of unease.

He reached the four who stood in various states of undress; their hair flowing as if under water. Stone expressions suggested gravity, gravitas; they suggested such confidence—or arrogance—that nudity did not diminish them; it did not make of them something to be gaped at, or even desired. No more did armor or cloth.

But when he came to the last pair, Jewel stopped breathing for one long moment. The woman on her left . . . was pregnant.

The Winter King's silence was one of incomprehension. What he saw made so little sense to him he was, for a moment, at a loss for words.

Jewel, however, didn't labor under the same confusion. She nudged the Winter King forward; he did not move. She wasn't even certain he could hear her. Instead, she turned to Kallandras, who had not yet approached the last of the standing pairs.

"Kallandras. Will the wild wind carry me for just a moment?"

"Do not be *stupid, stupid girl*," Shadow hissed.

The Senniel bard nodded, although he cast one backward glance at Celleriant before the folds of his summoned wind carried him to where Jewel sat mounted. As Jewel's, his eyes widened, his breath stilled. He spoke a word, and then another, and the wind lifted Jewel from the Winter King's back; he tensed beneath her, returning slowly to himself.

Terafin. Avandar, at the height of the arches, offered warning.

The wind set her down gently by Kallandras' side. Shadow landed beside her—between them—almost at the same time. It was clear that he didn't want to be in the presence of these statues—but Angel did. She met her denkin's silent gaze, held it for a moment, and then nodded.

As Celleriant had done before her, she approached a statue. And as the Arianni Lord had also done, she reached out to touch stone. Wind carried the scent of his burned flesh; her hand, however, was steady. There was something about pregnant women that made them seem like small miracles; that drew Jewel's attention. She did not have, had never wanted, children—but there was something about the creation of life, the intimacy of carrying it so absolutely close to the heart, that she had always found compelling.

One didn't, of course, touch the rounded belly of a random stranger—but something about pregnancy made all kinds of people approach an expectant mother. Even Jewel's Oma, a woman noted for her suspicion and hostility toward anything that didn't bear some trace of her familial blood, softened and drew near when evidence of encroaching infant presented itself.

"Do you know what you're doing?" Angel said; no one else spoke. Well, no one beside Shadow. The cat didn't approve—but he disapproved of everything she did: what she ate, how she ate it, what she wore, how she wore it, how she spoke, how she didn't speak, how she argued or didn't argue.

Jewel shook her head. She reached out and let her palm hover above the curve of naked, stone belly, lifting her head to meet the downcast eyes of a woman who appeared to be gazing at that swell of stomach. Her left hand cradled the lower part of that belly; the right rested at its height. There was, in this one statue, an absence of some of the condescension and arrogance that graced every other face; it made her look vastly more vulnerable.

Her hair, however, did fall in such a way as to hide exposed breasts, and it seemed, as Jewel watched it, that the wind moved its strands.

"Terafin?" Kallandras whispered.

"Have you ever heard story or song about these women?"

"No. I very much doubt that any living being has. One might ask the gods in the Between, but I do not think they would now answer."

"One god might."

"Yes, but he will not be found Between—and should he choose to grace the impudence of your question with answer, it is an answer you will pay for with your life."

She placed her hand against the exposed curve of flesh and jerked away almost immediately.

Shadow hissed. The hiss was soft, and it died into silence as Jewel's eyes widened.

Her hand did not burn. Burning might have been less disturbing. Shaking her head, she once again laid her hand against the rounded curve.

No, it had not been her imagination. The skin that she touched did not feel made of stone; it wasn't carved or worked. It was flesh, it was warm. She had once or twice touched pregnant women, just to feel evidence of the life they carried within them kick her palm.

Nothing else about the statue suggested life. Nothing. There was no movement of eye or lip, no disdain and no outrage—and had this woman been among the living, Jewel was certain there would have been, and that she would have deserved it for even daring to approach. "Adam." She exhaled. "Snow, bring Adam to us."

"I don't *want* to."

"I don't care. Bring Adam here."

"*Make* me."

"With your permission, Terafin?" Kallandras asked. "I do not think it wise to descend into argument with Snow. Not in this place."

"Not *ever*, but she is *stupid*," Shadow pointed out. He approached the feet—the bare feet—of the pregnant woman, and hissed at them, swatting them with unsheathed claws. Jewel heard the distinct sound of blade against stone, as if he were sharpening them. She didn't approve of his choice of stone, and made that perfectly clear.

He hissed.

Celleriant, however, had had enough of Shadow; if he now gazed at the statues with revulsion or even dread, the respect at his core was profound. Jewel caught the bright flash of blue out of the corner of her eye and turned. Celleriant now bore sword and shield.

Gods. "You deal with Lord Celleriant," she told the Senniel bard. "I'll deal with intransigent cats."

It was not a burden to Kallandras to step between Shadow and Celleriant; it was not, his posture implied, a risk to have the whole of his back exposed to Shadow's claws. What he said to Celleriant, no one else could hear—and Jewel thought, for no reason she would have been able to explain, that that was somehow right.

She dropped a hand on Shadow's head; it had been easier months ago when he'd been shorter. Adam came drifting down to where Jewel stood; he found the lack of ground beneath his feet far more troubling than she did. That should have given her pause. It should have been more significant. But studying such significance was a luxury that she didn't have time for at the moment.

"Matriarch?"

Odd that she could still find the time for immense frustration. She didn't correct him. Months of correcting him amounted to almost nothing whenever events became too strange, too wild. "I want you to touch this statue," she told him, forcing her voice to be steady.

He approached the statue the same way he had once approached the Serra Diora in the stretch of Terrean that led, in the end, to the Sea of Sorrows. He approached her as he had the same Serra on a desert night: the most beautiful mortal woman Jewel had ever laid eyes on. Then, he had carried a lute in his hands, as an offering of solace and comfort. Now, his hands were empty.

Empty, however, they had an entirely different power than they had possessed on the night he had carried Kallandras' lute.

Adam asked no questions. As the son of the Matriarch of Arkosa, he had learned that answers were costly; that questions were a burden and a danger that no one with any wisdom willingly risked. Matriarchs did not share their secrets; the living were famously bad at keeping anything secret, in the end. Angel tensed as Adam approached the statue. So did Shadow.

She understood why.

Adam was no more a child than she had been at his age—but neither she nor Angel were that age any longer, and at this remove, he seemed painfully young. The urge to protect him was powerful. But she had placed her life in his hands, and he had, at grave risk to his own, saved it. Child or no, it was his gift that defined him in this place.

His gift and her willingness to use it.

She saw his eyes widen in shock, but he didn't jerk his hand away as Jewel had; instead, he lifted his other hand, and placed it beside the first. His dark, southern complexion gave way to something almost green-gray. She reached out and gently placed an arm around his shoulder; he leaned back into that arm as if to brace himself.

"It's alive, isn't it?" she asked him. "The baby's alive."

"It's more—it's worse—" Adam whispered, in Torra. He lifted hands; they shook; nor did they stop shaking when he clenched them in fists. He wheeled, the lack of ground beneath his feet forgotten in his distress. He approached the woman who stood as part of this pair, reached for her hand. Healers needed to have skin to skin contact—but she was all of stone.

Jewel glanced at her palm. Stone.

Adam did not examine his hands; he had no need. Nothing in him doubted what his touch told him. He traversed the columns of statues, passing between each with increasing speed. He clutched the hands of the statues, where hands were exposed, or faces, where they were not. He did not speak a word; all of his urgency found expression in either motion or a frozen immobility.

Only when he stood at the foot of the columns did he stop.

Jewel moved toward him with no will of her own; the air carried her at the whim of the bard, and let her down gently beside Adam. He was tense, his shoulders drawn inward as if to ward off a blow; he was staring at a space beyond her right arm as if he must see something—anything—other than the statues themselves.

Celleriant drifted toward him, and with him came Kallandras; neither man spoke. Both had eyes for the healer.

Avandar.

Silence.

Do you know who these women were?

No. The Arianni are not known for their honesty, but in this case, trust Celleriant. If he does not know for certain, none among us—save perhaps your cursed cats—do.

Does the Oracle?

Of a certainty.

Did she mean for me to see this?

That, I cannot say. Even in my time, the Oracle's treachery was rooted in simple fact. Or complex fact. She did not stoop to lie; those who chose to take her tests did. It was the lies they told themselves, in the end, that destroyed them; the Oracle allows for no lies. Remember this. What you see here is.

I don't understand what I see.

Yes. That is the Oracle's curse. Or her gift. Philosophers were split, down the centuries, over which it was.

Would the gods know?

Yes. But I am not certain the gods would answer if you asked. There is a pall of tragedy over this place. You will not, he added softly, *reach the ears of the gods here. The lands between do not easily come into being upon the hidden paths.*

She set a gentle arm around Adam's shoulders. After a long, silent breath, he slumped, the tension leaving his back, his arms. The color did not return to his face, and his eyes looked almost bruised.

"Yes," he whispered, although she did not repeat her earlier question. "Yes, the child is alive."

She didn't ask him how that was possible, although she wanted to know. If these woman were Arianni in some fashion, childbirth might have rules that mortals did not share.

He turned to her, and she drew him into her arms as if he were a younger child; she offered him shelter, of a kind.

"What would you have me do?" he whispered.

"I don't know that there's anything you can do." She meant it. She spoke with conviction. But as the words left her lips, as they died into the watchful silence of too many silent men, she *knew* she was wrong.

She wanted to send him back, then. To send him to Finch, to Terafin, to *Averalaan Aramarelas*, where he might, for a small time, be safe from truths such as these that had no place in either of their lives.

That had had no place.

He knew. She was not one of nature's better liars; it was a skill she had learned only with time and effort, and moments of great vulnerability cut those lessons loose and set them adrift. She, therefore, chose her words with care. "What do you want to do?"

He understood what she could not put into words: her uncertainty. Her fear. She had asked the wrong question. She was the Matriarch, here. She accepted it, finally, and fully. She wondered if Yollana, that ancient, terrifying pillar of living steel, felt the doubts Jewel herself now felt. She wondered if Yollana had seen magics such as these. What would she do? What would she dare?

Yollana, like Jewel, was seer-born; unlike Jewel, she had never set foot upon the Oracle's path. She relied, for guidance, on the whim of vision that arrived without warning.

Jewel had had no dreams of these women. She had had no warning about these paths. "Are they all alive?" she asked him, her voice quiet, her arms steady.

He nodded into her shoulder.

There was a reason that Matriarchs did not allow themselves to be touched by the healer-born. A reason the Arianni likewise declined. A healer's touch was not simple touch; it could not be. While they healed the injured, they might touch unguarded thoughts; they might enter them, examine them. If the healed man or woman was dying, the possibility became a certainty.

These statues that were not flesh were not the stone they appeared to be. They were not—could not—be dying; what Adam touched in the brief contact could not bind him the way the dying did. She tightened her arms as if to say she wouldn't *allow* it.

"They are not mortal," Kallandras said, surprising her. She glanced up, over Adam's bowed head and curved back.

"They couldn't be." She bent her head again. "Can they hear us?"

He nodded.

"They're aware that we're here."

He nodded again.

"They don't understand us."

This time he shook his head.

Jewel, we must leave this place. We must leave it untouched, the Winter King said.

We've already touched it. And there's a baby—

That is why *we must leave. If these women are kin, in some fashion, to the Winter Queen, that woman, all appearances aside, cannot be with child.*

I think I know pregnancy when I see it.

Were she mortal, I would not deny that. But she is not. She was not, if she is as she appears. The Winter Queen and her kind cannot *bear children. They are Immortal.*

So? Gods have borne children. The firstborn are all, in theory, the offspring of the gods that walked this world.

Do you imagine that those births are anything like yours?

It had never occurred to her to wonder; birth was so much a part of life. When she heard the phrase "child of," it conjured instant images of that process. It made the gods seem more human. It also made sense: if mortals were somehow the creation of the ancient gods, that there would be echoes of that divinity in the much shorter, much smaller lives of the mortals they created.

You do not understand. Death is an artifact of birth. Where there is birth, death is inevitable. We use the word "child" or even offspring when we speak of the gods, of things ancient and immortal. We use the word "birth." Both are metaphors and both are inexact.

She's pregnant. There is nothing metaphorical about it.

Yes. That is very much what I now fear. But if she is pregnant, Jewel, she has not yet given birth. And if she does, she gives birth to death. Do not interfere in what you see.

"Adam, tell me—are they even sane?"

He nodded again. He trembled for a while and then grew still, lifting his chin from her shoulder, and lifting his own shoulders as well. Jewel closed her eyes; it was brief. "The mother. I have to ask one question about the mother."

He waited.

She struggled to find the words. She felt the shadow of the Winter King's fear as if she had swallowed it whole and made it a visceral part of herself. She did not understand what had happened here, but she understood that he was right: something would change, somehow, if things were not left alone.

"Did she want this child?"

He nodded.

"Do you—did they tell you what happened to them?"

He shook his head. "It's not easy to touch them. But her voice was clearest, to me. The others—they are all weeping. They are all lost." He hesitated, and then forged on. "When I call the dead back from the shores of the river, I find them because they are lost. They have not yet crossed the bridge; they have not yet found peace.

"They weep, like that. They weep and they hear me when I call. These women will never reach the bridge, but it's as if they're inches from it."

"They do not walk that bridge," Celleriant said. His voice held both ice and fire; his hands were not completely steady. Jewel wouldn't have been surprised to see his sword and his shield come to those hands; she was in fact more surprised when they didn't.

"No," was Adam's grave—and surprisingly steady—reply. "They do not.

They cannot see it; they will not find it on their own. They wander, instead. They speak a name."

"Do not speak that name here," the Arianni Prince commanded.

Adam frowned. "Why? It is a name you know. It is a name you speak. You speak it with reverence, and you speak it in sorrow." He turned toward the statues, and added, "it is not different, for them."

"If they are here, they are here at her whim. They betrayed her. This is the price they must pay."

"Did they betray her in the same way the Sleepers did?" Jewel asked.

Celleriant closed his eyes; platinum lashes rested against pale skin for a long moment before he opened them again. "Lord, I do not know. We are not mortals. We do not labor at the whim of the god-born Kings. We do not judge. There is no law but Ariane's. There is no justice but hers. You think of right or wrong as if they are a cage, a law, unto themselves. There *is* no equivalent, for us. She is not beholden to any external laws; she is beholden to her own, and her oaths, when freely given."

"Do you feel no sympathy for the Sleepers, then?"

"Does it signify anything?" Wind caressed his hair. He was otherwise motionless. "I understand why they made the choice they did. I also understand that there was a price to be paid for that choice. They knew what that price would be, and they accepted the cost."

"You have never seen this place before."

"No."

Jewel, be cautious. Two voices: Avandar's and the Winter King's.

If I were cautious, we wouldn't be here.

"How are the Arianni born?"

He glanced at her, his face expressionless. He then turned to Kallandras. "I am not certain I understand the question; do you?"

Kallandras did not smile.

"You speak, sometimes, of youth. Of your youth," Jewel said, trying again. "You speak of that youth as we sometimes speak of our childhood."

"Ah. We were young, once. All of us."

"As young," Jewel asked, "as these women?"

"Lord, *I do not know.* What would you have me say? Or do? If they are truly alive, would you have me destroy them?"

"No!"

"Would you have me offer them pity, then? If they are as old as you fear, they will not thank you; nor will they, in the end, feel anything but contempt or rage for me. Pity such as you counsel is an insult; it implies that I am so certain of my power they are irrelevant."

"There is a difference between pity and sympathy."

"I have not seen it. I have not," he added, when she opened her mouth, "made a careful study of mortals, but I have lived some months in your home. Mortals are noisy; they demand attention they could not otherwise merit, they are so inconsequential. They offer pity to each other."

"They do not offer *pity*. They offer sympathy."

"The difference must be subtle indeed."

"Pity is what we offer those who are so unfortunate we cannot conceive of living their lives. Sympathy is what we offer when we *have* lived their life, or when we've feared to have no choice but to live it. We offer it because we understand what the other person now faces."

"Ah. I do not understand what they face," he replied.

She surrendered. "Could she do this?"

"Yes. It is her work. You cannot see it."

Jewel shook her head, and then reached up to shove hair out of her eyes. "Do you see the woman at the head of the column?"

He said nothing. The wind grew stronger and colder while she waited for his reply. The Winter King's disapproval was cold in an entirely different way; she ignored it with effort. Her palm, resting against the side of her leg, ached.

She was not, now, the ruler Yollana of the Havalla Voyani was. She dreaded the day she must become that leader; she thought it would break her. And perhaps it had broken some part of Yollana as well, and she had sacrificed that part to preserve what she could of her kin. Triage was not a concept that Jewel welcomed; she understood it, when the figures were dry on paper and the people they affected were out of sight.

She was a seer. Out of sight meant different things to different people.

Her palm continued to ache; the pain grew stronger. She hadn't—she would swear she hadn't—been burned.

Even captive, the Arianni were not without power or influence. Where we were forced to fight them, we killed, the Winter King said.

I only touched—

Yes.

She turned, eyes widening, to face Adam. He had touched them all.

Chapter Nine

S HE WANTED TO SPEAK, but her throat was suddenly dry with fear. She had been silent this way many, many times in the past, but she never grew accustomed to it.

Adam was here because she had asked him to accompany her.

Adam had made contact with the statues of the Arianni because she had demanded it.

Yes, Jewel. You are Matriarch to Adam. He accepts your word as law because your only goal is the preservation of your kin.

She could have accepted that if she had asked him to take the risk with any deliberation; if she had moved him strategically; if she had had no other choice. But none of this was true in this instance. None.

Not none, Jewel. You are seer-born, and this is the path that will test you. It will break you, or it will be your making, as all such tests are.

They aren't, she replied, thinking of the ways in which everyone she knew had been half-broken; they'd retained enough of their sanity to remake themselves, but not enough to become whole.

That is the fate of humanity; we are fragile and simultaneously strong enough to keep moving. You are not here because you can see the end of every path you choose; you can barely see a yard in front of you now. You are here because you are seer-born.

Avandar, if he—

Yes?

She shook her head.

What, Jewel, will you decide to do?

She raised her hand, turning the palm up toward her eyes. She examined it for blisters, looking for evidence of an injury that would justify the ache. Her hand was untouched.

She offered it to Adam. "I'm not a Matriarch like Evallen or Yollana. You've already saved my life—at least once. There's nothing about me that you haven't seen. I touched the statue first. My hand aches. I can't see anything wrong with it because I can't look the way you can."

He exhaled. "My mother—"

"I know. And Yollana would have chopped off her hand before asking for your opinion. But I can't be either Evallen or Yollana; I wasn't raised to it." She thought of her Oma and grimaced. "I wasn't *consistently* raised to it." Exhaling heavily she added, "I think you're here because, in the end, Arkosa needs you to be here. What you can do, no other healer in Levec's experience can do.

"I don't know if Levec would have felt what you—or I—felt on touch."

Kallandras said, "Terafin, with your permission?"

"I think we've taken enough risks today."

But Kallandras was already moving. **It is not your risk, but mine. In this case, it is not for your sake that I make the request.**

"Kallandras—"

He flew swiftly beyond the reach of her voice, like graceful storm. The wind buoyed him, carried him, and dropped him ten feet; he laughed in delight, and she could not tell if it was feigned. But he came to a kind of rest in front of the pregnant woman, and he offered her a perfect, humble bow. Rules of etiquette differed by culture and class, as Jewel had found to her chagrin; she wasn't certain what the Arianni would make of the gesture, if she saw it at all.

He was a long time bowing; she thought he must be speaking. But he spoke—and listened—as bard, and in the end, he reached out and placed a very gentle hand upon the swell of rounded stomach.

She was annoyed to find she was holding her breath. But she could not apparently remember to breathe until he said, "She is stone, to me. Perfect stone. Had you asked, I would have said she was maker-made." He bowed again. The wind carried him back to Jewel. Or perhaps back to Celleriant. It was hard to tell.

"Your hand doesn't ache, does it?"

"No, Terafin. I might touch a wall in any manse save yours with the same effect. If there is life within these statues, it is a life felt by Adam, and by you."

"Celleriant also—"

"What he felt was danger and death, not life."

Avandar said, "There is an enchantment laid upon these pillars, which is to be expected given their location."

Kallandras nodded. "I do not believe Lord Celleriant felt flesh when he made contact; he felt fire and pain. These are not meant to be touched by one such as he."

And mortals, if the Winter King was right, hadn't existed. They had, therefore, never been a consideration.

"Was it a protective spell?" Jewel asked of Avandar.

"I would consider it proscriptive rather than protective, but the enchantment could serve either purpose. It is an odd question," the domicis added. "Is there a reason for it?"

"Adam said he felt sorrow and longing." Jewel understood both. "Not anger. Were I somehow entrapped this way, and capable of being both aware and sane for the duration, it's not sorrow I'd feel. I'd be angry."

"You do not serve the White Lady." Celleriant's voice implied that ice could burn. And maybe, for the Arianni, it could. "There is no anger in us— not for her. She could cast us aside, she could send us to our deaths, and we would fear only that our deaths would not serve her purpose. She could," he added softly, oh so softly, "order us to serve a mortal seer, and we would serve to the best and the fullest of our abilities."

Jewel closed her eyes.

"And we would do so, Lord, *because* she desired it. And while we did as she commanded, we would dream of the Winter Court, and the Summer, but in so doing we would not dream of our kin; we would dream of the White Lady. You are mortal," he said again. "You have seen the White Lady. You have faced her, challenged her, and you have survived. You think of her as beautiful. You believe that her beauty haunts your life; that it makes mockery of any other beauty."

Jewel swallowed, but nodded. "Beauty doesn't mean to me what it means to you," she finally said, as if this pale truth were somehow a defense.

"Perhaps not. Yours is a gray, empty world, full of squat hovels and inconsequential lives. You could not understand, could not *yearn* for beauty and live in the lands you do.

"If these women are, as you now fear, alive in some fashion, they once stood in the White Lady's shadow. They are kin to me, not to you; they feel their loss and their sorrow at the White Lady's absence. Sorrow tells you nothing about their fate; it tells you nothing about their crime.

"And it tells you less than nothing about the intent and the desire of the White Lady."

*   *   *

Jewel stood, now, at the back of the columns, not their head. She reached down and pulled up her sleeve. Twined around her wrist were three braided strands of hair, the braid so slender it should have been almost invisible. But it caught light and reflected it in a fine curved line, and where the wind was cold, a band of warmth lay against her skin. This, she thought, must be why she could touch the statues with fingers that failed to feel the stone her eyes saw.

She wanted to take the bracelet off, and almost did; Celleriant's hand closed around hers. He shook his head, mute, and she heeded the warning. "I only wanted to see if they—if they feel the same when I'm not wearing her gift."

"Do not part from that gift for any reason on these roads." His tone implied that the last part of the sentence was superfluous, and some hint of the passion that underlay his previous words remained with her. She knew, were these three strands of hair in his keeping, he would die before they left it. And he would kill.

She glanced at Adam, who had fallen silent and still while Celleriant spoke. The Arkosan boy now lifted his chin, awaiting her command. She had wondered what Yollana would do here. But even wondering, she knew. Yollana would touch nothing. She would allow no one else to touch anything, either. Her world was not *this* world; it was the world of the Voyanne. It was rough, and it had edges in the hidden and the ancient; she walked those edges only at great need.

The Havallan Matriarch had made sacrifices in order to walk them. She made blood plans against inevitable necessity. Kinship was not proof against need; no one, not even Yollana herself, could be certain that they would be spared should Yollana deem death and sacrifice essential. The Matriarch had lost sight in one eye as the price she must pay for the crimes—and gods, they were crimes—she had committed against a handful of her kin in order to preserve the majority.

Jewel understood that she could never be Yollana. She was grateful that Yollana existed—and more grateful that she was confined, in the end, to the Southern Dominion, a land that made harsh people and deserts. Choices made people; grim choices made grim people. Jewel understood that no matter how harsh her own childhood had been—with its loss and its abrupt end—she had never faced the choices that Yollana had.

She was almost certain she could not face them, now. She bowed head, inhaled, counting breath. One. Two. Three. In the middle of air that had no ground for mooring, standing in front of living statues created by a woman who was kin to gods, and perhaps more powerful than most of them, the faces that came to her were her dead: Lefty. Lander. Fisher.

Duster. Duster shrugged, as if to say fancy-ass statues weren't of interest. But she carried two daggers, and her spine was straight and tall, the way it had always been just before she launched into her own kind of battles.

Not her dead, then. But her living returned as well. It was Finch she saw. Finch. Teller. Arann. People who would never have come to her at all had she not been willing to make choices based entirely on a power that, itself, had roots in the hidden and the wild. Had she walked away from the things that were *not* her life and therefore not her problem, what kind of life would she have?

Not this one.

Not the life in which the family she'd built—kin, all, no matter what her Oma would have said—surrounded her, supported her, and, yes, loved her. She had brought only one of them with her, and she lifted her face to him now. Snow had taken to air again; he did not trust these statues, and given the rise of his fur, he considered them dangerous.

Night had not landed at all.

"Yes," she told Adam.

He said nothing.

"If you can help them, help. If you feel you can free them, free them." She heard Celleriant draw sword, and lifted one imperious hand.

Turning to face him, she said, "Am I your lord, Celleriant? Do I hold your oath?"

He stood, sword in hand, eyes glinting with the reflection of blue, harsh light.

"This is not the first time I travel a path that Ariane would not have me travel," she continued, when he failed to raise that blade—but also failed to answer her question. "It will not be the first time I choose to stand against her. Were it not for that choice—"

"I would never have failed her," Celleriant replied, voice low.

Jewel acknowledged this without evident sympathy, not difficult in this case because she felt almost none. "Perhaps not. If you kill me, you will fail her now."

His brows rose. She felt wind enfold her, tugging her hair up and out of her face; she expected to move—or to be moved. She wasn't. She was standing on thin air, her feet slightly separated, her hands stiff and straight by her sides.

"I am, as you often say, weak in the parlance of your kin. I don't doubt it.

I don't regret it. You hate the Lord of the Hells. The White Lady loathes him, as do I. But in your view of the world, hatred is almost meaningless. What he did to your kin—what he did to the White Lady—he had the *power to do.* You seem to prize power—all of you—without pausing to consider how it's used. You consider mercy a weakness. You have no concept of justice that I understand, when all is said and done. As long as bad things are not done to you or yours, you don't care.

"We do. Maybe because we're weak and we have to care. I don't know, and at this point, I don't care. You are bound to me by your own choice, is that right?"

His nod was tight and controlled.

"But I trust you less than I trust my Chosen."

That is wise.

It's not because he's powerful that I don't trust him. It's what he is. Who he is.

"You've said these statues should remain untouched. Fine. I'm not a servant of the White Lady; the most I could aspire to be is her slave—and I'm *never* going to be that. Tell me *why* I should walk away. And don't tell me it's because that's what she wants. Tell me why she wants it. Tell *me* why I should care."

"You *do not understand* what you see."

"No. I don't. What *I* see is a pregnant woman. What Adam sees is that she wanted the child she was carrying. What I'm *guessing* is that all twelve of these women are captive *because* that one woman was pregnant. I understand that in the lives of the Arianni there is only *one* woman. I've met mortals who felt very much the same way: they wanted—gods know why—all male attention, all focus, upon themselves.

"And I'm certain in one or two cases that the corrosive jealousy behind that desire did cause deaths. But this isn't death. It's true: the Winter Queen is peerless, in my experience. She is not the only child of gods that I've met— but she is, without question, the most compelling. The most beautiful.

"Yet I think it possible that these twelve, were they to move and breathe and speak, would be her equal. Is *that* why they're here?"

Terafin, the Senniel bard said, his voice so soft she might not have heard it were he not bard-born. **He does not know. This path was made for you—but what lies upon and across it was not. If I understand the Oracle at all—and I do not make that claim—this is your test. It is the first of many.**

"I don't want to make a mistake." Jewel did not look at the bard. "Celleriant, I'm seer-born. I've lived my life by my instincts."

"And your instincts have never failed you?"

"Of course they have. My instincts are not predictable; they're not under my control. They come and go as they please. I don't get to choose the warnings offered; I accept them when they are."

"And these vaunted instincts now?"

She looked, once again, to Adam—who had not moved an inch. "They tell me nothing, now."

Jewel, two internal voices said at once, with equal measures of dismay and annoyance.

"I've lived most of my life trusting instinct when it arrives. I don't even think about it. But I've also learned that where instinct is lacking, decisions still have to be made. In those cases, I rely on advisers and personal experience; I make educated guesses. Sometimes, it doesn't work out."

"You cannot compare the decisions you make in House Terafin with the decisions you will make here." He was struggling to contain his obvious disgust at the implied comparison.

She wasn't certain why he made the attempt.

No, you are not, the Winter King said. *But that is because you do not understand the nature of his vow; nor do you fully comprehend why he made it.*

You don't understand it, either, was her flat reply.

He chuckled. *In this, you are correct.* The amusement fell away from his internal voice. *I know who he served. You met her, much diminished, upon the hidden paths near Scarran. You have never seen her—and will never see her—at the height of her power; if you had, you would not so greatly fear the god the wise do not name. She was his equal upon fields of war, and in its many endeavors. You cannot imagine,* he continued, his voice growing remote, *that you are in any way her equal. You are not. You cannot be.*

Jewel felt no need to argue. The Winter King stated fact, no more.

You do not understand the cost to Lord Celleriant. It is my belief that he did not fully understand it, either; he thought of glory and war and death, because those are the shadows you now cast. He thought he saw—in your power—some path by which the White Lady might once again take to, and hold, the field. And she would do so in Summer, and it is a Summer that most believed would never come again.

Jewel was silent. The silence, as she met Celleriant's unwavering gaze, might go on forever. She was not, in the end, comfortable with silent spaces; they spoke to her of absence and death. He did not blink; she did, but this was not a contest of simple stares.

Adam surprised them both; he came to stand by her side. She glanced at him, and then immediately over his shoulder to the Senniel bard; the Senniel bard met her eyes in the same silence that held them all. But there were so many words beneath that silence.

She raised one hand; no one watching could mistake the gesture for a polite request for attention. Her palm was callused; it was not scarred—but unscarred or not, it had been cut, and blood had been shed, and blood mingled, to seal Celleriant's oath.

She had made no like oath to him. No explicit oath. But she had hoped, at the end of either her life or this war, he might find his way back to the White Lady.

"Things change," she told him quietly. "Even gods. I ask you again: tell me why I should not do this. Make me believe, given what you've observed of my life to date, that I would be committing a crime."

"You do not even know what you will do," he replied, his voice less heated.

"Yes, I do. I'll trust Adam."

Celleriant stared at the Voyani boy. His sword faded from view. "And if he does what I suspect he intends?"

"I don't know. They are not, and could not be, my prisoners; there's every possibility that freed, they would agree with you and attempt to kill me."

"We are not a people who are without a sense of obligation or gratitude," was his stiff reply.

Jewel said nothing. Adam spoke her name. She turned from Celleriant, Adam by her side, and she moved between the columns until they both came to rest in front of the woman who was with child.

"What does the wind whisper?" she asked the bard.

"A name," Kallandras replied. "But the wind fears nothing; it is, in the end, responsible to and for no one; the stories it tells are entirely of its context, and one must tease meaning out of them only afterward."

"What name?" Adam asked.

Kallandras smiled. "You will know it, if you can heal the damage done here. If you cannot, I will let the wind keep its secrets; they are not safely spoken of on this road. Or perhaps," he added, as he gazed into a distance of blue sky and scudding cloud, "at all."

Adam drew breath, exhaled, and turned to face Jewel; she placed one hand on his shoulder—whether to steady him or herself, she was uncertain. The bracelet on her wrist was warm enough now it was almost uncomfortable. She wondered if it would burn her, or if it would itself crumble to ash, and she felt a ridiculous pang of loss at the thought.

I never said, she told the Winter King, before he could speak, *that I did not*

*see what you saw in her. I never said I was immune to it. There are just things I want
more.*

There is nothing unique about what you want.

No. But unique doesn't matter.

Adam placed both of his palms against the curve of the woman's exposed
belly. Jewel hesitated before she did the same. She could not later say why she
felt compelled to do so. But this second contact was no less disturbing than
the first, even though she now expected visual stone to feel like warm flesh;
she felt movement beneath her hands. The child was alive.

She lifted her chin, looking up as Adam closed his eyes and bowed his
head; she looked down as his knees folded. He did not fall; the wind bore his
weight, just as it bore Jewel's.

Adam had touched many pregnant women before. He had attended births,
and on occasion, the resulting funerals of either mother or child. Childbirth
was desired as much as pregnancy was oft feared; it gave life, and took life.
But without children, the Arkosans were doomed to history.

Within the controlled environs of the Houses of Healing, under Levec's
curmudgeonly tutelage, he had—as healer—touched pregnant women. He
was not given leave to attend actual births; Levec did not trust him to remain
aloof. The dying, in the opinion of the old bear of a healer, were dying no
matter what age they were, and Adam did not have the fortitude to ignore
the imperative to bring them back.

This implied that Levec did, and Adam was privately uncertain that was
true. Levec could be—and usually was—unpleasant to outsiders. But he had
almost as proprietary a concern for the injured and the ill as he did for the
healers who lived within his domain. They were his responsibility, which
meant on some visceral level they were his.

So was Adam, but Adam had never minded it; he found it natural. Levec
in his very worst mood caused a shadow of the fear that Adam's mother had;
there was nothing the older healer could say or do that came close to some of
the decisions undertaken by the Matriarch. Some of the newer healers, on the
other hand, found him terrifying.

But expectant mothers did not. And Adam had never personally terrified
anyone, not even the small children it had been his responsibility to care for.
Visiting mothers to be were not common in the Houses of Healing, and they
were almost always well-moneyed; Levec used wealth as a barrier to keep
most of the many people contained in the city away.

Adam had been allowed to attend Levec during these visits. Adam had been uncertain why; he had, he told Levec, a lot of experience with expectant mothers.

"As a healer?" was Levec's gruff bark of a question.

The answer—which Levec knew well—was no. His gift had not yet appeared the last time he had lived among women who were with child.

"You will find the experience very different," Levec told him. "And if you still intend to return to your family—"

"I do."

"Then it will be valuable to encounter the difference in the company of someone who can answer the many questions you will have after the fact."

Childbirth was natural. Pregnancy was natural. The circumstances that surrounded either could be dire, tainting the fact of the child's existence. Adam understood this. The Voyani were matrilineal because one could be guaranteed to know who one's mother was. Knowing the father, given the violence of the clansmen and the lonelier stretches of life in the caravan, was far less guaranteed. But children were always considered good, even when the food was scarce and the lack of rains guaranteed that the coming months would be lean and harsh.

Children were the only future the Voyani had. It was not unheard of for the elderly to simply disappear into forests when the number of surviving children grew. All but the Matriarchs.

It had never occurred to Adam to question the fact of pregnancy or childbirth before. As he learned to use and control his power—although Levec was never entirely impressed by his efforts—it remained a simple fact of life, like breathing or sleeping.

Not until Levec invited him to attend an examination of Lady Bernice—a woman related in some fashion to the jovial and implacable Hectore of Araven—had that changed. It was not that the Imperial attitude toward children differed so greatly from the Voyani attitude—although it did, in ways that were both obvious and subtle; it was the physical *fact* of it.

There were two lives that were one. Meshed, entwined, they relied on the beating of one heart, the breathing of one set of lungs; this, he was familiar with. But they were not a simple, single body—if a body could be said, by a healer, to be simple.

They grew together, and simultaneously grew apart, the one waxing and the other waning. Levec had been unimpressed by his attempt to describe what his hands had touched, to wrap knowledge that his gift had given in words that might be understood by those not blessed by a similar gift.

Levec was so blessed, but he considered the attempt maudlin and sentimental. He was not a great lover of pets, but kept cats because they controlled the mouse population. He considered the pregnancy of *cats* to be similar. Adam was almost speechless. Almost.

But Levec had not finished, and Adam was able to chart the course of the pregnancy as it progressed. He was cautious, as Levec commanded, but curious. He could sense Bernice's thoughts; her tiredness, her annoyance at the size and shape of her own body, made foreign and strange by something that was nevertheless some part of it; her fear of childbirth and its possible consequences—to herself, and to the child.

Her fear of the child itself. Her hope for, her dreams of, that same child. These were the stories she told herself; they were almost carved in her flesh. But flesh was not stone; it shifted and changed with the passage of time.

"All things must," Levec told him. "This is the last time you will see Bernice unless she comes to visit after her son is born."

It was a son. Levec had not chosen to divulge that information to Bernice, although of course he knew. Adam was uncertain why, but Levec could be petty when annoyed, and apparently one of the relatives of Bernice had crossed some invisible line with the older healer. He contented himself with a rather smug silence.

Having since met that relative, Adam regretted that he had not whispered the truth to Bernice, although Levec would have boxed his ears. He could not speak of it after, because the baby did not survive. Bernice survived only with Levec's intervention; she was sent from the healerie as soon as she could be safely moved. Which meant, Adam thought, that she, too, had almost perished.

He did not understand.

"There are healers in the Houses. There are healers you consider more talented than you—why couldn't you have called one of us?"

"Us, is it?" Levec asked, the single line of brow rising into the deeper creases of forehead.

A frown was not enough to quell Adam's sense of betrayal and, yes, anger. "You have said yourself that my talent far surpasses yours, in your own opinion!"

"Your *talent*, yes. But you lack wisdom, Adam. You lack bitter experience. And so, because I am tired and weary, I will speak of my own experience."

This surprised Adam; had he not been so upset, it might have silenced him. "We walk different paths, Healer Levec. Your experience and mine are not guaranteed to be the same—and even if we face the same circumstance, our approach and our departure might differ completely!" He spoke in Torra.

Levec's Torra was not up to the task.

"When you touched Bernice the final time, you sensed the baby."

Adam folded arms tightly across his chest and nodded.

"Tell me, what were his thoughts?"

"We are not to touch the thoughts—"

"Spare me. I have asked you a question. Answer it." When Adam failed to comply, he said, "It is almost impossible for someone of your power to touch the body alone. What you touch you must never speak of—to *outsiders*. But I am your master, and you will answer *me*." Levec mirrored Adam's stubborn gesture; on Levec it was vastly more forbidding.

Adam inhaled. Exhaled. He had learned through bitter experience that one did not cry while speaking. Not when your mother was Matriarch.

"He had almost no thought."

Levec nodded. "But not none?"

"Not none. But there were no words—at all—for his experience, and his experience was so small. There was no ill will, and no good; there was no desire, no fear, no hope." Seeing Levec's expression, Adam added, "He has not *lived*. What thoughts would you expect?"

"Would that have changed, should he have survived?"

Exasperated, Adam said, "Yes!" Had they been in one of the rooms that Levec used for group discussions or classes, it would have stifled all conversation but Levec's. They were not; they were in Levec's private office—not the one into which he reluctantly allowed the nobility of this city.

"How quickly would that have changed, Adam?"

"I don't understand you."

Levec repeated the question in Torra. It was a simple question.

"I don't understand why you're *asking*. In order to have thought—to think, in the end, the way *we* think—"

Levec snorted. "The way *you* think and the way *I* think are vastly different."

"We think in words."

"Do you?"

"We can put our thoughts *into* words. We can make ourselves understood."

"Yes. We can. And that was learned. The infant could not learn that immediately. How long would it take?"

"Levec—"

"Longer than a day? Longer than week? Longer than a month?" Levec walked across the room and sat, heavily, in the chair on the other side of his desk. The desk, like the man behind it, was worn by use and time. "I was not always the man I am now."

"No. Once, you were an infant, too."

"Yes. But if I was not always the man I am now, I have some experience with healing. With healing," he added softly, "and its cost. It is why I built the Houses of Healing. It is why I find, and rescue, young healers. I have money, now—and power. It is not as hard for me to find them as it was.

"When I was younger, I believed that my power was a gift. It was meant to preserve lives and to spare others the losses I myself had endured."

Adam nodded.

"You are wondering how, or why, that changed."

He nodded again.

Levec smiled. It was a tired, weary expression; it contained affection, but absolutely no mirth or joy. "I founded this House so that others might hold on to that belief for longer. Healers are treated with respect in this city. They are treated with caution.

"In other cities and in other towns—the cities and towns of my youth—they were treated with similar respect in some quarters. But in others, they were treated as commodities. They were valuable—but in the way gold is valuable. Men kill for gold," he added quietly. "And when they find it, they hold on to it. Many a man has destroyed his life—and the lives of others—rather than let go.

"But you have heard this before, and it is not of this that I intended to speak."

Any healer that lived in the buildings that comprised Levec's Houses of Healing had, of course, heard worse. In the culture of the Voyani and the clansmen, healers were *not* valued. They were feared. The people of the Dominion understood that nothing was free; the more valuable the gift, the more onerous, and barbed, the obligation it incurred. There were those who chose to use their powers when those powers were discovered, but they were treated with suspicion. Except, of course, at need.

"When I was older than you are now—some decade older, so honestly, I should have known better—I was brought in secret to the house of a wealthy man. His wife—his second wife—was with child, and the pregnancy had been problematic. The delivery had been no easier.

"The midwives had offered him the choice of saving either the life of the mother or the life of the child; he was desperate for an heir, and he chose, without question, the child."

Adam said nothing. The death of a child in childbed was considered a tragedy; it was also a fact of life. If the mother lived, she might, in the end, bear other children and bring other life to the desert's edge.

"But the child was not delivered cleanly, for all that they made that choice. There was difficulty with breathing. I was brought to heal the babe, if it were possible."

Adam continued to say nothing, but now he felt uneasy.

"The child's birth had been compromised by the cord that bound it to its mother." Levec exhaled, shifting in place, his gaze firmly fixed to the perpetual clutter of desk. To anything in the room that was not Adam. "And so, Adam, I healed that child. I called him back from the bridge."

"Was he—was his mother waiting?"

Levec did not reply.

And that was answer enough, for Adam. But it did not offend him in any way. In his youth, the Bridge of the beyond, and the whole of the pantheon of the Northern gods, had been a children's story, if even that. The Voyani, a harsh people, understood only the Lord and the Lady; they knew that the winds that howled in the hottest and coldest of desert climes were the only fate that waited those who had once lived.

Only when the strange power he possessed had awakened did he understand that the Northern stories were true. But true or no, it was right that the dead wait and the living *live*. Even an infant.

Levec's expression disagreed. He was silent. He had started this discussion; Adam was surprised to see him falter; Levec seldom hesitated. But he understood, from that hesitation, that the child had not survived. He waited.

He waited, watching the older healer, seeing in the etched lines of his face the first sign of age's weakness, and not age's signal strength. Without thought, he crossed the room, passed the desk, and came to stand beside Levec's chair, where he gently laid a light arm across Levec's substantial shoulders.

"The child did not survive," he said. It wasn't a question.

"No. And not for the usual reasons. When we heal the dying, we must go to where they are. We call them. We find them. They cling *to* us, and we allow them to become some part of who we are; it is the only way we will find our own way back.

"They cling because they *think*, Adam. They have some sense of who they are; they have a very strong sense of their own isolation. They know that the mist and the fog in which they are lost—and often to which they come in some pain—is not life. They have fear. They have expectation. They have explicit desire. And they know profound loneliness.

"A newborn infant does not; not in the same way. They exist in the moment. In the moment that they know hunger, it is the whole of their world, but if fed, it passes; they do not retain enough to build causal thoughts. Not at birth. If an infant is lost at the foot of the bridge, his fear is visceral. He has no thoughts to drive that fear.

"And when found, an infant clings in a different way. His sense of *self* does not exist; it does not weather the contact with a healer—at least not with this one. I was fully a man. I had anger, perhaps even rage, and bitterness; I had seen enough of humanity to despise it. I had fears, and they drove me. My desires drove me. I am not in any way an invisible presence. Perhaps it would have been different had you been the healer to answer the summons."

"Tell me what happened."

"The child did not struggle; when I found him, he followed. He returned to life—and health—but the healing was difficult and long. I gave the infant to his father and the wet nurse he had already engaged in the event of an emergency. I did not feel the compulsion that normally comes when healing the dying. I thought, when I was paid, that I was done." He fell silent again.

But this silence, Adam understood. "Levec," he said, voice soft, "you saved my life. You brought me here. When you understood that this city—this home—was too confusing, you let me go to Finch and her den. I argue with you, it's true—but there was very little difference between argument and discussion among the Arkosans, unless weapons were involved.

"You do not need to tell me more. You have told me all that I need to hear. I trust you. I trust you as if you were kin."

He thought Levec was done, he was silent for so long. He was surprised when the older healer began to speak once again.

"Because infants have so little thought, they rely on instinct. They do not question it. They exist in single moments at a time. The only adults who do likewise are those who have taken severe injuries to their heads. An infant's instincts, however, are visceral. They have a strength that is *not* tempered by prior experience. When an infant is born to his or her mother, and the mother lives, the child forms an immediate attachment to her.

"In the case where the mother dies, they form that attachment to the wet nurse. This is both natural and expected." He inhaled.

Adam froze.

"You understand," Levec said softly.

And he did. "The child formed that attachment to you."

Levec nodded.

"And you did not know."

"No. I did not feel the same attachment *to* the child that a mother might have felt—or a father for that matter. As I said—perhaps, had you been the healer, it might have been different."

"You don't believe that."

"No, Adam, I don't. The babe would not eat. He did not form attachments the way a motherless child has throughout history. He *knew* only that I was absent, that I was gone, and that I was the center of the world. All that I accomplished, in the end, was that. The bond between healer and dying was strong enough to become rooted in the formless instinct of his mind.

"He would not eat. He lived the rest of his very short life in hunger, terror, and fear."

Adam swallowed. "And if you had stayed?"

"I cannot say. I do not know how much of the child's natural development was damaged by his exposure to me. Children are not adults. Infants are not children. It is possible that had I remained in that house, he would have lived. I do not know what his life would have been like. I do not know how *much* of me he retained—but absent any other experience, that might be all he was capable of becoming: a stunted, abandoned version of me.

"I believe a stunted, abandoned version of someone like you would be a far better choice—but—"

"You think the child would not adjust to its own life."

"I do not think the child would survive even you. And I will not expose you to that. I will not expose a completely blameless infant to it, either." Levec shook Adam's arm off. "I am far too old, and far too bitter, Adam. I cannot believe it would work well for either of you. I have seen many deaths. I have met many I would consign quite happily to that state. I have seen men and women I trusted *become* those men and women whose death would fill me with momentary peace.

"I will not say it is impossible that the outcome would be somehow beneficial in the end. But I will say that it is not worth the terrible risk. I could—barely—live with the knowledge of what I had done. I could accept it, learn from it, and move on. I do not believe the same could be said for you, and I am unwilling to hurt or scar you."

"If I chose—"

"If I offered you the choice, it would *be* no choice, Adam. There is only one choice, ever, that you could make. And you can damn well make it when you live in your *own* house."

"Ono Levec—"

"I am *not* your uncle." Levec pushed himself out of his chair. He seemed to understand that the visceral denial of the honorific stung, and took a longer, deeper breath. "You are a child, to me. Not my child, but *a* child."

"I am not considered a child by my people," Adam replied. "I am—"

"You're fourteen years old."

"Yes."

"You must forgive the elderly, boy."

"You are *not* elderly."

"It's all context. Compared to Sigurne Mellifas, I am a spring chicken. But compared to you? I have seen—and done—much, much more living. I want you to *have* a life that is not about regret and fear and isolation. You are," he said again, "a child. And when I look at you, I want to protect you from the things that scarred me. I know what I endured. I was tested by life. I am tested constantly by it now—especially my patience. I know, however, that *I* can endure, because I have.

"I don't want you to have the same scars. I don't want to discover that you're one of the people who can't endure. Before you argue, I've seen it happen. I've seen it happen many times."

Adam shook his head. "I should have called you Oma instead," he replied.

Levec frowned. "That means—"

"Grandmother. We can't be protected from life. We can—while we are very young—be protected from death, and any people that I have ever encountered attempt to protect their children from death. I *have* been given a gift. You've said that you want me—you want all of the healers you train—to believe that that gift is a blessing for as long as they possibly can.

"And Levec, I *do*. If it weren't for you, if it weren't for this smelly, loud, crowded city, I wouldn't. It would be a guilty secret, known only to my kin. But if I can't *use* it to help or save others, why was I given the gift at all?"

Levec glared. "You think there's a *reason* for everything?" he barked. "You think there's a reason that children are born blind or deaf or even dying? You think there's a reason that some are born to squalor and some to wealth? Do you have rocks for brains?"

"But—"

"But *what?*"

"You just said that you believed—"

"Because I was an *idiot*."

". . . And you want us to have the comfort of idiocy?" Adam asked, in honest confusion. "You are so much like a Matriarch in personality; you are nothing like a Matriarch in intent."

"I want you to be *happy*." Levec lifted a large hand and placed it—heavily—on Adam's shoulder.

"That is a sad definition of happiness."

Levec looked surprised.

"You believe that we cannot see the world as it is *and* know happiness. And so we must be raised and coddled in ignorance. Perhaps, if we never learn what a sword is, we will somehow never die at the end of one. Perhaps if we never learn that people do bad things, bad things will never happen to us?" He snorted. He could practically hear his mother's contempt, although she was dead and distant.

"Happiness is not all of one thing, and sorrow doesn't obliterate happiness. It might, if we were trapped forever in the moment of sorrow. If the rest of life couldn't touch us or warm us. But we're not. I have seen my kin die," he continued. "I have held children whom the fevers would not leave; I have held them while they screamed for me, because they couldn't *see* that I was there. And, yes, Levec—it was horrible. She screamed and cried—and me? I cried, too. I think I may have screamed."

"You should not have been the one responsible for—"

"*I* was the one she *wanted*. Should my mother have bade me plug my ears and run miles away so that I couldn't hear her? I would have hated her for it. I would never *ever* have thanked her.

"And maybe if I held that child now, I could *make her* understand that I was there, and that I loved her to the end."

Levec said nothing.

"But that child gave me many memories. All of her life. Some of the memories are good, and some have become better, with time."

The older healer snorted. "Fourteen years, boy, is not a lot of time."

"It is, to me. When I think of her death, it hurts. It's true. And it is true that if I thought *only* of her death, she would be pain and loss. But when I think of *her*, I don't just think of her death. I don't just think of our loss.

"You can't protect me from life. Not even the Matriarch could do that. You can help me to see life clearly. You can help me to see what's in front of my face, because sometimes the sun is in my eyes, and I can't. But you can't decide—for me—what my life has to be about, or what it has to mean, or what it *can't* mean. I am not you. You are not me."

Levec closed his eyes for a long moment. When he opened them, he looked weary. But he no longer looked angry. There was so much anger in Levec, Adam thought. So much anger—and so much love. Levec could never be Matriarch, of course; no more could Adam. But it was of Matriarchs he thought, now.

This man had taken the burden of Matriarchs across his broad shoulders. He had no living kin. Neither did Jewel or many members of her den. But both Levec and Jewel made family, and Adam understood family.

"My Ona Elena once told me something important," Adam said, hesitant now that the force of Levec's anger had deserted him. "Happiness is like a seed." Before Levec could speak, Adam lifted a hand. "She said that anger and hatred and love are like seeds as well. All the things we feel that endure, are."

"And we are?"

"Dirt," Adam replied.

"I might agree with that statement, but I'm certain you intend to go elsewhere with it."

"We are earth. But we are like different types of earth, in different climates. Not all seeds that fall from a tree take root. Not all things that take root survive. We cannot be *given* happiness. Only the seed of it. We might not recognize the seed," he added. "Because we can't see the tree it might become. We are surrounded by trees, and the seed in our hands looks nothing like them.

"For some, the earth is damp and fertile, and all seeds take root. But for others, the earth is hard, and water scarce. Elena believed that no man—or woman—starts life as a desert. But without trees, any man or woman can become one.

"She thought all things could take root in me, but she was my Ona," he added, with a trace of self-consciousness. "She told me it was important to take the seeds, to plant them, and to tend them. To water them, when water was scarce; to protect them from water when it was a deluge. She said that only by growing those trees in ourselves could we then have seeds to give to others.

"Rich or poor, child or man, anyone can plant such a seed."

"And the other seeds? The anger, the bitterness?"

Adam nodded. "Those, too, come from others. They are not gifts in the same way, but they require soil and if we are not careful, it is *those* seedlings we tend and shelter, and if those are the trees we favor, it is their seeds we pass on. And anyone can grow those seeds, just as everyone can grow the others.

"The seeds are all there. We can't choose, for others, which seeds they tend. We can only hope to make good choices for ourselves."

"And what am I giving you now?"

Adam smiled. "You are giving me worry, but it is a worry that comes from a place in which I feel safe."

"And will you heed my worry?"

"Always. But I will not always adopt it as my own. I know that you love me." Levec never liked to hear the word "love." "I know that your fear comes from experience; it is not idle. But I know it comes from your experience. A day will come, perhaps, when I will return to you and tell you that you were right."

Levec nodded, then. "The damnable thing is this. If you were not a person who desperately wanted to help others, I wouldn't care much for you at all. It's always the kind ones that break my heart, in the end. I cannot command you when you leave my home. I can ask. I will ask you, Adam: do not do this. Do not interfere with those who have not lived.

"Now, get out of my office. I have work to do."

Get out of my memories, Adam thought. *I have work to do.*

He was afraid. He had traveled with fear as a companion for so much of the past year. He had lost his mother because his mother could see no path to walk but the one that led to her death. She, like Jewel, was Matriarch; she, like Jewel, was gifted with visions that were woven into the fabric of reality.

He had lost his family in the desert—although they still lived. He had found a second family, hesitantly, within the Terafin manse, with its endless maze of walls, its lack of small, comfortable spaces, its lack of open sky or breeze.

But he had found himself, bitterly and in isolation, in Levec's broad, protective shadow. All of the healing he'd done, he'd done at Levec's command; all but one. Levec had taken credit for most of it, where credit was due, and Adam absolutely understood why.

He had, he knew, been blessed by the Lady; his life had been passed over by the Lord. He survived. He was taller, rounder; he did not face starvation or privation within House Terafin. Nor did he face the endless contempt of the clansmen—for he privately thought of the Terafin Council, and most of the people who bore its name, as clansmen. Jewel had even brought Ariel from the Dominion, a child missing fingers and family. He had, as he could, taken care of her, because feeding the children had been his most important job.

But there were no other children in the Terafin manse. Not children he could claim, in some small way, as his own. Not children whose survival depended, in any way, on Adam of Arkosa.

And this child—unborn, but alive—did.

I will ask you, Adam: do not do this.

He could see the older healer so clearly for a moment; he smiled and shook his head. He was afraid, yes. But he had learned to live with fear, and where he could, to manage it. There were very few decisions in his life that weren't shadowed in one way or the other by fear—and very few in which his fears were not at war.

Levec was the voice of one of his fears. But his own voice, his hands, and the power with which he had been blessed was the other.

They will not die if you leave them here, this shadow of Levec said, brow furrowed, eyes narrowed and darkened.

No, he thought. *But they will never live, either.*

What is life but the absence of death?

He froze for one long moment. The voice that he heard was not his. Nor was it Levec's. Neither man could have ever asked that question.

Chapter Ten

*N*O. *IT IS NOT a question you could ask. I have heard your voice, and the voices of your companions, since you first entered this hall. One of you speaks with the voice of the wild wind, and his voice is beautiful to my ear. And yet, at the same time, it is fragile and delicate.*

One of you speaks as kin speak; I hear the echoes of every syllable beneath my feet. And three of you speak like cats.

"They *are* cats."

And you consent to travel with them? That is not wise if you value either dignity or possession; they are capricious beasts. Ah, but it has been such a long, long silence, even their voices reach my ears.

Tell me what you are.

He blinked. "Pardon?"

What are you? You are not a cat. You are not my kin. You are not firstborn, and you are not the creations of the firstborn. Your voice is almost inaudible. The world does not move to give you room; it barely notices your passage at all. What are you?

"I am Adam," he replied. "Of the Arkosan Voyani."

That will not do.

"It is my name."

She laughed. Her laughter was like water in the desert—but Adam was Voyani; he knew that water in the desert could kill. *It is not a name. It tells me nothing at all about you. If I told you my name, you would understand much of me. But the telling is long and complicated.*

"It is a name. It is how I am known, by my kin. What do people call you?"

Ah, no. If you were not touching me, I do not think I could find you at all. But—
I have found you now. Come. Open your eyes, Adam.

He obeyed. He almost shut them again immediately.

Adam had never suffered a fear of heights, but he found the vestiges of that fear in him now—and it was unwelcome. He had, moments before, been standing—or kneeling—on thin air, high enough above the darkened stone below that he could barely see it.

He was not standing on air now; he stood on the slightly sloped peak of a mountain. He could hear wind howl; could see, hundreds of feet below, the snow-capped heights of lesser peaks. If anything grew here at all, snow buried it—but Adam suspected nothing did. The cold here was staggering; he couldn't be certain he could maintain his footing because he began to shiver. To shudder.

He turned slowly; he almost dropped to his knees just to have more contact with the ground, and less exposure to the open air. And he did fall to his knees, but not, in the end, for that reason.

"Welcome, Adam."

She was the most beautiful woman Adam had ever seen.

Her hair was the color of snow, and it fell down her body like a cloak so fine not even the most moneyed of clansmen could afford to own it. She was, as depicted, otherwise naked; as depicted, nudity did not make her self-conscious.

"Does it make you self-conscious?" she asked. "You are my guest. I do not understand your reaction, but if it will set you at ease, I will change." She did so, instantly, her hair falling into a spread of even, pale white, as if strands of that hair were weaving themselves into cloth.

That cloth covered her shoulders, her arms, the full fall of breasts; it draped over the rounded and prominent smoothness of expectant belly before reaching the ground. Her feet, throat, and hands, remained exposed to the biting cold, but the cold did not seem to affect this woman.

"I have always loved the heights," she said, as she approached the spot on which he stood. "No, do not move. It is, at the moment, impossible for me to fall. And a fall from this height would end my existence just as certainly as it would end yours." She held out a hand, almost in command. Adam came from a long line of autocratic women who were accustomed to unquestioning obedience.

He did not take the hand she offered because he was suddenly aware that his own hand was shorter, stubbier, and infinitely more dirty than hers had ever been.

Her brows rose in surprise; she laughed. The sound was the essence of both amusement and delight. "You are not a cat, then, although you have brought them with you."

"They didn't come with me," he said, almost defensively. "They came with the Matriarch. They are hers."

"We are *not*."

Although Adam never wanted to look away from the woman on whose mountain he found himself shivering, he did. Shadow, wings folded, was standing gingerly on an outcropping of stone that was sheer drop at his back. There was no sign of either Night or Snow, and no sign of the man Shadow had grudgingly agreed to carry.

He closed his mouth and glanced at the woman who made this mountain her home. She had lifted one perfect brow—at Shadow. "Who gave you wings?"

"We have *always* had wings."

"You have always been able to walk in the air, and you have always been able to survive landing when you insulted the winds in your hubris. I do not, however, recall wings before." As she spoke, she walked toward the cat, who sniffed and turned his head away.

Away in this space brought his gaze in contact with Adam's. Shadow growled.

The stranger laughed in response. "You sound like a kitten," she told the great cat as she placed a gentle hand on his head. "But the wings suit you. I would never have guessed."

"And where are *your* wings?" the cat demanded.

Her smile shifted, and what remained of it was both soft and melancholy. "I will never have wings again," she told the great cat, laying a hand, as she spoke, upon her belly.

Shadow hissed. He then leaped toward Adam, who almost jumped out of the way. He remembered where he was—and just how far above the ground— at the last minute; Shadow stopped just short of head-butting the healer's chest. "You can *do something*."

"You don't even like it when I touch you."

"*I* am not *her*."

"Do you know her?"

"Of *course* I do. *I* am not *stupid*."

"What do you think I can do?"

"What do you think you *are* doing?" was Shadow's surly response. It wasn't his only response, although the rest of it involved a lot of the word *stupid*.

"Shadow, I can't just touch her and grow wings for her!"

"*Why* not?"

"That's not the way healing *works*."

"It *is*."

"It's *not*."

"*It is!*"

During this exchange, the lady of the mountain approached. She watched; Adam was aware of her gaze, even when he couldn't immediately turn to meet it. "You call him Shadow?"

"It's what the Matriarch calls him."

"I see. And is your Matriarch as you are?"

Shadow growled. His wings rose, becoming rigid arches. "She is not for you," he told the woman. The almost omnipresent whine was gone from his voice; what was left reminded Adam of dream and nightmare.

"And you will keep me from her? How bold you've become." Her voice now reminded Adam of desert night. "I ask you to leave us. I will only ask once."

Shadow shrugged, the movement so similar to the shrugs of Jewel's den, Adam was surprised. "You can *ask*."

"And you will dare to ignore me?"

"What can *you* do? You are *here*." He turned his face toward Adam and muttered *stupid boy* loudly enough it could probably be heard from the foot of the mountain. "She is worried," he told the boy, when he'd finished.

Adam blinked. "The Lady is not—"

"Why does she *always* like the *stupid* ones?"

"I'm not sure," Adam replied, as he realized the "she" was Jewel. "But she likes the difficult ones as well."

The implication was lost on the cat, probably deliberately. "You will get *lost* here, *stupid* boy. You will starve. She will break, and it is *not time* for that yet." He turned, once again, to the stranger. "You will let him leave."

The woman's face was immobile; it was as frozen as this peak. "What is he, Shadow?"

"A *stupid* boy."

"Yes, I understand that. But not so stupid that he does not have a cat as his guardian. It has been a long, long time since I have had guests; will you deprive me of this one? I cannot reach my sisters, and the White Lady's voice is so distant I am not certain I hear it in truth; it might be a dream.

"But I have never encountered someone like this man before. I ask again: what is he?"

"He is mortal," Shadow replied.

Her eyes widened. "Mortal? He is born to die?"

"Yessss. All mortals *are*."

"All? He is not alone? There are more like him?"

"Yes. They are *everywhere*."

"And what great magics do they possess in return for the fate they have chosen?"

Shadow hissed. It was the laughing hiss. "They did not *choose* mortality; they were born into it. There are many, many of their kind who have been *extremely* stupid in an attempt to avoid their own nature."

"Born?"

"Born, Lady," Adam said. "Just as the child you carry will be born."

She was silent; her eyes traced the line of Adam's face as if she were attempting to read it. The language, however, was not her own; nor was it one she was familiar with. "What magic," she asked him, softly. "What magic compensates you for your fate?"

He started to say "none," because it was true. It was the truth of his kin, of his kind. "The power I have," he said, voice small, "was not granted to me because I am mortal."

Shadow hissed. This one was contemptuous. "It *was*."

"No, it wasn't."

The hiss grew louder. "It *was, stupid* boy. Not *all* mortals have your power. But you have it *because* you are mortal. You do not understand what it *means*."

"But I do," Adam said, irritated. There were very few things he understood, but his gift was one of them.

"Do you understand why I won't let you *touch me?*"

"You're a cat. No one understands how cats think."

Shadow blinked, looking for an insult in Adam's statement of fact. When he failed to find it, he snorted. "You can heal *her*."

"Jewel?"

"Yessss. Do you know why?"

"Because I'm healer-born."

Hiss. "Because *she* is mortal. I will not let you touch *me* because you will *change* what I am."

"But I don't change the healed—"

"You *do*. But mortals cannot be changed easily; even the gods had difficulty."

He thought of Avandar.

"You change them back to what they *were*. You cannot change what they *are*, except in that way. You *could* change her," Shadow added, this time pointedly staring at the Lady. "You could give her *wings*. You could make her *less* ugly."

Adam's jaw was attached to the rest of his face, or he would have lost it when it dropped. "She is *not* ugly!"

"She is not as ugly as *you*." He snorted again.

But Adam shook his head. "She is not what you are," he told the cat. "I have never been given leave to tend Lord Celleriant; I do not know if she is as he is. But, Shadow, if she were injured, I *could* heal her."

"You couldn't."

"I could." There was no doubt in his words.

"How *stupid* are you? She is *not* like you!"

But to Adam, she was. Mountain and ice and deathly cold aside, she was; except in one way. He had touched pregnant women before. He had been allowed to examine Bernice—until the disastrous delivery of the child. What his eyes did not see, his hands did. It had not occurred to him to wonder, until Shadow's arrival, whether his power should have sensed something different, or other.

"Yes," she said, although he had not spoken these thoughts aloud. "Although I did not recognize you—or your kind—you see the truth. I am, now, like you. I was not born a mortal; I did not exist to face death. If you release me from this place, I will die. There will be nothing to prevent it."

Shadow hissed. He stared at her protruding belly with recognizable loathing. Adam wanted to smack him; he almost did. But the exposed fangs were enough of a warning that he managed—barely—to refrain.

The Lady, however, smiled down at his expression of complete disgust. "Yes. You understand."

"*Why* did you do this? *Why?* You will *never* fly. You will *never* speak again with a voice that the wilderness hears."

"I could not bear this child and remain as I was."

"Why did you *need* a child? Why did you not make one the *normal* way?"

Adam said, without thought, "This is the normal way, Shadow."

"For *animals*." The irony of this angry, terse reply appeared to be lost on the cat. "For *mortals*, who are *like* talking animals!"

"But if she doesn't even *know any mortals*, how is this not natural?"

"*Ask* her. Ask her who the father is."

It was not a question the Voyani ever asked, at least not of the expectant mother. Adam was almost offended. "It doesn't matter. We know who the mother is. And we know that she wants this child." He hesitated. He had a hundred questions to ask, and none of them seemed appropriate. Shadow could speak of—and to—her as if she were no different than Adam or Jewel. Adam could not.

Any questions he might have asked—surrounded by empty sky and distant mountain peaks—slipped away the moment he met her eyes. They were silver in color, framed by white lashes that suggested a dusting of snow.

Only one question remained, and it slid out of his shivering mouth before it had fully formed. "What will this child become?"

Shadow hissed. There was no amusement in the sound, but no obvious anger.

"What he needs to be," was her serene reply, "in order to free our people." To Shadow she said, "If the child dies before he is born, it will make no difference to my fate. There is no way to change it, except this: I am trapped here, beyond Time's reach. Beyond the reach of any save the White Lady." She lifted an arm, and drew Adam into a loose embrace. "And a . . . mortal boy. You are cold." An edge of question adorned the observation.

"Y-yes, Lady."

"You are like plants, then. Like those with the smallest of voices; you perish so quickly, and at the slightest of provocation. You do not create your own warmth. Come, Adam. Here, at least, I can."

She spoke the truth; her arm, and the length of her sleeve, enfolded him. The wind's howl could still be heard; it could no longer be felt.

"Shadow says you are not for me."

The cat's hiss was louder, and it contained threat. The threat did not trouble her.

"I accept this, although I regret it. Tell me, Adam, how did you come to be here?"

"You brought me here."

She laughed. The sound was soft and gentle; it was as warm as he now felt. "You were already here. I could hear you, and when you touched me—and you are still touching me—I could sense enough of you that we could converse. But I did not call you to my side; none of us now have that power. We can hear the voices of the wind and the dreams of the sleeping earth, although even that, we do not touch; they cannot hear us."

"Can you hear each other?"

Silence. After a long pause, she said, "No. We are aware of each other, of course. Until recently, we could hear the White Lady. She sings," she added gently. Adam looked up; her eyes were soft, her lashes half-closed upon their silver. "She sings songs we knew and sang in our youth. But of late, she does not sing; we cannot hear her.

"We are truly imprisoned."

"Can she hear you?"

"I do not know. What had we to say, when we were by her side? We listened, Adam. You cannot know the miracle of her voice or her words; you have not heard them. When she sings, I forget, for a moment, all fear, all anger; I hear her voice alone. There is no song that can contain the whole of her, but when she sings, there are no other voices. Not the voices of gods, nor the wilderness that spawned them; not the voices of the firstborn, nor their many creations.

"We could listen to her song for eternity. We would sing for her—we sometimes did—but she was whole, without us; we were not whole without her. And we are without her now. Is that how you come to be here?"

He shook his head; Shadow growled. "She is not here," he said. "And he is *not* yours."

"I will not keep him."

"You *have*. She is *worried*."

"She is not my concern."

Shadow's growl deepened.

"Shadow," Adam said, afraid that the great gray cat—whose fur had risen an inch—would attack the woman in whose arms he was now standing. "How long have I been . . . gone?"

"*Too* long. Come *back*."

Adam swallowed. Nodded. To the Lady's shoulder, he said, "Did you choose to become . . . as you now are?"

"Yes. If you mean the child."

He shook his head. "You are—not here, but where I first touched you—made of stone."

"Is that how you see me?"

"Yes. It's how we all saw you, even—even Lord Celleriant."

She frowned. Even her frown was compelling; he wanted to reach up and smooth it away.

"You didn't feel like stone to the touch—not to me. But to the others . . . you did. You do. Your White Lady made statues of you. You don't even stand on the ground."

She glanced at Shadow. "Is this true?"

Not even Shadow could call this woman *stupid*. "Yesssss."

"Can you move?" Adam asked her.

"As you can see, yes."

"I mean—can you—" the words drifted away before he could harness them and drive them out of his mouth. There was nothing about this woman that was stone; nothing about her that was fixed and motionless. She was warm, she spoke; he could feel—and see—her breath. "You can't hear your sisters."

She shook her head.

"Would you speak with them, if you could?"

"It is not what the White Lady desired for us," she said. But the answer was long in coming, and thoughtful. She placed her free hand, once again, upon the curve of her belly. "I did not tell her what I intended. This life that I bear—you have seen others like it?"

Adam nodded. It was not entirely true.

"And could you care for him, Adam of Arkosa? Could you protect him and see him, in safety, to the White Lady's court?"

He froze. He did not want to deny this woman anything. "I do not think anyone can reach that court."

Something in his tone made her tighten her arm. "What do you mean?"

He said, "This is the business of Matriarchs, Lady. I do not understand it myself; I am not considered wise by my kin. I am considered too young."

She turned, then, to Shadow. The great gray cat's low growl was accompaniment to the howl of icy wind. "Of what does he speak? If he could find *us*, why would the Court of the Queen be impassible? Has he offended her? Has she reason to forbid his presence?"

The gray cat flicked his wings before folding them and muttering imprecations against the criminally stupid.

"Eldest, *please.*"

The single second syllable struck Adam as a blow. There was nothing— literally nothing—he would not have done to ease the fear and pain in her voice. But he could not answer her question. He understood it only superficially. He turned to look at Shadow, not to glare, but to join his wordless plea to her voiced one.

Shadow understood; a volley of opinion about Adam's usefulness and intelligence were the whole of his reply for what felt like minutes. His paws were, apparently, far more interesting than either the Lady or Adam for the next five. His subsequent sigh was almost thunderous.

"You have been *sleeping* for *too long.*" He flexed his claws as he spoke, apparently to them.

The Lady nodded. Her arm rested around Adam's shoulders as if it were made of stone.

"While you *slept*, she *changed* the *world*."

The arm tightened.

"While you *slept*," he continued, finally lifting his head to meet her gaze, "*She* met *Allasakar*."

"Shadow!" Adam didn't even try to contain his shock.

"What? He won't *hear* us."

"She met him long before we slept," the Lady said.

"Not in *battle*. She was *angry*. She meant to *destroy* him."

"What—what happened? What had he done?"

Shadow sniffed. "He called them. They *followed* him."

It was Adam who asked who.

"Her people. *Her* people."

"Eldest, you must be mistaken." Her voice had fallen to a whisper. Cold once again stung Adam's exposed face.

"I am *never* wrong," Shadow replied. "They called themselves *Allasiani*. They fought for *him*."

Silence.

"She couldn't *kill* him. Not *then*." He glanced at Adam. "She spoke to the wilderness. She was *loud*. And *boring*. She was *so* boring that the earth answered just to make her *stop*. The earth is even *more* boring," he added, with disgust.

"Shadow," Adam began.

"Yesssss?"

"If the Matriarch is waiting—"

"Yes, yes, yes." He flexed his claws again. "She *made* the *seasons*. She *bound* the world."

"I do not understand what you mean. The seasons—"

"Becoming mortal has made you *stupid*."

"No, Eldest. It has merely made me weaker. Weakness makes me more . . . tolerant."

"You *chose* weakness."

"I chose the White Lady."

"Because she *wants* weaklings?"

"Shadow," Adam said. "Please."

"She made the seasons *hers*. *She* is Winter. *She* is Summer." His gaze slid off the Lady's. "Winter was *long*. But Summer has not come. If there is no Summer, the White Lady will *never* leave her court—and you will never *find* it."

* * *

She closed her eyes. "Is this why you've come?" Her voice was a whisper.

Shadow did not reply.

"We have come," Adam replied, "seeking the Oracle. We did not know you were here at all." He swallowed and added, "We do not know *where* we are."

She opened her eyes, then, but they were narrowed, glinting slivers that reminded Adam of blade's edge. "The Oracle." Although she did not raise her voice, the two words resonated with bitter anger. "You do not wish to travel the Oracle's path." It was almost a command.

Adam said, "Not I, but the Matriarch. Her world depends upon it."

"Then I pity her world." The Lady frowned. "My pardon, Adam of Arkosa." Warmth once again seeped into him, especially his shoulders, where her arm still rested. "It has been long since I have had guests, and I forget my hospitality." Her fingers brushed through his hair, and he winced. His hair was not clean enough for her hand. It would never be clean enough.

The woman closed her eyes and stood a moment in the howl of wind that seemed to speak for her in the silence. "I spoke in anger. The Oracle did not mislead me."

Shadow growled. He did not speak.

"You have never cared for the firstborn," the woman said quietly. "And they have never cared for you." She turned, loosening her hold on Adam's shoulders. He wanted to cling. "I saw Winter," she whispered. Lifting a hand, she gestured, and the mountains began to sink. If Adam had witnessed it at a proper distance, he would have been awed. He was standing on them. Were he not standing in the Lady's shadow, he would have been terrified. As it was, he was merely apprehensive.

"I saw the Winter. I heard the silence of the forest. I saw the beauty of the ice. I heard the calling of the horns." As she spoke, Winter passed. Winter, and the mountain upon which Adam had first seen her. "It was beautiful and terrifying. I saw the hunters. I saw her people. I saw the Winter Queen.

"The Oracle did not show me the . . . *Allasiani*. Perhaps I judge the firstborn too harshly. I think knowledge of it would have broken me, then." She whispered a word. A name. "Winter passed. Summer arrived." She gestured again, and on the flats of stone that had once been mountainous peaks, grass grew. Grass, wildflowers, and trees. The trees were like—very like—the trees that graced the Terafin manse.

"I saw the Summer." For the first time, she smiled. But there was pain in the smile. Loss. Adam held breath until she spoke again. "I saw it pass. I saw Winter and Summer. You like the Summer, Adam?"

He was silent.

"Each time, I saw the Queen of the Hidden Court, it hurt me. You have seen her?"

Adam shook his head.

"Then you will not understand why. Eldest?"

Shadow hissed. "She was *always* ugly."

"You have grown bold indeed." Her voice cooled. Adam thought—for just a moment—that had Shadow spoken like this to her at the height of her power, the great winged cat would be dead. "Not dead," the Lady said. "But it would prove costly for him. He is bold; he is not foolish." At Adam's silent disagreement, she smiled again.

"I saw the last Winter. And I understood why the Oracle had approached me. She offered me truth—as the Oracle does. She offered me a choice. A chance to save what the White Lady had become. And even lessened as she was by the choices she had made, she was my world."

"But she imprisoned you here!"

"Imprisoned?"

Adam was confused. But the Lady's voice was warm now. "Did you—did you choose to become a—as you are now?"

"No," she told Adam. "This is not what we chose. We would never have chosen to be separated from the White Lady. We could hear her voice—but we could not see her, could not touch her, could not comfort her or defend her." She bowed her head; platinum fell across her shoulders like a liquid. "It is because of my choice that we are here."

"The child."

"Yes. She understood what my fate would be. My sisters . . . did not. Not immediately."

"Your sisters did not make the choice you did."

"No. It was not required."

"And your choice was necessary?"

"Yes."

"Then why did she imprison all of you?"

"Because she did not agree," was the quiet reply. "But we knew she would not. We chose among ourselves; it was not a decision made lightly."

"She imprisoned you—"

"It was not imprisonment."

"You can't tell me this wasn't meant to be a punishment!"

"No, and I will not try. But had she been willing to sacrifice us completely to her rage, we could not be here, you and I. Her anger, when it takes root, is vast and almost endless—but it is not, it is *never,* all that she is." She turned to Shadow. "Could you carry me from this place if you were willing?"

He sniffed.

Adam understood that this meant no; none of the cats were good at owning any form of incompetence. The Lady apparently understood this as well; she did not press him. His fur, however, remained ruffled.

She turned to Adam. "Can you, Adam?"

He could have pretended to misunderstand her; for the few seconds after she asked, he did. The shade of vast branches darkened his vision as he looked up to the skies. If he did not meet her eyes, it was easier to speak. "What will happen if I do?"

"Nothing will happen to you," she said. She might have said more, but he shook his head forcefully.

"Not to me, Lady. What will happen to *you?*"

"Nothing that does not also threaten you. I will die. I will die; time will kill me, if something else does not do so first. My sisters did not understand this, not immediately."

"You didn't tell them."

Her brows rose. "You are not as ignorant as you first appear. No. I told them only of the necessity. I did not tell them of the price.

"But I perceive that Shadow is correct; you cannot remain here. I do not understand how so slight a life, so slight a force, could be here at all, but I am grateful. I ask you again, Adam, could you carry me from this place if I asked it?"

Help us.

He looked at the Lady's face. Her lips had not moved; she was not speaking. He closed his eyes as an unexpected dizziness, a shortness of breath, robbed him of useful vision.

Help us.

Eyes closed, the growling of angry, fussy cat drew closer.

His hands felt warm. His hands, palms against flesh, fingers spread wide. Standing on air that was somehow solid beneath his feet, he had touched the statue that was not, to his horror, a statue—and he had come to the mountain. Shadow had followed him.

Adam knew he had never left Jewel's side. He knew that his hands had never left the curve of pregnant belly, the skin pulled taut by the demands of the growing life held within it. He knew that were it not for the contact between them—initiated by Adam—he would not now be here.

But he knew that, on the night Shadow had almost killed them both, he had never physically left Jewel's chambers.

Shadow growled.

Adam growled back. Surprise seemed to silence the cat, and Adam was certain he would pay for it later—but he needed to think.

Help us.

He needed to remember, as he had done when he had first approached a statue that he knew was alive, Levec's voice. Levec's words. All of Levec's *many* words. He was healer-born. He was, according to Levec, a healer with unparalleled power. It was not within this Lady's power to bring him to the cold, high peaks of a mountain; it was within Adam's. Adam's power had taken him to the dreaming in which Jewel had been trapped. Not hers.

It was the touch of the healer-born that had reached this stranger's thoughts. It touched what lay within living flesh. A corpse did not have thoughts, desires, or fears.

And a corpse did not carry—or nourish—a living child.

It was the child who spoke, now. And that, Adam knew, was impossible. Yet he understood the simple plea. He understood the words. He could repeat them.

The Lady, seen only with the power of the healer-born, felt like a young, expectant woman. He had no experience at all with the immortal; he had tried, only once, to touch one of the cats—and Shadow still hated and feared him because of it. Even when he had walked in the dreaming, he had touched nothing but mortals, or the essence of the mortals trapped there.

And she felt both unique and *of* them. Had he not seen her, had he come blindfolded into her presence, he would never have known otherwise. Her body had shifted and changed to accommodate new life, just as Bernice's had; he was certain that she could feed the child, when the child was born, because of those changes. If it was born, and if it lived.

Help us.

It.

No. He. If *he* was born. If *he* lived.

"If you can save this child," the Lady said, her voice distant but distinct, "and only this child, save him."

How could the child speak? How could he know words? He had not been born. He had not lived. He had not learned—as children do—the language of his parents.

I have learned the language of mine, the child replied. His voice was not a child's voice; nor was it adult; Adam could find nothing in it that was either male or female. It was both disembodied and wed to its physicality. Yet for all that, the child was a boy.

"How?" he asked, lips trembling with the effort to say even this much.

He sensed confusion. He could not see the child; the child made no attempt to look at him. And why would he? The child had not yet opened his eyes for the first time. He had not yet drawn his first breath, or uttered his first cry.

But he had listened to his mother's voice. He had heard her speak. Perhaps he had heard more.

I listen, the child replied, *to the White Lady. My mother listens. She cries. I will take my mother to the White Lady.*

And this, too, was wrong—but it was *less* wrong. Four-year-old children could speak with this guileless determination, this single-minded devotion.

Help us, the child said again. *My mother will never see the White Lady again, and she is sad.*

"I do not know if I can," Adam confessed. His voice was gentle, now. There was no hesitation in it. If it was wrong that this unborn child had voice, if it was wrong that he *could* speak, he was nonetheless a child. "I can try. How long have you listened to your mother?"

Again, he felt confusion. Time was not a concept the child understood. And perhaps, he thought, that made sense. The Lady had not been born mortal. If it was true that she had become mortal, her knowledge of that condition was not yet intimate; it was entirely theoretical.

"Did you speak to your son?" he asked her, without opening his eyes.

"Always."

"Did he always understand you?"

She was silent. To his surprise, he recognized the texture of the silence; it reminded him of Shadow's. He looked up, then, opening the eyes he had struggled to keep shut.

He said, in the softest of voices, as if she were mortal and frightened, "He understands you. He hears your voice; I think he has always heard it. How long have you been imprisoned here?"

"I do not know how you measure time," she replied—after far too long a pause. To his great surprise, she then said, "My child does not speak to me. I speak to him. I have told him, over and over, of all my hopes and fears and desires. I have told him what he must become, when he is finally born into this world. I have told him why he exists at all—and I have told him of the cost, to me." She hesitated, and then caught his hand; hers were now cold. "Is he mortal?"

Adam blinked. "Yes."

"You are *certain?*"

"Yes."

Her eyelashes formed a perfect fan of white; they were the color of Snow's fur. Her skin was almost as pale, now. "If it is true that you cannot touch the Immortal without changing some part of their essential nature, I ask that you do not disturb my sisters' rest.

"But as you have discerned, I am mortal. Free me, so that I may—at last—give birth to this child."

The child who could hear her voice. The child who had, in utero, come to understand enough of what he had heard over the long, endless period of his incubation. Centuries, Adam thought. Millennia.

Shadow hissed. "Do not do it," he told the boy. "The Winter Queen will *know.*"

"I don't care if the Winter Queen knows."

"You will not speak of the White Lady in that tone."

"My actions," he replied, "will speak more loudly than simple words. If this is what she wanted for you—" he stopped. He looked toward a bristling, great gray cat. "She will never die, if she remains here."

"No."

"And she will, if she is released."

"*Yessss.* She will die like *you* die. She will be *like you.*"

Adam said, softly, "She will be nothing like me."

The cat hissed. "She will be *almost* like you. She will walk in *time.* She will *age.* She will *die.* The White Lady will lose her—forever. If you leave her *here,* she will continue to *be* eternal."

"But this is *not life,* Shadow!"

"It *is.*"

Adam did not want the discussion to devolve into one better suited for squabbling children. Again. "And the child?"

"He will *never* be born." Shadow hesitated. "I do not *know* why she did not *kill it.*"

Adam uttered a brief Torran curse at the cat's contemptuous face.

"Destroying the child," the Lady said gravely, "would not save me. And perhaps she understood, in the end. I cannot say. I understand that my loss will cause the White Lady grief. It is an echo of the grief we ourselves might face should we lose her forever."

"*She* will not die."

"If she died," the Lady replied, "we would all die with her."

*   *   *

Adam did not understand the love that existed in these imprisoned women for the being who had imprisoned them. But he did not always understand the love—and the hate—that existed between any man and woman of his acquaintance, be they close family, close friends, or distant strangers. Love of a particular type was, and had always been, a mystery.

But life was not, now. Not to Adam.

Help us.

Yes, Adam said.

Something moved beneath his hands. He felt . . . surprise. Attention. Excitement. It was a child's excitement, not an infant's, and unlike the plea itself, it was not contained in, or by, words.

Adam moved away from the Lady. He held out one hand—his right—palm up. He was aware, as he made this gesture, that it was not his hand that moved; beneath his palm, if he concentrated, he could feel flesh. It was like dream or nightmare, he thought. During those, he lay abed, sleeping while at the same time running in terror, eating, hiding.

Yet, as in dream or nightmare, what *felt* true was the outstretched hand.

She regarded him as if from a great remove. No matter how close he stood, there would always be distance between them.

"If you will leave this place, if you will risk the heartbreak and sorrow of the White Lady who is your life, take my hand."

"It is to preserve what we have loved, it is to preserve the source of all that we are, and all that we might ever become, that I made my choice. I knew it would be irrevocable." She placed her hand in his; hers did not shake at all. "I was wrong, of course. You think of my current state as punishment, and in some fashion it was—but it was more, Adam. The White Lady loves as she loves, and she does not willingly surrender that which is hers. Not to time. Not to death. Trapped upon this mountain, I would remain hers for as long as she exists."

"But she does not visit." He offered her a second hand, and she took that as well. "If you are not what you were—if you are as I now am—the world itself will be strange and deadly; there is every chance that if you follow me you will meet death far sooner—"

"You mean, at all?" She laughed. Her laughter was warm and deep. "We know death," she told him; he heard her amusement but did not open his eyes to catch her expression—which was hard. "Our kin have always known death. But death is not an inevitability. We do not walk toward it. If we are powerful enough, skilled enough, fast enough, wise enough, we step out of its path; it might sweep the lands of all life but ours.

"It is of that death that you now speak, is it not? And not the one that awaits you regardless."

He nodded. He trusted himself to nod. He understood, listening to her while gripping her hands so tightly, what the distant White Lady desired: to preserve. To keep this woman safe. To hold her above death and time and the decay that came inevitably with either. Even childbirth risked that death.

Especially childbirth.

But Adam was a healer.

And if you can only save one? Levec asked, from a painful distance.

He did not answer.

Jewel did not lift her hand from the woman's belly; for her, the feel of it, the texture of perfect, taut skin, did not change. But she opened her eyes the moment she heard the sudden absence of all breathing, looking in panic to Adam. To Adam's hands, and to the flesh that lay beneath them.

He no longer touched a pillar, carved in the shape of an Arianni woman. He touched skin. He touched visible flesh. She understood, then, why the silence had grown so sharp and so thick.

She heard the sound of drawn blade: one. She knew who had drawn it; she almost told him to put the weapon away, but did not. She had seen the White Lady of Celleriant's life only once, but no part of her assumed that haunting beauty was without peril. It was, it had been, death.

And she had no doubt at all that he would attack this woman if she proved to be as deadly; the only person upon whom he would not—would never—turn that sword was Ariane herself.

You are wrong, Jewel. He would not raise sword against you except at your explicit command.

The stone did not give way to flesh instantly. The ivory-pink cast of skin traveled out from Adam's splayed hands, as if the stone were a curtain he was slowly and deliberately pushing to the side. It was not simple work; his brow was furrowed with concentration, his skin, in the cool air, beaded with sweat. Jewel's free hand held his shoulder, bracing him.

Shadow *roared.*

She startled, looking up; she could see the great cat, wings spread as he circled above these arches. Snow, riderless, replied in kind, and Night joined them. She could not tell what angered the cats—or if the cats were angered at all; they had never been shy about putting their feelings into actual words. There were no words now.

But she thought this might be the cat form of horns, of a type of complicated, sub-verbal heraldry or greeting.

Color spread up the woman's torso, down her arms, and down her legs; it turned marble hair platinum and lent it a weight and a sheen that Jewel's hair had never, and would never, have. She would have pushed her own straggly hair out of her eyes, but to do so she would have had to surrender her grip on Adam.

She surrendered her grip on the Arianni woman instead. Lids that had once been stone opened; lashes that had once been stone framed a very familiar silver gray. The first thing those eyes saw was Jewel Markess. They widened. Jewel placed a second hand on Adam, her palms shaking.

Adam, however, did not open his eyes; nor did he release the woman. The Arianni woman glanced down at his bowed head, and to Jewel's surprise, she smiled. The hand that had been raised to support an arch now fell, gently and slowly, to touch his hair.

"Adam," she said, and her voice was a shock of sound, it was almost a sensation. "Adam of Arkosa."

He did not reply. Her eyes narrowed. This was not a woman who was accustomed to being ignored. The cats above her head continued their three-part roar; the air shook with the force of their voices.

Silver eyes narrowed as the woman lifted her chin, turned her gaze upward, to the source of the noise.

"You are the Matriarch?" she asked Jewel, without looking down.

"It is what Adam calls me," was Jewel's evasive and unintentionally hushed reply.

"And these cats are yours?"

She coughed, which did attract the woman's attention. "They're cats. I'm not sure they can belong to anyone but themselves. But—yes, they're traveling with me."

"Do they obey you?"

"They're *cats*," she repeated.

"They obey her," Avandar said. He offered the lady—the naked lady—a perfect bow. In style it was Southern.

She frowned. Jewel half-expected her to call him by name, and was surprised when she did not. The lady glanced at Kallandras, who also bowed; if she could see Angel and Terrick, she made no sign; her eyes came to rest, at last, upon Lord Celleriant, armed—as Jewel knew he must be—with the sword and the shield of his people.

Her smile was brighter, sharper. It was not predatory, but it was not entirely welcoming. "Brother," she said.

He failed to bow. He failed to speak. He watched her for a long, long moment, his lips a thin line, his eyes likewise narrow.

Jewel exhaled. She started to speak, but Adam lifted his head; the lady's hand gently brushed his forehead. "I am in your debt," she told the kneeling boy. She lowered the other arm, and by some miracle of magic the arch above her did not come crashing down; it did not even teeter.

She then offered those perfect hands to Adam; he took them with obvious hesitation and she lifted him, with ease, to his feet. He was pale; dark semicircles sat beneath his eyes, and his lips were cracked. "The child?" she asked, in an imperious voice.

"He is well," Adam replied.

"Snow," Jewel shouted. The white cat's roar banked; she could hear sibilance take its place as he meandered his way toward her.

"*Yesssss?*"

"Adam is exhausted. I do not want him to fall here."

"Where *can* he fall?" the cat asked, with great interest.

Jewel placed a hand between his ears; the cat muttered. He glanced at the pregnant woman, huffed, and muttered some more. Most of it had to do with *stupid*, which meant, of course, Jewel. "You are never allowed to drop him," she said, "unless he specifically requests it."

Snow sidled up to Adam without quite meeting his gaze. This was made simpler by the fact that Adam had difficulty taking his eyes off the woman. The air carried her; Jewel wasn't certain whether she spoke to it herself, or Kallandras did.

She was almost the same height as Celleriant; her skin, her hair, and her eyes suggested immediate kinship. But she did not look particularly pleased by his presence. Since her look mirrored his almost exactly—absent armor and weapons—Jewel supposed this made sense. She didn't understand the Arianni. The lack of understanding made her feel human.

"I am Jewel," she told the stranger. "This is Snow; his brothers noisemaking above us are Night and Shadow, respectively. They carry two men, Angel and Terrick. You've obviously met Adam; the man who addressed you is Avandar, my domicis." The woman frowned. "My oathguard." The frown on her face cleared. The frown on Avandar's deepened. Jewel ignored both. "The man with the golden curls is Kallandras; he is a bard. Music is his strength and his gift.

"And behind me, you see Lord Celleriant. He is my liege; I am his lord."

She spoke to Celleriant in a language that Jewel did not understand. As she struggled to retain some of the syllables, she frowned. She had understood every word the stranger had spoken so far, and the stranger had clearly understood her.

Celleriant replied in kind. He did not set aside either his sword or his shield; this did not seem to give offense. As the woman spoke, she lifted Adam with ease and deposited him both firmly and gently on the white cat's back. She did so without apparently looking at him; her gaze was fixed upon Celleriant. Adam listed.

"What do you intend for the others?" Avandar asked the healer.

Adam shook his head. "They are not to be touched. The Lady feels that were I to somehow free them, I would pay with my life. She does not feel that my touch will mean to them what it meant to her; they will be as adamant— and as dangerous in their rage should I try—as Shadow.

"And the Matriarch does not command that I heal the sisters of the White Lady."

Celleriant's voice rose in outrage or horror; Jewel turned from Adam for just a moment to see the Arianni lord's expression. His skin was the color of his hair; his arm had fallen, and with it, the sword. He turned to Jewel as his shield and sword guttered and vanished.

"Do you know what you have *done?*" he demanded.

The practical truth was that she had done very little. She said, instead, "I have allowed a healer the use of the talent to which he was born."

"Do you understand who she is?"

"No. But you understand it and perhaps you will share."

Be wary, Jewel, the Winter King said. He had come out of thin air, as he so often did, to stand by her side, his tines raised. This woman was not the Winter Queen, but clearly, kin to her; he was drawn to her—just as Jewel was drawn.

"You are to travel," the woman said softly, "to the White Lady's court. If it pleases you, I will travel with you."

"And if it does not?"

"I will travel, regardless. I will not travel quickly, and perhaps not well; I am told I have a handful of decades in which to arrive, and speed is therefore of the essence."

She looked to Celleriant; he was rigid.

"I do not intend to travel to the—to the White Lady's court directly. I have come to find the Oracle's domain—and I don't have any clear idea of where it is."

"No, you would not. No one does, who has never walked the path to reach her. It is not simple to find; it is not simple to walk. Should she choose to remain hidden, she will never be found at all."

Jewel said nothing.

"But, Matriarch," she continued, frowning slightly as Jewel flinched, "I *have* traveled that path. Let us then come to an agreement. I will lead you to the Oracle if you agree, in turn, to allow me to travel with you to the White Lady's court."

"There is some chance," Jewel said, her voice too thin and too dry, "that I will not survive the Oracle's test."

The woman frowned. "You think she means to kill you?"

Shadow snorted; the woman ignored him.

"Not directly, no. I am not the first woman to walk the Oracle's path. But many who did so did not survive it."

"They died?"

"No."

Silence. Shadow hissed. The woman, again, ignored him. The great gray cat flexed his claws, and Jewel fixed him with a glare. It was wordless, but not even Shadow could pretend to misunderstand her meaning.

"Many have walked the Oracle's path," the Lady said quietly. "I have not yet heard that the Oracle destroyed those she chose, in the end, to grant audience. I am told the world has changed—has it changed so much?"

Celleriant's laugh was bright and hard. "If you are as you claim, it has changed almost beyond your reckoning." After a harsh pause, he spoke again in a language that was opaque to Jewel. There was less shock, less outrage, in his tone, and he did not draw sword.

Jewel thought the danger—whatever that danger might be—had passed, for now. *Do you understand her words?* she asked the Winter King.

His silence was almost reverent, which was answer enough. The wind tugged Jewel's hair, and she pushed it out of her eyes, even though those eyes remained closed for another long beat.

When she opened them, she lowered her hands—to her hips. Her pursed lips would have been a signal to her den—but only Angel was here, and Shadow had never come close enough that he could see them clearly.

It was time to leave. It was probably, she thought, past time.

And where exactly will you go?

Clearing her throat, she said, "I don't intend to die. Everything I care about depends on my survival and my sanity. If you will lead us to the Oracle's domain, we will escort you to the Queen's court." Although the two Arianni voices had not fallen silent, the Lady turned. "I do not think I can even find the court until I have undertaken—and passed—the Oracle's test."

Silver eyes rounded; platinum hair flew in the swirls of agitated wind. She turned to Celleriant, her voice raised.

He replied in Weston. "None can return to the court if they but leave it; the ways are closed; they are hidden to all." He then turned to Jewel. "On occasion, my lord sees things that are hidden. If she is to see what is hidden, she must subject herself to the judgment of the Oracle. It is for that reason that we have come. Whether you accept my lord's offer or not, it is to the Oracle that we must first travel."

"I do not have the time," she said, and for the first time there was an edge of fear or anxiety in that perfect, clear voice. "Did you not understand the truth of which I spoke? I will age and die. Your Adam has explained what mortality means, and I am mortal, now. I do not have the decades to undergo the Oracle's many tests—not again."

Jewel shook her head. "You don't have decades. *I* don't have *months*. Did Adam explain the difference between the two?"

She nodded. Adam, on Snow's back, looked foggy and confused. "I didn't—"

"The communication, Adam of Arkosa, is a bridge. You traveled to me, at my request; I, too, could reach across what you built. I understand your language—your two languages. I understand how you mark . . . time." She spoke the word as if testing it. "I understand what a healer is, and what you believe your Matriarchs capable of." She turned to Celleriant, who was now utterly silent. "I understand the gray simplicity of their tiny, brief lives—and the lack of beauty, the lack of wonder, that informs them."

"You are mortal?"

"Yes."

"You *cannot* be! Do you understand what you have done to yourself? You will be little better than—"

"*Thank you*, Celleriant," Jewel cut in. "You may, if it pleases you, discuss the taint and inferiority of mortality on your own time."

Chapter Eleven

NOW, JEWEL THOUGHT, standing in midair, the ground so distant beneath her feet it made her dizzy just to look, all that was left was logistics. She knew how much food they had; adding another person cut the number of days they could travel in safety without resorting to foraging. Given the wilderness, she had anticipated the end of safe food with dread.

But if it was true that this stranger knew the way to the Oracle, it might cut the travel time significantly—and regardless, Jewel knew she could not leave her here.

It might be wisest, Avandar said, but without much hope.

Yes. But wisdom didn't bring us here. Hope did. And fear. She failed to mention the fear. She did not understand what had happened; she would ask Adam in detail later.

"Snow, she's naked."

The cat hissed. "So *what?* We are *all* naked."

"I'm not."

"*Us.* The *important* people."

"Fine. Naked cat is far more attractive than naked woman."

"And water is *wet,*" the cat growled. "Fine. *Fine.* Carry Adam. Don't let him *fall.* Don't *make noise.* Don't *sharpen claws.* Don't *have any fun.* And now, *make dresses?*" His love of extended sibilants made the sentence much longer than it would have been had anyone else spoken it.

She sighed. "If you feel you're incapable of making a dress in these difficult circumstances, I understand." She turned to Avandar. "I think we can come up with something that might at least keep her warm."

Snow hissed. High above their heads, Night hissed as well, which didn't improve the white cat's mood.

The woman, however, stopped, arrested; her eyes opened—in wonder, not fear. Even Snow could not be immune to the shift in her expression—or the fact he had caused it. He preened. Jewel didn't even begrudge it; in his position, she would have done the same. No one had ever looked at her the way the woman now looked at Snow.

Snow sniffed and stuck his nose in the air, exposing the underside of his chin—something he very seldom did if his brothers were within swatting range. "What will *you* make?" he demanded of Jewel.

"Make? Nothing. We all brought clothing; she can wear some of ours."

The cat sputtered with his usual exaggerated outrage. Jewel was, in his opinion, the *stupidest* person it had been his misfortune to meet. Ever. *Stupid, stupid, stupid.*

White brows rose as Snow continued his rant. "You allow this?" The Lady asked Jewel.

Jewel shrugged. "They're cats. I've been called worse. Even by myself. You were aware that he makes dresses?"

"I was aware that, should the mood strike him, he *creates*, yes. I have seen only one or two of his creations, and one, sadly, was destroyed. Had any but the cat himself destroyed it, they would have perished for the crime. What price do you pay?"

"Pardon?"

"You have asked him to create; he has not yet agreed. What price will he demand in return for his gift?"

Jewel blinked. Snow sidled up to her, butting her hand with his head until she began to scratch behind his ears. "What will *you* give *me?*"

She looked at him, forehead bunching in lines as her brows rose. "Me? Nothing. I'm willing to find her something else to wear."

"Then why did you *ask?*"

"Because she's the only person I've ever met who I think would be worthy of what you can create."

Snow hissed.

"Not worthy of *you*," Jewel added; she privately thought no one deserved to be saddled with these cats on a continual basis. "Worthy of the *dress*. I would give her the one you made for me—"

Hiss.

"—But I treasure it. I value it. I would not be parted from it." This was mostly untrue. On the other hand, Snow was not generally suspicious of flattery; he expected all flattery was simple fact, where it involved him. "But I think most people would agree that it would suit her far more than it suits me. Perhaps she doesn't deserve it. But then again, neither did I."

"You are *Sen. She* is *hers.*"

"I will not command it."

"You *can't!*" Snow replied, in obvious outrage. Night hissed laughter; he had circled low enough he could stand on the height of the precariously supported pillar. The white cat glared at the black one.

Jewel kept her hand on Snow's head because he was warm, and when she touched him, she felt some of that warmth. The Lady didn't seem to note the chill in the air, given how poorly she was dressed for it.

She had told Celleriant she was mortal. Jewel couldn't quite force herself to believe it, although she was certain the woman spoke the truth as she understood it. The wind seemed at play in her hair; it was not a gale. She looked very like Meralonne before he joined battle: wild, pure, and inhuman.

"*You* just want to see *her.*"

Jewel reddened. "Yes," she said quietly, "I do. I want to see her in a dress of your making."

Snow hissed and muttered. Jewel simply waited.

The woman watched the cat; her brows took the shape of a frown, but on her, it was an elevated expression.

Snow pushed himself off the ground, shaking off Jewel's hand as he rose. His wings were spread, but he didn't flap them; they seemed to be caught instantly in winds that touched nothing else.

If he had complained about lack of material or tools, Jewel would have let it go; she had always suspected that Snow required neither to do his work. Haval had implied as much, and Haval noted everything. But she hadn't watched Snow work—and he had chosen to do the work now.

The Lady's expression changed as she watched him. He might have been the only other living thing in the area; even Celleriant was forgotten. From out of the folds of the air that carried them all so far above the ground, threads emerged. They were—or looked—white; white and gold. But as they continued to coalesce, they were joined by strands of black, of gray, of something the color of ash; of red, and the purple that red could become.

For a moment it seemed like a chaotic storm of colorful tendrils; it looked deadly, dangerous, wild. But the cat circled it, muttering—the word *stupid* had prominent position in every otherwise inaudible sentence—his movement somehow containing it.

She could almost understand why Haval treated Snow with so much respect. Gray threads and black, red threads and white, began to merge; the individual strands seemed to struggle to break free of the growing, whole cloth—but with little success. It awed Jewel. At the same time, it made her vaguely queasy.

As if in response to that, Shadow finally condescended to land. He almost knocked Jewel off her feet—and would have, if her left foot hadn't been part of what he was landing *on*. Angel took his life in his hands; he smacked the gray cat on the head.

Shadow hissed and said, "I will *drop* you."

Night hissed laughter. Night was doing a lot of laughing; Jewel was fairly certain he'd pay for it later. And it had better, her glare at the gray cat implied, be *much* later. She wasn't worried for Angel's safety. When the cats were whining and uttering dire verbal threats, they were harmless—unless you were furniture.

She did, on the other hand, place a hand on Shadow's head. "Who is she, Shadow?" she asked softly. The woman was so absorbed by Snow at work she didn't seem to hear. "Is she Ariane's sister?"

Shadow hissed softly. "You should not have come *here*," he told her. "She will be angry. *Everyone* will be angry."

"She seems to know you."

He nodded. "She went away," was his soft reply. "We didn't know where she went; the wind wouldn't *tell us*." He swiped, claws extended, at the air as he spoke. "*No one* would tell us. We tried to make *her* tell us."

"Her? You mean the *Winter Queen?*"

Shadow rolled his eyes. "She will be *angry.*"

"Yes, you've already said that. What should I have done instead?"

"She was *safe* here. The Winter Queen protects what is *hers*."

"The child," Jewel replied, "isn't hers."

"*Exactly*. I told you not to *trust* the Oracle."

Jewel nodded. "I'll remember that none of this is your fault." She fell silent as the threads at last became whole cloth; the cloth caught the gray, ambient light, and returned it, shifting as she watched. It folded in on itself, moving at wind that touched nothing; Snow's claws caught its lower edge and held it in place. Red seeped from his claws to the fabric; it was the red that she had seen as moving threads.

The white cat had fallen silent. He exposed his fangs as his ears rose to points; his body gained inches as his fur rose as well. He looked very much as if he were engaged in battle—until Shadow reached out and stepped on his tail.

"Shadow."

Shadow hissed. "We want a *dress*," he told his brother, ignoring Jewel entirely. "*Not* armor. Make armor for the *other ones*."

"This is *better* than armor!"

"It is *ugly*," Night said, descending as well.

"Ugly? *Ugly? You* are *ugly!*"

Jewel exhaled and glared at the three cats. If they'd been in the great room—or any of the guest rooms, including the one that was technically theirs—she'd be looking at furniture replacement and possible bloodstains.

She looked up at the woman and saw, to her surprise, that she was smiling. Before she could look away, the woman lowered her face, and met Jewel's gaze. "They have not changed, have they?" she asked, with genuine fondness. "I was not certain what to make of you; they have wings, now, and they did not require them before. And they seem smaller of stature."

"You should have seen them a month ago," Jewel replied. "They were two thirds the size they are now. Still trouble, though."

"You do not seek to confine them, then? But no, I can see you do not."

"They're cats. They more or less do what they want; they *mostly* avoid doing what I *don't* want." As she said this, she glared at Night, who hissed.

"But it *is* ugly."

"So?" Snow snarled. "*She* is *ugly*. It is not *as* ugly!"

Since the stunningly beautiful stranger seemed to find this amusing, Jewel didn't rush to her defense; it would have been embarrassing. She did clamp down more firmly on Shadow's head; Night was smart enough to remain out of reach.

"Kallandras?"

"Terafin."

"Is it safe to stand on the ground?"

"I believe that would be wise at this point. Your cats appear to be restless, bored, or both, and I am not certain the wind will not take offense soon."

By the time they made their descent, the dress was firmly between Snow's jaws. Jewel cringed, imagining cat saliva all over the folds of cloth. She didn't, however, say anything; cat saliva was probably better than no clothing at all, and in truth, Jewel thought any of her clothing that might fit the much taller, much more statuesque woman would only be an embarrassment—to Jewel.

Embarrassment didn't seem to be a concept that the stranger understood. Her nudity didn't bother her; nor did the cold. She seemed to regret the absence of the wind; Jewel mostly appreciated it, although she did offer thanks to it before it stilled. Terrick was embarrassed for her, and kept his gaze fixed on the ground, on the cats, on Angel—on anything, in short, that wasn't her. His cheeks were flushed, and Jewel kindly decided it was due to the chill.

Avandar was amused. *You are staring*, he told her.

Jewel reddened, because she was. But it was the stare she might have given a grand and distant mountain: like those mountains, this woman was a thing beyond desire. She invoked an awe that desire couldn't touch. Jewel had no words to describe her; even beautiful seemed too common, too inadequate.

Don't you see it? she all but demanded.

Yes, Terafin, I do. But it is merely beauty. If you cannot gather your thoughts and the tatters of your dignity when faced with this stranger, how do you intend to speak with Ariane herself?

Jewel shied away from even the thought; she occupied her hands by removing the dress from Snow's jaws and offering it to the stranger. "I'm not called Matriarch," she said, eyes drawn to skin that seemed warm and luminous.

"You are not?" She glanced at Adam, who was now asleep; Angel supported the bulk of his weight.

"Adam calls me that, yes."

"It is a title that conveys respect."

"For Adam, yes. It is not a title we use among my people."

"And what title do you prefer, seeker of the Oracle?"

"Jewel."

The woman frowned; even her frown could stop breath. "It is a . . . stone?"

"Yes, of a type. It's a name. It's the name I was given by my parents."

"It is not a name; it is a word."

"Yes. But if you shout it where I can hear it, I'll know you want my attention, as opposed to anyone else's."

"Jewel." She spoke the word as if testing it. She spoke it as if it were a song.

"Yes." Jewel inhaled, exhaled, and turned to the practical, as she so often did. "Lord Celleriant is called Lord Celleriant. If that isn't his name, it's used that way among my kin. What might we call you?"

Her frown shifted. "If the name signifies nothing," she finally replied, "You might choose a word. You have come to me, where none but the White Lady have ventured; I will therefore take no offense at whatever word you choose."

Jewel froze. She wanted, for one absurd moment, to shake Adam awake and make him choose. The Lady didn't seem to sense her discomfort—either that, or she didn't care. She donned the clothing Snow had made, and the rough collection of syllables that comprised a name fled before Jewel could grasp one.

The dress was almost white at the shoulders; as it fell to the ground, it gained color—but the color was stone or ash, darkening in the last yard to something that was almost black. The hem of sleeves and skirt were adorned with red embroidery, and delicate red swirls rested just beneath the line of her breasts; across the very obvious swell of belly, the cloth was a delicate gray. It was, in all ways, unlike the dress Snow had made for her.

What, she thought, should she call this woman? Lady, perhaps, but it seemed too prim a word. Jewel was certain that the hands that now ran along the folds of sleeves had carried swords before—and had used them. There was a harshness about her beauty, a distance, that offered wonder but no comfort and no safety. It made a mockery of the desire for comfort and safety.

She shook her head to clear it. "I understand that you are not as we are." She indicated the obvious mortals in their midst. "But every single Immortal I have ever met has a name by which they are known, or will be known, by us.

"I didn't name Lord Celleriant. I call him Celleriant because it is what his brother called him, and what the White Lady herself called him. Even the Winter Queen has a name by which she is known to mortals—Ariane. I wouldn't have the courage to call her anything else."

"You have met many?"

"No. I've met very few. Celleriant, his brother Mordanant, their lord." She did not repeat the Winter Queen's name. "Meralonne," she continued, after a pause. "Which is what he calls himself when he speaks to us. But the gods and the rest of the immortals call him Illaraphaniel."

Her eyes widened. "You have met Illaraphaniel?"

"Yes." She hesitated, and then added, "he lives in our city."

"And you yet live."

It was Jewel's turn to frown. The nameless woman turned instantly to Celleriant, as if for confirmation. At his slow, grave nod she said, "There is a story in this, and I would hear it. But perhaps it is best that we leave."

Jewel nodded. "We can't go back the way we came."

"No," the woman replied, as if the possibility had not occurred to her. She bowed her head for a long moment; her hair framed her face, lending it light, but no color. "Illaraphaniel.

"When we were young, he called me Shianne. It was a new name, a small name." She looked up, then, tilting her head, exposing her throat. "He was not Illaraphaniel, not then. And I have not been Shianne for so long the name is the barest echo in memory, even mine. I grew beyond it. I grew beyond it and I will never return; it is part of who I was—but it is not who I am. I . . . am no longer certain who I am." She did not look down; her eyes continued to seek the heights.

And then she lowered her clothed arms; silk fell like liquid to all but cover her hands.

She began to sing.

They froze at the sound of her voice; the first note, the fullness of it, almost deprived them of breath. She sang storm; she sang sunrise; she sang open skies and freedom; her voice rose and fell, hardening or gentling. Even the cats were almost still, although their tails or ears twitched.

It wasn't that it was impossible to move, but rather that if one looked away, if one allowed any form of distraction, some essential part of the song might be missed—and it would never be heard again.

And perhaps, just perhaps, that might be for the best. She did not sing in Weston; nor did she sing in Torra. Jewel couldn't understand the words themselves—if there were words at all. It didn't matter. She didn't need the language to underpin meaning; the meaning was plain.

Jewel wept. The tears were silent; they trailed down her cheeks. She couldn't stop them and didn't try, although she had long ago learned to hide the weakness of pain and emotion. This song was every farewell she had ever said, but more, every farewell circumstance had denied her: It spoke of love— not storybook love, but messy, complicated, conflicted emotion. She closed her eyes; she could see Duster front and center. Of course.

Behind her, Lefty, as he was the last day she'd seem him in the dim glow of magelight, far beneath the open skies. Fisher. Lander. She'd made a home with them, and their deaths had destroyed it, hollowing it out from the inside until it collapsed.

Duster, so difficult, had preserved what remained. But the act of preservation had destroyed her.

Just as it would destroy Shianne.

Jewel opened her eyes. Shianne was not Duster. There was no anger in her, no rage, no desire to destroy. For Duster, destruction had been the truest test of power; she'd spent too much of her life feeling powerless.

And this woman? Had not. She had none of Duster's doubt, none of her fear. She had all of her intensity, but it was turned, in this moment, with this song, to sorrow; sorrow and yearning. There was beauty in sorrow; beauty in resignation. And pride in both.

But surrounding them, elevating them, engraving them in some sense into a memory that was far too thin to fully hold them, her song.

Jewel was almost shocked when a voice joined hers, it felt so *wrong*. The voice was rougher, lower, less consistent in its strength and urgency; it should have clashed horribly with the eerie, almost overwhelming beauty of hers—but it didn't.

Of course not. There was only one man present who might have dared to draw breath and use it to reach out, to touch, to entwine himself inextricably with her song.

Kallandras was the youngest Master Bard Senniel had ever produced. What he sang now, he had not learned in Senniel College. He hadn't learned it in the streets of the hundred holdings, facing starvation and isolation; he hadn't learned it in the rooms of a brothel. Jewel knew because she had been in those places, and the loss he sang of now was Shianne's loss—but it was also his own.

It wasn't hers. She had felt a hint of it in the days when Lefty disappeared; she was shadowed by an echo of it whenever she thought of Duster's death. But the certainty of loss and separation—no. She was here to *find* Carver. She was here to do everything in her power to save him.

No part of that salvation meant walking away.

And yet, she heard in his voice—and in Shianne's—the certainty that only by walking away could lives—and love—be preserved, even if neither the bard nor the woman would ever be part of it again. Other lives. Other loves.

It wasn't a gift she could give. Surrendering the family she built for its own sake was surrendering the very thing that made her what she was. She accepted this as her own truth, and accepted, as well, that it was not a truth that defined either Kallandras or Shianne. They were, for a moment, beautiful in exactly the same way: the mortal man and the woman who had chosen to become mortal although she was, in all ways, of Ariane.

So she stood, listening, as each note shifted and changed, moving into the next note, the next lift of voice, the next breathless silence; she tried to gather the song into memory, to hold it for as long as it could be held, because she knew she would never hear it again; not this way.

The long hall spread out before them as far as the eye could see—or as far as Jewel's could. A ceiling that existed in shadow, if it existed at all, was supported by pillars whose heights likewise disappeared from view. The air was chill; breath rose in small clouds. Shianne had taken the lead, although she was sandwiched between Night and Snow; the two cats, for once, did not fight over the same position. They did complain, and as they were the only voices raised, the procession sounded as if it were composed of growling four year olds.

Adam woke twice while they walked, startling as if from nightmare; he subsided the moment Jewel spoke into his ear, her voice far softer in the echoing hall than it would otherwise be. She was worried, but worry was a constant companion. She knew the cost of overusing one's talent-born power.

"He is not suffering from mage fevers," Kallandras told her. She heard his voice, although his words were softly spoken and he was not beside her. Her own voice, to reach his ears, would have to carry, and she was hesitant to shout here. She didn't question the hesitance; she was seer-born.

You fear danger, here.

She almost laughed. *Yes*, she told the Winter King. *How could I do otherwise?*

We will not be attacked in these halls. He spoke with certainty.

You didn't even recognize the halls when we first arrived.

No. But if you listen, you will hear the Winter Queen's name; it is spoken in the silence. None but the desperate or the very, very foolish will seek a battle here. If I did not know better, Jewel, I would swear that we walked at the very center of the Hidden Court. The Winter Queen has not dwelled here for a long, long time—but she is everywhere within it.

"How long are these halls?" she asked.

Shianne paused and turned back to look over her shoulder. "I no longer have an answer for you, Jewel."

Jewel briefly regretted denying the use of the title Matriarch. There was something almost intimate in Shianne's use of her given name; the title—Matriarch—was far more distant. "Have they changed greatly?"

"Yes, as you must suspect. They are silent, now; the echoes speak of abandonment." She paused and added, "If you fear that we will find new residents, be comforted. Nothing that passes through these halls without the White Lady's permission would survive the night. No one dwells here save my sisters and I."

Angel cleared his throat. Shianne frowned. "I'm all for comfort, Lady. But—*we* don't have her permission."

"Without her permission, you would never have arrived at all."

Angel glanced at Jewel. Jewel glanced at her wrist. She did not lift her arm. "We did not travel here as others must have, in the past."

"No."

"We arrived because the Oracle sent us."

But Shianne shook her head; her hair moved like liquid lit from within. "You do not understand. The Oracle might open a door to this place; she is first of the firstborn, and there is no place, no matter how dire or distant, that she has not seen in her many, many visions. But such a door is not permission. Nor could she herself beg entry.

"If she chose to send you here as part of your quest, Jewel, she did so because she was certain you would be granted entry. Nor was she wrong."

"Is she ever?"

"Wrong?"

Jewel nodded.

"The meanings of the visions she grants are difficult to grasp, even by those who fully understand their context. She is not easily moved to rage or fear; nor has she ever been considered a creature of great pride. She has no *need* to be right."

Jewel noted that Shianne had not answered the question, and she almost let it go. But she had too much invested in this quest to do so with any ease. "I understand she has no need to be seen to be right. What I want—what I need—to know is whether or not she's ever mistaken."

"No."

Jewel fell silent.

Shianne laughed. The laughter was not kind, but it was not sharp or edged. "How can the Oracle ever be wrong? It has been said that she can see every possibility the future holds. Only one of those possibilities will become reality; only one will become the present, and from there, the past. Many, many are the gods and the immortals who have attempted, time and again, to use the Oracle to influence that reality in their own favor. Most failed. The Oracle could not be moved to choose one path or another; nor could she be moved to allow those who sought her aid in their endeavors to glimpse a present they could not otherwise easily see.

"She was considered a weapon."

"Most weapons aren't sentient."

Shianne's brows rose.

Jewel drew dagger, not as threat, but as demonstration.

The woman's eyes narrowed. "You cannot possibly think that is an example of a weapon." There was no question in the words; they were flat and dismissive.

The Winter King was highly amused. *In my time, Terafin, your knife would not have been considered a weapon; it might have been considered a tool of middling quality—if that.*

"The Oracle would indeed have been a potent weapon in the hands of the gods—or their offspring. Those who understood her gift, those who better understood the context of her visions, could have used her to sculpt, from the multitude of possibilities, the outcomes they most desired. We were," she added, "oft at war.

"But of course she knew—how could she not, who could see all things if she but bent her will toward them? But she was not neutral—and if you believe that someone who sees every possibility is neutral, you do not understand the Oracle." The words were bitter and softly spoken. "Like any of the firstborn, she forgets nothing, and her grudges can be long and harsh—but they are miracles in the making when she at last chooses to act—for when she does, she makes no mistakes. There are no last-minute reprieves for her enemies. She is thorough, Jewel—and perhaps she is because she is the only one who can see the entire game."

"Does every vision she shows serve her purpose?"

"I do not know. We ask, and if she chooses, she replies. She does not ask for our approval or our gratitude."

Gratitude was not what Jewel was feeling at the moment. Gratitude she thought, uneasily, was not what Evayne felt at the peak of her power. "It wasn't just the gods," she said. "Or even the immortals. I think, near the end, before the gods chose to leave, she saw mostly mortals. Mortals," she added, "like me."

"The gods chose to leave." She glanced at Celleriant. "We will have many a day upon the path you have chosen to walk. Tell me, then, about the gods and their absence. Tell me about their wars, and their victories; tell me about their defeats."

He was not comfortable in her presence. He was not as obviously awkward as Terrick, but that was impossible. He glanced at Jewel; she was surprised.

"I see no reason not to do so. Your knowledge—and Avandar's—far surpasses any of ours. Tell her what you know, if you choose." Jewel had often been curious, but she had never asked. His past was his past—just as Duster's had been her own. She had always believed that the past was irrelevant; it was the present and the future you looked toward that counted.

But she understood, as her arms tightened around Adam, that the roots of the present, and the roots of the future they would soon face, were planted in all ways in that dim and unknown past—the two could not be separated.

"Do not *trust* her," Shadow said, loudly enough that his words probably carried to the unseen ceiling.

Shianne glanced at the great, gray cat. "Trust," she told him, "is only an issue where there is an absence of power."

Jewel laughed, which caused platinum brows to lift. "It's always an issue, for me."

"Truly?"

Shadow was muttering to himself. There were a lot of sibilants.

"Yes, truly. If Celleriant chose to strike me down here, I would die."

"You would *not*," Shadow said.

"Absent all other interference, I would."

"Would *not*."

Jewel exhaled. "Fine. If I were alone with Celleriant and he chose to kill me, I would die."

Celleriant was not Shadow; he did not disagree.

"But he serves you?"

Jewel nodded.

"May I ask why?"

"Yes—but you'll have to ask him."

Shianne frowned. "Too much has changed," she said—to Celleriant. "Too much is strange. The halls seem empty of life and light; there is no sound, no song. Not even the wind plays here. What will we find beyond them?"

Celleriant said, "I do not know. I have not walked these halls. If they were ever spoken of at all, it was in ways so subtle I do not recall their mention. The wilderness was once a vast and endless space—but it was oft treacherous and unpredictable." He smiled; breeze moved his hair. It did not, however, touch hers. "And I have not wandered in halls of this size and grandeur since my youth."

"And how distant is your youth, Lord Celleriant?"

"Not as distant as yours." There was no insult—at all—in the words; indeed, there was almost the hush of reverence. "I was born in the Summer; I came of age in the Winter. When the Winter Queen called me, I joined her host. I rode in the Wild Hunt, over the endless winter landscape. If you do not know winter, you do not understand the beauty of the ice and snow and the cold, clear face of the watching moon; you have not heard the song of the horns."

She was silent and watchful, but her expression had softened. "And she rides at the head of the Wild Hunt?"

"Always," he whispered. "If you but close your eyes, you can see her astride her mount; she wears raiment of white and silver over armor of almost the same color; the horn is in her hand or at her lips and her eyes shame moon's light. Nothing escapes her; there is no place that her quarry might flee that she cannot pursue."

This was not entirely true, but Jewel did not interrupt. He seemed young and almost defenseless as he spoke. This was not the boy—if boy was the word—who had once sat beneath the boughs of ancient, Summer trees. And yet, she thought, he had loved those voices, too.

"Almost, I can see her," Shianne whispered. "Almost, you make me yearn for this Winter that I have never known. But you did not see her as she was before she was Winter and Summer Queen. She rode to war—"

"She rode to war when the gods walked," Celleriant replied, "Even in my time. The Winter and Summer roads were her power; not even the gods could move the lands against her when she stood upon them."

This, too, surprised Shianne. "She could hold those roads against the will of the gods?"

"Yes. She could not be moved from them, and they could not be altered or changed while she stood upon them. It was tried," he added, "but she spoke with greater authority to the ancient earth than even the gods themselves could."

Silver eyes softened; Jewel thought, for a moment, there would be tears. And there were. She had to look away—and then, to look back. If tears were a sign of weakness, Shianne truly felt no fear exposing it. Jewel wondered what it would be like to be Shianne.

You could not, the Winter King said.

I know that.

He was amused. *It is not that she is beautiful and you are not, although that is true.* He spoke without rancor or malice. *She is steel. She is edge. She is of the Winter Queen. On the most grim of your days, Terafin, you could not become as she is; on the best of your days, you would despise it utterly.*

You don't.

No—but that has long been a source of conflict between us. What I see as strength, you do not. You cannot. But I have come to understand, leader of your den, that what you see as strength is, in a fashion, strong. I could not take the risks you have taken. I would not have survived. But you have. Survival is the ultimate test. I had no desire to take the risks you take, when I ruled.

I know.

Yes. But when I was a youth, Terafin—no, even before that, as a child, I did. I had that desire; I took that risk. I was not wise; I lacked experience and the under-

standing that follows. I survived it. I only barely survived. I was mortal, as you are. But I did not come early into my power, as you did. You have seen me, in the dreaming, as I existed when I ruled the Tor Amanion.

Had I chosen the life you chose, I would not have been there. I think of you as weak, yes. But very few others see—or hear—the constant stream of fear and doubt that comprises so much of your thought. Do not attempt to change; Shianne is not an attainable goal for you.

Adam groaned; Jewel shifted her hold and whispered into his sleep. She wasn't certain what he heard; he murmured the word "Matriarch" before he once again fell silent.

"I do not know what your life was like," Celleriant told Shianne. "Nor, it appears, do you understand ours. She is the heart of Winter and Summer; she is not merely the detritus of the turn of the seasons. You knew Winter and Summer in your time."

". . . Yes. But not as you know them. They were deep things, the shift and change of a world that did not *break* the world itself. They marked the passage of time for those who must live, always, beyond its reach. Do you feel the passage of time?"

"Yes, Lady. And no."

"No more do I. I do not feel changed. I do not feel irrevocably wed to the march of both time and death." Her hand fell to the rounded curve that spoke of new life. "Will I, Jewel?"

Jewel wanted to say no. The desire was visceral. But she could not lie to this woman; she said nothing.

Shianne turned. As she turned, the cats who bracketed her swiveled as well. Jewel exhaled. Age was a fact of life, as was death. "Adam," she said, "is young. He is not yet adult, by our reckoning; he is a youth, not a man.

"And you?"

"I would be considered full-grown among my kin."

Shianne crossed the distance between them; the Winter King had halted. He allowed her to approach, lifting his head, raising the tines of his antlers higher so that they might be farther from her face.

Shianne's left hand remained upon the child she carried within; she lifted her right, offering it to Jewel. Jewel thought she meant to mount.

No, the Winter King said.

She's pregnant, Jewel replied, irritated.

Yes. But, Jewel—I will not carry her.

You're carrying Adam!

Yes. And I have carried old men and young before, at your behest. Had I found— had I located your Ellerson or your Carver, I would have borne them to you. But I will not carry this woman.

Why?

I would carry Lord Celleriant first, if you commanded it.

And if I commanded that you carry a pregnant woman?

A woman, yes. But that is not what she is. I will not—I cannot—bear Shianne. Do not ask it.

Something about his tone spoke not of distaste or fear or—as it would have in Jewel's case—embarrassment. He spoke with a certainty she heard only in herself, and only rarely. She swallowed. *Will you bear Adam if I am not—*

Yes. He will not fall.

She climbed down. It was awkward; she almost dragged poor Adam with her. Angel righted the healer, but did not join Jewel.

Shianne touched her face with the tips of cool fingers, as if reading it. She searched her eyes, and the shape of those eyes; she touched her lips at either corner, the line of her chin, her cheekbones. Jewel held her breath without conscious thought.

"You are older."

"Yes."

"And stronger."

"Yes. But in my kind, beyond a certain point, age is not strength."

"And in me, if I am truly mortal as you are mortal, it will likewise be a weakness."

Jewel couldn't imagine it. But then again, she didn't want to. Mortals were greedy, she thought, lifting a shaking hand to place it over Shianne's. There were so few perfect moments, they wanted to capture and hold them; to fix them in place; to force them to remain, forever, as they were.

"Yes," Celleriant said. He had not moved. Shadow had, muttering as his pads dropped far more heavily than they should have against the cold stone. He seemed both drawn to Shianne and afraid of her.

"Tell me about Winter," Shianne said—to Jewel. She allowed Jewel's hand to draw hers away from her face, but shifted her position so that their fingers twined. Celleriant's eyes narrowed.

"I mean her no harm," Shianne said, although she had never once ceased her scrutiny of Jewel's face. "If I understand what has happened—and I do not, not completely—I will not reach the White Lady unless I am by your lord's side." She might have said more, but her grip suddenly tightened; Jewel's hand went almost instantly numb. Before she could attempt to retrieve her hand, Shianne reached for her sleeve; she shoved it up Jewel's arm, quickly enough that the cuffs abraded skin.

Celleriant was between them in an instant. He caught Shianne's wrist in his left hand. She didn't appear to notice.

"Where—how—" she had, until this moment, spoken so smoothly and so perfectly it was hard to see her at such a loss for words. Even breath seemed to have deserted her. "Where did you come by this?" She attempted to lift Jewel's hand, to expose to closer inspection the slender strands of hair that were braided into a bracelet around her wrist. In this light, they were almost invisible—or they should have been.

"It is not for you," Celleriant whispered. "Nor for me. They were gifted my lord, and they will remain in her keeping." This time, he called his sword.

Jewel cried out, wordless; she yanked her wrist free. And then, before she could think or plan, she threw both of her arms around Shianne, exposing her back to Celleriant's edged blade. Blue light was reflected in specks of stone; nothing about it was warm.

Shianne was Winter, in Jewel's arms.

Her only answer to Celleriant was the sword she now drew; its light was not blue, but gold. The blue light guttered. The gold did not. Jewel tightened her grip, her arms; she could see platinum strands moving against her wrist, as if they contained wind, but only barely.

Kallandras began to sing.

His song was wordless; without words to channel its strength it felt strangely unbound, unconfined. Jewel's hair blew into—and out of—her eyes as the wind traveled toward the bard in response.

It was Angel who approached the armed Shianne and her mortal shield; Angel who gently pulled Jewel away. She did not resist him; nor did Shianne attempt to cling to her; she raised sword once, in Angel's direction. Angel could see Shianne's expression; Jewel couldn't. Whatever it was Angel saw, he hesitated only briefly before he drew Jewel away.

"Angel—"

Not now, he signed.

She fell silent. He drew her into the orbit of the Winter King who, unlike Celleriant, had not chosen to interfere. She looked back to see Shianne, sword in hand; she carried no shield, but the blade itself seemed to hold her attention; she was staring at it as if she had never seen sword before in her life.

Jewel had seen a sword almost identical only a handful of times. Avandar's sword.

Yes, Avandar replied. *And so, it is true. She is no longer as she once was.*

The sword's light dimmed as the sword faded from view. Shianne, how-ever, turned to Jewel. Angel stood between them, but not as Celleriant had done. "It has been so long," she whispered—although her voice carried. "So long. Jewel. Matriarch. What you bear, now—how did it come to be in your hands? I accuse you of no theft; such a theft would be impossible—even for gods—while the White Lady lived.

"But you do not understand what it is that you bear."

"And you do."

"Yes. I understand what it presages. I understand why—even if the White Lady is entrapped—you will be able to reach her. I do not know if any others will—the gift was given to you, and not to your companions."

"What does it signify?" Jewel asked.

But Shianne did not reply. Instead, she said, "Lord Celleriant, I do not know your Winter Queen; you do not know my White Lady. No one of us—not even my sisters—saw her in exactly the same light; she had subtle and different meanings for each of us. I assume that has not changed and I will not ask what she means to you; it is clear to me now that we are kindred spirits.

"Let me ask instead, one question, and only one. You have ridden with her host for almost all of your existence. You have seen her stand against gods. Tell me, in your existence at her side, how much did your numbers increase?"

He frowned.

"How many, Lord Celleriant, were born after you?"

Silence. The silence had layers that Jewel couldn't penetrate.

"None?" Shianne continued, her voice soft. "None in all of the long years you have served her?"

"I am the last Prince of her Court."

Shianne bowed her head for one long moment. "And what happened, be-tween then and now? Why did she choose as she has chosen?"

Celleriant's silence was rigid. It was shorn of dignity, shorn of defiance. Jewel had seen him like this only once. Without thought she moved to stand between the two members of the White Lady's court. She turned to face Shi-anne, whose gaze was anchored inches above the top of Jewel's messy hair. She shoved that hair out of her eyes.

"Why are you asking if you already know the answer?"

Shianne's gaze shifted; her silver eyes narrowed. "This has nothing to do with you."

"But it does. Because Celleriant serves *me*."

Adam stirred at the edge in Jewel's voice; the edge and the heat. He blinked, wobbled, and reached out to grab antlers. "Matriarch."

Jewel exhaled at the word. "Yes, Adam?" She kept her gaze upon Shianne as if it were a leveled weapon.

You will only humiliate Lord Celleriant, the Winter King observed. *He will not use a mere mortal as a shield.*

Jewel ignored this as well.

Adam leaned down. To Jewel, he said, "The White Lady does not bear children the way we do."

Jewel looked at the very ordinary swell of flesh that implied Adam was wrong. The Voyani youth slid off the Winter King's back, and the Winter King allowed this, although the boy's gait was wobbly and likely to end in a fall. He came to stand by Jewel's side.

"Is this true?" Jewel asked—of Shianne.

"Of course."

"How—how does Ariane bear children?"

"She does not *bear* children. We are hers; we are her offspring. We are the firstborn of the firstborn. But we did not begin our lives encased in her distended flesh." She spoke, now, with distaste.

Jewel, Avandar said quietly. *Have a care. There are some things you are not meant to know.*

Jewel also ignored Avandar. This was slightly easier; she'd had a decade and a half of practice.

"But we are not the White Lady; we are simply *of* her. What she creates, by will and desire alone, we cannot."

"What do you mean, can't? You're pregnant."

"Yes, Terafin," a new voice said. Shianne stiffened. So did Jewel. Maybe for the same reasons. Blue sword and shield came to Celleriant's arms almost too quickly as Jewel turned in the direction of the new voice.

Orange shields, visible to Jewel's eye as the artifacts of magic, surrounded her and Adam; she reached out and placed an arm around the healer's shoulder. She recognized the woman whose dusky voice now filled the hall with the wonder of its echoes.

Calliastra.

Calliastra, the daughter of the Lord of the Hells and the goddess of Love.

Chapter Twelve

8th of Morel, 428 A.A.
Terafin Manse, Averalaan Aramarelas

"JESTER?"

Jester was sitting in the arboretum that had been Alowan's quiet pride. Clearly Daine had continued the old man's regimen of care, although Jester noted no new plants. He was waiting with an easy patience, slouched across a bench, his back to the stone edge of fountain.

He'd been waiting for over an hour, figuratively cooling his heels. He did not trust himself enough to simply enter the healerie, but he needed to speak with the healer, and in this case, that meant Daine.

Daine was patrician, by look. Perhaps, in his youth, Alowan had been the same; by the time Alowan had met the den, it was impossible to discern the old man's roots. He had been nothing at all like Levec, the only other healer outside of Adam and Daine with whom Jester had more than a passing acquaintance.

Daine did not, at the moment, look happy. Nor did he look as if he'd slept much in the last few days. Jester knew better than to ask; Daine was at that age. At twenty, he was not a child—and the boundaries he set to define himself as adult were prickly.

Jester rose as Daine approached.

"You heard."

"In the right-kin's office. The Master of the Household Staff was the appointment before mine—and let me tell you she was *not* happy."

The sharp intake of breath told Jester more than he wanted to know, and he lowered his voice instantly, wincing. "Please tell me she's not in the healerie." When Daine failed to do so, he added, "No wonder you look a fright. How long has she been here?"

"Less than an hour."

Jester whistled. "How much less?"

"Not nearly enough."

"She's with—"

"Vareena, yes. Who is currently mostly sleeping. One or two of the more senior servants have dropped by as well."

"I'm surprised they dared."

"They didn't stay." Daine paused; he ran his hands through his hair, pushing it out of his eyes. Jester recognized the gesture; it was pure Jay. "That's not entirely accurate. Berald just left."

"Can you tell me what happened?"

"She was found in time and is likely to recover."

Jester froze for one long minute. He now understood why Daine looked so very haggard, and the ice became fire.

Daine caught Jester's arm; Jester startled. He had not intended to move. He had not been aware that he had. "Let it go."

Jester opened his mouth.

"Don't lecture me. Don't even think it. I *know* what Terafin men of power are capable of. That is not all of what's happened here."

"I want to know who was responsible for this. She's twelve—she's a junior servant!" Jester kept his voice level and quiet—but it took effort. He wanted to scream in fury.

It had been so long. So long. Jester exhaled.

"I know. But, Jester—it's political."

"It's—" Jester bit back the words.

"Jay was twelve when she started to gather her den. You have never thought of Jay as a child. Don't—don't make the same mistake now. What was done—was horrific. I believe it was meant as a warning or a message; I don't believe they expected Vareena to survive."

"Would she have, without your intervention?"

". . . No." Daine looked away. "In normal circumstances, the decision to expend the effort to heal would be made by The Terafin—"

"Who's not here."

Daine nodded. "It doesn't matter. These are not normal circumstances. I am—like Alowan—the master of the healerie, and the decision and its consequences are *mine*. I am not ATerafin." He tightened his grip.

"And you are not, in theory, *capable* of saving her life. You have just revealed—to men or women who are capable of sending *this* message—that the Terafin healerie is capable of—"

A sharp, loud, clearing of throat filled the arboretum.

Two adult men froze, and both turned, almost in unison. The arch now contained the most terrifying member of House Terafin, bar none.

"Vareena is waking," the Master of the Household Staff told the healer. "I believe she wishes to speak with you."

Daine swallowed. "I—"

"Now."

Jester was no longer twelve. But even at twelve he would have known better than to cling to the idea that there was strength in numbers. The Master of the Household Staff clearly didn't understand the difficulties healers faced when forced to call the dying back to their pain-racked, ruined bodies. Daine obeyed what was, in its entirety, a command; he walked through the arch of the healerie, leaving Jester to face the dragon on his own.

She folded her arms. He stepped out of her way—although he wasn't, strictly speaking, standing in it—to allow her to pass; it was a hopeful gesture. *Kalliaris* frowned.

The Master of the Household Staff did not make small talk. She did not chat. She barely had to open her severe, narrow mouth to send scads of servants fleeing in terror; talk was not therefore necessary.

Jester was, in comparison, the master of idle chatter—but attempting to generate successful idle conversation with this woman would be harder than trying to get the side of a cliff to chuckle. And he was too angry, by half, to humiliate himself by making the attempt.

"You don't want me to speak with her."

She evinced no surprise. He was wearing his House Council ring; she did not have one. She had the House ring, of course—but for a woman of her stature in the House, it wasn't required. Stature, however, implied hierarchy; hierarchy implied rules. Rules forbid the servants from speaking with people like Jester, and if those rules were stretched, they were stretched by men and women who knew how to be flexible.

"She is a member of the Household Staff. She is not your concern."

"Is she a permanent member of the staff?"

"I repeat, she is not your concern. The Household Staff is not your concern."

"And I will repent of all thought of interference if you tell me that the men—or women—responsible for her injuries are *also* members of the Household Staff."

She said nothing.

Jester, watching her, felt suddenly uneasy in an entirely different way.

"You are correct," the Master of the Household Staff finally said. "The healer is too young and too impulsive. But had The Terafin been present, she would have, in all likelihood, made the same choice—and the same mistake—before she could be brought round. It is not a mistake her predecessor would have made." These were more words—and more inappropriate words—than Jester had ever heard the woman speak. And he'd eavesdropped any number of times.

He stared at her. "You wanted her to die."

"No, ATerafin, I did not. But I accepted her death as a consequence of her role in this House—and the healer should have done so as well. He is not yet as wise or pragmatic as Alowan."

It was never wise, when dealing with dangerous men or women, to expose the weakness of fury; fury implied pain; pain implied vulnerability. To men or women who had proven themselves dangerous for a variety of reasons, compassion was almost as foreign as genuine sentiment. Jester, who understood what lack of power meant, understood best when to hide weakness.

He did not speak for a full minute. He expected the Master of the Household Staff to leave. She didn't. She stood in front of him, her eyes narrowed, her nose lifted. There was—and had always been—something vaguely martial about the woman; it was impossible to believe on any visceral level that she was a servant.

He could pull rank on her, in theory; he had that right. But might made right, and it was all on her side at the moment.

"Carver would have understood."

His jaw opened before he could stop it. The den didn't mention Carver. The servants, when in the company of the den, didn't mention him either.

"If you will not leave the healerie until I leave, I will leave." She walked past him and stopped at the door; Jester hadn't moved. He heard her exhale and could almost imagine, had she been any other woman, that she was praying for patience. Or luck. "Join me."

Jester did *not* keep company with the dour and the humorless. Had he chosen to break one of the more important rules of his social life, a less likely companion than the Master of the Household Staff could probably not be found.

But he followed, pausing outside of the healerie's door to retrieve his daggers from the wall-mounted wooden box into which all weapons must be placed.

The Master of the Household Staff did not likewise retrieve weapons, but she didn't require them. The halls were all but empty as she turned and made her way to the more secluded galleries; they were entirely empty when she reached them. It was not just Jester who was struggling with fury in silence.

He considered taking the nearest right and returning to the West Wing; he still held the report that Teller had handed him in one slightly shaking hand. But the Master of the Household Staff turned her glare on him at exactly the right—or perhaps wrong—moment, and he gave up on that plan. Whatever she intended to show him, he was going to see. He doubted very much that she intended to speak more than a few cursory words.

He almost lost his jaw a second time when she approached the entrance to the back halls. She glanced down the gallery at a section of paneling between two of the public function rooms, and when no discernible guests appeared, turned and opened a door. It was perhaps two inches taller than she was; she was not a short woman. It was taller than Jester.

She stood to one side and indicated that Jester was to precede her. Jester considered unsheathing one of his daggers, but decided against it; it took a surprising amount of effort. There were sixteen different ways that the servants could kill him, each of them less incriminating. He entered the narrow, short hall and stepped aside as she closed the door at her back.

The halls were not well lit; they did not—as the far side of the gallery did—boast windows and daylight. Magestones did not grace ceilings; lamps did. The uneven flickering of the light made it clear that they were entirely natural. In many ways, these halls reminded Jester of the alleys in the hundred holdings, except for the lack of sky. The floors were stone, although in some sections of the servants' quarters, proper wood had been laid. Footsteps echoed; no rugs absorbed noise. Even breath sounded strangely enlarged.

He waited in silence as the Master of the Household Staff once again took the lead she'd momentarily surrendered, no doubt to make sure her victim wouldn't turn tail and run. He was surprised at her use of the back halls; she was at the very head of the Household Staff, and had quarters for her use in the main house.

Unless, he thought, as he followed, it was not to her quarters that she now led.

"It has long been my contention," she said, in her stiff, chilly voice, "that the entire West Wing has been coddled to the point of near imbecility. Arguments in favor of the West Wing have been made, and while I believe you are collectively about to prove my point, it is not an argument I now have an interest in winning. There are far too many members of your wing embroiled in all levels of House Terafin."

Jester stopped walking. So, after a brief glance back, did the Master of the Household Staff. "Who was she working for?"

One iron brow rose. "Perhaps," she said, "you are capable of actually learning." She didn't speak with any notable approval. "You will not, of course, ask that question of any—*any*—of the servants. I am aware that there has been a lowering of general standards where the residents of the West Wing have been concerned; in the absence of The Terafin, those standards could be raised."

Jester smiled and shrugged. "It's not a bet I'd take."

This caused predictable narrowing of eyes. "Vareena was a very junior servant, and she was assigned to tasks appropriate to her seniority; she has been with the Household Staff for a little over a year. She had no prior history of service to one of The Ten; she had, however, been apprenticed to the staff of one of the more significant merchant houses. A background check—which is, of course, always conducted—did not raise any flags, and Vereena showed an admirable commitment to her duties.

"She was not brought to my attention by a member of the House. You will understand that, in the climate as it existed a year past, we were far more reserved in our external hiring practices."

"You expected—"

"Difficulty, yes. The Household Staff does not embroil itself in the affairs of the House Council; the House itself must continue to run, and run smoothly, regardless of the politics in the front halls."

Jester thought of the page who had stumbled—artfully and deliberately—in just such a way that she might deliver a message to the only man present who would be inclined to catch her before she fell. He said nothing.

The Master of the Household Staff noted this, but did not add to what was by no stretch of the definition a conversation.

"Vereena did not live in the manse itself."

Jester was silent for a couple of yards. "She was too junior."

"Indeed. She was expected at work at six in the morning six days a week. She was expected at noon on the seventh. She has, to my knowledge, never been late."

"Not something I could say of myself."

"No. But you answer to a different master." And the Master of the Household Staff, her voice implied, *had* standards. Jester had no difficulty remembering why he avoided her—or why most of the servants did.

"Yes, sporadically," he replied. He had recovered enough that he could once again offer her the lazy, nonchalant smile for which she had so little use. It bounced off her expression and fell beneath her notice.

They continued down halls that were conspicuously empty. Jester didn't have Carver's familiarity with the back halls, but he frowned. They had taken the first right, which put them somewhere in the vicinity of the small ballroom; he could see two doors that aligned roughly with the neatly linened side tables from which lighter fare was served. He did not expect that they would emerge from either of those doors, given the hour and the fact that the room was not in official use.

Nor did he expect that they would emerge in the rooms that lay beyond it; they were rooms that were also meant for the use of servants when the small hall was used for entertainments. But she continued past that room, and past another junction that would have led to a different exit in a more well-traveled gallery.

"Why aren't you angry?" he asked. He hadn't meant to ask anything serious, and would have clawed back the words if it were possible. She didn't appear to hear them, on the other hand; he couldn't decide if she was attempting to be merciful or dismissive.

She surprised him. "I am obviously discomposed," she eventually replied, "or I would not be speaking with you. My staff is well enough trained not to notice the breach of etiquette." She continued to walk. He followed, curious in spite of himself. She considered Vareena's injuries—injuries that he had not himself seen—a matter of politics, and at that, politics that did not or should not involve the Household Staff.

But she was not averse to removing impediments to the safety of that staff in other circumstances. These were therefore not the right circumstances. He let go of some of his fury as he considered what the wrong circumstances might actually be. For all her stiff, cold condescension, she was not a woman who respected power except in matters of etiquette; the formal separation demanded by rank was a duty she expected both sides of the equation to support.

For that reason, she had never been well loved by the residents of the West Wing. In the august presence of the Master of the Household Staff, servants who were otherwise friendly—or even friends—became stiff, formal, and almost invisible. The den was certain that, were it up to the Master of the Household Staff, there would be *no* interaction of note that did not involve servants' duties.

Or the den had been certain of it. Jester, in this narrow, cold hall, felt some of that certainty crumble beneath his feet as he walked. It had been assumed—by all—that The Terafin had been responsible for the choice of servants that graced the West Wing; for Merry and Viv and their small band of friends and rivals. It had not occurred to him to wonder how The Terafin had ascertained that the men and women chosen would, in fact, be flexible enough to aid the den in the little ways that had become, over time, so important.

He wondered now. Echoes of the earliest of the rumors that had reached the den—mostly through Carver—came back to him, following the rhythm of their footsteps. The small garden plot the Master of the Household Staff kept. Her rumored use of its contents.

Jokes abounded about servant deaths—but most of them involved fear. Of this woman. None involved poison. She *was* terrifying. But Jester doubted that she had ever been moved to murder a member of her own staff; that would, no doubt, be too merciful.

The guests and members of the House did not interfere with the senior servants. For one, those servants were not in easy reach; they were surrounded by the various detritus of their responsibilities as supervisors and instructors. Some guests and some members of the House had attempted to interfere with the junior serving staff—it was considered inevitable. Merry and her friends had ways of avoiding those difficulties; they were a hazard of the job.

Jester accepted it; he *expected* it. Firm in his loathing of the rich and the powerful, it had never occurred to him to question its truth.

Too much, he thought, had never occurred to him.

Some of the junior servants, he was certain, had fallen prey to House Council members. But they had been too ashamed to speak up. They had brought no complaint to the Master of the Household Staff; they feared the loss of necessary employment because they blamed themselves.

And yet, rumors of the actions taken against members of the House persisted. And Jester believed them.

How, then, to reconcile the fear of the servants with the truth of those rumors?

He thought of Vareena, and had his answer. Some offenses could not be hidden. Vareena would be dead were it not for the intervention of the healerie. And it was an intervention of which the Master of the Household Staff did not approve.

Jester was not certain how far they had walked by the time the Master of the Household Staff came to the end of the hall—and it was an ending, not a junction. She opened the door—which was, in all ways, an ordinary door;

it was not built to be relatively invisible. It was also locked, and the lock required two keys.

If someone was to enter the back halls, they weren't doing it from this door. But given the number of entrances and exits, Jester wasn't certain why it was relevant. He half-expected the door to open into a dungeon, replete with shackles and implements of torture.

It opened, instead, into a sunny, light-filled room. He blinked, his eyes adjusting. As they did, he cataloged what he saw: windows—large windows—occupied the wall to the left of the door's frame; they were, at the moment, covered by lace curtains that hung from rods just above the window's frame. They were not the magnificent bay and bow windows that afforded a view of the grounds to the House Council's various members—but they were fully glass, and at least one opened to allow breezes to cause the curtains to sway. On the wall opposite the door was another door, and to either side of it, cabinets, most of which appeared to house dishes or glass.

And opposite the windows were shelves. The Master of the Household Staff appeared to be a voracious reader. Glancing at the titles, he grimaced; if she read, she was not particularly interested in lurid adventure stories. Of course not.

She was interested in etiquette, in history, and in The Ten families; she was, it appeared, interested in the merchant houses and in the heraldry that the pretentious boasted. He remembered, as his eyes scanned spines, the early years of the den, when Teller and Jay had undertaken Rath's equally pretentious lessons; he could *hear* Jay's invective so clearly he grinned.

But he could hear, as well, Teller's curiosity, his avid interest, his almost tangible yearning. He was certain that Jay would have quit in disgust if she hadn't been aware of it as well.

He had not thought of Rath in years. Ironic, that this room—otherwise the antithesis of any rooms Rath called home—should bring him back so sharply.

Someone cleared her throat, and Jester's grin deepened. He was certain that he was now at the heart of the dragon's den: it connected the two facets of her life.

"By all reports, ATerafin, you have a day of leisure ahead of you. I, however, do not; given the actions of the healerie, my day has become infinitely less pleasant. Do you understand that Daine's life is now at risk?"

"Because the rest of the House will know he's healer-born."

Her curt, sharp exhalation implied either disgust or impatience. Or both. In that moment, she reminded him of Haval, the man he had been avoiding.

"I'm already getting this at home," he said, his back toward her. "I'm not sure I need it anywhere else." He turned; the one thing that was notably lacking in any of the glass cabinets was liquor.

Drinking in the presence of the Master of the Household Staff might be amusing. Or suicidal. "Or because, in healing someone that close to death, he now knows as much about her life as she does."

"You understand."

He didn't. But he was beginning to, and it made him uneasier than even the bizarre and isolated walk with the Master of the Household Staff.

"You assume that I do not approve of either you or your friends in the West Wing."

"I did."

"I see."

"Who was Vareena working for?"

Jester felt the temperature drop as the breeze shifted. He turned to face the dragon, his hands clasped loosely behind his back. Her expression offered as much warmth as it usually did.

"You chose the servants."

"I choose all of the servants, yes. I understand the duty of a host to guests. I understand service. I understand, further, that this House does not stand without the service of the men and women who bear its name—in *any* walk of life. I am, of course, ATerafin. Do I appear young, to you?"

This was, among the older women of his acquaintance, often a signal. Jester could not imagine that the Master of the Household Staff wanted either comfort or stroking. "No. If it helps, I don't believe you've ever appeared young—even when you were."

"Whom would you expect this opinion to help?"

"Clearly not me." He grinned.

She didn't. She was far more brittle in her annoyance than Haval; there was no humor in it.

"Does my age imply anything to you?"

Only the good die young. His grin deepened, although he kept the words on the right side of his mouth. "You were alive during the House War that saw Amarais Handernesse ATerafin seated."

"Indeed."

"You weren't—"

"I did not occupy my current position at the start of the war."

"You were given your position afterward."

"Yes."

Jester frowned. The tone of her voice was off, somehow; he tried to recall what he'd heard of the last internal conflict for control of Terafin—but nothing came to mind when he thought of the servants. "You didn't support the previous Terafin in her bid for the seat."

"No."

"You didn't support any of the contenders."

"No."

"Did the previous Master of the Household Staff?"

The silence, and the obvious reluctance that framed it, was longer. "Yes. Before you ask, he did not throw his support behind the woman who did, in the end, take the seat."

Jester continued to think—and he resented the effort; he wanted a drink. Or three. The Master of the Household Staff approved of Iain; Jester would have bet money that should Iain evince interest in the seat, she would back him.

But he was no longer certain he would win. Amarais had valued the Master of the Household Staff; Jay both resented and respected her. Neither of the two would have presented an ultimatum, overture, or threat, to gain her support—and her support could be invaluable.

He had, he thought, learned much about her various attitudes toward the House Council, most of it conveyed by small shifts in her facial expression. Aside from Iain, he could not think of one of whom she approved; she was at quiet war with Barston, and had been for a decade.

"You've never involved yourself in the politics of the House."

"I have never involved myself in politics," she replied, in a tone of voice that made politics a step below any other form of illegality. "The Household Staff is necessary for the smooth functioning of the House; it will be necessary no matter who sits in the seat."

Jester's glance shifted toward the window; there was only so much of the Master of the Household Staff's stiff, condescending gaze he could take. He almost pinched himself; the day had not started particularly well, and it had traveled in directions he would never have predicted.

He missed Carver.

He missed Carver, and he was almost certain Carver, like Lefty, Duster, Fisher, and Lander, would never be seen again. The lack of certainty was a sharp, painful gift. Hope always was. What would Carver do? This entire discussion, bizarre and unpredictable as it was, would have been Carver's responsibility.

"How do you prevent your staff from becoming involved in House politics?"

"How does The Terafin prevent her House Council from becoming involved in external politics?"

She didn't. "Why are you speaking to me about this at all?"

"Because The Terafin is not present. She does not occupy her seat. You assume I do not approve of her; you are not entirely in the wrong. She does not understand service—not as it pertains to, and arises from, the Household Staff. She does not fully comprehend the extent to which familiarity breeds contempt.

"But she has survived this deficiency—or rather, my staff has—because of the extraordinary way in which she ascended the seat. I do not question her absence," she added, although it was clear she was doing exactly that. "And I admit a certain gratitude at the way she averted the deaths that must come with any martial struggle.

"I wish you, of course, to speak with the healer. You have a vested interest in the fate of Terafin, ATerafin. And you have connections the Household Staff does not. I will not," she continued, "support your faction should the specter of war rear its head. But I will not support any other faction, either. I will ensure that the House continues to function."

Jester, silent, slid hands into his pockets. "You terrify the servants."

"Do I?"

Jester nodded. "In the same way The Terafin did."

One iron brow twitched. "I believe you are confusing respect with fear."

He shrugged. "How will you explain Vareena's injuries?"

"I will explain nothing; there will be no need."

"You terrify them," Jester said, repeating the phrase as he considered it, "but they trust you. They do not trust your mercy or your flexibility."

"With good reason."

Yes. She offered neither. "But they know what to expect from you. They understand that you have free reign among the Household Staff. You are the first—and last—resort. But they understand that the Household Staff is yours. No one who bears the House Name interferes in any obvious or detectable way with the servants." The exception, of course, were the cooks, but Jester felt no need to point this out; she was no doubt aware of it.

She said nothing, and Jester almost dropped the conversation. Almost. "Vareena is not ATerafin. She *is* a member of the Household Staff. News of what was done to her—and you are aware of the details, where I am not—will spread through the back halls before sundown. If you do nothing—"

"You are concerned about my standing among the Household Staff?" Both brows rose. She wasn't shouting, but she might as well have been.

Clearly this was a bad idea. Jester did not reply.

"I will deal with the Household Staff. You, however, will deal with the House Council."

"Of which I'm not a member."

"Of which," she agreed, "you are not a member."

"What will happen to Vareena?"

"I will deal," she replied, "with the Household Staff."

"She's *twelve.*"

"Age is irrelevant." For the first time since she entered this light-filled, hushed room, she moved. Jester expected her to throw him out the way he'd arrived—although she had very, very strict rules about the use of the back halls. His presence broke all of them except the first, but it was the only one that would count. The Master of the Household Staff had granted her personal permission.

She did not, however, usher him out. "Touch nothing," she said curtly as she moved toward—and through—the door that led into what he now assumed were her rooms.

He was left alone in a small, sunny room, a hint of breeze touching his face. His hands remained behind his back; he was certain at this point that if he even moved, she would know. But she had not told him to remain as he was; she had merely advised him that nothing was to be touched.

Therefore, he touched nothing; he did look. The dishes in the cabinets were of an unfamiliar make and pattern, and many looked old—too old to be used respectably in food service. The lace of the curtains was an ivory that spoke of age and use; the books were likewise worn. He glanced at the rug that softened his footfall, and frowned.

A similar rug graced the right-kin's office.

What did he know about the dragon? Not, he thought, enough. He had no doubt that the similarities between the two rugs did not stop at appearance. It had never occurred to him that servants would require the specific type of magical protections that the right-kin did.

No, he thought, with a trace of his usual bitterness, it had never occurred to him that the needs of servants would matter to those who could afford those protections. On the other hand, had he encountered the Master of the Household Staff in any other situation, he would have scoffed at the very notion that she could be a servant.

House Terafin: where even the *servants* were patrician and terrifying.

Shaking his head, he approached the closed door through which the Master of the Household Staff had disappeared.

"—If you expect gratitude, you have failed to understand my role as Master of the Household Staff."

The door was a solid, thick door; the Master of the Household Staff was not shouting; Jester had never heard her raise her voice. She was a woman who valued control, and that control extended to herself in all ways. He should not have been able to hear her, but he did.

"I understand the role well," her visitor said. His voice, as hers, was smooth and chilly. It was also familiar. Rymark. Rymark ATerafin. "You are to see to the efficient and smooth operation of this manor and its properties. The situation is, of course, beyond you."

Jester's surprise made clear that he had expected Haerrad to be behind the death. Or the near death, as the case was.

"The girl was a member of the Household Staff."

"Yes. And her presence in the manor implies a sorry lack of security in our hiring practices."

Silence.

Rymark was not a man who had ever been easily intimidated. Jester had assumed this was because Gabriel ATerafin, the former right-kin, was his father. Gabriel's rather clouded resignation had done nothing to change Rymark's attitude. Jay's ascension had—but, as expected, the change was superficial; it was a mask turned in the direction of The Terafin, and discarded everywhere else.

"I have not yet seen proof of your claims, ATerafin. Even had I, she was a member of the Household Staff, and my responsibility."

"You understand that The Terafin is on urgent leave."

"I am not fully apprised of The Terafin's business, and as it is not my concern, I would appreciate if no more were said of that matter in these rooms."

"And you understand that at this time, the House is in a delicate political position. It is my suspicion that at least one—if not two—of the previous attempts on The Terafin's life came at the directive of the *Astari*."

"That is not my concern. It is not the concern of the Household Staff."

"It is the *concern* of *every* member of this House." Rymark's voice rose.

"No, ATerafin, it is not."

"An example must be made, and a message sent, to the *Astari*. We are not to be trifled with, and we are not without power and resources of our own. The death of the girl achieves both. We are not cowering in terror; we are not looking over our shoulders. We are not victims of espionage and deadly political games."

"Again, ATerafin, you have no proof."

"I have proof, if it is required. It will be tendered to the House Council, not the *servants*."

"It will be required," she replied. "I have books to which I must attend, and a duty roster. If you have nothing further to say, ATerafin?"

"I have a great deal—"

"A figure of speech. You have nothing relevant to say. I will, however, tender a reply to your statements. If, as you claim, you have incontrovertible proof that a junior servant was in the pay of the *Astari*, ejecting her via the trade doors would have served to send the message you desired sent. If you wish the *Astari* to understand that they are vulnerable and their operations understood, her death was not a necessity.

"Had you come to me with this proof, I would have dealt with the situation. In future, remember this. She was *not* ATerafin. Her death could cause the rules of exemption to be revoked in their entirety, and the whole of the House laid open to the Mysterium and the Magisterium's truthseekers, should the *Astari* desire it.

"And in this Empire, ATerafin, being a member of the *Astari* is not considered a capital crime."

Jester, no fool, had not waited upon the return of the Master of the Household Staff; he had heard everything he needed to hear, and possibly a great deal more than he wanted. He exited the way he'd arrived, and without escort, which he considered a positive. He took one wrong turn on the way out of the back halls, which brought him into a far less abandoned section, but most of the servants were willing to turn a blind eye. One or two asked briefly about Carver.

He had nothing to say. The fact that Jay had gone in search of him—that she was the only possible way he'd come home—he couldn't share. Jay to the servants was The Terafin. The Terafin did not abandon the rest of her duties for the sake of *one* man, no matter how important—and Carver, in the scheme of things, was not one of the fundamental pillars upon which the stability of the House depended.

The servants pointed him in the direction he wanted to go, and eventually he arrived in the great room of the West Wing; it was empty. He took the opportunity to pour himself a drink, and grimaced; he'd grabbed the wrong bottle and was not in the mood for the sweetness that hit his tongue.

He emptied the glass and headed over to the long couch, where he dropped like a soggy rock, Teller's report still clutched in one hand. He glanced at it, wondering how quickly it would put him to sleep; given what the purported report contained, it shouldn't, but Jester suspected that Guillarne could manage to make demonic magic a simple foil for his own imagined brilliance and cunning.

Which was not entirely fair to Guillarne, whom even Finch respected as a merchant negotiator—but Jester was not in a mood to be fair, and Guillarne was not present, and therefore unlikely to feel insulted.

He tugged off boots and set them on the carpet before falling over and stretching out. He needed to think. He needed to talk with Teller—which would have to wait; he needed to talk to Finch, and as he definitely did *not* need to speak with Jarven, that would have to wait as well. Jester had never called kitchen, but felt, at this juncture, it might be necessary. He'd let Finch decide.

Jester didn't make a habit of lying, although he had nothing against it; he *was* lazy. Guillarne's report looked like nothing but work. Yes, if he teased information out of the carefully self-serving, ego-strewn words, he might satisfy his curiosity about the disaster at the guildhall, but he wasn't certain to pick up all of the implications contained within.

He wanted another drink, but didn't want to get up. The drink wouldn't come to his hand on its own, more's the pity. He lifted Guillarne's report, paused, and then smiled. As smiles went, it wasn't particularly friendly. Yes, it was work. Yes, he wanted a drink. And he wanted a bit of amusement.

For amusement, on a day that had held less than none of it, he was willing to live with a little bit of discomfort. He stood, walked over to the cabinet, poured himself something that was far less sweet, and, glass in hand, headed out the doors.

Jester knew that Haval had gone to the Merchant Authority at about the same time as he was asking Barston for an appointment with the right-kin. At the time, he had hoped—prayer being a little beyond him—that Haval would then go to his *own* house, to be castigated by his very direct wife.

He was certain that fate had not been that kind, and at the moment, appreciated what would otherwise have been typical bad luck. He walked, glass in one hand, report in the other, to Haval's workroom. Haval was to prepare mourning clothing appropriate for work in the Merchant Authority for Finch, which gave him an excuse to be present—not that he needed a fortuitous excuse; he was perfectly capable of coming up with a believable, practical lie.

Having no free hands and no convenient page, Jester kicked the door instead of knocking. He heard a muffled reply, and kicked it again. The third time was the charm; Haval, looking about as irritated as one would expect, appeared in the doorway. He was wearing an apron through which various pins had been placed.

He looked pointedly at the drink in Jester's hand, and less pointedly at the report, which was not as pristine as it had been on receipt. "I do not need to tell you to touch nothing. I will, however, tell you to watch your step. I am almost at the point where I am willing to surrender some part of my tailoring duties."

"You're on death's door?"

"I may well be soon—of apoplexy." He waited until Jester had entered the room—which given the state of cloth and bolts strewn on the floor was more time-consuming than it sounded—before he closed the door. "What are you carrying?"

Jester handed it to Haval and slid one hand into a pocket. Haval noticed; Jester was subtle, but subtlety failed where Haval was concerned, and given the contents of the conversation to follow, was pointless.

"Guillarne's report of events at the Merchants' guildhall." He left the document in Haval's hands and attempted to find a safe chair to occupy. Given Haval, that was a challenge.

"Your appointment with the right-kin was productive, then." It didn't sound like a question; it was. Jester was silent, considering and discarding a variety of responses.

Haval did not immediately return to the cutting of cloth; he found a chair more quickly than Jester had, his prohibition on touching things not, of course, applying to himself. He read Guillarne's report, as Jester had intended. Jester watched his expression; there was none. No lift of brow, no twitch of eye, no shift in the corners of his mouth; no tightening of hand, no change in breathing—nothing.

"You have read this report?" he asked, without looking up.

Jester failed to answer, which did draw the clothier's attention. Jester shrugged. "It looks like a lot of work."

Unblinking, Haval stared at him.

"Look, have you ever *met* Guillarne?"

Haval exhaled. "I find your lack of curiosity astonishing." Voice firewood dry, he added, "Much information comes from gossip; gossip grows out of the need to have information important to your social context, coupled with the need to impress others with that knowledge." He handed the report back to Jester. "You will read it."

Jester smiled. "You can't blame a lazy man for trying to shift the burden of unasked for work."

Haval ignored this. "A reasonably intelligent man could be forgiven for assuming that your presence here indicates a desire to discuss Guillarne's statement. I count myself reasonably intelligent. You, however, did not come to discuss its contents, yet you are here, interrupting what is not, in the end, optional work.

"I will assume that you are not lying; you have not read the document in your hands."

"Not that you would have any problems with a lie."

"Not the ones that do not waste my time, no." His posture shifted, which is as much expression as he allowed himself. "In an effort not to waste what is apparently a scarce resource, I will come to the point. Why are you here?"

"If you haven't had the pleasure of Guillarne's company, and the report did not instill a visceral desire never to do so, you are a stronger man than I."

"My time, Jester."

"If you don't know Guillarne," Jester continued, enjoying himself but aware that things would get serious very shortly, "I'm certain that you *are* acquainted with Duvari."

Haval didn't react to the name at all.

"Some key members of the House Council believe that Duvari was responsible for one of the failed assassination attempts on The Terafin."

"Significant members?"

"That's a judgment call."

"Yes, and I suppose I should not expect such discernment from you."

Jester laughed. "That's harsh."

"It is not. I can, however, be harsh if you feel a need to appreciate the difference."

As he'd finished the drink, Jester set the empty glass beneath the chair and raised both hands. "I am getting to the point. I am not aware of how many of the House Council believe this; I don't think numbers are relevant. There is nothing about the belief that is ridiculous."

"No."

"I've heard rumors about Duvari—most of them occur whenever a suitably rich or politically powerful patrician meets their end. Most of the rumors are exactly that—another way to take a public swipe at a universally detested man."

"It is a miracle to me that you have survived Jewel; I admit that I would not have thought she had the patience."

"Fine. Duvari has spies within at least all of The Ten. He has spies here."

Haval's expression changed, then. Jester found Haval's use of expression disconcerting. The clothier did not speak.

"If one of his spies were discovered—and killed outright—would Duvari attempt to use the death to his advantage?"

"Please tell me this is a hypothetical question."

"You don't like lies that waste your time."

"Duvari attempts to use all events to his advantage. It would not be the first time a member of his *Astari* died in service to him. He will not take the House to task; he will hold a grudge, but as you suspect, the difference will not be notable in his actions."

Jester wanted another drink. Haval did not keep alcohol in his workroom.

"If a member of the *Astari* were to perish here, Duvari would in all likelihood see to that member's replacement. He would, however, be extremely concerned with the discovery itself. It implies incompetence on the part of the deceased, or superb competence on the part of the discoverer."

"What if—purely hypothetically—the assassination was attempted, but the spy failed to perish?"

"Depending on the injuries sustained, Duvari would repatriate."

"Let's say, for the sake of this discussion, that this occurred. The *Astari*, dying, was discovered and taken directly to the healerie."

The silence went on for a beat too long before Haval removed his apron.

The early dinner hour came and went. Jester was flopped on the couch in the great room; the low table in front of it contained two glasses; one empty, one almost entirely full. Haval had agreed to a drink in principle, but had failed to actually enjoy it.

Word had been sent to the healerie; word had been sent to the right-kin's office. Word had not been sent to the Merchant Authority, because traffic to and from the Common was heavily congested; Jester felt that Finch would arrive at the Terafin manse before the message reached her hands. Haval did not agree with this exaggerated assessment, but was willing to let it be; he had said very, very little since exiting his workroom.

The only person Jester wanted to speak with at the moment was not coming home any time soon. He held his peace; he had asked Haval a dozen questions, interspersed by awkward silence, and as no answers had been offered he contented himself with rest.

Finch arrived first, and she arrived early. There wasn't, at the moment, enough significant work to keep her in the Merchant Authority offices; too many people had perished, and the lines of communication were being re-built slowly. The richer holdings were awash with funeral preparations. She entered the great room to find Jester lying on his back and Haval sitting in the spine-stiff upright position he preferred when not working. A greater contrast could not be found.

Jester, who had opened one eye at the sound of the door, closed it again. "You're early. Get yourself a drink; you're going to want it."

"I've been working with an agitated, excited Jarven for the past week. If Jarven hasn't driven me to drink anything stronger than tea, I can't imagine your news will. I have news of my own," she added. At her tone, Jester opened both of his eyes and propped himself up on his elbows.

Finch was dressed for the Merchant Authority, which never looked comfortable. She had not paused to remove the netting and the pins that kept her hair out of her eyes. "What happened?" she asked, looking pointedly at Jester's feet until he moved them. She sat on the end of the couch and leaned into the armrest. In this light, she looked fragile and exhausted.

Jester searched for words. One glance at Haval told him that if he didn't find them, no one else in the room would. "We have a problem."

"We?"

He nodded. "I spent over an hour in the company of the Master of the Household Staff while you were safe at work."

Given the events of the week, safe was a very dubious description—but Finch cringed on his behalf anyway. Finch worked with Lucille, who was terrifying in an entirely different way, but Lucille didn't bring out the big weapons until someone had actually managed to offend her—not that that took much effort.

"What did she want?" Finch asked, as if spending an hour in the company of that ancient dragon was a casual event.

"She wanted to let us know that a twelve-year-old junior servant who was almost murdered should have died."

Finch blanched. Jester loved her for it, inasmuch as he loved any member of the den. "She didn't say that."

"She did. In slightly more condescending, vastly more chilly language."

"When you say almost—"

"She was found before she died. She was taken to the healerie—to Daine."

"He saved her."

"Yes."

Finch did not evince any particular relief. Instead, she turned to Haval, who had listened without comment—or movement. When Haval failed to interrupt or offer his usual dry sarcasm, she massaged her forehead. "You said she was twelve."

"Yes."

"She hasn't been given the House Name, then."

"No."

"Let me talk with Teller."

Jester blinked. "Jay's not here."

"Jay doesn't handle most of the paperwork involved with adoption into the House. The biggest difficulty we might have is the Master of the Household Staff; the usual route to adoption for servants comes entirely through her recommendations. If she felt the girl deserved to die, she's not likely to make that recommendation. I think she can be talked into accepting it."

Jester was still blinking.

"I assume you're concerned because she falls outside of the Laws of Exemption. She *could* refuse the House Name if she wished to invite magisterians into the Terafin manse on her own behalf—or her parents, if they're clever and want money. But if she does that, she will never work for The Ten again in any capacity, and she probably knows it; the Master of the Household Staff doesn't hire fools."

Haval nodded, his expression neutral. "Admirable, Finch. You are missing one key piece of information, but your solution is sound."

Finch inclined her head, brow furrowed.

"It is our working belief that the junior servant in question was—is—a member of the *Astari*."

Silence. Jester counted three long beats before Finch said, "and she was taken to Daine."

"Yes."

Finch rose. "I'm going to get changed if I can pry myself out of this clothing. Grab Teller and Arann when they get in. I need to pen one quick message before we call kitchen. And," she added, "I need to eat something." She stopped in the doorway and then said, "Two messages."

Arann was excused from his duties, as he still worked the later shift. He had, as Finch requested, brought Torvan and Arrendas with him. None of the three wore the armor of the Chosen; all of them carried the swords. Arann was about as relaxed as he could be, given Jay's absence and the events surrounding her decision; Torvan and Arrendas, however, were not. Finch seldom asked to speak with them informally, and when she didn't use the normal channels, it was never good news.

Daine was not in the West Wing. He had taken to sleeping in Alowan's old rooms. Finch approved of the decision in principle; she understood that he needed to make the healerie his own in the eyes of the House. She was now feeling far less sanguine.

Teller, not surprisingly, arrived last. He and Barston had taken late dinner together, and Teller arrived with an armful of documents which were, no doubt, pressing emergencies. He had not been expecting a kitchen call tonight.

Only when Teller had entered the wing did Torvan and Arrendas leave to fetch Daine.

Although magelights were no longer prohibitively expensive for the den, they seldom used them in kitchen meetings. These meetings had been at the heart of the den in the most cramped of quarters, and in the most dire of situations—sometimes the meetings had been held in the dark because there had been no money left over for cheap candles, and daylight hours had been necessary for scavenging.

They used lamps, now. There were three.

Daine was drawn and almost jaundiced when he arrived with his escorts. He took the seat nearest to Finch. He set his hands flat on the surface of the table and slumped in the chair, and Finch slid her chair closer so she could wrap an arm around him. He leaned into her shoulder.

So, she thought, giving up the scant hope that the events of the day had been misunderstood by Jester. Daine had, in fact, used his healer-born gift to save the life of a person on the outer edge of death. Given his pallor, he had not yet recovered. He was not, however, in the grip of the mage fevers that plagued any of the talent-born who pushed their powers past their natural limits.

No, she thought; he was in the grip of the compulsion to remain joined with the patient, from whom he must be separate if they were both to recover. She said nothing; she simply strengthened her arm.

No one around the table spoke; they were waiting for Finch. Finch had not taken Jay's seat, but she had taken—for the evening—the responsibility and the weight of the kitchen. "Torvan, Arrendas, be seated. You are not the guards on duty."

They did as she asked in silence. She then turned to Jester and said, "Can you separate Haval from his nefarious clothing and bring him here?"

"I'm not sure we want him." He signed *don't trust*.

"I'm not sure we do, either," she replied; she felt no need to lie to her den, and no need to manage them. "But if anyone has information about what we're likely to face, it's Haval."

"Daine will have that information," Jester countered, bringing up the point of the meeting in an oblique way.

"I don't believe he will." She signed *trust me*. She thought, watching him, that he would refuse. She would have gone herself, if she weren't holding Daine upright, and her glance told Jester as much.

He exhaled, pushed his chair back—loudly—and left.

"Do we want Meralonne?" Teller surprised her by asking.

"I don't believe so. If we need him, we can find him. He won't sit in the kitchen without smoking his pipe, and I don't have the sentimental attachment to pipes that Jay does." She hesitated and glanced at Daine, whose eyes were closed. "And I'm not entirely certain his expertise is relevant."

"Are you certain it's not?"

"Sadly, no."

Haval entered a relatively quiet kitchen, which served as something of a warning. His glance swept the room and came to rest, briefly, on Daine. The boy was pale and his pallor was appalling, which lent credence to Jester's claims. Haval, however, had wasted very little time doubting Jester, and only a small amount of hope.

He took the chair that Finch indicated and sat in it; Jester had turned the back of his to face the table, and leaned across it, arms folded beneath his chin. He looked extravagantly bored. He wasn't, of course; he didn't generally take as much trouble to appear that way when he wasn't expecting conflict.

Given the way Finch glanced at him, Haval understood that this posture was for the benefit of the interloper—Haval himself. He accepted it, as he accepted all else: with observation and no obvious reaction.

He returned attention to Daine, the healer-born boy. At age twenty, he had the bearing of a patrician—and Haval understood why. He had been forced to heal a man decades his senior. He had not been prepared for the experience—if one ever could be—and he had come away from the experience with rather more of that man's thoughts and outlooks than was good for anyone. Even the man himself, who had shortly thereafter died of unrelated injuries.

But he had also brought Jewel back from the edge of death. In so doing, he had burdened himself with another person's outlook and experience. The two could not be more different. Haval had heard—although it had taken effort to be in a position *to* hear it—that Daine had been sent at Alowan's request for just this reason: he hoped to set Jewel's view against the view of the unnamed Terafin patrician, and thus give Daine the balance necessary to navigate the scars left by the act of healing the dying.

And Jewel, of course, was not content to leave it at that. She kept the boy. She kept him here, in the West Wing, with the remnants of the den she had doggedly gathered. Had Levec forbidden it, Daine might have chosen to return to the Houses of Healing—but Haval thought it unlikely.

After the death of Alowan, Daine had stepped into the healerie, taking the duties of the older man and making them his own. What Alowan might have refused to do, Daine could not; he carried too much of Jewel in him. A dying child had been given into his keeping, and he had wrapped his power around her, pulling her out of death's hands.

And to do so, he had to see her clearly; to do so, he had to open himself to her inspection. For as long as it took, they had to be one. Vareena, the junior servant, was *Astari*.

Daine knew. He knew what she knew, and he knew what the cost might be—both to himself, and to the girl who had failed.

Finch gestured. Arann's reply was slower to come; even in the secret language of the den—a deplorably open secret if one had eyes and half a thought to spare—his use of words was sparse.

"We're here tonight for a number of reasons."

Daine shifted, pulling himself to an upright position when in Haval's opinion he should have been abed—and sleeping—hours ago. He stared at his reflection, his gaze so focused it seemed to exclude anything else in the room.

Daine knew. He had not, to Haval's eye, decided how he would handle himself—or Vareena. Vareena could, with little effort, leave the healerie unless she were heavily restrained—and Haval very much doubted that Daine had ordered such restraints.

But given Jester's impromptu meeting with the Master of the Household Staff, Haval thought escape or disappearance would offer more difficulties for Vareena than she might otherwise expect. He had not yet decided how best to handle the situation, himself.

"Do not look for mercy or protection from the *Astari*," he said, speaking to the young healer.

Daine's chin lifted fractionally, his eyes sharpening.

"Duvari does not choose randomly when he chooses those who enter his service."

"They do not serve Duvari, but the Kings," was the young man's stiff reply.

"That, sadly, is not true. The Kings, if pressed, could not name Vareena—if that is, indeed, her name. Not even were she presented to them now. She was chosen by Duvari; she was tested by Duvari, and she survived. She was not placed in this House as an agent of the Kings; she was placed as *Astari*."

Slowly, slowly, Finch gestured.

Haval shook his head. It had not escaped his notice that the den themselves were not comfortable when he chose to speak in their particular tongue, and he did it only at need.

"She serves *the Kings*," Daine said, in a lower—but far more intense—voice.

"And the Kings command her to kill?" Haval replied. "Do the Kings now accept and witness the oath of allegiance all *Astari* must swear?" He pressed, allowing his focus to develop an edge; allowing knowledge and certainty to show.

It was, of course, a lie; all of it.

"The *Astari* swear their oaths to *the Kings*, and the Kings accept them; the Kings themselves make clear what that oath must mean. It is the Kings' honor that is upheld or debased—and the *Astari* are aware of this. They must act in the best interests of the Empire, even when they are far away from the heart of its power; they must make choices that reflect those vows."

"And the Kings then command them to kill? To assassinate those who might prove a theoretical danger in some dim future? Is that what you claim?"

"The *Astari* are not commanded to kill. And only a select few—a very few—expect to survive such assassinations, should they be deemed necessary at all. It is the Kings—the god-born—who decide."

Haval closed his eyes. "Ah, yes," he said, his voice once again the voice of the tailor. "So they do. But it is Duvari who decides which crimes are to be brought to the Kings for judgment, and it is Duvari who decides when the security of the Kings' protectors has been compromised.

"It is often the case that those compromises also break inconvenient laws—but Duvari is, among the *Astari*, a law unto himself. He has the Kings' trust."

A rigid silence had fallen over every other occupant of this table; Jester's pallor was unfortunate, given the color of his hair. Only Finch seemed unmoved; Teller was too still.

He met, and held, Finch's gaze.

"We cannot afford to surrender the only healer we have." She surprised him; she was a constant surprise. "And if I understand what you have implied, Haval, and what Daine has all but given away, we may be looking at exactly that."

Daine's gaze returned to Finch as if she were an anchor.

"Vareena will not be content to remain here. She may not consider Daine a threat."

Daine said, softly, "She does."

"She would have to," Haval said. "If you know what she knows, you are."

"I don't know everything she knows." Daine's voice was lower and fuller; more his own. "But I know enough."

Haval nodded. "There is no way to hide it; if Vareena leaves, she will leave with that information, and it will travel to Duvari, as all things eventually must."

"How do we preserve Daine's life?" Finch asked.

"There are two obvious and immediate possibilities if your goal is to preserve Daine. The safest and most obvious, you will not countenance."

Silence. He did not elaborate; there was no one in the room who did not understand. Not even Daine. Perhaps, at this moment, especially not Daine.

No one asked Haval how he could speak with such certainty. No one argued against it. He had considered a less direct approach and discarded it. He did not understand what had happened with Vareena, but knew that the den was not involved—or had not been, until she had been brought, dying, across the healerie's threshold. He knew Duvari as well as anyone present could claim to know him.

But he knew Jewel at least as well, and he knew that the den had been informed by her views and her beliefs. Not until they began to perish would they shift ground easily—if at all. He glanced, briefly, at Jester, and then returned to Finch.

"The second is far less reliable; it requires a great deal of finesse and information which would otherwise be difficult to uncover."

"Are we agreed," Jester asked, "that the first option is *not* an option?" He placed a hand on the table. This, Haval had not observed before, but it was clear in context that he was calling for a vote. And no one voted against him; Daine's hand hit the table in a fist, and spread. Haval did not presume to vote; neither, he noted, did the Captains of the Chosen. If they were expected to do so, no one informed them.

Jester turned, somewhat belligerently Haval felt, to Haval. "What's your second option?"

"You will want to consult with the House Mage to execute the second option. The House Mage is not the most reliable of allies."

No one disagreed. No one spoke. Haval did not find this frustrating, although he did exhale heavily and pinch the bridge of his nose. "I do not know how many questions you are willing to answer, Daine. But you must answer at least one."

Daine said nothing; Finch's arm tightened, briefly, as the young man shuddered. He looked up at Haval, composing his expression so perfectly Haval could almost see the *Astari* training take hold. "What question?"

"I believe you are already aware of what I will ask."

Daine's nod was measured, controlled. His expression was almost as neutral as Haval's; he had not chosen to dissemble or hide behind his obvious distress, his obvious discomfort. He was assessing Haval as if Haval was the largest threat the room contained. He did not spare a glance to the captains. Haval, observing him, considered the chances of success to be far lower than he had at the start of the evening.

The tailor set his hands upon the table and gestured; the gesture was fast, brief, and aimed in its entirety at Jester. *Watch. Do not speak.*

"Understand that, for Vareena, the worst has already happened. She was discovered. You understand what that means to—and for—her. I do not think she will be thankful that you saved her life; it was her dying that exposed—to one who has not sworn the oaths she has—her knowledge and her identity. She is too young to be fully apprised of the composition of the *Astari*, but what she does know, you will know. I expect her to attempt to kill you."

"I don't," was Daine's stiff reply.

"If you wish to lie, lie. But perhaps attempt to be less obvious. I assume that you have no wish to die; please correct me if that assumption is in error."

Daine inhaled; he appeared to be counting. "She doesn't deserve to die."

"Better. It is both the truth as you perceive it, and the truth, period. It is, however, irrelevant. Death comes to us all, deserving or not."

"Not at twelve, it doesn't," Jester cut in.

"Sometimes far younger than that. You have all had some experience with death. You wish to preserve Vareena; you wish to protect what she protected. Given the healing, that is no surprise. I, however, was retained to protect what Jewel wished to protect. One of those things, Daine, was you. Who attempted to kill Vareena?"

"Why do you want to know?"

Haval once again brought fingers to the bridge of his nose. "Because if we are to preserve you both, we must have something to offer Duvari. Vareena was a junior maid. She has, if I am correct, spent her entire life in Duvari's service. She has, quite possibly, served the *Astari* as spy prior to her placement here. Her knowledge of the inner workings of the Kings' protectors is nonetheless, in my opinion, slight.

"It is not slight enough that Duvari will not consider Daine a threat. Daine, however, is the lesser threat."

"The greater threat being Vareena's discovery."

"Yes. If I am correct, Daine, she has no idea—at all—how that discovery occurred."

Daine nodded slowly.

"She, therefore, does not have the information that we need. What we need to give Duvari is the breach in his security. Not less—and certainly not more."

Chapter Thirteen

TELLER CLEARED HIS THROAT. Finch kept an arm around Daine's shoulder. Both the right-kin and the director of the Terafin Merchant Authority offices now looked concerned, which came as a relief to Haval. They were—the entire den was—sentimental; they habitually allowed sentiment and attachment to color their decisions. In the worst case, the sentiment overrode any other concerns. That they were aware that there *were* other concerns was of some comfort. Haval did not expect further comfort to be found this evening.

The Captains of the Chosen were silent in an entirely different way. They did not interrupt. They waited for Teller to speak.

"If we assume that Vareena's assassination was at the hands of a member of the House, we're compromising our own security. If we have methods—within the House—of ferreting out Duvari's spies, they are not something that we can casually turn over to the *Astari*. It will work against our future interests."

"Indeed." Haval glanced at Jester, who said nothing.

Finch was not likewise silent. "Those methods clearly exist." She spoke, in theory, to Teller; her gaze, however, fell to the captains. "Torvan, Arrendas, are you aware of what they are?"

Silence. Torvan finally said, "No."

"I am not, as House Council member, apprised of them, either," Finch said. "Teller, as right-kin, are you?"

"I am aware of many of the precautions taken to keep internal matters within the House."

"And do you believe that those precautions exposed Vareena's affiliations to whomever chose to kill her?"

"I don't have enough information to determine that."

"And if you had that information and you made that determination, what would you then do?"

"What," Jester asked, "would Jay do?"

It was, of course, the only question that now occupied the den. To be fair, it occupied the Chosen as well; the den's Jay was their Terafin.

Finch said, clearly, "Jay's not here." And the absence was felt. "We are. We'll have to take our best guess and proceed from there. She left the House in our hands, and we can't wait until she returns—we don't have the luxury of time. Not in this." She then turned to Haval. "I would appreciate it if political games played in the House not be played in the kitchen; I have enough difficulty with Jarven in the Merchant Authority as it is, and I'm not looking to add to them."

Haval smiled and inclined his head. "Very well. I have some interest in your answer, but you are not, as you point out, my student. Were Jewel present, she would face the same difficulty that I have posed to you all; I believe she would handle it with markedly less grace, but I believe I know what answer she would tender. Daine is one of her den. She would accept the possible future disadvantage if it would preserve his—or any of your—lives.

"I do not believe, however, that the breach in Duvari's security can be laid at the feet of the precautions the House itself takes. This poses a different set of difficulties."

Finch looked predominately relieved; she was already moving to catch up to Haval. "We don't have the information required to give to Duvari."

"Exactly." Haval once again turned to Daine. "And to get that information, we require you to answer the question I initially posed."

Jester glanced at Haval; he said nothing. Haval doubted that anyone else had noticed; they were now watching Daine. Jester had dropped the pretense of boredom; he was listening with just as much care as anyone else in the room. To Haval's surprise, he gestured quickly, the movements of his hand sparse; he might have been drumming the tabletop.

He must be old and out of practice, Haval thought, as he inclined his chin slightly. Too much surprised him, these days. It was not a good sign. Jester had signed: *thanks*.

Daine hesitated.

"Daine," Finch said, once again taking the kitchen's occupants in hand. "We will not kill Vareena."

"Duvari might."

"If Duvari wants her dead, there is nothing you, I, or anyone else can do to preserve her." Finch's voice remained soft; it was only the words themselves that showed an edge.

The healer accepted this as truth, which was unsurprising; it is what Vareena herself would no doubt believe. If she was competent—and in Haval's opinion, she must be—she was twelve; her experience was focused, but lacked depth.

"And if you somehow think you can discover what Vareena didn't discover in time, stop now. Vareena may have been working in isolation in Terafin— but first, I doubt it. I highly doubt it. And second, you are *not* Vareena. You are not *Astari*. You are a part of this den, and we have your back. Don't walk away from us. Don't get lost in Vareena."

Daine reached up and caught Finch's hand. He inhaled, exhaled, and straightened. "I'm sorry. I'm sorry—you're right. I don't understand what happened, and I've been unable to really think about anything else."

Haval nodded. "You are afraid to let the information out; you do not wish to give any warning to enemies that you clearly did not anticipate and cannot identify."

"You should have been *Astari*," Daine replied, wincing.

Haval's expression soured instantly; it was not entirely an act. "I will attempt not to take that as an insult. Given the hour and the urgency of my other duties, I am likely to fail if the statement is ever repeated."

Finch laughed. As Haval's expression grew more pinched, Daine joined her. Teller smiled, but the smile was genuine. Haval allowed them the moment, no more. "We are not your enemies. The only man in this room who has not proved worthy of trust is, in fact, me. If you wish to relay this information in my absence, I will leave."

Daine shook his head. "Someone will tell you anyway. You wouldn't be here if Finch didn't want you here, and I trust her judgment."

Of course you do, Haval thought. He left the words unspoken. "Who almost killed Vareena?"

"Sabienne."

Jester did not look surprised; he was. Everyone in this room knew that Sabienne had thrown her obvious, public support behind Haerrad. Only Jester knew that it was Rymark who had chosen to intervene with the Master of the Household Staff. The name he had expected to hear, given his eavesdropping, was Rymark's.

No one else at the table blinked. "How?" Finch asked.

"Poison."

Jester frowned. Poison—the right poison—could be hidden. It would be very suspicious if a junior maid collapsed and died in service—but the first thought in anyone's mind would not be murder. Yet Rymark had taken it upon himself to visit the Master of the Household Staff—which seemed almost an act of desperation when considered with care.

"That is not the whole of the story," Haval said. "If Vareena collapsed, she would not be taken immediately to the healerie; the Master of the Household Staff would no doubt be summoned first. Yet Vareena was taken to the healerie—and rumors suggest she only barely arrived in time."

"She had been poisoned." Daine's reply was defensive.

"I do not doubt that. What I now doubt is that it was the poison that was responsible for her state."

"It would have been."

"Ah. But it was not."

". . . No."

Jester rose; the motion was almost involuntary.

Sit, Haval gestured. The younger man failed to note the signing—and Haval was not at all certain that this failure was deliberate.

"The poison," Finch said, "I could see. Haerrad has no love for Duvari; he positions himself opposite the *Astari* so loudly it is a wonder that Duvari bothers to send his spies at all. Killing a spy he'd discovered would be, in his mind, a reasonable response—and a safe way of slapping Duvari in the face.

"But if he plays at enmity loudly, he is capable of subtlety; he must know that the girl was not ATerafin, and her death—if Duvari so chose—could open Terafin up to the very type of investigation that would weaken it significantly in the eyes of The Ten. He did not support the current Terafin, but he did not vote against her."

"Only a fool would have done so, after The Terafin's funeral," Haval said.

"Haerrad can be a fool; he is always dangerous, regardless." Finch frowned. "But I don't understand. Sabienne poisoned Vareena—or at least Vareena assumes it was Sabienne; it's unlikely that she saw the poison in use. Did she?"

"It is the only possibility. Sabienne asked for her aid."

"Specifically?"

"No. She met Vareena while returning to her rooms to change; she was to meet a member of the Makers' Guild, and she wished to don appropriate mourning, given the losses the city faced with the destruction of much of the Merchants' Guild. Vareena was concerned; the request, however, seemed reasonable on the surface of things. Sabienne did, indeed, leave Terafin to meet with a member of the Makers' Guild—on House business. I had it checked."

Haval coughed.

Jester resumed his seat. "The reason Haval is coughing," he said, as he examined his fingernails, "is the unusual interest you've shown. How, exactly, did you have this information checked?"

"I sent a page with a message for Sabienne. I did not," Daine added, "send a message in my name—but yes, I approached the page."

"Well, don't in future. Finch and Teller can afford to look suspicious. They are part of this game. You aren't—and you can't afford to be. There's some chance that some members of Terafin don't actually know you're healer-born. Granted, it's small—but it's not zero. The *last* healer that worked openly in this house was assassinated in order to isolate The Terafin. If it worked once before, it might be tried again.

"Don't open yourself up to anything that looks even remotely political. Not now."

"The page returned to say that Sabienne was otherwise engaged."

"Sabienne left Vareena."

"Vareena left Sabienne and returned to her duties—she was seen by other members of the Household Staff after her encounter with Sabienne. She realized what had happened, and attempted to return to the back halls. She collapsed in one of the small rooms used by the serving staff.

"She was found; she was carried elsewhere. At this point, her vision was failing. She is . . . not aware of the injuries she sustained when she lost consciousness."

"The injuries?" Haval asked.

"Were severe. They look to be the work of a madman. There was no possibility that her death could be mistaken for an illness or an accident; it was pointlessly brutal. I consider it a small miracle that the servants who did find Vareena had the presence of mind to call me."

"Wait. They called you—they did not move her?"

Daine hesitated, and then nodded. "I'm sorry. I thought it best—for the House—to claim that she had been carried to the healerie. She was, but only after." He was pale as he closed his eyes. "They had the presence of mind to send someone running to the healerie. I do not think they would have maintained that presence of mind had they been forced to carry Vareena. Her body lacked structural integrity. It's nothing short of a miracle that she survived for as long as she did."

"Have you spoken at any length with the servants who found her?" Haval asked. Jester understood then why Finch had wanted Haval in the kitchen. He asked the questions that had to be asked—questions that would have been very, very difficult for anyone else. It was difficult just listening.

"Only one."

"And that servant?"

"Berald ATerafin. He is one of the senior staff. He won't talk to you, though," Daine said. "The Master of the Household Staff made clear that this incident is closed."

Haval's frown was like a line carved in solid stone; at any other time, Jester would have enjoyed it. But one thought was running through his head, and he could not dislodge it.

Why kill the girl in this fashion if she was already dying? No, that was the wrong question. Why kill the girl in this fashion at all? What would be gained? Slitting her throat would have achieved the same effect: it would make clear that this was incontrovertibly a murder.

Given Daine's information, simple murder was not the end goal. Murder, on its own, upset and unsettled people; it caused existential fear. It caused . . . fear. The injuries done Vareena would cause a depth of fear that a simpler, cleaner death would not.

Fear.

And the attack on the Merchant Authority, the near-slaughter in the Merchants' guildhall, and one isolated spy's death collapsed together, structure shifting, into one clear picture.

Jester rose, and this time Haval did not gesture him back into his chair.

Instead, the clothier rose as well. The words Jester might have said, Haval now took from him, as gracefully, as bloodlessly, as he had carried all of the questions it turned the stomach to even think of asking.

"Henden," Haval said. "Henden of 410." He turned to Teller. "I believe that now would be the time to summon the House Mage."

Torvan rose. He had not spoken a single word to this point; nor had Arrendas. "I'll go."

The date had an effect on every person in the room. On the Captains of the Chosen, one of whom was even now heading for the door; on every member of the den present for this impromptu—but necessary—kitchen meeting. On no one was the effect more pronounced than Finch. Finch had traveled to the Common every day of that Henden. Finch had walked back across the bridge, to the relative sanity of the silence provided by living on the Isle.

Finch still had nightmares in which she was once again sixteen years of age and working with Jarven and Lucille in the Merchant Authority. But in those nightmares, the voices of the tortured dying were voices she recognized. She was, in her nightmares—as she had been in the Henden of 410—powerless.

Facing demons now, she would still be powerless—but not in the same way, please, *Kalliaris*. Never in the same way again.

Jay. Jay, where are you?

There was no answer. But Finch had some experience with both the desperation of the thought and the inevitable silence that followed it. Why? Why now?

She failed to ask the question aloud. "Demons attacked—and attempted to destroy—the Merchants' Guild. They had limited success—but it was limited in large part because of the Order of Knowledge's timely arrival. Losses are still being reported; many of the merchants present during the attack are still being treated for various injuries. The fire that gutted the great hall and a large portion of the building is now known to be magical in nature.

"An attack of this nature on Terafin seems almost too small and too random by comparison." It was an attack that could not have happened had Jay been here. "The Terafin is not in the manse—but great damage could have been done to Terafin—and as a consequence, to Terafin's various concerns; such damage was not even attempted.

"What we know of the intended victim is that she has been a junior member of the Household Staff for a period of approximately a year, and that she was placed on staff by the *Astari*. What purpose would her death serve?" She looked up at Haval. "We need to think like demons."

"I will attempt to take no offense at the direction of your final words."

"None at all was intended. I would say exactly the same to Jarven, were he here."

"I will not remain in this kitchen if you attempt to cajole Jarven to join your meeting."

"That was in no way my intent. I am uncertain why, Haval, but I feel your presence here does not compromise our future safety; I cannot be so certain of Jarven."

"And I have distracted you. A pity. Do please continue."

"How was the *Astari* apprehended? We must assume that Haerrad gathered the information."

"That is in error."

"How so?" Finch intertwined the hands she had placed upon the table's surface.

"One can assume that Haerrad had the information—although even that is a stretch. Sabienne serves his interests, yes, but she does not move in lock-step with Haerrad."

"You don't believe that someone came directly to Sabienne with the information?"

"It is a possibility you must entertain. I think it less likely; Sabienne is far more publicly neutral about the activities of the *Astari* than Haerrad has ever been. If one wished to cause disruption, and one wished that disruption to be certain, it would be better for Haerrad to be the recipient. However, assuming that this is—or was—the case, what does Haerrad have that would induce Sabienne to commit murder?"

"Is this relevant?" Teller asked. He was not as neutral as Haval, but that had never been his way; Finch, who knew him well, knew how much the turn in the conversation had distressed him. But she thought, given Haval, that he would be aware of it as well.

"You would not—any of you—be induced to commit such a murder yourselves."

Jester lifted a hand. "It wouldn't take much to persuade me, given the right target."

"Do not be tiresome. We have some little time before the House Mage presents himself—"

"We may have more time than you think," Arrendas said. "The House Mage is not famously interested in petty politics, and his disinterest can make him quite difficult to find."

"Be that as it may. Consider Sabienne's role and character in this."

"Your own opinion?"

"I have very little to offer. Sabienne is not one of my clients, and her sphere of influence overlaps my own humble shop very seldom. I am not attempting to distract; I am attempting to map out some small number of avenues that indicate the complexity of the situation. If we are dealing, in truth, with the demonic—and I allow it as a very real possibility—some of the complexity can be set aside.

"If we are not—and again, I allow it as a very real possibility—you set it aside at your peril."

Finch exhaled. "Very well. If we are looking at external difficulty, what purpose would it serve? Haerrad—or those in his faction—clearly considered the *Astari* a danger to be disposed of. Assume Haerrad's faction had the information. They did not elect to bring it to the attention of the House Council in Jay's absence.

"It suits everything I know of Haerrad to attempt to deal with the difficulty himself. He might bring it up in future as a measure of his efficiency at protecting the interests of the House from enemies, even if the enemies are within our own ranks." She considered this scenario with care. It was the simplest explanation of the first part of Daine's story.

"If Haerrad had an informant, the informant would be aware of who, precisely, the *Astari* was. If Haerrad's security measures were entirely his own, he would have the same information, regardless." Frowning she glanced at Teller, to see a similar frown etched in the corners of his lips.

He lifted his head, and she ceded the table to him. "Everything would make sense except for the butchery. Finding the collapsed corpse of a junior maid would cause distress among the Household Staff—but little of that distress would communicate itself to Haerrad. Except, of course, for the Master of the Household Staff. I would not have heard of the incident had she not arrived in my office looking like murder itself. It is just possible she thought that I might be responsible for the attempt."

"She's not that much of an idiot," Jester said.

"In the absence of The Terafin, the right-kin's office adopts the responsibilities that would otherwise devolve to the head of the House. She understands the form of hierarchy, and she will follow it if it kills us all. My reaction would probably make clear that I had no hand in—and no knowledge of—Vareena's death."

"She didn't die," Daine said.

"Yes, apologies. Of the attempted assassination. Haerrad is not a man who is intimidated by the Master of the Household Staff; it would practically be beneath him to address her complaints."

On this, everyone could agree.

"A more obvious murder could work to the advantage of the *Astari*—but whatever else one can say about Duvari, I don't believe he would allow his people to be killed simply to cause that kind of difficulty. If Duvari was not the target, we circle around. An obvious murder benefits no one. It certainly doesn't benefit Haerrad or his faction. Haerrad is therefore not the likely target—this won't harm him. It won't come back to him.

"It's too much of a coincidence that Vareena was poisoned—and dying—when this occurred. Haerrad would not have her killed if he had no proof."

"Say rather that Sabienne would not have killed her without same," Finch added. "Haerrad is not a man who feels that the death of a servant has far-reaching consequences."

Teller obviously concurred. "We are agreed, then, that everything makes political sense up to the poisoning."

"Haval?"

"Yes. I might quibble with details, but in this, we are of the same mind."

"I can't believe," Finch said, "that the demon was unaware of her status."

"*Astari?*"

She nodded. "I am almost inclined to believe that the demon itself is some part of Haerrad's information network—at least in this regard. If Haerrad has somehow become aware of Duvari's operations here, that would be a blow to Duvari. But if the leak came not from Terafin, but from within the ranks of the *Astari?*"

Silence. Finch found herself watching Haval, which was fair; Haval was watching her. His glance strayed—in a familiar way—to the rest of the occupants of the kitchen, but when it came to rest, it stopped on her. He reminded her, in many ways, of Jarven. Haval, however, had no sense of humor that Finch could discern. Given the things that generally amused Jarven, this was probably for the better.

"The death would then serve two purposes. It is not—in any way—the type of death that sustains the purely political; it engenders fear, and raises questions about the very people who would otherwise be perceived to benefit from the death."

Haval's brief nod was encouragement. Finch knew she was old enough—powerful enough—not to require it. Or she should have been.

"But those who *did* benefit from the death—those who might have otherwise caused it—will be stymied. They cannot draw attention to themselves; they cannot be certain that one of their own did not, in fact, commit this crime. The servants found Vareena; they brought you, Daine. I would be extremely surprised if the Master of the Household Staff had not had the room in which she was found cleaned—and everything incriminating burned or otherwise destroyed—the minute Vareena was moved."

"That doesn't necessarily aid her, if she wishes to apprehend the person responsible for the death."

"No. But it means that the panic that might otherwise wash over the House itself will be momentarily contained. Haerrad and his faction will be silent. If this is the case, the death will not reach Duvari's ears. But if there had been *no* healer, what then?

"Vareena's body—what remained of it—would be found. It would be seen. Some word, surely, would reach Duvari."

"Word would reach him regardless of the manner of death."

Finch, however, was frowning. "Yes. It would. But no matter how pragmatic Duvari is, this death would not be like any other death. Daine?"

He shuddered and closed his eyes. "No."

"Haval, I have a request to make."

The clothier smiled. "And that request?"

He already knew what it was, Finch thought. But then again, Jarven might have known as well. "Your sources of information are more diffuse than ours."

"If you mean the den's, possibly. If you mean Jarven's, unlikely."

"I meant the den's. I wish to know how many junior servants or minor dignitaries in any of The Ten have likewise perished recently."

"That is not a small request, ATerafin."

"No. If this death was aimed above our heads at Duvari, it might serve two purposes. If it is just within Terafin, it implies—heavily—that there are demons within Terafin, *and* that they serve the House interests."

"Dangerous. Historical examples of butchery exist absent demons."

"Yes. The second reason we are now waiting upon the House Mage. If there are demons within Terafin and The Terafin is not here, it opens the House to the inspection of the magi and the Mysterium. If the intent is to weaken the House in the absence of its ruler, and to strike at Duvari, this accomplishes both goals."

"If there is a demon."

"Given the week we've had, Haval, I would be very surprised if no demonic presence was found. I remember Henden," she added, voice hardening. "And I remember what the demons wanted from us: Fear. Despair. Horror. And we gave it to them because we're human. I *hated* to react the way they wanted. It felt like a loss.

"But to have no reaction to something like this is, in the end, the greater loss."

Jester, however, was frowning. He glanced at Daine, whose eyes were still closed.

Finch gestured.

Jester's hands remained motionless. His expression was unreadable, not because it was as neutral and masklike as Haval's, but because there was too much in it to easily find one overriding reaction. Jester was thinking and didn't particularly care for any of the resultant possibilities.

But she knew him well enough—if anyone did—to discern one thing. "Whatever you're sitting on, share it. There are times to go it alone. This isn't one of them. Jay's not here. We have what we had when she went to the South: each other. What I'm afraid we don't have is a margin for error."

"The Master of the Household Staff knew."

"Pardon?"

"She knew that Vareena was *Astari*."

Truth?

Yes. Truth.

"Teller?"

"She didn't say as much to me. At all. I think she expected me to have some idea of why Vareena had been attacked. If you're asking if I agree with Jester, I have to say yes. Yes, I think she did know."

"She wouldn't have passed that information to Haerrad."

Teller shook his head. "She has enormous respect for hierarchy—but so does Barston, and they can't stand each other. Haerrad has no respect at all for the Master of the Household Staff. She might, if she had the information and was concerned, take it to Iain—but in the end, I doubt she would. The Household Staff is hers. She would take care of the difficulty—by ejecting the servant—on her own. She wouldn't surrender sovereignty to the House Council where it concerned the Household Staff."

That was Finch's read, as well. And Vareena had clearly *not* been ejected. "How did she know?"

Jester shrugged. "The most obvious explanation is that she knew from the start."

Finch cursed—mostly with her hands. "This is not something we need."

"There are members of the House who were accepted as Terafin even though they were *Astari*," Jester pointed out.

"I'm aware of that. If it weren't for the disaster that befell the Merchants' Guild, I'd be speaking with one of them now. But having a member of the Royal Trade Commission who only barely keeps rooms in the manse work side-by-side with the *Astari* is in no way equivalent to having the Master of the Household Staff be in league with them—if that's what you're suggesting."

"There is no way that woman is *Astari*," Jester replied, folding arms across the back of his chair and leaning into them with his chin. "She owes loyalty—obvious, open, unquestionable loyalty—to *Terafin*. Nothing will change that short of her death. Or, you know, everyone else's, which is probably more likely."

"But you think she knew."

"I *know* she knew," Jester replied. "She told me. Where by 'told' I mean bit my head off in cold, crisp fury at the incompetence of our den. Daine, for saving Vareena's life; me for being enraged by word of her injuries. She made clear that Alowan would have let the girl die."

Daine was uncharacteristically quiet. Finch expected him to leap to

Alowan's defense; when he didn't, she accepted Jester's opinion as truth. It was unsettling, but not beyond belief.

"Daine, what did she say to you?"

Daine swallowed. "She said that only with very, very careful maneuvering could we avoid being plunged into a war we could not win. And she told me never to interfere with the Household Staff again without her direct permission." He hesitated, and then added, "Even Vareena found her terrifying."

"That's the first sensible thing I've heard about Vareena." Finch wanted to let her hair down—literally. The more pronounced, expensive netting was pulled too tight, and she was suffering predictable end-of-day headaches. "Does it matter if we think she hired Vareena strongly suspecting her affiliations? Does it change the parameters of the issue we're facing in any way?"

"Not ours, no," Teller replied—when no one else did. "We expect that Duvari places his spies within each of The Ten Houses; probably further. I would like to know why Vareena was not dismissed if the Master of the Household Staff was certain—but that's a problem for the future. The problem for now is that we have a twelve-year-old *Astari* who probably wants both herself and her healer dead. That, and the possible presence of a demon who is attempting to wave a huge banner which proudly proclaims his existence.

"Jay will lose all her hair if the Master of the Household Staff quits before she returns. Or quits at all. I don't actually see Jay being upset about Vareena-as-*Astari*."

"She will not," Haval interjected, "be best-pleased."

"No. But she wouldn't have the girl killed; she might have her tailed, and she might put her in the way of disinformation. If," Jester added darkly, "she had ever been informed." No one at the table thought that that information would have been forthcoming from the Master of the Household Staff.

Finch's eyes narrowed. She was on the edge of exhaustion; she was not at her best. "Jester."

He met, and held, her gaze.

"There's something else."

"Yes. There is." He smiled. It was a lazy smile. "If it's true that Sabienne was likely responsible for the poison—and would have therefore been responsible for Vareena's death without intervention, something makes no sense to me. I told you that Master of the Household Staff told me, in no uncertain terms, that she considers us all incompetent. She didn't give me a plan for avoiding future ugliness; she didn't make clear what she thought that ugliness would be. I assume she's concerned with Duvari's possible reaction.

"But the thing that makes no sense," he said, given the subtle shift in the line of Finch's mouth, "is that Rymark ATerafin approached the Master of the Household Staff and pretty much laid claim to responsibility for the girl's death. He knew she was *Astari* as well."

"Rymark ATerafin." The word dropped like a stone—a big, ugly stone—into still water. Arendas stiffened in his chair; he refrained from speaking. If he wasn't here as Chosen, he wasn't here as den; he occupied a space between the two.

"Rymark," Teller said, "would never claim responsibility for a death if it didn't give him a strong political advantage."

"No. And there's no advantage to be gained by this. And the girl's not dead."

"Is he aware of that?"

"Apparently he wasn't when he spoke with the Master of the Household Staff; she didn't choose to enlighten him, either." He shrugged. "She may have accepted his claim of responsibility; it's unlikely Vareena told her anything, so she's unlikely to have other feet to lay it at. She was about as happy as you'd expect." Jester rose. He paced along the kitchen wall.

"So: Sabienne knew that Vareena was *Astari*. And Rymark knew. That implies that either Sabienne has switched allegiance and is now working with Rymark, or that both Haerrad and Rymark had the same source of information."

Finch nodded, but withheld her opinion on which was more likely. It was very seldom that she saw Jester think. He frequently claimed that thought was too much work—and for the most part, in Jester's life, it was. But he had always been observant.

"I think it unlikely that Sabienne would choose to support Rymark's faction at this point in the game. Faction is too strong a word; there *is* a sitting Terafin, and given the obvious presence of demons, she's a compelling one. She can't, to my mind, be killed by the common—or uncommon—assassin. Elonne and Marrick have accepted that."

"Haerrad and Rymark have not."

"Neither has made any open or overt moves since she took the chair."

"No. If someone who was considered trustworthy were to approach either Elonne or Marrick with the information that Vareena was *Astari,* I very much doubt they would have acted. They may—or may not—have chosen to share that information with The Terafin."

"Who isn't here."

"Who isn't here. They would not, to my mind, have had her killed."

"You think someone gave that information to all of them?"

"I think it's possible. Haerrad and Rymark are the only two who might have taken the bait." Yet he frowned as he said it. "But—it doesn't make sense. Neither of them would have slaughtered her in an obvious, horrific way."

"Let's go back to the demon hypothesis," Finch said. "Assume that there is at least one demon within the manse. He would have to have arrived before Jay returned, or after she left again. But I think it has to be the latter."

"Why?"

"Because she claimed she could sense demons on her land, and Vareena was killed—was almost killed, I'm sorry, Daine—on her land. If the demon had been here before she chose to meet with the Oracle, I think she would have known."

Teller nodded.

"Which means the demon would have arrived only after her departure. Jay's departure isn't public knowledge, yet. It will be; there's no way to avoid that—but it's not open knowledge. Had this occurred three weeks from now, it would trouble me just as much—but confuse me less. The demon is almost certainly a new arrival. But he is a new arrival who could ask for, and expect to receive, the ear of at least two members of the House Council.

"And that, at the moment, terrifies me. Jester, stop pacing or I'll start. We've faced this before: the demons can, and do, look human. They can—and have—occupied living people, using them as a disguise. The person in question could well have been a loyal and upstanding member of the House Council—of the House itself. If the demon were at all careful, there would be no suspicion. And Jay's not here." Jay could see the strangeness.

"I could tell you," Daine said quietly, "who the demons are. I would need physical contact with them."

Finch shook her head. "We have a House Mage for that. You can be decapitated in an eyeblink—and Meralonne can't. I'm not sure death would take him if he offered himself, weaponless, with open arms."

"That is harsh," the mage in question said. He was standing, unlit pipe in hand, in the doorway; no one had heard the door open.

Finch managed, with effort, not to glare at his pipe as he lit it and sauntered—there was no other word for his movement—into the kitchen. Jester resumed his seat. Finch indicated that the mage should take a chair, but without much hope. Meralonne was, in all ways, like a cat. He did as he pleased; you could possibly cajole him or bribe him or distract him—but command? No.

Meralonne surprised Finch; he sat. "To my thinking, you have overlooked one possibility."

"I've probably overlooked two dozen."

"None of any significance."

"How long have you been listening in?"

"Only long enough—thanks to the impatience of your captain—to hear the last string of suppositions."

"Do you believe a demon could be planted here?"

"Yes; they have already demonstrated that ability." He blew smoke rings as he tilted his chair back on two legs and propped his slippered feet on the table. "Consider this scenario: Rymark is aware that the demon is present. It is just possible that Rymark is attempting to claim responsibility for the death because he is afraid of compromising either himself or the demon in question."

"What would the demon gain?"

Meralonne smiled. "Pain. Sustenance."

"Not from that death," was Daine's quiet, intense rejoinder. "She was unconscious throughout."

"Ah, now that *would* be frustrating. There have been no similar deaths?"

"None." None yet, Finch thought, grim now.

Haval exhaled. "Very well. You have always suspected that it was Rymark who was responsible for the demon that killed Amarais Handernesse ATerafin."

No one in the room spoke for one long beat. When someone broke the silence, it was Jester. "We didn't suspect," he said. "We *knew*."

"It would not, then, be a stretch to say that Rymark is aware of—possibly in league with—demons?"

"None."

"Do you assume that Rymark is the summoner?" Haval's question was flat, unadorned.

"We don't exactly know much about demonology—it's a *forbidden art*."

"I believe Finch is attempting to keep Terafin on the right side of Sigurne's famous vendetta against the ancient arts of summoning and control," Meralonne said.

"Finch," was her reply, "is merely being honest."

Meralonne raised one platinum brow, which had the effect of making him appear to be even more dismissive. "A pity. If you are certain that the demon who assassinated The Terafin was there at Rymark's behest, than Rymark was the summoner."

"He could have been working with—"

Meralonne waved pipe smoke in her direction. "Do not mince words. What should, at this point, be your chief concern is this: Rymark would not have chosen the manner of attack that *was* chosen. Either he has summoned a demon beyond his control—which would in almost all circumstances cause his death—or he is not the summoner.

"But he is aware that the demon is present—and he does not wish its presence to be revealed. It may be that he has chosen to serve The Terafin, and to cut ties with former allies." His smile was slender; he was amused. "And he is discovering that those ties are binding in ways he had not foreseen. If he does not control this creature—and it seems clear to me that he does not— who does?

"And why was it sent here?"

"It was sent," Arann said quietly, "Because Jay's not here."

"Yes. If they are attempting to destroy the economic wheels of the city by killing all of its significant merchants, they are no longer attempting to hide their presence; they have come in force. Now."

"Because Jay is absent?"

"That is my supposition. I will look for your demon. It seems clear to me that, if you desire that information, the fastest way to get it is through Rymark ATerafin himself."

Finch shook her head. "Haerrad had that information. Which means that the demon will—no doubt—be masquerading as someone Haerrad is willing to trust."

"Haerrad," Jester said, "trusts no one. He may consider the source of information reliable." He rose.

"Where are you going?"

"Drinking with Marrick," Jester replied. He did not look like he was in much of a mood for carousing. "If Marrick was given the same information, it will have come from the same source—and we'll know that they were targeting specific individuals on the House Council. The ones with significant power.

"If Marrick doesn't know, so much the better. Haval, will you do as Finch requested?"

Haval nodded quietly. "I am concerned," he said at last. "I feel that you have been intellectually thorough, given the information at hand. Demons are very like the mage-born in their abilities. The West Wing—and its kitchens—are secure; no information will escape into the wrong hands from here. Not magically. But the servants clean, and they require access.

"The information therefore comes from somewhere. Vareena was not a normal child. Duvari doesn't allow untrained children into his service. She would therefore be both pragmatic and careful; it is unlikely—in my opinion—that she was to do more than listen to servant gossip while doing her duties as a junior maid."

"She wasn't a maid," Daine said.

"Apologies."

"She was too junior."

Finch winced, and caught one of Daine's hands in hers; he crushed it. She focused most of her attention on Haval. "In other words, her duties as a probable spy were very, very light."

"Yes. I believe the first order of business is to find—and dispose of—the demon, if it exists."

Meralonne blew rings. Concentric rings.

"The demon's presence here is more problematic. The demons, however, are straightforward. I assume that he is to prepare for Jewel's return, and to kill her the moment she sets foot on these grounds."

Finch exhaled; she was almost out of patience. "It's been tried, Haval. And given the guildmaster's reaction—the Guildmaster of the Order of Knowledge—if the last big demon didn't succeed, nothing will."

"Yes. That is my concern." He turned to the very indolent mage. "Member APhaniel?"

"I will attempt to ferret out your demon. If you are asking in a roundabout way why the demons might expect, with preparation, to have greater success this time, you fail to understand what Jewel is, and where the manse itself is situated. This is understandable; I do not believe Jewel herself fully realizes it. It is willful, expensive ignorance.

"She is not invulnerable. If control, however brief, can be wrested from the absent Terafin, what she faces will not be a single demon, no matter how powerful; it will be a small army.

"It is not clear to me that Rymark ATerafin is fully ignorant of these plans. He is a man who is concerned with both his own survival and the power he can accrue while accomplishing it. He is aware of the power that a god—even a hobbled one—wields. He may—"

"Wish to commit to both sides, and await the outcome of that battle?" Finch asked. Her hands were shaking.

"It would be the prudent course of action." Meralonne's smile was slender and cold. In spite of this, it was clear that he found Rymark amusing.

Finch didn't.

"You are angry, ATerafin."

She said nothing.

"You are not the only one whom this attitude angers. It is my guess that Rymark has been given the opportunity to fully commit. If he fails to make that commitment in a fashion that satisfies his former allies, they will force him to do so by revealing his connections to the demons, thus giving him little choice. He is unlikely to survive for long if Sigurne has any proof—at all—that he has too great a knowledge of the forbidden arts.

"He has survived thus far because he has been adept at keeping these activities hidden. Should a demon wish to threaten Rymark, this is how he would do it." Meralonne frowned.

Probably because Haval was.

"The demon is not preternaturally omniscient. If we assume that demons do not require food, shelter or sleep, they are nonetheless wed to physical form. They cannot—without magic—pass through walls; what I have seen or heard of demons implies that if they did, there would no longer be a wall. How, then, did this possible demon have the information about Vareena?"

"You are certain it was correct?"

Finch said, curtly, "Yes." She didn't want to have the same conversation a second time; not with pipe smoke driving clean air out of the kitchen.

Haval stood. "You will excuse me, Finch. Teller. Jester, I would like your aid. If I am to return to my shop for a period of a few days, I cannot leave the fabric and tools here."

"Going out drinking, remember?"

"And far be it for an old man to interfere with your evening of pleasure; it will not take much time."

Finch's eyes narrowed; she said nothing. She was surprised—and uneasy—when Jester shrugged and followed. She didn't dwell on it. She was now concerned about many other things.

Well, two. Daine and Teller.

"Daine, I want you to remain in the West Wing. I understand why you took up residence in the healerie—and why Jay let you. But there were no demons here when Jay left, and she wouldn't have let you out of her sight if she'd even suspected they'd be here."

"She doesn't live in the West Wing," Daine pointed out.

"Yes. But I do. I want you here. These are—with the possible exception of the right-kin's office and The Terafin's personal chambers—the most secure rooms in the manse. We don't have House Guards; the only guards here are Chosen."

He looked as if he would argue; Finch could see, clearly, that he wanted to do so. But he was exhausted. His color was horrible; his hands—and his shoulders—were shaking. He was terrified for Vareena, and afraid *of* her as well. She caught his free hand in hers and drew him round to face her. "We won't survive this," she said, "if you die. They couldn't kill The Terafin until they'd killed Alowan first. Things are not normal. You can argue with Jay when she returns. But don't argue with me. Please. I don't think I could stand it tonight." When Daine failed to reply, she said, "Captains, please—escort Daine to the healerie to collect anything he might need."

They nodded. They were grimmer by far than they had been. They didn't, however, move. They exchanged one silent glance before Torvan rose and addressed not Finch, but Teller.

"Before you all adjourn, we would like to discuss your current guard rotations."

Finch gently helped Daine out of his chair.

"Apologies, Finch—but that was a plural 'you.' Teller's detail would have been considered acceptable a scant five years ago. Yours is nonexistent. You have protection *only* when you are in the West Wing; you do not have protection of any note traveling to—or from—the Merchant Authority."

She opened her mouth, but before she could speak, Haval chuckled. She looked at him. It was hard to tell what Haval was thinking at any given time, but she was *almost* certain he was genuinely amused.

"You have been given the opportunity that any responsible leader dreads," he told her. "You are being asked to lead by example."

Torvan and Arrendas exchanged another glance. If they were amused, it didn't show. "We're not asking," Torvan said quietly. "We would prefer that neither of you elect to humiliate the Chosen by refusing to cooperate with the changing of guard—but we will accept humiliation if there is no other way to carry out our duties."

Finch opened her mouth again.

"If Rymark is being pressured to somehow demonstrate commitment, ATerafin, there are very few significant ways in which he could accomplish this. He cannot assassinate The Terafin; she is not present. He can attempt to take control of the House in her absence.

"The only way to do that is to kill both of you. Neither of you are The Terafin; The Terafin left us strict orders which you do not have the authority to countermand. We will now follow them to the letter."

Finch nodded, as if this was not unexpected. In truth, it wasn't. She had called Torvan and Arrendas in for a reason—her reason largely being Teller.

But she knew that Teller would accept what she would accept, if reluctantly. She was concerned, and growing steadily more so, about Teller.

She lifted a hand and laid it against the table, signaling an end to the meeting. "When you work out the details, inform us. We will do our best to keep you apprised of our movements, should those movements shift."

Torvan nodded. He didn't salute. But Finch was fairly certain that formality would, as of this evening, be added to their routine. She glanced at Arann; his hands moved briefly, but he smiled. It was his usual, quiet smile—but Finch was almost surprised to see it.

She returned it, even though her head was pounding. "Thank you, gentlemen." She was not entirely looking forward to work in the morning, because Jarven would be in what he cheerfully described as transition.

Jarven would be at the head of the Merchants' Guild, unless something was done. She had some idea of what that something would be.

"ATerafin," The pipe-smoking mage said. "With your permission, I will now begin a hunt of my own within these halls. Inform the Household Staff that they are not to interfere."

"The Household Staff is unlikely to interfere with you under any circumstance."

He nodded, bored. "Indeed. They will summon the House Guard. Who will, in turn, summon the Chosen. The Chosen and I have our routines in place; we understand each other. I will not, however, be guaranteed the luxury of waiting upon the chain of Terafin's command if you are to see the demon apprehended or destroyed. It is not clear to me that the demon would choose to remain within the manse."

"Jay's not here."

"No, she is not. She is not, however, completely ineffectual; there are rudimentary protections built into the earth upon which the manor stands. I do not know the extent to which those protections are allowed free rein—but it is best to proceed with caution. I am the first line of defense."

Finch was never going to escape the kitchen. She drew her shoulders back, lifting her chin in almost unconscious imitation of the former ruler of the House. "I have seen you fight," she said, voice cool. "And I wish the manor and its various walls to remain standing. The repair of the foyer the last time you let loose within the manse was fiscally ruinous."

White brows rose; pipe smoke trailed from bowl rather than lips.

There was a tense, still silence. Finch raised one brow, as Haval so often did.

The mage *laughed*. "You may recall that on that one occasion my intervention preserved The Terafin's life," he said, his grin wide and disturbingly youthful.

"I do. But The Terafin is not here. There are—at least that we know of—no gods present, either. Should a god happen to enter our foyer, I will repent of the harshness and inflexibility of my command."

"Command."

"Command." She inclined her chin. "We face one demon, possibly two. I have confidence that you can manage them with a minimum of structural damage."

Jester allowed Haval to open the door to his wretchedly messy workroom; he followed the old man in. Haval also closed the door.

"You really are paranoid, you know that?"

"It has served me well," Haval replied. "It will serve you equally well should you adopt similar, basic precautions."

Jester nodded. "You want to speak with me?"

"Yes. I did not, however, lie; I will spend some time in my shop. It is a far better conduit for the general information Finch seeks. You will speak with Marrick?"

"Yes, and possibly Elonne; she's not particularly fond of me."

"I cannot imagine why."

"Will you speak with Duvari?"

Haval pinched the bridge of his nose. "That is not the way these conversations are conducted."

"That isn't a no."

"Neither is it a yes. I am unwilling—at this moment—to approach Duvari directly; you have access to Devon ATerafin, and I suggest you use it."

"Not my access," Jester replied. "If we're desperate, Finch will speak to him—but she's not kidding. Every element of the Merchanting in this city has been thrown into total disarray; Devon is extremely busy. I believe he is currently resident in *Avantari* for the duration."

Haval shrugged. It was almost a mirror of the gesture that defined Jester on most days. "Allow me to point out that I consider this, in its entirety, to be your problem. Yours personally."

"Haval—you implied that you might actually train me."

"Yes. I did. Consider this the first of your assignments."

"This is hardly training."

"It is, in the end, the only training of value. I would hold your hand if you were a child younger than Vareena. You are not. We are both aware that there are other methods of approach should you feel it necessary."

Jester had had a long week. He did not see an end to it in the near future. "You believe that Duvari's *Astari* have been compromised."

Haval said nothing. He began to gather bolts of cloth and straps that contained both pins and needles of various sizes. He gathered threads and beads as well; Jester had never been fond of beading. "Do you believe it?"

Did he? Jester began to gather beads that had escaped their containers; there were more than a few. "It depends."

"On what?"

"On the information you can ferret out."

"Do you gamble?"

"Yes."

"Gamble now."

"Yes." Before Haval could ask for embellishment, Jester continued. "Yes, I think there's a very high probability that Duvari's *Astari* have been compromised. I don't know enough about demons to tell you how."

"And you don't wish to dwell on what you do know."

"It's too much work."

Haval's eyes narrowed; Jester thought he was actually annoyed. It was a symptom of the day that this made Jester feel triumphant, but he kept it to himself. Or maybe not: Haval was a sharp man.

"Let me tell what I know," Jester said. "It's probably all old news to you if you've grilled Jay."

"I have, of course, spoken with Jewel about her past experiences. I would be pleased to hear what you've observed."

Jester began to talk as he worked. By the time he was halfway done, given Haval's intent questions, he had mentally rescheduled his plans to spend an evening getting pleasantly drunk with Marrick ATerafin.

Chapter Fourteen

9th of Morel, 428 A.A.
Terafin Manse, Averalaan Aramarelas

BIRGIDE VIRANYI WAS OCCUPIED in the gardens behind the Terafin manse. She had accepted employment with the Terafin Master Gardener, and if he respected her knowledge and ability—and he did—he also considered her his hierarchical inferior. She did not, in any way, attempt to rise above her given station; she accepted it. In no other way would she be given access to the Terafin grounds. She had been in situations in which she was treated with far less respect; inasmuch as she could be, she was content.

Or she had been.

She looked up, and up again, to the boughs of the great trees that made a forest of the estate. She knew—better than almost anyone alive—that the Kings' trees did not grow in any soil but the soil of the Common. When her expertise in flora was not required by the *Astari*, she studied clippings, leaves, even the exposed roots of the Kings' trees. She had thrice been granted royal permission to secure their living branches—at considerable expense to the Order of Knowledge. It was said that there wasn't a plant that the Viranyi woman could not grow.

She had not expected to like The Terafin, and regretted it. Although Birgide was no longer young enough to believe that all power must be inherently evil, she understood that all power was a weapon; sometimes it was sheathed, sometimes it was not. Weapons could be turned in any direction the wielder chose. At most, one could hope to have influence in the choice of the wielder—but people were changeable. Treacherous, yes—but not all treachery was a product of greed; at times it was a product of love, of fear, of a desire for greatness.

Which was, of course, irrelevant. Birgide bent to pick up a single, white-fringed leaf; it was larger than her hand. She had not seen it fall. Its stem was too strong, too green, for that; she heard no wind in the leaves above.

But this one leaf had fallen nonetheless, and it had fallen at her feet.

Birgide Viranyi had spent a fruitless decade in an attempt to grow the Kings' trees in any other soil but that of the Common; she had even taken that soil with her in her attempts in the North, the Western Kingdoms, and the Southern Terreans of the Dominion. No amount of attention, of care, no base analysis of the soil or the conditions that surrounded it, had yielded success; the failure had stung her pride.

Over the years, the sting faded. She could not, therefore, explain her continued attempts; she considered herself one of nature's pragmatists. She considered the odds of success—after a multitude of failures, some public and some private, depending on needed funds—close to zero. And that, of course, was as large a lie as she allowed herself. Lies were meant to face outward, like a mask; no one wise turned lies inward.

What Birgide had failed to do, The Terafin had done in the course of one evening, without conscious thought or deliberation. Where Birgide had cajoled or commanded the aid of both magi and maker-born, The Terafin had relied—in all measured reports—on nothing.

It would have been hard for anyone in Birgide's position not to envy the woman. Harder for many not to resent her. Perhaps in her youth, Birgide would have done so. But youth had led to this place, this forest that seemed endless, although it was bound on all sides by the properties of those powerful enough to claim a permanent home upon the Isle. The grounds overlooked by the Terafin manse would not have been considered significantly large anywhere but the Isle.

Dimensions did not appear to make a difference. The forest in which these trees were situated was far larger—on the inside—than the grounds marked in the archival maps contained within *Avantari*. Such maps were not always precise, but no plausible lack of precision could explain away the difference in perceived size.

So, Birgide thought. This was magic.

She was, of course, familiar with magic. She was familiar with its use, although she was not, herself, talent-born; she had spent many of her formative years as a student in the Order of Knowledge. And many more as a member of the *Astari*. Nothing she had learned in the Order's many halls had prepared her for this.

But nothing, she thought, would. Sigurne Mellifas feared that this—this inexplicable forest that existed in a space it could not possibly occupy— might become the new norm; that events to the West, beyond the Free Towns, implied that such changes were already occurring. Sigurne argued that The Terafin was not the cause of such transformations—that the events within and around Terafin were simply precursors. Early warnings.

Duvari did not trust Sigurne.

He was, however, inclined to believe that she did not lie. This did not mean she could not be in error. He had made clear—to Devon, to Gregori, to Birgide, and to the two who served in the back halls—that they were to establish reasonable grounds for acceptance of—or rejection of—Sigurne's report.

Birgide did not feel that Devon was objective enough. Duvari, on the other hand, was so famously narrow in his suspicion that simple objectivity often looked like dissent. She did not confer with Devon ATerafin while she worked in the grounds; nor did she cross paths with Gregori.

She had not, in fact, been informed who the *Astari*-planted servants on the Household Staff were; nor had she asked. She was relatively certain that neither Devon nor Gregori knew, either. They were not, at the moment, her chief concern.

The forest was. The forest, and now, the single leaf she held in the palm of her hand. She had gathered leaves before, both here and in the Common; this one was different. She could see no reason why it might have fallen; the stem was too new.

Birgide did not believe in fate. Nor did she believe in lucky coincidence; in her experience, coincidence of a fortuitous nature was generally the product of an enormous amount of work, planning, and execution.

None of which explained The Terafin's forest. None of which explained the shadows cast by the Kings' trees. Had she somehow cobbled together a dry and academic explanation for either—and she was certain that she could, although it would take an enormous amount of thought and work—she could not likewise create an explanation that would encompass storybook trees of silver, gold, and diamond. She could explain the artifice used to create one of each, although the cost to do so would be staggering, in Birgide's opinion.

To explain the artifice in creating a small forest of each, no.

Yet even these paled in comparison to the lone tree of fire that burned at the heart of these woods. That tree did not shed leaves. It shed warmth. Birgide had not—yet—been foolish enough to touch the actual branches, although she had poked one or two cautiously with both wood and glass. The wood did not, to her surprise, burn; the glass did not melt.

But she was certain if she was willing to visit indignity upon such a tree, she could cook over its fire, or beneath it.

She had found this tree on her third day of exploration.

And on that day she had surrendered the pragmatic—for a long, hushed, hour—to the wonder and the growing sense of awe she felt.

Birgide had never truly belonged anywhere. Her interests, her focus, and her travel had made it difficult to find or make lifelong friends—but she had not required them, and did not generally note their absence. She was fully capable of fitting in anywhere she chose.

Or she had been.

She was aware, in this forest of silver and gold, standing beneath the burning branches of a tree that defied reason, that she could not fit in here. It was ironic. She had made the study of unusual flora her life's work; if there was anywhere she should feel at home, it was in a forest.

But not this one.

Something about this forest reminded Birgide of The Terafin.

"The Terafin," a familiar voice said, "created that tree. I think it's the only tree here that she created deliberately."

Birgide turned as Jester ATerafin sauntered toward her. The dark circles beneath his eyes implied an appalling lack of either sleep or self-restraint. "I did not expect to see you here," was her neutral reply. She was disturbed by his presence; Birgide had not heard even the hint of footfall.

"No?" He shrugged. "I, on the other hand, would have been surprised to find you anywhere else."

She smiled, acknowledging a hit. Birgide found Jester ATerafin difficult. He professed to be lazy and unambitious—and she agreed with this assessment, to a point. Nothing she had seen in her time in Terafin led her to believe that there were reserves of commitment and dedication that Jester kept carefully hidden. He was not political, and although he was one of Finch ATerafin's advisers, the quality of his advice was dubious.

She did not consider him a threat. And yet, he was perceptive, in his fashion; he was cautious in a way that implied competence.

"Have you heard the news?" he asked, clasping his hands loosely behind his back as he turned his unfortunately pale face toward the fire.

"I doubt it. I've been in the forest." She lifted the single, fallen leaf. "I am perhaps not attending to the duties for which I'm being paid. Is it news that will amuse or enlighten me in some fashion?"

"You've heard about the events at the Merchants' Guild?"

Not amusement, then. She nodded. "One could not fail to hear of those events unless one were no longer breathing. Have all of the surviving Terafin merchants returned?"

"The right-kin has their reports; the Guildmaster of the Order of Knowledge had them transcribed for us."

"That's unusual."

He grinned. "Guillarne made clear that he was unwilling to describe the events at the guildhall if a transcription of the entire interrogation was not given to him personally."

That very much fit with what she knew of Guillarne.

"He knew he'd have to answer all of the questions a second—or third or fifth—time, and *his* time is of value." The grin faded.

Birgide nodded. "You said that The Terafin created this tree?"

He laughed. "Rumors of demons, magery, and unheard-of slaughter do not engage your interest?"

She grinned "You mentioned the tree to distract me."

"I did. And I shouldn't have—but I couldn't resist." His smile faded. "I have a question to ask. I have danced around how I might ask it; I have even considered anonymity."

Interesting. "And you want an answer in return for the information about this tree of fire?"

"No. I don't know much more than what I've already told you—and that's not worth barter. One of the junior servants was attacked in the manse yesterday."

She was silent for a beat. Jewel's closest allies took an interest in the Household Staff; the Household Staff took an interest in them. It was unusual, but not unheard of. News about an attack would therefore reach the den swiftly.

"The attack occurred because the servant—Vareena—is a member of the *Astari.*"

Birgide did not waste time dissembling. Jester had made no accusation. He left her nothing to deny. She considered removing him and decided against it; Jester was not a man who showed initiative. If he was here, he was here at the behest of another. Given the absence of The Terafin, Birgide could think of very few who had the ability to send Jester on an errand of this nature. Finch ATerafin, perhaps; she had both the authority and the political power. "Vareena survived?"

"Yes."

"Is she still in the ranks of the Household Staff?"

"For the moment, yes."

"What do you want?"

"In exchange for Vareena?"

Birgide shook her head. "Duvari does not barter for careless operatives. If Vareena were to be tortured for information, she would offer very little of value; she would be unlikely to survive the attempt. I would expect you to understand this; it is therefore not to return Vareena that you have come."

Jester nodded as well. He was, to her surprise, frowning at the leaf in her hand.

"It fell of its own accord," Birgide said. "I am aware that I require permission to remove anything—at all—from the forest."

"The Master Gardener has probably given you carte blanche."

She smiled. "Yes. But there is almost a sentience in this forest, and I do not wish to anger it."

"You think the trees are *sentient?*" he asked, astonished.

"You have trees of silver, gold, and diamond, ATerafin. Sentience is somehow a stretch for you?" She lifted a hand to branches of fire. "If these trees had mouths with which to speak, they would speak; I am almost certain of it. Do you wander this forest often?"

"No. I don't dislike it, but there are no taverns, bards, or amusing people in it. To listen to rumor, sometimes there are demons. And worse. I try to avoid them," he added.

She glanced at him; his perpetual grin was absent. "You haven't answered my question."

"About what I want?"

"At least you remembered it. I am attempting to discern what you want, ATerafin. I do not believe this was entirely your idea."

"I'm hurt."

"Not noticeably." She started to speak, and stopped. This was a conversation it was unwise to have. "When you say demons entered this forest—"

Jester ran his hands through red, red hair. "I've only got The Terafin's explanation—and frankly, I'm not a mage."

"The Terafin is not notably available to be questioned by people who are."

"Have you *spent* any time with actual mages?"

She couldn't repress a smile. "My work as a botanist does not demand it."

"She's spent a fair amount of time with the Order's guildmaster."

"I was not aware of that. Before you ask, I am generally unaware of most information that does not directly impact my duties."

Jester watched the tree of fire for a long moment; its flames, which consumed nothing, were silent. "We will release Vareena. I don't believe she will survive, otherwise." He was silent for another long moment—and Jester was not generally silent. Birgide knew; he had followed her around in her various inspections like a chattering, bored dilettante. Had the majority of his many, many questions not shown a hint of genuine curiosity and an intelligence he seemed to resent, she would have found some way to discourage his company.

But she understood that he was suspicious; it was natural. She accepted the suspicion because she was not here on Duvari's orders; she was here for almost purely personal reasons. But she had been in Duvari's service for most of her life—and one did not simply discard the habits of a lifetime, no matter what else one might be doing.

She glanced at the leaf in her hand. The habit, she thought, with some rue, of a lifetime. She had come halfway across the continent—at speed—because of the *Ellariannatte*. She had come to study this miracle—and in so doing, had discovered others: the silver, the gold, and the diamond. She had discovered the tree of fire. She had discovered three delicate wildflowers that she had never encountered before, in any of her many treks. She had been given permission to take samples, and she had potted several.

None survived an hour outside of this forest. She could not test her theory by taking them to the Common—where they would eventually be trampled by small children, if not malice—because they had not survived that journey. There was much, indeed, that was magical in this forest.

She had walked into story.

As a child, she had daydreamed beneath the boughs of old trees; as an adult, she studied them. She was a pragmatist. How, then, to explain the hush of the awe invoked by places such as this? She had often walked in that hush like a hopeful child; she worked, but when her eyes were caught by unexpected shadows, she turned, caught in the moment by echoes of her childhood. Life had been grim; forests had been her only escape.

She had not come to this one seeking escape. She had come, she said, seeking knowledge. She knew that she could sell her field notes to fully two dozen of the magi in the Order of Knowledge—for she had been given permission they had been denied. She wouldn't even have to endure their condescension, they would be so eager.

What they wanted was not so different, in the end. They wanted to walk into story. She closed her eyes. "What do you want?"

"I want there to be no reprisals," he replied.

She frowned. She did not dislike Jester, and knew that she should pay this conversation more attention; had she been standing anywhere else, she would have. "Do you not feel," she said, ignoring the words he had forced himself to speak, "that you walk in story?"

When he failed to answer, she turned; he was staring at her, arrested.

"Have I surprised you?"

"I've spent three *weeks* digging whatever dirt you point at. You've never struck me as the fanciful type."

"No. I have never struck myself that way. But—here, I feel it. I feel almost disarmingly young again—but not in the ugly, helpless way of childhood."

"I didn't live in a forest."

"No. I didn't, either, more's the pity. But it was my retreat. It was the only place it was safe to dream. I do not know why I speak of this now—and to you, of all people." She shook her head, turning her back on the tree of fire. She could not see how flames framed her, but was aware of the effect her positioning would have. "Duvari does not, except in the most extreme of circumstances, engage in pointless reprisals."

"That is not what is said."

"No, of course not. And you perhaps do not have a window into the ranks of the *Astari* to observe the facts, and no reason to trust my evaluation. I am concerned, Jester."

"Oh?"

"You are disconcertingly serious; I feel that I may have misjudged you."

He shrugged. "I take no offense."

"No. You don't care enough to take offense. And yet, you care enough to be here. How does this affect the right-kin and the director of the Terafin concerns in the Merchant Authority?"

"Did I mention that I'm not fond of intelligent women?"

"Frequently."

"It has never been more true." His face was the color of fire, reflected fire. His hair was that color regardless. She had thought him young and feckless, but in the firelight realized she had underestimated his age. "Is it true that Vareena knows little of value?"

"She would know the manner of her own placement. She would know how any information that requires or merits attention would be conveyed. Beyond that, no—and the circumstance of each would—as you can imagine—be individual."

"And were this information to be shared or discovered, Duvari would not consider it too much of a threat?"

"He would consider her discovery a threat—but once discovered, he would assume the compromise was complete." She was silent for several beats as she digested the conversation—and her own almost inexplicable part in it. "Tell me, ATerafin, you said Vareena was attacked?"

"I may have let that slip."

"How severe were her injuries?"

He looked above her head to burning flame, his expression momentarily unreadable. "You understand my difficulty."

And she did.

"I understand that Duvari considers The Terafin a threat."

Birgide lifted a hand. "Do not do this, Jester. I am not here as *Astari*. I will not carry any threat you make, and it is clear to me you mean to threaten."

"Is it a threat to give warning? There are people within Terafin that Duvari might dispose of—for his own reasons. The Terafin might be angered; she might be relieved. But there are people it is best to leave *well* alone unless you have disposed of The Terafin first. Duvari has never struck me as the type of man who takes things personally.

"Has The Terafin struck you, ever, as someone who doesn't?"

Jester watched Birgide. She had turned her back upon the tree of fire, but even in the midst of their conversation, her eyes were drawn to it. And away. To, and away. What must it be like to serve two masters? Jester wondered. He could not with certainty say he had ever served so much as one. But he had a rare moment of clarity, watching her. He understood why he had found her so quickly. He even understood why he had found her here.

"I am the only man associated with the House Council—however tenuously—who will speak with you. I am perhaps the only member of The Ten who will do so. For reasons which are so glaringly obvious they require no explanation, The Ten do not exchange information with Duvari."

"And yet, you seek to do so?"

"No. I'd sooner die than be stuck in a room with Duvari. I have a personal dislike of people who never smile. Have you ever seen him smile?"

She laughed. "No. Never."

"Were it not for his line of work, he would be the very definition of uninteresting."

"But his line of work absolves him of that status?"

"It does. People loathe him. People resent him. People fear him. All of the social fortifications they might otherwise employ against minor dignitaries like me, they turn toward him instead."

"And they are, therefore, more careless than they would otherwise be."

"Around me, yes—but I am, and will remain, insignificant."

She was once again glancing at the tree.

"It is seldom that I am less interesting than a plant."

"There is no one—not even Duvari on most days—who would interest me more, if that is any consolation."

It wasn't, but he didn't come to people expecting consolation. Or kindness. Jester saw the world clearly. "We don't believe that Vareena was discovered through any competence on the part of either our House Mage or our surveillance."

She didn't even blink. But this time, when she turned toward the tree of fire, she turned fully. Her back was stiff, straight; her hands fell to her sides and remained there. He knew that she could kill him; she could not kill him easily. "What makes you say that?"

"We'll know within the next few days whether or not Vareena was an isolated incident. I imagine Duvari will know first—but not by much." He wanted a drink. He wanted a drink, his bed, and some idiot waking him to tell him that he'd overslept. At this point, even if that idiot was Haval, he'd take it.

On the other hand, if this pleasant fantasy did somehow become the new reality, Haval would no doubt inform him—in that pinched, humorless voice of his—that the day's events had been even more of a nightmare than the current reality's. And he'd probably still be talking to a woman who seemed to prefer the company of plants and dirt to the company of people.

Jester—at this particular moment—had some sympathy for that preference; hours of dirt would no doubt whittle it away.

"It will be difficult for me to carry word to Duvari."

"I would speak with Devon," Jester replied, taking the first of the no doubt hundreds of risks the day before him demanded. "But he is currently seen almost exclusively in the company of Patris Larkasir—at the behest of the Crowns. You are the only alternative available. Trust is not required; you may do nothing with the information and wait to see how events unfold. I must, however, ask that you refrain from denuding the House of necessary members."

"I will refrain—but it is not, of course, to me that you wish to make this request."

Jester, watching her, said, "I think you underestimate your own importance."

"Hardly. I am aware of my standing within the ranks of Duvari's many agents. He is not best pleased with my presence here. He could not—unless my services were urgently required elsewhere—forbid it. Not unless he felt that my presence would compromise the safety of the Kings. He wished The Terafin to forbid it, and made clear to her that I served him. She did not hold this against me."

"Do you think the forest—the forest as it is, now—would survive The Terafin's death?" he asked, looking at the height the tree's flames reached. The question sounded idle; it was not.

That he'd asked it surprised her enough that she turned, once again, from branches of fire. "Do you?"

"I am not the expert. You are. You've spent time studying within the august halls of the Order of Knowledge—but you wear no medallion, and you are not among the rolls of its mage-born."

"You *have* been busy."

"The information, as you suspect, was given to me without so much as finger lifted on my part." This was, of course, a lie. Jester would have dearly loved for it to be the truth, however, and he had learned to gild his words with whatever truth he could find. "It is not possible to study within the Order without gaining some knowledge of—some appreciation for—the talents of the mage-born. Not for a woman of your character. I'm almost certain that part of your education was, in fact, the clear and careful gathering of that information. You might ascertain who was promising, and who powerful; you might learn which of the mage-born have accepted—or at least applied for—the right to accept a patron.

"And this is conjecture on my part; it is idle."

"Yet you are here."

He shrugged. "You have as much working knowledge of magic as one who isn't mage-born could be expected to have." He kept his voice level and even, which was difficult. The branches of the tree were shifting in place. He thought at first this was due to the haze caused by rising heat—but he was never going to be that lucky.

And he was curious. Birgide had found this tree; without Jay's active consent, locating it should have been almost impossible.

"The magics involved in the creation of this forest are not magics that any of the mage-born—any—could facilitate. Given that fact, even my conjectural replies hold no weight. The god-born sons of Teos have offered speculation, no more; their god is strangely reluctant to engage them in matters that concern The Terafin."

Jester frowned.

"But if you insist, I will offer my opinion. The forest in its present form will not survive without The Terafin. Such a forest would not have been considered a remote possibility by most of the mage-born without objective proof of its existence. Indeed, they argue about it in frustrated ignorance, even now. But you have, as House Mage—exclusively, and rumor has it, free—Meralonne APhaniel himself. He believes that the forest is real; he believes that it came into existence exactly as The Terafin claims.

"How much do you know about Member APhaniel?"

Jester shrugged. "He smokes a pipe which irritates any number of patricians; I have long suspected that it's almost the only reason he does. He is as fractious as the rest of the magi—but far more arrogant. He doesn't give a damn about anyone's opinion but his own, and means it, unlike a majority of people who make that claim. He fights like a demon."

"An interesting choice of words."

"Is it? I stay out of his way."

"His area of speciality is ancient—and legal—magics. If he feels a claim is credible, it lends that claim both weight and authority. It may also bring a certain amount of resentment; the magi are famously political."

"Everyone with power is."

"Meralonne APhaniel believes this forest is real. And Meralonne APhaniel treats The Terafin with unheard of respect. The power of First Circle mages has never moved him to offer either respect or consideration. The power of your Terafin does. Do you know where she has gone?"

"Not exactly, no. I wouldn't tell you if I did—but I don't."

Birgide nodded, as if both the question and the answer were pro forma. "It is believed that she is to be instrumental in the survival of Averalaan. In the survival," she added softly, "of the Kings."

"You don't want to share who it's believed by."

"It might come as a surprise to you, but any answer I give you would be pure conjecture. I am told—as are we all—what Duvari feels is necessary for my duties. No more and no less."

"And you are not here as a member of the *Astari*."

"No. But of course, as I am here, and as I am considered an expert in botany and its many branches, I will be asked to offer my opinions about the composition of this forest, its soil, and its various impossible trees."

"Will Duvari listen to you?"

"Yes. He will not listen happily, but he will listen. It is for that reason that it is necessary for my replies to be definitive and objective." She exhaled. "And there is very little objective fact to be found in this forest. It is a wonder of a place. And the heart of it must be this tree. I cannot guarantee that Duvari will listen to reason when it comes to the safety of the *Astari*, and there are costs in even the attempt to have such a discussion. He has survived these decades because he is, at base, suspicious of everyone and everything.

"The *Astari* have been compromised before."

Jester's eyes widened. He held up a pale hand; it was golden in the fire's extended glow. "Please do not continue in this vein. It is making me feel distinctly less safe."

She didn't smile. "Is it not why you came to find me? To inform me that the *Astari* had been compromised?"

"Yes. And I am reconsidering the wisdom of that as we speak."

"You are not. It is not to save Duvari and the *Astari*, nor to save the Kings or the Empire, that you sought me out. You are afraid for your former den. You are worried about Finch and the right-kin. You are concerned about Jewel's reaction should Duvari attempt to secure knowledge by removing a healer.

"Regardless, it is not the first time the *Astari* have been compromised."

"And those compromises were demonic in nature?"

"Once. Once that I'm aware of."

Jester whistled. He shouldn't have, but stiff protocol had already been abandoned by the simple decision to be here with Birgide at all. He felt himself relaxing in the warmth of the tree of fire. Had he been Haval, he could have feigned relaxation without actually condescending to enjoy any. "I feel I've wasted your time," he told her.

"Don't. If I appear unruffled, the news you have carried is disturbing. You feel there is a demon in our midst—a demon who is aware of the *Astari* and its methods of communication. Aware, as well, of the least and quietest of its members. That implies an infiltration of a higher order."

"You don't think it could be Duvari?"

"No. We are demonstrably still alive. If Duvari had somehow been taken, we would stand no chance at all."

"But you'd fight, anyway."

"Yes. I love this forest," she confessed. "And these trees. Silver, gold, diamond—but most of all the *Ellariannatte*. I owe your Terafin a great debt; Duvari told her, point-blank, that I was *Astari*, and she elected to allow me to join her Household Staff."

"Could you speak with Vareena?"

"That would not be wise."

"I'm afraid she'll try to kill the healer."

Birgide closed her eyes. "It is not, I am sorry, the healer who concerns me. Nor is it Vareena herself. Tell me, in exact detail, what happened."

"Will you make certain to lie about your source?"

"It is never wise to lie to Duvari. If you mean for me to speak with him—and you do—I cannot dissemble." She folded her arms, waiting.

Jester cursed her genially. "There are days it is not wise to leave one's bed. I accept that. But I feel it unreasonable that there might be whole weeks—or months, more likely—where that is the case. This is vastly more trouble than I am accustomed to dealing with."

"But you are here."

"To dump the difficulty on the shoulders of someone vastly more responsible."

Her eyes rounded; he could almost see the fire through them. Her genuine outrage, unvoiced, made him laugh. It felt surprisingly good. He held his amiable silence until her eyes narrowed. "Do you know Devon?"

"I know of him."

"I'll take that as a yes."

Her arms, still folded, had tightened.

"Devon is *Astari*," Jester continued, when she failed to interrupt him.

"That is not commonly known."

"It is not *widely* known, but it is known. I do not," he added, "discuss it often. I discuss it now for a reason."

"I hesitate, given your attitude, to ask what that reason is."

"You stand at the heart of The Terafin's forest," he told her. He walked closer, moving quietly and almost diffidently. "You've crossed a continent to study The Terafin's trees. Duvari would not have introduced you as *Astari* if he had meant for you to remain here. But remain here, you do. I think it will take a full-on emergency to pry you from your position here."

She said nothing.

"But you are, according to the Master Gardener, a woman of great fame in the circles he occupies. He speaks of you with healthy, glowing respect. He is beside himself with joy at your current position—you are working *for* him. On our grounds."

The nothing extended, although Birgide's eyes narrowed.

"If Devon can be both ATerafin and *Astari*, why can't you?"

Outrage had vanished into silent watchfulness. If a woman could be said to be bristling with suspicion, this one was. Jester was aware that he should not be enjoying himself *quite* so much, but felt that he had earned it, given the week so far. "Apologies," he said, with the usual amount of sincerity. "Suggestions such as this aren't usually considered a threat."

"Or an insult?" was her chilly reply.

"Or that. I've more experience with that one, though."

This pulled curiosity out of her otherwise rigid expression. "Oh?"

"Angel. You're probably aware of him."

She was, and didn't dissemble. "He did not, that I'm aware, take the House Name. It was offered?"

"Yes—at the same time as the rest of us. He wouldn't touch it for years."

"Something changed his mind?"

"The Terafin died."

"I see."

Jester shrugged. "We were here because Jewel was. Taking the House Name didn't change that, for us. She wanted us to be ATerafin; we were ATerafin. Angel, not so much."

"What did Angel want?"

"Angel? Who knows. He's got some pretty Northern ideas of honor and allegiance."

"Implying that I do? Or that I don't?"

"I don't know."

"Jester—" She exhaled. "I have half a mind to strangle you."

"I'll take the other half."

"You won't prefer it." Her grin was sliver thin. "You do not have the authority to offer me the House Name. You clearly have the gall."

"I have the authority to offer the name provisionally," was his easy reply. "But it's not a provisional offer. You are not here as *Astari*. We don't require you to be *Astari* while you're here. Devon's work with the Royal Trade Commission is genuine. He serves the interests of the Twin Kings, where interests collide; they seldom do. When they do not, he serves Terafin."

"And Terafin's interests would be served well enough by a botanist?"

His eyes widened in deliberate mimicry of hers. "Consider where you're standing."

She failed to reply; he expected that.

"While The Terafin is absent, I think you'll do whatever you can, within reason, to preserve her forest. You might as well get something out of it."

"We are talking about a House Name, ATerafin, not a handful of coins or a future commendation."

"Yes, we are. Let me tell you what I've gleaned from listening to Member APhaniel. The forest is our protection. While demons do—and can—move within the manse itself, they must do so with subtlety."

"His opinion is also conjecture."

"I've seen him fight demons," Jester replied. He didn't bother maintaining the easy, nonchalant smile with which he'd made his offer. Birgide wasn't wrong; he didn't have the authority to make it. But he knew, if she accepted, it would be affirmed. Jester wasn't Chosen—but he didn't need to be. He needed Jay to come back, and he needed—as they all did—that she have something to come back *to*.

"You have?"

"Yes. Before I was ATerafin. His fight destroyed the foyer. I don't know if you heard about it; you'd've been what, sixteen? Our age? It was during 410. Just before Henden. He was terrifying. He seemed to know the demon; the demon seemed to know him. Conjecture or no, I'm willing to believe him."

"That is disturbing."

Jester shrugged. "He says there is a chance—small, but real—that the demons and those who've summoned them might momentarily wrest control of these lands from Jewel in her absence. And if they do, her chances of surviving her return diminish."

"I don't understand this forest. I don't—and I've no wish to—understand your obsession with it. I look at the trees and think of selling leaves in the city streets, and I imagine the trees know it."

Wind crackled through burning branches. Jester forced himself not to take a step or ten back. Birgide watched.

"I want two things," Jester continued. "I want you to call Duvari off. Take Vareena or don't—I don't care. But I want him to stay well clear of my den."

"You can't imagine that I can give orders to Duvari."

"No. I can imagine the Kings can—but it is costly to approach the Kings with demands of this nature. I am not, however, patrician. The right-kin and Finch would, no doubt, reject outright any attempt to contact the Kings. But I don't particularly care what such an approach would do to the rest of the House."

Both of Birgide's brows rose. She didn't completely believe him. Jester shrugged. Her belief wasn't his problem. "The second thing?"

"I want this forest to be standing. I want this forest to be Terafin's. I can't stand against demons. Some of the *Astari* can, but not many. I don't know if you're one of them or not. I don't think you need to be. Whatever you need, it's already here."

"I am not mage-born—"

"Neither is The Terafin, if it comes to that."

"No. But her understanding of her lands is instinctive and visceral; I do not possess it. No one, I am certain, does, with the exception of The Terafin herself. I don't understand what you expect of me, Jester."

"I told you—"

"Apologies. I had not realized you were a pedant."

He chuckled. "I've been called far worse."

"I do not understand why you expect that I can do these things." She held up a hand as he opened his mouth. "Yes, I understand why you feel I can approach Duvari. I have not agreed to do so—but you suspect that I will, agreement aside. I suspect I will, as well.

"But the other? The forest? I am here as an expert *tourist*, ATerafin. I am here on sufferance because I could not—if any opportunity presented itself—stay away. I have already earned Duvari's stiff disapproval; he has not forbidden my presence. The Terafin did herself no favors by accepting my request."

"Nothing she could do, short of suicide, would sway Duvari's opinion."

"No, perhaps not. It is not in his nature to trust. But that is beside the point. I am not an expert. I am not The Terafin. I am not ATerafin. Why do you feel that I can materially affect the forest in a positive way?"

"Do you gamble, Birgide?"

"In the sense that a life lived in service to the *Astari* does not end quietly or peacefully, yes. But in a more casual way, no. I am not a seeker of excitement."

"It's a gamble."

"You cannot offer the House Name as a *gamble*. The Terafin would be appalled."

"She let you stay. She knew; she let you stay. For reasons I trust I don't need to explain, The Terafin has always relied on her instinct. And the rest of us? We survived by it. Literally. Our instincts have never been gold-plated—but hers? Always. She *let you stay*. You spend more time in the forest than she does."

"That is not all."

"I really loathe smart women."

"And not smart men?"

"They're fewer in number, and almost never interested in me."

Birgide laughed. "I have never been interested in you; I thought you feckless and lazy."

He bowed. "At your service."

"I have rather enough feckless and lazy in my life. What are you hiding?"

"Hiding is a harsh word." He had no idea what Birgide could now see in his face; Haval would probably be outraged were he in the vicinity, eavesdropping. "You carried the leaf."

"The leaf?"

"Yes. You were holding one of the leaves from the Kings' trees."

"The *Ellariannatte*."

"I prefer the single syllable words if they get the point across. The leaves don't fall here the way they do in the Common. But you held one in your hand. And you were standing in front of the tree of fire. Do you know where the fire came from?"

"No. And I am not certain, at this juncture, that I want to. You are all too casual in the information you offer. You have spent a decade drinking with the patricians—you, at least, should know better."

"I might lie."

"You are too lazy to lie. You feel safe here; you feel that I will not harm you—or that I will not be allowed to harm you, should I make the attempt."

"I'm not at all certain that's the case—but I suspect it is, yes. I'm not certain that you would ever risk your life, your livelihood, your vocation, to preserve The Terafin's life. But I'm not sure, at this point, that you wouldn't. What I'm certain of is that you'll protect these lands to the best of your ability—if you make that commitment. I'm asking for that commitment."

"And I must be ATerafin?"

Jester shrugged. "I think, if you do this, you'll have earned the name—but oddly, I don't think it's necessary. The leaf didn't fall at your feet because you're ATerafin. The path didn't open to this tree because you're part of the House."

She turned toward the burning tree. "This is not what I expected of my day," she told him. "Any of it. Demons. *Astari*. You. I think you might be the largest surprise, and it is not entirely pleasant."

"No. Believe that I'm not enjoying it either—but I've been told to earn my keep, and my current lifestyle is expensive."

"Let me consider your . . . offer. And your request."

She expected no argument, and received none. She doubted—very much—that Jester had the authority to offer her the House Name. But the current

Terafin was not comfortable with authority, and she did not doubt that should Jewel Markess return, she would confirm what Jester had offered.

No one within Terafin had the power to compel her to speak with Duvari. The Terafin herself might have that power over Devon, who walked the thin line stretched between two masters—but Birgide believed that if Devon were available, Jester would not have come.

Except, of course, he had. She was pragmatic. She did not believe in fate; she did not believe in destiny. But she would not have believed in this forest had she not seen it with her own eyes; had she not walked beneath the branches of the impossible, and touched trunks of silver, gold, and diamond.

She turned, now, to face the tree of fire. She had not touched its branches; she had not placed palm against its trunk. If the flames did not burn the undergrowth, they were hot enough to suggest fire, and not the artifice of its appearance. She had seen fire used by the magi on one or two occasions; it had never taken this form.

She regretted cutting Jester's story short. She wanted to know—even if he lied—what he might claim the origin of this tree to be. She turned again, to say as much, and stopped as a flicker of fire, more gold than red, caught her attention.

It was a leaf.

It was a falling leaf.

Without thought, she reached out with a cupped palm—her left hand, although she could use both. The breeze which caught this floating bit of heat was slow and hazy; the leaf descended.

She knew she should let it fall. She knew it was of fire. She knew what fire did to flesh it touched. And she understood, watching the trail of red-and-gold light, that this was the moment of decision. No thought of politics, no thought of power struggles, no calculated, pragmatic examination of circumstances was to be allowed her. She could catch the leaf or she could let it fall.

The leaf from the *Ellariannatte* had fallen. She had retrieved it from the ground. But this leaf? No.

"Birgide—what are you doing?" Jester's voice was sharper, louder, than it had been. She didn't begrudge the question; it was the very one she asked herself. But if her hand shook, if her arm trembled, she did not withdraw.

"I am," she answered, unmoving, "being tested."

She thought he would rush forward and grab the hand she held aloft, pulling it out of the path of danger. Perhaps, had she been one of his den, he might have. She wasn't. She was not now, nor would she ever be, his responsibility or his kin.

The leaf of fire reached her open hand.

And it burned.

Jester cursed and closed the distance between them, recognizing the way her entire body tensed, and recognizing, as well, the smell of burnt flesh.

Birgide—being the person whose flesh it was—didn't appear to react at all. She didn't lower her arm. She didn't attempt to divest herself of the fire.

And the fire began to spread. Jester yanked his jacket off and lifted it to throw it over the hand that held the leaf. He was rendered speechless when she closed her fingers in a fist around it.

"Leave it be," she said, through clenched teeth—the only certain sign that the burning was not his imagination.

"Birgide—"

"I mean it. This is nothing." She grimaced as the fire spread from her closed fist; her eyes teared.

"Birgide." Jester stepped back, his coat folded over his arm, his face pale.

"Did you think," she asked, in evenly spaced, controlled syllables, "it would be as simple as a single word?"

"Yes, actually."

Her laughter sounded like a hiss of pain. "Sometimes," she said, through teeth that remained clenched, "you are astonishingly naive." But was he really any worse than she was? She had learned to endure pain. It was a matter of both pride and survival. In the latter years, mostly pride. She had learned, in the earlier years, to evince pain, to play it up, to give people the fear they wanted—it put them off their guard. It gave her chances to strike or escape. In almost all cases, escape had been her choice.

But not all. She had never run from Duvari. He was not a warm man; not a friendly one. He was not kind, and his form of mercy involved quick death. He was harsh, exacting, suspicious, judgmental, and deadly. Always deadly.

And he served the Kings.

Birgide did not remember when that single, clarifying point had become the reason for her existence. When she had first encountered Duvari, she would have scoffed at the motivation. She did. She recognized everything dangerous about him in the first two seconds of their meeting, and she knew men like Duvari did not serve; they ruled.

When had she started to believe otherwise? Not when she entered his service. Not when she trained. Not when she learned to imbibe small quantities of the poison to which she had been subjected in later years. Not when she had first killed a man—in self-defense. If Birgide was sent out to kill, it was not meant to be so obvious a death.

When?

She could not recall. Her hand ached. She thought the flesh in the center of her palm must be damaged enough by now that the pain would pass. Fire had spread from her clenched fist down her arm in a trail that was more vine than branch. But this fire did not burn. She had taken a risk. Had made a gamble.

The pain did not recede; it wouldn't. Not immediately, and not for days. She would have to tend the burned and blistered flesh; she could not afford the infection that often set in after a burn. She did not open her hand. Did not attempt to retreat.

Tendrils of flame continued to emerge from between her clenched fingers, as if they were liquid and couldn't be contained by so faulty a vessel. They followed her arm, and then spread across her shoulders, her collarbone, the underside of her chin. She felt warmth that threatened to become heat; she thought blisters—obvious ones—would be left anywhere the fire touched her skin.

And still she endured.

It would not be the first time.

Jester's lips were white, when Birgide turned to look at him. His skin was the same color. She was honestly surprised that he stood before her, bearing witness, his own hands curved into fists. "You don't," she told him softly, "have the sense you were born with."

"It was beaten out of me," he replied, his casual shrug made difficult and awkward because he couldn't relax into it.

"So was mine, apparently." She closed her eyes, inhaling rapidly. Forced them open again. "It's a brand," she told him.

"A what?"

"The fire is branding me. It's leaving a mark."

"*Why?*"

"What do brands normally mean?" she asked him. Frustration took the edge off pain. Or pain made frustration sharper. She wasn't certain which, and didn't care. "Ownership. Slavery."

"Both of which are illegal in the Empire."

"So is murder. Murder still happens." She was afraid when the weave of flame tendrils rose to cover her face. A scar was nothing new in her life. But she needed her sight. She needed her vision.

Jester reached out and caught the hand that did not hold the leaf of fire. She could have shrugged him off. She didn't. Instead, she gripped the hand he'd offered; given his sharp intake of breath, she thought he might regret it; she wasn't certain that she hadn't cracked bone.

But it helped. It helped.

Jester turned toward the tree itself. "Cut it out!" he shouted, as if that would make any difference at all. "Jay would never demand this. She'd accept the offer of service or she'd reject it—but she would *never* allow this!"

In spite of herself, Birgide was impressed. "You really *are* an idiot."

"My middle name. One of the few that's useful in polite company."

She tightened her hand as he moved toward the tree. "It may have escaped your notice, but your Jay is *not here*. She doesn't get to decide the terms by which I am accepted or rejected."

"She would, if she were here."

"And she is *not here*, Jester." Birgide gulped down air.

"No. She's not. But *we are*." He yanked his hand free, or tried; Birgide's grip was far too solid. She wasn't certain she could voluntarily extricate her hand without work; it was almost numb. Where Jester walked, she followed, stumbling.

He reached the tree and came to a stop inches from its flaming trunk. His skin was orange and gold, his hair the color of fire; his eyes, reflecting flames, were the same. "Is it worth it?" he asked, voice low.

"What?" she responded, confused.

"I never swore an oath to Jay. She never asked for one."

"But you served her anyway?"

"I was found in a brothel. Most of us were."

Birgide fell silent. The pain in her hand was throbbing and dull now. But the fire was a mask in front of her face. She closed her eyes. If the forest decided to reject her, the eyelids wouldn't save her vision.

"We had two choices: die in a fire, or escape with her. Not really much of a choice." He was staring at the fire now, as if he could see the flames of the past. "We had nowhere to go. No one who wanted us. No one who wouldn't sell us back, or worse. She was our age. Another orphan. But she had friends. Friends with swords. She crawled through the brothel looking for one person. That was Duster. You probably don't know about her; she died the day we arrived at the manse.

"If she hadn't died, we would have.

"She found Duster." Jester sucked in air, and reached out toward the trunk. His hand froze an inch from its surface. "And she found the rest of us as well.

She took us all. She wouldn't leave us. And some of us were too damaged to follow quickly.

"I never understood it. I didn't argue and I didn't demand explanations—not then, not later. Not ever, really. I didn't want to ask questions. She was a miracle. I wanted to believe in her. I didn't. I couldn't. Not at first."

The heat across Birgide's face became warmth. Simple warmth. Fire as salvation, and not destruction.

"But years have a way of dulling the edge of suspicion and fear. Was I cynical?" He reached out again, and again his palm stopped an inch from the tree's flame. "Yes. Bitter. Angry. Weak. Enraged by helplessness—I mean, by mine. I didn't particularly mourn the people who did die in that fire." He was white. Whiter than Birgide had ever been. Even the reflected firelight didn't change his base color.

She wanted to ask him what had changed that, if anything had. She didn't. She knew, if she waited, she would have her answer. Her hand was no longer the very definition of pain; it had numbed into a constant throbbing, as if her heart had momentarily moved into her palm.

"But she kept us. She kept Duster, the worst—and the best—of us. She kept Lander, who wouldn't speak a word for months on end. She already had Lefty—a right-handed kid who'd had fingers lopped off. She had Finch—Finch, who escaped the brothel, and who led Jay back to it. And Carver." Jester swallowed. Birgide thought he would kick the tree, and froze.

Jester apparently thought he would kick the tree as well; the fire flared, reddening the gleam of polished leather. He wasn't—quite—a fool, but even intelligent men had moments of temperamental weakness. Carver's absence loomed so large in the den, it might as well have been a death.

Jester exhaled. "She kept us going. When the money ran out—and it did—she kept us all moving. No one starved. There were enough of us that we wouldn't freeze to death in our sleep—not given the room we lived in. We learned a thing or two about her. About her hunches. We trusted those—even when we couldn't bring ourselves to trust *her*.

"I would never have died for her. Not then. Not even when Duster did. Duster was the worst of us—but in spite of it, facing death is what she did. It's not what I did, unless I had no choice. And when given a choice, I'd bolt first.

"But I came to understand that Jay would have died for any of us. Then. Now. She thinks we're one happy family." His lips were a twist, a grimace laid over a smile, as if he couldn't quite decide which was more appropriate. "And maybe we are. We're happier than my old family ever was, before Dad disappeared. But we depend on her. It's like—gods, this is embarrassing—she's our mother or something."

"She is," Birgide felt compelled to say, "your lord."

He was staring at the fire, and failed to answer. "Maybe. She's *a* lord. As patrician in title as the lot of them." His smile was wan, but genuine. "And as lords go, she's better than Duvari."

"No comment."

He laughed. She liked the sound of his laughter far better than the intensity of his anger—because Jester was angry. Looking at him, she realized for perhaps the first time, that Jester was always angry. "There's a difference," he said. He took a deep, sharp breath, and before Birgide could react, reached out grabbed the trunk of the tree. "There *has* to be a difference. This is *not* what Jay would want, and this is *her damn tree.*"

And just like that, the pain was gone.

The pain left; the fire did not. The mask it had built over the whole of her face remained in place; she could see the world through the tint of the fire's glow, just as she saw Jester. She released his hand—and as she had suspected, this was work. He didn't apparently notice, but he turned toward her, his hand pressed against the trunk. Absent was the smell of burned flesh; the fire had not harmed him at all.

"Thank you."

His brows rose. After a moment, he shrugged. "If I tell you it was nothing, will I be accused of undervaluing your life?"

"I don't know. Try it and see." She opened her clenched fist in front of Jester's watchful eyes. The palm was scarred—or appeared that way on cursory inspection. Birgide's inspection was not cursory; nor, she thought, was Jester's.

In the center of her palm was a white patch that seemed solid; it wavered at the edges as if it were cloth. No, not cloth; it had the borders a leaf might have. A small leaf. As she moved her hand in the light shed by the burning tree, red glinted off this new scar.

Jester said, "It's metallic." It wasn't a question.

She probed the mark gently with her fingers. The touch itself caused no pain. She felt her fingertips; the sensation was distinct. It was normal. What was not normal was the scar itself. ". . . Yes. Yes, I think it is."

"It's the shape of the leaves."

"It is the shape of *a* leaf, yes. Not the leaves on this tree." She shook her head. "Not the silver, the gold or the diamond. I think it's meant to be *Ellariannatte* in miniature."

The difference in Jester's posture made clear how tense he'd been. She would not have otherwise noticed it. Duvari had never been particularly complimentary about her powers of observation—not when she was actually focused upon duties that had nothing to do with the Kings. Looking up from the mark, she said, "I will accept your offer."

He laughed. The laughter filled the clearing made by fire and fire's unnatural heat. "This," he told her, as the laughter faded into a worn smile, "is why I will never be a merchant."

"Oh?"

"You've made clear—the *forest* has made clear—that you'll serve Terafin, name or no."

"Ah, you misunderstand me. I am not even certain it is deliberate. Yes," she said, gazing up at the tree as the lines of the masking fire slowly, slowly faded. "I will do everything in my power to preserve this forest. I will not," she added, "do it for The Terafin's sake; I will do it for my own. I would do it," she continued, "if Rymark himself took the House Seat and ruled from it."

"That is never going to happen," Jester said, the edge in his voice cutting the smile from his face.

"That is a House matter, and I am not—yet—of the House; I will not discuss it further; you understand the point I attempted to illustrate, no?"

"Use a better illustration."

"I am not a politician; it is not one of my many skills. I mean only that the forest exists—for me—separate from the ruler of the House."

"It doesn't—"

She lifted her scarred hand. "Do you ever let people finish a sentence?"

"Not unless they're committed to it." He grinned. It made him look younger. It made her feel older. Objectively, there couldn't be more than a handful of years separating them, and she was uncertain that she actually was the elder. "I'll be good."

"If the forest exists separate from Terafin, it is joined to it by the woman who presides as the head of the House. I will serve—in what limited way my oaths to Duvari allow—Jewel Markess ATerafin because to serve her *is* to preserve what lies at the heart of her grounds.

"But I could do that without tendering the aid you require. I could do that without approaching Duvari. There would be no need on my part to interfere in matters that exist between the Kings and The Ten."

"And you will?"

She stared at her palm again. "Yes. Jester—what color are my eyes?"

He frowned. "Pardon?"

"What color are my eyes?"

"Last I looked? Gray."

"Look again."

"Birgide—" The rest of his words deserted him as he obeyed. ". . . They're not gray."

She nodded. "What color are they?"

"In this light?" He hesitated, which was unlike him, but given the day, it was a minor inconsistency. "They're—they're kind of a reddish brown."

"How brown?"

"In this light," he repeated, with more irony in the emphasis, "they're red. I think they could pass for brown if they weren't reflecting so much fire."

"You're lying."

He gave up. "Yes. I'm lying. You think this is an artifact from the tree."

"Yes. The forest doesn't speak to me in the way you and I speak to each other. But I think, having decided to accept my service—and it *is* service, Jester—it has offered me tools with which to do my duties." More than this, she did not say aloud.

Chapter Fifteen

INTO THE FADED, pale day of the abandoned, ancient halls stepped one of the firstborn whose images had been engraved, in the passage of seconds, into the basement of one room in *Avantari*: Calliastra.

She had eyes, at the moment, for Shianne. Celleriant seemed to be beneath her notice. So, too, the cats.

Only the cats cared. Shadow hissed. Night hissed. Neither sound implied laughter or amusement, and in case their displeasure was somehow not apparent, their fur rose inches, changing the shape of their backs and faces. Shadow stepped closer to Jewel's side; he placed one paw on the top of her foot and pressed down.

Jewel glanced at the top of his head, at the height of his ears; she was surprised to see that her hand was still attached to his fur.

Stand well back, Avandar said. His magics, orange and gold, colored the air around the whole of their party.

I know. She glanced, briefly, at her arm; at the arm that bore the Warlord's sigil. It was not, however, for herself or her domicis that she feared. Angel was here. Terrick. Adam. They were all at risk, should Calliastra's focus waver. Kallandras was mortal as well, but Jewel could not imagine that he could be caught in Calliastra's grasp; she was, in fact, certain he could not.

As usual, she couldn't say why, and as usual, she didn't question the certainty. She knew it was the artifact of the talent to which she'd been born—the talent that had led, in slow and winding steps, to these grand and haunted halls.

Terrick dismounted. He dismounted and, to Jewel's surprise, armed himself.

Jewel frowned; Angel frowned as well. Angel, however, dismounted and drew sword, taking his lead from the older man.

Shianne—armed—had not caused this reaction in Terrick; Terrick's gaze had been as awestruck as Jewel's whenever it had fallen on the Arianni woman. It had fallen on her only slightly less often. It was hard, despite Shianne's claims of mortality, for Jewel to look at anything else.

Or it had been. But Calliastra, daughter of gods, was compelling in her own right. She was beautiful, yes—but it was not a beauty that spoke of mountains and the vast heights and depths of a natural world that counted mortals as nothing; it was a beauty that spoke of desire. Desire, darkness, and death, as if one led naturally into the other, like dusk into night.

Night, in the eyes of the child of gods, was endless.

"She is not for you," Celleriant said, coming to stand between Shianne and the daughter of their ancient enemy.

"She was not, once. She might be, now," Calliastra replied, smiling. Her lips, full, her eyes, dark, implied both warmth and smoldering heat. If Shianne was distant and untouchable, Calliastra was her opposite.

Jewel swallowed.

She had faced Calliastra once, in the Stone Deepings; had it not been for Avandar, she would have died there. Willingly. It angered her to remember it, but she accepted it: she was mortal.

The Lord of the Hells, and the goddess of love had birthed Calliastra. Jewel had met almost no one who did not desire love—even if they failed to trust in its existence. And Callistra stood, now, in the ancient remnants of the Winter Queen's first court: she had power here.

Shianne, however, inclined her chin. She evinced no fear, and no particular suspicion. "I am not," she replied, "for you."

"You have chosen," Calliastra replied, "to do the unthinkable. You have tied yourself to the rhythm of life and death." She gestured at the baby, still enfolded in the center of Shianne's body. "Summer and Winter are not for me; they never were. But life and death? They are mine, Shianne."

"And I," Shianne replied, regally and distantly, "belong to the White Lady. If you seek to touch me, if you seek to destroy me, understand that I have already made my choice; there is nothing that you can offer me that will change it. I am, as I have always been, *of* Ariane."

"Yes. Yes, you are." Calliastra smiled. Her voice, soft and sensual, was almost a purr. "And you carry within you the seeds of her death."

Shianne stiffened.

So, too, Celleriant.

"Do you think she preserved you for your own sake? She was foolish; she was sentimental. Sentiment is *my* domain. You are evidence of her weakness. She should have destroyed you, at least. Instead, she kept you here; she kept you hidden.

"But the roads are changing, Shandalliaran. They are shifting. A god walks this world once more, and every step he takes reminds things wild and hidden of the life they once knew. Ariane is trapped in her hovel of a Hidden Court, and I? I am free to roam as I please.

"I heard your song. It moved me. It drew me from the vastness of my home." She did not seem particularly moved, to Jewel.

"It drew you," Shianne replied, "from its emptiness. Why have you come?"

"To see the beginning of the end, little niece." She smiled. Her smile could melt ice.

It could not, however, melt stone; Shianne was stone, now. She said nothing.

Calliastra turned. "Viandaran. I see you have not yet tired of your consort."

"She is not my consort," Avandar replied. He was quiet, his tone chilly; his stiffness, however, was natural. "She is *Sen*, Calliastra. Perhaps even you will remember what that once meant."

Avandar.

It is necessary. I do not know if Shianne divested herself of all power when she made her choice.

Jewel thought of the golden sword. *I doubt it.*

As do I. But she is not, here, a match for Calliastra. We might stand against her for some small while; we might drive her off, if the cats choose to be useful. We cannot destroy her. Not yet.

When?

He didn't answer.

Why is she here?

She did not, in my opinion, lie. She is here to stand witness to the beginning of the end.

What end? Silence. *Avandar?*

"Listen to *him*," Shadow growled. "And do not be *stupid*." He hissed at Calliastra. The child of gods failed to notice him. Pointedly. She did not, however, fail to notice Jewel; she turned.

Jewel remembered the starless night of the Stone Deepings; she remembered the velvet of a voice that promised everything. Her mouth was half-open, her lips dry, as she met Calliastra's eyes. They were Duster's eyes.

It angered her. She attempted to hold on to the anger, to shore herself up with it. But she knew it was too feeble; Calliastra engendered emotion—emotion itself was no shield against her. It was purchase. It was anchor.

Yes, the Winter King said. *She was ever a danger to our kind, even when the Cities were at the height of their power.*

She is no danger to you now?

No. She cannot take what is already claimed. I will die if the Winter Queen decrees my death. I will die if the Winter Queen dies. There is nothing she can take from me; nothing that will feed her endless emptiness; nothing that will calm her ancient sorrow.

Sorrow.

Sorrow, Jewel. She did not understand, when young, that love must lead inevitably to death. And she could not easily accept that she could not control the hunger that drives her to feed.

You pity *her.*

I do. You do not—and it is safest for you. She is firstborn. What she wants is not, and has never been, pity.

What does she want?

What she can never have: love. Warmth. Belonging. She is Allasakar's daughter. She is Laursana's daughter. How that union came to be, I will not guess. But it has made her the creature she is. You think her monstrous.

She did.

And so she is. But she is wed to her monstrosity; short of destruction, she cannot escape it. And Jewel: she has tried. There are lays and legends—lost to you and your kin—that speak of her tragedy.

Jewel's frown creased the corners of her eyes and mouth as she turned her glance toward the Winter King—and away from Calliastra. *You want me to ask her what she means when she speaks of the end.*

Silence. It was a thin silence; it could not hold. *Not I alone. Look at the Lady. Look at your liege.*

Jewel did. Shianne was the height of distant mountain in the coldest of winter; her expression gave nothing away. So, too, Celleriant. A flick of movement caught her eye. Angel was signing.

No, she signed back. *Stay where you are.* She glanced at Terrick and added, *hold him back.*

Angel cast a very dubious look at the grim and bearded Rendish warrior; he signed again. Jewel almost laughed.

Calliastra chose that moment to reach out to touch Jewel's face.

Celleriant was in the air before the firstborn's perfect fingers grazed Jewel's wind-dark cheek. The wind howled, speaking all of the words he could not or did not choose to shed. His blade, blue lightning, traveled in the heart of his storm; he landed.

He landed and drove Jewel back. Calliastra could not be moved. As a testament to the value of his service, it wasn't promising. The Winter King's flank caught her back before she could hit the cold stone beneath all of their feet.

The cats converged, hissing, claws scraping stone as they pounced and landed.

Calliastra was the very mountains; the cats *bounced.* "Will you," she said, voice of ice and shadow, "deny your lord what she herself *chooses?*" And even as she spoke, her expression was shifting and changing, until she stood before Jewel wearing more than just Duster's eyes.

Duster. Duster who was, who would remain forever, sixteen years of age. Memory couldn't contain that truth. Jewel's sense of Duster aged with her. She *knew* that Duster had died in the streets of the holding when the rest of her den had arrived at the Terafin manse. She knew that was half her lifetime ago. But she couldn't hold the image of *this* Duster in her mind.

This Duster was all of sixteen. She had swallowed rage and pain and humiliation; she had made loss her personal grail. And she had carried both to Jewel, offering them, time and again, with only the barest glimmer of hope to alleviate the darkness of all her early lessons.

And Jewel had been sixteen as well. She'd *had* hope. Hope.

Calliastra, she saw clearly, had none. She cursed the Winter King in the silence of thought, because she saw, just as clearly, that even gods did not live without hope; it grew again. It grew, no matter how much it cut and destroyed when it once again failed to take root. Love. Death. Loss. All loss.

The anger she felt at Calliastra's use of Duster's appearance guttered. It couldn't warm her, couldn't hold her back. She saw Duster in this woman— and woman was the only word she had for her; she couldn't truly imagine that gods could feel this kind of pain. Gods were what they were. Calliastra . . . was not. The Winter King said she had struggled, in her youth, with the knowledge that all love—for Calliastra—led inevitably to death.

And Jewel could *see* that. She could see it in the ferocity of Duster's expression.

She is not *your Duster,* Avandar said, voice sharp, harsh. Jewel's arm began to throb, like a second, beating heart. She knew it was bleeding.

"No," she said. "She's not. Shadow, *cut that out.* You're just going to sand your own claws off."

He hissed. "You'll be *stupid,*" he told her.

"Stupid, *stupid, stupid,*" Night agreed.

Calliastra laughed. The sound of her voice—it was Duster's voice. Duster's harsh, edged laughter. A flicker of genuine amusement ran through it, but it was slender, and it implied pain. Other people's. "They are not impressively respectful."

Jewel grimaced. The voice—the voice wasn't Duster's. The words weren't. She tried to hold on to this fact, and failed. Because she understood, looking at this scion of ancient gods, that at heart—at heart, the two could have been the same person. "They're impressive."

"And you allow it."

"They're cats. I'm not sure why all of the Immortals seem so surprised—I can't exactly change their base nature."

"Why not?" Calliastra's brows rose. "They are, if I am not mistaken, yours—and you are, according to Viandaran, *Sen*. You can change their base nature. You can alter the shapes they wear. You can redefine what service means to them. Perhaps they did not tell you this?

"Or perhaps Viandaran did not. The Sen cannot alter mortals—but the rest of the world is their canvas if they but accept the whole of their power."

Jewel let the words sink into her, hearing them, understanding them in a way only a seer could. "Avandar," she said, speech giving the words a weight that the internal voice could not, "is this true for *all* Immortals? Could one who is Sen do this?"

Shianne's voice rose above all of theirs. "What is Sen?" she asked. It was only barely a question.

"I can't answer that," Jewel replied. "I don't completely understand it myself; the word was used when the gods walked the world—and only then."

"Until now."

"According to Calliastra, a god now walks *this* world. Avandar."

You are playing by her rules, he said. It wasn't an answer, and they both knew it.

"I'm not. I'm playing by rules I don't understand. I ask because I accept my ignorance. I want to alleviate it. Could I change the cats?"

Shadow hissed.

Snow sneezed.

Night hissed—at Snow.

"Yes. It is my belief that you could alter the cats."

"Could I alter Celleriant?"

"You could try," Celleriant replied. "But you would fail."

Jewel nodded. "Because you are Ariane's."

"Because I am the White Lady's, yes. Sworn to you, lord. Sworn to you while you live. But I am—and will be—Arianni. It is my nature. It is my existence. If the White Lady were to perish, I would perish with her—as would all of my kind."

"All?" She frowned.

"All."

"And I could not alter Shianne."

"No, lord."

Calliastra's smile had fallen from her lips, and her lips, thinning, lost the fullness of Duster's anger, Duster's youth, Duster's constant rage. "You cannot believe," she whispered, in a voice that would have been a hiss had she chosen other words, "that *I* could ever be subject to *your* pathetic, mortal powers?"

Jewel did not reply. The stone beneath her feet cracked; the crack extended from beneath her boots across the length of the hall for as far as her eyes could see. Calliastra stood astride it—as did Jewel herself; the cats launched themselves into the air.

"Viandaran—if you wish to preserve your consort, you will educate her."

Avandar was silent, in all ways.

Calliastra turned her chin toward him, her eyes darkening until they were all of black. Black velvet, Jewel thought: death, but not unwelcome. Not to Avandar. As if she could hear this, Calliastra said, "He is beyond me. His curse was the punishment for his hubris; the god who granted him the immortality he craved is ash and dust and memory. But he remains a testament to the power of the old gods and the old ways.

"I cannot grant him the death he desires; he cannot grant me the life I require—or the life I once desired. And, child, he cannot preserve you should you choose to throw your life away."

But he had. Jewel's arm ached enough that had she needed a reminder, it would serve. But his power pressed against her, she thought, with no intent on his part. He was silent, angry, watchful; he feared the effects of any words he might offer her.

And well he should.

Why, she could hear, at a remove of decades, *did you keep Duster?* Rath's voice. Not her Oma's, as it so often was, decades after the old woman's death.

She labored under no illusion; Calliastra was not Duster. She was the child of gods; Duster was a child of the streets. Those streets had swallowed her whole and spit her out gods only knew where; her body had never been found. Jewel knew. She had searched, the power of House Terafin at her fingertips, even if her ability to use it effectively had yet to be honed. But the compromised magisterial guards and their damaged and lost missing persons' files had led to nowhere.

No one believed that Duster had survived. Jewel was certain she had not.

It was not, therefore, of Duster that she should have been thinking when facing a woman who was, to all intents and purposes, a living, walking god.

But she did. Duster had never been convenient, and apparently death hadn't changed anything.

"I don't need to believe it," Jewel replied, as the crack widened. She had a small terror of heights, but also had a bard who could speak to the wind on hand; she could—with minor effort—ignore the possibility of falling to her death. "I only need to *know*. Perhaps, in your eavesdropping, you failed to understand why we are in Ariane's ancient halls. If you think we came to rescue Shianne, you are mistaken."

"Rescue is not the word I would have used," Calliastra replied, drawing herself up to a much fuller height than she'd occupied in Duster's form. Or in any form, really. Shadows coiled in her eyes; shadows curled around the contours of her cheeks, her cheekbones, falling as if it were prehensile hair down her back. "You have killed her; only your own mortality prevents you from understanding this."

Jewel nodded, as if this made sense—because, when Calliastra spoke the words, it did. She seemed a goddess as she stood, chin lifted, in her raiment of night.

And it seemed, to Jewel, that the children of gods must be lonely creatures. "Shianne," she said, although she didn't look away from Calliastra.

"Matriarch."

She barely flinched at the use of the word. "If I understand correctly, you are—all of the Arianni are—the White Lady's children."

"Yes."

"But you were earliest."

". . . Yes."

"I don't understand the concept of children and offspring as it exists for the gods. But you understand the concept as it exists for the White Lady."

"Yes."

"Explain it, to me."

Silence.

"The child you carry now, I understand. But bearing children doesn't kill us. It doesn't require our deaths. Could you have children in any other way?"

Shadow rumbled beneath her palm. "She could."

Shianne, however, said, "No."

"You *could*," Shadow insisted.

"Your truths are vast and flexible, ancient," Shianne replied—which was more a shock than it should have been, given the day so far. "Ours are not.

The White Lady was firstborn; she survived the wildest of the ancient days, bound as she was to the lay of the ever-changing land." Silver eyes met brown, assessing them. "Had I decided to attempt such an act of creation, every single being thus created would have been the palest imitation of me. And I? I was already the palest of imitations of her. An echo of her song.

"But that is not, I divine, what you are asking."

Terafin, the Winter King said. The single word was all of his warning. Jewel understood. But she continued.

Jewel nodded. "I want to know why. Why did she create?"

"You must ask her, Matriarch. I am part of her thought, but not—never—the whole of it."

Jewel was almost certain she would never have the courage to ask. If Ariane was the daughter of two gods—and she must be—they were vastly more forbidding in their combination than Calliastra. "I think," Jewel said softly, "she was lonely."

Silence.

In the hush before it was filled, Jewel heard the keening of the wind. She felt the rumble of the earth. She heard the hiss of at least two cats; the one beneath her palm was, it appeared, holding or husbanding his breath.

Calliastra laughed. The shadows that framed her and granted her a cold, beckoning majesty shifted as she once again stepped toward Jewel, ignoring the cats and the Arianni Prince who stood in her way. Celleriant brought his sword to bear; she reached out, without so much as a frown, to brush it aside. And it went.

Jewel, the Winter King said, changing tactics.

She wasn't this powerful the first time I met her, Jewel replied.

She was vastly more cautious on those roads.

Clearly. Then again, Ariane is unlikely to ride through these halls while the Wild Hunt carries her standard. But even as she spoke the words, she knew that Ariane's absence was not what made the difference. Calliastra's strength was evidence of Allasakar's growing dominion.

"What," Calliastra asked, as she continued to walk, "do you know of loneliness?" Her words were cold but not brittle; she spoke as if ice could burn. "You live a handful of years. Less, if you are foolish. A handful of years in isolation? It is *nothing*."

Jewel stood her ground. Shadow had fallen silent beneath her hand; no hiss, no criticism escaped his lips. Night and Snow did not land. Celleriant leaped again, into folds of silent wind; he brought his shield to bear as he landed.

"Do not," Calliastra said softly, "stand between us. I cannot take you; I *can* destroy you."

Jewel could see only Celleriant's back, but she knew he would be smiling. She was uncertain that his death was inevitable; she was certain that while she stood exposed, he would not run from it.

No, she thought, he would leap toward it, testing himself. Always. "Lord Celleriant."

He said—and did—nothing. Shianne, however, whispered his name; he turned toward her. Jewel couldn't see his expression.

Calliastra was not concerned. Avandar's shields grew bright; orange blended with gold in a wall that hugged Jewel's body, sliding beneath her feet. The domicis did not otherwise move. Nor did the Winter King. There was a hush of held breath and stillness, as if everything in the great hall that was not Calliastra had become backdrop.

To Jewel, they almost had.

What had she seen, in Duster? In the girl that she had slapped in rage, in the girl that she had wanted—many days—to push out the nearest window? What had she seen that had caused her, time and again, to risk everything just to make a home for her?

I was twelve, she thought. *Twelve. I believed in everything.*

But had she? She couldn't believe in love that lasted forever; she had been an orphan. She couldn't believe that the universe was either just or fair; her parents had done nothing at all to deserve their deaths. They had struggled with poverty and long, lean, very cold months for all of Jewel's life with them.

There had been no magic in their lives. No great, grand halls. No women of stone who were nonetheless women of flesh. No gods, except in their prayers—prayers which fell on no ears, at all. There had been no forests of silver, gold, and diamond, and no burning trees. No winged cats. No Arianni princelings. No immortal men who longed for death, for the peace of an ending.

Just Oma, and father and mother and Jewel herself. And Jewel's curse. Jewel's gift.

Oracle.

"Yes, Jewel Markess. Oracle."

Calliastra froze, then. She froze, her arms outstretched, her fingers inches—if that—from Jewel's shoulders.

The Oracle stood, robed, hooded, her arms by her sides, not two yards from Calliastra's back. "I am late. Forgive me."

"You are late?" Calliastra said, turning, her hands falling into fists. "If so, you are late by design; nothing is accidental in your life."

The Oracle did not deign to reply. She turned, instead, to Shianne—who was about as friendly and welcoming as the daughter of darkness had been. "Well met," she said.

Shianne inclined head. "It is said that despair is your shadow; despair and loss."

"The events which bring either despair or loss are not of my making, daughter of Ariane. You know, perhaps better than anyone present, how short my reach is. I would never have chosen to lose you. I would never have counseled you to so much as glance at the road upon which you have chosen to walk."

Shianne's heavy lashes fell briefly. "Were it not for you, I would never have known the path existed. I would never have seen the need to walk it."

"And in this new age, would you now recant? Would you choose to ignore that road?"

"Why do you even ask? We can but walk forward; there is no road back."

"No. Not even for one who can walk the different branches of time, seeking always for some path that will bring her, at last, to the present."

"You speak of Evayne," Jewel said.

"Yes. Of all of those blessed—or cursed—by the gift of vision, she is dearest to my heart. Her life is a dim, dim echo of mine, and it will be brief in comparison. It is to speak with Evayne that I have come, but I do not see her among your party. And yet it is perhaps good fortune indeed to find you here, sister," she said at last, to Calliastra, who was standing before her, shadows once again wrapped tightly about her, arms drawn in and crossed.

Family, Jewel's Oma said, *is complicated.*

Calliastra said nothing. She really did remind Jewel of Duster, now that she looked nothing at all like her.

"I am uncertain what brings you here," the Oracle continued, "but I have a few words of advice."

"I am not paying the price for your advice—no matter how wordy it might be." Duster would have said: *I don't need your damn advice. I don't need* anyone's *advice.*

"No. You have not asked; it is a gift. A warning, no more."

And just as if she *were* Duster, she bridled, the shadows leaping around her in frustrated, silent anger. She said nothing, waiting, her hands carved, white fists. If the threat were offered *to* her directly, she could cope. She could laugh, could mock, could show everyone—show the world—that she wasn't afraid.

But that, Jewel thought, was not the way this was going to go. As she'd thought it before, in the dim past.

"You are in danger," the Oracle told Calliastra.

Jewel's expression was stiff, neutral; she held it that way with the ease of long practice. No, she thought, not long. Duster had been with her for only three or four years, half a lifetime ago. But . . . practice, nonetheless.

Calliastra's expression was neither. Her eyes almost literally sparked; would have, if shadow had been flame. "I?" she asked, voice the same burning ice. "*I* am in danger?"

The Oracle was as impregnable as Jewel—but with, in Jewel's opinion, significantly less effort. "Yes."

Silence rarely held so much anger. Clearly it couldn't contain it. "And what do you consider a threat *to me?* Am I now to fear death, as if I were an insignificant mortal?"

"Gods have perished," the Oracle replied.

"Fools have perished!" Calliastra snapped—just as Duster might have.

She is not your Duster, Avandar said.

No. Of course not. Jewel exhaled, glancing, briefly, at the rest of her companions. Angel's hands danced in the air; Jewel almost laughed. *Yes*, she signed back, bearing the full brunt of Avandar's disapproval. *Like Duster.*

She is not harmless.

No. But neither was Duster.

He didn't believe her, of course. He couldn't. A streetwise orphan who had died running headlong into demons was insignificant to Avandar. He was wise enough to refrain from pointing out that she should have been just as insignificant to The Terafin; it was a fight he couldn't win.

It is not a fight—

But it was.

Jewel believed in fate. She didn't believe that fate was immutable; she believed that it could—with work and blood and terror—be shifted by inches, if it could be changed at all. But she had lived under the storm clouds of her peculiar gift for almost as long as she could remember, and she understood what it told her, now.

Or maybe life was always like this. She could draw a line between her experience as The Terafin and her experience as a seer; she could make it solid. But life leaked across those boundaries, in either direction. And she knew, watching this scion of gods, that if it was at all possible, she would keep her.

She would keep Calliastra, who was walking, inevitable death to those who learned—however possible—to love her.

"I did not venture here to argue with you, sister," the Oracle said, in her gratingly reasonable tone. "And I offer the warning as a gift to you, in your hour of need."

Had Calliastra been Duster, the Oracle's face would bear the marks of her hand. Or worse. And Jewel thought the Oracle knew this.

"You cannot possibly believe that *anyone* here has the power to harm me!"

"I did not speak of harm," the Oracle replied. "But if it eases you at all, I will. Uncertainty is oft the bane of our kind."

Calliastra spit shadow.

Jewel lifted a hand. "Oracle," she said.

Both women—if they were that—turned to look at her. Only the Oracle was smiling.

"Calliastra does not require your warning or your concern."

"Concern is not a requirement," the Oracle agreed. "But it is mine to give. As with any gift, any true gift, what is given is gone from the giver; what the gifted chooses to do with it is beyond me. But you must understand, Jewel Markess, that you are Sen.

"There is a reason that the Cities of Man were feared, even by the gods."

"I hunted in the *streets* of those Cities," Calliastra said.

"Yes, sister, you did. But you did not—ever—hunt the Sen."

And Jewel said, "But she did."

She would have clawed the words back the instant they left her mouth, but that was impossible; they hung in the air as if they hovered on bright, sharp wings. Every eye was turned toward her; she felt, briefly, as if she had stepped into a familiar nightmare, and was now standing naked in the middle of the hall.

The Oracle inclined her head almost graciously at the correction. "So she did."

Calliastra, however, was staring at Jewel.

"She is seer-born," the Oracle said, answering the question that the daughter of Allasakar hadn't asked.

"She sees less than you."

"I am willing to entertain your polite fictions, and perhaps—if she survives—Jewel Markess will be likewise willing."

"You think she's the danger." The words were flatter. And because they were, they carried far more threat.

"No, sister. Not directly. She is only mortal."

Calliastra laughed. It was a bitter, bleak sound. It was—gods—Duster's

laugh. "I am the daughter of Allasakar and Laursana. I understand temptation; I understand the price paid if one surrenders to it; who else could understand it so well as I?" Her laughter was low, velvet, and angry. Jewel had
heard angry laughter in her life—in politics it was often hard to avoid—but
no anger was as raw as Duster's. Or as deep. "You think that *she* could offer
me anything that would tempt me to harm or destroy myself?"

The Oracle, perhaps wisely, chose not to answer.

And it was far too late, regardless. She'd insulted Calliastra. Calliastra was
not Duster—but for just this minute, she might as well have been. "I am not
afraid," she all but snarled.

No, no, she wouldn't be. Not of death. Not of pain. Not even of Jewel, not
yet. If fear came at all, it would come—as it had for Duster—later. And all
Jewel had to do was survive.

A bit hard, when the threat was a god. A bit hard, she thought, when she
had so little to offer. Duster had at least needed food, clothing, a roof over her
head. What did a god need?

"That, indeed, is the question, is it not?" the Oracle said.

Calliastra couldn't look more incensed. She didn't try. Instead, she turned
to Jewel. "It appears our discussion will have to be postponed; the nature of
all such discussions is private." Her lips, full and red, curved in a hard, harsh
smile at severe odds with the texture of that mouth.

"The Oracle," Shianne unexpectedly said, "sees all. If it is secrecy you
desire—"

"I do not care what the Oracle sees; she is so addled she is barely able to
differentiate between reality and possibility."

"She has no choice; she sees. I don't think she has any way of averting her
gaze." Jewel was only slightly surprised to realize that the voice was her own.

"Do not think to tell me that she suffers," Calliastra replied. "She who
stands at the heart of all possibilities, and understands, before they occur,
what their cost is, large and small."

"She suffers," Jewel replied. "She sees the end of all things before even the
smallest beginning."

"I see the end of all things," was the bitter reply. "And none come to me
seeking solace, advice, or wisdom. None come seeking company." As if becoming aware of the words that had just left her, she straightened. "And I
require none of these things."

Jewel said nothing. The Oracle was likewise silent, her words having had
their effect. Calliastra was rigid for another long, held breath, and then she
slowly relaxed. "You do not intend to leave us immediately."

"No, sister; I have come for a purpose, and I have not yet fulfilled it." She had inserted herself between Jewel and the daughter of darkness; how or when, Jewel could not later say.

Jewel glanced at Kallandras; he was silent and watchful. So was Shadow. Jewel found only one of these disturbing. She didn't enjoy being told she was stupid—but the silence was unnerving. It was loud in all the wrong ways.

The great, gray cat rippled in place, bright sheen of fur traveling out from Jewel's hand as if he were a pond into which she'd dropped a large stone. This was more disturbing than even his silence; she withdrew her hand.

He growled until she returned her hand to its resting place.

"I do not understand cats," she whispered.

"Because you are *stupid*." He added, his voice a rumble, "Your stupidity is not *our* fault."

"It *is*," Snow said, from somewhere above the ground. "It is *your* fault." His voice was not notably deeper.

"Her *ignorance*, maybe," Shadow conceded. "But her *stupidity* is her own."

Calliastra's eyes had become rounder with each growling insult. She looked above Shadow's head to meet Jewel's gaze. "Why," she asked, as if admission of curiosity was being dragged out of her against her will, "do you tolerate this if you have any choice? Do not tell me 'because they are cats.' This is not the first time I have encountered your cats, and it will not be my last—that blessing does not exist in any world or time."

Shadow was rock steady—and silent.

Snow and Night, however, were indulging in the type of rambunctious catcalls that were safely made at a distance. It was embarrassing. But given her early life, and given the suspension of rules that now governed her current one, Jewel could live with embarrassment.

"Were the cats different?"

"They were, no doubt, different when you first encountered them, were they not?"

Jewel almost couldn't remember. "They were stone," she said slowly. "But . . . they weren't different until they were in the presence of the Winter King."

"And then?"

"They were silent."

"Exactly. If you cannot force them to alter their base behavior—and you are only mortal, after all—you can force them to conform to your status as their lord."

"I have my doubts."

"It is precisely because you have those doubts that they are free to run roughshod over any dignity you might otherwise possess. And you will require that dignity, Jewel Markess. You have very little else of value in this place."

"I wasn't aware that mortal dignity had value."

"Ask Viandaran." She finally condescended to look directly at Shadow. "Why, Eldest, have you condescended to serve a mortal?"

Jewel, behind Shadow's face—and exposed fangs—couldn't tell if he reacted at all. He certainly didn't answer. "You can," she said, in the lowest of voices, because she was curious to hear the answer herself.

"He doesn't *want* to," Snow shouted down.

"They are brave," Calliastra said, "when they are at a safe remove." She lifted one white, shadowed hand; her fingers were long and graceful; they lacked the calluses and the scars that Jewel's shorter, stubbier hands had picked up over the years. "Come here."

"Don't *want* to," Snow replied. "*Make* me."

"*Make* him," Night agreed, swooping in low.

"With your permission?" Calliastra now said, to Jewel. Jewel was so shocked she had no words. The silence intensified when Calliastra brought her arms down in a sudden lunge that apparently ended with wings.

Great, rising pinions and arches that seemed all of black or obsidian glittered in the uneven light and the falling shadows of pillars.

Snow and Night hissed. Shadow was silent. So was Jewel, but she expected the reasons for it were vastly different. Calliastra had always been compelling. She caused heat to rise in all the wrong ways just by speaking a syllable or two. She promised—everything. The implication of that promise made even the inevitable death that followed seem trivial and inconsequential.

Jewel had met her only twice, and it had been true both times.

This was different. As the wings grew, so did their owner, becoming, as she unfolded, something that could never be mistaken for human. She was—had been—statuesque; she was not, and had never been—except when she took on forms and shapes that weren't hers—small.

Now, she towered. She was ten feet—maybe twelve—in height; her wings, as they snapped open, were double that, taken tip to tip. She was night's daughter, here; one could not see the influence of the other parent at all.

And Jewel understood, viscerally, *why* people followed *Allasakar* to their deaths. If he was even a tenth as majestic and compelling as his daughter, what choice would one have?

Jewel's fingers curled around Shadow's fur—which had risen. He hissed, which brought her instantly back to herself. No, she thought, as Calliastra lifted her perfect face toward the heights of these endless halls, she *was* herself.

She had met gods before.

She had met gods in the Between, where gods and mortals might safely meet. Until today, she had never understood why the word "safely" was spoken in that context. But the air enfolded raised, black wings, bearing the scion of gods aloft, and Jewel had to force herself to breathe again at the sight of her flight.

Shadow growled.

"Oh, shut up," she told him, still captivated—as all must be—by the sight of Calliastra in flight. "It's not as if she can catch them."

"She is *dangerous*," Shadow replied, his voice rendered less lovely by comparison to Calliastra's. "She is dangerous to *you*." He exhaled and shook her hand off, padding away. When he was three or four yards distant, he lifted his head and roared. It was as if he'd swallowed a dragon.

He took to the sky as if attacking it.

"Shadow!"

The Winter King was amused. *You are afraid that he will damage her?*

No—but—

He has no sense of his own dignity, and consequently none whatsoever of hers. It is the reason that cats are oft despised by those who have the power to survive their constant companionship. Only the powerful and the focused can force them to behave in ways that are unnatural to them.

Then why did she seem so surprised that I couldn't?

Ah. She was surprised at the extent *of the insolence you allowed. Even mortals were capable of forcing almost acceptable behavior when the cats were in their presence. You are their lord while you live—and they might as well have* no *lord, given the respect they show.*

And she's going to teach them respect? The goddess—and she could think of no other word that suited her at the moment—moved as if she were ebon lightning. Snow was not the strategist that Shadow was; nor was Night. She understood why Shadow had taken to air when he dove *into* his pale brother an instant before Calliastra's wing bisected him.

And it would have.

She thought of the Warden of Dreams, then.

You seemed certain that she could not kill the cats.

I was. I am. But certainty in the face of Calliastra in this here and now seemed a very, very tenuous thing; it was hard to hold.

Night avoided her wings, which should—given their size—have been easy. It wasn't. She needed no weapon in the air—the wings were deadly. The Warden of Dreams had wounded both Snow and Night—with ridiculous ease. That had been in the dreamscape.

That was, and is, his seat of power, the Winter King replied. *In these halls, or in the Deepings, he would have posed little threat. Here, she is his equal in that place. Perhaps his superior.*

Jewel turned to Kallandras. Before she could speak, Celleriant did.

"No," he told her. "If you mean to ask him to ask the wild wind to intercede on behalf of your cats, it is unwise."

Since Jewel had meant to do exactly that, she fell silent.

"Kallandras' control of the wild wind is very like your control of your cats. He cajoles. He encourages. He plays."

"I don't do any of those," Jewel pointed out.

"You do not *command*, except when your reflexes overtake your thoughts. It is my belief that you could—but only for short periods."

"They would make my life a living hell if I did."

"Yes, lord. So, too, the wind. It will accept brief orders, brief controls, brief entrapment—just as the cats do—but the wilderness has its own sense of pride and dignity. Calliastra is in the air, now. She commands. Disobedience is only barely possible—and reminding the wind of its helplessness is never wise.

"Reminding any immortal of helplessness is never wise." He glanced at Kallandras, but felt no obvious need to remind the bard of the basic facts he now offered Jewel. Then again, the bard probably didn't need it.

"She is angry," Celleriant continued, voice softer, face raised. "I have only once seen her in full fury, and it was long, long ago." His eyes were almost literally alight. "I feel young again, in this place; it is almost as if it is the ancient Deepings in Summer."

But Shianne, who had come closer to where Jewel stood, said, "That was unwise, Matriarch."

"Please, just call me Jewel. Which part was unwise?"

"All of it, I fear. I was willing—barely—to approach the Oracle. Not even when I was immune to the death she carries within her would I have dared Calliastra. She is too willful, too unpredictable, and too spiteful; her malice is frequently petty, but the means by which she expresses it, less so."

"Will she kill my cats?"

"No—although she will try. She blunts the edge of her fury, here; if I did not know better, I would say she chooses to do so deliberately. Her anger is unlike yours—or mine; when it reaches a point beyond her endurance, the manifestation is as you see it now. Thus, the anger of those born to gods." Her voice held no revulsion; it held the faintest tinge of awe. "But I, too, remember.

"If she sorrows, however, you must be well away. Nothing, with Calliastra, is safe: not her fury, not her contempt, not her desire. Even her love is deadly, it is so twisted and impure."

"You may be mortal," Jewel replied, "but you don't know much about mortal love."

"We are not speaking of mortals," Shianne said.

". . . No," Jewel replied, tearing her eyes away from the aerial, deadly, dance. She signed. Angel approached; she had maybe half of his attention. Fair enough. Given Calliastra and the cats, she knew she didn't merit more of it.

Duster, her fingers said.

His eyes narrowed, subtly altering the contours of his face; she could see the shadows of the former spire of his hair. *Not Duster*, he signed, emphatically.

Duster, she said again. Her fingers rose, making a question of the name.

He hesitated, and turned, again, to the sky. "I can see it," he said, choosing to forgo den-sign; it wasn't meant for subtleties. Experience lent the gestures weight and meaning, but sometimes, not enough. "But, Jay, she's not."

Jewel nodded. It was not in agreement.

"Is it worth the risk?" He didn't speak of the cost—to Jewel—of Duster's eventual acceptance of the den. He knew it only secondhand.

"Yes."

"It's not a small risk."

"No."

"She's a—"

"Yes. Like a goddess. She's lived forever. She'll outlive us both."

"As long as she's not the reason she does," he replied, with a tight, crooked smile.

"You don't like it."

He shrugged. "I didn't care much for Duster, truth be told."

"She saved your life."

He nodded. "She wasn't the type of person it was safe to care much for; she'd take it badly."

Jewel grimaced; it was true.

"She's like Duster, that way."

"I think she's like Duster in a lot of ways."

"And you think we need her."

Jewel hesitated. Angel marked it.

"Will you survive her?" he asked instead.

When Jewel failed to answer, he turned to the Oracle in her dark gray robes; they drifted in a breeze that touched nothing else—at least not on the ground. Her hands hung by her sides, but they were curved in loose fists as she watched Calliastra rage across the heights.

"Angel—"

He stepped past Jewel toward the Oracle; she glanced at him. "You do not want to ask me a question, child."

"I do," he replied. Terrick proved that he could pay attention to two things at once; he lessened the distance between Angel and himself, coming to stand at his back, ax in hands.

"You do not. Understand that your Jewel has come this way seeking only to ask me a question."

"She wants more than that."

"No. But to ask it, she must endure more."

"You answered Teller's question."

"He did not ask a question. He asked for a glimpse of what I see, no more. Tell me, do you think he has benefited from it? What he sees he does not understand; he knows only enough to fear it. Fear of the future does not—and has never—stopped it from arriving.

"Fear casts a shadow long and dark, and he has chosen—perhaps unwittingly—to walk within it." She lifted her left hand, uncurling the fingers and exposing a very scarred palm. "It is costly to afford those born without vision a glimpse of it."

"He doesn't want to look," Jewel told the Oracle.

"He does. He wishes to know if you will survive the choice you make today."

"I've made no choice, today."

The Oracle smiled for the first time, a hint of genuine approval in the lift of lips.

"But I understand why you're here. I understand—I think—what you want."

"You might understand some small, small part of what I want—but you are mortal, Jewel. I have called you Sen; you are not. Not yet, and perhaps not ever. You have set foot upon my path; you have not reached the heart of my home. You hope to have Shianne lead you there. You understand why it is impossible for her."

"I don't."

"Her question is not yours. Her choices—like your Teller's, or your Angel's—are likewise unique to her. What she loves and what she fears, what she hopes to lose and what she cannot bear to let go of—all of these things are defined by her existence and her experience."

But Jewel shook her head. "You might not choose the whole of the path I walk—but you chose where it started. It started here. You meant me to find Shianne and her sisters."

"No, Jewel. I knew that you would. But there were many, many choices you might have made when presented with this forgotten footnote in our ancient history. Many." She turned, then, to where Adam listed against Kallandras. "The choices he might make are fewer. He is young. But I did not choose him as your companion; you did. Why?"

"Because I think he needs to learn whatever this path of yours has to teach. I can't learn it for him. I would, if I could."

"Yes. That is your besetting sin, if you can be said to have only one. You understand much, and yet, do not know that you understand it."

"I understand one thing."

"And that?"

"You want me to keep Calliastra."

"She is my sister," the Oracle replied; she did not deny it.

"What does that even mean to the children of gods? You don't share parents. You weren't raised the normal way—not according to Shianne. They're *all* your siblings. Ariane. Coralonne. The Warden of Dreams—both of him."

"Yes. Tell me, Jewel, did you love your Duster?"

Angel sucked in air; it whistled across his teeth.

Jewel lifted her chin, no more.

"Given what she cost you, given that it was in part her hand that pushed you into Lord Waverly, given the difficulty she caused the weaker and more vulnerable members of your den—"

"Enough."

The Oracle nodded gravely. "More than enough, I think. Your answer is yes. And it is no. And it is yes. It revolves, evolves, shifts. It is built on the folly of hope; it is shredded by frustration and despair; it is tainted by guilt and grief. And yet, at its core, it remains. You are mortal, and yet you contain these complexities with ease."

"It was never easy."

"Let me ask you a different question."

"Can I demand something in return?"

The Oracle's eyes narrowed. Something about her expression reminded

Jewel of Jarven, of all people. "What would you have in return for the simple, spoken answer that is all you have to offer?"

"At a time of my choosing, an answer to a like question. A simple answer."

"You are bold."

"No. I'm a merchant. I don't need to answer your question. You don't need to ask it. Neither of us will starve or die."

"And how will you enforce compliance? I might receive your answer and choose to withhold my own."

"I'll trust your word. Words seem to have meaning, for you."

"Do they?"

"Yes."

"You are certain."

"Yes."

"You have grown since you last walked the Stone Deepings. Very well. Yes, I will accept this exchange. I cannot guarantee you will like my answer—but you cannot guarantee that I will appreciate yours. And if you fail to answer it, for reasons of your own?"

"An answer for an answer," Jewel replied. "Your question?" She cringed at the sound of metal against stone, and did her best to ignore it; Angel didn't. If the hall was about to lose support pillars, she trusted him to tell her.

"Why have you considered taking Calliastra as companion? You are aware that you can neither command nor control her; you are aware that her love is death. There has never, in her long history, been an exception. If she travels with you, all of your companions—saving only the Arianni and Viandaran—will be at risk. She has never been master of her base nature; she will keep no promise she makes to you, even if she intends to do so.

"You understand this. You are not fool enough to lie to yourself, even if you paint pretty pictures with words for the benefit of your followers."

Jewel nodded.

"Why, then? She is as you see her now: rage, fury, and death if you are not powerful enough. You are not," she added, in case this needed to be said. "Yet you stand beneath her long shadow, and you do not see her power. You see the similarities to a mortal girl, dead over half your lifetime ago. Am I mistaken, Jewel? Do you now tell yourself pretty, mortal lies? You cannot believe that you need her, as you once claimed to need your Duster."

"You know a lot about our lives," Angel said.

Jewel lifted a hand in sharp den-sign. He subsided, but it clearly took effort. "No," she said softly. "I would like to believe that I need her. I would like to believe that this—this impulse—is an artifact of my talent."

"By which you mean it is not."

Jewel exhaled. She didn't even consider lying; she did consider silence. "I didn't understand the nature of the Stone Deepings when I first walked them. I didn't truly understand them when I held the road against the Wild Hunt."

"You do not feel you understand them now."

"No. But I understand that it's not just because I'm seer-born that I can walk this path. It's not because I was seer-born that I could walk the Stone Deepings. I thought, at the time, it was because Avandar showed me the way. Avandar could have held the road against Ariane; I'm certain of it."

"He would not be so unwise."

Jewel ignored this. "He couldn't have held the road the way I did. And he couldn't have walked this path."

Avandar said nothing.

Jewel exhaled. "He couldn't follow me into the dreaming. He can't follow me into the forest unless I consciously desire it."

The Oracle inclined her head, watching; she didn't blink. It was hard to pin her eyes down to a single color, and Jewel gave up trying; the color of the Oracle's eyes was almost entirely irrelevant. The contours of her face, the lines—or the lack of lines—that defined it were likewise irrelevant. Calliastra's winged shadow passed over them both, accompanied by the growls and hiss of the three cats.

"I walk these paths. Even this one. I don't know if the others could without your direct—and continuous—intervention."

"If you refer to those born in the mortal world, Viandaran could," the Oracle replied. "But it would be costly."

"For him, or for you?"

The Oracle did not answer.

"I don't walk these paths because I'm seer-born."

"You most assuredly do."

"And all seers walked them?"

"Terafin," a familiar voice said, "you play the Oracle's game. It is costly in ways that even you, with your experience, cannot imagine."

Jewel turned. To Evayne she offered what she hadn't offered the two first-born: a full bow.

Chapter Sixteen

"**W**ELL MET, TERAFIN," the seer said. Her robes—the same deep hue of midnight—looked at home in these ancient halls, cats squalling like vocal storm overhead. They caught her attention and earned a grimace, no more.

"Well met. Before you ask, I have no idea what the date is."

Evayne's smile, glimpsed briefly as she drew her hood away from her face to rest across her shoulders, was sharp but genuine. She glanced, once, at Kallandras, who offered her a bow that put Jewel's gesture of respect to shame.

This Evayne was the older Evayne. "You walk a path of the Oracle's choosing. You walk in her shadow. You no doubt intend to take and pass her test."

"Will I succeed?" she asked, bluntly.

"I am not the person of whom you must ask that question," was her counter. "But it is, as you suspect, a pointless question, here." She turned to the Oracle, who waited. "I did not expect to find you here." Her tone, as Shianne's, was chilly.

"You did not look," the Oracle replied. "But you seldom do."

"For you? No. If you require my presence, you will find me."

"And did you expect to see Jewel?"

Voice even cooler, Evayne said, "I do not know why you persist in playing these games. I thought I might—might—meet Shianne, and I see that she is here."

Shianne was silent.

"My apologies, Lady." Evayne bowed. "I am Evayne. Evayne a'Neamis. I walk, with my lord's permission, across the paths carved by time. I recognize you because we have met before—in my life. In yours, we have not."

"A'Neamis?" She turned to Celleriant and spoke. His reply, soft, was almost inaudible.

Shianne turned again to Evayne; her face was still. Her eyes, however, were unblinking. "You . . . are the child of a god?"

Evayne nodded, grave now. "I am. But I was born as your child will be born, not as your Lord was."

Shianne said, to Celleriant, "I do not understand."

Celleriant replied, but not in Weston. Before Jewel could ask him what he'd said, the Oracle spoke again.

"You have not yet answered my question."

Evayne turned. She lifted a hand, and let it fall as Jewel drew breath.

"I want Calliastra because I see something in her that I might—just might—be able to reach. I want her because yes, she's deadly, and yes, she's dangerous. I'd say I want her in spite of that—but I'm not sure it would be true. She is beautiful," she added softly, "but not because she offers death or temptation; she's like—like this place. This ancient, empty hall.

"She's like my forest. She's like my rooms. None of these things is of me. None of them are part of how I perceive myself. But they respond to me, regardless. The strength of my own belief—or my anger—defines how and where I walk in these spaces.

"It defines how I touch the dreaming. And it defines how I touch people—like me—who are trapped there."

"And is that the answer, Jewel Markess?"

"Yes. Because if I had met her when I was twelve years old, I would have offered her a home. It would have been hard. It *was* hard, the last time I tried something similar. I would have offered anyway, knowing it.

"Calliastra is not the only daughter of darkness I've met."

The Oracle stilled.

"And I offered a home to the last one, as well. She even accepted it, for a brief time."

"And you offered for the same reasons?"

Jewel shook her head. "I offered because she was sixteen years old and alone in my city, and the Kings had been advised to execute her simply for existing. I offered because Sigurne Mellifas spoke against that execution. And I offered because yes, she reminded me of Duster. I couldn't save Duster. If I could go back in time, right now, I *wouldn't* save her. Because to save her would be to lose everyone else." Jewel closed her eyes for a long second. Opened them to see that the Oracle hadn't moved. She wasn't the color of stone—but she had all of its substance.

"I gave her orders. She followed them. It killed her. It saved everyone else."

"My sister will never follow your orders; she will never obey your commands."

"No."

"You seek to expatiate your own sense of guilt?"

"Who doesn't?" Jewel countered. "Who among us doesn't? Only the people who feel no guilt at all. I can't bring Duster back. I can't save her life. She's dead. She will be dead for the rest of my natural life. In that regard, no.

"But it's not as simple as that. Calliastra has come to me twice as Duster. Twice. Duster is not the only person I've loved—and lost—in my life. If you asked me on a calm day, I'd tell you she's not even the most important. It's said that Calliastra takes on the appearance that is most beguiling and tempting to her victims."

The Oracle nodded.

"Not a single member of my family would tell her—or you, or anyone— that *Duster* is my temptation or my secret desire. And, Oracle, I wouldn't either. If there are faces and voices that have that power, Duster's not one of them. She puts me on my guard. She reminds me that I need to keep perfect control of everything I do while in her presence. I can't lose my temper. I can't lose *control*.

"Did I love Duster? Yes. In the complicated way you love people who cause damage on most days just by opening their mouths. Not in the way you love people in whom you want to be lost—forever. And yet, Calliastra chose her.

"There are only two reasons I can see for that. The first, that Calliastra's ability to discern love or desire is weaker than myth or legend claims. I don't believe that. I believe she has that power. Yet if she has, she uses it poorly against me. The second is more complicated."

"I would have your complicated answer."

Of course she would. "She chose Duster because she understood what Duster meant to me. She understood that I saw Duster as she was. Not as she *could* be, although I saw that, too—but as she *was*. She understands enough about people to know that I did love Duster—even as she was. Did I want her to change? Yes, probably. I wanted her to be happy.

"But if she had never changed, if she could never be happy, I'd've kept her until the end anyway."

"You did."

Jewel nodded. "That's most of the answer," she added.

"But not all." There was no question in the Oracle's tone.

Jewel exhaled. "Not all. In the Stone Deepings, I had Avandar. He knew that road. He found it, and if I understand what's followed, he kept it hidden. Not from you," she added, "and not from the other firstborn.

"I should have died there. Had it not been so close to Scarran, I would have. But it was. I survived. I survived because I could root myself in my own life. My life is not yours. It's not Shianne's. It's not Angel's—although his is probably closest. But it wasn't my life in Terafin that I drew on; it was the life that drove me, in the end, to the manse.

"Duster was part of that life. Everything I wanted for her. Everything I feared. And I need those things, going forward. Not just about Duster—but about everything else. I won't survive this place, I won't survive your test, if I lose sight of who I was. It's the root of everything I am now. It's the foundation for everything I hope to be."

"And everything you fear to be?"

Jewel nodded. Shadow could apparently fight, hiss, growl, *and* eavesdrop—and he let her know exactly how impressed he was by her admission of fear.

The Oracle actually smiled at that. "My sister is not wrong; you let them run far too wild."

But Jewel shook her head. "I'm not Calliastra or Ariane; I'm not you. I only have the time for so many battles in a day, so I have to choose the right ones. I've been called far worse than stupid in my life; it's mostly harmless."

"An interesting approach."

"It's the only one I have. I don't know what I'm doing. I don't know where I'm going. But I know who I am, and I know why I'm here. And I have to remember both." She lowered the hands she had lifted; she often gestured when she talked.

"You have fulfilled your end of our bargain," the Oracle said. "But I think it wise, for the moment, to draw my sister away. She will return to you," she added. "But in her current state, it is likely that she would kill at least three of your party; she seldom rages so openly. I will admit that I am curious."

"Will you admit that you've seen how it ends?"

The Oracle inclined her head. "I have seen how it ends in all its various permutations, for good or ill. I will admit I have my favorites. But my ability to affect the outcome is slender."

Jewel frowned.

"I cannot force anyone to walk my road. I could not force you to do so. I did not meet your Duster; I know of her, of course. I can see the way her story is still tied to yours. The effect you had on your Duster, I cannot have on my sister; I can anger her, irritate her, sting her pride. I cannot move her in any other way."

"How do you intend to get her to leave, then?"

"As I said: I can anger her. And I am likely to survive it." She lifted her arms. Jewel had just enough warning to turn away before the Oracle's hands plunged into her own chest; from there, she pulled the crystal that Jewel thought of as her heart.

"Follow the road you deem wisest," the Oracle said, as she lifted the crystal in both hands. "There is—as you have come to understand—no other way to reach me." She spoke three loud, thunderous words; her voice—always measured and always soft—rose above wind and cats and angry daughter of darkness, drowning them all.

From out of the crystal itself, lightning flew. Pale, white, it dimmed all other light in the hall. It dimmed the darkness of Calliastra. It grew wings as it traveled; wings, shape, form. Calliastra turned, cats forgotten; the cats themselves yowled as lightning branched without warning and hit them all.

"*How DARE you?*"

No mistaking that voice. There was nothing of velvet or desire in it; it was pure, raw, rage. "Angel!"

Angel nodded, although his gaze was fastened to lightning, shadow, and howling, enraged cats. He spoke to Terrick in Rendish. Terrick, like Angel, was instantly wary.

Avandar.

I have been ready to depart for some time, he replied, his inner voice so dry it should have caught fire. *Well done, Jewel. There is some hope, in the end, that you will survive this.*

Winter King.

The Winter King knelt. Jewel did not give orders to Kallandras, but they weren't necessary. He braced—and settled—Adam upon the Winter King, and the great stag rose, bearing his weight. Any other mount would have dropped him.

"Celleriant—we're leaving."

He, too, implied that he had been waiting. But he turned to speak, briefly, with Shianne before he joined her. Shianne followed, gathering the skirts of the dress Snow had made for her. Jewel almost told her it wasn't necessary, but stopped; she suspected Shianne knew. The woman who had once been Arianni seemed to appreciate Snow's work in a way that Jewel herself probably never could.

"Evayne?"

"With your permission, I will accompany you. I cannot say how long I will remain by your side."

"I know. But permission in this place is not mine to grant or withhold."

"But it is, Terafin. You understand these byways on a visceral level; understand them in a more deliberate fashion, now. You accepted the Oracle's invitation; the path you walk is in some small part yours."

Terrick and Angel retrieved the packs; they slung carriers over the Winter King's haunches. The cats had served as mounts, but Jewel didn't call them down from the literal storm above; she saw them in brief flashes as lightning continued to break the darkness. She was certain they would survive.

She was far less certain about the fate of the rest of her companions.

Adam was snoring; she'd sidled toward him to place the back of her hand on his exposed skin. He wasn't hot.

"Mage fevers," Kallandras said quietly, "seldom kill the healer-born."

"Seldom isn't never."

"No."

"How long do you think he'll sleep?"

"He will wake if wakefulness is required. I do not have vast experience with mage fevers; I recognize them in most cases. Adam is merely exhausted."

Winter King, Jewel said. *Will you not carry Shianne?*

I have told you, I cannot.

Will you not try?

If you command it, I will make the attempt. But I will not do so willingly.

Jewel surrendered. She also repented of abandoning the cats to their momentary lesson.

She is young; she is strong. The fact of pregnancy—beyond its cost to her—does not diminish her. She will not thank you for your concern; she is not weak.

I don't want her to go into labor while we're on the road.

I fear you have little say in the matter. You are not, and were not, midwife. You will have to trust her assessment of her own condition. The child and its health are of great value to her; she will do nothing to risk its safety. You have a healer on hand, he added, *if her understanding of her own condition is poor.*

Jewel hesitated.

You are not her servant. You are not her liege. You are not, in any way, responsible for her well-being. You wish to be kind; I will not belabor all of the ways in which this is a weakness. But understand that her world was—and is—the White Lady. Your attempt to be kind will make her wary and suspicious, at best; it will not make her comfortable.

And how do I make her comfortable?

See her as I do, he replied. *She is beautiful to you, yes—but even that is not a comfort; her concept of beauty is foreign to you.*

But not, Jewel knew, to the Winter King. *I don't understand how you see her.*

Then see her as Terrick does. She is worthy of awe, yes—but she is deadly. Even stripped of power, she will always be that. You have some experience with containing the deadly; use it here.

Jewel started to answer, although she wasn't certain the words would actually go anywhere, when Angel stopped walking. She clipped the back of his boot with the front of hers and drew to a stop. The stone-slab floor beneath their feet ended, not in a doorway or a t-junction or any of the normal, architectural cues that denoted change.

They simply stopped. Jewel turned; the floor beneath her feet—and behind them—was solid. The floor three yards ahead was not. As if the hall itself had been cut in two by the blow of an impossibly large ax, it led into . . . nothing.

Celleriant was armed by the time Jewel reached the sharp edge of cut stone. Beyond it, all that could be seen was a kind of dull gray. It didn't look like fog; fog had shape and variations of color that this gray did not possess.

"Lord?"

"Do you see what I see? Gray?"

He lifted a brow, but nodded.

"Angel?"

"Same."

Winter King?

There is no path that I can see.

But you've said you can travel any *path that Ariane has traveled.*

Yes.

"Terafin," Evayne said, stepping forward. "Perhaps I can help." She carried a crystal cupped in her palms; the light it shed traveled up the underside of her chin, emphasizing her bones and facial structure in a way that made her seem forbidding.

Jewel glanced out at the nothing that waited.

Shianne said, "Perhaps I can be of aid. There is a path."

Evayne's hands stiffened; her expression froze. She otherwise said—and did—nothing.

"I am not certain that I can walk it any longer," Shianne continued. "I have not tried. But it is an old path, and it was not meant for use by any who were not servant to the White Lady." She looked at Jewel's wrist.

"Where does it lead?" Jewel asked.

Shianne frowned. She turned to Celleriant and spoke briefly.

Celleriant responded in kind. If he spoke in a tongue that Jewel had never learned, her ignorance in this case was not an impediment; his response was cold and as emphatic as it could be. Only a battle cry would have been more obvious.

Shianne nodded in quiet assent.

Jewel, however, did not.

"Terafin," Evayne said.

Jewel ignored her. She walked past the seer, whose heart was so obviously exposed, and toward the two Arianni. She stopped once at the sound of falling rock; it was distant. It wasn't distant enough. "Celleriant."

He was grim and silent; Jewel was almost surprised that he condescended to acknowledge her at all. That should have been enough of a warning. In some ways, it was. She turned to Shianne. "Tell me," she said, speaking as if to the leader of one of The Ten. "Where will you lead us, if you lead us to an exit?"

"These halls," Shianne said, "are ancient. They are older than I; they are not older than the White Lady."

"Did she not create them?"

"I cannot say. I do not recall ever asking. It was," she added softly, "my home. We rode out from these halls into fair weather and into storm; we were safe when the earth was angered, and safe, as well, when the water and the air raged. We saw sunset, between the eastern pillars; sunrise, between the western. We looked seldom to the North.

"What was in the north?"

"If you must ask openly, do so here—but even in these halls, safety is not guaranteed. I will not answer, not now. If we find ourselves, against all odds, in the Hidden Court, ask again; I will answer there, willingly." She glanced at Celleriant. "It is to the South that we travel, if you rely on my knowledge." She turned back the way they had come.

"I counsel against, lord," Celleriant said.

Jewel looked, pointedly, at the total absence of anything an inch from the end of floor.

"The seer believes she can give you the information you require to traverse it."

Terafin, the Winter King said, choosing the formal title, as he was wont to do when the matter was weighty. *Take what the seer offers.*

Jewel reached up and pushed her hair out of her eyes. "You believe I can forge a path out of this place, starting here. And you also believe that it is the preferable option. What do you think we will face, if we follow Shianne?"

"The Oracle's test," Evayne replied.

"But it's to *take* that test that I've come."

"Is it?"

Jewel's words were the truth. But they were not all of the truth.

"You are strong in ways that I never was," Evayne said, when Jewel did not reply. "But it is the strength of diamond, of crystal. The right blow—or the wrong one—will shatter you. Absent that, there is almost nothing that you cannot endure if you but choose to endure it; nothing that you cannot accept if you choose to accept it."

"That's true of anyone."

Evayne ignored this. "You are in the high wilderness, although you cannot recognize it. You are in the cradle of the ancient world. I cannot build the path on which you must walk—but walk it from here, and you will, regardless, face the Oracle. You will not leave this place if you cannot." She held out the seer's crystal again, cupped in both palms. "Terafin, there are some choices—as you have said—that you could never make."

"And it's to avoid offering me that choice that you've come."

"No. I do not choose the timing of my arrival. I could not know, until I arrived, that you would be here. Or that I would. But we *are* here." Her voice had dropped. "We are here. I did not walk these halls when I went to the Oracle the first—and only—time."

"Then you don't know what I'm facing."

"No."

She was lying. Jewel *knew* it. She turned to Shianne. "Lead," she said quietly. "Lead, and I'll follow."

Shianne nodded, although she cast one narrow glance at Evayne. Celleriant was, for the moment, invisible to her, as was the Winter King. "The risk," she said, "is to Jewel, and no one else?"

"She risks all by simply being here," Evayne replied. "Even you."

"She cannot harm me more than I have harmed myself, and she will not—ever—harm the child. If I understand what I have seen, she is meant to reach the White Lady. If the child survives to reach the court, everything I have done—everything, no matter how bitter—will be with cause."

"But if you perish, you will never see the White Lady again."

"And that, perhaps, would be a kindness," Shianne replied, her voice soft, her expression neutral. "For I am not as I was; I have cast aside the better part of her for reasons she would never accept while she drew breath. But if I am part of her—if I was—I was not all of her, nor she all of me; the choice, as the Oracle said, was mine to make, the consequences, mine to bear."

"Jewel," the seer said, as Jewel straightened her shoulders. "You do not understand where you will walk if you follow her lead."

Jewel pushed hair out of her eyes again. She felt that she had aged ten years in the space of minutes. "You're wrong," was her quiet reply.

Angel lifted a hand in den-sign.

Jewel mirrored the gesture.

Carver.

The seer, to Jewel's surprise, smiled. It was not a mirthful smile; there was no joy in it. It aged her face—but age never weakened Evayne. It made her more powerful; it made her more dangerous. "I do not pity you," she said, voice soft. "Remember that. I could not make the choices I now believe you will make; there is too much for which I am responsible.

"You have always been both more and less ambitious, Terafin. I believe I hear your cats; if you are to be away, you must move quickly. The gray one is particularly sullen."

"Why did you offer me the choice, then?" Jewel asked, as Evayne fell in beside her. Without the cats to contest ownership of Jewel's personal space, Evayne's presence caused no comment.

"All choices made out of hope and desperation are evil," the seer replied. "And all, necessary. I had hoped to spare you pain."

"I don't believe you."

"It is, nonetheless, true. Understand that your pain, and its effects, will be profound if you cannot control it, unless you intend to remain absent from your home, your den, and your city."

"I can't."

"Not if you wish any of them to survive, no." Evayne's crystal had once again vanished into her robes; midnight blue rustled as she walked, folds billowing in a breeze that touched nothing else. "Jewel—" she exhaled.

I believe it would be wisest, Avandar said, *to accept Evayne's initial offer.*

I know.

Jewel. He had seen her brief gesture. He had seen Angel's.

She did not answer.

"What do you fear?" Shianne asked Jewel. Jewel had paused to check Adam as they skirted the edge of the great hall, moving, at last, to the South. Adam had not woken.

Jewel looked to Evayne.

Evayne shook her head. "I will not take him from here."

"You've done it before."

"Yes. At need, and at great cost. I will not take him now. Where you go, he must go. I believe you will need him, Terafin." She looked at his sleeping face. For a moment, they all did.

Adam was, in sleep, painfully young. He was not yet sixteen, but he had reached the age of majority among the Voyani.

"You are not horrified at what you faced when you were his age."

"I don't think I was ever his age."

"You were. If you will not trust your own impressions, trust mine. What you did then, only you could do. What he must do, only he can do. Age is not a shield. We are at war, Terafin."

Jewel said, "Not yet." But her mouth and lips were dry.

"Understand that you are not making this decision for him; no more am I. He chose to come, and I believe, in the end, he will understand that choice far better than even you." She lifted her hands and raised her hood. "I will not leave you while I have choice; I believe I know where you will walk." She hesitated again, and then said, "There is another way."

But Jewel shook her head. "There is *no* other way. I came to take the Oracle's test because I had hope that *if* I passed it, I would be able to find my kin."

"Jewel," was the soft reply, "if you travel this way, he will *be* your test. It is not necessary; choose—make—a different path."

But Jewel shook her head. She smiled; it was a wan smile. "Help me strategize, Evayne—or go away. If I could build a path of my own, if I could forge one out of nothing the way I could in the dreaming, this *is* where I would go."

Celleriant and Shianne spoke quietly and at length as Shianne once again took the lead; before they had finished they were forced, by the hissing fury of flying cats, to raise their voices. Jewel couldn't see the three, and felt guilty at having left them behind. That guilt troubled no one else, not even Angel.

Kallandras joined Jewel; Avandar ceded the position to Jewel's left. Her domicis was silent in all possible ways. He offered no advice, no opinion, no argument.

The Winter King listened to the two Arianni. He was likewise silent—but his disapproval grew. Jewel felt the weight of it.

Understand what it is that you do.

I understand what I risk, she replied. *But I am* taking *that risk.*

Once or twice Shianne's voice rose in obvious anger or dismay; Celleriant's did not likewise join hers. Jewel let them speak; the world in which Shianne now walked was not the world she had left, and she needed to know what some of the differences were.

She needed to know, Jewel thought, if she was going to answer any of the questions they had.

Meralonne had seemed almost certain that to find Carver was to alert the Sleepers, whose sleep, so necessary to the survival of her city, was now so tenuous. He had been certain that if he traveled to where Carver now stood, *he* would wake the sleepers. They would be aware of him—but he would not be in danger.

She was not certain how they traveled. She had never pressed Celleriant on the issue, and the Winter King's explanations left much to be desired. But she needed that information, now.

And if Meralonne was not here, Shianne was.

"Jewel," Avandar said.

She turned.

Whatever he had intended to say when he caught her attention, he kept to himself; he met her gaze, held it, and then slowly inclined his head, no more. *I ask for one thing, if we are to continue down this path.*

Jewel waited.

Accept the consequences as they occur. Do not mire yourself in pointless regret. Do what you must do, and continue.

She nodded.

I will remind you, Jewel. Where you go, I am now committed to go. I will walk your path while you live. It is a consequence of one rash decision, he added, *on my part. I accept it.*

Shianne was waiting for Jewel, or so it seemed. Celleriant stepped, without comment, to the left to allow Jewel to walk between them. They spoke in their mother tongue; she found the spoken language hypnotic and beautiful, even absent obvious meaning. It was like song; like bardic song.

And it was not what she needed now, but it pained her to interrupt. "You knew Illaraphaniel, whom we call Meralonne."

Shianne nodded. Both of her hands rested upon her belly as she walked.

"Did you know the other three?"

"Yes. Lord Celleriant has informed me of much that has passed in my absence."

Given Celleriant's expression, the information hadn't gone only one way. "You understand, then, that the White Lady ordered these four to accompany a mortal to kill a god—and in the end, they failed."

"They chose to fail," was her reply. "But, Jewel, so have I." She glanced at her hands, and at what lay beneath them.

Jewel shook her head, frowning. "Why can you speak my tongue?"

It was Shianne's turn to frown. "I do not understand."

She speaks, the Winter King said, *as she speaks. What you hear is dependent on her, but it is not deliberate on her part; thus speak the firstborn and their offspring. Thus, the Kialli.*

"Have you ever met another who speaks in a tongue that you cannot understand?"

Shianne looked to Celleriant.

"They do not hear language as we do," he replied. "Mortals cannot even make themselves understood to each other, unless they first learn the correct words. It is not a limitation we share." To Jewel he said, "there is no mortal tongue that the Winter Queen cannot speak; no tongue that she cannot understand. Shianne speaks as we speak; she speaks as the White Lady speaks."

"But surely it is not to ask that that you are here?" Shianne said, once again turning her attention to Jewel.

"No. No, sorry. You knew Meralonne when he was one of the four. Before he was one of the four. I am not afraid of Meralonne; I trust that he will not destroy my home in my absence, no matter what occurs." She grimaced, remembering a fight in the grand foyer of the Terafin manse on a dark, dark evening a lifetime ago. "He won't deliberately destroy it.

"But Meralonne felt it likely that the other three *would.* And I won't be there to prevent that, if they waken. I'll be here."

"There is nothing you can do to prevent it, should destruction be their desire," Shianne replied, her brow creasing at the utter absurdity of that hope. "Nor could Lord Celleriant; not even I, at the peak of my power, could stand against three. I could hold ground against one, perhaps. But not now. Never again." Her hands trembled as she spoke. "There is only one who might—and she is trapped in the Hidden Court."

Jewel nodded. "I understand that. I understand that in order to secure the safety of my home I must find a way into the Hidden Court—and open a way out—before the Sleepers wake. I have to bring the Winter Queen to my city—and before that, I have to have every ancient assurance that she will command the Sleepers to do no harm while doing no harm herself.

"I've seen the Wild Hunt," she added, her voice dropping. "Let loose in Averalaan, they would do as much damage as the Sleepers."

"I do not think that possible," Shianne replied, "given what Lord Celleriant has said. And I do not think you can bind the White Lady to such a promise. You are too desperate."

Jewel nodded; she was a merchant. She understood the burden need placed on a seller. "I'm desperate," she agreed, a hard edge to her tone. "But not, in the end, as desperate as she is."

"Oh?" The question was chilly.

"She'll be trapped in the Hidden Court if she won't negotiate. If my city is to face destruction no matter what I do, I'll be damned if I help her."

Celleriant lifted his head.

"Don't," Jewel told him. "I mean it."

"I am aware of that," he replied. "But aid is not wed to you or your survival."

Stop him, the Winter King said.

It was too late, and they both knew it. "It is," Jewel countered. Years of difficult negotiations—many of which came with veiled threats of unspecified harm—had left their mark. She lifted her wrist, pulling her sleeve back to expose the almost invisible strands of hair braided and knotted around it. "You cannot use it. Nor can Shianne." The words were the truth; they were immutable. "The way is closed to both of you. If a path exists, it is a path I will create, and I create it with her tacit permission. What I bear otherwise is necessary—but it will never reach her if I am dead."

"Once you reach the Hidden Court, that condition no longer applies," Celleriant said.

Jewel nodded. She was aware of this. She had not yet decided how best to counter it—if it could be countered at all. Evayne had sent Kallandras to her, bearing a slender sapling.

A Summer tree. The last of its kind. Without it, there would be no Summer. Without it, there would be no road for the White Lady to travel, for Winter was over.

Jewel knew her own weaknesses. She accepted them. She carried them with her now: Angel, Adam. Grimacing, she added the names of the rest of her party to that list, saving only Avandar. Avandar whose desire, in the end, was death. His own death. She knew Ariane could use any of her other companions against her.

Yes, the Winter King said.

She had not yet come up with a plan. Depending on the gratitude or the mercy of the Winter Queen was not, and could not be, part of it. The Winter King acknowledged this with a faint hint of approval.

The great hall continued for what felt like a mile—or perhaps longer. The pillars that rose to either side seemed like great stone trees in an orderly, sculpted forest. She wondered, briefly, if she would see leaves of stone; if they would fall at her feet with a heavy thud and lay there, for gathering.

Leaves of stone had existed in the undercity, in the stone garden. She had never had the temerity to take them—if they could be removed from their stone stems, their stone trellises, at all. She wondered what she might have planted in her forest, had she.

Whatever it was, it couldn't have grown into this. This was not a monument; it was an edifice, as natural as distant mountains or storms at sea. Men had not labored for decades to create it; it was like—very like—the architectural changes wrought by the wild earth in *Avantari*.

It was like the rounded, domed room with its carved statues; there was a sense that, at any time, the stone might move, shifting position and composition at its own convenience. She could not walk here without awe.

But she did walk, Shianne by her side. She forced herself to remember that the Sleepers were *of* this hall, this place, this hidden world. They were majestic; they were beautiful; they were death.

"If we anger them enough, will they come here first?" she asked.

"If what Lord Celleriant has said of your city is true, they will not need to," she replied. "He says there is no magic, no strength in your walls or your mortals—not to withstand the oldest of the Princes."

"We have Meralonne," Jewel replied, without much hope.

"Yes. And he understands the strengths and the weaknesses of your kind in a way my brethren will not. But he stands in isolation, riven from the life that made him—when I knew him—what he was. If they have slept since their failure, they will not wake greatly changed." She smiled; it was a soft, hollow expression—what wistfulness would have been had it been sharper and harder.

"How do we make them come to us?"

Shianne did not appear to understand the question. She spoke to Celleriant; Celleriant stared straight ahead, as if he had heard neither her question nor the one that had preceded it. Avandar added nothing; nor did the Winter King.

They walked in the silence of a funeral procession; only Terrick and Angel spoke, and neither was chatty.

They might have walked this way for hours, but ahead, at last, was a wall. It was bone white and entirely unadorned; there were no pillars, no statues, no carvings and no engravings; the wall rose up, and up again, marking an end.

*   *   *

Jewel knew, as Shianne continued to walk, that they had reached the end of these halls; the end of the shelter that kept most of the wilderness out. There were no visible doors in that one wide stretch of wall that seemed to travel to either side for as far as the eye could see. But there wouldn't be, here; doors would be too easy.

Shianne did not slow at all.

"Lady," Terrick said, his voice softer, the hesitance at odds with his weapon and his general stance, "we do not see a door or an arch through which to pass." His Weston was oddly accented, but clear. Jewel almost told him to speak Rendish, as Shianne would understand it; she didn't, because she wouldn't.

Shianne frowned. To Celleriant, she said, in clear Weston, "Do you see no exit?"

He was silent for a few seconds. "No," he finally said. "If there is a pathway here, it is not visible to my eye."

I see no path, the Winter King said, before Jewel could ask him.

Kallandras glanced at the wall, and offered Jewel a very slight shake of the head. It didn't surprise her. She took a deep breath, exhaled, and reached out to touch the wall her shadow fell against.

She felt stone. It was smooth and hard against the flat of her palm. She felt, in a different way, the relief of her domicis and the Winter King, although neither spoke. Shianne watched her in silence. The Arianni woman almost spoke, but stilled before words left her lips; the hesitance in someone so exquisitely perfect was jarring.

It shouldn't have been. She was far from kin, wandering the ruins of what had once been her home. And she was pregnant. Jewel had never had a baby; there had never been an infant born to anyone who lived in the West Wing. She couldn't say when the baby would come—and that worried her. She wasn't certain what a baby required, either, but she was fairly certain Adam was. Was counting on it, in fact.

But she knew Shianne would not remain in the safety of the halls. If Shianne had given up both power and eternity, she'd done so for a reason, and she would never accomplish it here.

"Matriarch."

She was surprised by the sound of Adam's voice. Adam had been softly snoring the last several times she'd checked on him.

She turned slowly, pulling her forehead away from the white stretch of pale stone. She opened her eyes. She did not remember closing them; she didn't remember the moment at which she had leaned her head against the wall.

He was standing beside her, his arm around her shoulder. His eyes were narrowed in concern. Her confusion must have shown. She glanced past Adam to Angel.

Angel lifted hands in den-sign; his expression was shuttered and neutral—which meant worry.

Avandar—how long have I been standing here?

Four hours.

Four hours. Four hours for a few simple thoughts. The hall was as cold as the realization that her hand now rested against something that was no longer entirely flat.

"Did you at least eat?" she asked them, in aggregate.

Angel stared at her.

"Did the cats come back?"

"No," Avandar replied. "And that is possibly as much mercy as the halls will show us, today."

"Then you might as well eat. This is probably as safe as we're going to be for the next little while."

Terrick was already tending the packs. This wasn't the life he was familiar with—it couldn't be, given their location—but he was possessed of grim, Northern practicality. After a moment, Angel joined him.

Jewel looked at the wall.

It was no longer flat; like the room in the basements of *Avantari*, it was carved. Trees of stone, flowers of stone, and beings that Jewel had seen, briefly, in dream stretched down the length of wall in either direction.

In its center, yards from Jewel's hand, was a single, simple, stone arch.

Chapter Seventeen

FINCH DISLIKED THE dresses Haval had made. The fabric itself—a deep burgundy and a dark blue, each with a distinctive, nubbled sheen—was appropriate to the station in which Jarven had dumped her. If current necklines were immodest, this dress clashed with them all; she felt as if she were wearing armor. With skirts.

Which was why Finch disliked them. The dress she wore today had not, by the second or third hour of wear, faded into the background the way her regular clothing did. She was constantly aware of its presence—and of its value. The value made her wretchedly nervous, although it was almost immaterial; no one who did not know the cloth itself would remark on it. Likewise, the reason the cloth was so valuable. No one would know but Finch, Haval, and Jarven. Finch, however, was the only one wearing it.

It reminded her constantly of all the ways in which her life might end.

The deaths at the Merchants' guildhall had yet to be fully tallied; men and women were still listed as missing by their various families, and the excavations required by both the Mysterium and the Magisterium had whittled that list down every few hours.

This made the office empty and quiet enough that she could think, with discomfort, about something as frivolous as clothing.

The skirts had been designed to allow full freedom of motion; they sported pockets hidden across their various seams. The pockets were not, at the moment, empty; they were full of small stones. Each stone had a slightly different texture, and each could be activated by touch. She would have carried the stones regardless of clothing; years under Jarven's tutelage had made clear why such stones were necessary.

Silence. Misdirected conversation. Light. Shadow. Warmth and coolness. Memory.

The last stone was one she very seldom used, and never when she was not in attendance; she had no need of it, then. Magically captured conversations were, of course, useful—but magic could be manipulated. It was not safe to trust the contents of a stone when one's presence could not confirm its accuracy.

She rose. Her desk—twin to Jarven's—was too large and too sparse; Jarven disliked mess. Finch, however, lived in it while she was working; stacks of paper, spare quills, half-empty inkwells and open ledgers covered the surface of any desk she called her own. Until now.

Lucille was at her own desk when Finch opened the door. "He's not back yet," she said.

"He'll be back soon. I'm going to make tea."

"Might as well." This in reference to the utter quiet that had descended on the Terafin offices. Finch had, for a change, one appointment today—and as that appointment was with Hectore of Araven, it wouldn't be productive in traditional merchanting terms.

Guillarne had sent one letter. In it, he was polite, but direct.

Had he sent the letter to Finch, she would have answered it in the same style; the letter, sadly, had been addressed to The Terafin. Since Barston was the first destination for any correspondence in the House, he saw it; since the right-kin was the next stop, should the correspondence merit it, Teller had seen it, and since Teller lived in the same wing of the building as Finch did, Finch had heard of it.

Guillarne was not a happy man. He invited The Terafin to consider the wisdom of acceding to Jarven's obviously senile demands; Finch's placement could not, in Guillarne's mind, have occurred in any other fashion. To give him his due, Finch agreed. He stopped short of threatening The Terafin with his departure; not even Guillarne was that foolish.

Finch had not intended to threaten Guillarne; she had not considered the necessity of keeping him in line. He was flamboyant, yes—and not to be trusted—but he tended to utilize scraps of the truth in his quest for success, and he could charm the dead back to life if it served his purpose.

Finch had never liked him; he had barely acknowledged her existence. But she was well aware that there were far worse fates than simply being ignored. And she had never considered Guillarne a threat to the House—or rather, to Jay's rulership of the House.

Had Jay been in residence, things would be different. She wasn't. If Guillarne was to be answered at all, it would be through Teller. Guillarne would accept it, but not with grace; she turned what she knew of the merchant over and over in her mind. It wasn't useful—but she was, at the moment, severely under-occupied. Making tea for Jarven was so much a part of the daily routine it was almost peaceful; it certainly didn't cause stress.

She did, however, take the expensive dishes. Lucille had insisted that she use nothing else from now on—for two reasons. The first: that she was now at a level with Jarven in terms of title, and that she would, of course, be granted far less respect. She needed to dress, speak, and accouter herself appropriately—even to the tiniest of details.

The second was the real reason: someone had already attempted to poison Finch. Finch's attempt to make clear that she was certain it would not happen again fell on the selectively deaf ears of an increasingly mutinous Lucille. Therefore, Finch used the cups. She knew a battle that she couldn't win with any grace when she saw it, and in truth, she didn't like to fight with Lucille. If it made the Authority dragon rest easier, it was worthwhile.

And, to be fair, the entire tea set weighed significantly less.

She lifted the tray and carried it to her office. Lucille disliked seeing her do it—for the first reasons, not the second—but Finch felt safe ignoring this. It was grousing. Lucille had never, in all of the years they'd worked together, taken any great pains about her own reputation. She wasn't concerned if people condescended to her or attempted to ignore her. No one with any sense did it once; no one, period, did it twice.

She had, however, always been protective of how Jarven was seen by the people who frequented the office. And Finch was now part of that office. If anyone could protect that reputation, it was Lucille.

Finch, if a sometimes reluctant student of Jarven's, had learned from him nonetheless; she was well aware that reputation was a shifting target. It was useful. In Jarven's case it was now useful as misdirection. Experience was vastly preferable to hearsay.

On some days Lucille opened the office door for Finch. She did so today. Jarven was behind his desk.

Finch glanced at Lucille. Lucille pursed her lips.

"Do not blame Lucille," Jarven told her. "If you were not paying enough attention to notice that I had arrived, it is hardly her fault. She is not paid to warn or prepare you for inconsequential—and expected—events. Don't just stand in the door; I have had a very trying morning, and I want my tea."

Finch smiled.

"And do not give me that smile. Did I mention the morning was trying?"

"You did." Finch came and set the tea tray on Jarven's desk. She pulled a visitor's chair to her customary position, ignoring the desk that she occupied when visitors of any stripe arrived for a meeting. This did not make Jarven's mood any sweeter; Finch thought he might send her scuttling for her own desk, given the shape of his brows as they folded.

Instead he leaned into his chair, tilting his head back until it rested almost at right angles with the rest of his body. He closed his eyes, lifted his fingers to the bridge of his nose, and held it between them for three long breaths.

"You are not, of course," he said, eyes still closed, "to blame."

Finch nodded, although he couldn't in theory see this. She poured tea, and set biscuits aside, while she considered the weathered, lined face of the man who was her mentor. Lucille was worried for him. She was also worried about him; they were not the same.

But he had lost weight, to Finch's eye. His color was off. He had been using his cane as if it were a necessity and not an artful affectation. And although he indulged in the characteristic petulance that defined so much of his interaction in the office, his heart wasn't in it; he did not take his equally characteristic enjoyment from the reactions it invoked.

"Please," she said, "Do not tell me that you are bored."

He lifted his right eyelid. "I am weary."

"Yes. And in my experience, you are never so weary as when you are bored."

He did smile, then, raising his head and shifting in place so that he might pick up the tea that was steaming almost beneath his nose. "I am not, as you suggest, bored. I cannot, however, believe that I could *ever* be so much the fool that I envied members of the governing body of the Merchants' Guild their power. And yet, I am somehow uneasily certain I *was*.

"It is a very good thing that I cannot travel back in time and give my younger self the dressing down he so richly deserves." He shook his head. "And here you are, of an age with that cocky, aggressive young fool—and no such dressing down is required. It embarrasses me."

"Please don't be," Finch replied quietly. "I know who suffers when you feel embarrassed."

He laughed. It was a dry, thin laugh. "Not, I hope, you."

"Not overmuch. But Lucille takes it badly."

"Lucille," he said, somewhat acerbically, "takes everything badly."

"She doesn't, and you know it." Finch sat back in her chair, cup and saucer in hand, steam embellishing her view of the ancient Terafin merchant.

"I do," he replied. "But I had hoped, by installing you in your present position, I would shift some of the onerous burden of her worry onto your shoulders."

"I am perfectly capable of behaving in ways that will not cause Lucille additional stress."

"Indeed. It is not, however, your actions that will cause her worry." Jarven took one loud sip of tea before setting the cup aside. "Has young Guillarne been causing difficulty?"

"Not more than I can handle."

"That is hardly an answer, Finch."

"And yet it contains all the correct components: it is factual, it is a statement, and it touches upon the possible concerns you have raised."

He chuckled. "Guillarne would be a fool to take you on."

"He would be a fool not to," she countered pleasantly, "if he desires your position. I will never be as uncertain in my post as I am now. I have never particularly liked Guillarne, but I have never said he was a fool. You have," she added, as he opened his mouth. "But at the moment, we have lost enough."

"We have lost more than enough." He fell silent. It was a quiet, steady silence, shorn of petulance and complaint.

"Is it as bad as you feared?"

"It is worse. I had almost forgotten how mendacious merchants could be; Patris Larkasir is almost beside himself with rage."

"How many of the merchant houses are attempting to take advantage of the current situation?"

"Too many," was his curt reply.

"Guillarne is not among them."

"Not in the sense that the idiots who claim membership in the Merchants' Guild are, no. I am generally tolerant of the games merchants play when the situation is relatively stable; I understand the urge to find something interesting with which to pass time."

"Boredom is not generally deadly."

"It is specifically deadly to me."

And Jarven, of course, shared. "You said you were not bored."

"I *am* bored. I am sick nigh unto death of writing letters and playing politics with what remains of the governing council of the Guild. I'm tempted to poison the lot of them and fill their positions with people who will not demand so much of my time for so little result."

"Hectore?"

"He is, of course, being reasonable."

"Jarven—you *wanted* this."

"Yes. But I do not desire to be a crutch, and at the moment, that appears to be my only function. Oh, don't make that face. I am *doing* it, regardless, and if I am to do the work, I am allowed the luxury of complaint." He lifted his tea again. "If Guillarne is not causing difficulty, who is?"

She hesitated.

He marked it. "Well?"

"We are not entirely certain. Have you spoken with Ruby?"

"Ruby is not causing you difficulty; she is causing *me* difficulty. She can, I admit, be unpleasantly cunning—but she can only be in one place at a time—and believe that that place overlaps with much of my day outside of the haven of my office. Your Jewel chose a very inopportune moment to abandon us."

Finch nodded. "I am aware that Ruby does not feel that she is appreciated enough by the House. Much of her power resides outside of its very closed doors. I can," she continued, "deal with Ruby."

"You are welcome to her." He frowned. "You have wasted at least ten minutes in hesitance. What have I said about that?"

"I honestly can't remember."

"You *are* worried." He set the cup down, shifting position once again; his elbows now adorned the surface of his desk. His hands, steepled beneath his chin, emphasized the attention he now paid to Finch.

"Yes."

"It is not a merchant matter."

"I am uncertain, Jarven. What occurred at the Merchants' guildhall was not, in the end, a merchanting matter—but more than a hundred lie dead in its wake. No merchant of any power could raise effective arms against what was encountered there."

"You've read Guillarne's report."

"I have."

"It is not just Guillarne's report."

She exhaled. "No."

"You are not certain you wish to inform me of the events that *do* trouble you."

"Of course I'm not."

His smile was Winter in a face; slender, unadorned, chilly. "I would say

that you are wasted here." His voice was soft. "But I aspired to this very position with almost everything I had at your age—and I dislike thinking of
my own life as a waste."

"Jarven," she said, sipping tea and studying his glacial expression, "What
I am, I am in part because you taught me. It has never been inconvenient for
you because you have never aligned yourself against my interests." Before he
could speak, she added, "Nor will you do so now. You understand me. You
understand me far better than I understand you; there is very little of my
actual history that you do not know.

"But you have always, *always*, encouraged me to be cautious of men in
power; to do otherwise, with you, would be an insult that I will not tender."

His expression cracked as he laughed; the ice melted. Finch did not
react—but she did, once again, sip tea. "I take it back; you *are* wasted here."
The smile once again fell away, but the chill did not return. "Demons?"

This time, she set her cup down in the saucer and grimaced.

"Finch. You cannot expect that I would have *no* idea, surely? The manse *is*
my residence—when I am not forced to ride herd on the short-sighted and
mendacious."

"At the moment, while demons are, of course, a pressing concern given
events this past week, I am worried about Duvari." She was certain the distaste the name produced was not feigned.

"If you must mention that name in my office—"

"Our office, surely?"

One brow rose in a white arch.

". . . Or not." She laughed. "I am certain actual poison could not produce
the expression on your face right now. I almost want to call Lucille in."

"I am certain actual poison would be far less difficult and far less
dangerous—at least to me. I would," he added, in a slightly more plaintive
tone, "rather hear about demons. Duvari is one element of the entire Merchant fracas that I have managed to be adroit enough to avoid."

She rose, restless, and began to walk the edge of the carpet that fronted the
two desks.

He tsked behind her back. He considered pacing to be an almost political
failing; it showed worry or impatience, either of which could be a besetting
sin. Since Jarven was often whiny and petulant when impatient, Finch
thought this unfair—but Jarven correctly pointed out that *his* foibles were
disguises. Hers were not.

"How important do you consider Duvari to be?" she asked.

Silence.

"Jarven?" She turned and almost missed a step.

"I have, as you often point out, taught you. I have, in my opinion, taught you *well*. Not even the most foolhardy and aggressive of my early protégées could have asked me that question with a remotely straight face. And yet, here you are. I believe I am *almost* disappointed—but I am certain there are extenuating circumstances which you will, in all haste, explain."

She folded her arms, but stopped pacing. "It was, in its entirety, a serious question. You can complain about Duvari for hours—I've heard you do it, admittedly in front of the right audience. I have seldom heard you speak of Duvari in terms that are not derogatory. I have," she added, "seldom heard anyone of note speak of him in a remotely complimentary fashion. I do not interact with Duvari often."

"You do not," he replied, "interact with Duvari *at all*."

"We are not going to have that option."

He exhaled. "Sit. Watching you pace is making me dizzy."

Finch sat. She tried not to fidget with the skirts of the dress she so disliked.

"I have taught you to play games; many of those lessons were indirect; I forced you to observe, and I have allowed you to draw your own conclusions from those observations. Where necessary—in my opinion—I have encouraged you to think more deeply; to see the advantage to be gained in any situation, even the most dire. You have, of course, no such experience with Duvari.

"I tell you again, Finch, you will not interact with the Lord of the Compact."

"And who will, in The Terafin's absence? You? Teller is set to call a House Council meeting in five days—or perhaps three, if the situation becomes too complicated. At that time, we will introduce you as a provisional Council member; we expect complaints, and some measures to stifle them have already been put in place.

"But even so, Duvari accepts the hierarchy of the House; he will, in the absence of The Terafin, defer—if he even understands the word—to the right-kin."

"To your Teller."

"Yes."

"And why should this be a problem?"

"Demons. I meant to tell you," she added, which was half true. "But I thought we might wait on Hectore; he is to visit this afternoon."

"He will be late."

She frowned.

"As, I'm afraid, will I. The Merchants' Guild is under investigation by the

Magisterium and the Mysterium, and we are to speak with the Guildmaster of the Order of Knowledge."

"Was the head of the Merchants' Guild ever found?"

"Given the urgency of the request, I believe the answer is yes. My own concerns are, unfortunately, more mundane. More than a dozen of the guild's guards—in guild tabard, no less—were working in concert with the creature that almost destroyed the membership."

"And they would need to be paid."

"And fed, and clothed, and housed, yes. Were it not for the Order of Knowledge, we might have had one or two of these men in custody, where we might question them at our leisure. As they were careless—"

"They *were* somewhat occupied with a demon."

"As was I," he countered. "And I would not have made that error."

"You never believe you can die."

"On the contrary, Finch, I believe I can die at any time. I have not recovered from steps taken to insure that I survived in the halls behind the guild's lamentable kitchen. While it is true I emphasize my age to my advantage, it is not all pretense." He winced.

"That, on the other hand, you did not purpose."

"Yes. It is useful to blend truth with our fictions; it makes the whole much more convincing. And you are, of course, attempting to change the subject."

"I am thinking the subject through. Were these guards hired by the guild-master?"

He smiled. "That would be my current supposition."

"Was the guildmaster not himself?"

"That would also be my supposition; confirmation will have to wait upon Sigurne Mellifas—as difficult and shrewd an old woman as any I have ever met. She shows an alarming interest in The Terafin."

"Who is not, as you've pointed out, present. I am unwilling to let Teller navigate Duvari on his own."

"I think that wise. No, do *not* start pacing again. I happen to be fond of that carpet; it deserves better. Sit."

Finch inhaled. "Did you have much personal experience with Alowan?"

"The former healer? I did."

"His assassination was tactical."

"Of course. You are concerned for your Daine? Finch, *please* make a fighting attempt at self-control. I will begin to feel guilty if you do not."

"I would almost like to see that. Is there anything you don't know?"

"There is much that I suspect; suspicion outweighs evidentiary proof. I am, however, content with suspicion, where it is reasonable and where it fits available fact. Daine is an open secret, among senior members of the House; he is certainly an open secret among the Household Staff.

"I fail to see how this relates to Duvari."

Probably, Finch thought uncharitably, deliberately. "No, you don't."

He watched her; she met—and held—his steady gaze. "You are making more work for me."

"You're aware that a random servant was attacked; you're aware that the results were messy and completely obvious. Whoever attacked the girl thought her dead—and they wanted the entire House to know it. They wanted news of their butchery to travel—and Jarven, it has. The entire Household Staff is on edge—and they should be. It was a savage, brutal attack. The girl should not have survived. She was possibly lucky: she was discovered by someone who kept enough of her wits about her that she sent—immediately—for Daine.

"Daine was able—at cost—to save her life."

She expected some petulant complaint; Jarven offered none. He watched her, fingers beneath his chin, his expression remote.

"The girl was not a random target."

"Ah."

"She was a member of Duvari's *Astari*." When Jarven failed to comment, she continued. "We are relatively certain she was chosen because of that affiliation. What we cannot ascertain is how that information was gained. Some preliminary investigation has been done."

"Results?"

"Not promising."

"Terafin was not the only House to suffer such an attack, then."

"No. It may not be widespread; we have had only a few days, and inquiries of this kind have to be handled with care." Or, in Jester's case, with alcohol. She failed to mention this. "We know that at least two other Houses suffered shockingly similar deaths and dismemberments—but in both cases, the victims died. There was no chance at all that they could be saved; even had a healer been on hand—and I am not familiar with the disposition of the healer-born in other Houses—they would have been unable to preserve the victims."

"Which means the knowledge of the Terafin girl's survival is known to the assailant."

"That is the supposition we are now working with. We cannot, of course, be certain that the victims in the other Houses were also *Astari*."

Jarven nodded. "You suspect that they were."

"None of the victims were inherently powerful; none occupied positions of note within their Houses. They were the type of desultory spy that one expects Duvari to place all over the Empire as a matter of course."

"Which is not an answer."

"We would have suspected nothing of the sort, had the Terafin servant not survived. We would have had other concerns, of course. We have already launched an internal investigation. It is . . . not going smoothly."

"And this is why you are concerned."

"We're almost certain there is some demonic or magical involvement. And Jarven? I am done with demons. I could live a hundred lifetimes absent their presence and it wouldn't be *long enough*." She lowered her head.

"You are afraid that Duvari will kill your healer."

"Yes. We have taken some precautions—but I'm unwilling to give up the healer, and Jay—The Terafin—would stand behind that decision with her life."

"If, by stand behind that decision, you mean she would attempt to neutralize Duvari, she would lose."

Finch said nothing for one long beat. "I will take the matter to the Kings, if any harm—*any*—befalls him."

"That would be politically costly, as you well know."

"Yes. But it is a price I am willing to pay. I will take the matter to The Ten as the Terafin regent, and I will demand justice. I will not play games of proof; I will not dance in the shadows with Duvari and his *Astari*. He is what he is—but he serves, and answers to, the Kings—and I will make the Kings answer to Terafin."

"You will not have the support of The Ten should you choose to do this."

"I will have the support of some of them, and if they would be wisely unwilling to attach their names to my petition, they would welcome it. Duvari has long been a thorn in everyone's side. To see him leashed or muzzled would delight them; they will not stand in my way to curry favor with the Kings."

"Well," Jarven said, pausing to snap a biscuit in half, "I better understand your sour expression. You *have* been thinking."

"I am unwilling to pay that price if it is not *necessary*. But I will demand everything short of Duvari's death if Daine dies. And Jarven—I mean *everything*. The Ten tolerate Duvari; the Crowns tolerate the laws of exception. If Duvari killed me, if he killed Teller, we would accept it as part of the bitter cost of power."

"But not your young healer."

"No. I would accept Jay's death. I will not accept Daine's."

"And you are telling me this because?"

"You asked. I would prefer that this be dealt with through the regular channels, of course." She exhaled, losing inches and anger as she spread her palms in her lap. She did not take up the cup again because her hands were too unsteady. "Let me ask you again: How important is Duvari? Or rather, how important are the *Astari*, and could they function without him?"

"Given the rest of your speech, I am not certain it is prudent to answer that question. But I will attempt to maintain some faith in you, although I confess it badly shaken.

"The *Astari* are necessary; they protect the Kings. I do not know what the *Astari* would be should Duvari die—but it will not, for the first few years, be pretty. He is strong enough to dispense with both charm and lie; he curries favor with no one. He will not bend—but, Finch, he does not break. I do not think there is an assassin alive who could kill him; there are very, very few of any quality who would accept the commission were they offered it. He is, as you know, a necessary evil."

"And if the *Astari* have been compromised completely?"

Jarven rose. "You almost make me feel old, Finch. May I point out that I do not enjoy the sensation?"

"Yes." She rose to pour more tea. Jarven, at least, had been drinking his.

"There is only one way that the *Astari* could be completely compromised."

"That," Finch replied quietly, "is what I now fear."

"You will not take this to the Kings."

"No. If I am willing to go to war against Duvari, desperation drives me; I am not desperate to preserve either the *Astari* or the Lord of the Compact in a similar fashion. I will, if resources permit, approach such matters through the regular channels. One of which was meant to be my appointment with Hectore this afternoon."

Jarven sighed theatrically. "We will be here as soon as humanly possible; given the merchants, even I cannot guarantee that we will be on time. I would," he added, voice softer and vastly less frail, "leave Hectore in control of the Merchants' Guild if that struck me as the wise option."

"Hectore is highly respected; he is a merchant of long-standing and credible wealth."

"All of that is true. He is also better at dealing with the wheedling and the self-aggrandizing."

"But you won't."

"I do not believe, at the moment, that it is in our best interests."

"Who is 'our' in this case?"

"Mine, of course." His smile was thin. "We are, at the moment, working in grudging lockstep. If Hectore was to take the leadership of the tattered guild into his capable hands, I am not certain that that would be the case. And, Finch, Hectore is no fool. He would just as soon grab fire and hold it in cupped palms, had he any choice."

"I disagree."

"You, my dear, have not been present at the council meetings. Perhaps I will send you in my place."

She failed to smile in response.

His smile—which was a thin edge of an expression—faded. "Have you chosen to approach Duvari?"

"Word has been carried."

"By a messenger you trust?"

"By a messenger who has not been compromised, yes."

"And that is why you are wearing that dress."

She exhaled. "Yes, Jarven. Tell me one thing."

"And that?"

"Will the Kings survive if the *Astari* have been infiltrated by demons?"

"Not if their point of entry is Duvari. When will you know?"

"It depends on how clever demons are," Finch replied. "But they know that we suspect, and some precautions outside of the purview of the *Astari* have been taken. I can only see two routes to take, in this situation."

"You can see more than two."

"Given our history with demons, I can see only two that are likely. The first—and the one that we hope for: the demons attack us, in the Terafin manse."

"And the second is that they attack the Kings."

"They've done as much damage to this city with the attack on the Merchants' Guild as they could have done with *armies*. More, I think. But it was not subtle; it was bold; loud. They did not expect to fail."

"They did, however."

"Yes. But there is an arrogance that assigns failure to the incompetence of others, and not to the competence of the targets."

"Very well. I concur. They are capable of subtlety. They are capable of perfect mimicry."

"It's not mimicry."

"Oh?"

"They inhabit the bodies of their victims. I don't believe all demons are capable of this—but those that are can be incredibly effective. They have access to the memories of those victims, although it is not said to be perfect access; they can inhabit a dead body for a day or two, if the victim did not survive."

"It is not said by who?"

"The Terafin House mage. The mimicry is subtle, yes. But when they cast it aside they do so in the loudest and flashiest way possible. The House mage believes it is almost impossible for the kin to view mere mortals as serious threats."

"And that is our only advantage?"

"No; we have others. But he considers it a large advantage. Before you make that face at me, *none* of this has been discussed by the House Council. So access to the House Council seat would not materially change the information you now have."

"I am attempting to manage my resentment in constructive ways," he replied. "It would have been useful to have this information before the events at the guildhall."

"Meralonne feels that people are far too prone to panic, and the Kings apparently agree."

"He is not wrong. Panic, however, is a useful tool when wielded correctly."

Finch was not surprised by his response. "It is seldom wielded correctly by anyone but demons—and I would prefer that there be some distinguishing, mortal characteristics that divide us."

He nodded. "It is, in the end, far less harrowing than the Henden of 410. I remember you, then. You seemed so fragile I thought Lucille would actually hit me when I told her I would not see you sent home. Do you honestly think that Duvari himself has been compromised?"

Finch hesitated. "Not yet."

"Why or why not?"

"Jarven, now is not the time for lessons."

"All of life is a lesson, Finch, as you should well know. The most valuable things you have learned from me were not explicitly taught; they were derived entirely by observation and experience. I intervened only when I thought the cost of your decisions would be too high—for you. But I am not, now, playing games." At her expression, he added, "Yes, yes, I realize we use different definitions for those words.

"Tell me."

"The victims. If multiple people are taken out in an obvious, violent fashion—and if those victims are all *Astari*, it's possible that Duvari has been compromised, and the *Astari* are being eliminated from the bottom up. But that makes no sense, to me. By doing it, he alerts every person who isn't compromised. He increases the precautions that must be taken."

"That is true only if the Kings are the actual targets."

Finch nodded, lost in thought. "If, however, they are aiming *at* Duvari, the deaths make perfect sense. They isolate him; they isolate the *Astari*; they sow a level of distrust and discord that the *Astari* probably don't experience often. If Duvari's *Astari* are paralyzed—" She stopped. Frowned.

Jarven glanced at the corner of the room, where his coat, his hat, and his gloves were neatly put away. "It is time for me to make my way to the Order of Knowledge."

"The meeting is there?"

"We have been given a lecture hall within the main building until the investigation is done." He glanced at Finch, who sat quietly in her chair, turning scenarios over and over; examining them for flaws, rating their probability. She looked up when he cleared his throat.

"Apologies," she said, as she retrieved his coat and his walking stick. Whatever advantage she accrued from her new position, Jarven still expected her to wait on him.

"Finch."

She looked up.

"Be careful."

"I could offer you the same advice."

"First, it is not advice. It is an order. It merely sounds like advice because you have chosen to misinterpret my tone. Second, death—while not to be desired, especially if the death on offer is painful and long—is coming for me anyway. If I sit this out and do nothing, I will merely prolong boredom and ineffectiveness. This is not the case, with you.

"At my age, I an unlikely to find or train new protégées. You are, therefore, my only hope of lasting legacy."

She handed him his walking stick only after he had donned—with her help—his fussy coat. "You don't care about legacy, Jarven."

He chuckled. "Perhaps. I do not like the direction your thoughts have taken in the last five minutes; they make me uneasy."

13th of Morel, 428 A.A.
Avantari, Averalaan Aramarelas

Birgide Viranyi stood in the inner offices of the Royal Trade Commission. The office was only skeletally staffed; the crisis that had, in one evening, damaged the city so badly necessitated Patris Larkasir's presence in the Merchants' Guild, and he was old enough—and angry enough—that it was not deemed wise to have him travel alone.

Devon was, of course, by his side. As the man considered most likely to succeed Larkasir in his role with the Trade Commission, he was privy to all of the relevant economic discussions; if he had duties to the *Astari*, they would be left untended in the near future. Devon served the Kings, and the Kings had decided that his work with Patris Larkasir superseded all other duties.

Birgide glanced at her hands and grimaced. There was dirt under her fingernails, and her attempts to remove it had not been entirely successful. Duvari met with people from all walks of life—but in his own way, he was fastidious. He would notice. The man noticed everything.

Her discussion with Jester—and her wordless acceptance of the responsibility laid across her shoulders by, of all things, a *forest*—had had subtle, but immediate effects. She experienced one of them now: she glanced down at the rows of desks, bound on three sides by standing cabinets that served as demi-walls, and saw webbing. It was very fine, and reminded her, on first glance, of the complicated but delicate strands spiders wove.

First glance, however, yielded a second. The strands were not the pale white of webs meant for insects; they were colored, and they shone faintly, from floor to the height of ceiling or cabinet or desk. They had no physical component; she could, with ease, pass through them without causing them material damage. But as she did, they thrummed like struck strings, as if they were parts of an instrumental whole.

Birgide was a botanist, not a bard; if she heard musical notes, she couldn't make sense of them; she had the suspicion that a song could be played—but she lacked the necessary tools. The notes were pleasant, for the most part; arranging them meaningfully was, at the moment, beyond her.

They did not alarm her. She was almost certain that they implied the presence of relatively normal magic; the Terafin manse was likewise adorned with similar webs. Only in the right-kin's office did they approach this density; if anything, it was stronger, there.

She had undertaken an informal tour of the Terafin manse, Jester ATerafin by her side. His presence eased her passage; if the Household Staff looked askance, most of their raised brows or stiff lips were directed at the red-haired, flamboyant Jester. She almost faded into invisibility by his side, and because she had, she was free to leave it; to wander, in silence, studying every entrance, every exit, and every hidden door.

They encountered both House Guard and Chosen; Jester was familiar with, it seemed, every member of the Household involved in service. If the guards were not friendly, they were, to Birgide's eye, less alert—with the exception of the Chosen. They responded to Jester, but they did not lose sight of her. She wasn't, at this point, concerned.

She asked Jester only a few questions; given his expression, he considered them random, but relatively harmless. And so: she had a view of the Terafin manse that she had never had before. She stopped only once with open concern.

"Where does this lead?" she asked, her hand hovering above a section of wood paneling in one of the function rooms.

Jester frowned. "The back halls, normally."

She raised a brow.

"Have I offended?"

"In general, you put more effort into your evasive answers."

He laughed. "This is going to be a problem," he told her.

"Your evasiveness?"

"My lack of same. You are indirectly correct; I tell the truth so seldom I am unaccustomed to putting much effort into its delivery. Truths," he added, "are seldom interesting, and people misuse them so frequently."

"It is to be hoped that The Terafin does not share this assessment."

"The Terafin lives in a mound of political paperwork while spineless rats nibble at her skirts. No, as you suspect, she does not. All attempts to shift her position with regards to truth have failed utterly; she is honest or she is silent. She is not," he added, an odd smile changing the shape of his mouth, "silent often enough."

"She is not terribly chatty," Birgide replied.

"Why are you asking about this door?"

"I do not believe it currently leads to the back halls. Would it be safe to test that theory?" When Jester failed to answer, she turned from her inspection to see that his skin—unfortunately consistently too pale—was a shade of something closer to gray than white. "I will assume that the answer is no."

Jester nodded. "You will have to excuse me," he said, offering her a perfunctory, distracted bow. "If I may leave you here, allow no one to enter this door. If someone exits it, that's fine—but they are not to return to the back halls the same way."

"Where are you going?"

"To summon the House Mage," he replied, his words flying over his shoulder as he began to sprint down the gallery.

"Wait!" She turned toward one of the House Guard. He was perhaps a year or two older than Birgide. His expression had hardened, his eyes had narrowed, his skin had paled. Whatever had caused Jester to seek the House Mage, this man understood.

Jester cursed. To Birgide's surprise, he cursed in street Torra, and he didn't scruple to do so under his breath. "Have you got this?" he asked the guard.

The guard's nod was grim. "Get the mage—I'll make sure no one uses this entrance until it's dealt with."

Birgide was aware of Meralonne APhaniel's existence. As a function of her role within the *Astari* and her placement—albeit it to study the finer points of botany—she could name, without fail or pause, every First Circle mage within the Order's active rolls. She could also name all of the Second Circle, as well. Knowledge of, however, was not acquaintance; being talentless, she was generally considered a nonentity as far as mages were concerned. The magi were cautious to the point of paranoia about each other. They were not as careful around people like Birgide, whose utter lack of magical talent meant she would never be a threat to the prominence of their position in the only important hierarchy.

Meralonne, however, was different. Even among the Order's many magi, he was unique. He had been, as far as Birgide could determine, a member of the Order of Knowledge for decades; he was, in theory, older than Sigurne. No one was willing to acknowledge this; Birgide had never understood why.

But Duvari had cut short that avenue of research—which had raised flags that Birgide was not aware, until that moment, had even existed.

Meralonne APhaniel was the Terafin House Mage. She considered this even as she followed Jester at a run. She was surprised when he came to a skidding halt in front of The Terafin's personal chambers. Two of the Chosen guarded these doors, a clear indication that the rooms were not occupied by The Terafin herself.

"We've got a door problem," Jester said to the woman on the left, without preamble. She nodded, stepped to one side, and allowed Jester to yank the doors open. Pages often performed that function for guests and important dignitaries; clearly, Jester was neither.

"She's with me," he added, as he stepped through the doorway.

Birgide had never been invited into The Terafin's personal quarters; nor did she ever expect to be so. She hesitated for a second and Jester disappeared. Literally. The doors appeared to open into a high-ceilinged library. He was not, however standing beneath that ceiling; nor was he walking across the library.

She glanced at the silent Chosen. Neither of the two, man or woman, appeared to be alarmed. They were well enough trained that alarm would be almost invisible, but Birgide detected no unusual tension. No surprise.

She walked quickly through the open doors.

Jester was, to her surprise, waiting for her on the other side. The doors through which she had walked no longer existed at her back; instead, she was framed by a wrought iron structure that implied the existence of a gate, without actually containing one.

Birgide looked beyond Jester ATerafin. Beyond and above. There was no ceiling here. There were no obvious walls. There were shelves, but closer inspection—even at this distance—indicated those shelves were also . . . trees. The flooring was a pale, unstained wood; she would have sworn it was a softwood, which was in no way suitable for the chambers it occupied.

Except that nothing in her experience would suit these chambers. Nothing except the *Ellariannatte*. She almost closed her eyes, so strongly did she sense their presence.

"Sorry," Jester said brusquely. "I have to admit this is not my favorite part of the manse these days."

"Was it ever one of them?"

"Sure. I was never summoned here, so anything that occurred here was guaranteed not to be my problem." As she raised brows, he added, "Lazy, remember?"

"We all have some measure of laziness—we're human. But yours, given your position in the House, is taken to ridiculous levels."

"Not ridiculous. Merely self-serving. I'm perfectly happy to acknowledge my multitude of personal weaknesses."

"Because you hope they will disqualify you from having to actually be useful?"

He grinned. "You see? You're coming to understand me better as the days pass."

Birgide smiled absently, her attention once again drawn away by amethyst skies that seemed to stretch out on all sides with no visible end. "Are we staying here?"

His shoulders slumped. "I hoped so. But he doesn't appear to be arriving to meet us."

"Does he usually?"

"Yes. He's taken up residence here, and he's ferocious about defending the space. The Chosen keep a very skeletal guard—but I don't think it's for his benefit. We don't want to lose any of the Household Staff to the wilderness." He began to walk to the right of the fence, toward the shelves. Birgide was almost afraid to touch them.

The thin strands of light that were scattered throughout the Terafin manse were nowhere in evidence in this room. Or perhaps, she thought, following in Jester's wake, they were so much part of this landscape they could not be separated from it; she heard music, distant but distinct, every time she took a step. If Jester heard the same, he gave no sign.

Nor did she ask; as she considered the wording of the question that was forming, she was distracted by the sharp, harsh illumination of lightning. Pale, white-green streaks flashed across the whole of the sky, changing both its texture and its color.

Jester exhaled. "We've come at a bad time," he said, as if such obvious magic was commonplace here. "No wonder the path was allowed to finish forming there."

"Is it a common occurrence?"

"It's not common. It has happened. It's how we lost Ellerson and Carver. Meralonne is—can be—aware of when doors within the manse become strange, and he usually deals with them."

"How?"

Jester shot her a look.

"You didn't ask. Of course. Never mind."

"I didn't," he added, "ask you how you knew, either."

"No." She didn't volunteer the information; she didn't understand it well enough herself. "But you did accept that I did."

"I saw what happened in the forest," he replied. "At the moment, I'm inclined to trust your instincts."

Lightning flashed across the sky again. It was accompanied by a roar that literally shook the floor beneath their feet. Jester was understandably tense; he was not, however, frightened.

"Does *this* happen often?"

"I don't know. I don't ask the House Mage—"

"Questions. You really are remarkable."

"You don't say that as if it's a good thing."

She could not help it, she laughed. "I have always thought you feckless and lazy," she told him, when she stopped. "But I must admit that your dedication elevates it into an art." She frowned. "That last flash of lightning was different."

"The blue one?"

"Yes."

Jester nodded. "I don't know about you," he said, "but I've been walked off my feet this afternoon. I'm going to sit down." He looked up at the skies as amethyst once again reasserted itself. To Birgide's ears, so did the subtle, insistent song, the whisper of leaf against leaf and branch. She followed Jester down a row of shelves, glancing at the spines of the books; the language, which began as familiar, modern Weston, devolved into Old Weston, and from there, into languages with which she was not familiar. So, too, the style of bindings.

She did not touch the shelves, although the temptation was strong. Instead, she walked clear of them. As if they were a literal forest, there was a clearing in their center: a thing of floor, table, and chair. Beyond these, she could see a fountain, a clear, primitive font of stone and wood; lilies in pale pink and violet adorned the slightly rippling water.

Jester pulled out a chair and sat, leaning back in a lazy sprawl. She was not particularly surprised to see him put his feet on the table's surface. The table itself was home to a small stack of books and a single, silvered mirror of the kind that one found in modest dressing rooms.

"You might as well sit," Jester told her.

"We are waiting?"

"For Meralonne. When he's finished—and assuming he's survived—he'll join us here. I hope you don't mind pipe smoke."

"He still smokes?"

"Only if it irritates someone. I don't really mind it," he added. He folded his arms and tilted his face toward sky. "Did you see him much, when you were a student in the Order?"

"No. He was, however, infamous for both his pipe and his general demeanor. Most of the mage-born are arrogant and dismissive when dealing with the lesser students. Meralonne was arrogant and dismissive when dealing with anyone, which somehow made it easier to bear."

"I disliked the waste of my time," the mage said.

Birgide blinked. Meralonne APhaniel was floating some ten feet above the table, his hair a spread of unfettered platinum that adorned his shoulders and fell across the whole of his back. He wore no other cape, and at the moment, carried no weapon.

But seeing him now, seeing him this close, she felt, viscerally, that he was *of* this place, and not the halls that existed beyond it, be they Terafin manse or Order of Knowledge. The wind that touched his hair carried him down to the floor.

"You are Birgide Viranyi," he said, surprising her. He almost shocked her by tendering her what appeared to be a very respectful bow. His smile, as he rose, acknowledged this. "My apologies, ATerafin. I was much occupied."

"I can see that," Jester replied, taking his feet off the table and pushing himself, reluctantly, from his chair. "You're bleeding."

He was. Birgide had both cataloged it and failed to find it either disturbing or inappropriate. He looked much like any warrior come directly from the field of battle, save for the lack of weapon. "It is inconsequential. Come. Let us attend to the disturbance in the main hall." He turned to Birgide, and, if the events of the day had not already passed beyond the bizarre, pushed them into the surreal: he offered her his arm.

She was aware, accepting it, that her own hands were dirty, callused; that she was dressed as a gardener and not a dignitary of note; that she was scarred, her nose once broken, her hair shorn. Even when it had grown, it had never grown as his did. All of these things were true any given day of the week—or year—but she seldom felt them so keenly. Interesting.

"You will not often see me in the manse itself," he told her, as he led them back the way they'd come. Jester walked to her right, in silence. "In the absence of The Terafin, creatures grow bold, and these lands are not well-defended." His smile was sharp. "Or they would not be, were I not here."

"Your duties are somewhat more mundane."

He spoke as if he knew.

"The Terafin as she exists now is bound tightly to the world you inhabit. But the roads that lead to her are also hers; because she cannot acknowledge them fully, there are weaknesses in her defenses. You are meant to stand where she cannot stand in her absence. I am both surprised and unsurprised."

"You *do* know."

"Of you? Yes. The forest speaks your name. Serve The Terafin," he added, his voice cooling. "Serve the forest, if you must. But serve as the Chosen serve. The ancient world is waking, and it is wild. There is beauty in it such as you and your kin—talent-born, god-born, mighty or insignificant, have never witnessed. But there is danger in it. There is no malice, but service does not mean to the ancient what it means to mortals."

"The cats," Jester pointed out.

The mage grimaced, his eyes narrowing at the mention of The Terafin's chaotic winged retinue. "What they offer is no one's definition of service, on either side of the divide; it is possible that mortals might consider it acceptable. It is not. I would not suffer them to exist in any space I claimed as my own."

"I believe the cats care about The Terafin."

Meralonne APhaniel exhaled. "Yes. Inasmuch as it is possible for those feckless, dangerous infants to care about anything other than their momentary entertainments, I would agree. That did not prevent one of them from almost ending her life."

Birgide had not heard of this, and did not ask. If there was time, it would come later. She was concerned with the mage's knowledge of the role she had only just accepted, because she felt suddenly certain he had a far better understanding of it than she did. "What does service mean to the forest?"

"It is entirely dependent, at this point, on you. If you are careless, that will not remain true. Service is an artifact of power; the powerful rule; the powerless are ruled."

Birgide frowned. "Is that not always true?"

He laughed. "Mortals play at power. Money is power. Prestige is power. Talent is power. Should the Kings desire it, however, they could not level this city in a day. They could not level it in a year, if they met with any resistance."

"And you are claiming the forest *can?*"

"Look at the library through which we now walk," he replied, "and understand that the whole of it—what you can see, and what you cannot—was created in minutes, if that. You have walked the paths lined by trees of silver, gold, and diamond—and they, too, took root in a similar span of time."

"Neither of these things happened in isolation."

"No. They happened because of The Terafin. You have some experience with changes wrought outside of the boundaries of the Terafin properties. Or perhaps you do not; accept that I do, and they have. Those changes, like these, occurred in a span of minutes."

"You are saying The Terafin is a power."

"Yes."

"And if I serve her—"

"She did not take your oath of service; the heart of her forest did. If you will take advice—and it is freely given and quite possibly worth only what you pay to hear it—you will offer your formal oath to *her* the moment she returns. She has limitations that the high wilderness would not even begin to understand—but what she accepts, the forest will accept." He reached the iron arch. "And now, we must attend the difficulty in the manse itself."

"APhaniel."

"Yes?"

"What causes the difficulty?"

He did not answer.

Chapter Eighteen

BIRGIDE HAD STOOD BY the side of the House Mage while he examined the section of wall the House Guard now forbid anyone to touch. Anyone did not include Meralonne, of course; he gestured them away, and they went. To Birgide's eye, they were grateful to be relieved of the task. She stepped back so that she might watch both the mage and the paneled section of wall.

"You're staying?" Jester asked.

She glanced at him.

"Suit yourself. I find staring at walls unentertaining at best, and I'm heading back to my rooms."

Birgide nodded, turning back to Meralonne. Even in this room, which was in all ways more mundane, he looked as if he belonged to some ancient, wild magic that she could witness, but never approach or use.

Where strands of colored light graced the room, they were concentrated for the most part at the level of the lighting and the windows themselves; there was very little to be found at foot level. The strands were violet and orange, the colors blending and diverging as strands traveled.

Only around the paneling that the mage now faced were they different. It wasn't the color so much as the texture; the strands were thicker, the weave tighter. They emitted no sound when touched—or at least no sound Birgide could hear; she was reluctant to test the limits of her newfound perception, given Jester's reaction.

Meralonne touched nothing. He studied the gleaming wood grain as if the lines there told a story only he could read. "Do you see what I see?" he asked softly.

"No."

"And yet you see that something does not belong here."

She nodded.

"How does it differ, to your eye?"

"I can't explain it," she replied.

His eyes, which remained focused upon the paneling, narrowed. If he was petty and aggravating to many of the magi within the Order, he was sober, even grave, here. Birgide watched as the thick, dense weave began to unravel, threads moving as if they had will and purpose of their own, and seeking surfaces to which to cling.

He allowed them none.

"How is this dangerous?" she asked.

"I am almost not of a mind to answer the question, given your own evasion," he replied. He exhaled, and—later than Jester had predicted—drew a pipe from the folds of his robe. She blinked. He had not been wearing the robe when they had met him in the library above; nor had he been wearing it when they had descended into the manor proper.

Meralonne had never been of a mind to answer any irrelevant questions— where relevance was based entirely on his own interests, whatever they might be. Birgide, accustomed to this, fell silent.

He surprised her. "It is not clearly understood by most of the citizens of Averalaan, but the city itself is situated on dangerously unstable ground. You spent some time recently in the Western Kingdoms?"

She nodded.

"And, no doubt, you heard rumors of strange happenings along the roads?"

She nodded again, this time more slowly.

"The world is changing, Birgide. No power exists which will stop that change; small pockets of power exist which might mitigate the damage it causes. I would be one of those small pockets. The Terafin would be another. In my opinion," he added, lighting the pipe he held in his hands, "She is the only significant one. What the Kings, the Exalted, and the rest of the Order combined might achieve is insignificant in comparison.

"And Jewel's reach is defined by borders of the city. They know," he added.

"They?"

"Those who serve the Lord of the Hells, and those who have lived for far, far too long in the shadows and the hidden byways barely acknowledged by your kind at all. They know she is absent. But even absent, she is connected to these lands. Do you understand the connection?"

"How could I, Member APhaniel? I am not mage-born. I am not a historian; I am not one of the more enterprising of the bards. Even the wise do not understand how she was able to intervene on the first day of The Terafin's funeral rites; they know only that her intervention was necessary.

"I have seen trees of silver, gold, and diamond. I have seen a tree of fire. I have seen amethyst skies and trees that *grow shelving*. There is nothing in any of this that can be rationally explained by the logical mind. And yet I do not doubt what I have seen."

He blew rings of smoke in reply. Birgide did not particularly care for pipe smoke. She was, however, perfectly capable of tolerating it as if it were the most wonderful aroma in the Empire when it came, as it did, from one of the most dangerous men she had ever met.

"Do you understand why you were chosen?"

"No."

"Because you are not one of her den. You are an outsider."

Birgide had been an outsider for all of her life. She was used to it. It did not sting. Or so she told herself.

"You came to her through channels that are political—and dangerous. On an instinctive level, she understands the games you play; she accepts the risks you have made an intrinsic part of your life. She did not know you when you were twelve, or fourteen, or even sixteen. She did not know you before she became Terafin.

"She can, therefore, believe in your competence."

"If Jester ATerafin is any indication of the competence of her friends—"

"He is not," was the bored, slightly irritated response, "as you are well aware. She is willing to see you take the risks you have chosen to take in her service. She is, on a very fundamental level, reluctant to risk her den. I believe this was made clear to you."

"You were listening?"

"I do, on occasion." His smile was sharp. "Understand that they are, at the moment, necessary. If the Kings die—"

Birgide held up a hand.

Meralonne, being magi, ignored it. "—They will be replaced. Their sons are young, but capable. Once or twice in the past, the Queens have served as regents until the princes came of age; it would not even be necessary at the present time. It signifies little. The Kings, in any combination, cannot do what must be done to preserve your city and empire."

"And The Terafin can."

"I did not say that. I have doubts—but if there is to be any hope, it lies with her."

"And she is not here."

"No," was his grave reply. "You are. Deal with the difficulties as you see fit, if you accept my assessment—but do so quickly."

"She is unlikely to know if damage is done to her informal council in her absence."

"Is she?"

And so, Birgide planned. She did not discuss these plans with Jester; there was no point. Nor did she discuss them with the vastly more organized and competent Finch. She did not communicate with Duvari through the regular channels open specifically to her; she no longer trusted them.

She was not certain she trusted the Lord of the Compact, and that was a bitter thought. But the logistics of the operation, while largely unknown to Birgide, were known to others. The likelihood that they were the source of the breach was not zero; it was the only thing that offered hope for the future of the *Astari*.

While Birgide planned, she worked. She tended the mundane grounds at the direction of the Master Gardener; she tended the wilderness when the work that could be easily inspected by any passerby was finished. In both cases, she was silent and solitary. The gardening staff, predictably, viewed her with some suspicion; she had vaulted above them in seniority almost instantly, and that never encouraged collegiality. With time, she would earn a place among these men and women—or perhaps not; she did not have the time to build a collegial base from which to operate.

She was not, however, unfriendly; she was neither arrogant nor condescending, although she could use either to her benefit should the need arise. Had she not accepted Jester's offer, she might have been unconcerned.

She had, and therefore, she was. Meralonne's dismissal of the importance of the Kings and their future role sat poorly with her; she did not ascribe his attitude to the magi or the Order of Knowledge. She ascribed it, she thought, as she lifted her head and stretched beneath the boughs of the *Ellariannatte*, to the wilderness. The thought brought no comfort.

Between her feet was a planter. In it, she had carefully culled a cutting or three, as she had done many times during the past decade. The soil in which those cuttings were now loosely planted was from the forest.

She did not believe that these clippings would fare any better than any other clippings she had taken from the great trees in the Common, but they were both her comfort and her pretext. She intended to go to *Avantari*. She intended to plant them in the Kings' gardens; she had, in fact, standing permission to do exactly that, should her long research at last bear fruit.

The standing permission was, of course, meant to be handled with appropriate care; it was not to be abused. There were channels through which she must go; if the Terafin Master Gardener was proprietary and difficult with regards to his own domain, he was one tenth as protective as the Master Gardener responsible for the grounds of *Avantari*, who would, no doubt, be prickly and almost beside himself at her effrontery.

She would not, however, grovel. What she had been willing to endure for a chance to work beneath the boughs of the *Ellariannatte* here, she would not be willing to endure from the gardeners of *Avantari*.

It was inconceivable that Duvari would have no knowledge of her arrival. She was not certain how this would be interpreted, given that she had made no formal request of him. She hoped that he would interpret it correctly, but allowed for the possibility that it was already too late for Duvari.

"I see Jester did not exaggerate."

"Does everyone who happens to work within the manse learn to walk so silently they offer no warning?" Birgide asked. She did not cease the careful arrangement of cuttings and soil; nor did she immediately rise; her hands were dirty.

"My apologies," the unexpected visitor said. "I am content to wait while you finish."

"I assume that you consider the visit itself of some import."

"I seldom interrupt someone else's work for trivial reasons, given how little I appreciate such interruptions myself."

Birgide wiped her hands clean—or as clean as they would be without soap, a brush, and warm water. She then extended her right hand to the older gentleman who stood at a distance. He glanced at her hand with the slight lift of brows.

She kept her hand extended. "I am, as I suspect you know, Birgide Viranyi."

He took it. His grip was firm, but brief.

"You are?"

"I am Haval Arwood. I have part-time residence within the West Wing as tailor and dressmaker."

Had Jester mentioned a resident older man? Birgide offered him a neutral nod as he withdrew. He stood just outside of her natural unarmed combat range; he stood outside of her armed combat range, as well, although she was not visibly armed.

"I'm sorry," she said, "but I'm not attired to entertain."

"Meaning you would like me to leave you to your very necessary work."

"Without intent to insult or offend, yes."

"Intent is always a tricky thing." He smiled.

The smile was disturbing. Birgide found herself unconsciously shifting position.

"I did not come here with intent to harm. I am not certain," he added, glancing at the branches of the tree beneath which she stood, feet planted and slightly apart, knees almost imperceptibly bent, "that I would have found you, otherwise. These parts of the grounds are . . . difficult to navigate."

"You've tried?"

He nodded. "I have always managed to find my way out. I do not believe this is guaranteed."

She frowned. "Why did you try?"

"Because this forest is at the heart of The Terafin's power, and I desired to have a better understanding of it."

"And did you gain that?"

"No. But there are things beyond my ken at work."

"And today?"

"I believe you intend to visit *Avantari* later this afternoon."

Birgide nodded. She saw no point in denial.

"I would like you to carry a message for me when you go."

"To who?"

"An old acquaintance. I do not guarantee that he will be *pleased* to receive it, however; it is not without some attendant risk."

She revised her opinion of Haval Arwood in that moment; she would have to do some research—quickly—when she reached *Avantari*. "I am not, that I am aware of, often tasked with the duties of a messenger."

"No? I foresee a future in which you will become accustomed to being so." He handed her a scroll case; it was simple; it was also sealed. Birgide did not recognize the seal.

"To whom would you like this message delivered?"

He raised a brow but did not answer. Instead, he removed a leather satchel with narrow straps from his side. "This is for you, in payment for the favor I have asked. You may find it useful. You may not—and I would, in all honesty, prefer the latter. If it is not useful, keep it; if it is useful, return it."

She frowned. She was not naturally trusting; had she been, Duvari would have beaten it out of her years ago. But she trusted her instincts, and Haval Arwood did not strike her as a threat.

"Is it valuable?" she asked, taking the satchel.

"Yes, but not in the traditional, mundane sense of that word. Honest dirt will not devalue it. My apologies for any delay my presence may have caused you." He bowed. It was a neat, crisp bow.

Birgide glanced, briefly, at the satchel; the leather was worn and shiny; it was not new.

"Ah," he said, pausing without turning back. "If you do, indeed end up speaking with him—and in the very worst case, you will not—tell him that he is, in my opinion, a smokescreen. The danger, should it arrive, will arrive here—in House Terafin—and not within *Avantari*. I have no proof, but I have uncovered information which strongly supports that supposition."

"He'll ask what it is," Birgide said, reluctant to join this conversation, but equally reluctant to allow him to just walk away.

"No. He won't. There is, however, a large possibility that we will be seeing more of each other in the near future."

Birgide could easily carry a small satchel; she carried a large backpack, and several planters, in a small cart. She was not dressed as a dignitary of any note; nor was she dressed as one of the many, many servants within *Avantari*'s complicated hierarchy. She was, however, recognized by the part of the palace staff that had the responsibility for the interior grounds, and directed to the trade entrance.

The trade entrance of the palace was, however, militantly guarded. Birgide did not find this alarming; nor did she find it inconvenient. Today, in fact, it was the height of convenience. She stated her business and waited in a room that was only barely part of the palace's interior. Given the attack on the Merchants' Guild, the increased level of scrutiny was to be expected, and Birgide was not at all surprised to see a middle-aged woman, escorted by Kings' Swords, enter the waiting area.

She wore, openly, the medallion of the Order of Knowledge, with the distinctive elemental symbols in a quartered circle. She was mage-born.

The Kings' Swords were armed; one carried a crossbow. This was new, but it was, again, an acceptable precaution; she did not imagine the Sword who wielded that crossbow was particularly pleased to be doing so. Birgide had never understood the ways in which weapons were viewed by the royal guard—but she had never aspired to become one. She could wield a short sword should the situation demand it; she could wield a long sword, but with considerably less proficiency. In his place, given the possibility of demonic threat, she would have been far, far more comfortable with a ranged weapon.

She was a very good shot.

The mage stepped forward; she held out what appeared to be a slender gold-plated book. "Apologies," she said, with an evident lack of sincerity, "but I will ask you to place your hand upon the cover of this book."

Birgide examined the book. She could see, across its cover, the golden glow of strands of light. Gold was a color she had not yet encountered in her traversal of the Terafin manse. Without hesitation, she did as asked.

To her surprise, the lines of gold grew warmer and brighter at the touch; she could almost hear the snatches of a melody as the book was withdrawn. It was familiar music, in a bone-deep way, although she did not recognize it at all.

"Thank you for your cooperation." The mage withdrew.

The Swords did not; they passed her into the main building itself. *Avantari*'s visitor galleries were grand and intimidating; the service entrances and hallways could not compare. They were, however, fully stone, and the ceiling, if lower, was vaulted. Manors in the hundred holdings could boast public halls as grand as these, although admittedly the decor in the palace was usually more impressive.

These halls lacked that decor; they lacked the runners and the long carpets; they lacked the paintings and the ornate weaponry that many seemed to feel were appropriate ornamentation. They had, on the other hand, gained the Kings' Swords, in a single line against the wall to Birgide's right. She moved past them; her cart—which was inspected carefully—echoing loudly in the high-ceilinged space.

First, she would do what she had come to do. Then, with luck, she would speak with Duvari.

As it happened, she was met by Sancor Littleton. He was not the Master Gardener, but answered directly to that august man, and he greeted Birgide with the weary, frustrated tolerance she had come to expect. When he saw the clippings, he frowned.

"You are not trying again, are you?" he asked, although the answer was so obvious he clearly asked to hear himself speak.

Birgide's smile was self-deprecating. "I have been allowed access to the Terafin grounds," she replied. "And these cuttings are from the trees that now tower there. I have some small hope that the results might be different."

Sancor ran hands through his beard. "The Terafin Master Gardener is, at the present moment, an insufferable braggart."

She laughed, although she considered the description unkind. "He is justifiably proud of the Terafin grounds at present; let him have his small moment of glory."

"We would be content to let him have, as you call it, a *small* moment. He practically crows at every opportunity. He even has *you* working as part of his *staff.*"

Since Birgide suspected Sancor would bite off his own tongue before he condescended to offer her an actual position among the palace gardening staff, she made appropriate noises. All pretense aside, she *did* have hopes for these cuttings. If she had used that as an excuse to be here, it was nonetheless also true.

And to be fair to Sancor, if he disliked her, it was almost a matter of principle. She was, after all, an outsider; she was not the child of one of the servant lines that otherwise graced the staff. He would be beside himself with almost unequaled joy should these cuttings, against all prior experience and the odds that arose from them, take root.

The *Ellariannatte* were, after all, called the Kings' Trees. If they could grow anywhere in the Empire, it should be here. Birgide, however, was content to have them grace the Common; in *Avantari*, they would be seen by vastly fewer people. She suspected that the reigning Terafin felt the same. Or perhaps felt it more strongly and more viscerally, given her background.

Sancor passed her through the Swords that were on duty, and accompanied her to the Courtyard gardens. These gardens were not, strictly speaking, in a courtyard, but they were bound on all sides by the various buildings that comprised *Avantari* proper, and all of those buildings looked out—and down—upon them.

There were small pavilions, small viewing platforms, artfully surrounded by standing trees; there were small ponds, small running brooks and multiple fountains. The flower beds closest to the trees implied wilderness, but did so artfully; Birgide preferred them to the geometrically precise flower beds and grass at the edge of this so-called courtyard.

She wheeled her cart very carefully along the small and perfectly laid paths, abandoning it there; she could walk into the interior, and did so, taking only the planter with her; her tools hung belted around her waist.

There was no sign of Duvari—but there wouldn't be, not yet. And while she waited, she worked.

Choosing a spot in which to plant the cuttings was an act of deliberation akin to moving armies, at least in *Avantari*. She had made some educated guesses when she informed Sancor, by letter, of her intent, and he had—as expected—

vetoed all but two instantly. Every patch of ground here was personal; Birgide, who was happy to remain apolitical, nonetheless understood this.

In almost all cases, the cuttings would be planted in the various hothouses that fed into the gardens; the growth in the courtyard itself must imply perfection on all levels—and not all successful growth was perfect. Birgide was therefore sidestepping at least three different protocols to be here at all, and Sancor had made clear—odiously, condescendingly and desperately clear—that there would be ructions if her work interfered with his—or any of those under his direct command. Since Sancor would be the one called on the carpet if such damages took place, she had some sympathy with this—but she had chosen Sancor for a reason.

He was vain, he was arrogant, and he always felt slightly uncertain about his positioning on the staff, although he was much closer to the top of the hierarchy than Birgide could ever hope to become, all of her expertise notwithstanding. And he knew that she was now a member of the Terafin staff—and that, in Terafin, the *Ellariannatte* grew. She had standing permission to continue her various attempts to cultivate the trees here, but seldom invoked them as a right—there was always an unspoken cost to invoking rights people didn't feel you ought to have been granted in the first place.

She worked. Hands that had been painstakingly cleaned once again adopted dirt; she often thought that fingernails served no actual purpose except to accrue evidence of the labor that divided the patricians from the working class.

Birgide was not a chatty person, except when necessity forced it upon her; she worked, as she lived, in relative silence. She was surprised to find herself humming as she cleared a very careful amount of dirt, adding the water she had personally prepared. She had no fond memories of lullabyes; no fond memories of most human voices. She, like anyone who could hear them, enjoyed the work of the bards—but she did not seek them out; she accepted invitations to gatherings at which bards were guests. Bards were often found in the Western Kingdoms; they, like she, traveled widely in pursuit of their goals. She offered no offense to the bards, ever.

She did not know what kind of voice she had. She had no interest in choirs or singing. She could not, therefore, name the tune she was humming. She could stop, and did, but as she focused on work, on the familiarity of a pursuit that almost everyone—Birgide included on most days—felt was chasing rainbows, she took up the tune again, without intention, without deliberate thought.

She paused a second time, frowning.

This time, she looked at the cutting. It was, she thought, glowing softly; its light was gold. There were no strands around it, nothing to imply that there was an enchantment cast upon it by an external mage; it was simply golden. It reminded Birgide of summer.

When she began to hum a third time, she let it be, as if the song itself, wordless, was her only method of communicating with the *Ellariannatte*. And so, she hummed and planted. Her knees joined her fingers; although she had brought a mat on which she might kneel, unrolling it had entirely slipped her mind. She knelt upon the ground, her knees making rounded dents, as if, in some measure, she were temporarily planting herself.

There were days, in her distant childhood—a childhood she had escaped and would never return to—when she had dreamed of just that: to be buried someplace in the forest that was her only refuge. To be part of it. Of course, she had assumed she would be dead when and if it happened—but death had seemed like peace, because there had been *no* peace.

She almost never thought of her childhood. But it was true that the personal meaning of forests—the trees, the weeds, the wildflowers—came out of that childhood. Where there were no people, there was no pain. As a child, she could easily confuse lack of pain with joy; joy was absent. It was not something she experienced. Relief could make her giddy. Relief could give her small moments in which the act of existence was not a cosmic injustice in the eyes of people who were larger, and angrier, than she.

Training with the *Astari* had involved pain, injury, and not a little humiliation, but the pain was predictable and consistent; if she failed, if she did not learn quickly enough, she suffered. But she suffered *only* then. It had been a relief. It had not been like pain at all.

But joy? Joy had been the absence of pain. She developed pride in that absence as well: it meant she was stronger, smarter, swifter. It meant she had learned.

What, then, did planting and nurturing and tending have to do with joy? Pain was absent, yes; pride was present—when the careful nurturing and planning actually worked. But it was more than that.

These were alive. They took root, they grew, they aged—and yes, they died. They did not war; they did not politic; they did not rage. They existed, and they offered—to those who could grasp it—peace. And yet, even that was not quite right.

She hummed. Her hands were warm. By definition the earth was dirty, but it was a clean dirt. She could, with time, effort, and careful application of nail files, wash it away with nothing but water and soap. It did not stain her; it did not linger. As she worked, she smiled.

She could not honestly say she cared about the fate of Jewel Markess ATerafin one way or the other. By her very position, she was in the middle of every deadly game that the patricians could play. Somehow, playing those games had failed to kill her, but very, very few of the leaders of The Ten died a peaceful death; one could not count on winning.

What she cared about—what she had cared about the moment she first left the Terafin manse and entered the grounds—was the forest. The Terafin had given that to her. If The Terafin had not understood just how much it would mean to Birgide, that was fair; Birgide herself had had only the barest inkling.

She paused to examine her hand. It was—she was certain—burned to bone; the burn had not scarred. It did not, to the eye, exist at all. It did not pain her, although from time to time she could feel a tingle of something in the center of her palm.

She felt it now, as she worked. She felt it as she handled a cutting imbued with a golden warmth and light she had never seen before. She was almost certain that that light had existed in every other attempt; the ability to *see* it had come with the Terafin grounds. With the forest that could not exist, except in idle daydream and visceral yearning.

She knew, as she worked, that she would give her life to defend The Terafin because The Terafin stood at the forest's heart—and only because of that. But that, she thought, had been enough. She looked, once again, at her hand.

With the meticulous care that characterized almost all of her work, she finished. She had left space in which to erect a tiny fence around the cutting, but the materials remained in the handcart. She rose, brushed specks of soil off her knees, and headed toward the cart.

The ground beneath her feet shuddered.

The carefully laid path, narrow and winding as it was, broke; stones rose, scraping against other stones as the path itself was shattered.

Sancor, she thought, with genuine panic, *is going to kill me.* Or die of apoplexy on the spot. She turned, and when she did, the gardening spades she carried fell out of almost nerveless hands.

The cuttings she had planted with such care were gone. What now stood in their place were two full-grown trees, with leaves of ivory-edged green that now dangled well above her upturned face. The artful implication of wilderness had been likewise obliterated, but from this vantage, the obliteration looked deliberate.

Birgide bent and retrieved her tools; she must have, because she held them in her hands. But she had no conscious memory of the action; no physical memory of it, either. She saw the trees, and saw the shadows they cast—but also saw, in the heart of the Courtyard gardens, the light. It fell in translucent, golden strands, from height to ground, anchored in earth and stone, twining around brass and plated iron, blending with the blue of carefully sheltered magestones.

It was, she thought, the same light that imbued the wilderness behind the Terafin manse. She passed her hands through it and heard notes; they were similar. Her hands caught on nothing; she felt the shift of temperature, no more, and even that was so slight it might have been imagination.

She heard shouting somewhere in the distance; she heard footsteps. She knew, within minutes, she would no longer be alone at the foot of the *Ellariannatte* she had struggled to grow here for much of her adult life.

She felt no triumph. She understood that this was not, in the end, her success; it was not through dint of will and trial and error, through repeated failures and repeated attempts, that she had finally experienced a measure of success. She understood, and felt a pang of something that was almost disappointment. But no disappointment could survive the sight of these trees.

They did not magically alter the rest of the Courtyard gardens, which was a profound relief. If Sancor was grateful that she had succeeded—and she had no doubt he would be—he nonetheless had to deal with every other artist that toiled here, one of whom would be justifiably unhappy.

Sancor arrived first. Behind him she saw Almette, and behind Almette, three under-gardeners; the three were younger, and their jaws were hanging open. Only Almette was bold enough to breach the distance to hug Birgide; to, in fact, lift her off her feet, squealing in wordless delight.

Sancor would have died first, but even Sancor looked cautiously pleased, although on his sun-weathered face, this barely shifted the line of his brow. Cuttings did not become full-growth trees in seconds. Not even in the Kings' gardens. But if it could happen in Terafin, his expression implied, it could—and should—happen *here*.

He had not, of course, considered the implications of what it meant should it happen here. And he should have: the entire Palace Staff had been in shock when the supporting pillars—of stone—had magically been transformed into something entirely unfamiliar. So had sections of floor.

It was not spoken of, even among the servants.

If Sancor did not consider the implications, Birgide knew at least one man would. She was not at all surprised when the Lord of the Compact walked down the badly jarred footpath. He didn't sprint, as the others had; nor did he gape at the two *Ellariannatte*. He barely glanced at them, his measured gaze was so focused.

The gardeners, however, were immediately ill at ease. Duvari had that effect on everyone, regardless of their station.

"Where," he asked, "did these trees come from?"

No one answered, which surprised Birgide. She would have expected Sancor to throw her to the wolves.

"They are here," Sancor said stiffly, "with permission."

"That is not what I asked."

"That is all you require. You are not the Lord of the Courtyard; you are the Lord of the Compact. If you have concerns, address the Master Gardener."

Duvari did not look surprised; Birgide was. She failed to stare at Sancor because she could control surprise or shock with relative ease. She, however, had no desire to throw Sancor to the wolves at this particular moment. "With the permission of the Master Gardener, and the Kings themselves, I brought cuttings from the Terafin manse to the Courtyard; if there is blame or suspicion, it must fall on me."

Duvari nodded. "When did you bring the cuttings?"

He, of course, knew. She was certain he knew to the minute when she had been granted access to *Avantari* and, further, to the Courtyard gardens. She answered his question, regardless.

"Very well. I would like to speak with you further on the subject of these cuttings. Those are your possessions?"

She nodded.

"They are all of the possessions that entered *Avantari* with you?"

She nodded again.

Sancor was annoyed; he was far less adept at hiding this than Birgide. He was Head Gardener here, and junior to no one except the Master Gardener, who was not, in fact, standing in Duvari's shadow.

"Head Gardener," Duvari said, before Sancor could speak. "This is not a matter of pretty plants; it is a security matter. You may answer to the Master Gardener in other concerns; *everyone* except the Kings answers to *me* in matters of security."

"I am not," Birgide quietly pointed out to Sancor, "a member of the gardening staff. Given the circumstances, his concern is reasonable; I am not offended."

"You have clearly not spent enough time with the Lord of the Compact,"

Sancor replied, somewhat acidly. "But if you are determined to obey, I will accept it. I will be *certain* to mention this to the Master Gardener," he added.

Birgide did not want to be anywhere near that conversation, but given the slight tautness of Duvari's expression, wouldn't be. He was angry. "Will you quarantine the cart?" she asked him.

"The magi," he replied, "are here. They will, no doubt, be interested in the trees themselves."

She wilted. Sancor swelled. There was, she thought, no activity in any walk of life that did not, in the end, become political. On the other hand, the war that the gardening staff could start did not generally involve bloodshed and bodies.

And so, she stood in the back office of the Royal Trade Commission. Her gardening tools and her handcart were impounded; the magi were inspecting them, no doubt with disdain and gloves to protect their hands from simple dirt. She had not been subjected to the magi, beyond the cursory entrance scan; she was certain they were demanding that right somewhere beyond her hearing.

On the other hand, the magi did not care for Duvari, nor he for them; he was not inclined to give in to any of their demands, as it set a bad precedent. They would have their work cut out for them.

Accordingly, she had time, and silence, to consider both the office and the events of the afternoon. She had left her handcart; she had not, in fact, left either the satchel or the scroll she had been given. Nor had she surrendered either to Duvari, along with the cryptic message that was to accompany the scroll. No, she thought, the message had not been cryptic. The opinion offered was extremely clear.

She waited. The interior office was empty and would, no doubt, remain so; the front office was staffed by two young men, who looked professional but somewhat harried. The heightened precautions that had caused the number of Kings' Swords present to swell had had effects everywhere.

No one wanted a demon to burn down a large portion of *Avantari*. Demons had recently entered *Avantari* with the intent to assassinate the princes, and while Duvari was aware no security could have prevented that attack, he was also aware that there were other occasions in which demons had chosen to enter through the front door or the service entrances. If he could not make their presence impossible, he could make it more difficult.

She smiled, thinking it. Duvari was, all vehement diatribes aside, a man.

One man. He was not mage-born; not, to Birgide's knowledge, talent-born at all. But she could easily imagine Duvari going toe-to-toe with the demons. She could rationally assess his chances: poor. But she could not viscerally believe what the rational mind insisted was true.

She did not believe that Duvari was the source of the security breach. She acknowledged that she was not impartial; she had preparations in place, should those beliefs be proved wrong.

As she waited, she gave in to a restlessness that would—in her childhood—have been grounds for severe punishment: she walked. She moved through this one room, touching strands of light above standing cabinets, desks, innocuous workbenches, listening, as she did, for the notes that touch invoked.

She wished, briefly, that golden strands graced this office; the sounds of the violet and blue were lower, resonant base notes. The orange was of a medium range; she wished, again, that she had studied music. She hadn't. She could play what sounded pleasant to her—but she suspected that the bards could have created a symphony of sound, dancing across the room between clusters of finely tuned strings.

She wondered what the result might be.

"I see you are restless," A familiar voice said.

She turned as the notes stilled. Duvari had come, and he was not alone. To his right stood a man she had met perhaps twice: Maures ADonlan. He was Duvari's contemporary; he, like Devon, was part of the Royal Trade Commission. Unlike Devon, he was not junior enough to be at the beck and call of the aging Patris Larkasir—but he had no desire to run the office. He handled specific routes between the Empire and the Dominion, and he handled them with a quiet, graceful competence; he spoke at least three languages, each of them so fluently the small mistakes translation could inspire were absent.

And none of that was important information at present.

No information about Maures was, or would be, relevant again—not in the same way. Where the magic cast by the magi—at the direction of the Lord of the Compact and the Mysterium—was colored and delicate, the nimbus that now surrounded Maures was not; it was thick and dark, like the black smoke that rose from burning flesh. She looked at him, nodded coolly, and turned to Duvari, wishing for one long moment that she still cradled the cuttings of her precious trees in her arms. They would form a shield between her and what was left of Maures ADonlan. Where he walked, the strands she thought of as evidence of magic seemed to bend or twist to avoid his touch.

They did not avoid Duvari in the same way. It was the only relief she felt, and there wasn't enough of it.

"What," Duvari asked, "have you done in the Courtyard gardens?"

"At the request of the Master Gardener—the repeated, public request—I brought cuttings culled—with permission—from the Terafin grounds to the Courtyard. I worked with both permission and supervision. I have done nothing against any protocols."

"Do not," Maures said, "play games."

Birgide raised both brows; she had never quite learned the art of lifting only one. "I am unaccustomed to games," she replied. "I am a botanist. I have little—very little—to do with politics of any stripe; my concerns, when I pursue research or studies within *Avantari*, are entirely the rules and protocols of the *Master Gardener*. If I have offended in some way—and apparently, I have—the people with whom you must raise your concerns are the gardening staff." She had stiffened, shifting position; this, given the chill in her tone, would not be remarkable.

But she listened. She listened to Maures' voice. It was deep and rich and multi-layered—as unlike her own voice to her ears as the music she plucked from translucent, magical strands. Duvari's was also thin and unremarkable.

Maures glanced at the Lord of the Compact; Duvari was impassive. He demanded no further explanation, but he did not attempt to leash his companion.

"The *Master Gardener*," Maures said, "did not cause trees to magically reach their full height in a matter of minutes. This has occurred in no other lands but the estates Terafin controls—and you have come from the Terafin estates. I ask again, explain yourself."

"I have tendered all of the explanation I can. You are not, that I recall, Lord of the Compact; if I am to answer to anyone for this, it is he."

"Then answer," Maures said.

"Maures."

The man subsided. He did not do so with any grace; Birgide thought he was genuinely enraged. It gave her a measure of confidence; nothing else, at the moment, did. She shifted her stance again.

"Birgide." Duvari turned his attention to her. "Please answer the question."

"I came with cuttings, as I have said, from the Terafin grounds."

"You have been given leeway to do research there that even the Order of Knowledge has been denied."

"I have The Terafin's permission, yes. It is, of course, dependent upon the Master Gardener of Terafin; I have not been given carte blanche—there or here—to proceed entirely at my own whim. The grounds at the back of the manse appear to be unstable; they are certainly remarkable in ways that simple magery cannot explain." As Duvari opened his mouth, she continued, her voice even, her expression neutral. "There are trees of silver, of gold, and of diamond. They shed leaves that are, in shape, appropriate for trees—but they are not, in any sense of the word, organic."

"And such trees could not be grown or created by magic?"

"I think the Artisans might be able to create one of each, with time and effort. But a small forest? No. I chose to approach House Terafin because rumors reached me of the *Ellariannatte*—but they are the least of the wonders that are to be found there." She could not keep the smile off her lips as she spoke; nor did she try.

"The least?" Maures said. Birgide would not have dared, not when Duvari was so close and had—in his quiet way—made his position clear. "We have been concerned," he continued, when Duvari remained silent, "about Terafin and its interference. The Terafin has clearly already caused damage within *Avantari*, the extent of which remains little known only through strict vigilance on our part."

What, Birgide thought, had Haval said? What exactly?

"She is dangerous," Maures said to Duvari, before he continued his angry lecture. "And you have brought some part of The Terafin's workings with you into *Avantari*."

"They are trees, ADonlan."

"They are not simple trees; simple trees do not reach their full growth in a matter of minutes."

"I am not certain they *have* reached their full growth," she countered. "I have studied these trees for all of my adult life. There has never been an instance in which they have been harmful in any way. I do not expect—sudden growth notwithstanding—their presence here to cause any difficulty."

Maures opened his mouth. Birgide, however, watched Duvari.

"That is not your decision to make."

"No. I believe, in this instance, it is the Master Gardener's. Or perhaps, the Kings themselves." She walked, slowly, across the room, toward the area in which the translucent strings were at their most dense. Toward, she thought, the windows in this office, which faced the Courtyard gardens, and therefore, the *Ellariannatte* themselves. Through spotless, clear glass of a serviceable nature, she had to lift her chin and expose her neck to see their heights.

She did. Thus occupied, she said, "If it is necessary, I will tender my resignation immediately." She watched Maures in reflection; she watched the

Lord of the Compact. Sliding her hands to the workmanlike, shiny satchel, she waited for a response.

It was not long in coming. "You intend to resign?"

She turned, once again, to face Duvari. Her hands were loose by her sides; fingers trailed through violet and orange as she nodded.

"Effective when?"

There were only two phrases she might use in such a circumstance; both made her feel young. Youth had had very, very little to recommend it in Birgide's experience. The first was *If the current crisis had not commanded so much of your time, I would have left the service sooner.*

It was the second she chose. "Right now."

"You understand," Duvari continued, as if she had not spoken, "that there are very few acceptable ways to retire from the service? You've sworn an oath to the Kings; they have accepted it."

Birgide nodded. "It is my belief that they will accept the resignation."

"They are the Kings," he replied. "I am the Lord of the Compact. You have spent too much time within Terafin if you think the *Astari* have the rights of the Terafin Chosen."

Birgide glanced at the door that led to the outer offices. She glanced at Maures. Maures did not seem overly concerned with her resignation; he did not seem overly concerned with Duvari's reaction to it.

So, she thought, it was true: demons did not absorb all of the memories and experiences of their victims.

Duvari turned to Maures. "I will have words with the magi," he said, his voice as quiet as death. "You will take care of things here."

Maures nodded. And, of course, he smiled.

Birgide's hand now rested upon the hilt of an awkward dagger. Haval Arwood's gift. Her palm, as she tightened her grip on the dagger, grew warm. Unlike the flame of the burning tree, this warmth caused no pain; it reminded her, instead, of summer rocks. Of Summer.

But winter was white misted breath, not thick, dark smoke; winter was blinding snow, and falling flakes and silent port; winter was reddened cheek and chapped skin. What imbued Maures now was none of these things. Could be none of these things. The Summer and Winter Birgide Viranyi knew were anchored in human experience.

Duvari turned as he reached the doors that opened to the outer office.

Birgide lifted one hand and passed it through the strands of magic: orange and violet, all. The notes reverberated, in a very rudimentary music. Maure's eyes narrowed; she wondered what he saw.

"You cannot possibly think," he said, Duvari forgotten, "that you can stand against me?"

"Stranger things, by far, have happened," she countered. The notes she had struck stilled. But the notes she had not now took their place as she stood in the tall, wide windows that faced the Courtyard gardens.

What she had read of demons—and the reports were closely guarded—was scant. She knew only that they were deadly, that they were often immune to simple steel, and that they were *fast*. They were not immune to magic, but they had magic of their own with which to counter that school of attack; they were not bound by simple things like gravity.

Or flesh.

They were powerful enough that they did not feel the need for caution when they chose to attack. And they were rumored to be capable of exactly this: they could assume the appearance of the living. They could inhabit them, speak as them, and gain some part of their knowledge.

But Duvari trusted no one completely. Birgide was certain that the only person who understood the network of *Astari* spread across this Empire—and occasionally beyond it—was Duvari himself.

Duvari, who was armed. Duvari who could wield any weapon Birgide had ever seen with equality facility. Today, he carried short daggers; they had fallen into his hands with a flick of the wrist. Hers had not; she understood that the gift given her by Haval Arwood was to be her best chance in what was to follow.

But it was not, she thought, as the sound in the room grew louder—and brighter, if sound could be said to have any visible component—her only weapon. She felt, of all things, joy—a giddy, boundless joy. Joy, in Birgide's life, had been ascribed to the absence of pain. It would never be relegated to that, again.

Because here, facing demon—and grieving, in a quiet way, the loss of the man he had absorbed—Birgide was in her forest. She was in the forest of her childhood, when everyone in her life had been composed of rage and fury, and the power to lash out, again and again. She was not—would never be—as physically strong as the people who had made life unbearable.

She was not, and would never be, as powerful as the creature she now faced. Not in a pure fight, not on her own. But she understood, as the sun streamed in through the window at her back, that she was not alone. She had chosen the peace and the power of her solitary life in the forest, and its echoes returned as voices. Every stolen moment of harbor, every brief escape, every temporary respite, had been a seed, and those seeds had grown roots. She stood, rooted, solid, shorn of fear.

But she understood, as the Lord of the Compact *moved*, that those moments of safety had not been the only safe moments; that more than one seed had been planted, and more than one had taken root. Maures did not notice Duvari—not immediately; his attention was solely riveted upon Birgide.

And Birgide knew she would have seconds—if that—free from that attention. She shifted her stance, standing at ease, hand in satchel, sun warming the back of her neck. Maures—or whatever he had become—cast shadows as he walked; the shadows were multiple and only one of them suggested humanity. She thought she could trace the outlines of his demonic form in the fall of that darkening: four arms, tines that rose from the shoulders, too sharp and slender to be wings; broad chest, and a height that even the tallest of men could not naturally reach.

He carried no weapons. The shadows implied that simple weapons would be superfluous; his hands were long, and seemed bladed or clawed; the reach of those protrusions was greater than Birgide's reach with dagger or sword would be.

And she should have been afraid. Should have.

But having brought the *Ellariannatte* to *Avantari*, she couldn't be. Because the forest was here, and because Duvari had taken, from her defiance, the only message of import. She didn't flinch or blink when the Lord of the Compact drove both of the small knives he carried into Maures' exposed back. His strike was too low for organs. Birgide thought he had attempted to sever spine.

And it would have worked; she was already in motion.

She was not prepared for the sudden flight of desks and shelves in the office, and aborted her planned attack when a chair bounced off the window two feet above her head. The windows did not break. Nor would they, without a more concerted effort.

Maures stiffened, stumbled and fell. But even as he fell, the shadows that had been clear only to Birgide's vision shifted and solidified; hands that had been, upon entry into this office, human, shed flesh—and blood, and bone—as longer, thicker arms broke through. And yes, claws—long, slender, curved blades. They shredded carpet as the demon pushed himself off the ground, unfolding.

Half of Maures' face fell away; half clung as demonic face expanded. Shadows for eyes, ebony for fangs; nothing about what emerged from the cocoon of a familiar body looked remotely human. The ribs that surfaced from the clothing Maures had worn extended a foot to either side, like a shattered cage.

It was a blessing. It was death. But Birgide had lived in the shadow of death for as long as she could remember; only her chosen field of study had celebrated life in any form. And even that study had been undertaken because plants could lead, in the end, to death.

Always death.

And who else should face demons? Who else? She stood; light streamed in from the window; Duvari moved like a man possessed. As he moved, the sound in the room shifted; watching him, *listening* to him, she understood that all of his movements were augmented in subtle ways. For a man who was at best coldly suspicious of the magi, this should have come as a surprise.

Duvari always used the tools at hand. He was gone as the demon sent both of his arms back; the sound of blades hitting blades filled the room, but the demon did not even turn; he faced Birgide. Birgide reached up with her left hand, intercepting sunlight and air and transparent strands of magic.

The demon growled; his voice was not Maures' voice. Birgide thought he must have literal eyes in the back of his head—or the sides. He rose—and rose again. He did not attempt to strike Duvari with his long, clawed hands a second time; he gestured, and a desk rose. Two. Birgide had no illusions; she could not survive the crushing weight of either.

She started to leap to the right and froze, her left hand tightening in the sunlight, her fingers becoming numb. She held the hilt of an awkwardly shaped, unbalanced knife in her right.

The demon smiled. It was hard to look at his face, because half of it was now the obviously dead skin of a man, but she thought his smile held genuine amusement. "I know what it is you hold," he said, as the first of the desks went flying backward, toward Duvari. "It is only effective if you can strike me—and, Birgide, you can't. You were never the most competent of combatants."

The second desk flew toward her.

She watched its slow, ungainly flight. She heard it as magic asserted itself in the air of the room, and she watched as it arced, at last, into the falling beams of light. There, it came to a sudden stop, suspended above the ground in the strands of a golden, bright net.

Summer.

The demon's expression rippled, shadow melting into flesh. His eyes—defined only by a shift in texture somewhere in the high midpoint of his face—had rounded and deepened. He spoke a word. Two. Neither were in a language Birgide recognized.

Her hand, still entwined in light, tightened; the light itself developed texture and weight at her touch. She pulled on the strings and the desk swayed in midair. In the distance, she was aware that the first thrown desk had landed; wood cracked and shattered, as if it were glass.

Her cursory glance past the demon's sharp, open ribs did not reveal Duvari, and she could spare no further attention; the demon was not concerned with the Lord of the Compact. He leaped toward Birgide, and she shifted her weight, bending into her knees and raising the dagger she carried.

But she did not strike; his leap was a feint. The beginning of the jump implied a direction and velocity that he did not choose to travel. Rumors were true: the demon was fast. The floor beneath Birgide's braced feet cracked; she couldn't see what had broken it.

This time, when she leaped, she moved; the sunlight didn't hold her in place. Strands of light trailed behind her, twined visibly around her hand; they didn't restrict motion, which was good. She hit the floor, rolled to her feet, and leaped again as the shadow passed—narrowly—over her moving body.

The floor held; the demon's reach was vastly greater than her own. His arms were deceptive in length; they elongated, and his claws shrieked against the floor; sparks rose as he hit stone supports. He did not intend, as he'd said, to give her opportunity to strike him with the dagger that Haval had gifted her.

He had enough of Maures' memory to know that armed combat had never been her strength. She could fight; she could leverage her size—or lack of size—to advantage, hiding her strength. Hiding had been one of the few trained activities that had earned her neither bruises nor humiliation. They were refinements on rudimentary lessons she had already learned.

Maures understood that size was not the measure by which the *Astari* were judged. He had overseen some part of her training. No one, however, oversaw it all; no member of the *Astari* could be aware of another's full measure. Maures, alive, would have been more cautious.

Maures, alive, did not have the arrogant confidence the demon did. He was sloppy; all of his gestures were, as he himself, large and forceful, as were his attacks. Where the desk had failed, he gestured another into the air; as he did, she could see new strands of gray attach themselves to the desk's surface and legs. The desk flew, and as it did, the demon joined it, leaping up and across the room to the left of where Birgide stood.

Birgide could not stand to fight when too much of the room could be used against her. The floors were not thin, the supports were not fragile, but neither had been designed or built for a conflict such as this.

She leaped to the right, rolled, and leaped again. Claws broke wooden planks inches from where she'd come to a stop as he followed. Had he minimized the ferocity of his blows, had he minimized movement, practiced restraint, she was almost certain she would be dead. To avoid him at all, she had to avoid injury; there was no room for error, no room for the loss of speed injury often caused.

The demon struck. Only when he embedded hands into flooring was he slowed, but even the resistance of breaking floor couldn't hold him in one space for long. There was a pattern to the attacks themselves; he struck and leaped, struck and leaped. He was not in one spot for long enough that Birgide could stab him with the dagger she carried. Ornamental, heavy, jeweled, it was also useless; it could have been sword or club, with just the same effect.

She could not continue this for much longer, and knew it. She could not stop, could not assess the threat with any detached rationality; she could move, and move, and move.

Even so, she was planning as she dodged. A ledger struck her shoulder; it was the only thing, so far, that could. Her arm numbed; she was certain she would be bruised should she survive. Duvari did not join the fray. Nor had she time to look to see where—or if—he had fallen. Every motion flowed from every other motion; the first decision—to leap to the right of the demon's lunge—dictated every other decision.

She carried the strands of golden light that had briefly trapped her hand. She had noticed, as she rose from the first almost acrobatic leap, that those strands seemed to anchor themselves to whatever she touched; for the most part, that was floor. The office was not small; it was meant to house dozens of men and women. Had the wall been closer, she would have made her way there; it was not.

She therefore used the floor, and only the floor. She moved, where she could, to the right; if she had to backtrack—and she did—she reversed course as soon as it was feasible. An erratic, oblong circle began to emerge. Golden strands of Summer light, anchored at intervals a few yards apart, took root; they were a taut, bright weaving.

They were a large, insubstantial net. The demon failed to notice their existence. Twice, perhaps three times as the length of what could hardly be called a battle grew, he passed through them; his presence did not uproot them—but it did not destroy them either.

Some of the strands became enmeshed in flying debris. The demon's instinctive sense of her speed was good—too good; he could anticipate where she would land, where she would rise. The objects thrown fell short, regardless. They fell short, caught in webs of golden light, and slowed in their trajectory. Thus chairs, shelves, bookends, struck floor a foot away from their intended target. Glassed doors shattered; shards made the wreck of the floor trickier to navigate. Cut hands would not kill her, and she did cut both hands and leg; none of the cuts were deep enough to slow her down.

Not until she took that last injury across the mound of her left palm.

Birgide's hands were callused; she was accustomed to the minor injuries expected when working with plants. This cut was deeper, but not by much. But the left hand held the summer light, in its complicated net of strands. Blood pooled slowly in the creases of that palm, and when it touched strands the room shifted.

Light flared, bright, gold—but this light, the demon could see.

And in it, she could see the demon clearly. The whole of his body was ebon; his ribs, the tines that rose defensively—she saw that now—from his shoulders, chitinous and gleaming. But his shadow—his shadow was no longer demonic; it did not reflect the contours of his body or its visible shape.

It was slender, yes, but not extreme, and as the light in the room grew, the shadow solidified until it was almost a thing unto itself, joined to the demon only at the feet. The light intensified; as it did, the strands solidified. So, too, the shadow itself; dark and solid and so similar in shape to a man that she wondered if it were Maures.

Wondered, and yet, knew. It was not. She stepped back as the demon's musculature tensed; he knelt, his knees immune to shards of glass and splintered wood, his hands uncut. His eyes, as they widened, were gray. Gray passed into silver as those eyes reflected light. "Impossible," he whispered. "The Summer is gone; it will never return."

"It is Summer magic," Duvari said. His voice came from behind and to the left; Birgide did not look away from the demon.

"It is not," the demon replied. "Are you so impoverished that you cannot *hear* it? The Winter is come to an end; Summer waits."

Birgide said nothing.

But Duvari said, "if I understand events in your world, you have destroyed the Summer trees; if Winter is at an end, what is left?"

The creature roared. No syllables broke the singular sound: a mixture of triumph and pain. To Birgide's surprise the roar ended in a strangled, terrible laughter, which was just as raw. "I curse you," the demon said, in a voice that was almost human. "I curse you to love, Duvari. To love, and to love, and to be torn between the two until one—or the other—destroys you utterly.

"You have never known fear. You have never known pain. Even the pain that *we* can cause is nothing in comparison." He roared again, and the sound of it—oh, the sound; Birgide's hands were halfway to her ears just to lessen it. She lowered them, her hands shaking as they fell to rest at her sides.

The demon, tensed, roared a third time. Before the almost animal sound had echoed into silence, he leaped.

Birgide stood her ground. She heard Duvari shout her name, but it came at a great remove, overwhelmed by the sudden rush of sound, of Summer song. There was warmth, in this room. Warmth and the promise of life.

And there was death as well—but this death was not for her. The demon ran through the bright, golden strands, arms extended in the gaps between their placement. He would kill her, if he could.

But he couldn't. The strings tightened, the net closed. Warmth became heat, and heat gave way to a fire that was at once all the colors flame knew: Blue, orange, gold, white, red. Red. He did not scream.

But his shadow did, before the disintegration of his body swept it away.

Chapter Nineteen

"**Y**OU WILL EXPLAIN YOURSELF."

Birgide knelt in the ashes, sifting through them. Nothing of the demon remained; nor did anything of Maures. She nodded, sliding the unused relic back into the well-used satchel before she rose. As she did, she withdrew the scroll case that Haval Arwood had handed her.

"I did not intend," she said quietly, "for the *Ellariannatte* to bloom and flower here. But I will not lie to you. I hoped."

Duvari was leaning against one of the standing cabinets, his arms folded, his chin inclined. To Birgide's surprise, his eyes were closed. "I was once told that it is best to allow the brilliant their eccentricities—and the careful culling and planting of the *Ellariannatte* was yours." He lifted chin, opened eyes.

His face was bruised. She could not tell if he had sustained any other injuries, and did not make the attempt; what Duvari was unwilling to share was best left unnoticed.

"I have read every report that referenced your progress in the Order of Knowledge," the Lord of the Compact continued. "Not one indicated any competence in magery."

"No. I was not talent-born."

"And yet the demon has been destroyed and you have not."

Birgide nodded.

"He was destroyed by spell."

She shook her head. "I have made the quiet study of the mage-born a large part of my life. This was no magery—not as it is understood *by* mages." She walked carefully across the floor, avoiding glass and splinter; it was not a straight path. Too many cabinets had fallen, too many desks. The Royal Trade Commission had standards; none of the carpentry was poor, and none of the wood soft. Birgide did not envy the man—or woman—who would have to make excuses for this disaster. Given current events, it was likely to drive poor Patris Larkasir mad.

"How did you know what he was?"

She failed to answer immediately. Instead, she extended the hand that carried the scroll case, her expression neutral.

Duvari's eyes narrowed. They were almost shut. "Where did you get this?" he asked. He did not reach out to take the case. Birgide's arm was tired. She knew the whole of her body would ache half a day from now. But aching or no, she could not now withdraw.

"In the Terafin manse," she replied. "I was asked to deliver it to you, today."

"The dagger you carried for most of the fight came from the same source?"

She nodded.

Duvari took the scroll case. He did not break the seal. He did not even examine it. So: Duvari knew Haval Arwood. Or knew, rather, the seal that Haval had chosen to use. Birgide had not recognized it herself. "Was there a message?"

She thought him angry, although she could not say why; there was no shift in tone, and no change in facial expression; his body did not tense. "Yes."

"Deliver it. I am expecting a pompous Master Gardener to intrude on my report to the Kings."

"He feels the attack upon the *Astari* is a feint."

"Does he? And did he say why?"

"No. He understands my position within the *Astari*. He believes that the attack, when it comes, will center on House Terafin."

"Terafin was not the only House in which members of the *Astari* were lost."

This was news to Birgide—and news, at that, that Duvari would not usually share. It did not make her bold; it made her nervous. No doubt that was Duvari's intent.

"I have been offered the Terafin name."

Duvari straightened. Without a word, he walked toward the window that faced the Courtyard gardens; he stood, staring out, the scroll loosely clasped in one hand. Birgide could see his reflection returned to her in glass.

"You will take it," he finally said. It was not a question. It was not, by tone, a command.

"Yes."

"What else can you see, Birgide? What else can you divine? I have known Maures for half his life; there was no deviation, no unusual behavior, no hint of otherness in him. Yet he was lost. We cannot know how much information he shared, nor with who." He paused. "The trees are surprising."

Birgide waited. Five minutes passed, perhaps more. Duvari's mood was strange. But in the end, he turned to face her. "There are no mages among the *Astari*."

She nodded.

"But you are not, in your own estimation, a mage. Could you detect the demonic in just this fashion anywhere within *Avantari*?"

"I believe so."

"Then do so. I will not surrender you to Terafin while I have need of you. But Birgide—you are now a Terafin weapon."

And Birgide said, "Accept that The Terafin is now the only effective shield the Kings will have, Lord of the Compact. Accept that The Terafin is the Empire's weapon. She will not depose the Twin Kings. It would never occur to her to try."

"Will she obey them? Will she obey their orders?"

"I have met The Terafin only once. I cannot say with certainty."

"And will you obey her orders, or mine?"

"If you do not order me to act against her, if you do not order me to kill, I will obey you in all things."

But he shook his head. "You are young. You were always young. You believe the words you speak."

"I believe them because I *mean them*."

He raised one brow.

"The Terafin," she said, lowering her voice, "is the heart of the forest. It is because she is here that the *Ellariannatte* grow."

"But she is not here. Not even the gods know where she now resides."

She was surprised. "You asked?"

"The Kings did. They are concerned. They believe what you believe. Belief, however, is not my duty. It is not my responsibility. Vigilance is. Come, then. We will travel the halls of *Avantari* before you return to Terafin."

She nodded.

"I also expect a report."

Of course he did. He was practical; he did not ask her to sit down and write it immediately.

"If this strange power you have introduced to *Avantari* causes harm, I will kill you myself."

She nodded again. It was almost a comfort to hear him speak the words aloud.

Duvari left her for half an hour, during which she righted fallen chairs. She did not have the strength to right either desk or cabinet, and at least two of the desks would not stand regardless, having lost legs in the fray. She did, however, collect pieces of glass and splintered wood. The floor was gouged, and the rugs that had covered it, rent; these she left.

She made stacks of the books, or started to; Duvari interrupted her. He returned in formal dress, his skin powdered in such a way that the bruises did not immediately show; they were obvious to Birgide. She doubted they would be obvious to many others; very few made a habit of studying Duvari's face.

To her surprise—and dismay—he began his inspection of the palace in the Hall of Wise Counsel. She did not immediately realize where he was heading until they were almost upon it. She was not dressed—in any way—to meet the Kings, the Queens, or their sons. Dirt was once again wedged into her nail beds, and her hands were flecked with dried blood. She was discomfited enough that she attempted to point out the severe breach of etiquette.

Duvari was not amused.

Then again, when had he ever been? The various men and women who had undertaken much of her martial training had been prone to harsh words and a grim, almost humiliating humor. Duvari, never. Humiliation came with you and left with you; he spent no words or obvious effort to cause it. Had he caused pain?

Yes. Bruising. One broken arm, one fractured leg, both training accidents. But compared to the life she'd known before, they were nothing. She understood exactly *why* the injuries had occurred. She knew what she had to learn to avoid them. They were consistent.

The height of the ceilings now loomed above her like judgment as she made her way through the standing ranks of Kings' Swords. The last hall was thick with them; they occupied both walls at intervals of four feet. They did not appear to notice Duvari—but they noticed everyone else; Birgide was certain that even had she been expected, she would have been stopped at multiple checkpoints.

The Kings' Swords did not interfere with Duvari. The passage through these heavily guarded halls was therefore the briefest it had ever been for Birgide, not that she was a frequent visitor. Duvari was stopped when the doors of the Hall rolled open and his presence was announced. He was required to place his hand upon a golden tome, twin to the one that Birgide herself had touched as a prerequisite for entry into *Avantari*.

Birgide was required to touch it as well, and did, surprised at the hands that carried it: the Guildmaster of the Order of Knowledge.

Sigurne Mellifas smiled. "Birgide," she said.

"Guildmaster."

"Yes. Today, yes, I am. I imagine you are surprised to see me."

Birgide, however, shook her head. "You came for the trees."

"Yes. They were your doing?"

"No, Guildmaster. They were, in their entirety, The Terafin's gift."

The older woman's gaze sharpened. "You have spoken with The Terafin since her departure?"

"No. But the forest is The Terafin's, and the forest is now, in some part here. It is here, on the Isle. I believe—although I have yet to visit to confirm my suspicions, it is present in the Common as well."

"Enough, Guildmaster," Duvari said. "We will speak of these things with the Kings and the Exalted. I do not wish to waste time in needless repetition."

Birgide fell silent, as did Sigurne.

The Kings entered the hall from the sculpted wall farthest from the doors. The Exalted entered with them. Although the Kings were dressed in Court finery, they were not dressed to hold audience; the Exalted wore the robes of their office, but had ventured forth with only a single attendant each.

Those attendants—priests, all—set about lighting the incense braziers that masked smell—among other things. The Queens were absent, as were the Princes; the only other people in this vast and silent hall were *Astari*.

The doors at Birgide's back rolled open; Birgide turned.

Solran Marten, the Bardmaster of Senniel College, stood in the open frame. She met Sigurne as an equal, and placed her hand gently upon the book in the older woman's arms. "Sigurne," she said. "I should have expected you. I must apologize for my tardiness. The Guildmaster of the Makers is some half a hall behind me; he had some questions, and I could not easily disentangle myself."

"Gilafas ADelios will also attend?"

"Yes, if that is acceptable to the Kings and the Exalted; he seemed to feel that he had been invited."

Given Gilafas' rank, an invitation was not, strictly speaking, required to open most doors. And given that Gilafas was a maker, disorganization was almost expected.

Duvari looked as if he had swallowed newly broken glass, although he nodded curtly and left the three women to speak, briefly, with the Kings themselves. Duvari was one of the very, very few in the Empire who could approach them so casually.

"The trees?" Solran Marten asked.

"In a manner of speaking. Duvari was not best-pleased to see them in the Courtyard gardens; he offended the Head Gardener present for their planting."

"If he did not have them clapped in chains and carted off," Solran said, laughing, "he must have been in a very good mood."

"I confess, with Duvari, it is difficult to tell," Sigurne said, offering a reluctant smile to the bardmaster's generous laughter.

"The trees are impressive, though. They are your doing?"

Sigurne shook her head. "Not, sadly, ours." She lifted her head as Gilafas ADelios entered the room. A young woman followed closely behind; Sigurne asked them both to lay palm against the book she carried.

Birgide, however, was now unconcerned. None of the men—or women—in this room were possessed. The room itself, however, was unlike the Royal Trade Commission's offices. Streamers of color decorated every wall, concentrated around the windows; the runner that led from the doors to the dais upon which the thrones were placed was a deep, vivid turquoise—a blend of blue and green.

The wall through which the Kings had entered was a tapestry of tightly stacked colors; she counted eight.

But it was the Kings and the Exalted themselves that were arresting. Telltale signs of magery could be found on their persons in the colors Birgide had come to expect, predominantly orange, which she now classified as protective.

But the light that shone in their eyes lent a golden sheen to their exposed skin that made them strikingly compelling—and terrifying.

"Birgide?"

She nodded. "It has been years since I last set foot in the Hall of Wise Counsel; I am, perhaps, admiring overmuch, given the circumstances."

"It's a little empty for my tastes," Solran said. She offered Gilafas ADelios her arm. "The Kings are waiting, Guildmaster."

The Guildmaster of the Makers nodded. "You see the sculptured facade," he said to Birgide.

"Yes. It was almost certainly maker-made."

"If an Artisan can be considered a maker, then yes. Yes, it was." The young woman at his side stepped back, allowing Solran to guide Gilafas. The Guildmaster was neither as old nor as frail as Sigurne; he was, however, far more easily distracted. The distraction came and went; on some days he was so sharp at his business the overconfident did themselves major injuries; on others, he could barely stay on topic for a sentence, which caused frustration or rage, depending upon the person.

Given the compressed lips of the young woman who had escorted him, Birgide guessed that today was one of the latter.

The Exalted never seemed put out by Gilafas. Today was no exception. He was greeted warmly, almost as if he were kin and not the guildmaster of the most moneyed guild in the Empire; a chair was called for, and Gilafas took it without blinking.

No like chair had been summoned for either the bardmaster or the Guild-master of the Order of Knowledge—nor would it be. Both women approached the seated Exalted and offered perfect obeisances; Sigurne's was shorter, but no one expected a woman her age to hold an exacting social bow for too long.

Birgide, however, knelt. She was the only person in the chamber to do so; Gilafas' aide had retreated to the wall closest to the door. Had the doors been open, she would have departed to wait outside.

Nor did the Exalted or the Kings tell her to rise.

"Birgide Viranyi, of the Order of Knowledge," the Mother's Daughter said. "You ventured into the Courtyard gardens this afternoon with cuttings taken from the Terafin *Ellariannatte.*"

Birgide, on one knee, lifted her chin and nodded.

"You planted them."

"In the wildwood quarter of the Courtyard gardens, yes. I have standing royal permission to attempt to cultivate the *Ellariannatte* in the gardens and grounds."

"So we have been informed. You have made the attempt some fifteen times, at irregular intervals, over the past decade."

"I have."

"This is the first time you have had any notable success."

Birgide nodded. She did not glance at Duvari; his expression was dour, but it gave nothing away. She could almost believe that he wished to censure her, or to see her censured—but no. He feared what the presence of the *Ellarian-natte* presaged—but he was pragmatic enough to consider the demons the greater threat.

"Do you understand why you have had such remarkable success today?"

Birgide exhaled. The layer of carpet between hard stone and bent knee did not make kneeling notably more comfortable. She could not, however, rise without permission or command. "Yes."

This surprised the Mother's Daughter. "You will explain it."

"I am groundskeeper for The Terafin's forest, the boundaries of which cannot be circumscribed by simple surveys—or complex ones. It is my belief that the forest itself extends across the whole of Averalaan. The trees that grow in the back of the Terafin manse might be planted successfully anywhere the forest touches."

"That is an interesting supposition. Guildmaster Mellifas?"

"You are aware, of course, that The Terafin has not given the Order of Knowledge permission to study the forest of which Member Viranyi now speaks. If you wish my comprehensive opinion, the Order of Knowledge must be granted that permission. If you wish my considered opinion, I concur."

"You have reservations, Guildmaster?"

"Where unknown magics are concerned? Of course I have. I am however, more interested in the reason for the guildmaster's presence. Guildmaster ADelios?"

The guildmaster was staring out the window. Or rather, staring at the window; from this vantage, out should have been rendered almost invisible by thick colored glass. Sigurne and the Mother's Daughter exchanged a glance.

King Cormalyn answered the question, since it was clear Gilafas would offer none. "The guildmaster arrived shortly after Member Viranyi did. He referenced the trees." The King glanced briefly at the man to his right. "Ah. He said, 'The trees, the trees, I must see the trees.' He demanded immediate access, and if immediate access was not to be granted, an immediate audience with the Kings."

Birgide was seldom shocked. Seldom, clearly, was not never. She could not keep her glance from straying to Duvari's face, just to catch a glimpse of his expression, although she knew her own would betray nothing.

Duvari's eyes were narrowed as he stared at Gilafas ADelios. The Kings, however, motioned him to silence, and he obeyed.

"We have therefore granted the audience," King Cormalyn continued. "We wish to ascertain that it is safe for the guildmaster to, as he requested, see the trees." As he spoke the last words, he turned to Birgide, who had remained upon knee. "Rise."

She did so with the fluid grace developed by training. Turning to the Guildmaster of the Makers, she asked, "What, exactly, do you intend to do?"

He did not appear to hear her question.

Sigurne Mellifas caught his elbow in one hand and his shoulder in the other; she guided him away from the windows and toward Birgide Viranyi. This was not, clearly, what Duvari had envisaged for the afternoon. Birgide herself was not entirely certain this was preferable. But she tendered Gilafas the bow his station—and wealth—all but demanded, even though she was certain he wouldn't actually see it.

He didn't. He did, however, see Birgide. "How very odd," he said, pulling himself free from Sigurne's steadying grip. He approached Birgide as if she were a sculpture. "Very odd." He turned to King Cormalyn and said, "Did you send the poor girl from your side to serve The Terafin?"

Birgide's glance, when it fell to Duvari again, was far less casual.

Duvari's, however, was not. "What," he asked, voice deceptively soft, "do you mean, Guildmaster?"

"She has come with the trees," Gilafas replied. "And it is for her they will grow and flourish. I seek leaves and branches with which to make a floral crown. I will work in *Avantari* if the Kings prefer it, but I believe I will do better work in Fabril's reach."

"Did you arrive here from Fabril's reach?"

"Of course."

Birgide had made the acquaintance of the guildmaster only twice in her life; she did not recognize this scattered, strange man at all. So, she thought; rumors of the madness of the maker-born were not simple, or petty, malice. Birgide, who felt protective of the forest and its many, many trees felt no fear of this man at all. "I am sorry," she told the guildmaster, "but I am unaware of the significance of Fabril's reach in this context."

"And so shall you remain if you do not wish to stand here for four hours listening to words that make no sense whatsoever," the Exalted of Cormaris cut in. "Suffice it to say that the guildmaster has probably sent the magi scurrying about the palace in near-panic, and leave it at that." His gaze, golden, was Summer and light in Birgide's vision. She could not help but smile.

Joy was not consistent across the *Astari;* Duvari's face resembled frozen stone at the end of this brief speech. He watched the Exalted, his gaze cutting between them, as if waiting for more.

"If you wish it," Birgide said, "and if I am granted permission, I will take you to the trees. They are new," she added. "And when you arrived, they had not yet been planted."

Gilafas frowned, as if attempting to understand a language with which he had only passing familiarity.

"We will allow this," King Reymalyn said.

The Exalted of Reymaris stood. "I am uncertain of the wisdom of this action."

"And as you are not the son of the Lord of Wisdom, accept that we are King, here, and we have made the choice. Lord of the Compact?"

"The choice is, of course, yours," Duvari replied. "Allow us to inspect the Courtyard gardens first."

The King nodded. Duvari turned on heel and strode—at speed—toward the closed doors; they opened before he reached them.

"Birgide Viranyi," the Mother's Daughter said, the moment the doors had closed.

Birgide inclined her head. "Exalted."

"You have chosen to serve The Terafin."

"I have chosen to accept employ as a gardener upon the Terafin staff."

"So." The Mother's Daughter turned to confer with the son of Cormaris and the son of Reymaris, their voices muted although they sat not ten feet away. The private discussion was long enough that Duvari had returned by the time they once again turned their attention upon Birgide.

"Do you work under the auspices of Meralonne APhaniel?"

"No. I report to the Terafin Master Gardener."

They once again spoke amongst themselves. At length, the Mother's Daughter stood. "You are not what was expected," she said. "We will attend with the Kings and the Guildmaster of the Order of Knowledge."

"May I be bold enough to ask what *was* expected?"

"A herald," the Exalted of Cormaris replied, his voice crisp and on the chilly side. "Or a squire."

It was difficult to speak in the hall itself, and only in part because of the presence of the most important men and women in the Empire. Gilafas appeared to be humming; the humming stopped only when he thought of something to say. He did not speak with any particular dignity; had he been among makers, his conversation—a mixture of the autocratic and the delighted—would have been cause for amusement, not concern.

He was, however, in the company of Kings. As the Kings chose to take no offense—and offense at this point could be taken with ease—no one else could. The *Astari*, however, looked pinched and annoyed, to Birgide's eye.

The Swords, however, did not appear to consider Gilafas' behavior a reflection on the Kings' dignity; they considered him harmless. If he was not, he was harmful in an entirely political way—and politics was not the duty of the Kings' Swords. They formed up around the Kings; Birgide thought they resembled a human turtle.

The presence of the Kings—indicated by the standard which was carried at the rear—meant the checkpoints discreetly vanished; there was nothing between the moving body of Swords and the exit into the Courtyard gardens. Nothing but yards of stone over which tapestries and paintings had been hung. The runners that protected the floor from heavy feet were a coal black, thickly edged in white and fringed in gold. Thus did *Avantari* pay respects for the merchants who had been lost to the demons in the guildhall. The full tally had not yet been made; work continued, and would continue, until the magi were satisfied that all answers had been extracted from the guildhall's ruins.

Gilafas ADelios was a man possessed. It was a happy possession, and as the *Ellariannatte* came into view—which occurred the moment the party set foot upon the least ornate of the garden pathways—his eyes crinkled at the corners; every line sun, wind, and age had carved there was put to use, and yet the effect lessened, rather than added, years.

Birgide was surprised when he turned to her and offered her the deepest and most reverent of bows. The unexpected show of respect reminded her, conversely, of the dirt beneath her nails and the coarseness of her clothing. But she was now in her element, Kings and the god-born and the Lord of the Compact notwithstanding.

"Welcome," she said, as she offered the guildmaster her arm. "To the Courtyard gardens."

Above her head she could hear the rustle of leaves—all of the leaves of the Terafin forest: sounds of crystal, metallic wind chimes, and, yes, leaf in high breeze. She lifted her face, as Gilafas lifted his, and leaves fell, pulled in desultory dance toward the ground. They landed at the maker's feet.

Not Birgide's. She heard breath stop as the leaves fell, but was not surprised to see them settle: gold, silver, diamond—and crowning them in delicate life, *Ellariannatte*.

She exhaled and turned to the maker, who stood, staring at his feet, which were surrounded. Birgide had never seen so many leaves fall at once; she had, in truth, never seen unattached leaves of silver, gold, or diamond; those had shied away from her hands, as if the trees were sentient.

None of those trees grew in the Courtyard; none graced *Avantari*. And yet, here, at the feet of a maker, their leaves assembled.

She could see the shadows of tall trees across the footpath, but nothing to cast them. The footpath, in any case, was in disarray.

"This is acceptable to you?" Gilafas asked.

He did not, directly, speak to Birgide, but she understood that the older man was asking—with humility—for permission. And she understood, as he watched her, that it was her permission to give. It was an odd feeling.

"Yes," she told him softly. "Do you know what you will make of them?"

He stared at her as if she had, once again, begun speaking in a foreign tongue. And then he gathered the leaves. He had come with an empty satchel; he filled it. His aide attempted to offer help, but he shooed her away without seeming to see her.

Birgide offered a sympathetic glance; the woman shrugged in response, shaking her head at Gilafas as if he were a much-loved, and much-coddled child.

"I will return to you," Gilafas surprised her by saying. "But I ask one favor, if I may ask it."

Birgide waited. She was long past the age where the desire to please drove her to agreements that were in the end impossible.

"Watch for butterflies. You will see them soon, I think. Do not harm them, do not capture them—but watch. And listen."

The Guildmaster of the Guild of Makers then turned and pushed his way through the gathered dignitaries as if they were of no consequence. And, in truth, given his expression, they weren't.

The Kings exchanged few words; the Exalted, more. Birgide felt as if she were in a bubble whose walls only she could see. Duvari joined her; she thought she preferred the bubble.

"That was astonishing," he said, voice soft. "I have known the guildmaster for many years, and I have only once seen him driven by his talent. He is accustomed to decrying its power and strength."

"You've seen him like this?"

"Never in such illustrious company; I am somewhat surprised that he ventured beyond Fabril's reach. But, of course, he would. The materials he required could be gathered in no other way."

"You've seen makers at work before." It wasn't a question. Birgide herself had not.

"I have seen Artisans at work," was Duvari's almost gentle correction. "I do not envy their minders; they are akin to the youngest of children; they walk, but they see nothing of the world in front of their eyes; they are caught and pulled by the drive to create. They can forget to eat, to bathe, to clothe themselves; they will work their hands raw to bleeding. Their talent creates priceless artifacts and treasures—but it consumes them." He exhaled. "You wonder why I share this with you."

Birgide nodded.

"If I am not mistaken, he will come to you again. He will walk in the forest you guard and nurture. There is only one thing—beyond the maker-born urge—that moves his weathered heart. I will not speak of it further except to say this: if you encounter the butterflies of which he so artlessly asked, you will report—directly—to me. If," he added softly, "you are allowed to return to Terafin at all. The Exalted are unhappy."

"More or less unhappy than the Lord of the Compact?" She knew, by Duvari's tone, that no one would hear either his words or her own.

"Significantly less."

She glanced at him, surprised.

"I am ill-pleased with the *Ellariannatte* and their sudden incursion into the heart of my responsibility. You must have expected that."

"If I had thought they would grow—like this—for me, I would have. But Duvari—I am not The Terafin. I am not the forest's lord."

"No. If I understand what has occurred, you are guard and guardian. But you are also one of mine, Birgide. You understand the responsibilities of the *Astari*. You owe loyalty to the Kings. And at the moment, you can see what none save perhaps Meralonne APhaniel and The Terafin herself can see: the demons. I would keep you in *Avantari* for the foreseeable future—but it is my suspicion that my decision would meet with some resistance.

"Therefore, serve. I will require your presence within *Avantari* on specific days and at specific times, which will be made clear to you in future." He glanced at her and added, "I would advise you to avoid the man who now calls himself Haval Arwood, if at all possible."

"Why?"

"It is very easy to forget that he is a dangerous man. In part this is because he does not wish to be one. I would however say that he is far more of a danger than the demons who have infiltrated Terafin in the past. If, however, he does approach, do not attempt to harm him. You may give him a verbal message."

"And that?"

"Tell him that, for the moment, I agree."

She did not ask what the subject of agreement was, because she did not want to know.

"I believe we are to return to the Hall of Wise Counsel. Do you understand what is to occur there?"

"No. I assumed you wished my presence to ascertain that the Hall itself was secure."

"The Hall—and one other—is secure. If demons arrive in *Avantari*, they will not enter the Hall of Wise Counsel. Nor, should they be foolish enough to flee there, will they leave it."

The Exalted resumed their seats, the Kings their thrones. Duvari chose to stand—as was his right—between the two thrones, three steps back. The Kings, of course, noted this. The Exalted did. No one spoke against his presence.

Birgide knelt.

This time, the Exalted of Cormaris bid her rise. "It has been brought to our attention that you have been in combat recently, within *Avantari*."

Birgide nodded.

"The nature of your opponent was demonic."

"Yes."

"The demon occupied a position of both trust and responsibility. He worked undetected by his closest companions. Yet you were aware of his nature instantly. We are informed that you are a member of the Order of Knowledge in good standing, but you are not, yourself, mage-born. This would be correct?" He added, looking to Sigurne.

"Birgide Viranyi is a member of the Order of Knowledge. As all members are, she has been extensively tested for signs of mage-born talent; she has evinced none. She is, however, better known in the Western Kingdoms than those who have that talent, and she has increased the visibility of my Order—and the respect in which it is held."

Birgide was surprised, but said nothing. Sigurne was the guildmaster, but it had never appeared to Birgide that she had any interest in those who were not mages. She clearly had enough interest to at least take note of those who were externally respected.

"Thank you, Guildmaster." The Exalted of Cormaris turned, once again, to Birgide. "My father wishes to speak with you now."

Birgide did not ask if she had the right of refusal. In theory, she did. Theory was always tenuous in politics, and given the presence of the *Ellariannatte*, she chose not to assert that right. She was, however, nervous. Although it was common knowledge that the god-born could bespeak their parents, she had never witnessed it personally. "I would be honored."

Braziers were lit.

The white smoke of burning incense filled the room. Instead of rising, as smoke generally did, it wafted toward the ground from the height of braziers set up in several places on brass tripods. Priests attended to the burning; the Exalted remained on their thrones. The Kings, however, rose.

To Birgide's surprise, the smoke impacted the visibility of dense strands of colored light; they thinned as she watched. This meant, she thought, that the transition to the Between was a more literal transition than she had previously assumed. Then again, while men and women of power might speak—with care—of the results of such a transition, they seldom described it.

In one day, Birgide had seen—and fought—demons. She had seen Duvari injured—something that had literally never occurred during her training—or anyone's, to her knowledge. She had planted *Ellariannatte* in the grounds of *Avantari*, and they had not only taken root there, but had instantly grown.

Their presence implied much about the nature of the forest behind the Terafin manse, and to underscore this, the Guildmaster of the Makers had come, and he had gathered leaves and retreated with them. Any of this might have led to the interview with a god, but she suspected that it was only the latter that mattered.

She could no longer see her own feet. Since she was relatively certain they were still attached, she was not concerned. But she could no longer hear the forest, either—and only in the silence of this gray, other world did she realize that she could, in fact, hear it constantly, no matter where she stood.

She was surprised to see the mists roll over Duvari; surprised as well to see Sigurne Mellifas fade from view. Even the Kings had absented themselves from this meeting; only the Exalted remained. In the thick, formless mists of the Between they seemed larger than life, the golden light emanating from their eyes a fire which, left to burn, shortened mortal lives.

And the god-born were mortal.

Emboldened by the lack of the three men who ruled her life, Birgide said, "Why am I here, Exalted?" She directed her question to the Mother's Daughter, although it was the Exalted of Cormaris who had demanded her attendance.

"Do you not know?" was the quiet reply. "In all the years that my temple has resided upon the Isle, there have been none who have chosen the responsibilities that you have, perhaps in ignorance, undertaken."

"No," Birgide replied. "In the life of the Isle, I do not think the forests of Terafin existed."

"They existed. But we were not able to walk them until very recently. I understand that you do not feel they are a threat." The comment made clear that the Mother's Daughter did.

"In what way are they now considered a danger, Exalted?"

"Ask that question again after the guildmaster has returned to your side. And be careful when you treat with him; he has long been obsessed with a single quest, and in you, he believes he might—at last—achieve it."

"What quest?"

The Mother's Daughter exhaled. "I should not speak of it. Were I not here, I would not."

"I would counsel caution regardless," the Exalted of Cormaris added, in a clipped, reproving tone. This surprised Birgide. She could not imagine a time in her life when she would have dared; nor could she see one in the future.

"Your counsel is duly noted," the Mother's Daughter replied. Her smile was gentle. It was also somewhat condescending. "Gilafas ADelios accepted guardianship of a wild child. He lost her to the wild roads and the Winter Queen, and he has searched—without hope or peace—these many years for some way to retrieve her.

"In you, Birgide, in your fallen leaves and your *Ellariannatte*, he sees the beginning of a road that will end with that retrieval."

"I would not think the guildmaster would—"

"She was an Artisan. And it was her hand, and hers alone, that remade what Fabril gifted the first of our Empire's Kings, in the hopes that they might continue to rule in the war that is to come."

"That really is enough," the Exalted of Cormaris said.

"She will know it, and far better than we or the gods, by the end—if she survives. If she does not, there is no harm in the information. She has been trained to hide and guard her secrets. Come, let us not be quibbling like children when your father arrives; he is unlikely to be impressed."

"The quibbling of mortals," a vast voice replied, "is merely part of their conversation; it does not concern us. Indeed, in such minor fractures of social grace, they reveal much their words would otherwise hide."

The ground that Birgide could not see shook beneath her feet as the voice—the multitude of voices—filled the very air. The god was commonly depicted as male, but Birgide understood, hearing the roar of a crowd, that the depiction was flat and far too simplistic, for there were women's voices in the mix—young and old, quivering and strident—and children's voices, too. There were voices that were a thing of gravel, and voices that were velvet and honey. In a crowd of any size, those voices blended, syllables becoming as undistinguishable as the individual voices themselves.

Not so, the god's voice. Although each sound was a precise concert of syllables, each voice could be separated from the whole. Or rather, the sensation of hearing each. Birgide had fallen silent not from awe, but the simple attempt to dissect and catalog what she experienced; this had oft been considered a social failing.

The Exalted of Cormaris raised both chin and face; the Exalted of Reymaris and the Mother lowered their heads. Birgide did neither; she watched the moving folds of mist as if they were a curtain—and at that, one made by a madman. Her wait was rewarded, in a fashion, as the curtain finally parted.

The god was, in her estimation, eight feet in height, or perhaps even nine. His face was not one thing but many; it was very like his voice. It should have been disturbing; it was instead strangely compelling. In watching the shifting structure of jaw and lip and cheekbones, of forehead and hairline, of skin color and even gender, Birgide thought that gods might not be so terrifying: they encompassed so much more than a single, wayward woman, surely their understanding was equally vast? Who could judge so readily something that was part of their essential nature?

He met her eyes because she had not lowered them, and she almost repented of her curiosity, then. She could not, however, lower the eyes he now met; he held—he demanded—the whole of her attention. He acknowledged his son; she heard him speak. But he walked between the Exalted and past that son, to where Birgide now stood, pinned.

"So," he said. "It is true. What did you offer, Birgide Viranyi?"

She lifted her hand. In the fog of the otherworld, she could see the scarring that fire had caused; it was a glowing, pale light—not gold, not white, but some color that hovered between the two.

"You have chosen the path of pain," the god said.

"Pain," she replied, without thought, without filter, "is what I know. Pain and the peace of the forest."

"There is no peace to be found in the wilderness; not for you and your kin." The god bent—he would not kneel. He reached for the hand, cupping its back in his giant's palm. "You serve."

She nodded.

"I see The Terafin's name in this mark. Do you understand what she is?"

"No." Birgide wanted an honorific with which to address a god; none came to her, and she therefore offered none. She was afraid, now. But then again, fear was familiar; it was her earliest emotion. Everything else had come later.

"My son tells me that an Artisan approached you."

Since Birgide had been standing beside that son and had not once heard him speak, she frowned. But she answered. She did not think the ability to refuse was in her. "Yes."

"He asked your permission to take the fallen fruits of your domain into his keeping."

"Yes."

"Do you understand why it was you he approached?"

She started to say no, but the word froze on her tongue, and she could not speak again until she had swallowed it. "I did not consciously understand it," she said, instead. "Nor do I now. But he required my permission to take the leaves, although the leaves did not require my permission to fall."

"Tell me, Birgide, do the trees in your forest converse?"

She blinked.

"Do they converse with you?"

"Not—not in words, no. I have made the study of plants my life."

"And you have made the study of the *Ellariannatte* your life's work."

"Yes. Before Terafin, that work was considered as realistic as unicorn hunts. It was tolerated, sometimes affectionately."

"That work, as you call it, is why you are here now. You are, to my knowledge, the only mortal who is not Sen whom the wilderness has chosen to bespeak. You are harbinger, although you do not understand it, of war and death. There will be no peace in your forest, Birgide, if you falter at all. We are concerned."

She was silent.

"We have never seen the position you now hold given to anyone mortal, save the Sen. But we see it in you now; you are Warden."

"I was not given a title."

"No. And a title is not required; it does not materially change who—or what—you are. Those who see it will know; those who do not will never take the necessary information from the title itself. Gilafas ADelios is an Artisan. He will see you. He will see what you represent. But he is not the only one.

"Those who walk the endless wilderness will see and know you as well. You are not Warden of the entirety of the hidden path; none could be, and survive the burden and the price demanded. But in the city in which my children are at the height of their power, it is unnecessary.

"I would ask you to lay the burden you have undertaken down, if I thought it a possibility. You will not. Nor will the forest now revoke what it has accepted unless you fail in your duties. But you are too mortal, Birgide. Your concerns are too small and too quotidian. You are wed to your concepts of justice, of power, of necessity. You must learn to expand them if you mean to be effective."

"I—"

"They are concepts created by mortals for mortals. Mortality encompasses the god-born and the talent-born, but there are, with rare exceptions, limits to the power. The demons, of course, confound that expectation—and yet, they have been contained; they have not been more of a danger than the rogue magi themselves.

"Until now. Now, Birgide, things wake which were never part of your calculations of either decency or power. You have played the games that the *Astari* play. You have observed the games that patricians play. You have seen war, you have seen death, you have caused it. But the scale was—and is—mortal. Human. You have not played the games we played at the dawn of your world."

Silence. She glanced at the Exalted. They were uniformly grim. None of this was a surprise to them.

"My sons were afraid that you presaged the ending that was once foreseen. Let me set their worries at rest. You are not the herald of the end of days. You are merely a symptom.

"And you are a surprising symptom. You are not of the wilderness. The wild is not your breath, blood, and bone. You cannot speak to the high wilderness and be understood—it must stoop to listen; it must stoop to translate, encasing the whole of its meaning in a way that you can—if you struggle—barely comprehend. We do not understand why you were chosen.

"Do you?"

Birgide frowned.

"Do not fear my wrath. There is little you could say that I would find insulting; to insult, there must be intent."

She glanced at the Exalted of Cormaris; his lips compressed. Clearly he did not agree with his father on matters of etiquette—and it was the Exalted who would be coming back to the world with her, not the god.

"It is possible," she said, choosing words with care, "that I was chosen because I had The Terafin's permission to enter her forests and tend to her gardens—either of them. And possibly because of what the forest itself—as a concept—meant, and means, to me. But if I had to offer a rational guess, I would say that I was chosen because the Immortals you seemed to expect aren't here now.

"Except for the demons, and I don't think—"

"The dead cannot serve the living forest," the god told her. "And in any meaningful sense, the *Kialli* and their servants are dead."

"Yes, but they're here. And standing against them, we have mortals, mortals, and more mortals. The Terafin herself is not immortal. She is not god-born."

"She is Sen," Cormaris replied. "And the Sen, like the Artisans, exist very tenuously in your world. They are human, but mortality fits them poorly, and in the end—" He shook his head. "To my sons, I will say only one thing: the Sen did not rule the great Cities of Man. They founded them, but they did not rule. They could not remain in the world the living occupied as a matter of course without altering it irrevocably.

"Your Terafin charts a course the Sen would never have charted. She is determined to remain true to what she perceives herself to be. But that perception, in our experience, is faulty. The world will break, Birgide. Lines will fracture. Things will seep into your mortal cities that have not walked the face of the world since the sundering.

"I have delivered this message to my sons and daughters. I deliver it now to you. You are the first sentinel. If things change, return to me."

"Can you not tell us, now, what to expect?"

"No. I can tell you what we experienced—but it would take years upon years, even here, and I do not think you would gain useful information from the telling. There is a mage in your city, a Meralonne APhaniel."

"He is, at the moment, resident within the Terafin manse."

"He has walked the loneliest of roads. Do not trust him."

"He is the House Mage."

"He is, perhaps, the House Mage—but not for much longer. Do not trust him, Birgide. Do not allow him to speak with the trees at the heart of your forest."

"He has been granted the same permission I have," she began.

"No, he has not. If you mean The Terafin's grant of passage, you do not understand the role you have taken. You are Warden. He is Prince. There is only one place you could hope to stand against him, and you will not be able to stand against him for long."

"Why do you assume that I'll have to stand against him at all?"

"We have had word: the heralds are on the move."

This meant nothing to Birgide.

It meant something to the Exalted. "It is too soon," the Mother's Daughter said. "We are not prepared."

"No. But were they to arrive a century from now, my children, you would not be prepared. The only hope you have—in our opinion—rests upon the shoulders of your Sen—and she is too new, and too timid to do what must be done." The god bent to Birgide; she thought he meant to bow, and would have collapsed to the supine position of absolute inferiority had she not feared the mists.

She was, however, mistaken.

"Our sister could not be present for this interview, but asked that we bestow a gift upon you, if we deemed you worthy of it. We do not know, yet, the full measure of your worth—but having seen you, we are both apprehensive and relieved. The Terafin is The Terafin. She is in control of her power; her power does not yet ride her. She chose to trust you. You have chosen, in your fashion, to honor that trust. The heart of the forest understands both of these things.

"We therefore give you the gifts one gives a gardener. We cannot tell you which of the seeds will grow and flourish and which will fail to take root, nor can we tell you what the outcome of successful growth might be. The wilderness is not an Imperial garden, even so fine a garden as The Ten are reputed to keep. There is a sentience to the sleeping earth, the gentle breeze, and the towering trees that the plants in your city have never—and will never—achieve. And yet you labor over them regardless."

"Without them, we face starvation."

"Starvation is not a concept the Immortal come to easily," he replied. "The Mother understands it fully in a way few of her brethren do. These seeds are from her many, many gardens; they grow nowhere in the world to which you were born. Take the Mother's gift or reject it; the decision is yours. She will take no offense should you decide to leave them with us."

"And what does the Lord of Wisdom counsel?" she asked softly—as softly as she might have asked a similar question of the Lord of the Compact.

"Be true to your vows as you understand them. There are many responsibilities and many oaths sworn in a mortal lifetime—and the oaths are binding only inasmuch as the oathgiver desires. But there will come a time—and soon—when one who can oathbind will enter the world of men. You will see deaths then. Mortality is small, Birgide, in its passions and drives. Mortals do not focus on one thing above all others.

"The Arianni are defined by their Winter Queen. No other love, no other loyalty, is proof against that definition. Mortals, however, are torn, always: they love their families, their friends; they are responsible for their work, where work is available. They feel, on occasion, responsible for their neighbors, their pets, and their horses. They do not, and cannot, choose one thing with any ease.

"But now, you have so chosen. The oath that you gave was not given to mortals, who might view your circumstances with compassion or forgiveness. Serve as Warden, but understand if you wish to survive that no oath has the weight or the meaning of the oath you have offered your forest. Do not look to the Kings and falter. Do not look to the Lord of the Compact and falter.

"The gift you have been granted is, for the moment, singular: the Kings will not find another like you. But it is hopeful as well. If you are too small and too weak in the end to bear burdens such as these for long, you are also mortal; you are only required to bear them until you dwindle into age and death."

Birgide listened impassively, understanding that she spoke with a god. Or that she listened to one. When he was done—when the multitude of voices had once again settled into silence, she held out one hand. The scarred hand.

Even here, in the mists of the Between, she could see that the scar was large and deep; it was also golden, as if the metal had pooled, forever, in her palm. Light eddied off the surface of her skin.

The god looked at her empty, exposed hand for a long moment, and then he exhaled. There was thunder in his breath and across his brow, and she saw, for a moment, the flicker and tightening of a thousand mouths, superimposed one over the other.

Into that hand, he placed not seeds but a basket; the basket was workaday, the workmanship of twined, shaved wood very much what one would see in the Common. It was, however, smaller and lighter. "Understand the ground you now walk upon, and stand your ground there. When The Terafin returns—"

"Will she?" Birgide asked, ignoring the pinched expression that briefly crossed the face of the god's son.

"If she does not, there will be no ground to stand upon," was his reply. "There is no certainty. The desire for certainty drives us all—but it is a chimera. We prepare to fight the battles we can foresee; we think, we work, we plan. But The Terafin was no part of those early contingencies, and I see, in the hand of Gilafas ADelios, that those plans must be revisited.

"Remind my sons again, as I have reminded you: the Cities of Man were not ruled by the Sen, although they were built by them." He frowned. "You are not a scholar of history, I see."

"Even were she," the Mother's Daughter said, "the Cities of Man are some part of history that has been lost to us—at the discretion of the gods." She hesitated and then said, "Will the Sleepers wake before The Terafin returns?"

Birgide turned, then, to stare at this scion of god and mortal. She had, of course, heard the phrase "when the Sleepers wake" many, many times in her life; she had used it some handful herself. But it was clear to her that the Mother's Daughter did not intend the phrase to mean what it had meant to Birgide. Not "never."

Both the Exalted of Reymaris and Cormaris turned to stare at the Mother's Daughter. She might have asked the god about his sex life to lesser consternation. Birgide could not demand explanation about the Sleepers from anyone present. Not even the god. So she did what she did at gatherings of the political and the powerful: she listened.

"That cannot yet be determined," was the quiet reply; the voices had hushed, although they were audibly present. "We have hope, daughter of my sister. Teos has sent his children into the streets; he has sent the one or two who can travel to the edges of the dreaming. There are those within your city now who might stand, for some small time, against the firstborn princes— but it would be best for everyone who cannot if such a confrontation never occurred.

"Where our children can, they attempt to mislead and misdirect the heralds." He gazed at Birgide again. "In my opinion, it is folly."

"Who can stand against the Sleepers?" Birgide now asked. It was perhaps the only question that seemed relevant. She didn't ask who or what they were.

"One, you have met: Meralonne APhaniel, whom we call Illaraphaniel, in the old style. But he is not a match for the three."

"The other?"

"It has no name. It has no known form, or all forms. We called it, in the Old Weston style, *namann*. We did not know that it was resident in your city until the *Kialli* attacked your Merchants' Guild. One of the magi present was a son of Teos, and what he saw, Teos saw. And now, we know. There is danger in its presence.

"Look for *namann*, but search with care."

"It was seen at the Merchants' Guild?"

"Yes. In the company—at least briefly—of Jarven ATerafin and Hectore of Araven. We must release you to the world you have left, but I have taken none of your time. Go, with our blessings."

Chapter Twenty

JEWEL HUDDLED BY THE side of a rounded indentation in the ground, a shallow rock pit that seemed—or so Terrick claimed—to have been created for just that purpose. The decision to build the fire had been hers, and it had been arrived at with a great deal of angst and anxiety not usually reserved for fire itself.

"The wood is dead," Shianne said. "It is silent. The forest will take no offense at either the gathering or the burning." She glanced at Terrick and added, "but take care. Do not take your fine, fine ax to the wrong tree, even here. The forest has a long memory."

"Living trees do not make good firewood," Terrick replied somewhat stiffly. "They are too damp, and we do not have the time to let them dry on their own."

Shianne laughed. Terrick reddened further, which Jewel tactfully put down to the wind here, which was ferocious.

They had exited the arch she had chosen. She had stepped onto the carefully cut, flawless stone path. So had everyone else. But the small road ended abruptly a mile or two away from the ancient halls. It was impossible to judge, because the halls themselves had vanished the moment they had cleared the arch. They were stranded in the middle of trees, trees, snow, and more trees.

Terrick had found a wide stream—he disdained to call it a river. Although Jewel was nominally in charge, she surrendered the lead to the Northerner. Avandar placed himself in the rear, although it was highly unlikely that predators could approach without being noted by the flying guard of winged cats. The cats had joined the party, careening wildly overhead.

And bragging. Loudly.

Hours had turned them into voluble, *bored*, winged cats.

The reverse was also true: they could not fail to be noted by anything that was paying even trivial attention.

Angel went with Terrick, who teased him about his soft life in the South; clearly the cold of this winter landscape reminded Terrick of youth and vigor, not freezing to death in the streets of the hundred holdings. Adam, however, remained with Jewel and Shianne. His initial wonder at the snowscape and the white, white forest gave way, quickly, to the cold.

"I forget," he said, in quiet Torra, "that endless snow is like endless sand. They are both deserts."

He was quietly helpful whenever he approached Shianne; he was far less tongue-tied than anyone else, except for Celleriant, whose reluctance to speak was far harsher. The Winter King was absent; he had gone to scout ahead on the nonexistent road. He was, as Celleriant, restless and ill at ease; the cold reminded them of the lives they had once led.

Lives that meeting Jewel had irrevocably destroyed. She was aware of it more keenly than she had been anywhere but the Stone Deepings.

Shadow landed. He didn't appear to leave paw prints in otherwise pristine snow as he padded his way across some of it.

"Don't be *stupid*."

She had not voiced the thought aloud, but was not surprised to have it criticized anyway. "We're *bored*," he added, and dropped his head in her lap.

"It hasn't even been a day, Shadow."

"It's been a *boring* day."

"You got to play with a child of the gods."

He hissed.

"We've got nothing here that even comes close. I'm sorry."

"We've been bored *forever*." He batted her hands with the top of his head, and she settled into scratching behind his ears; he was warm. He was warm the way the Winter King was warm.

"Where is Kallandras?"

Snort. "Who *cares?*"

"Obviously I do, or I wouldn't have asked. Is he at least with Celleriant?"

Shadow mumbled. Jewel took this as a yes.

"I don't want anything bad to happen to them."

"You don't want anything *interesting* to happen to *anyone*."

Shianne, seated across from Jewel on the other side of what would, with luck, become a fire, laughed again. Her voice was deep, but it was clear and high; Jewel loved her laughter. So, too, did Adam; he gravitated toward it.

"She is doing it on *purpose*, stupid girl."

"I don't much care," Jewel replied.

"You *should*."

"Why? I'm going to help her, anyway. She's pregnant. If she's using some sort of magic to make herself astonishingly beautiful in order to encourage me—all of us—to be happy about what we're going to do anyway, where's the harm in that?"

"I believe he is concerned that I will bespell you and you will do, in my name, things you would never otherwise consider."

"There's probably not a lot I haven't considered. I'm in the middle of an endless tract of forest in the snow in the middle of nowhere, with no obvious way out, and no clear idea of where I'm supposed to be going."

But Shianne shook her head. She had rested her arms around the curve of her belly as if the child she carried within was the only thing that mattered. "You know where you are supposed to go, Jewel. But I think you know, as well, where you should not. You have not yet decided—and because you have not, we are here."

"And when I do decide?"

"It is still hard to carve a path through the wilderness, but it is my belief we will find one. I find it cold," she added.

Jewel attempted to shove Shadow's head off her lap. "Go sit with her," she whispered.

The cat hissed. "People have babies *all the time*, stupid girl."

"Yes. And a lot of the time, it kills them. I don't want her to freeze to death on my watch."

Shadow lifted his head and roared.

One white cat came crashing—literally—through the tree cover above, dumping snow and dry branches across the landscape. "What? *Whaaaaat?*" Snow growled at his brother.

Shadow once again dropped his head into Jewel's lap. "She wants *you* to *sit* with Shianne."

Shianne smiled, shaking her head; platinum framed her perfect face. "She is afraid that I suffer the cold in a way that you and your brothers do not."

"Of *course* you do."

"And she wishes you to lend me some of your warmth."

Snow hissed.

"I want you to *sit with her*," Jewel added. "I have no idea what you think she meant, but that's what *I* meant."

"Oh." Snow sauntered across the landscape, taking swipes at fallen branches and buried leaves. His feet, unlike Shadow's, made a mess. He didn't, however, drop his head in Shianne's lap; Jewel thought that not even the cats could be so bold or so casual with this woman.

Mortal or no, something about her made the idea uncomfortable—at best. He did, however, curl around her in such a way that she could lean into his side if she so chose. Her eyes widened slightly. "I repent," she said to Jewel.

"Of what?"

"Every uncharitable thought I have had about your governance of the ancient. Your Snow *is* warm."

"He's not," Shadow said. "It's just that *you* are *cold.*"

"Oh, hush," Jewel told the great, gray cat. "I'm cold and you don't complain about that."

"I complain about your cold *feet*," he replied, sniffing. "But you're asleep, then."

Shianne stilled. "You guard her dreams, Elder?"

"Yesssssssss?"

"And not you?" she asked Snow.

Snow growled. "Her dreams are as boring as *she* is. Do *you* dream?"

"I do not know. I have not slept as mortals sleep, and had I done so in the great hall, my dreaming self would be unassailable. I do not believe that even the Warden of Dreams could have found me or my sisters were he to bend all of his considerable will upon the search."

"You are *not* in your hall *now*," Snow pointed out.

"No. I am curious. I have some power, still. I was told that I would not. But the cold is less pleasant than it once was, and even the air itself is . . . stinging. I do not particularly fear death," she added. Her voice was so soft it almost invited sleep. "But I do not wish to face it until this child is born and safe."

Safety was illusion. Jewel knew it. She suspected Shianne knew it as well.

"Even time seems different, somehow."

"Does it? I've never had personal experience with anything but mortality, so I can't compare."

"Do you fear age?" Shianne asked. Snow hissed laughter.

"Not yet. I imagine I will as I get older." Jewel glanced at Adam; he was, to her surprise, watching her, not Shianne.

"Because of the infirmity?"

"Yes. No one wants to be weak. No one wants to watch the slow diminishing of the strengths they once had. We accept it because we don't have much choice."

"Not *all* mortals are so *accepting*."

"Yes, well."

"Some mortals seek immortality?"

Something about the tone of the question made Jewel tense. But she answered. "Some of our oldest—and goriest—stories involve men who were desperate to unlock the secret of eternal life. They believed that it could be had in exchange for any number of things."

"What things?"

In Torra, Adam said, "The sacrifice of other lives. Some believed every year of life they destroyed they could somehow consume. It didn't work. The sacrifice of precious stones, of precious plants or very rare animals. The drinking of blood. And, of course, the bargains with demons."

"You speak of demons, as does your Matriarch."

"Yes."

"Tell me what these demons are."

Silence. Shadow hissed his laughter, which joined Snow's. And then, without warning, Shadow lifted his head and roared. It was a long, loud sound that shook branches. It shook more. He continued this for minutes, during which Jewel covered her ears.

Shianne, already pale, paled further as she listened; her arms tightened, her lips became, for the moment, the color of the rest of her skin, as if somewhere, she was bleeding out the remainder of the life her choice had left her. Jewel rose before Shadow had finished, reached the Arianni woman as the great, gray cat drew breath, and caught both of her hands in her own.

"I understand," Shianne whispered. She closed her eyes. "I understand the White Lady's endless rage and sorrow. You cannot know the harm—the eternal, endless harm—done to her. And these demons, as you call them, can grant this immortality?"

"Oh, no. Of course not," Jewel said—in the same Torra in which Adam had spoken. "I think that once, gods could—when they walked this world. Speak to Avandar, if he is willing to converse, and ask him about eternity before you think—in any way—that it is a gift for my people."

"I am not your people," Shianne replied.

"No. And perhaps, for you, it would not be the burden it is to Avandar. I cannot say. I can only say this: he was born when the gods walked the world, and the only thing he desires of the gods—of anything now—is death. His own," she added.

"And not even the firstborn can grant it," a familiar voice said.

Jewel closed her eyes briefly; she then stood, releasing Shianne's hands. Shadow was already on his feet, and his fur had risen at least an inch as a very familiar woman entered the clearing that surrounded the stone pit. "Calliastra."

"The same. I once thought Viandaran could give me what I needed, but he could not."

"No."

"Is it not a mistake you would have made?"

"I don't need what you need," Jewel replied. "But I need things that are probably just as painful when denied."

"The needs of mortals were never as pressing, although they were oft more immediate." She smiled as she spoke; it was both exquisite and unpleasant. She glanced at Shianne. "The Lady has condescended to entertain the Elders. For simple warmth. It is quaint."

"*We* have *condescended*," Snow corrected her. He did not move, although his fur had also risen. As had his wings. Their ridges were high. Jewel had once seen him break a man's arm with the downstroke of those wings.

"You did not win that fight," Calliastra said, eyes narrowing. "You *fled* it."

"You were *boring*," Snow growled back. His wings rose higher. Adam quietly came to Shianne's side, and as the cat shifted position, led her away; he did not go far. Shianne did not seem alarmed—nor did she seem particularly offended. But she slid an arm around Adam's shoulder and her hand tightened enough to cause a shift in Adam's expression. He was, however, watchful.

"I would counsel you against continuing your fight." Celleriant had returned. He stood between Jewel and Calliastra, his blade and shield facing the firstborn. "What the ancient halls contained, the forests will not."

"They are noisy enough to wake the dead," Calliastra said, still glaring at Snow.

"The dead would not be a concern. But other things sleep in the wilderness, and not all will be grateful to be awakened."

"I am not afraid of waking even the earth itself," Calliastra snapped.

Of course she wasn't. She wasn't afraid of anything. And she made it as clear as Duster once had. "It's not for you he's worried," Jewel said quietly. "It's for me. What you can survive, I can't."

Calliastra's eyes couldn't narrow further without closing; her hands could ball into tighter fists, and did. "Do not seek to humor me. You have survived greater threats—I witnessed one. You have found ways to stand your ground on ground that is not, in theory, your own. There is no threat that would instantly cause your death."

It had been so long, Jewel thought, since she'd lived with Duster. And both she and Duster had, themselves, been young. Young, raw, and lacking in experience. "You're right. I'm unlikely to die. But as it's not my death I fear, it doesn't matter. There are people here who are far less likely to survive rampaging, angry dragons than I am. I have Lord Celleriant. I have the Winter King. I have Avandar.

"And I have the talent I was born with. They don't. If you need to set violent ground rules with the cats, you need to do it somewhere else. I'm sure they'd be fine with that."

Shadow hissed. This was not the laughter hiss.

"And you two—and Night, if he's listening, and he probably is—I mean it. Most of the creatures that know you on sight, or know of you, probably *avoid* getting embroiled in your company, just for the sake of peace and quiet. They won't avoid Calliastra in the same way. They probably won't avoid Celleriant, either. You have a freedom none of the rest of us do."

"It's not freedom," Calliastra said. "It's lack of dignity, lack of gravitas. They do not suffer the consequences of either their hostility or their trespass."

"It doesn't matter why. They're indulged. Or ignored. Or despised—but people don't often close with them. They don't seek them out. If they know you're here, they'll come."

"Not if they are weak, they won't."

"They don't have to be strong to kill Angel or Terrick." She didn't mention Shianne or Adam; she knew that almost nothing short of instant decapitation could kill the young healer. "They just have to be fast."

"Why did you bring them, then? You didn't honestly intend to take the Oracle's test while accompanied by vulnerable encumbrances, did you?"

"Clearly I did, because they're here."

"You tie yourself down."

"Always. But that's what friendship and companionship *is*. Ties. Bindings. I could cut them all loose, if that's what I wanted. I could set them *all* free. But if I did, what would I have left? What would my motivation *be?* I've come seeking the Oracle *because* of those ties. Sacrificing one of my friends in the almost vain hope that I can rescue another isn't a good trade.

"Look—you're the daughter of gods. I get that. I'm not."

"You are Sen," Calliastra said.

"I have no idea what that means." She exhaled mist as Calliastra opened her mouth. "No, that's not true. I have some small idea of what it means to other people. I have no clear idea of how to leverage it. I'm not here because I'm Sen. I'm not even here because I'm seer-born."

"Why, exactly, are you here? You are far from your home, and in my opinion, it is likely that you will never return to it."

Jewel shrugged. "Maybe not. But I'd like to keep the odds from declining, which is why I don't want you to go all out with the cats anywhere near us." She folded her arms as she spoke.

In her current form, Calliastra wasn't much taller than Jewel—if she was any taller at all. She wasn't terrifying. She was compelling, of course. She was not distant, cool, unapproachable. She didn't stand on a pedestal; she invited touch. She invited interaction.

And of course, accepting that invitation was death.

Calliastra gave Shadow the side-eye, which was fair; he looked like he wanted to rip one of her limbs off, and wasn't particular about which. Jewel felt the breeze lift her hair, and she exhaled, loosening her arms.

"I don't need anything from you," the gods' child said. "I don't particularly want anything, either. You are not attractive. You are not powerful."

Jewel nodded as if she didn't care. Largely because she didn't. "Do you need the type of food half of the rest of us do?"

"No."

"That's all that's on offer. We'll feed you if you want to eat with us. If you're bored, you can keep us company. But no one here is food."

"And you think you can *stop* me?"

"Yes, actually."

Dark eyes rounded. Calliastra laughed. The laughter contained both derision and genuine amusement. "And how, exactly?"

Jewel shook her head. "In my position, would you share that information?"

"I don't believe you *have it*."

"Your risk to take. I'm willing to alleviate your boredom. I'm willing to give you something to do while you wait for the end of the world—"

"The end of *your* world."

"—But all of that is off the table if you make any attempt to harm anyone here. I'm not a saint. I'm not going to tell you to starve to death. But you don't feed off your companions, and that's what the people here will be for as long as we travel the road together."

"*Stupid, stupid, stupid girl*," Shadow said, hissing on all the sibilants.

"You let them run far too wild," Calliastra replied, speaking to Jewel, as apparently Shadow was now beneath her.

"So I've been told."

*   *   *

In case the great, gray cat had been too subtle—in his own estimation, of course—he muttered the word stupid at every opportunity, or at least every opportunity that involved Jewel. Snow was unimpressed, but took it less personally. Night remained at a distance. Celleriant left off exploration of the surrounding forest with the introduction of Calliastra, and had the Arianni Prince been as unconcerned with dignity as the cats, would probably have been spouting the same words Shadow was.

Shianne, however, appeared to find Shadow's ill-humor amusing. Regardless, she kept herself between Adam and Calliastra at all times. There was very little she could have done that would have endeared her more to Jewel. Adam, on the other hand, kept trying to move.

The Voyani were ruled by Matriarchs. Their sons were raised in an environment in which governance—and power—belonged to the women. But the future of the clan was its children, and Shianne was pregnant. Being protected by a woman whose pregnancy was visibly advanced was just too much.

Terrick returned; he stopped for a long, quiet moment when he saw Calliastra. She smiled. It was a red-lipped, heavy-lidded smile that made Jewel's cheeks redden—and it wasn't aimed at her. Terrick, however, appeared to be made of the ice and snow in which he was raised.

He built a fire in tight-lipped silence.

Sleeping arrangements were disorganized and problematic. Jewel had not considered winter travel with any more care than choice of clothing. In the hundred holdings, winter had been met with dread—but defense against it was simple, if money could be found. When money couldn't be found, it was still simple; it involved bedrolls and very, very tightly packed rooms. Shelter existed, regardless, if one could scrape by on rent.

Shelter, however, did not exist in the wilderness. Open branches did not provide protection against the wind or the snow. Terrick once again took over. He gave instructions to Angel, Kallandras, and Adam. He also gave instructions to the cats, although the instructions were entirely different and mostly consisted of growling to warn them to play elsewhere.

At the end of hours of work, during which both Angel and Adam rotated toward the fire and back, he had dug what looked like a cave out of heavy snow. "That," he said, with quiet satisfaction, "is where we'll be sleeping." And that, for Jewel, was a problem.

It was dark. The ceiling—such as it was—was low. There were too many people to fit comfortably, but Terrick insisted that with nightfall, that many people *were* comfortable. "You need to respect the cold," he told Jewel firmly.

Celleriant did not require the snow cave. Calliastra did not require it. The cats offered to demolish it by landing on the roof, which Jewel instantly forbid; Snow and Night howled their boredom to the skies. If there were wolves in this forest, she hoped it would keep them away. Wolves had figured prominently in the stories of Northern climes she had heard on her Oma's knees.

But snow caves hadn't.

"Terafin," Terrick said.

She sucked in air while Calliastra mocked her.

But the Winter King came to her rescue. *I will stay with you,* he told her. *You will not freeze. While you are with me, simple weather will not be your death.*

She realized, as he spoke, that the cats could serve the same function. Shadow pretty much insisted on it, by shouldering the great white stag to the side. The Winter King was not pleased—but like any other immortal present, he considered the cats a natural pestilence to be endured, if not enjoyed.

Jewel therefore remained outside of the cave when it came time to bed down. Shadow hissed at Calliastra, who frowned. "I will tend the fire," she surprised Terrick by saying. "I require neither sleep nor heat. Mortals require both. Even men such as you."

Terrick glanced at Angel; Angel shrugged and nodded. No one else offered any argument, although Kallandras whispered a question that only Jewel could hear. Well, that she and the cats could hear. Shadow growled. Had he not otherwise been his usual, whiny self, it would have been a terrifying sound.

Kallandras, however, accepted it without apparent concern. He nodded once to Celleriant, who returned the silent gesture; the bard then disappeared into the dark, cramped hollows as if this was familiar to him. It probably was. Jewel had never seen Kallandras out of place anywhere. Clothing didn't define him; language didn't define him. Battle didn't define him.

She wondered if anything could, which was an odd thought. She curled up around her great, gray cat; he lifted his wings and folded them over her, sitting at attention, his unblinking gaze scanning the forest as night truly fell. Jewel couldn't imagine sleeping in such a cold, exposed space—but it had been a long day; it was almost certain to be a long day tomorrow.

Tomorrow came in a way she had not expected.

She couldn't say for certain when closed eyes and unnatural warmth gave way to natural sleep. She could, however, say when sleep gave way to dream, and she understood why Shadow had peremptorily shoved the Winter King to one side. In this dream, she watched Calliastra tend the fire. She didn't tend it the way Terrick did—that would no doubt be so far beneath her she wouldn't understand the how of it. The why—that it was necessary—would likewise escape her.

The fire's light harshened the shadows; Calliastra's hair blended with the line of her back, trailing down her shoulders and moving in a way that suggested hair had a life of its own. She spoke to the fire. Jewel could hear the murmur of syllables as a blend of voices, an echo of the voices of gods. The fire whispered back.

That was the first sign.

Shadow lifted his head on a low, deep growl—which, given proximity, could be more felt than heard. That was the second sign.

"We meet again, Jewel Markess." The voice itself was the third, although Jewel felt it was unnecessary. The figure that had once been Calliastra rose, hair spreading to the sides and out in a snap, and becoming, in that motion, wings of black shadow.

Jewel rose. She place a hand firmly atop Shadow's head, which did nothing to lessen the low, deep growl she found so disturbing. She was, however, very surprised to see Night and Snow saunter in from the sides.

The last time she had had all three of the cats in her dreams, she had almost died. If Adam had not been present, she would have. If Adam had not been a healer, *he* would have. And yet, for all that, she felt safer surrounded by them.

The cats, however, said nothing. They shared a growl, but all of their hostility and focus was directed at the Warden of Dreams. And that probably made sense. If they had nothing personal against killing her, they took offense at being controlled and manipulated, and they were both on their guard and vengeful.

"Are you both here?" she asked.

"Yes. And both awake. But you are not in your own small demesne; you have wandered, in ignorance, into ours."

Jewel would have folded her arms had she not been forced to collar Night—in a figurative sense—to keep him from moving toward the standing child of gods. Or children; Celleriant's previous reactions had made clear that he accorded one respect, and the other, enmity; the fact that they existed in the same body didn't seem to trouble him at all.

For Jewel, it would have been a difficulty. To kill one—if that was even possible—would be to destroy the other, who probably didn't deserve it.

Shadow hissed, lifting his voice an octave. Jewel shook her head. He was obviously concerned about the Warden; he didn't call her stupid. He didn't step on her foot. He was, however, unimpressed with the direction her dream thoughts were taking.

"It wouldn't be the first time I've wandered onto roads like these. You are the Warden of Dreams. But you are not the Winter Queen and the Wild Hunt, and I survived both. If you're here to deliver nightmares, it's a waste of your time. Nothing you can do to me here is any worse than what I can come up with on my own. It's probably more visceral, but it's not more real."

Except that she had almost died the last time. She failed to note this, but was certain they did not.

"Perhaps. Do you understand the way in which dreams are a prison? Perhaps you do not. Perhaps you depend on waking to unlock the cage and set you free. And if you were in the world to which you were born, it would be. But here?" His wings, dark, widened and rose.

Jewel was reminded that beauty and death were synonymous in this place; he was beautiful. Admiration was only safe at a distance. "You can't cage me here," she replied, keeping her voice as even as she might have in a very frustrating meeting of the House Council.

"No?"

"No. Unless you wish to meet the Oracle. It is not my path I walk, but hers, and I think you know it."

He laughed. His laughter, like the rest of him, was glorious; although she knew better, she felt something akin to pleasure at giving such a creature cause for genuine amusement. "You have not walked these roads long if you feel that we cannot interfere with each other."

"She knows we can," Calliastra said. She was standing to the right of the Warden of Dreams, looking as dark as his wings.

His eyes narrowed, amusement dropping from their corners as he turned. "I did not think to find you here."

"Clearly, brother."

The word, like the firstborn woman who spoke it, annoyed. "You are wasting your time with this one," he said, indicating Jewel as if she were just another tree in this vast, winter landscape. "She is not for you."

"Oh?"

"She is seer-born. I have walked the edge of her mortal dreams for the whole of her short life. I know what she fears. I know what she desires. Nothing you can do can give her either. Leave."

Jewel would not have dared to speak to Duster in such a dismissive way.

She knew Calliastra was not Duster—but there were enough similarities in their reactions she would have known better.

Clearly, the children of gods did not have an edge in observation and derived wisdom.

"If I have chosen to spend time in her company, that choice *is* mine. Your opinion of my effectiveness means less than nothing."

The bristling fur of three great cats began to flatten as they watched. It was almost comical; their heads drifted between the two firstborn as if they were watching a game of ball. Jewel switched a hand to Snow's head when his tail began to twitch. He hissed. Night yawned.

He yawned loudly. He then set about grooming his paw while staring balefully at the firstborn. To Jewel's surprise, this caught their attention.

"What did you wish to show her?" Calliastra asked the Warden, her voice stiff and deep and yet still compelling.

The Warden frowned. "You are here in the dreaming, where you should not be. The dreams belong to me—and to Jewel. You are no part of them."

Snow hissed. It was, unfortunately, the laughter hiss. The Warden's gaze felt, as it turned on the cat, as if it could kill. Snow, however, wasn't bothered. "She is not afraid of *you*," the cat said. "And *we* are not afraid of *anything*."

"She is afraid," the Warden replied. "You merely distract her from fear."

"If she is not afraid of *us*," Shadow growled. "She is not *allowed* to be afraid of *you*."

The Warden was silent for one long beat, and when he spoke again, Jewel knew that one brother had retreated—as he so often did—in favor of the other. "She is not afraid of me," he said, to the great cat. "And has no reason to be so."

"You did not visit. *He* did."

"That is true, but I am here now. Jewel, why do you remain in the wilderness? The dreams and fears you encounter on this road will scar you; you will never escape them while you live. Without intent, will, desire, no one walks these paths for long; they are swept off them, there to wander in broken sanity for the time that remains them."

"One of our brothers was lost here, once."

Jewel frowned. "Firstborn?"

"Yes. And no."

"That creature is no brother of mine," Calliastra said, with evident disgust.

"You are unkind, sister."

"Always."

"No, not always, and that is your tragedy."

Calliastra clearly preferred Nightmare to Dream—but Jewel thought she understood why. Hope was painful when it was dashed, and it was always dashed.

"*Yes,*" Shadow said, hissing quietly. "But despair is always broken, time and again, by *hope.* The two exist, circling each other. No matter how strong one is, the other cannot be avoided. It is like—*very* like—the Warden himself."

Calliastra turned the malevolence of her glare on Jewel, who had not spoken. Jewel did not, however, deny that she was the source of Shadow's comment; there was no point.

"I was thinking of my own life," she offered instead. "Not yours."

"Think *quietly,*" Calliastra replied. "Where your odious cats won't hear you."

"In the dreaming, that would require me not to think at all."

"And if you are not a fool, you will understand that is *exactly* what you must do in the dreaming. You give him permission—both of him—to play with your heart and your mind if you open either to him."

"No mortal's heart is completely closed," the Warden of Dreams said. "Unless they are dead. The mortal dead do not dream. But it is true; I have come to carry both nightmare and dream to you. It is necessary," he added. "The *Allasakari* intend to march upon your fragile, mortal city. If you cannot make a decision, it will be moot, soon."

"And you'd care?" Calliastra demanded.

"The *Kialli* do not dream, little sister. The mortals do. Even the darkest of their fears sustains us—but if they are exterminated, I will have nothing. Yes, I would care."

Jewel swallowed. "What dreams and what nightmares?" she asked.

His smile was soft, if pained. "That is not the way either work. A dream is an experience—as is a nightmare. In the case of one seer-born, the separation between dream and reality is thin; one world affects the other, if only peripherally. What you dream has relevance and meaning to the fate of your world. And yes," he added, as Jewel drew breath to speak, "the meanings are not plain or clear—to you. That is also the nature of dream and nightmare."

"We will retreat, if that is your desire; your guardians have a power here that they do not—and cannot—have in the mortal world."

Shadow growled.

The Warden of Dream smiled. "You guard her dreaming, yes. But you cannot control where she walks in that dreaming; you cannot control what she sees." He turned, again, to Jewel. "In sleep, you are at your most vulnerable, and mortals must sleep. There are places within the high wilderness where you might sleep in peace—but you will sleep long, and the world will turn beyond you while you do.

"You have heard the stories of Lattan and Scarran?"

Jewel nodded.

"They come, at heart, from those experiences."

"Tell me," she said, as she once again grabbed Night by the scruff of an admittedly tall neck, "Why do the dreams come? Who sends them? You were said, once, to be a messenger—"

"Yes. A messenger of the gods."

"But the gods are gone."

"Not all of them, little Terafin ruler. Surely you must acknowledge that."

She stiffened. "And were you sent here, tonight, or did you just happen to wander across our path?"

"The paths in the wilderness are multiple and shifting. Understand that. No distance you cover in the march of a long day is guaranteed to remain behind you when you wake. Each small dell, each small land, has rules and boundaries—but you are mortal and you walk in ignorance of what either are."

"That wasn't an answer," Jewel replied.

"Very good. Nor will I provide one, this eve. There will come a time when you and I will converse almost as equals. That time is almost upon you, although you cannot see it. I will show you the dreams and the nightmares that lay at our own hearts, and you, Jewel, will show us things that we have not seen for so long we have almost forgotten."

"And we forget nothing."

Shadow was at a full-on growl by the time the Warden lifted his wings. They were, Jewel thought, coal gray—but in the night, it was hard to tell. She thought she could see stars.

"She really is a remarkably stupid mortal, isn't she?" Calliastra asked Shadow.

Shadow, however, surprised Jewel; he did not reply.

Jewel closed her eyes. Shadow hissed and hissed and hissed. There were words in it.

Jewel.

Winter King.

Your cat is not wrong. Do not close your eyes in this place.

I'm sleeping.

Yes. By your own choice. Even I find this inexplicable and foolish, and I have grown accustomed to your risks. Why do you take this one?

Because Shadow is with me, Jewel replied, although the answer was not the answer the Winter King wanted. She had no answer to give him, but said, *because I believe I must have this dream, in this place. I don't know why.*

For some reason, however, this unhelpful explanation eased him. *Understand that the power of the talent-born is not lessened by their departure from the world of man. It is strengthened by it. You cannot see it as strength because almost every creature that can speak in the world you now walk is more powerful than you are.*

Should I wake the others?

No. Those of us who can sleep in safety must. The dreams your companions have are not the danger your dreams are. But they will be stranded if you are lost. If something you see or hear propels you to act, they must be woken. If you leave them, there is no definitive path you might walk to return to their sides. Remember these words if you remember no others.

She nodded.

The quality of the hissing to her left changed. She opened her eyes to fire.

It was not the fire of a camp pit; not the fire of logs, confined and consumed for the purpose of providing heat or warmth. It was a raging, building consuming fire—and it was burning in the Common. Her breath caught smoke and debris as she stood immobile for one long minute; she recognized the building at the heart of the rising flame: the Merchants' Guild.

People streamed around her as if she were a rock in the center of a rushing current, shouting in their flight. She didn't even attempt to stop them; instead, she began to move through the crowd, toward the fire itself.

She understood that this was a dream or a nightmare. But she *knew* that in some fashion it was real; it was truth. What she could not know, did not know, was the *when* of it. As she approached a building both familiar and privately despised, she saw that the fire had flown, in patches, to other rooftops, other buildings. There were no magi in the streets, nothing to contain the spread of that fire. She saw, looking up, that fire adorned the branches of the standing *Ellariannatte.*

Movement in the sky caught her attention and held it: the magi that were not lining the streets in an attempt to contain and control the fire were, of all things, flying.

She could breathe again. She understood that this was not her battle, not her fight; that she could bear witness and hand over the responsibility of it to those far better equipped to deal with it.

And that was good, because fighting to one side of the building—and fighting at its peak—were *Kialli.* She recognized both because neither looked human. They had adopted forms meant to terrify and demoralize—although for Jewel, those forms had the opposite effect. She *knew* who they were, where they were, and what they were doing; they did not attempt to abuse trust by assuming the guise of friends and allies.

The streets had emptied in the sudden way streets can in dreams; the screams and shouts panic raised had dissipated. She turned to the demons who remained; they were fighting.

They were, she thought, fighting while an audience, pressed against the outer wall of the Merchants' Guild building, watched. For the most part, they were dressed as servants, but among their number were two men she recognized instantly: Jarven ATerafin and Hectore of Araven. Although she stood nowhere near them, she could hear their quiet conversation. Jarven was offering the Araven patris a wager.

Jewel had never liked Jarven. She was certain, at the moment, she never would. She didn't, and couldn't, trust him. But Finch had a soft spot for the old Terafin merchant.

Jewel did, however, care for Hectore. And that was just as soft a spot as Finch's; she knew it. She had found no information about Hectore that implied he could not be trusted—but really, given the position Araven held in merchanting matters, she was certain she could if she was determined. She wasn't.

This had been the hardest thing to learn and accept about people: that they could be both incredibly cruel and mendacious, and *also* incredibly generous and kind. They were not all one thing or all the other. It shouldn't have been hard to learn; after all, she was like them. But—it had been.

Hectore was far less amused than Jarven appeared to be. Even in dream, he could not be compelled to take the bet Jarven offered, although he didn't punch or slap him, which Jewel would have been severely tempted to do. Instead, he paled and turned, his mouth opening slowly around syllables too attenuated to be understood. He was shouting to or at someone.

She turned in the direction of that someone and saw two things.

No, she saw more than two things, so much was happening all at once: she saw a demon, winged, weaponed, a thing of flame and shadow and beauty, and she saw something attacking him. She could not, now, say what the creature was. Its form, which seemed, at base, to be almost human, shifted and blurred; it grew wings, but even those wings were not fixed and solid, as the demonic wings were; they weren't leather or feather; they weren't scaled or furred; they weren't even of a single fixed length.

The form of the body was likewise indeterminate, and she realized, watching, that Hectore shouted at this creature, and that she had seen it before. Once. In the great, rounded room of carved reliefs beneath *Avantari*.

She might have spoken. She opened her mouth.

But light appeared behind the demon's wings, sharpening their outlines, and as the light grew, she realized that a new combatant had joined the fight. He was in form as tall as the demon; he carried a sword of blue lightning. He had swallowed that lightning; it was of him. It was reflected in his eyes, in the trailing edge of his hair. He was not the heart of the storm, but the storm itself, and what he struck—earth, air, the fire that had seeped from the guildhall itself—he destroyed.

The demon called him by name.

And she knew the name. Of course she knew it. But there was nothing connecting any prior experience to the creature of blue lightning and destruction that stood before her now. The fire in the guildhall was inconsequential. The men and women within the hall would die, yes, and that would be tragic under any other circumstance.

But this man? This man would walk across the city, and even the most casual of his steps would break earth; the sweep of his sword would bisect buildings and anything that happened to shelter in them. She knew he intended no harm.

She thought him incapable of causing none. As the demon perished—and it did—the earth in the center of the Common itself rose, breaking, and breaking again; a spire rose from beneath the earth, displacing everything above it as it reached for the sky.

Meralonne turned toward it. He turned, then, and called wind, and it seemed to Jewel as the spire continued to rise he dwindled in power and majesty before its height. The wind caught his hair, drawing it from his face as if the elements were valets.

"Terafin," he said.

As the ground broke beneath her feet, the air caught her, holding her aloft.

"They are come. They are come; where is the White Lady?"

And Jewel said, "I don't know."

"If you have not located her yet, you will not locate her in time; come home. Come home while any of that home still remains. I will stand while I survive. I will defend what can be defended."

She wanted to tell him that he had destroyed half the Common in his socalled defense. The words wouldn't come. Even in dream, this Meralonne was not the one she knew. She could no more imagine him smoking a pipe just for the petty pleasure of irritating patricians than she could imagine him as any part of her life.

"Meralonne—"

"No. But I remember being Meralonne, Terafin. You have no time. Choose, and choose quickly."

This was the point at which nightmare would give way to a darkened room within any bedroom of her life. Instead it gave way to roaring cat; Shadow flew in from the left, knocked her off her feet and managed, somehow, to break her fall at the end of its wide arc. He was about as happy as she could expect.

She was not awake.

"*Stupid stupid* girl!"

She stood in the ruins of city—or rather, Shadow did; she was mounted. Snow and Night were absent, as were Calliastra and the Warden of Dreams. The Merchant Authority was a smoking ruin; the great trees that grew—or had grown—exclusively in the Common were the only standing structures in sight—and many of them were damaged or dead.

She knew this was not real, but was afraid to examine the ruins too closely. She didn't want to see her dead. She didn't want to see the wreckage of Helen's stall or the ruins of Farmer Hanson's. She didn't want to find bodies, because, given nightmares, she knew whose bodies she was likely to find.

Shadow hissed. He remained angry. But there was a tenor to this anger that tasted of fear.

"Where are your brothers?" Jewel asked. Her voice shook.

"They are *too smart* to be here," Shadow replied. His voice was a thin whisper. "You don't dream."

He snorted. He muttered about stupidity under his breath. Very much under his breath. Jewel slid off his back, and he allowed it—but only barely; his wings were high and he spread them at her back as she made her way toward one of the standing trees.

If this was a nightmare, it was also a dream: she recognized the tree. Or rather, she recognized the paint on its bark. Although it was illegal to "interfere" with the trees in any way, people proved, time and again, that fear of the magisterial guards wasn't incentive enough. Especially not when love, alcohol, and ego were placed firmly on the other side of the scales.

The current act of defacement was a carefully painted infinity symbol with a name on either side. One of the names was Rendish, which was unusual; the other was Torran. As declarations of the permanence of love went, it was actually tasteful.

Scattered beneath the defaced tree were leaves; they were newly fallen and Jewel, without thought—or with as much thought as one ever had in dreams—bent to retrieve one. She had gathered these leaves as a child, her Oma standing close by in the street, keeping an eye out for magisterians, not that the guards ever stopped the children from gathering those leaves. Her Oma trusted no one but kin. To Jewel's young eye, she didn't much trust her kin either, but her Oma insisted there was a difference between incompetence and malice.

"You've no kin here."

"I know," Jewel replied. She was not surprised to hear her Oma's voice, it returned to her so often. Leaf in hand, she rose.

Jewel knew this was a dream, but it was a waking dream. Even if her Oma's expression was at its most thunderous, she was grateful to see the old woman, it had been so long. Her voice was a constant; her words—often harsh and bitter—one of the foundations on which Jewel stood. But her face, like so many things last seen in distant childhood, had grown dim, slipping through the cupped palms of memory.

The pipe in her Oma's hand was lit, and a thin stream of pale smoke rose from the embers of burning leaves.

"You've no kin in the city," her Oma said again.

"You've no kin," Jewel replied, "Except me. I'm the only one left. But me? I have family here."

"You don't."

"I do. As much family as my parents were to each other."

"They had you to bind them."

Jewel nodded. "But if I'd died—if I'd been the one to go first—they would still be bound regardless. They were my parents, yes—but they had each other, blood or no. Blood's not everything, Oma."

"Without blood, what is family?"

"Family," Jewel replied. She folded her arms, but refused to retreat. She'd felt the slap of the old woman's palm more than once, and had hated it. But she'd learned early that fear didn't make the punishment any easier. And she wasn't afraid, now. She knew that her Oma wouldn't have accepted the den as kin. But when her Oma lived, she'd had blood-kin. Relatives. Son and daughter and grandchild.

Jewel, absent the family of her birth, had built one. And it meant as much to her as blood relatives had meant to the cantankerous old woman.

"Do you think calling them kin makes them kin, girl? Is that what I taught you?"

Jewel exhaled. "What you taught me is what kin *means*. We eat at the same table. We talk—and laugh and argue—in the same kitchen. We sleep under the same roof. There are those who'd die for me. There are those who already have. They've faced cold, and hunger, and worse, by my side. Any road I've traveled, they've been willing to travel.

"They're my home. They're as much my home as you once were."

"And the rest of the city?" the old woman asked. She lifted a pipe to her lips and bit down on the end—a bad habit she'd had when annoyed. "You've moved up in the world. You think you're any better than you used to be? You think you're better than your Oma, now?"

"Yes." Jewel's arms tightened. She had, seconds ago, wanted to hug this elderly, critical tyrant. Seconds. "I am better than you, now—because I'm *alive*. You're not. You died on me. The dead don't get a say, anymore."

To Jewel's surprise, the old woman laughed. It was a familiar rasp of sound that ended—ah, gods, as it had always ended in the last few months of her life. With a hacking cough.

"You understand that I'm not here?" she said, when the coughing had quieted and the embarrassment of being so infirm in public—which meant, in her Oma's case, in front of anyone else, ever—had passed.

Jewel nodded. She was dreaming, and she was not dreaming. Dreams had their own, internal reality—but she couldn't quite fit herself into them here. Her Oma was dead. Her Oma was, no doubt, terrifying people in Mandaros' Hall.

"Was I really all that terrifying?"

"Yes. Always."

"Well. Well, then. That's probably why I'm here." She coughed again. "What are you wasting your time on, girl? Wandering around in a daze with those great, noisy creatures of yours?" She turned and pointed, with the pipe's stem, at Shadow.

Shadow sniffed.

"What have you promised?" she continued. "And have you failed yet?"

Jewel was silent.

"You understand what you've seen. You understand what it means. You can't pretend it's opaque or confusing. You're not an idiot. Well, not mostly an idiot. I didn't want this for you. When your mother came home with the story about the dog—I didn't want it. You understand that?"

Jewel swallowed. Nodded.

"But it's never mattered what I want. And it doesn't matter what you want, either. You are what you are. You became a power because you wanted to keep your family safe. Well, fine. We all want to keep our family safe. I'll give you yours. You didn't have any other choice, and it's better than nothing."

Jewel bridled, now, but managed to keep her silence. It was surprisingly difficult, and not made easier when Shadow hissed laughter.

"And you, shut up. If she'd listened to me, you wouldn't be here, either. Cats are a useless lot of parasites."

Shadow growled.

So did Jewel's Oma. "You can kill me if you want," the old woman told him. "All you'll do is traumatize her. Nothing you can do—nothing at all— can hurt me now." She turned back to Jewel. "All you want now is to hide from the choices you've made. It would be nice if life worked that way; it doesn't. Never has. You're Matriarch, now."

"We *don't have* Matriarchs! We're not Voyani!"

But her Oma shook her head. "Don't you recognize this place, girl? This is death. It's what will be if you do nothing."

"I'm not doing nothing—"

"As good as makes no difference. We all die. It's what we do. But we build as well. If no one stepped in to continue the building and the repairs, this is all your Common would be: ruins. And trees. You always liked the trees," she added, her voice softening inasmuch as it ever did. "Had no one succeeded the first of the Twin Kings, the same. Had no one stepped in to fight during the Henden of 410, this is what you would have—or maybe worse.

"You are Matriarch. Understand what Matriarchs are, and what they do. No one can make the choices you will have to make for you. No one can absolve you of them."

"If I make a mistake—"

"Yes. Large choices have large consequences. This is what power *is*. Oh, you can argue that power is force or violence, and I won't disagree. But it's not *your* power. I shouldn't be here," she added. "I didn't raise an idiot. You know what you need to do."

"I—"

"You don't want this, is that what you mean to tell me?" Her Oma spit to the side. "You should have thought of that sooner. But you'll think of it now," she added, turning again toward the gates that led out of the Common. "Because he's coming."

Shadow roared. He hit earth with his forepaws, and the ground beneath Jewel's feet shook. Stones, loosened by time and disaster, fell in the distance.

Jewel heard them, felt them strike ground, wished—for one long, silent moment—that they could strike her, instead.

Or that lightning strike. Or that dragon breathe. Or that earth break and swallow her. Anything, anything, but what she *knew* would follow.

And of course, nothing killed her. Nothing struck her. Nothing removed her from this nightmare that was, in the end, of her own making. She had been so careless, and it was not—it was never—she who would pay the price.

Breath deserted her as she stood, wreathed for a moment in pipe smoke and the lingering growl of shadow cat.

Carver came down what was left of the main west road of the Common.

Chapter Twenty-One

H E WAS PALE. His hair hung over one eye—that hadn't changed. But his clothing was dirty and torn in at least one place, and it was brown where blood had dried; brown and stiff. Exhaustion made his desperate run a series of stumbles and backward glances; he was being pursued, but his pursuers were far enough behind that Jewel couldn't see them.

"Yes," her Oma said quietly. "Do you understand? You have no time, Na'Jay. You have no time."

She could not speak a word. She couldn't raise voice, let alone arms; she couldn't feel the ground beneath her feet, couldn't feel her feet themselves. She was frozen between one breath and the next. Everything she had ever feared was contained in this moment. Gods and demons and firstborn had haunted her dreams and her nightmares, and none, in the end, could hurt her as this one did.

And would.

He looked up as she stood, immobile. He looked up, and across the distance she could see his visible eye widen. He stopped. He stumbled. She moved. She moved without will or thought, her slow single step breaking into many, all of her decision—her choice, the *only* choice—forgotten in the visceral need to be there to catch him.

Her arms were open, and then, closed; she felt his ribs, the slight weight of him, the brush of his falling hair over her own as he lowered his head into the crook of her neck. He shook.

Or perhaps she did. They were silent and inseparable for the space of several breaths.

It was Carver who pulled away first. That was the only mercy she was given. He drew back, placing both of his shaking, cold hands on her shoulders; she could see hints of the eye that was almost always covered as he looked down at her.

"Jay. Jay. Why are you here? I told you not to come."

She had to look away. She had to look away because she was afraid to close her eyes. Her throat was too swollen for words. Any words. She knew this was a nightmare. It was only a nightmare. But clearly she knew Carver well enough that there was no difference between the waking and sleeping versions.

"I'm sorry," she whispered. And then, because she couldn't speak, she lowered her head into his chest. "I'm sorry, Carver. I'm sorry."

"Jay, stop." His hands tightened. "Stop."

Because she stood in the ruins of a city, and not in the Council Chambers of *Avantari* or the House she ruled by name, she shook her head. She wanted to weep, but fought it; if she started, she would never stop.

"What's happened? Is everyone else safe?"

She almost laughed. But it, too, would have been on the edge of tears, and it would have pushed her over.

"No *one* else is *safe*," Shadow said. Jewel had forgotten the gray cat in her rush across the ruins of the Common. "Not you, not *any* of her kin."

"Then why are you here?" he demanded, ignoring both the interruption and its source.

"She is here because *you're here*. She is as *stupid* as *you*."

Carver exhaled. "We have to leave," he said. "I don't know how you got here—but I hope you've got an escape route planned. We're not going to have much time." He pulled her, shifted his grip, started to head out the other side of the market circle.

She stopped him.

"Jay—I mean it—"

"I know." She closed her eyes. "I know. I thought—I really thought—I could find you and save you. I thought I could make a path that led straight to where you landed, and I could bring you *home*." She looked at her hands; she had left the Terafin seal in *Avantari*. But the weight of the title was never, had never been, about simple golden seals. She swallowed. "I agreed to walk the Oracle's path. I agreed to take her test. I knew that unless I passed it I couldn't. Find you. Find a way to reach you.

"That's where I am, now. In a bloody winter forest in the middle of nowhere. This is a dream."

Carver had stilled.

"It's a dream. A nightmare. Carver—"

He lifted his hands, then. He released her and stepped back. As if he couldn't trust his voice, he signed. He signed *go now.* And she couldn't. She couldn't wake. She couldn't stop speaking.

"The Sleepers are waking. That's why the closet opened somewhere else. That's why I'm actually here. I need to be able to find the only living being they might—just might—obey. And I need to do it yesterday, because they've been sleeping under our city. Under the hundred holdings. And when they wake—" She glanced around at the ruin of the Common.

Carver clearly didn't see the ruins as she did. She wondered if he even saw the trees. Without thought, she handed him a single leaf, the one she'd retrieved. Hands shaking, as silent now as he was, he opened his hand and took it.

"I can't find her if I can't pass the Oracle's test. I'm not certain that finding her will be enough; she's trapped somewhere. She can't leave—and I need her to leave. I need her to *ride.*" She closed her eyes. "But I can't—I can't find you. I can't save you. Carver—" she opened her eyes again, because she was weeping; she was bent with the weight of emotion that tears alone couldn't shed.

He looked down at her. He looked down, and then he lifted his hands. He didn't touch her; he touched, instead, something at the back of his neck. A necklace, Jewel thought. A pendant.

"Take this," he told her. "Take this and give it to Merry."

Her own hands opened to take what he offered.

He smiled. There was pain in it. "What will happen to the city if you don't leave?"

"They'll destroy it."

He nodded. "Everything I care about is in that city."

"Everything *I* care about *isn't.*"

"Almost everything you care about is. In that city. Teller's there. Finch. Angel—"

"Angel's here. With me. I mean, he's in the forest where I am when I'm awake."

Carver's smile deepened, losing some of the edge of pain. "You know what you need to do. You told Duster to—"

She lifted a hand and covered his mouth. "I told Duster to die," she said.

He nodded. His hands signed *yes.* But he added, "She chose, Jay. She chose." He exhaled. "Tell Merry I'm sorry. I should've told her—" he shook his head. "Did you find Ellerson?"

Jewel blinked. She had almost forgotten. ". . . No." Before she could say more, she heard hooves in the distance, and she saw Carver pale. He pulled away from her. She couldn't let him go. Her nerveless, shaking hands opened the pouch she had carried from *Avantari*'s hidden basement on the wild trek she'd undertaken.

Leaves, leaves, leaves.

And beside them in her bag, the one leaf she had been given in a different dream: blue, metallic, like and unlike the *Ellariannatte*'s leaves. She *knew* this was not the place it was meant to be. But she knew, as well, that this was all she had to offer the man she intended to abandon.

He stared at it.

"Take it."

"It's a leaf—"

"I *know* what it is. Take it, Carver. Take it and go."

"What am I supposed to do with it?"

She shook her head. "You're not awake. No matter what you think, you're not awake. Take it and find the strength to use it."

"And do what?"

"Plant it. I don't know. I'm not awake, either."

Shadow roared. The rhythm of hoofbeats changed as the sound of his anger died into stillness.

"Go," she said again. "I'll wake. But until I do, let me buy you whatever time I can." She signed: *go now*, and he nodded, and he turned. Just as if they were both sixteen again, in the streets of the twenty-fifth.

She wanted to grab him. She wanted to grab him and hold him. She wanted to follow. And she *knew* that she could. In this moment, she could walk that path. She would abandon every other person who had followed her to this place, because none of them—not even Avandar—could follow where she led; not yet. But she knew that if she followed Carver here, she would wake where Carver was.

And she knew, as well, what the cost would be.

And she couldn't pay it. That was the truth. She could not bring herself to pay it. Carver was *one life*. One. And in the balance was the life of every other person she loved, or had loved. In the balance were the Kings and The Ten and the mage-born and the makers and the bards—all save Kallandras himself. At this moment, they didn't matter to Jewel. Had they been the only losses, she would have suffered them willingly. But in the balance, as well, were Merry and Lucille and Barston. In the balance were all of the children very like Jewel herself had once been: powerless, hungry, and lost. And in the balance, at the very end, the rest of her den: the people who had survived the twenty-fifth and The Terafin's assassination, and the demons.

She fell to her knees; Shadow growled.

But she had fallen for a reason, had allowed her grief to bear her down with purpose; she gathered the fallen leaves of the *Ellariannatte*, and rose. As she had done once in the gardens of the Terafin manse, she set the leaves free, throwing them, with purpose, into the waiting breeze. And the breeze *was* waiting, in this dreamscape.

Wind took the leaves and carried them; their flight ended in earth. Where leaf and earth touched, the *Ellariannatte* flowered. These were not trees of silver, gold, or diamond. They were not trees of blue metal—and she wondered, then, if the leaf she had left Carver could be planted here at all.

They were the trees that had girded the Common.

Where disaster had killed or injured those trees, new trees sprouted, reaching up, and up again, as if straining to achieve their full growth in time. What approached those trees—if anything did—she couldn't see. She didn't want to see. She wanted to believe that Carver would somehow escape them. That he would live without her aid. That he could somehow buy her time.

Time to visit the Oracle. Time to find the Winter Queen. Time to save the rest of her home.

And she didn't, and couldn't, believe it. She knew it was a miracle that Carver was still alive. She *knew* he was. But the only miracles Jewel had ever been able to count on in life were generally the ones best left for nightmare.

The trees were a small forest in the ruins of what had once been the center of her life. She turned; Carver was gone. So was her Oma. Only Shadow remained, and he watched her with wide, unblinking eyes.

She failed to move.

Shadow closed the gap between them. He said nothing. He didn't even tell her how stupid she was, or had been—and she had, and knew it. There were leaves on the ground, and she bent and retrieved one, as if she were a child again.

She held it in one palm; in the other, enclosed in the fist her hand had become, was a pendant. To give to Merry.

She was grateful that she was not resident in the manse. It was the last thing Carver had asked of her. It was one of the only favors he had ever explicitly requested. And she was coward enough that the thought of fulfilling it crushed her.

But this was a dream. It was a nightmare and it was a dream. Even in the wilderness of her current waking life, she would wake. She would wake and leave as much of it behind as she could.

"It is time," Shadow told her.

Jewel nodded.

She woke to campfire and Calliastra; to Celleriant and the Winter King. She woke surrounded by gray fur and gray wings; the first sound she heard was the hissing of angry cat; it was the closest thing to her ear.

Waking was awkward. Even Calliastra's normal hauteur had broken, and the uneasiness that replaced it looked so foreign on the firstborn face that Jewel almost failed to recognize her. She rose, and as she did, she opened her hands.

From the right fell something that sparkled in the early morning light. From the left, a leaf that no tree in this forest had shed.

She stared at them. She stared, and then bent, stiffly and slowly, as if she had aged decades in one night. Her hands trembled as she lifted the pendant from packed snow and dirt; she held it aloft. It caught light. It was a simple thing, really: a locket in the shape of an oval. She had no doubt that if she opened it, at least one half of the two sides would be filled.

But she didn't.

It wasn't meant for her.

Nothing, this morning, was. She lifted the chain in trembling hands, and lowered it over her head; it caught in strands of her hair and she tore at them. She would wear this—it was the only way she could be guaranteed to keep it safe.

When Angel woke, he knew something was wrong. He signed—to Adam— and Adam shook his head, his lips thinner than usual, his gentle smile completely absent. No one appeared to have gone missing during a night spent in the admittedly warm but very cramped hole they had dug out of snow that was probably, from the looks of this forest, older than Angel.

Calliastra was tending the fire. Celleriant was beside her, at a cold but respectful distance. Kallandras was preparing food, with Terrick's help—or perhaps the reverse. Shianne sat opposite Calliastra; she was the only person present who didn't seem to be aware of the raven-haired, disturbingly attractive child of—if Jay was right—gods. No; her eyes were on Jay; she was watchful.

She was, Angel thought, worried.

Jay was pacing. She stopped when Angel caught her attention—mostly by stepping into the path her feet had crushed into the snow. He froze—it was cold enough for that—when he saw her eyes.

They were red.

"Jay?"

She started to speak, stopped. Three times. And then she inhaled and lifted shaking hands instead. Her hands were mittened—mittens being the piece of Winter clothing she most disliked—and seeing this she bunched those hands into fists instead.

"What happened?"

She said nothing. A long nothing. And he remembered the long days spent in the old apartment in the twenty-fifth, waiting. Waiting, first, for Fisher, and then after, for Lefty. Her expression reminded him of those days, because the only thing that was different about it was the years that had passed over her face in the interim.

Jay was not Duster. She'd never been Duster. You could talk to her, argue with her, be fearful in her company. You could weep, and she accepted it. But she and Duster shared one thing: they didn't cry in public. They could rage, yes. Duster could threaten your life sixteen ways before the sun had truly cleared the cover of buildings. Jay could throw pots and cups. They could curse.

But tears? No.

The obvious evidence of those tears left Angel stranded. He retreated, stepping on Adam in the process. Terrick muttered something under his breath. The only person present that Terrick felt comfortable criticizing was, in fact, Angel. It was, however, Adam who apologized to the older Rendish man. And to Angel.

"It's not your fault he can't watch where he's going," Terrick snapped.

"He doesn't have eyes in the back of his head."

"His ears don't face forward—you weren't exactly silent."

Angel lifted a hand and in den-sign begged Adam to stop. Adam glanced at Terrick, and then at Jay. He lifted his own hands. His den-sign was only slightly slower than Angel's, but Adam was the age they'd been in the twenty-fifth, when den-sign had been half their public talk. He took to it as easily as they had, back then.

Adam seemed so young to Angel. But Adam had saved The Terafin's life, several times, before the assassination that had made Jay The Terafin. He wasn't a child.

But he wasn't the fourteen-year-old youths of the Free Towns, either. He had no awkward strut, no need to brag; he tended to children and aged women with a gentleness that Angel saw almost nowhere else. Life in the South, among the Voyani, must have been very, very different.

Jay had said that the leader of one of the Voyani clans was the most terrifying person, without exception, she had ever met. The name of the woman escaped Angel, but it didn't matter. Adam called Jay Matriarch. And Adam, without the long history of the den to hold him back, was waiting for her.

Angel lifted a hand, signed.

Adam glanced at him and shook his head. *I'll wait.*

What do you think happened?

Adam's hands were still for a long second. But he signed a name at the end of that silence.

Angel's eyes widened; he turned back to Jay, stepped forward; Adam's arm caught him—to Terrick's further disgust—in the chest. The boy didn't swing it; he merely held it out, as if he were a slender, human gate.

But Jay grimaced, seeing them both. To Adam, she signed, *it's good.*

Adam glanced, again, at Angel. He swallowed and nodded and retreated.

"The Voyani," Jay said quietly, "are ruled by their Matriarchs—and it is death to know too much of a Matriarch's business unless you are her heir or, as Adam, her actual child. I think he means to spare me the necessity of killing you." She smiled as she said it, but the smile was a window into pain. "You'll note he hasn't stayed, himself."

"He would have."

"Adam is always willing to risk his own life. He does it with a quiet purity—you can almost *see* his desire to be helpful or useful. I don't think I was ever Adam. Certainly not at his age."

"Jay—"

She had taken the time to gather her thoughts, to find the control to speak. Adam had, intentionally or no, given her that much space. "I don't understand the mechanics of the Oracle's test. But I understand why Evayne speaks of it with such loathing. Remind me, if we meet again, to ask her what her test was."

"Would you answer that question if she asked it of you?"

Jay said, voice low, "I'm not certain, yet, what the whole of the test comprises." But she inhaled, held breath, and exhaled white mist. "And I know how little time we have to reach her."

"Did she ever tell you what happens to you if you fail?"

Jay shrugged. "No. The implication was insanity or death. Mostly insanity."

Angel fell silent. "How bad was it?"

"Was what?"

"The dreaming?"

"Bad. Bad enough that we'd be sitting in the kitchen for hours if we were back home."

"I'm no good at transcription."

"You're no good for *anything*," Shadow said. He stepped on Angel's right foot as he shouldered him out of the way. "Be *more* useful or we will *eat* you."

Jay, however, dropped a hand onto gray fur. "You will eat him over my dead body."

"But he can't *do* anything. You don't *let* him do *anything*. What is *he* good *for?*"

Jay started to speak, stopped, and met the gray cat's unblinking eyes. "Does it matter?" she asked—and to Angel's surprise, the question was grave.

"Look at *where you are*, stupid, stupid girl. *Everything* matters. Why did you *bring* him?"

"He wasn't willing to stay behind."

Shadow growled.

"What? That's the truth. I promised I wouldn't go where he couldn't follow—and he could follow, here. So he did."

Shadow snorted, turned, stepped on Angel's foot again, and stomped toward the campfire. Angel glanced at Jay. Her hands were free of mittens. She signed: *Carver*. Just as Adam had done.

She signed the name again, and this time, she met his gaze and held it. This time, she let tears trace the line of her cheeks and chin. She couldn't speak. He wouldn't have demanded words, regardless. He was frozen for one long minute, and then, because he had nothing else to offer her, he crossed the distance that separated them. He wasn't certain if he was offering comfort or seeking it. She wasn't certain, either.

He was aware when Adam rejoined them; aware as well that no one else did—or would. Adam was new to the den, but Adam was of them—the only person that had come to the West Wing at an invitation other than Jay's. He asked no questions, but slid his arms around them both, and bowed his head, and after a moment, sang a very quiet, very short song. It was Torran; more than that, Angel couldn't tell.

Jewel rode the Winter King for half of the first leg of their journey. She walked for the other half, to the Winter King's amusement.

I wish you would carry her, she said, for the hundredth time that morning. But he wouldn't unless she commanded it. Command—resolute, no-nonsense command—was not her strength in any situation that was not a matter of immediate life or death. He knew this, as well.

What he did not completely understand was the guilt riding caused her. No explanation resulted in comprehension; he found it mystifying. In his defense—not that he needed one—Shianne found it equally mystifying. Guilt, apparently, did not come easily to denizens of the ancient world.

Respect does. If you are to be worthy of respect, you must be seen to be a power. You can be a power, without the obvious trappings—but you will have to prove that power, time and again.

This was a conversation they had had multiple times during her brief reign as Terafin. They occupied the same positions at the end of such arguments as they had at the beginning. Today, she clung to it because of its familiarity. But she clung to it, for the most part, while walking. Terrick had fashioned rackets that were tied to her feet. They were awkward and cumbersome—but as promised, they made walking less exhausting.

Terrick said they would make everything less exhausting; Jewel couldn't imagine running in them.

If there is need for flight, the Winter King said, in his most severe internal voice, *you will not be touching the ground.*

Jewel laughed almost bitterly. *I will not be riding away while we abandon a* pregnant woman.

She is not a woman, he replied, which was also a familiar refrain. *She is mortal by her own choice—but her death—*

No.

You do not understand what she presages.

No? Possibly because no one has explained it. I'm willing to bet you don't understand it, either. It makes you uneasy, but you can't tell me why. And I'm terrible at making hard choices when I do *know the reasons for them; I won't even consider it when I don't.*

"Matriarch?" Shianne said.

Jewel had become accustomed to this title from Adam, but cringed every time it left Shianne's mouth. Admittedly, this happened less frequently. The Arianni woman only used it when she wished to catch Jewel's attention—and as it was hard not to notice Shianne, Jewel's attention was generally already caught and held.

She blinked. She noticed, as she looked around her, that the moving company had, with two exceptions, come to a halt. The two exceptions were Terrick and Angel, who forged on ahead.

Shadow, who walked to her right, had dropped into a low growl, exposing fangs. His wings rose, rigid, above his shoulders.

The growl caught Terrick's attention; the older man turned. One look at the cat, and his ax was in his hands; Angel's sword joined it as the two men once again turned to look in the direction they had chosen.

Jewel looked to Shianne.

But Calliastra, silent—and unencumbered by the snow-rackets and heavier winter clothing that was a necessity for the merely mortal—lifted flawless throat as she peered into the network of branches above their heads. "I fear," she said softly, "we have entered the gauntlet."

"The gauntlet?"

"You can well imagine that my sister would be of incalculable value to *any* who could either control her, suborn her power, or prevent its spread. This is true in the hidden world, and will be true until the end of days—or the end of her. The firstborn are not," she added, "invulnerable. They are not deathless. They are not subject to the vagaries of time—and the age that graces mortals—but they can, in theory, be destroyed.

"And many, many are those who have made, and will make, that attempt. Even now." She smiled. It was not an edged expression, and made her look far younger. "I feel almost nostalgic, it has been so long. It is a grand game, to attempt to cut the Oracle off from any possible avenue of escape. She is, as you can imagine, hard to plan against.

"Many of the seers who attempted to take the Oracle's test never reached her side. That, in and of itself, is a test." She glanced ahead, at the backs of the two who now served as scouts. "It would have been best for you had you come alone."

"Alone isn't a possibility, for me."

"No. You have Lord Celleriant and Viandaran. You have the Winter King. You have the cursed, squabbling—"

Shadow let it be known what he thought of the coming description. Loudly.

"And perhaps—perhaps, you would have had me. I feel almost as I did when the world and my place in it was new. There is possibility in the very air."

And, apparently, lightning.

Calliastra's smile brightened, her eyes widening, as that lightning struck branches not yards from where they now stood.

Kallandras took to the air immediately, a reminder—if one were needed—that walking across the snow was an unnecessary courtesy. Branches, struck at the heights of the crowns of winter trees, didn't break so much as shatter; splinters and chunks of leafless bark fell like black rain.

That rain, however, failed to land upon the people directly beneath it; wind caught the detritus and shunted it to one side or the other, serving, at the bard's command, as an invisible roof.

Jewel, the Winter King shouted—and it was a shout, although no one else could hear it.

Jewel, however, had turned to Adam; she grabbed both of his shoulders, turned him around, and told him to mount. The Winter King was not happy. Jewel didn't give a damn.

I have lost enough, she told him, and if thoughts could burn he would have been cinders and ash. *I will not sacrifice anything else when I have* any *choice!*

He is a healer—he is unlikely—

Carry him. Carry him as if he were me. Protect him and keep him safe.

Lightning punctuated the internal words, and the Winter King accepted her command; he knelt. Adam looked to Shianne, however, instead of mounting. Jewel wanted to scream. She understood why he hesitated. She wasn't climbing the back of the Winter King, either. "Adam, get on the Winter King *now*."

His body obeyed her tone, and she was—for perhaps the first time—grateful for his upbringing among the Voyani.

"Snow!" she shouted, into the debris strewn sky. The white cat descended, landing on snow without breaking any of it.

Jewel turned to Shianne. "Lady," she said, with as much respect as urgency allowed. "Snow will carry you."

"Why *me*. She is *heavy*. Why do *I* have to carry *her?*"

"Because I said so!"

"But then I can't *fight!*"

Shianne ignored the cat's whining. She lifted the skirts of the dress he had made and approached his side. His wings were high, and in the way; he tensed them. Jewel promised she would strip his wing of flight feathers if even one of them so much as grazed Shianne, which caused white hackles to rise and gray cat to snicker.

Shianne, however, was looking toward the sky, her perfect lips compressed in a frown that implied confusion. "What is attacking?" she asked, as she seated herself.

"I don't know. Calliastra?"

Calliastra smiled. "I would say, if I had to guess, that the *Kialli* do not wish you to reach the Oracle's side. But the *Kialli* are not the only danger you will face. Unless I am mistaken, you carry upon your person a pendant of some value?"

Jewel's hands curved into fists.

She thought of Carver; her hands rose to cover the golden locket. Calliastra's mercurial frown was a thing of passion and beauty. Also contempt. "Not *that*. That is an insignificant mortal trinket. The other. If you value your life—or the lives of your other companions—you will not touch it, not yet. Perhaps not ever.

"I do not know how it came to be in your possession, but it is, or was, a part of my brother's collection. Perhaps you have heard of him? Mortals called him Verasallion, in my youth. He does not like to lose what is his. But if it is my brother you face, you will perish here. Do you see or sense your own death?"

"No," was the bitter, bitter reply. "My own death would be an end to pain."

"Only an end to yours, little mortal. Do not—never—forget that." Turning to Shianne, she said, "the sky is not safe."

Shianne said nothing. To Jewel's surprise, she closed her eyes and lifted her face; a rain of ashes missed her delicate skin. Fire joined lightning. The skies, which had been a cold, even gray, were lit, for a moment, from within: they became white and red and black.

It was beautiful.

Avandar approached from the rear. "You might consider lowering your voice." His entire body was shimmering with light, predominantly orange. But there were hints of other colors: violet, blue.

"I think they know we're here."

"They know that something approaches, certainly," he replied. "They cannot—or could not—be certain what, or who."

"Is Calliastra right? Are we facing demons?"

"I am standing beside you," was his mild response. "If we faced Verasallion, you would know; he would cover the sky with the span of his wings and the storm would destroy the forest and everything beneath him. Let us hope for demons."

Any day that involved hoping for demons was not a good day. Jewel started forward; Avandar caught her shoulder. "Not you."

"I want to see—"

"You will be seen. You are unarmed. This is not your fight."

"We're not in the normal world. If it's not my fight, then whose?"

"Those more likely to survive, Terafin. You are not upon your own ground, here. The elements will not obey you. The fire will not protect you. You stand in wilderness that has never been claimed. I invite you to consider why."

Calliastra was watching this exchange with a growing—familiar—
impatience. Jewel was not surprised when she sprouted wings of shadow. "*I
will scout,*" she told them both. "I hear your Night, and I would not leave all
of the fun to him." She leaped toward the sky as if the sky was her enemy.

Avandar released Jewel's shoulder; he met, and held, her gaze. "We follow
Terrick and Angel. They are the two most likely to be lost, here."

Terrick's movements had slowed. He grunted, adjusting the weight of the ax
as he slid behind the trunks of standing, barren trees. Angel's sword caught
light and reflected it as he found different trees; their progress was marked by
the hide and seek the den had perfected in streets of a city.

Lightning perforated the gray sky above their heads; it seemed aimed at
their backs, where Jay was. But there was nothing in flight; no shadows cast
upon snow to indicate that the combat was aerial.

The den's hide and seek had often been a matter of survival—but they had
faced people. Lightning had been no part of the deadly games the dens played
among themselves. Nor had fire. Not this fire.

It erupted across the tree line a hundred yards ahead, and it spread, flames
consuming winter wood as if the trees were dead and dry. Terrick pulled up,
as did Angel. They could see no visible sign of enemies. The lightning itself
seemed to flash in place, as if Terrick and Angel were so inconsequential they
weren't worth the bother of killing.

And given the attitudes of the various immortals whose paths Angel had
crossed, they probably weren't. Unless the mortals in question provided some
sort of sustenance, the way hunting prey did for humans. Angel lifted a hand
and signed; Terrick frowned.

"Let's head back. We can stay on the outer periphery, but I don't think
we're going to find anything that Calliastra doesn't find first."

Angel was worried about their supplies. Dead people didn't require food or
shelter—but lack of either in this place just meant death would come anyway.
He, like Terrick, had shrugged himself out of the heavier pack that encumbered
movement; the fire forced them to retreat. The retreat took more time, not less,
but Angel lost some hoisting the pack by one strap onto his shoulder.

"Smart boy," Terrick murmured, doing the same. He stopped speaking
when a shadow sped across the snow, broken by branches and geography in
its passage. Both men glanced up.

"I think that's ours," Angel said quietly.

"It is not the cats."

"No. I think it's Calliastra."

Terrick watched for a moment longer; the natural shadow ran into the fire, where it was lost to easy sight. "I don't like it."

"I don't, either. But I trust Jay. If she's willing to accept Calliastra, I'll accept her. I don't have to like her."

"She is death, boy."

"Yes." Angel nodded in the direction from which the shadow had come. "But at the moment, what isn't?"

Terrick chuckled. "This isn't the fight I was trained for. Those cats, the death goddess, wind that moves at a man's command, and fire that spreads across living trees as if they were kindling. I can't fight at range; I can't throw the ax."

"We would make a mile a day, if that, without you," Angel replied. "And you know it. The winter is your element."

"Aye, and maybe it is. I feel young again, in this place. There is your lord."

Angel nodded. "I've never questioned your sanity."

"But?"

"You seem happier to be here than you ever seemed in the Port Authority."

Terrick nodded. "I am. I saw your father surrender his life on what seemed a mad, pointless quest. He died beneath the shadow of loss and failure. But, boy, he made you. He trained you. He did what he could to prepare you for this life. The mad quest? Doesn't look so mad, now.

"This is the reason Garroc left Weyrdon. And I waited for Garroc, and then, for Garroc's son, to have an ending to the long, tangled story. To have peace. All I have to do is obey the few commands your lord gives, and protect her.

"I can do that. And you, boy? It's the only responsibility you've ever truly accepted. Yes, I'm happier. When I finally meet Garroc across the bridge, I will tell him your story. And mine. He will understand." He shifted his grip on his ax and grinned. "And I will see dragons. I know it in my bones. I will see frostwyrms and gods and demons. I will see things that there are no Weston words for. It is enough. It is more than enough."

Jay met them as they headed back to camp. The familiar, pinched set of her lips eased as they came into view. Angel sheathed his sword, which probably meant Terrick's lips were just as pinched, if for vastly different reasons.

"There's a ring of fire spreading across the forest," Angel told her. "No sign of what caused it."

Avandar frowned.

"Adam is with the Winter King; Shianne is with Snow. You might have heard that last bit."

"The complaints?"

"Apparently, he can't fight with a pregnant woman on his back."

Terrick was not Angel. He didn't sheath the ax; he held it, watching the sky. "Are we safe?" he asked Jay, although he didn't look back at her.

"At the moment? Yes. Kallandras and Celleriant have taken to the air as well. I'm not sure there's going to be much left for the cats, though—Calliastra took off after Night. If they start another brawl like the last one, they're going to level huge swaths of forest."

"And us?"

"Probably—but that would be less intentional."

"Calliastra passed over the ring of fire," Terrick said quietly.

"We're going to head that way as well. Stay in range of Avandar; if magic is used here—and frankly, the ring of fire—he can protect us from the worst of it."

"Not the worst," Avandar replied. "If something chooses to wake the wild earth here, we will be in some danger." He glanced at Jay; her brows folded a moment as she considered his words.

"Not yet," she finally said. She began to walk toward the fire that Angel had spoken of—but that wasn't hard; he was certain all paths would lead to fire.

Lightning struck trees as they walked. A rain of bark—and larger branches—fell to either side of the path Terrick chose. Jay didn't expect to be hit; she did glance up from time to time to see which tree had been struck, to better gauge the accuracy of whoever their unseen opponents were. The lightning was clearly aimed; the fire had been laid down as a precaution.

Given the cats, Calliastra, and the two men who fought in the air as if they weighed less than hummingbirds, it wasn't much of a precaution.

To Avandar, Angel said, "Can you carry us through or over the fire?"

Avandar's response—and a response wasn't guaranteed—was lost to the roar of a very angry cat. The sound was thunderous; it belonged in the air, with the lightning. Angel couldn't differentiate the voices of the cats.

Jay, clearly, could. She had paled. "That was Shadow," she said.

Of the three cats, Shadow was the tactician. Angel signed. Jay signed back. The sky, less full of obscuring branches, gave them no line of sight on the cat—or any of the combatants. They picked up the pace that Jay now set.

She was worried. Angel was less worried; he privately suspected that nothing could kill the cats. The cats, on the other hand, were perfectly capable of ending lives, and had demonstrated this with authority.

*   *   *

Kallandras hovered. His movement was not flight; it had none of flight's grace or deliberation. The air was alive. Lightning flew with the grace and power that he denied himself for a moment, striking trees and perhaps ground beneath his feet; he had removed the snowshoes that Terrick had provided. No battle in the wilderness was going to be fought on the earth.

To the west, Celleriant was likewise anchored in air; the Arianni Prince was armed with both the sword and the shield of his kin. In his hands, at the moment, they resembled the lightning that flew, uncontained. His hair curled in currents at his back; no strands escaped to obscure vision.

As if aware of Kallandras' regard, Celleriant smiled. At this distance, his eyes were silver light.

Kallandras drew his weapons. A gift from Meralonne APhaniel, they were artifacts of a bygone era; Kallandras believed they had last seen use during the age of the Blood Barons. He used them only in combats in which his opponents were likely to be talent-born or inhuman, and even then, he handled them with care, will, focus.

They were the length, at the moment, of long daggers; the hilts were of a piece with the blades, and the blades themselves meant for parrying or thrusting; they were not edged in the Southern tradition. Or the Northern, for that matter. But the shape they held now could change if he had the will to command it.

They could change, more treacherously, if he did not.

He had not drawn them since he stepped through the portal in the basement of *Avantari*; he had not been certain whether the surroundings would affect the strength of the weapons' will. The blades had been crafted by an Artisan with the materials he had had at hand.

The materials he had had at hand included demons. Meralonne was not apprised of how they had come to be in his possession—or how he had survived it; no one completely understood how Artisans worked. Not even Artisans themselves. But they could work, and did.

And they had crafted blades that existed for combat; that were drawn to fear and pain. For that reason, Kallandras did not use them often. He had learned that that temptation ended lives among the brotherhood. He had seen it, during training. He had learned to value death, and to respect it—but to crave it? Never.

The wind moved him before he reasserted control over its flowing currents. Control, in any battle, was necessary; one surrendered it only when one had no other option; lack of control was failure. Or death.

In this place, the wind was stronger, its voice clearer.

And in this place, for the first time, he heard the voice of the blades. It was a singular voice, which surprised him, for there had always been two weapons. It spoke—as the *Kialli* did—in words; the wind did not.

And it spoke with force, yet its voice was velvet. It was almost more of a sensation than a sound.

Let me go, the weapon sang. *Let me fly. Let me meet the dead and grant them some small measure of peace. LET ME GO.* As it spoke, both weapons shuddered. There was very little traction in the air; Kallandras had taken the equivalent of five steps when he regained control of them.

Here, to be mastered by the blades was death—in all likelihood, his own.

The wild wind was like—very like—a child. It required cozening, praise, appreciation; it could be commanded and forced to obedience, but the sullen resentment it felt lingered. It was best, always, to allow the wind to believe that it had choice and the freedom to make decisions; best to convince the wind that the wind itself had chosen the enemies it faced.

Locomotion was not a matter of life or death, as far as the wild air was concerned; it was just as happy to pick Kallandras up and carry him in its currents as it was to remove the roofs of buildings.

The weapons, however, were not like the wind. The wind knew mercurial anger—fury—and equally instant joy; it sang or it raged or it whispered, hiding behind Kallandras while playing with his hair.

The blades twisted in his hands, bending toward him. They had done so once before, in the silence of Meralonne's tower; they had drawn the slightest of blood, no more, before acquiescing to serve him; they had taken a shape and form with which he was familiar and even comfortable.

They lost that form as they struggled for mastery.

He held them, regardless. He could have dropped them—he had that much control—and in truth, he considered doing so. In the wilderness of this winter landscape, they might never be found again.

But no weapon he now carried in this place was their equal, save for perhaps the wind itself—and the cost of rousing wind to fury was too high, here where the earth slept beneath their feet, waiting provocation.

He tightened his grip and spoke. He spoke with the voice to which he'd been born, and into which—at so much peril in the South of his birth—he had grown. Bard. Bard-born.

Stop.

The blades, folding, shuddered to a trembling halt. The length of each didn't straighten; they strained against the imperative in a command no one else could hear. He struggled with their sudden weight.

They spoke to him.

They spoke of death. They spoke of loss. They spoke of rage and bitter betrayal. They spoke—ah, demons—they spoke of their lost brethren. Brothers, all. And at their head, a Queen. They were sundered forever.

Just as, they whispered, Kallandras himself was forsaken.

He was no longer a young man. That man had believed that pain would never lessen, never end. That love's sharpest edges would cut forever. At a remove of decades he had learned that those beliefs were true. But he had also believed that the rest of his life would remain static; that nothing would fill the emptiness, nothing would speak to the loss.

And that had proven less true.

His life had not been static. His affection, reserved and withdrawn, had nonetheless been hesitantly, slowly offered, growing roots so quietly he had not himself been aware of their existence until his trek through the Sea of Sorrows at the side of the Arkosan Voyani. His gift, trained in service to the brotherhood, had been repurposed in service to foreign Kings, through the halls of Senniel College, the most respected of the bardic colleges.

You were trained to sing death, the weapons said. *And we were created, to* cause it. *We are not your enemy. And here, bard, you have many. Some you will see. Some you will hear. But some will take you unaware. Give us free rein. We might be allies.* The blades twisted in his hand, becoming longer and more slender in shape; the hilts—all of a piece—retreated.

But these weapons, Kallandras had also learned. He smiled; the weapons sensed genuine, if bitter amusement in the expression; it did not please them. Their struggle intensified. Even trapped as they were within the confines of simple weapons, the arrogance of the immortal could not be underestimated.

"Brother!" Celleriant shouted.

The weapons momentarily stilled, listening—as the bard did—for a voice that was familiar.

"You will miss your chance if you hesitate; we not only have the cursed cats, but Calliastra herself to contend with—and neither are inclined to share glory."

The *Kovaschaii* did not kill for the glory of any but the Dark Lady. And yet, Kallandras thought, shifting his grip. And yet. He did not relish the challenge of battle the way Lord Celleriant did. He did not seek to prove himself against the wild and elemental; nor did he seek to control any element but the air itself. As a mortal, the elements were beyond him; only Myrddion's ring allowed him to speak with the wind as if he were . . . Celleriant. Or Meralonne.

In both, when they chose not to guard their voices, he could hear a loss that resonated with his own. But his loss was not their loss; his choice, not their choice. It was therefore one of the oldest—and most familiar—of voices that returned.

Only a fool carries weapons he cannot master.

And how many times, Kallandras wondered, had that same master called him a fool? Too many to count, although with effort and will, he could. The sting and humiliation of those early lessons had left no scar. What he was, now, was in large part the legacy of those difficult years.

He had mastered the weapons that he had been given; they were many.

He had mastered the dark; he had learned to fight, where necessary, in water, and across the sands of the desert. Snow, however, he had come to on his own. Snow, and air.

You cannot name us.

"It is not required. Here, you serve my purpose or you lie in the snow beneath us, there to wait until you are found. You are unlikely to be found by mortals in this place; your desires will count for even less against those who now claim these lands."

No one claims these lands.

A roar shook the air. Literally.

Kallandras grimaced; he sent a benediction to the wind. Gratitude came easily and without effort; placation was more difficult. The wind, however, did not require that effort—not yet. Soon, Kallandras thought, as Celleriant once again called him.

"Make your decision; make it quickly. I am generous enough to offer you that choice; there will be no finer weapons to be found in this stretch of sky, for this particular battle."

It was not, of course, over; not even when the blades once again returned to the shape they had held since he had accepted them. This was a fight he would have, over and over, until he abandoned the weapons or returned them to the magi.

But, he thought, as he called wind and leaped into its folds, that was as it should be.

The sky was winter clear, the air cold; the wind at the heights above the trees that covered ground for as far as the eye could see was bitter and sharp.

The wind could moderate the chill, but it could not destroy it; nor did Kallandras ask.

Where lightning struck trees, the debris wafted in currents not under the bard's control; they rose and swirled in dense, temporary clouds. He suspected, but could not be certain, that The Terafin stood on the ground beneath them; had all combat been aerial, that would have been the safest.

Some combat was aerial.

Kallandras could see the sweep of wings in the distance—wings he'd missed on first glance because they were the exact hue of the sky itself. So, too, the creature's neck, its head—but the interior of its jaws were the dark shade of crimson when those jaws opened.

They opened on lightning and anger.

As lightning flared, Shadow roared, folding his wings in a dive; streaks of pale blue-white brushed his feathers on the downward arc.

Had Calliastra not taken to the skies to confront the creature, it would have been hard to gauge its size, the perspective of clear sky offered so little for rough comparison. But she had. The creature was large; much larger than the cats or the firstborn.

A second set of jaws opened, longer and wider than the first. Kallandras approached slowly, skirting the highest of the nearest branches. He was wrong. The creature's body could not be easily seen, and if it had eyes, they also blended with the sky in which it fought.

Chapter Twenty-Two

"**W**HAT ARE THEY FIGHTING?" Terrick asked.

Jewel said nothing for a long breath. "I can't tell. I can hear it—but I can't actually see it. Avandar?"

The same. He was, however, uneasy.

"You don't think this is natural." When Terrick coughed, she added, "For the wilderness."

"No, Terafin. Whatever they fight now is casting lightning bolts toward the trees. There are creatures that could, once, do this—kin to the dragons, but separate from them—yet I assure you, were we fighting one of those, you would see it. You might see it seconds before you perished—but you would see it."

"Do they fight on the ground at all?"

"Yes. The forest is not ideal for that. If enraged or determined, the creatures will land regardless—but the trees here are not fragile, mortal trees, and such a landing might wake them."

"And the lightning won't?" she all but demanded.

"The lightning might. It is deep winter here. The forest sleeps." He hesitated, and then added, "I did not dwell in forests in my youth. I did not have the patience to learn to hear them speak. Or the time." His smile twisted into something grimmer. "And when I had the time, and knew I had nothing *but* time—" he shook his head. "You travel with Lord Celleriant. If the trees wake, he will know."

"In time to explain that it's not us that attempted to destroy them?"

A roar broke the flow of conversation.

Jewel closed her eyes. "Angel?"

"Yes?"

"Did you hear that?"

"I think we all heard it."

"Did you understand it?"

Silence.

"Avandar?"

"No, Jewel. I heard what I suspect Angel and Terrick did: a roar. A roar that implies a set of truly impressive lungs. You heard words?"

Jewel nodded, grimmer now, her lips set in so thin a line they were almost invisible.

"Is he saying anything unexpected?" Angel asked.

"What, exactly, would you expect him to say?"

"I don't know. Food! Die!"

"I'd be happier with that, because I think he's attempting to give commands to the elemental air."

The roar of an all but invisible creature was thunder. Not to be outdone, the cats replied—but their familiar voices, at this distance, were dim echoes. Dim, insulting echoes.

Lightning replied; lightning, anger, aimed not at treetops or Jewel, but at moving, taunting targets. Jewel saw that one of those targets was Snow—and that Shianne was now in the air, perched on his back. All of her outrage was silent; she didn't have ready words available to vent it, and had she, no target.

Avandar, however, nodded grimly. "It is not a tactic that many would have used in such encounters in my youth—but Calliastra is correct. Dignity is a sign of the certainty of power. Let the cats fight as they fight; it buys us time."

Jewel didn't even ask for what; she knew. Terrick did not give Avandar the lead; he took it. And he led them directly to the fire that he and Angel had encountered.

The Rendish man had called it a ring. It seemed, to Jewel, to be an apt description; it stretched in a thin line that curved slightly—very slightly. A circle. *Is it alive?* she asked her domicis.

You cannot hear it.

No.

And yet you can hear the voice of the creature above us as if it spoke language.

Clearly. She was impatient and struggled not to show it. Or not to show more of it.

Yes. It is elemental fire. But it is contained and restrained at the moment. It longs to leave the circle; it longs to burn the forest.

And that would be a bad thing?

For us, yes.

She shook her head, frowning. *For them. For whoever is attempting to kill us or pin us here. It's possible we could survive the fire—we can, in a haphazard way, fly. But the trees can't.*

No, Terafin.

Burning or harming the trees wouldn't be in the interest of whoever controls this fire. It wasn't a question.

That would be the safe assumption.

There was no safety. "We can't call air anywhere near this circle without breaking it, can we?"

"No."

"The forest isn't the concern, then. It's the earth."

"The earth would have to be sleeping very, very lightly to notice a fire as small as this; the wind has come and gone to no effect."

"The trees here are rooted in earth. I think some of the trees here are—or were—sentient, at least in a way Celleriant and Shianne would understand. If the earth is slumbering deeply enough to ignore the small voice of this fire, I'm betting it won't ignore the screams of the trees whose roots are buried so far down." She exhaled. "Can you douse or separate the fire to let us through?"

"Yes. I think it unwise, however."

"Because they'll know?"

"They'll know where the break is, yes. And they'll know, for certain, where you are."

She glanced pointedly at the canopy of sky that was now filled with combat and furious cats. She could see the slender, winged outline of Calliastra as well, but the firstborn voice was mercifully silent. "How long can she fight like that?" she asked, voice almost hushed.

"A fair question. Until this journey, I had never seen her take that form; it was not to her liking. It reminded her too much of loss. I do not know what it signifies."

"You think her father is here."

"I think her father's power might influence her, yes. But she is not her father; she has will and choice. You are not foolish enough to mention his name here."

"No. I'm not angry enough, either." She shook her head. "If the earth won't help them, it certainly won't do us any good."

But Avandar smiled. "I believe I can speak with the earth. I was one of very, very few mortals who could—and I could not master that until after I had been granted the god's gift. It was the work of decades."

She hesitated before she shook her head. "Not you," she said, in the softest of voices. "Not unless we have no choice at all."

"Celleriant can speak with the fire, if he desires it; it is not his natural element. He cannot do so from the air, however."

"Kallandras can control the wind, if necessary."

"You do not understand the elemental air if you think the matter that simple."

Nothing, Jewel thought, would ever be simple again. She had learned to play games of power in the last decade of her life, and she had used those games, to greater or lesser effect, in the last few months. But no study of trade routes, no study of houses, no intelligence offered her even obliquely, was of use here.

Power, of course, was—but the definition of power had shifted dramatically the moment she had accepted the Oracle's invitation and set foot through the portal in *Avantari*. And yet, she was not without power, here—she just didn't understand the rules. She didn't understand the etiquette, if raw displays of power, such as Calliastra's, could be said to have etiquette at all.

The Immortals seemed to do whatever they wanted; the only thing that stopped them was the possible fear of death. And even then, Jewel thought, they were arrogant and feckless enough not to fear the challenge. They lived forever; they never starved, never grew ill, never grew old.

None of these things would ever be true of Jewel. She *could* starve. She could succumb to illness—absent Adam's presence—and she would age. She had already aged. But she had power.

You lack the will to use it, the Winter King said.

No, she replied. *I lack the will to use it as you used it. I don't know what mortality meant to you in your day. I don't know what it meant to you at the height of your power. It probably just meant weakness, if Avandar's experience says anything. But I am mortal. It's part of what I am. It's part of the power I have.*

It is not—

It is. Only mortals can be Sen.

The Winter King's silence was not assent, and he broke it after a significant pause. *You do not understand what it means to be Sen.*

No. But you don't, either.

No. If you wish to traverse the fire, I can take you past it.

And the others?

If necessary. Viandaran cannot be stopped or killed by so negligible a display of power; it was almost certainly set in place to trap and confine you and your less powerful companions. It would stop neither the bard nor the healer.

She stiffened at the mention of **Adam**.

I am not advising you to send him into combat; I am merely pointing out that he will survive it. What will you do?

I want to know who's controlling the fire. It's not the creature in the air.

No. If you will allow it, I will scout ahead. I will leave Adam to your care. I can bring you that information.

She didn't want the Winter King to die.

He surprised her. He laughed. *You do not understand the enchantment laid upon me. I will die with the White Lady's permission and leave, and only then. Some part of me is bound to her, and it returns to the form she gave me upon the end of my Winter reign.* He appeared some ten feet away. *What would you have me do?*

She signed to Adam, who nodded and dismounted. *Go.*

When the serpent roared a third time, no lightning left his lips—and lightning would have been preferable to what did: Kallandras heard the command in the rumbling thunder. The air upon which he balanced grew uneven—worse, it grew wild and angry.

He was familiar with the wild wind; he knew its mood well. He knew, also, that the wind would not casually destroy him unless he attempted to force it to behavior not of its own choosing. This, he did seldom for that reason. When the wind fought him, the ring that allowed his voice to be heard by the wild element burned; the diamond at its center scorched skin and flesh. He could—and had—fight through pain and injury, but it was his last choice.

His first?

Song.

The most famous bard Senniel College had ever produced—and he had no false modesty—lifted his bard-born voice in song. He did not sing for the wild element, but for the serpent whose flight and fight depended on that element as much as the bard's did.

He chose a simple song, to start. A Southern cradle song, one etched into memory by a voice he had not heard for decades, a gift given him by the talent that had defined his life, had caused his family's death, and had given him a home in Senniel.

He sang in Torra, the language of his childhood. The words themselves were containers for the power he now put into the song: he could make himself understood even if language was a barrier, not a bridge.

"Is that Kallandras?" Jewel asked Angel.

Angel nodded. He lifted his hands in den-sign; she caught the familiar movements as she glanced toward him.

"No," she agreed, her hands stiff by her sides. "It wasn't smart at all." But even saying it, she smiled.

"What is he singing?"

"A song my Oma used to sing." And of course it was never in song that her Oma's voice returned to her.

The serpent listened. It fought; the cats and the firstborn wove in and around what Kallandras assumed was the length of its body—as if they could see it. But Celleriant was now more cautious; he stood, armed and watchful.

Kallandras saw clear, cloudless blue until the serpent opened at least one set of its jaws; then he saw red and black and white, a wound in the flesh of sky. He was not surprised when the serpent roared, as if to drown out the song. Had Kallandras not been bard-born, it would have worked; he was. There was nothing, short of death, that could dampen his song if he desired it to be heard.

And he desired it. He sang.

He noted that the gray cat folded wings and plummeted toward the trees, but did not otherwise track his progress; he doubted that any of the cats could be killed by a simple fall.

"What are you *doing?*"

"Thinking of ways to strangle one of your brothers."

Shadow hissed laughter. "*She* told him to fight," he pointed out.

"And *I* told him *not* to fight."

"Sssssssoooo?" The great, gray cat snorted. "Why are *you* playing here?"

"You're playing up there."

The snort shifted into a low growl. "You *never* want *us* to have *any fun.*" He stomped toward the fire, crushing snow and dead branches. It was deliberate; he generally didn't condescend to touch the ground otherwise. Apparently, the snow made his feet wet—or cold, depending on the whining—and cats didn't *like* that.

Only when he stalked past her did Jewel realize where he was headed.

"Shadow, don't—you didn't like it when you singed your whiskers in the fire."

The cat hissed. "I liked it when the *stupid* cat singed *his* tail."

"According to you, there are no stupid cats here. What are you doing?"

The cat reached out with his left paw, claws extended. "I am telling the fire to *go away*." He roared.

The fire roared back. It was very disconcerting. "Shadow—"

"*You* should be doing this."

"I can't tell the fire what to do."

"You *can*."

"Shadow—"

"You tell *everyone* what to do!"

"Yes, but most of you don't *listen!*"

The fire, however, shocked Jewel; whatever it heard in Shadow's voice, it obeyed. As she could make sense of the roar of the creature above, she expected to make sense of Shadow's command in a similar way—but he sounded like an aggravated, giant cat to her.

This was what made the wilderness of ancient and immortal magic so bloody difficult. Nothing made sense. If there were rules to its use at all, they were rules that were invisible to the merely mortal. Regardless, the circle of fire dissipated all at once.

Avandar looked down at the gray cat. "They will know," he said quietly.

Shadow snorted and looked up at the sky. "They know we're here *anyway*." He glared at Jewel. "Why are you *standing* there?"

"We're not alone," she replied.

Shadow growled and turned in the direction that had once been guarded by a wall of fire. Standing ten yards from the great cat was a lone man.

"You are not terribly difficult to find," he said.

Shadow bunched and gathered. Jewel quickly ran forward to place a hand on the top of his head. "What *now?*" he demanded.

"Don't kill him. Don't kill him yet."

The cat yowled in outrage.

And the man's brows rose. "Well met, Jewel ATerafin. Well met."

"Are you in command of the serpent in the sky?"

"And perceptive, although that is less of a surprise. I am not, as you guess, its captain at the moment. Nor is it entirely happy to serve those who control its flight."

Avandar was almost instantly beside Jewel; she saw the flash of orange light that spoke of protection; bands of blue overlay it. She couldn't remember immediately what blue meant—it had never been used against her in any combat that also involved magic. Nor, she knew, was it relevant now. She recognized the *Kialli* lord who stood, waiting.

"And Viandaran," the man said. "Well met, indeed."

"Isladar."

"Terafin. You have had much success since our last encounter."

"If we don't count the dreaming, the last time we met, you tried to kill me."

"Indeed."

"I could forgive that," Jewel continued, her hand pressed into the top of Shadow's head. "I can't forgive the child you victimized to draw me in."

"Or the man who serves you?" He glanced at Angel, and away. Angel, whose distinctive hair was now like any other hair. Jewel was surprised Isladar recognized Angel. And yet, at the same time, unsurprised.

"The child," she replied, "had no choice. Angel was foolish; he did."

"He saved your life."

Jewel shrugged. "I'm aware of that. If the serpent is not yours, why are you here?"

"I wished to speak with you," he replied.

"And not to assassinate me?"

"Greater hands than mine have made that attempt in recent mortal months, or so rumor implies. No. The harm I feared you might do has already been done; I cannot undo it by the simple expedience of your death. Viandaran, do not make the attempt."

"If the Terafin is willing to forgive, I am not."

"You were never a forgiving man. In your youth you were the epitome of its opposite. But she is your master, and if she does not desire my destruction, you will not make the attempt." He spoke coolly, his voice shorn of doubt.

"*I* might," Shadow said, voice low.

"Eldest," Isladar replied, "I ask that you grant me mercy." He bowed—to the cat. If Jewel's jaw had not been attached to the rest of her face, she would have lost it.

This mollified Shadow—but not by much. Jewel could feel the tension beneath her palm.

"Eldest, I did not know that you would become her companion. I would not have raised hand against her had I understood her import."

He was lying. Jewel knew it immediately; she was certain Shadow did as well. But the cats were particularly vulnerable to flattery. Shadow, the tactician, was no exception. "Why are you here?" she asked.

"I did not lie. I am here to speak with you, for however long you allow. You are aware that you are in danger here—although it was never danger to yourself that formed the core of your intent. Kiriel is not with you." It was not a question.

Jewel answered it anyway. "No. She was AKalakar, not ATerafin, but she remained in the South at the end of the war."

He nodded as if this was not a surprise; Jewel doubted it was.

"Do you see it, Viandaran?" Isladar asked, looking up to the sky, his lips curved in a smile that was too cold to be nostalgic, but implied nostalgia anyway.

Avandar did not reply. Jewel glanced at Angel; he was armed with a dagger. An ornate, consecrated dagger. What Jewel was willing to forgive, Angel was not. She signed. His hands remained still; his expression made clear his intent. But she trusted him; he would not move unless she commanded—or at least allowed—it.

Isladar frowned. "Is that Calliastra?" His voice was sharper, the edges more apparent.

"It is," Jewel replied.

Her voice pulled his gaze from the vault of sky. "You are still determined to shelter the children of your greatest enemy."

"Calliastra isn't Kiriel. She doesn't need shelter."

"No. I had thought you wiser than this. She will be your death, or the deaths of those you protect." He paused, and then, to Jewel's surprise, said, "What of Ariel?"

It was easy to forget, in this winter place, the maimed Voyani child Isladar had abandoned on the edge of the Sea of Sorrows. Adam had taken care of Ariel, and Shadow had tolerated her remarkably well—but she remained in the Terafin manse, under the watchful eyes of the rest of the den—men and women who did not have a single child between them.

"She is safe."

Shadow growled, then. Before Jewel could finish drawing breath, he lunged for the *Kialli* lord who had almost broken Kiriel di'Ashaf. Kiriel, Jewel thought dispassionately, who had both hated and loved him. She *knew* then that Isladar's fate was not in her hands, but in Kiriel's. Jewel's near-death was not personal in the sense that Isladar cared one way or the other about it; it was merely another tool in a demon's arsenal.

He had meant to hurt Kiriel. To hurt her and, in a perverse, demonic way, to protect her.

Isladar was not a fool; he was yards away from where Shadow landed, and he moved damned fast.

"She is not *yours*," Shadow growled. He had crushed snow and broken the branches that sheltered beneath the winter blanket.

Isladar looked genuinely surprised. "Ariel is mortal," he told the great, gray cat, as if that fact would not be obvious to him.

"She is *not yours*," the cat replied, and leaped again, without visible warning.

Isladar leaped as well. All of his movements were defensive; he made no attempt to harm Shadow. All of the aggression at the moment was squarely in the gray cat's court. "This is unwise," he told Shadow, as Shadow once again broke the crust of ancient snow and ice with the full force of his landing weight. "I am not your enemy here, but enemies gather; they search. You were clever; the fire is gone, and there is no clear direction for the breach—but they will find you if you continue."

Above, the serpent roared.

"They will *not*," Shadow growled. "There is *too much* noise." He gathered himself again, but this time, Jewel had had enough.

"Shadow!"

The cat hissed his displeasure.

"He is not wrong. We do not know what we face here—but we'd like to avoid it. You'll survive. Some of us won't."

Shadow's expression immediately sank into the exaggerated lines of cat sulking. He tossed his head back and forth and expelled a litany of sibilants, most of which were wrapped around the word "stupid." This, Jewel could live with.

Isladar could live with it as well; he didn't even seem to be surprised by it.

I agree with your cat, Avandar said grimly. *This is not wise.*

You think he's lying?

No. I think truth, in this case, is irrelevant. Of the Kialli, he is the most opaque, to me. He cares little for the dignity that even Calliastra maintains; he is willing to bend—to bow—to your cats. I do not think it would matter which of the three. He is willing to speak with you, treat with you, as if you were an equal. You do not understand the threat in this.

No, I really don't.

He would be considered dangerously insane by his own kin.

"Lord Isladar, I will speak with you if you will answer one question."

"And that?"

"In the air above us, in which the combat so far has been largely contained, there is a woman upon the back of my white cat. I do not know if you can see her from this distance."

"With effort—and without the intervention of your gray cat—I can. Your question?"

"Do you recognize her?"

Isladar glanced at Avandar. "Did you, Warlord?" His question was cool, casual.

"No."

"And yet, your lord expects that I might?"

"I have not asked; I am not privy to all of her thoughts or her moods."

"But you suffer them, regardless?" Isladar's smile was thin, but genuine. "I understand mortals as well as any of the kin." The kin, Jewel thought. Not my kin. "I raised one from birth."

She stiffened. The words that came to mind, she kept to herself, although it was hard. She could not imagine a demon raising a mortal child—even a child like Kiriel. And yet, Kiriel was demonstrably alive. She understood why a demon might—just might—keep Kiriel alive. But Ariel was, as he himself told Shadow, a mortal child. There was nothing about her at all that made her remarkable; she might be food for demons, but no more.

And yet, Ariel was also alive.

"Yes," Jewel said quietly, "you did. You did not raise Ariel."

"No. I . . . found her. She was surprisingly costly, to me. Tell me, Terafin, would you throw away your House to protect the life of a cat?"

Shadow growled.

"Eldest," Isladar replied, bowing. "I speak of mortal cats, as you must well know. Your preservation is not in the hands of The Terafin."

Jewel said, "I don't like cats, much. Even if I did, no. No, I would not." And she thought of Carver, and she stilled. "Not cats."

Isladar's gaze fell immediately to Jewel, and it remained there for a long, long beat—as if he knew. And, of course, she thought, he did. He couldn't know what caused the pain—beyond the fact that it wasn't him—but he could sense the pain itself. It was what demons *did*.

"You have grown," Isladar said quietly. "You are not, now, what you were when last we met, and even for mortals, the time between has been almost insignificant." He offered her the same bow as he had offered Shadow, which struck her, of all things, as funny.

She kept this off her face, as well. "My question?"

With effort he looked away, toward the aerial combat. "It is difficult to see much; I do not believe Calliastra is best pleased to have your cats as comrades."

Once again, he smiled. "But it is rare to see her so unaffected. She lacks caution, here. Any of those who now hunt you will recognize her the moment they lift eyes, if they are old enough. I would not be surprised if she is conversing—in a fashion—with at least one of them, even as she fights. She is not, I think, angry. Not yet."

"She's *always* angry," Shadow said, unwilling to be left out entirely.

Isladar said, "To the *Kialli*, what she feels is not anger."

"*You* are *always angry*," Shadow replied.

Isladar raised a brow, although he had not once looked down. His eyes narrowed; his lips pursed in a brief, slender frown. His expression was human and familiar, which put Jewel instantly on her guard.

She remained there when he whispered a single, long word. "Shandalli-aran." But she looked away. She had to look away. Something in his face was too bright, too *open*, to countenance for long.

"So," he said softly. "It has come to pass." He lifted a hand, as if in greeting, or as if to grasp this one glimpse of a distant, perfect woman.

"She is mortal," Jewel told him, gentling her voice.

"She would have to be. Even from this distance, I can see that she is pregnant." He closed his eyes; closed, he could then turn again to Jewel. "You are unkind," he said; it sounded like praise. "I would not have thought it of you, when first we met."

"Is it unkind to give some sort of warning?" she asked.

"Perhaps not. The bearer of bad news, among the kin, offers that news with some pleasure."

"I don't consider mortality a besetting sin or weakness."

"Ah, no. Of course not. You are one. But mortality—to us—means many things. Mortality is loss, Terafin. Mortality is always loss. One cannot capture a mortal in time unless one chooses to kill them, and even then, one discovers that much is lost. It is why those who kept mortals in a time when the Cities of Man were at the height of their power were considered at best strange. What we conquer, we keep—but we cannot keep you for long and every day is surrendered to time." He lifted his chin, opened his eyes, and said, "I would not be here when she lands—but curiosity was *my* besetting sin. I wish to know how much she has changed; how much she has retained, and how much she has cast aside."

Jewel said, softly, "Are those who hunt us now *Kialli*?"

"Yes, Terafin. It is possible you will recognize one or two, but perhaps not. Their presence in your world and their presence here differs, often greatly."

"You appear the same, to me."

"Yes. I have that ability—but it is not trivial. We were not meant to return. When we do, the plane surrenders form and flesh for our use—but never willingly. We anger the earth, the water, and the air; if we have power and will, we can force them to obedience—but we cannot easily cajole or ask. And that is not why I came." Almost, he turned to the sky again.

"Would she recognize the *Kialli*?"

His eyes narrowed. "You have spoken to her at length."

"I have listened where she is willing to speak, yes. She has been willing to speak with us."

"She seeks the Winter Queen."

Jewel saw no point in lying. "Yes."

"You do not understand what you have set in motion."

"I set nothing in motion. I am not the father of the child."

Irritation changed the cast of his features. "She is here. You are here. The overlap cannot be coincidental. I do not believe that you understood what you were doing; no more do I believe you understand it now. But you have changed, in one motion, the entire face of one long, long game. You understand only in part who she is.

"But understanding who she was and how she came to be here is more relevant. I should not have come," he added. "There is enough, here, to confound my brothers should they do as I have done."

"And that?"

"Look," he replied. "Observe."

"She has not encountered the *Kialli* before. If they are old enough, she might know them."

"Yes." His smile was sharp and therefore felt more familiar. "You called her mortal. She is not, however, as you are. She is not as Viandaran is. There is no place in Mandaros' long hall for one such as she."

Without thinking, Jewel said, "And her child?"

"That would be the question," he replied.

"Why did you come?"

"To offer you safe passage, for a time," he replied.

"You tried to kill me."

"Yes. As I said, your death, now, would serve no purpose. I *am* of my kin. If your death was painful and extended, it would offer me sustenance—but it is not a sustenance I require. Kiriel is not part of this game."

"Which game is she part of?"

He smiled. He did not answer.

Jewel.

I don't trust him.

Of course not. What he wants, almost by definition, is not what you want. But if he intended to lead you into a trap, you would know. Does he?

. . . No. It was a grudging admission. *Not me.*

Kiriel is not here. She is not, as he said, part of this particular game. Nothing you say or do at the moment will either protect or harm her.

He will. He'll do both. And saying it, even privately, she *knew* it for truth. *He only tried to kill me to hurt her.*

Yes. And he is Kialli.

Did you know him?

No. In my youth, the Kialli did not exist.

But you knew Meralonne.

There were very few powers who did not know the four Princes of the White Lady by name, if not on sight. On sight, it was easy to mistake one for the other. If you do not trust him—wisely—he has offered an alliance of a sort. I would consider accepting it.

"What game, Isladar? You serve the Lord of the Hells. Nothing he wants is anything *I* want, and if he perished tomorrow, I'd celebrate with the full financial backing of my House. I'd line the streets with banners and open the stalls in the Common to anyone who was hungry for at least a full three days. I am, in any small way I can be, your lord's enemy."

"Yes. And sadly, it is, at the moment, a very small way. I want *war,* Terafin. I want war, and to have a war, there must *be* powers that can stand in opposition. As you are now, you will be crushed beneath my lord's feet."

Jewel's hands formed tighter fists.

"He may—or may not—notice you before your death. That is all."

"I've survived stronger *Kialli* than you."

Do not let him provoke you, two voices said simultaneously.

"Yes. You have survived. But we have never been free to act with full power in your mortal city. Here, we are not so constrained."

"Neither," Jewel said quietly, "are we. If you have constraints, so do we. We don't want to turn our city into rubble. We don't want to kill people who have none of the obvious power that we've gathered here. Our hands are just as tied as your own."

One brow rose as he considered her words. "Perhaps," he said, the single word smooth and uninflected. "Will you now abandon your companions to their aerial battle?"

The serpent roared, as if in response; Kallandras was no longer singing.

"How are they controlling the serpent?" she asked.

"Carelessly." Isladar's frown shifted the lines of his face; he looked colder and far more autocratic. "The serpents are old and wild; they are not, however, earth or air. They can be reasoned with; they are willing to negotiate."

"What have you offered it?"

His smile, on the other hand, was beautiful. Jewel thought all deadly things were, in their own fashion: they were compelling because they were dangerous. "Freedom, Terafin."

"He seems pretty free, here."

"Yes. To you, it would seem so. But these lands are not your lands. It may surprise you, but the wilderness is like an echo of the world in which mortals have been left on their own. Pockets of landscape, pockets of geology, pockets of weather. Each domain its own. Some are claimed, Terafin; some are not. The only place they once met was in the lands you now call the world.

"Those lands were the backbone of the ancient. They were, in their entirety, the crossroads between the various enclaves. The old bindings are crumbling; they have promised the serpent that he will be—finally—free to roam as he pleases, unconfined by the walls the gods put in place before they withdrew."

Avandar, is this true?

It is not the whole of the truth—but the whole of the truth would take you years to understand; it is materially correct.

Then how in the hells are we to find *the Hidden Court? How are we to reach Ariane?*

As if he could hear the question she would not ask out loud, Isladar said, "I am here. To venture here, I came from lands you yourself might once have traversed; to leave, I will return to them—as will you, if you survive. If I am not mistaken, you will seek other remote locations in the wilderness.

"Understand that they are not all one thing, and not all the other—but to find them, you will have to touch—at least peripherally—the lands in which mortals now reside. Once," he added softly, "before the worlds were sundered, all lands overlapped." His smile was cold and unpleasant. "But when they did, mortals perished. Their existence was confined to small enclaves; they were pets. Much like the pets mortals now keep—your cats, your dogs, your birds—they were cherished by those who sheltered them. Those that were not so lucky died.

"And died, Terafin. Only in the Cities of Man did mortality flourish—but even there, life for those on the ground was difficult and short."

"Not much different in our own cities." Jewel was stiff, now. Bending would have probably broken her.

"It was very, very different. Men lived, in those days, by the rules that govern all races."

"Power," was her flat reply.

"Indeed."

She had seen, in Avandar's dreams, some of the Cities of Man, and she didn't doubt him. She thought she would have *hated* those cities, had she lived during their reign.

This amused the Winter King, who agreed with her assessment.

"What will you do? You have come to find the Oracle. My brethren have come to stop you."

"Do they know that they're hunting me, personally?"

"Yes. You were unwise in your display of raw power in your capital. They do not believe that you can stand against them unless you undergo the Oracle's test. They do not," he added, "understand the test itself."

"And you?"

"I believe that you could, indeed, thwart us without confronting the Oracle. I have studied mortals for much of my life; I understand why, as a body, they are insignificant, but it is never wise to dismiss them all out of hand. They believe that the Oracle will give you what you require."

"And you do not."

"No." He bowed again, which surprised her. "If reports are to be believed—and I am not privy to the reports directly—you are Sen, Terafin. I believe that my brethren have miscalculated here. They do not want the Cities of Man to rise again. Effort has been expended—fruitlessly—to make certain that does not happen. You are aware of one such failure."

She said nothing.

"But they do not understand *why* your ascension would serve as an advantage to us. They think that they can stop the Sleepers from waking."

She was cold. She was so cold.

"Ah, yes. You are aware that your fragile, mortal city will not survive such a waking. We, of course, do not care. But the Sleepers were a danger when they walked the world; they will be a danger if they walk again. The Cities of Man were proof against even gods at the height of their power. Or some of the Cities were; you will not, of course, know of those whose ambitions overreached their abilities.

"Nor is it relevant. I believe you have the ability to protect your city should the Sleepers wake in its midst—but it will be costly. I do not believe you can do *that* without the Oracle's guidance. You hope to avoid paying her price," he added, and again, he smiled. "You are mortal. You have lived in a barren, powerless world—and that is changing, even as we speak."

The serpent roared again.

Shadow hissed.

"You disagree, Eldest? I mean to give her warning, no more. I am *Kialli*. You will, of course, fail to trust me; all of my words will be suspect. But I offer advice—and no comfort. Power in the ancient world always demanded a price. Mortals were oft foolish in their attempt to transfer their accrued debt. I believe some of your stories still exist, but if you will not seek them out, let me tell you that those attempts did not work out well—either for the mortals or those they hoped to sacrifice in their own stead.

"Power has a price. See it. Pay it. Or walk away from the power you require." He bowed again.

"Why are you doing this?" Jewel demanded. "What advantage do you hope to gain?"

"I did not lie; I want war. We will be enemies in the future, as we have been in the past; my goals and your goals can never, in the end, be the same. But I am in your debt."

Jewel folded arms. She did not, and would never, trust the man who stood, silent and without the obvious arrogance that graced most immortals—even the stag—but he wasn't lying. "You are so not in my debt."

"I had nowhere else to leave the child."

"How did she even—"

"It is of no material consequence. She came into my keeping; I agreed to keep her safe. I could not, in the end, achieve that in the Shining City. I could not take her to Kiriel, for reasons that I am certain are obvious. I could leave her nowhere else."

"Why do you care?"

"Does it matter?"

"Yes."

He met, and held, her unblinking gaze. "Understand that the *Kialli* do not condescend to truth; it is a vulnerability, a weakness."

Jewel waited.

"I am not like my kin. I remember, Terafin. I remember much. I do not know why it is of import to me; I have no plans for the child, and see no future for her but the future that plagues the mortal races; she will age, she will die, and she will be unremembered. She will make no mark of greatness in the future. She will influence no great powers, and play no role in the war to come. She is unlikely to survive that war at all, as it currently stands. She is missing fingers. She was, from all accounts, the scion of poor, but free, clansmen.

"There is nothing in her that is relevant at all."

"You saved her."

"Yes." He smiled. The smile did not suit the cast of his features; Jewel found it disturbing, although she couldn't say why. He looked, once, again, toward the sky, as lightning changed its color. "I told you: mortals, your distant kin, were very much like the pets adopted by mortals now; they are like your horses. No, they are like your cats. They have no utility on the surface—and possibly no utility beneath it, as well. The most powerful of mortals might own such creatures; they are irrationally fond of them, for no obvious reason.

"It is my suspicion that Ariel is much like a cat, and I, like the mortals who might own them in your lands. I cannot, however, say with any certainty; I studied mortals, but I did not attempt to imitate them."

"So your answer is: you don't know."

"Indeed."

She exhaled. "Ariel doesn't belong with you."

"No. That is why she is currently in your keeping. Or in the keeping of your den. You will not take her on the road to war while your home is left standing. Does it surprise you that I have a similar inclination?"

It did. Nothing about the *Kialli* lord in front of her made sense to Jewel. Not even the fact that, inasmuch as her gift could determine, he spoke truth.

"Let me *eat* him," Shadow growled.

"You won't like the taste. He'll just turn into dust and ash in your mouth."

The great, gray cat snarled. In as low a voice as he ever used, he said, "But he will *bleed* first."

"Doesn't matter. The rest of it will be ash, and you've tried that once."

"That was *Snow!* Snow is *stupid!*"

Isladar raised a single brow. Although he didn't appear to be watching the cat, Jewel was certain he was aware of the movement of every, single one of Shadow's whiskers. "Yes," she said quietly.

Shadow yowled in outrage. "We don't *need* him!"

"Do you mean the Sleepers to wake?" she continued, over the caterwauling of angry cat.

Isladar joined her, but began to walk. "Can you speak with your companions in the air?"

"I can send Shadow."

"I won't *go*." This verged on growl. He did not like Isladar.

The serpent roared. The ground shook. The tremors continued when the roar itself was no longer even an echo. Shadow fell silent, then. Everyone standing on the ground did.

"Please don't tell me," Jewel said quietly, "that the earth is waking."

Isladar's smile was cool. "It is not yet awake. But if you will accept my help, we must leave this place. I can no longer safely fight on the ground—nor can any of my kin." He glanced once at the sky. "The serpent is not *Kialli*. He is not of the dead. The wilderness hears his voice when he chooses to speak with it at all.

"It hears ours," he added, as he picked up the pace without apparent effort, "and it attempts, where it can, to destroy us; we are no longer of this world. The elements took our choice as desertion and betrayal—and they are not the only ones."

"It is possible you will not be the safest of guides," Avandar said.

Isladar smiled. "If I cannot cajole the earth as I once did, I can speak in such a way that the earth does not immediately attempt my destruction. It was," he added softly, "the work of silent decades."

"Decades that your comrades have not spent."

"No. Where rejected, they reject—or destroy. The earth, of course, cannot be destroyed; it can be subjugated."

"Not easily."

"Of course not. But where things come easily, they are not, in the end, of value. Not to you, Warlord. Nor to me. I can pass above the restless earth; I can silence my voice and my presence. But I cannot fight with any power. Nor can my kin—but they are likely to survive the waking earth. Some of you will not." He froze as a roar once again broke the stillness of sky above.

This roar was higher; it didn't sound like a force of nature; it contained too many syllables.

A name, Jewel thought. And she recognized it.

Isladar's smile deepened, sharpened. "They have seen her. I do not know your intent in this, Terafin—but you chose well. We are *Kialli*. We remember."

Above them, in the air, Shianne replied. She spoke, as the first voice had, and there was as much pain, as much surprise, in the names she called.

"But memory, in the end, is not as visceral as experience. Knowledge at a distance is a dull shock, a dull pain, in comparison." His smile deepened. "You cannot feel what they feel."

"No. I can . . . hear it."

"It is not the same. This, Terafin, is what we have become; it is one of the few pleasures left to those who must mind and tend the Hells. Even the pain of our own kin feeds us. Remember this."

"Isladar?"

"We must run," he replied.

"Would she recognize you?"

"After this day," he said, "I do not think she will recognize any of the kin should you encounter them again. Our choice—such as it was—would be an unthinkable betrayal to her, and she is encountering that grief and that loss for the first time."

"*We* told *her*," Shadow growled.

"Yes, Eldest. But rumor, while painful, does not have the teeth of truth."

Shadow would not leave.

"I need someone in the air. I need you to carry a message—and I need you to lead them to us when—and if—we find safe harbor."

Shadow could converse—as most Immortals could—in any language known to man. Certainly in any language known to Jewel. He failed to understand the words, while simultaneously finding them insulting.

The Winter King quietly rejoined the group. *There is no fire in the direction you are heading; there are no demons.*

Good. I need you to join the rest in the air.

You could force the cat to your will, the great stag said, with only a trace of his usual disgust. He was—there was no other word for it—excited, somehow. Born mortal, he had become something other. Or perhaps that otherness had always existed at his core; Jewel didn't know how a Winter King was chosen. She had never asked.

Nor did she ask now. *Yes,* she replied, rescuing the packs the Winter King so effortlessly carried. *I could. But it's costly, and he'll sulk for days. I don't think we can afford that.*

You do not want to suborn his will to yours.

She didn't, but changed tactics. *You want to be there,* she told the Winter King. *And I need someone to be there. Go.*

I cannot speak as your Shadow speaks.

You're smart enough to make yourself understood. When we come to harbor—if there is one to be found—you'll have to lead the others to where I am. There's no one in the sky now who won't be able to follow you.

And you?

We're following the demon, she replied. *He doesn't intend us harm.*

He will not fight if harm presents itself.

For us? Probably not. But given anything else we're likely to encounter, I'll take the lack of intent. Go.

The Winter King was not Shadow. He obeyed.

Jewel didn't count steps. She had no idea how long she'd run—only that she had run, one heavy pack strapped to her back. Shadow hissed and growled when she'd saddled him, metaphorically, with the others. What was good enough for the Winter King was clearly very far beneath him.

"You could have joined your brothers," she told him, while he tore new runnels in the ground. "But no—I had to send the Winter King."

"And the Winter King obeyed you," Isladar noted. "You have indeed traveled interesting paths since last we met."

"Yes. And none of them managed to kill me, either." She finished buckling a slender strap around Shadow's underbelly, and rose. Isladar began, at once, to run. It wasn't a sprint—he set a pace that Jewel could match. But as distance grew, the pace became punishing.

She listened as she ran, her breath escaping slightly open lips in a thin, pale stream. The earth's rumble shifted, and after a long stretch, stilled.

But the creature roared again, and echoes of his voice remained beneath her feet when the voice itself fell silent.

She had seen what the earth could do. She had marveled at it. But she knew that earth, awake, here, would be deadly: the bard and Celleriant could not easily maintain their footing in an air made wilder by anger.

She turned to shout a warning to Kallandras and stopped. She wasn't bard-born. If she could—somehow—make herself heard, she would be heard by all: her companions and the enemies who had erected a slender barrier of fire to trap her here. Had she been alone, she would have done it, regardless—but she wasn't.

She had never wanted to be alone again. She'd built a life, with all its resultant compromises, that ensured that she wouldn't be. And those compromises stung now. What she might survive—on instinct, on talent—Angel would not. Neither, she thought, would Terrick—although she felt a twinge of something that disagreed with that assessment. She didn't question it. Didn't evaluate it.

Avandar wouldn't die. He was the only man here who would greet death with joy.

I would prefer the passage to be as painless as possible, he replied, a hint of dry humor in the words.

I need Kallandras to speak—

No, Terafin. No, Jewel. He cannot safely do so from the air—if he can do so at all. His command of the one element is a gift of the ring he now wears—a ring that cannot be transferred or removed except at his death. If then.

I don't need him to speak to the earth. *I need him to sing to the serpent.*

Ah. That, I can tell him.

She didn't even ask how. She merely cursed herself for not speaking sooner. She had never ascertained the full range of Avandar's capabilities—in part because she was certain he would hide most of them behind pretty—or angry—lies. She regretted it, now.

Isladar's stride had widened; the pace he set went from uncomfortable to painful. Jewel sensed no pursuit; if demons were present, she thought their full attention must be, in the end, upon the serpent and Calliastra—her form, the full shadowed width and breadth of her wingspan, was visible in a way the serpent, strictly speaking, was not.

Shianne's voice cut across all roaring—serpent or cat. It was as strong, as clear, as pure as Kallandras' voice, when raised in bardic song.

It stopped even Isladar in his tracks; Jewel knew, because she ran into the stiff, hard line of his back.

Shadow hissed laughter. Jewel almost kicked him. She moved to the side to avoid contact with the demon lord, and saw, for a moment, his expression: the width of his eyes, and the slow way they closed; the stiffness of his arms and the shudder that took his hands before he curled them into fists.

She had never seen a demon in pain, before.

"No," Isladar said quietly. "Our own pain does not feed us, except in one way." His hands remained fists as he turned, again, to look at the height of the contested skies, where every voice but one, and one alone, fell silent. Not even the serpent roared, Shianne's voice was so powerful.

Jewel couldn't understand a word of the song itself. Not a syllable. And she was grateful for her ignorance, because tone alone conveyed too much. She didn't cry in public, but regardless, tears escaped her eyes—nor did she attempt to brush them away, to deny them.

Because to deny them was to deny Shianne when she exposed a part of herself that Jewel would *never* have willingly exposed to any—not even her den.

She was surprised when voices joined Shianne's. The first, she recognized instantly. Shadow. It would have been hard to miss, because he'd come to stand on her right foot. His singing voice resembled the voice one might expect from a yowling cat—at least in texture. But it managed, in spite of that, to contain actual notes.

Snow and Night joined him from on high.

And then, surrendering for a moment to the force of Shianne's stark voice, Isladar smiled. It was a bitter expression that spoke of loss—but more, it spoke of resignation that had once again slipped away, revealing everything that could not be accepted: loss, death, consequence.

He sang.

He sang, and had they been running, it would have been Jewel who would have frozen midstep, as if running or walking—or even breathing—consumed too much will, too much thought.

She saw him—before she turned away—not as demon lord, not as *Kialli*. Nor did she see him as Arianni, although the resemblance was there. She saw him, instead, as ghost, the grief of past losses too overwhelming to be laid to rest.

And if this ghost was deadly—and he was, as were all of his kin—if he could destroy the living, in this one simple moment, that almost made sense. Grief could, and did, destroy the living if the living couldn't somehow make peace with it.

But there was no peace to be made with this grief: it was too raw, too new, too fresh. It invoked loss in a way that even Lefty's death had not. She felt slight, insignificant, almost invisible, as he joined voice to Shianne's.

And he was not the only one. Although she could not see them, could not pin direction from the sound of their voices, they joined him: his kin, his brethren, the demons he meant to betray by leading her through this gauntlet of trap and death.

She wondered, then, as she would wonder in future, what love meant to demons. She had seen his hand in Kiriel, and it was dark and scarring. But she could not imagine pain such as this coming from that place. She could not imagine that Isladar could grieve—truly grieve—Kiriel's loss; Kiriel was pawn or Queen in a game of complicated chess.

He would never sing for Kiriel as he sang, in this single moment, for Shianne. But he *could* sing thus; it was humbling. She bowed her head; she meant to give him privacy, the sense of awe was so large.

But she had no time for privacy, because she understood what this song— what this complicated, terrible outpouring was: a gift of time. She did not touch or approach Isladar; she did not speak to him. She signed to Angel, and Angel passed word to Terrick; she signed to Adam and he joined her. Avandar nodded.

They began to move.

Shadow slapped the demon lord with his right wing.

The humility, the grace, the respect that Isladar had offered Shadow was entirely absent as he turned in sudden rage, lifting an arm. To it came sword: red sword.

"You will *wake* the *earth*," the cat growled. He did not seem particularly intimidated by either the weapon or the rage itself. For one long second, Jewel thought the earth no longer mattered to Isladar. The earth, his chosen mission, his game—all were dwarfed by the enormity of the experience and the memory that he had almost involuntarily chosen to honor.

But the sword wavered as Lord Isladar's arm fell, once again, to the side; it was gone between one blink and the next. He retreated from a song that had not ended. "We are *Kialli*," he said, his voice remote. "We remember. But we choose the memories that we honor in the end, and there are some to which we do not return." He whispered her name, raising his face as if he could see hers, at this distance.

Chapter Twenty-Three

15th of Morel, 428 A.A.
Terafin Manse, Averalaan Aramarelas

"**I** NEED TO MEET WITH JARVEN."

Jester's brows bunched together over the bridge of a lightly freckle-dusted nose. He didn't bother to lose the expression; he was speaking with Birgide. If the expression had hit his face—and it had—it had already been noticed. As Jester was famously lazy, he refused to put effort into what was already pointless.

Birgide, however, had become strange. In the past few days, he'd noted a shift in her personality. This took no effort; he was certain even those who paid passing attention would note the difference. She was not exactly open; she was neither welcoming nor friendly. But there was a difference in the wall of her face; a window had been constructed.

Or an arrow slit.

"Why do you need to meet with Jarven?" he asked, looking at the surface of his drink—which was receding rapidly.

"You don't trust him." Birgide's reply was about as informative as Haval's generally were.

"No."

"Why?"

"Clearly you've never met the man." And thinking of Haval, Jester rose. "What happened in *Avantari*?"

Birgide smiled. "I planted *Ellariannatte* in the Courtyard gardens, and they grew."

"Tell me they didn't grow the way the trees in our gardens did."

"I have no idea how the trees in your garden were planted; I cannot say that with any certainty. They grew, however, as fast."

"Do you want a drink?"

"No, thank you. I can drink, but dislike the taste of alcohol."

"Must have made you great fun at parties."

"It wasn't a job requirement."

Thinking of Duvari, Jester grimaced. "Given your boss, I'm not surprised. He probably chooses for lack of great fun. Or any fun."

"Fun is not one of his criteria, no. On the other hand, he doesn't require the obliteration of either charm or sense of humor. Where are you going?"

"It's a conversation I'm going to have to repeat, and I don't have your training. I'll botch something."

"Repeat?" Her expression cooled, but Jester couldn't pinpoint the changes that gave him that impression.

"Yes. To Haval. If you feel you will be constrained by his presence, he is a simple tailor."

She lifted a brow. "What position does he hold within Terafin?"

"He's a tailor. You may have heard of him—but then again, maybe not. Being a tailor isn't a front, as far as I can tell. And frankly, I can't. But he's known Jay for half her life. She trusts him."

"You don't?"

"I don't trust anyone. I distrust Jarven." He exhaled as he reached the great room's closed door. "But you'd be hard-pressed to find anyone who would support Jay in the same way."

"And me?"

"I trust you more now than I did two days ago."

"I have not been dismissed from service."

"You couldn't have been."

"Oh?"

"You're demonstrably not dead."

She did smile, then. "I am willing to speak in the presence of Haval."

"You know something about him I don't?"

"I know that he was allowed to find me in the forest."

Haval was sewing when Jester interrupted him. He looked up. "Well?"

"She wants to talk to Jarven." This pronouncement had no notable effect on the tailor's demeanor.

"Why?"

"She hasn't said."

"What did she say?"

"That I didn't trust him."

"Ah." Although the room was a sea of tailoring chaos, Haval himself was fastidious in the care with which he set aside his work. He was aproned, and did not choose to divest himself of that. "She is in the great room?"

Jester nodded.

"You are not, of course, telling me everything you know."

"I'm not in the mood for tests today."

"Or ever?"

"Or, generally, ever, yes. You're nothing but a constant test—a battery of tests. If you feel the need to test someone, you can work on her."

"You expect me to work with her."

"Yes."

"Why?"

Jester exhaled. "Because she's the chosen guardian of the forest."

"Chosen?"

"It's complicated."

"Of course it is." Haval waited, his posture perfect and almost without character.

Jester hadn't lied; he was not in the mood for tests. "I'm to lunch with Marrick today, if you recall."

The clothier condescended to nod.

"At your suggestion."

"It was not a suggestion. Birgide?"

Jester exhaled. He then told Haval what had occurred in the Terafin forest. Haval listened without comment—and without expression. Only when he was certain Jester was done did he nod.

"Very well. I will speak with Birgide." The hint of a smile shifted the corners of his mouth. "I imagine Duvari will be ill-pleased."

"At her?"

"That requires no imagination whatsoever. I thought you disliked the Lord of the Compact."

"Anyone sane does."

"Ah. A pity; you are certain to be seeing far more of him in the near future."

They found Birgide by the fireplace; she appeared to be inspecting the mantel. Nor did she leave off that inspection when the door both opened—and closed—as they entered. Jester immediately walked to the cabinet which housed alcohol meant to entertain guests. As he opened the door, he thought of Ellerson; as he closed it, his thoughts strayed to Carver.

He didn't want them to stay there; he picked up the two drinks, glanced once at a tray, and shrugged. Neither Haval nor Birgide were guests, and Birgide wasn't drinking anyway.

"You delivered my message," Haval said. He took an armchair as the question—which was not actually a question—drew Birgide's attention away from her inspection.

She nodded. "There is surprisingly little information about you in the palace archives."

"You checked."

"I made that attempt. I did not have time to be more thorough, and I may be denied access to the full archives in future."

"A fair precaution."

She took the chair across from Haval. Her posture implied business.

"You have stated a wish to meet with Jarven ATerafin."

Birgide nodded. "Wish is perhaps the wrong word. I believe what I said was that I need to speak with him."

"Curious. Why?"

She met, and held Haval's gaze. The intensity of the scrutiny on either side bored Jester to tears. "I seek information."

Jester almost choked. "You'll get, at best, half of what you want—and probably the useless half."

Haval glanced in his direction. "While overly dramatic, Jester is essentially correct. You will not obtain useful information from Jarven unless you have information to trade—and even then, there is no guarantee. The information must have some amusement value, or some relevance to his interests. I assume you have no obvious merchant connections through which you might push."

Birgide nodded.

"You cannot use Duvari as a conduit or a threat; Jarven is perhaps one of a handful of men in the Empire who does not consider the Lord of the Compact—or his many *Astari*—a danger. On the wrong day, he finds Duvari an irritant; on the right day, he finds him an amusement. He will give Duvari nothing, or less than nothing."

Birgide exhaled. "That is unfortunate. Jarven, however, is one of two men who might lead me to the information I seek. I assumed, as Jarven is ATerafin, that he would be easier to approach."

Jester coughed again.

Haval frowned. "And the other?"

"Hectore of Araven."

"Hectore of Araven is generally the more approachable of the two. He does not condescend to fake extreme age or its inevitable effects."

"Will he see me?"

"I am not his personal secretary; I cannot, of course, say. If, however, he agrees to any meeting, this will pique Jarven's curiosity, and he may allow a meeting to satisfy it. Why these two men?"

Birgide glanced at Jester. Jester almost missed it.

But the question in that glance surprised him enough that he considered it with care. He didn't particularly care for Haval, but considered him almost trustworthy; he understood that there was some history between the tailor and Jarven ATerafin that was almost certain to remain hidden. He knew that Haval's former profession did not involve selling expensive dresses to the moneyed—but everyone had a past.

"Inasmuch as any man in Terafin—outside of the den and the Chosen—can be trusted, it's Haval. He's a bit like Duvari, but Haval, at least, is rumored to have a sense of humor. He will do nothing to harm The Terafin or her chosen causes; he will, at best, absent himself from those he disagrees with. If you're concerned for The Terafin's security, don't be.

"If you're worried about Duvari, on the other hand, I've got nothing."

Birgide surprised both men present; she closed her eyes. It was a full minute before she opened them again. "I spoke with Cormaris."

Haval's left brow rose.

"Cormaris spoke of the Sleepers and their heralds."

Jester rose, picked up his empty glass, and headed to the cabinet for a refill. Back to the room's other occupants, he said, "Will they wake any time soon?"

"According to the god, yes. You don't seem surprised."

Jester shrugged. "Did he happen to give any hints how we might stop them?"

"You aren't surprised."

He drank. "I'd like to be, if that counts."

"Do you have any idea where they are?"

Jester didn't answer. Birgide accepted his silence.

"The god spoke of heralds."

"Makes sense. The Sleepers were—when awake at the dawn of time—four

Princes of the Hidden Court. Having heralds wouldn't be much of a stretch. Did the god say the heralds would be responsible for waking them?"

"Not in so many words. He seemed to feel we could delay their waking by confusing or misdirecting the heralds."

"Did the god say who these heralds are?"

"No. If they're coming now, my best guess is that they are not mortal. But I believe Cormaris feels it's only a matter of time—and no, before you ask, I didn't ask how much time. I'm not sure gods experience time the way the rest of us do.

"He cautioned me—us—against trusting or relying on Meralonne APhaniel."

Jester poured, emptied his glass, and poured again. "Did he say why?"

"I didn't understand the full import of his answer, no. He seemed to expect that the mage would somehow change. Meralonne has always been chaotic."

"I don't suppose Duvari has actually discussed this with the Guildmaster of the Order of Knowledge."

"Not in my presence." Birgide's smile was slight. "If I am not actually present, Duvari does not consider the knowledge to be of relevance to my duties—and no one asks Duvari for information, regardless. If the guild-master feels that Meralonne will remain reliable, which Cormaris considered a remote possibility, he said that Meralonne could not stand forever against the three. But he also said that there was one other in the city who might be of aid in preserving *Averalaan* should the Sleepers wake."

"She's not here."

"He did not refer to The Terafin. He referred to someone—something—he called *namann*, and he said that this creature was seen, briefly, in the company of Jarven ATerafin and Hectore of Araven. Cormaris told me to seek *namann*." She hesitated; this was more measured. "I intended to approach the two god-born sons of Teos who reside in the halls of the Order of Knowledge—but they are west of the city itself, seeking information for their parent. I have asked contacts at the Order about *namann*, but," and here she frowned, "was told that if this was an emergency, the scholar of choice in such matters would be Member APhaniel."

"And Jarven and Meralonne are both, in theory, in residence in the manse." Birgide nodded.

Haval had let Jester do the talking; Jester resented it. He turned to the tailor and said, succinctly, "Your call."

"I am not a member of the House Council."

"Neither am I."

Haval lifted both brows in open criticism. He then turned to Birgide. "I will ask you to discuss this with Finch before you make your choice. She has served as Jarven's aide for a number of years; she knows him well enough to gauge the risk you take. She has also built some connection with Hectore of Araven."

"Your advice?"

Haval looked surprised. Jester thought the surprise might even be genuine, although with the old man, it was impossible to be certain.

Birgide, however, accepted the expression at face value. "My position at the moment is difficult. I serve the *Astari*, but I will, in future, serve it as a member of House Terafin. And I will do nothing—not now, and not ever—to endanger the forest at the heart of The Terafin's hidden lands. But I lack expertise in patrician games."

"I cannot believe that," Haval replied.

"Your belief is not relevant. I am, of course, aware of those who hold power, and those who exercise it. I have not been trained to interact in any way with the powerful and the patrician. I do not have the ear of the Kings or the Queens. I do not rub shoulders with the powerful among the guildmasters. I am aware of the internal workings of the Order of Knowledge because I am one of its many non-talent-born members.

"Jarven ATerafin is a notable power. I know some of his history and some of his activities, both before he was offered the Terafin name, and after. I know that Duvari dislikes him—but the dislike is superficial; he does not consider Jarven a threat. Or rather, he does not consider him as much of a threat as he does The Terafin herself.

"I know very little about Meralonne APhaniel—but what I do know is disturbing."

"And that?"

"He has been a member of the Order for a very, very long time. He was a member in good standing—and a First Circle mage—when Sigurne was brought from the Northern Wastes. His power is, and has always been, considerable. He was not, however, considered a credible threat. And I find that extremely unusual."

Haval said, "It is."

"What do you know about Meralonne, then?"

"Less, I am certain, than the Lord of the Compact."

"And more," Jester cut in, "than either of us."

Haval surprised Jester; he shrugged. It was an economical movement given how little he'd moved for most of the conversation, but it clearly meant *of course.* "He is not, in my opinion, mortal. He is classified as a First Circle mage; he is, again in my opinion, far beyond that. His power appears to have limits. But—again, opinion—I believe those limits have greatly lessened with the passage of a few years."

Birgide's attention was now riveted upon the tailor. Jester's was, on the other hand, squarely on his almost empty glass.

"My research, of late, is limited," Haval continued. "I am certain that the informal House Council—which you know as The Terafin's den—has more information than they have chosen to share. Speak with Finch."

This time, Birgide nodded. "You don't trust Jarven."

"A fool—and only a fool—trusts Jarven," Haval replied. "I am vain enough not to classify myself as a fool, although present circumstance appears to stretch that vanity almost to breaking."

"And Duvari?"

"I trust Duvari." His smile was slender. It seemed unguarded, which instantly put Jester off his drink. "Understand, however, that the use of the word 'trust' is entirely contextual. Duvari is consistent. He is intelligent. Given a map of the various conflicts we face, positioning Duvari upon that map will yield specific results."

"You think him predictable."

"Ah, no. I think his *motivation* is predictable. His flexibility and intelligence create a large margin of error when it comes to determining his next move."

"And Jarven?"

"He is, and has always been, a feckless, dangerous gadfly. His raw intelligence is, in my opinion, easily the equal of Duvari's—or mine. But his compass is simple amusement or boredom, and it is impossible to clearly predict what he will find amusing. He is just as likely to spill an important secret to watch the panic it causes as he is to hold it to his chest. He forms attachments that are loose and easily discarded. In some cases, he appears to work against his own interests. He does not. His interests, however, are not the predictable, patrician interests.

"He is not a fool. He might as well be. Fools are frequently dangerous because they cannot be predicted; they cannot be trusted to act in their own interests because they cannot be trusted to *see* them. It is best, with Jarven, to keep him off-balance. When he is occupied, he has less time to indulge in his brand of chaos."

"And is he off-balance now?"

"Sadly, no. He has taken over the governance of the Merchants' Guild—and that type of bureaucracy breeds boredom and frustration."

Birgide glanced at Jester. Jester shrugged. "I've never liked him," he offered. "But Finch always has. I think it unlikely that he would deliberately harm Finch. I don't think he gives a rat's ass for The Terafin." Jester emptied his glass. "He hates to lose. I don't think he ever truly considers that he has. At the moment, he's aware of the demons and their intent, and he considers them interesting enough he's unlikely to cause havoc in our camp."

"I will speak with Finch." Birgide rose. "And I will speak with Meralonne APhaniel."

"He's in The Terafin's personal quarters."

"Yes," Birgide replied. "I know."

"What," Haval asked quietly, when Birgide left the West Wing, "has happened to her?"

Jester shrugged. "I already told you. Your memory isn't *that* bad."

The tailor's lips thinned. "I am willing to allow you to express the laziness for which you are so well known—but only to a point."

Jester exhaled. "I offered her the Terafin name."

"Under whose authority?"

"Jay's."

"An authority, in other words, you do not have."

"I talked to Teller about it," Jester replied. It was more or less true. "Teller is right-kin; he has that authority."

"It is, at best, a provisional authority."

"Jay's not going to say no. Not now."

Haval exhaled. "As she is not present, she cannot. I ask again: what has happened?"

"Does it matter?"

"Clearly, or I would not be asking. If I am to serve as adviser, the quality of the advice I offer is directly related to the facts I have at hand."

"I trust her."

"As much as you trust any outsider, yes. That's clear. I would like an explanation as to why."

"Because the forest chose her."

Haval pinched the bridge of his nose. "That is not what I wanted to hear."

"But it is what you expected."

A rare smile graced the tailor's face; it was sharp and bright. "You are becoming more observant. Will she find APhaniel?"

"Yes."

"If he is still resident within the Terafin chambers, she will not be able to pass the Chosen."

Jester smiled his signature, lazy smile. "Well, it's not much of a test otherwise, is it?"

Birgide understood tests, she had passed so many of them. She had failed a number, as well, but the failures were fewer now than they had been. The cost of failure was too high.

She was willing to walk to the upper reaches of the Terafin manse in part because she did not wish to tell Jester or Haval that there were other ways to reach it. She herself wasn't certain of the time it would take to navigate the forest to reach the internals of the manse—but she knew that The Terafin's personal quarters were only tenuously part of the manse itself.

And she knew this until she approached the grand, double doors that led to those rooms. In size and shape they were of a piece with the older decor in the central manse; they were guarded by two of the Chosen—which meant The Terafin was not currently in those rooms.

Birgide stopped in front of the doors as the Chosen faced her. "I am here to speak with Meralonne APhaniel."

"Meralonne APhaniel is not accepting visitors in these quarters," the woman to the left replied. She was older, and as Birgide herself, visibly scarred.

"Is that by command of The Terafin, or his own decision?"

"He is not accepting visitors," the woman repeated firmly.

Birgide nodded, but did not move; she was staring, now, at the doors themselves. The walk through the halls of the manse provided glimpses into the paranoia—or defense, depending on one's context—of Terafin itself. The colored strands of light that ran like translucent streamers from height of ceiling to the floor were far denser from the height of the stairs than they had been anywhere but the right-kin's office.

But they had not prepared her for the door itself. She was almost certain that nothing could have. Birgide could see the door she was certain the Chosen saw—but only with effort, and that effort had to be sustained. Without that effort, the door was not a door in any way. Nor was it a tunnel or a hole, although those were the first words that came to mind.

Golden light illuminated the hall, shed by the doors themselves—a light that reminded Birgide very much of the *Ellariannatte*. And why?

Why had she not seen this the first time Jester had dragged her here?

Like the great trees that had dominated Birgide's adult life, the doors were alive. The light that shone from their core was not translucent; nor did it take the form of slender, weblike strands; it was rooted. What emanated from the core were branches and the glittering, shimmering shape of light-imbued leaves.

One of those branches slowly bent toward her; one of the leaves curved up, as if it were a celestial hand. She reached out with her left hand—always the left, as she favored the right—and pressed her palm against that leaf. It did not burn her; she had not expected it would.

But she had little idea of what to expect, and was as surprised as the Chosen when the doors that were not doors to her eyes rolled open. She was not, however, alarmed, and the Chosen were; swords left scabbards, and a faint tint of light in the hall made clear that one of the two had invoked some silent alarm.

She lifted her hand from the leaf and stepped back immediately, lifting her chin as well to expose the line of her throat. "I mean no harm," she said, her voice low and even. "I did not intend to touch the door." She was certain she hadn't. She took a step back, but stopped three feet from the wall opposite the doors, her hands still exposed.

The guards, for their part, did not threaten her or give commands; they watched.

Only when the Captain of the Chosen—in this case, Arrendas, although there were two—came down the hall did they shift some small part of their attention. Arrendas ATerafin joined them.

"Report."

The woman who had spoken now nodded in Birgide's direction. "The doors to The Terafin's chambers opened," she said.

The captain understood immediately everything that had not been put into words. As a unit, Birgide found the Chosen quietly impressive. He turned to Birgide instantly; he was wary.

Birgide thought he knew who she was, and who, on the outside of the manse, she served. She reevaluated The Terafin's relationship with her Chosen in that instant, and made decisions of her own. "I made no attempt to open the door, Captain," she told him. "But I do not perceive the doors in the same fashion you perceive them. Jester ATerafin has some rank within the House; he bid me speak to Meralonne APhaniel."

"The mage did not open the doors for you. Nor did the Chosen."

"No," she agreed.

"Will you tell me, then, that the doors opened themselves?"

"Yes."

He turned to the woman. "Did she touch the doors at all?"

"No. She lifted her left hand—slowly. She uttered no words; she did not appear to be giving commands at all."

"And the doors opened."

The woman nodded again. She was no happier with this than the captain.

"There are no doors within The Terafin's chambers that would not open for this woman should she desire entry," a new voice said. New, at least, to the conversation. Unheard and unremarked, Meralonne APhaniel had stepped through those open doors.

The Chosen exchanged a glance; it was the captain who spoke. "On whose authority?"

"The Terafin's," Meralonne replied.

"The Terafin is absent, and she did not leave such instructions with the Chosen."

"No. These are not instructions that could have been left with the Chosen."

"They were left with you?"

"Of course not." Meralonne pulled his pipe from his robes, which had an instant effect on the Chosen; they relaxed. This was subtle; there was no change in their stance or the height of their weapons; no shift in the direction of their focused gaze. But it could be heard in the slight change of breathing pattern.

Meralonne, smoking, implied a lack of present or immediate danger to them. To Birgide, it did not, but the context of Terafin was not the context of the *Astari* or even the Order of Knowledge.

"APhaniel," the captain said, terse now.

Meralonne lifted silver brow, but failed to otherwise respond. He did, however, light the leaves that now lined the bowl of his pipe. "You do not understand the position Birgide Viranyi was offered; nor do you understand that she accepted it. In truth, I am not certain The Terafin herself does.

"But I understand it. She is, to the gardens behind the manse, what the Terafin Master Gardener is to the rest of the grounds."

"And that?"

The mage frowned. "She is their defender and their keeper. She cannot materially decide what will, or will not, grow—or rather, she can, but it is subject to The Terafin's whim."

"The Terafin is not present," the captain repeated.

"No, of course not." He glanced at Arrendas as if he was reevaluating the captain's intelligence—and not to the benefit of the captain. "But the forest has taken a shape and growth that is *of* her. In her absence the forest does not significantly alter its character, nor will it unless she returns and her intent has changed."

"What, exactly, were you offered?" Arrendas demanded—of Birgide.

Birgide said, quietly, "The forest."

"You are Warden," Meralonne added. It was not a question.

"I'm not certain what that means," she replied. "But it is not the first time I have been called that."

"It will not be the last. You wished to speak with me?" He glanced at the Chosen. The Chosen resumed their posts. The captain, however, said, "How does this position affect The Terafin?"

Birgide did not hesitate. "While The Terafin is absent, the forest itself is vulnerable in ways the Chosen cannot alleviate." She spoke without heat, and almost without inflection. "Not all of the Chosen can enter the forest. All *can* enter The Terafin's personal chambers; there is a path between these . . . doors and the functional rooms. But stray from that path, and it is my belief that the Chosen might have difficulty finding the way back to the manse."

Arrendas looked to Meralonne, who nodded and blew concentric smoke rings.

"I can enter the forest. I can always find my way out. I can," she added, with a smile she could not entirely contain, "find my way to the single tree that defines its heart. I am tasked with protection of the domains into which the Chosen cannot easily enter or exit.

"I am tasked with attempting to detect intruders who might enter the Terafin manse or properties from the wilderness. In the past, those have been demons. I am not certain what might attempt such trespass in future, but I have been given the tools to sound the alarm when such alarm must be raised." When the captain failed to nod—or move—Birgide said, "I am to speak with Finch ATerafin either this evening or in the early morning before she makes her way to the Merchant Authority. Finch habitually retains Chosen when within the manse; no doubt the Chosen will be present for that interview.

"Jester ATerafin, however, was the only witness to my investiture."

"And he accepted it."

Birgide nodded quietly. To her surprise, the captain appeared to relax. Or relent. Birgide would not have assumed Jester's name could have that effect on anyone outside of the den. "I came to speak with the House mage on behalf, indirectly, of the Twin Kings."

Meralonne raised both brow and pipe. "I am seldom called by the Kings."

"You have been called far more frequently than a lowly botanist."

"Indeed. What brings you to me? I am in the exclusive employ of Terafin; general inquiries may be delivered to the guildmaster in my absence."

"I am tasked with seeking *namann*."

A long pause followed; tobacco burned in the pipe's bowl, undisturbed. "That is neither safe, nor wise."

"No. The gods felt that you would be aware of his—or her—existence. They did not tell me what to look for."

"They understand *namann's* nature, up to a point."

"He was sighted in the city."

Meralonne said nothing.

"During the attack upon the Merchants' Guild."

"He was no part of that attack." There was no doubt at all in Meralonne's voice—and Meralonne had been a large part of the city's defense.

"They did not imply that he was; merely that he was seen, and that he was of interest—of necessary interest—to the city itself."

"And so you seek *namann*."

"I seek, at least, information about him."

"Has it occurred to you that the creature you seek might have no interest in the city, or its defense?"

Birgide nodded. "I am, however, a simple botanist, and when the gods give delicately worded commands in front of their sons, I hasten to obey." Her smile was slight, but it invoked an answering smile from the mage. And pipe smoke.

To the Chosen—without a glance—Meralonne said, "We will converse in the inner chamber. In future, Birgide Viranyi is to be given access to all areas of the manse that are readily available to me."

"That is not your purview," the captain predictably replied.

"I will, if necessary, speak with the right-kin and the regent."

Regent. The word hung in the air for a long, silent moment, untouched. The captain did not concede; he retreated. The mage offered Birgide a surprisingly deep bow. "It is merely a matter of pride," he said, pipe stem briefly pressed between lips. "I could not stop you from entering this domain while you live—and I suspect your death would be very, very difficult for even a First Circle mage to achieve." This, he offered as the Chosen listened. Birgide suspected it was as much of a concession as the mage was willing to make; they would, of course, hear, and they would, of course, report.

Birgide once again stepped into the heart of the Terafin manse. She felt, as she did, that the description was literal: here, the wild, ancient magics with which the forest itself was imbued were at their peak. She could hear the muted whispers of moving leaves in the ancient trees as if she was standing beneath their boughs; she could hear the gurgling flow of brooks or streams in the distance.

And she could see Meralonne APhaniel as she had never seen him; it was Meralonne who drew and held her attention.

His working robes had vanished, to be replaced by raiment of silver and gold, and his hair—white and striking in its length—was platinum, its fall unimpeded. His forehead was unbroken by adornment, but Birgide expected to see a crown or circlet across his brow.

His eyes, like his hair, were platinum. Age had never defined the mage; his age had long been a guessing game among the young and the naive who had entered the Order's doors by passing their many tests, most written.

But seeing him now, she knew that he was ageless. No lines, no blemishes, no touch of sun disturbed his perfect features. She reached out to touch him, her mouth half-open, and stopped before she could lose her hand.

But his smile deepened, as did his amusement, and the pipe in his hand—worn, weathered, and clearly well-loved—did not change at all. "You are not the Warden I would have chosen," he told her quietly.

She struggled to find her voice. What she found instead was Duvari's. She knew exactly what he would say, should he venture upon them now: Meralonne APhaniel, a First Circle mage, and Birgide, one of the *Astari*, gawking like a pampered young noblewoman. It grounded her.

"The forest," she replied, with quiet dignity, "is not yours. It's not your decision to make."

His smile was brilliant, unfettered, unlined; he glanced, once, at his smoking pipe. She almost—almost—offered to hold it for him. "No, indeed. Do you understand the nature of the power granted you?"

"No."

"You are remarkably honest. I am not certain such honesty is wise."

"There are two cases in which honesty is irrelevant."

"You're quoting."

"I am. In any situation in which the power and knowledge resides entirely on one side, honesty is irrelevant. It makes no difference."

"You do not believe that you hold all of the power."

"No. You do."

"Do not be rash," he replied. "You make assumptions based on your certainty of your own ignorance. You are not without power here. It is my belief that your power, in this place, is the greater power. If I were to leave the manse, it would no longer be undefended."

"And will you?"

"Not yet, Birgide. Not yet. You have spoken with gods, and the gods have answered—but as with any beings of power, they have expressed their intent and desire poorly. *Namann* is unusual. It would be best if you left off your search."

She said nothing.

"But if you will not, there are things you must know. *Namann,* in the ancient anals, was considered of the firstborn."

"Firstborn?"

"The scion of the wild gods, born when the gods walked the plane and mingled, however briefly, with the living. You have heard of the Wild Hunt? The White Lady who rides at its head is of the firstborn. The Oracle is firstborn. There are others," he added, pausing to inhale a stream of smoke.

"You don't believe *namann* is firstborn."

"In keeping with his existence, he is—and is not. No restrictions were placed upon his form; nor were restrictions placed upon the power he received. The gods in their youth created him, in concert. He did not have a single parent, or even two, but many. Not one of the gods withheld their power. He is the only proof that gods long dead existed. He can never be all of one thing, or all of another. The gods did not tell you what to look for; they offered no description. They could not. *Namann* defies simple categorization.

"In the eyes of mortals, he might take any form; he might take parts of any form—but those parts would not appear cohesive or whole. His appearance has always unsettled those who view him. Were he within the city, believe that you would know."

"If he can take any form he desires—"

"You do not understand. The form he takes is only tenuously wed to his desire; he is pulled, constantly, by many shapes and many powers, and he is torn between them almost literally. If he has come to be in the city, do not assume that he has lived here disguised and in isolation. If he has found some method or manner of securing a physical form and you interfere, the damage that might be done to the city is incalculable."

"You know where he is."

"Perhaps, perhaps not. I know that he is, like tidal waves or storms at sea, unpredictable; he is a force of nature that cannot be invoked or controlled, even at his own behest. What function did the gods feel he might serve?"

Birgide fell silent.

Meralonne nodded.

"May I ask if you are, in some fashion, like *namann?*"

Brows rose; pipe stilled. It was almost as if he could not decide whether to take offense at the question. "In what way?" he asked at last.

"You have labored beside Sigurne Mellifas for the entirety of my life; if the various members of the Order are not mistaken, you have served, more or less diligently, for longer." Given the petty jealousies endemic in the Order—or in any body in which people gathered—more or less was generous. "The Guildmaster of the Order appears frail, delicate, forgetful; the polite fiction among those of the Order who will condescend to speak with the talentless, is that this description is accurate. She is accompanied by Matteos Corvel; he is her right hand. He is, however, upstanding. In matters of delicacy, he will not move hand or foot across the line of his own ethics.

"And yet, members of the Order with overweening ambition have perished."

Eyes glinted like sword edge.

"I believe that you have some small attachment to the guildmaster, however poorly it is expressed. She is known for her war against the demon-kin. You are known for the part you have played in it. I cannot conceive of Sigurne Mellifas rejecting the responsibilities she has almost single-handedly made the focus of the magi—but if she does not, what would compel you to do so?"

"A good question." The response was mild, if chilly.

Birgide waited. When it became clear that no further answer was forthcoming, she shrugged. She meant to ask Meralonne about the Sleepers, but the words would not leave her mouth; there was no politic way to ask the only question she suddenly felt was relevant. Not directly.

"If you have no advice to offer in regards to *namann*, I will take my leave. While you consider the search unnecessary, the gods disagree, and I am beholden to at least one son of Cormaris."

"Would it surprise you to hear that I do not know?"

She froze.

"I cannot see the future; I cannot revisit the past. What I remember of days ancient and almost forgotten is stronger and more visceral than the decades I have spent in pointless labor within the Order. The world as it exists for you is not the world of my youth."

"No. Change is a constant."

"You are Warden, Birgide. It is not possible for petty illusions and polite fictions to fool you, unless you choose to be deluded. The world of Sigurne's youth is not the world of mine, as you have long suspected." He gestured, and the pipe vanished. "*Namann* is a creature from the time of my youth. The warnings I have offered are meant as an act of generosity." Wind rose beneath the amethyst sky, touching only the mage's platinum hair. "Listen, when you walk in the forest. Listen to the wind; listen to the leaves; listen. I do not know if you will ever hear the forest's true voice—but the forest, clearly, has heard yours." He glanced at her left hand; she lifted it, exposing the palm, that he might better inspect it.

He reached out; the tips of his fingers stopped just short of a scar that was both luminescent and somehow metallic. In a voice far softer than she had yet heard from him, he said, "There is still wonder in this world; there are still surprises. You are mortal, Birgide, and yet you *are* Warden.

"What do you understand your duties to be?"

"I am guardian of the forest—and the wilderness—of Terafin. I am not The Terafin's personal guard. She has no need of that—she has the Chosen, and they are far better than I would be."

"You are mistaken."

"No," she said quietly, and with a sudden, visceral conviction, "I'm not. They occupy spaces that she will never allow me to occupy—and that is as it should be. I don't know yet how I am to fulfill the duties I've accepted; I know only that I will find a way." She hesitated, and then added, "I have never felt so strongly about anything in my life."

"No?"

"No."

"Odd. Mortals experience a depth of instant emotion it is otherwise difficult to achieve. You spoke with the gods."

"I spoke only with Cormaris." She hesitated. He marked it.

"The Lord of Wisdom is concerned about the Sleepers. There is no other reason he would impel you to seek *namann*. You have so little time."

She made a decision, then. "He also spoke of the heralds."

"To you."

She nodded.

"They are coming." It was not a question.

"So the gods believe."

His smile was as bright as his eyes. "Do not ask me to interfere, Birgide. Not even Sigurne would be so foolish. But I will tell you this: if any can impede their progress now, you can. You must understand what Jewel herself refuses to see: Terafin's vast forest, its hidden pathways, the whole of its waking, wild majesty, are not confined to the simple, architectural plans of a manse and its lands.

"There is a reason that the *Ellariannatte* grow in the Common—and until recently, only there."

Birgide was silent for one long beat. "Why do you think she refuses to see this if it is true?" She did not accuse the mage of error. Had he been a mortal First Circle mage, such an accusation would have offended him for life. "She is a power. She is one of The Ten, arguably at the head of the most powerful House. Anything that increases that power preserves the House and its stability."

"That is, no doubt, what the rest of The Ten—and the Lord of the Compact—feel. Their feelings are not materially relevant. What she will not acknowledge is nonetheless truth; acknowledge it and work with it if you are to preserve what you have vowed to preserve. More than that, I cannot or will not say."

"What do you want, APhaniel?"

"From you? Nothing."

"At all."

"Would it surprise you to hear that I do not desire the destruction of this vain, gray mortal city?"

She was no longer certain.

"Three of the heralds will travel along the ancient roads. You are not conversant with the lay of the hidden land; before they approach this city, you will not be aware of their existence. But when they do, Birgide, if you listen carefully and mind the small perturbations in your preserve, you will know. You cannot, I think, kill them; nor can you bar their passage permanently. Jewel could, if she were present and she were focused—but she does not walk the whole of her domains, and because she does not, they are less secure than they might otherwise be.

"You are therefore left with few choices and few options. You may misdirect them. You may, with effort, shift the paths they walk. The forest itself might bespeak them—I cannot say. It has not chosen to directly speak with me, and I have wandered beneath its many boughs."

"There is a fourth herald."

"Yes. But he will not walk roads you can directly influence yet. If he is to be stopped at all, he will be stopped by the mortal guards and bureaucrats who gather in this city's many buildings like rats. And because he does, and can, he is not, in the end, to be feared."

"What purpose do the heralds serve?"

"They will wake the Sleepers," Meralonne replied, "when they reach their sides. They will carry the regalia of their forgotten office; they will remind them of everything they have lost. In loss, they will be at their most dangerous."

"What will stop them?" she asked, her voice dropping to a whisper.

"The Terafin, if she returns." His tone of voice was wrong; it was grim and edged.

"Meralonne—"

"Enough. I have said enough. Leave me." It was a command. Nor did Birgide disobey it—not immediately. But she turned as she reached a standing, wrought-iron arch. Flowers bloomed across its height, as if it had been designed as a trellis and not the gate she now knew it was.

"What will happen to The Terafin?"

"I cannot answer that question with any certainty. She will arrive, either alone, or in the company of the only being alive who can command the Sleepers and expect to be obeyed. If she arrives alone, there is only one path open to her if she is to save the city that is at her heart."

"And that?"

Softly, so softly Birgide thought she should have missed hearing the reply, he said, "She is Sen."

15th of Morel, 428 A.A.
The Placid Sea, Averalaan Aramarelas

Jester found Marrick difficult because he was a hard man to distrust. Absent his actual presence, it was much simpler: Marrick had a web of connections through the patriciate, the merchant Houses, and the guilds. He had a sizable amount of money, and a personality that inclined all but the most suspicious to be of aid to him where it was not too costly.

In person, Marrick was amiable, friendly, and disinclined to the type of betrayal that characterized a man like Ludgar. Or Rymark. Jester's visceral dislike of patricians came to his rescue—but only barely.

Marrick lacked Elonne's sophisticated polish; he lacked Haerrad's aura of brute, physical strength. What he donned, instead, was the patina of a distant, but much loved uncle—the man to whom you went for fun, rather than discipline. He wore it now, in the Placid Sea. He managed to get things done, his demeanor implied, by raw luck. As if a life like Marrick's could somehow be stumbled across by a friendly, unthreatening, older man.

They had been given a table suitable for Marrick's rank within the House—but it was not in an entirely private room. The owner of the Placid Sea was proud to have a senior member of the Terafin House Council as his customer, and wished his custom to be known. Had Marrick demanded a private room, one would certainly have been made available—but in keeping with Marrick's easygoing, public persona, he was willing to be put on display if it was of aid to the owner.

Jester chatted with Marrick while food came and disappeared; he chatted while wine did the same, at slightly lesser speeds. Marrick's laugh punctuated the low level conversation of the rest of the dining room, and heads turned frequently on the off-chance that some glimpse of whatever caused this good humor might be afforded at a distance.

In the case of the last laugh, it was the stone that Jester placed on the table. He looked rueful as he activated it, and this was genuine. Haval had conveyed it to Jester with curt, but specific, instructions. Since the stone itself did not contravene the laws of exception, Jester had grudgingly accepted it. He had no objections to the stone itself.

What he disliked was the conversation that was to follow. Jester did not, as a rule, speak about anything important. He disliked the pretension. He disliked the target it made of him.

But he was going to be wearing a target regardless, in the foreseeable future; he was Finch's adjutant on a Council that was about to be crashed by no less a person than Jarven. The reactions of every *other* member of the House Council to Jarven's presence were possibly the only thing about it that Jester looked forward to seeing.

"What," he said, removing his hand from both stone and table, "would you say if I told you we have definitive proof that Rymark was responsible for The Terafin's death?" He grimaced, and added, "Amarais Handernesse ATerafin."

"You're still not used to the change," Marrick noted.

Jester shrugged. "The current Terafin refers to Amarais as The Terafin. I doubt that's going to change in the next year. Or five. If it doesn't offend her, I don't worry about it."

The easy smile remained on Marrick's face. "Do you have definitive proof?"

"The Terafin does."

"Would that be the reason Rymark has chosen to throw his lot in with hers?"

It was Jester's turn to laugh; his laughter was unusually bitter. "*You* threw your lot in with hers after The Terafin's funeral. Rymark serves himself, and only himself. You must be aware that he's already starting to make waves in the House Council."

Marrick shrugged. It was an easy, natural motion. Jester's shrug clearly needed practice. "The hummingbird doesn't change its wings. You are not, I note, concerned about Haerrad."

"Haerrad is what he is. He's relatively predictable. He acts in what he views as his own interests, but he hates to lose. Making a war unappealing for a man like Haerrad is simply a matter of making it appear to be a losing battle."

"While appealing to his self-interest?"

"I don't think it matters. Haerrad won't trust anyone as far as he can spit them. He assumes that everyone approaches him with their own self-interest in mind; loyalty is a matter of how strongly the interests coincide."

"You are being surprisingly expansive this afternoon."

"Lack of solid drink," Jester muttered. "You haven't answered my question."

"It seems, at this vantage, to be purely speculative. I assume there is more to it than that. If you wish me to wax philosophical—and given it's you, I will contain my shock and consternation—I can do so. You've never been one for such discussions."

"I admit they put me off the lunch I'm paying for, yes."

"Well, then. What would I say? Probably, 'Let me see your proof.' Given your expression, this would leave the rest of the conversation hanging in the air—although your attempt to start it implies that you may have brought proof with you, if that were possible. Rymark is cautious. You are too famously lazy to manufacture proof, and The Terafin—your Terafin—is too scrupulous to allow it, regardless. Humor an old man, Jester. What is your angle, here?"

Jester and Haval had argued to a standstill on three separate occasions. It galled Jester to have to cede the tailor any ground. "I am out of angles," he replied—as Haval had advised. "There have been two separate attempts on the life of Finch ATerafin."

Marrick's smile hung, empty, on his face. It did not, as it had for Jester when he'd first heard the news, vacate that face entirely. "Since The Terafin's leave of absence."

Jester nodded.

"Word of these attempts has not reached the House Council."

"I should hope not. It only barely reached the den."

"And Finch has installed Jarven upon the House Council to counteract the possible threat?"

Jester laughed. "Finch was opposed to the idea from the beginning; The Terafin acceded."

"She seems wiser than that."

"She doesn't trust Jarven, no."

"And Finch?"

"Finch knows him better than any of us—and she was the one who advised against it. But there's no possibility, in my mind, that Jarven is responsible for the attempts. Had he been, she'd be dead."

"You're certain."

"I've never been more certain of anything in my life. Inasmuch as he can be, Jarven is now looking out for Finch. But Finch is capable of looking out for herself."

"And that's why we're here?"

"No. We're here to discuss the fate of Rymark ATerafin—and the regency."

At that, finally, Marrick's smile deserted his face. "Why the regency?" he asked. If the smile had vanished, the easy, indulgent tone had not.

"Finch intends to hold it."

"And not the right-kin."

"The right-kin has his hands full, and he wasn't trained by a wolf to preside over a den of overweening sharks."

"It did not occur to Finch to bring this to my attention herself."

"No. She has no idea I'm here."

"And why are you here, then?"

"Because I'm lazy. I don't want her power. Or The Terafin's. Or even yours. I want a better drink than the Placid Sea offers important guests at lunch. I want to sleep in until dawn is well past me. And I want Finch to survive." Jester leaned back in his chair, studying Marrick's lined face. "I don't know how many people you actually trust; you certainly don't trust me. Haerrad trusts no one. Rymark trusts no one. Elonne trusts a select handful."

"And me?"

"As I said, I don't know. I trust no one outside of my den. I trust my den absolutely. What Finch takes, as regent, she will hold in trust. When Jay returns, she'll step aside. She'll do it happily. My other suggestion was you."

Marrick laughed, then. "Me?"

"You. Even if you want to hold on to the power you claim, you'll surrender it for the sake of the House. I won't ask."

"You are an interesting young man," Marrick said, lifting his wine glass. "An amusing, interesting young man. What position will Jarven hold?"

"He will hold a senior Council seat."

"Greater in theoretical power than the seat Finch herself holds."

"His pride is overbearing. He has been a singular power in the House because of his duties at the Merchant Authority; he will not stoop to halve his power for a lesser consideration."

"I admit that I have had few dealings with Jarven. It is not always considered wise where it is unnecessary. If you mean to ask me to support Finch as regent, I cannot answer immediately."

"Of course not. You'll have your list of demands."

"Concessions is the word generally used."

"By the well-heeled and well-educated, yes. But if I'm not to play at being a gadfly, I don't have the energy to prettify."

"You, of course, have asked for nothing."

"I've asked to have things resolved as quickly as possible so I can return with good conscience to the dissolute life."

Marrick's answering smile had a different texture; Jester couldn't quite put his finger on the difference. He didn't doubt his own instincts; the difference was there. "I am flattered, I admit. Why did you choose not to ask me to accept the regency?"

"Haerrad would gainsay it immediately, as would Rymark. I suspect—I'm not certain—that Elonne would support you; given the alternative, I believe she'd prefer it. But you won't do it."

"Would I not?"

"No. Not unless the House were under external attack, or the lack of a regent would cause it irreparable harm—in your opinion. It's all of the work, but comes with very little of the public benefit."

Marrick did not laugh. He folded his hands across his chest, and leaned back into his chair, waiting. "You expect that I would not—as you put it—stand aside."

"No, *I* expect that you would."

Brows rose slightly. "Why, exactly, do you have this impression?"

It was Jester's turn to evince surprise, although in Jester's case, he could be certain it was genuine.

"The expression on your face is priceless." Marrick lifted his glass and smiled. "I won't even say you're mistaken. But power is a funny thing, Jester. We grow accustomed to it. We change the nature of the power we hold by small and slow degree—and it changes us. I understand that you now want two things. You are, and will of course, remain loyal to Jewel. Not even Haerrad could doubt that. You don't personally care about the House. I'm surprised you're willing to talk to me, given your general disdain for the powerful."

"Is it that obvious?"

"Not obvious, no. But it's there. You wouldn't take the House if it were offered to you."

"I took the name."

Marrick nodded. "I didn't say you were a fool."

"What do you want?"

"I want my position on the House Council guaranteed. I want information, when it becomes available to The Terafin. I will never be right-kin; I don't have the patience for it. The office is too small. So. The first thing you want is to preserve what your Terafin has built. I accept that. She is not ambitious enough—but she is new. In time, she will be.

"But the second thing is more interesting."

"And that?"

"I am, in some ways, a betting man. Gambling, however, has not destroyed me, where it has destroyed many. Do you understand why?" It was a rhetorical question. Jester waited. "I accept a loss with the same grace as I accept a win. I do not want what you want."

"And that?"

"Revenge."

"I think we prefer to call it justice."

"I don't believe you. You know there's no such thing. You are not here to ask me for support for Finch. If Finch felt she required my support, she would have arranged to meet with me herself. She is causing quite the stir in the Merchant Authority."

"I *am* here to ask you to support Finch as regent. To support an actual regency. You know what killed The Terafin. If Rymark is actually responsible, you know that it is not a matter for House law." Jester glanced at the wine in Marrick's hand; he really hadn't had enough to drink. "The Kings and the *Astari* already watch Terafin like hawks.

"Rymark was willing to accept the current Terafin. But he won't be willing to accept a regent."

"You are certain the others will?"

"I don't care what the others do. With everyone else, it's a matter of politics—and if I can't wrap my head around it, there are people who can. With Rymark, it's more. We can't see the whole of the game he's playing. But we saw one of the definitive moves, and it involved a demon. None of the den are talent-born." He exhaled. "I don't care if you promise to support Finch. If I'm wrong, I'll be the only person to approach you.

"If I'm not, I won't. I'm willing to bet that overtures have already been made. I want to know by who—but it's not necessary."

Marrick laughed. "You are a gambler. What, then, do you want from me?"

"There are a dozen people with middling to impressive power who might want to see Finch dead; it is possible—barely—that the assassin was sent by one of them." But not, his tone implied probable. "There's only one who is guaranteed to succeed."

"He has not succeeded yet."

"No. But Finch isn't The Terafin. It's only a matter of time. Yes, I gamble. But there are some stakes I would never put on the table."

"You are certain of your so-called proof?"

"Yes."

"And so you will wage war while The Terafin is absent." Marrick's expression was devoid of warmth or humor. "Understand that we are all ambitious."

Jester nodded.

"And we are, in a fashion, cautious. We steel ourselves for war and its many, many losses. Do you think there was no relief when Jewel was acclaimed House ruler? Don't answer that question; I see from your expression that you do. We were willing to fight. We were willing to risk everything to gain the prize.

"Now you tell me, indirectly, that we will have war, but without the incentive. Participating at all will involve the losses we did not take—but winning gains us very, very little. What do you offer?"

"Let's go back to what you want. You were all willing to politic to achieve the House Seat, a seat only one of you could occupy. In the event that all four of you were left standing—"

"It would not have happened."

"—What did you expect to take away from the attempt? If not the seat, what?"

"I wasn't guaranteed to survive," Marrick replied. "I didn't intend to lose."

"You didn't have plans for loss?"

"No. I was committed. You are not a fool. You've always tried to be wary—even today. I am exactly what you see in front of you, but it's never been all that I am. Give me a reason to fight this war, Jester, and I will fight it. I did it once, for Amarais. I will never feel for Jewel what I felt for Amarais; I am not, and will never be, her den. I will never be her counselor—she'd be a fool to have me, and her instincts have always been sharper than either of ours."

Jester hated risks. But he'd come to the table to take them. "Rymark ATerafin wasn't interested in the Terafin seat."

One brow rose. Marrick looked amused, but in a condescending way. Jester expected it, but hated it anyway.

"He expected the Empire to fall. He was to take Terafin in order to undermine both The Ten and the Twin Kings. To that end, he allowed demons entry into Terafin. He may have—and this we have no proof for—been responsible for the demon that appeared during the victory parade. Demons are not a matter for Terafin alone—I understand that.

"But Jewel is now the heart of the defense against the coming army of a walking god. What she did on the first day of the Terafin funeral rites, she must do, on a larger scale, when that army arrives."

"She doesn't require the Terafin Seat to do that."

"Yes," Jester replied, "she does." Marrick did not look convinced, which was not unexpected.

"I will consider what you've said," Marrick eventually replied. "If I do not choose to join you—and there is every possibility I will not—I will at least commit to neutrality."

Chapter Twenty-Four

15th of Morel, 428 A.A.
Araven Manse, Averalaan Aramarelas

"**H**ECTORE, you will pace a hole in the carpet."

"The carpets can be replaced."

"Spoken like a man who doesn't oversee their replacement." Andrei lay inclined upon the long recliner. The room was devoid of servants, and Hectore did not have House Guards. Had he, he might have chosen to act with his usual equanimity. Here, however, he had no reason to hide anything.

He glanced, like a nervous mother, at the recliner. "Do not even think of standing. Until our guest arrives, you will *rest*."

Andrei's brows gathered briefly, but no rejoinder left his mouth. He was, to Hectore's eye, pale and exhausted; his skin was not sallow, but seemed, rather, to be almost translucent. The cut that adorned his cheek had healed—as all such injuries always had.

But Andrei was not fully himself, and they both knew it. Hectore headed toward the door.

"You've put her off three times," Andrei said. The recliner creaked slightly as Hectore's most important servant pushed himself to his feet to follow. "She won't stand for another; the fourth time, she'll come with the Magisterium. Or Duvari."

"You have not fully recovered," Hectore replied, back to Andrei, hand inches from the door.

Andrei knew better than to lie to him. He knew exactly how little comfort Hectore would take from the attempt. He did not, therefore, make it.

Hectore missed his sarcasm. He missed his complaints, which was more surprising. Traveling through Averalaan without Andrei was like leaving some essential part of himself behind. Andrei reminded him, in a hundred different ways, of who he was.

"That's not the way it works." Andrei's voice drifted closer. "And you know it." The familiar accusation was as much comfort as Andrei could offer. "You have met and spoken with the guildmaster on a number of occasions. There is no reason to believe that this one will be any more of a disaster."

"There is every reason to believe it," was Hectore's grim reply. He turned. "She was there. The servants—the ones who survived—will forget what they saw. They'll forget the demon, the fire, the fighting. People do, when things are unpleasant. Sigurne's life has been the study of the unpleasant. She has spent decades being relentlessly vigilant. She will forget precisely nothing."

"She has no legal recourse to question you; you have broken no laws." Andrei coughed and added, "or rather, no laws about which she would have any concern. She is not political."

"It is not her first choice, no. But she can politic with patricians should she decide it must be done. Can she harm me? No, not directly. She can light fires it will be difficult and taxing to put out. It's not me I'm worried about." .

"I must ask you to worry less about me."

"Might as well ask me to stop breathing, while you're at it. I am telling you now, Andrei, if I find out who summoned those demons I am going to strangle him myself. Eventually."

Andrei rolled his eyes. "I know who will end up with that task if such information is discovered."

"Not this time," Hectore replied. "You can wait your turn."

Andrei's smile was quiet, but present. "In the decades I have known you," he told his erstwhile master, "you have not changed."

"I like to think I've mellowed."

"And I like to think that you will learn the error of your ways and stop coddling your fifth grandchild. I expect neither are actually true; such is the nature of daydream. I am almost fully recovered. I am not afraid of the guildmaster."

"Then your version of fully recovered and mine differ significantly. You have never been a fool before."

"That is not what you have said historically."

"I said you were persnickety, demanding, and overly organized; I do not recall questioning your wisdom."

"Your memory is clearly kinder—to you—than mine."

Hectore chuckled. The tight, bunched lines of his shoulders relaxed. He looked at his oldest servant, remembering how and when they had first met. He had been a younger man; a gambler. But the risks he took were calculated. Andrei had been one such risk.

But no, it was not just that. Hectore was sentimental; he liked, on occasion, to view himself as charitable or even generous. He was aware that a vast amount of delicate ego was involved in such views—but he considered it minor in the overall scheme of human nature.

"You only need be who you are," Andrei told him.

"And you?"

The answering smile was bitter but resigned. "I only need be what I have been, by your side, for decades. Come. I hear Matteos Corvel in the grand hall."

Matteos Corvel was standing in the smaller visitor's room of the Araven manse, at the side of the diminutive Sigurne Mellifas. She was seated almost strategically in the most elegant—and simple—of the arm chairs the room contained. Age, Hectore knew, was often her shield and her excuse; she had been "old, delicate, frail" for two decades. He had been willing to humor her; his belief in her frailty—or lack thereof—being irrelevant. Even had it been relevant, Hectore had manners. People's lives were composed of various polite fictions; it helped them move through the days. Hectore had, he was certain, many.

There were two reasons to choose the smaller room as the appropriate place to meet. It was well-furnished and well-decorated, it was within easy reach of the kitchens, and it was well defended. In this room, should Hectore feel trusting enough to meet his many rivals or possible allies, very little harm could be done to either the lord of the manor or the room itself.

There were other reasons, of course.

Sigurne made to rise, and Hectore immediately bowed and begged her to sit. "You are a guest in my home," he said, as she resumed her seat, her left hand on the handle of a very simple cane.

He glanced at Andrei, who took up his customary position by the door. Andrei could, when he chose, disappear while standing in place. He was the consummate servant. Present when needed, wordless, absent—and forgotten—when not required.

Sigurne accepted this, although her glance went immediately to Andrei. So, Hectore thought. His glance did not stray from her once.

"We are grateful for your cooperation in the very difficult and ongoing investigation," she told him, as he took the chair closest to hers, gesturing for Matteos to seat himself as well. Andrei left his post by the wall, and walked to the liquor cabinet; in this case, it would be entirely for show. Sigurne very seldom drank anything but water—and if Hectore was any judge of her character, today was not to be one of those rare exceptions.

Matteos, however, was willing to indulge in a social drink. Of the two, he looked the more exhausted to Hectore; his eyes were ringed in dark circles and his cheeks looked gaunt, even hollow. If Sigurne was no longer young, Matteos, her junior, appeared to be teetering on the edge of the age that had never consumed her.

"I am, where possible, happy to cooperate," Hectore replied. It was entirely truthful. Sigurne understood this; she understood, as well, that "where possible" was a large, wide line over which it would be difficult to push the patris of House Araven.

Andrei brought a tray, which he set on the small table; he handed Matteos a drink, and offered Hectore one, as well. For Sigurne, he brought water. He then stepped away, returning to his silent and watchful position against the wall.

Sigurne did not appear to notice. Matteos, however, grimaced.

"You have been a difficult man to reach in the past few days," the guildmaster said.

"And you have, as is your wont, been persistent. But I am here, now. How may I be of aid?"

"You were always fond of a gentle game," Sigurne replied. "And had I time, Hectore, I would play."

"You were never fond of games."

"We play for different stakes, you and I. I can no longer afford to dally for my own amusement. Your wealth and success are, of course, the envy of many patricians. But among the wealthy and powerful, it is wealth that has been of particular interest." She smiled. "You have—and have had, for many years—Andrei." She did not look at the servant. As he was behind Hectore, neither did the Araven patris. "People have asked, often, where you found him. They have traveled to the Domicis to ask for information, as most believe that is his function.

"Their curiosity has never been appeased. Nor would it be," she added, "if Andrei were, as rumor suggests, from that guild."

"I should hope not."

"But he is not, of course. Nor is he *Astari*, or formerly of that group, although his survival has often implied it."

"There appears to be a great deal of curiosity about a man who is a simple servant."

She nodded. "Such curiosity has long been idle. The time for that has passed. For my part, I regret any discomfort this may cause." She glanced at Matteos. Matteos clearly disliked her silent request; it was almost a full minute before he chose to reply, and he spent most of that drinking.

If, however, Andrei was Hectore's obedient, chosen servant, Matteos was Sigurne's. He rose, and from the interior of his rumpled, unremarkable robes, he drew a scroll case. It was the color of aged ivory, but that was not what caught Hectore's attention. The seals did that. He recognized the symbols of the Twin Kings.

When it suited Hectore, he could affect nonchalance; in this case, he considered it unnecessary. He was surprised. He was also not amused. Both had value in what had become a much more difficult negotiation than he had expected. He accepted the scroll case. He then lifted it above his shoulder.

Andrei left the wall. He was almost silent; Hectore knew he had moved because of Matteos Corvel. Sigurne herself did not condescend to notice; nor did she appear to be at all concerned. She did, however, place a hand—gently—on Matteos' still arm.

Andrei examined the scroll; it took him all of ten seconds. "It is, as you suspect, genuine."

Matteos did not look outraged—but it was close. Sigurne, however, accepted the cursory inspection as if it were both necessary and expected.

"And the enchantment?"

"It will open for you. There is no other enchantment—beyond the usual restriction of form—placed on the exterior of this case. There are faint traces of magic that imply that the scroll would not otherwise fit; it is possible that you will hear the Kings speak when the scroll itself is in your hands." He handed the case back to Hectore.

He did not, however, resume his position. He stood behind the chair Hectore occupied as if he were his shadow.

Hectore did not open the case immediately. Instead, he met Sigurne's benign gaze. "This was unnecessary."

"That," she inclined her head, "is the opinion I offered the Kings when asked. The scroll was both enchanted and sealed by me, if you wonder at Matteos' expression. The Kings however may ask advice—or demand it—without any obligation to heed it."

"Hectore," Andrei said, which surprised everyone in the room. His voice was gentle. "Open the case."

Hectore said—and did—nothing.

"I am not afraid of what it contains."

"I think," Hectore replied, "you have far less to lose." He rose, case in hand. "Are you instructed to wait for a reply?" His voice was deceptively soft.

Matteos Corvel bridled anyway. Sigurne's hand—which had not, Hectore noted, left his arm—tightened. "I was not sent purely as a messenger; the palace retains men and women whose work that is. It is assumed, however, that you will cooperate with the Kings' request, and I am here to facilitate that cooperation. If, however, you choose not to do so, I am not empowered to act as the Kings' agent. I would consider it a great favor if you did not force that role on me."

"You are very, very good," Hectore told her, feeling both admiration and a tinge of uneasiness. "Had you desired money or power, it would have been yours. It is not," he added, to Matteos Corvel, "an insult."

"The guildmaster is due a measure of respect," was the tight, but heated, response.

"I have, I trust, given her that." He considered the consequences of returning the case unopened. They would be high, but not impossible to weather. But he considered, as well, the attack on the Merchants' guildhall. Dozens of men and women—old rivals, new rivals, and friends—were dead in the wake of an attack that was inconceivable, except perhaps in the darkest of nightmare. The governance of the guild itself had been left to Jarven ATerafin— and that leadership had taken up the majority of Hectore's time and thought.

He could handle Jarven; he had in the past. But the demons were a battlefield beyond him. They had changed, in one action, the nature of Hectore's reality. "You don't understand what you're asking," he told Sigurne.

"No. I don't. But I have my suspicions. Thus, my advice to the Kings." She rose as well; Hectore felt a twinge of genuine guilt—but it was not enough to drive him to sit. He wanted to pace. He wanted to throw the case across the room at the nearest wall or fireplace; it was an act of petulant defiance, and it would not harm the message itself. In this room, in front of his guests, he could do neither.

"Hectore," Andrei said again. Into the silence that followed his spoken name, Andrei added, "you have not failed me. You have never failed me. But you have seen yourself that change is coming."

"I see no opportunities in this change."

"And that is unlike you. Come. Even Jarven is excited."

"Did I not have a rule about mentioning his name in my house?"

"Several, that I recall."

Hectore glared at his servant in much the way he might have had they been alone. He took each end of the scroll case in hand, and twisted. The seal cracked. No sign of magic followed. He removed the top of the case, handing it Andrei, who accepted it without comment.

The official document was wider than the length of the case, and thicker in diameter, the seals affixed to the bottom of the document adding weight in all senses of that word. Hectore read its contents.

The events of the past month have left a lasting shadow across the city. The loss of the merchant heads of many families have contributed to a shortage of necessary supplies, and people fear a return of the Henden of 410. In the current tense atmosphere, it is of utmost necessity that daily business be conducted in as smooth and reliable a fashion as possible.

Were such daily business to be our chief concern, your part in these discussions would be unnecessary; you have always been exemplary in such circumstances. The events of the 7th are not events that exist in isolation. Changes are occurring across the breadth of the Empire. Changes are occurring within Averalaan as we write. If not handled with care, the consequences will be far more disastrous and far-reaching than even the worst of the events this city has historically faced.

The Mysterium and the Order of Knowledge have long been tasked with the protection of the Empire. But in their considered opinion, the power and knowledge they currently possess is not equal to the task of continuing to do so in the near future. Our parents concur.

We are aware that during the incident at the Merchants' guildhall, on the 7th day of Morel, in the year 428 A.A., you were instrumental in preserving the lives of those who work in the back halls. Word has reached us of the presence of an individual who was capable of meeting the demons in combat. The Lords of Wisdom and Justice have tasked us with the finding of this individual. They feel this individual could be just as instrumental in the survival of the Empire.

This was not as bad as Hectore had feared. He glanced up, quickly, at Sigurne; she was watching.

There is some belief that you have some information about the individual in question. The gods were not able to give a detailed description. They were, however, provided information about witnesses. We do not consider the individual a threat, and have no wish to harm or incarcerate him.

Hectore snorted.

But it is imperative that he be found. To this end, Sigurne Mellifas has undertaken a difficult conversation. At her request, we have left the particulars of that conversation in her hands; there are very few people, in the upcoming conflict, who can be trusted to handle such conversations with the appropriate caution. She is one. She will attempt to make clear the concerns of the Crowns, and the reasons for this search.

The information is to be considered a matter of security; its spread, an act of treason. We welcome your input and your cooperation in these very difficult times.

Hectore set the gently worded edict aside. "You did not speak frankly to the Kings," he said quietly, his eyes upon the guildmaster.

Matteos, already annoyed, looked even less pleased.

Sigurne said, "I spoke frankly, Patris Araven. But I am not a god. I cannot speak with the certainty that the gods possess. I made clear only that I thought of the two witnesses, you were capable of giving us the information we required. I was not privy to the contents of the Kings' letter. I was, however, asked to come to speak with you on matters that are not directly concerned with the investigation itself.

"Will you listen?"

"At the Kings' command," Hectore replied. He returned to his seat. By silent assent, Andrei returned to his post by the back wall. He was going to be insufferable, Hectore thought, because he had been right.

"Tell me," Sigurne said, lifting the glass of as yet untouched water on the table, "what you know about the Sleepers."

Two hours later, Hectore escorted the elderly guildmaster out of the Araven manse. He offered her his arm and she accepted it; she seemed tired and careworn. Matteos had thawed slightly in the intervening time, and allowed Hectore the privilege of that escort. Andrei tidied the guest room; he was waiting for Hectore's return.

The news that Sigurne imparted troubled Hectore; he had no reason to hide it. Sigurne did not feel that the combined power of the magi—all circles—would be up to the task of defending the city from the disaster she was certain was approaching. She acknowledged, at Hectore's behest, that there were members of her magi that were fully capable of fighting all but the most powerful of the demons; she considered these mythical Sleepers more dangerous, by far, than even the demon that had appeared without warning at the heart of the victory parade some months past.

She considered the demons that had appeared in the Merchants' guildhall to be a much lesser threat. And at the hands of a much lesser threat, so many had perished.

"She is not wrong," Andrei said, as Hectore opened, and closed, the door.

"They were powerful enough."

"Armies are not composed of demons, but an army of mortals, with no significant individual power, is just as terrifying if you have no like army prepared to meet it." He offered Hectore wine—a pale, white wine that was sweet and cool. "What will you do?"

"Do you believe in the Sleepers?"

"Yes."

"Do you believe they will wake?"

Andrei closed his eyes. "Yes, Hectore."

Hectore paced in tighter and tighter circles. "Get dressed," he told his erstwhile recovering servant.

Andrei raised a brow.

"We are heading to the Merchant Authority."

"You do not intend to speak with Jarven. The Kings have said this is a confidential matter of security—"

"Jarven, I am almost certain, already knows. I do not intend to speak to him about the matter in any direct fashion. But he knows." And he, Hectore thought dispassionately, could do what Hectore himself could not: he could question Andrei, if it proved necessary.

The Merchant Authority was not empty. If the events at the Merchants' guildhall had cast a shadow over the city, it was a shadow in which people still moved. The wheels of commerce might wobble, but they very seldom ground to a complete halt. People had to eat, among other things.

"Andrei." Hectore did not even attempt to keep irritation out of his voice.

"Yes?" Andrei was on high alert. He was always perceptive; he had always been observant. But in certain situations he reminded Hectore of Duvari. It was a reminder that was distasteful enough; Hectore resented it.

"At the moment, there is no building in the entirety of the hundred holdings that is more secure."

Andrei, predictably, failed to respond.

"I am going to send you home to continue to convalesce if you do not relax." Hectore briefly considered sending him home regardless. If Andrei could relax—for a definition of the word that had, no doubt, been at home during the time of the Blood Barons, if then—within the Merchant Authority, he would not relax in the Terafin offices. He had never liked Jarven.

He had never understood why Hectore did. And that was fair; on the surface of things, there was very little to actually like about a man who had, on a whim, attempted to ruin him. Perhaps, had Jarven succeeded, Hectore would feel as Andrei did. Or perhaps not. They had both been younger men, and they had both played games of ambition with everything they had.

Hectore made his way up to the Terafin offices, noting, as he did, that the crowded building was thick with guards in various tabards—and of varying competence, in his opinion.

He was surprised, however, to see the Terafin doors adorned not by House Guards, which could be expected, but by the Terafin Chosen. There were two.

"It appears that I am not the only person who feels caution is required," Andrei noted. He said this before the doors opened; guards were, like servants, invisible.

Hectore frowned—at the Chosen. "Do not be tiresome. I have to speak with Jarven; I think that's burden enough for one day." The doors opened to the sight of Lucille ATerafin, which brightened Hectore's otherwise stressful day. She did not smile when their eyes met; the habitual frown of the Merchant Authority's most well-known dragon appeared instead.

She reached for a wide, squat book. "Patris Araven."

"Lucille," he replied. "ATerafin."

Her brows folded in the middle.

"I am certain it has been a trying week." Before she could speak, he added, "I offered to take the governance of the guild; Jarven rejected my suggestion out of hand."

"You didn't argue forcefully enough," she replied.

"That is slightly unfair. You have known Jarven for at least as long as I, and you know what he is like when he has decided on a particular course of action."

"I know what *you* are like when you've likewise decided."

Hectore chuckled. "I admit I offered out of a sense of responsibility. Herding the terrified is not something I relish."

"You don't appear to have an appointment today."

"I could offer the polite fiction that I have confused the days, but I won't. If Jarven is not involved with guild affairs, and if he has a moment, I would like to speak with him. If he is or does not, I will stand in line and make an appointment."

Lucille exhaled. "You have a standing appointment with Finch," she said, in a much lower voice. She could be quiet; it was not an ability that saw much cultivation at the front desk of an office such as this.

"I would prefer to speak with Jarven on his own, if that is at all possible. I am very fond of Finch; I do not desire to see her trapped between two old, bitter men."

An answering laugh could be heard—barely—from behind the closed doors of the most important office in the Terafin suite. Lucille could obviously hear it as well. She rose. "I believe that Jarven is free."

* * *

When Lucille opened the door, Hectore saw—to his surprise—that the office was otherwise occupied. Finch rose as she caught sight of him. Jarven, of course, did not. But either of these two could be expected to be found in this room; a third person was present. From the looks of her clothing she was not a merchant; from the looks of her visible scars, she might once have been a caravan guard.

Or a soldier.

She was the first to rise, the first to offer a bow that was, in form, completely servile—and in execution, curiously distant. Jarven's smile was expansive. "I am surprised and delighted to have your company at this particular moment," he said. His delight was genuine; it put Hectore instantly on his guard.

But it also evoked a smile that was, in some small way, nostalgic. Jarven noticed it immediately, of course. His eyes were that too-bright hue peculiar to Jarven when he was spinning his many, many webs. He could see the lay of the political and economic landscape with a clarity and a ruthlessness that most men simply did not possess. He had always had an enormous sense of his own worth, but he had, simultaneously, a lack of the ego that required others to believe it.

Hectore took a chair. Andrei took up his familiar position at Hectore's back, against the wall nearest the doors. Finch did not sit; she headed out.

"Let Andrei get the tea," Hectore told her. "In your position, Finch, you cannot afford to be seen fetching and carrying."

Her smile was as genuine as Jarven's. "It is the only chance I have to escape the confines of this office without guilt." She glanced at Andrei, and brief uncertainty marred her otherwise pleasant expression. "If that will not step on your toes?"

Jarven exhaled loudly. In case this was missed—and how it could be, Hectore didn't know—he also lifted his fingers to the bridge of his nose.

"What have I done wrong this time?"

"You do not address a man's servant, Finch. You *know* this."

Finch's smile was just as bright as Jarven's. And, Hectore thought, marveling, just as hard. "I address mine all the time," was her cheerful, deliberate response. "And only two of them despise me for it."

"You see?" Jarven said to Hectore. "This is what I have been enduring since I was foolish enough to cede office space to young Finch." He made a shooing motion with his hands.

Hectore, however, inclined his chin, and Andrei exited the open doors in

Finch's wake. "It is no small wonder to me that she has not attempted to assassinate you."

"Finch is rather direct. Were she angry enough to desire my death, she would want to personally cause it. Assassins are not her style. And my manners are deplorable."

"Unusually self-aware today, aren't you?"

Jarven settled back into his chair, folding his hands across his chest; he looked as if he intended to take a nap—a nap, his posture implied, that was long overdue and well-deserved. He did not, however, close his eyes. Instead, he said, "May I present Birgide Viranyi? She is a member of the Terafin Household Staff, under the wing of the Master Gardener. She requested an appointment, and I admit I was curious enough that I granted it. Birgide, I have the pleasure of introducing Hectore of Araven."

Birgide bowed again. "Even I recognize the patris," she told Jarven quietly. "Much is said about him in the back halls."

"Of Terafin? I admit some surprise," Hectore replied. He, of course, had never heard of Birgide Viranyi.

"Terafin is not the first House I've served in this capacity." Her smile was slender; it appeared genuine.

"Birgide came to ask a few questions," Jarven continued. "Coincidentally enough, the second person on her very short list was you."

"Short list?"

"She wished to speak to either—or both—of us. I am being magnanimous; she will not have to waste time either repeating her questions or appealing to your own overworked staff in order to grab a minute of your time."

"Please," Hectore said, gesturing. "Sit. If Jarven is rude enough not to remember that you are a guest in his office, I am not—I will begin to feel exceedingly self-conscious about sitting, myself."

The Terafin gardener took a seat. She was silent for one long moment. When she spoke, Hectore wished she had remained that way.

"Patris Araven—"

"Hectore, please."

"Good luck with that," Jarven added. "I believe the only reason she uses my name is the confusion it would cause should she choose formality. The office is otherwise littered with ATerafin."

Hectore was, of course, curious. Household Staff of any stripe did not enter this office; they certainly didn't enter it the way Hectore or any of the more powerful merchants likely to be found in front of Jarven's desk would. Yet she was here, and Jarven was not bored. He had questions of his own for Jarven, and he did not intend to ask them in front of an unknown gardener. "I am comfortable being addressed formally, if that is more to your liking."

"Thank you. I am a gardener. In the Order, I am called a botanist. I have accepted a position of permanent employ with the Terafin Household Staff."

A glance at Jarven's expression made clear to Hectore that he was surprised. His eyes were bright and slightly narrowed.

"I am known—among gardeners—for my attempts to transplant the Kings' trees. In more than a decade I have seen dozens of failures. I have had precisely one success. That success, however, was both recent, and in *Avantari's* Courtyard gardens. My success there led me indirectly to two men: Jarven ATerafin, and the Patris of House Araven." She glanced, once, to the door, exposing the defined lines of her profile.

"She has come," Jarven said, when she fell silent, "to interrogate two old men."

"I do not think of myself as old," Hectore replied. "And if it comes to that, I think of you as ageless."

Jarven laughed. "Come, Birgide. We are both famously busy men. Tell him the rest."

But Birgide shook her head. "Patris Araven, how long has your servant been in your employ?"

"I see," Hectore replied, "that this is going to be one of *those* days. You are not the only person I have seen today who has expressed an interest in my servants—although given your position on the Household Staff, your curiosity is less of a breach of manners."

"Is that how you answered the other person's query?"

"No. Unfortunately for me, it was not a discussion I could easily deflect or avoid."

"Which is not to say that he did not do so," Jarven pointed out. He rose with the aid of a cane, and made his way to the bookshelf. There, he withdrew one slender tome, nestled among ledgers that had never been intended to serve as decoration. He returned to his desk. "If Birgide will not be more direct, I will. She has come to question us because of our part in the defense of the Merchants' guildhall. Apparently, one of the defenders was noted."

Hectore nodded. He dispensed with the cultural habits of life as a merchant, and shuttered his expression. Men and women with any wisdom did not push Hectore when he wore that mask. The Terafin gardener understood this in an instant, which deepened Hectore's curiosity. He did not tell Jarven to continue. He was done with that particular game.

All of life was a negotiation. Some negotiations were pleasantly familiar.

Arguing with the owner of a small stall in the Common sometimes invoked nostalgia.

But there were some things the Patris Araven would never buy, and some he felt—strongly—were not, and should never be, for sale.

"You intend to bore us all," Jarven said, noting correctly the cast of Hectore's expression.

"You are here; your very presence and general attitude should cause any who complain of boredom to reconsider their stance." To the Terafin gardener, he said, "For what reason have you come?"

"To ask questions," she replied, "that might lead me to the man who chose to act in defense of the guildhall." The door opened; Hectore had spent more time in defensive silence than was his wont.

Finch entered the room, widening the gap between door and wall; Andrei followed her, carrying a tray. On it was the usual expensive tea set, with its enchanted paint and its less expensive tea. But there was also a stoppered, square bottle—an equally expensive one, and short, squat matching glasses to one side. Frowning, Hectore met Andrei's glance—or tried.

Andrei was, however, looking at the Terafin gardener. And the Terafin gardener was looking at him. Truly looking at him. Until this moment, Birgide Viranyi had displayed the cautious neutrality servants generally showed in the presence of patricians. Her eyes, however, were rounding, the narrowed edges lost to a genuine surprise.

Or horror.

It had been a long, long time since Hectore had truly considered killing a man. He considered it now. But if the Terafin gardener died, Hectore would still be left to deal with the magi and their implacable leader. And even if the power to end Sigurne's life resided in his hands—and most things did if he was willing to pay the price—he knew himself well. He would never be able to look himself in the eye again—not that mirrors were a great boon, in general—were he to exercise it. She was dignified steel, but of an age where respect was her due and her right; he could no more bring about her death than he could murder a child.

What would you do to protect your family?

Old, old questions. Old, terrible questions.

Anything. It was a young man's answer. It had been spoken with a young man's helpless certainty, and a young man's drive and focus. And had that been the whole of his answer, the whole of his truth, he would not be in this room today, thinking these dark thoughts. *Anything that I could share with them after the fact.*

I don't understand.

You and most of the merchants I've had to cross pens with. If, to save my wife, I had to, for instance, kidnap or kill the child of a rival, I could never tell her. I could never look her in the eye again. You haven't met my wife. Many feel that she is almost feral when threatened—and there's some truth in that. But she exists within a tunnel. The walls that define what she will, and will not, accept are not permeable; they are not weak.

It is not of your wife that I speak.

No, of course not. Most men don't. But it is relevant because she is *my wife.* His first wife. His first wife, buried and mourned decades past. *If I saved her life in that fashion, she would assume that she was responsible for the act that preserved her. That it was not my hand that—let's stick with kill a child—committed the crime; it was hers. Without permission, without intent, without consultation, she would be a murderer. She would, in her own mind, be a criminal of the type she has mercilessly and tirelessly fought.*

Silence. Not Hectore's, of course. The young man he could remember being was full of word and thought and humor and fire. Yet his words were a bridge to the past. His words were Hectore's. They echoed; they had never left him.

I am not, in my own estimation, a "good" man. I have killed. I will, no doubt, kill in the future. But there are limits to what I will do. There have to be limits. If, by choosing the wrong action or making the wrong decision, I preserve my family, I will also nonetheless destroy it. And if it is *to be destroyed, it will, gods willing, be destroyed by someone else.*

But in this hypothetical case, your wife would still be alive.

Yes. But she would never again be my wife, and what exists in the spaces between us? It would be worse than ash. It would be pain and guilt and betrayal.

Betrayal?

Hectore nodded. *I am not the man I was when I first met my wife. She is not the woman she was. I like to think that we are more, or better. But the seeds of what we are now? Those were always within us. Men believe that if they are not quicker, smarter, and more cunning than the men who gather around them, they will never succeed. Or worse, they will fail utterly. Do you know why?*

Because it is true?

Because they want *it to be true.*

That is not the case.

It is. If it is the truth, they are free to do as they please without recourse to guilt or conscience. If they can believe that all *men must behave in a certain fashion, they are no better—or worse—than the men surrounding them.*

And you?

I don't believe it. I look. I see. Not all successful men are contemptible. For those who believe all men are, those men are simply considered more accomplished liars. They are smoother and more charming. And in some cases, that is the truth—but not all. If they look at those who appear, on the surface, admirable, they see everything that they are not. It's a tricky thing. I've met men and women who are *admirable. And also powerful.*

Silence again.

All men change, Hectore said, in that dim past, whose roots went so deep they could not be unearthed.

"Yes. All men change." Everyone in the room, excepting only Hectore, was surprised by Andrei's words. "Change is inevitable."

"No two oak trees are alike," Hectore replied. "But they are recognizably the same type of tree. I want to change the way an oak sapling does. I want to grow deeper roots. I want to grow thicker branches. I don't want to become an apple tree or a rose bush or whatever else other people value. So: I will change, Andrei, because I am a man, and all men change."

"And you will remain constant, because you are Hectore, and you will always be Hectore."

Hectore smiled fondly. "That is the mistake you make. You think 'Hectore' describes one thing. It does not. All men—all people—are many, many things. Monstrous men are capable of great acts of kindness, kind men, of monstrous selfishness. We don't want *one* thing; we want many, many things, all at once, some contradictory. We are not like you, but we contain multitudes in our own lesser fashion.

"And we decide, in the end, which of those we will strengthen, and which we will discard. Yet even then, we are shadowed at times by regrets and desires that make no sense at all to us. Do not agree to serve me because you believe that I am free of the constraint of foolishness or greed or desire; I am not. Agree to serve me, if you will, because you understand the way completely contradictory desires pull and twist a person, and you value the struggle to remain true to ideals that are, by their very nature, impossible to achieve."

"You do not see yourself clearly," Andrei said. "And you never have."

"I see myself clearly," Hectore countered. "It is those on the outside of me who cannot. They see the actions, but not the struggle to reach the decision that prompted the actions. They see generosity and assume that generosity was the only impulse."

"I did not say that you were particularly generous, Hectore."

Hectore laughed.

"But I see you have decided." Andrei then set the tray down on the small, exquisite table meant for use by visiting dignitaries. Finch did not, as Jarven had, seat herself behind her large desk. She sat beside Hectore, instead.

"Would it help you to know I have fears?"

"Only if they do not involve your grandchildren or godchildren and the foibles of their respective youths."

Finch laughed, which surprised Hectore.

"You are embarrassing me in front of the joint heads of the Terafin's merchanting operations." But he spoke with an easy, relaxed smile. He was fond of Finch. He was fond of her Jewel. He was not a young man. He had not, in truth, been a young man for decades. But Jewel? She was young. And Hectore thought that she was one of the very few who could accept Andrei's service. Hectore could—and had—amass a fortune; he could leave endowments for the children and grandchildren he had watched for the entirety of their short lives.

He could leave no such thing for Andrei, because in the end, that was not what Andrei needed.

Andrei served tea; Finch tried to do so, but retreated, as if understanding that the role that defined Andrei was necessary this afternoon. Or perhaps she simply accepted that in service such as this, she was nowhere near as competent as the Araven servant.

He, therefore, took tea to Jarven; Jarven accepted it without his usual complaint or cheek. He was assessing every man and woman in the room the way a merchant assessed a contract.

When Andrei carried tea to Birgide, however, he bowed. The bow was not, in style or even substance, a terribly Weston bow; it was not the bow offered between equals. Hectore was not familiar with the protocols of the back halls, but knew enough to know that this gesture was not among them.

Birgide seemed almost as discomfited by the gesture as Hectore felt. Jarven, of course, was neutral. Finch was not. She looked to Birgide, and Birgide turned toward her. It was a brief and unexpected display of uncertainty. What surprised Hectore was that she sought reassurance of a kind from Finch.

And that Finch could, in fact, offer it. She turned her neutral, pleasant gaze on Andrei, Hectore's erstwhile servant. "Have you come," Finch asked him—directly, and against all protocol, "to offer us aid?"

Andrei met Finch's gaze; his own flickered, briefly, to Hectore—as Birgide's had previously gone to Finch. Birgide was paler; her scars more pronounced. She had looked away from Andrei.

Hectore understood why. Again, he thought of having this woman killed;

this time the impulse was stronger, clearer. But Andrei had bowed—to her—as if he somehow recognized her. As if she was part of the shadowed world of his life before Araven and Hectore.

"He is my servant, a fact that appears to be lost to the lax protocol of this particular office," Hectore said, without rancor. "I hold you blameless," he added, when Finch turned her surprised expression on him. "You have been left to Jarven's sensibilities for far too long, and Lucille has never been one to stand on formality."

The mention of Lucille caused Finch to relax. Jarven, however, grimaced.

"As a servant, he is not here to do anything but see to my needs. He is invisible—among people with manners—until his service is required; he becomes invisible the moment it ends. Servants," he added, his tone becoming more severe, "do not, in general, bow to strangers in an office such as this."

Andrei had unfolded, returning to the posture that defined him. The fact that he was not standing against the wall changed nothing. But there was a peculiar tension across the line of his shoulders, a tightening that implied held breath.

"If you can, perhaps, explain why this singular bow has been offered, the rest of us can stop gawking like awkward youths."

Andrei's expression shifted into something more familiar—irritation. "Even servants are expected to bow to the Kings."

"She is not, unless something has radically changed since our meeting with the guildmaster this morning, one of the Kings. Were she—or, failing that, given gender, a Queen or one of the Exalted—your bow would be remarkable only for its lack of servility."

Finch exhaled. "Birgide?"

The Terafin gardener nodded. She was paying attention to Andrei—but she had not, since he rose from his bow, met his gaze. To Hectore's surprise, she did so now. Her eyes were clear and unblinking; they were also the color of rust. Hectore rose. Finch and Jarven remained seated.

Andrei smiled. It was a slight smile, a shift of lips. Hectore had seen that expression on his servant's face a handful of times over the march of decades; he had not clearly understood what it meant on any of those occasions. He did not understand it now.

"Warden."

Birgide nodded. "I am Warden of the Terafin grounds."

Andrei shook his head. "You are Warden of the lands upon which the entirety of Averalaan, great and small, resides. The forest does not exist solely within the boundaries of Terafin—and you must know this. You planted the Kings' trees in the Kings' garden—and they grew."

"You were aware of this, as well?"

"As well?"

"You are aware of the position of Warden."

He nodded. "You will not be the first Warden I have encountered. Will you attempt to kill me now, or drive me from this city?"

Her surprise was visible, visceral; her response, when she spoke, was so mild it was at odds with everything else about her: tense, wary, readied. "Gardeners are seldom called upon to kill anything but harmful insects and weeds. I am not—have not been—familiar with you, but given your association with House Araven, I believe I can trust you to be neither."

She had surprised him almost as much as his question had surprised Hectore. Nor had she finished. "Did the other Wardens?"

"I was not welcome in their domains."

"Why?"

"You must see, in me, some of what they saw. You are mortal—but you are Warden. What you see is not what any other in this room sees. It is not what the citizens of Averalaan see when they encounter me."

"Is it what the Patris of Araven sees?"

"You will have to ask him," Andrei replied. Not yes, but not no.

Birgide turned to Hectore.

"I see Andrei," Hectore told her quietly.

"Do you understand what he is?"

"He is among the most valuable members of my Household Staff."

Birgide fell silent instantly. What she heard in Hectore's voice was there; he had taken no trouble to hide it. He could accept threats to his financial empire; he could accept attacks meant to undermine it. He could accept with a certain equanimity the overtures of assassins and the ambitious who hoped to replace him.

No one who did not have a death wish threatened Hectore's *family* personally. It had not historically ended well for anyone foolish enough to try.

Andrei, however, lifted a hand. "Hectore."

"I wish to make clear," Hectore said, his eyes on Birgide, "that you are, in all ways that matter, family to me."

"Hectore," Jarven added, "is, and has always been, sentimental. He is, and has always been, exceptionally intelligent. Only in matters involving sentimental attachment does he set aside his interests—but he does so with remarkable ferocity. I have tangled with the Patris Araven when neither of us held the positions we now hold—and even in that youth, I was not foolish enough to threaten, attack, or otherwise endanger his family. It was known, even then, to be an act of almost literal suicide.

"And I was fond of his wife at the time, I must admit." He idly flipped the pages of the ledger he had placed upon his desk. Birgide watched his movements, and the turn of the pages, as if she could read what was written there, and did not care at all for the contents.

This was obvious enough, it amused Jarven. Hectore's concern for Andrei was sufficient that he welcomed Jarven's amusement.

Andrei, however, did not. It often amused Hectore to note just how tightly Andrei held his grudges. He would, no doubt, find it amusing when they were quit of the Merchant Authority, but it was inconvenient at the moment.

"Hectore," Andrei said again. He was smiling. It was the smile of resignation, almost of surrender. Hectore hated it on sight, it so seldom graced Andrei's face.

The Patris Araven turned to Birgide, but was surprised; Finch stepped between them. She reached out to touch Hectore's arm, and it fell immediately into the accommodating position one assumed when one offered to escort a young woman. He started to drop his arm; Finch's hand tightened, briefly, over it. "Birgide," she said quietly, "is special. She is newly ATerafin, at my discretion."

Jarven frowned. "That is not your right."

"It's Teller's right," she countered, in a tone of voice so soft and so reasonable only the truculent could pursue disagreement. "Jay will either confirm or deny it when she returns."

"If she returns."

This caused Finch's lips to thin and her hand to involuntarily tighten; in no other way did she acknowledge Jarven. Hectore had her attention. "You've seen The Terafin's cats."

Hectore nodded.

"You saw the dress she wore on the first day of the funeral."

"I considered it both a privilege—on my part—and a coup, on hers. I do not think, however, that she intended her clothing to be the political statement it most certainly was." He smiled fondly at the memory.

"And you saw the trees."

"We all saw the trees."

"The forest in the back of the manse is forbidden to visitors. It is Birgide's belief that, should the wrong person intrude, they might never find their way out again."

Silence.

"But Birgide has been to the heart of the forest. There is nothing in it she has not seen. You took dinner with The Terafin in her personal quarters."

Hectore nodded slowly. "The forest is like those rooms?"

"Yes. Birgide has been chosen by the—" she hesitated. It was rare to see hesitation of this kind from Finch. "—Spirit, I suppose; I don't have a better word for it. She has been chosen by the spirit of that forest to stand as its guardian."

"She is not simple guardian," Andrei added quietly.

"No. I didn't assume it was simple. But she serves as the go-between. She is tasked with protecting the forest, and she has been given the tools with which to achieve that in some small measure." She hesitated again. Jarven was utterly still, his face a mask. He had shifted position in his chair, although he did not rise. "She sees what we can't see.

"I don't know what she sees when she looks at Andrei. I don't know," Finch added, turning to face the Araven servant, "what she sees. I see Andrei, as I have seen him by your side. I understand his import to you."

Hectore thought, given the softness she forced into her voice, that she saw a great deal more than that. He was not Jarven; he had not made a practice of hiding himself; nor did he shift personality at whim and his own convenience.

"I understand, as well, that his expertise is, in some fashion, the greater when it comes to things that are best left in the hands of the talent-born or the god-born. But what we face, we will *all* face—talent-born, god-born, King or commoner. A threat to the Empire, a threat to the city itself, threatens us all. We would not—ever—attempt to deprive you of Andrei's service. Given his forbearance to date, I'm not certain that's even possible.

"Instead, we ask that you consider our circumstances and decide how much you wish to be involved in them. If, in the end, you consider it unwise, both of you will be free to go."

"The Kings might have a different opinion," Jarven said. He had slid into a quiet, steady voice; it was shorn of amusement or the petulance of his aged, infirm act.

"Not even the Kings would be unwise enough to confront Hectore of Araven directly," Finch countered. There was steel in the reply. "Nor, in my opinion, would they choose to accuse Terafin of malfeasance. That would require the consensus of The Ten." Her tone made clear that she thought the probability of consensus among that august group to be approaching zero.

"I have some idea," Hectore replied, "of what the city now faces. I am not at liberty to discuss it; I have been informed that the discussion itself would be considered an act of treason."

Jarven laughed.

Andrei pinched the bridge of his nose. Giving amusement of any kind to Jarven was not his life's ambition. Finch offered the servant a sympathetic look, which Jarven could not fail to note.

"He is dangerous," the Terafin gardener told the Terafin House Council member.

"Yes, of course he is. But he's served Hectore for all of my life."

"You cannot be certain of that."

"I can be as certain of it as I am of anything."

Jarven coughed.

"I am not you, Jarven," Finch replied, as if the obvious criticism had been spoken aloud. "I need some certainty in my life. The Terafin met with Hectore. She could not, therefore, avoid meeting Andrei. She said nothing; she offered no warning; she felt no danger.

"She was in command of her forest, even then. Had Andrei been the danger that either you or Birgide perceive, I believe she would have."

"You and The Terafin have different skills."

"We always have. She taught us to trust even the most difficult of people—and Andrei has never been that."

"ATerafin—" Birgide began. She shook her head. "Councillor."

"Finch."

"Finch. I feel this is unwise."

Finch nodded, unruffled. "Your objections are understood."

"No," Birgide surprised Hectore by replying, "they are not. What you see before you is not human."

Finch shrugged. The motion was economical, and to Hectore's surprise, unforced. "He wouldn't be the only occupant of the Terafin manse who is not."

"He is *not* an occupant of the Terafin manse while I live and breathe," Hectore interjected.

"It was a figure of speech. Is he demonic?"

Birgide's hesitation was marked by everyone in the room.

"Birgide."

". . . No."

"And what is he, then?" Jarven asked. He chose that moment to rise, shedding, as he did the patina of weakness that generally came with age. He was like, and unlike, Sigurne.

Birgide closed her eyes. Hectore struggled not to feel offense on Andrei's behalf, but gave up; it was not a struggle worth having.

"You are like a doting parent, Hectore," Jarven observed.

"That has never caused me harm, before."

"It is not, generally, the parent who suffers."

Andrei's expression soured further. His attitude was in line with Jarven's, and, of course, it pained him. He looked entirely like himself. Even the injuries that had troubled him seemed to have gone the way of Jarven's age-induced weakness.

"I was once considered of the god-born," Andrei told Birgide. "Although it is my suspicion you are aware of this."

"I met recently with Meralonne APhaniel," she replied. "And his mastery of things ancient was considered unsurpassed within the Order. Grudgingly. I believe he was aware of your presence in a way that the rest of the city was not."

"And he did not speak of it."

"Not until today, no. He considers any attempt to communicate with you both dangerous and unwise."

Hectore cleared his throat. He was accustomed to receiving attention the moment he desired it; it was slow to come, today. "You are saying that Member APhaniel *knew* that Andrei was in the city, and did not choose to mention it to the Order—or his guildmaster—at all?"

"I am not privy to the communications between APhaniel and Sigurne Mellifas," was Birgide's careful reply. "My tenure at the order involved very little casual contact with the magi." A politic answer. An answer that demanded other questions.

Finch inhaled once. The silence of her breath lasted three beats before she exhaled. "Patris Araven, I would like to invite you to dine with me, on an evening of your choice, in my quarters in the Terafin manse." She did not mention Andrei. She did not even look at him. Hectore had been fond of Finch—one could not help feeling the deepest of sympathy for anyone trapped in an office under Jarven—but this single decisive action on her part was so graceful and so unexpected, fondness gave way to something stronger.

He had agreed to aid Jewel—The Terafin—because he thought of her as an unofficial grandchild—the daughter of Ararath, the most heartbreakingly difficult of his many godsons. Jewel had sent him to Finch. And in this office, Hectore accepted that he would offer aid to Finch should Jewel no longer require it. Finch was not Jewel. She had no discernible magic, no inborn

talent. She was forced—as Hectore had been—to navigate the shoals of in-
fested, political waters with nothing but guile, ambition, and will.

"I am offended," Jarven told her quietly.

"Oh?"

"You have never invited *me* to dine in the West Wing."

"I have—I believe I invited both you and Lucille to visit."

"I note you are not inviting me now."

"I suspect that I won't be able to keep you away unless I wish to cause
significant internal embarrassment to the Merchant Authority offices." Her
brow furrowed. "Very well—but can you *please* stop teasing Jester? It makes
him uncomfortable, and I have to live with him."

"Given your current situation in the House, you most certainly do not.
Quarters would be made available for your personal use—and yours alone—if
you but asked."

"Don't change the subject. If you will treat Jester as an intelligent, capable
peer, you are welcome to join us."

"I could treat him like the Twin Kings and it would only increase his
hostility and suspicion."

"Much of which, you must admit, you deserve."

"You wound me, Finch." He smiled.

"Not noticeably." Finch smiled as well. "Patris Araven? Would dinner
with Jarven suit you?"

Andrei looked like he had swallowed glass. It was immeasurably comforting. "I almost cannot imagine doing this without him," Hectore confessed.
"Although I would be greatly obliged if you managed to finagle an acceptance out of Lucille. Jarven is at his best when he is with her."

"He is not."

"He is—all of his mischief in her presence involves his dignity alone; it is
otherwise benign."

Finch laughed. "She is not terribly fond of you."

"No, and that's a pity. I bear her no ill will; I have admired her—at a safe
distance—for decades."

"When do you think you will be available?"

"Given Jarven's command of the Merchants' Guild during this time of
crisis, I have remarkably little to do. If you felt it appropriate, I could join
you tomorrow evening."

"The early dinner hour?"

"I would be delighted."

Chapter Twenty-Five

THE SILENCE WAS BOTH cold and heated as they jogged. Jewel could manage to run in spurts—but not for long. The attachments Terrick had fashioned for the feet of those who could not skirt above the snow's surface made her widen her stance; Terrick had said it was unnecessary, but she still hadn't developed the knack of moving naturally. The pack she carried slowed her down; Avandar took it. Terrick and Angel were already encumbered; Adam, on foot, bore tenting which had seen almost no use in the winter landscape.

Shianne's song continued for some time. The earth shifted twice beneath Jewel's feet, a rumbling that made her knees feel like water. She understood that earth, air, and water in their wild, elemental forms, had voices; she had never heard them speak. Even in her own land, on her own ground, she had been aware of them as presences—but as intruders, as unwelcome guests.

No, she thought, stumbling as the ground shuddered again.

On some fundamental level she felt, about the elements on that day, the way she felt about her great, winged cats. She had been angry. Beyond angry. She would have been just as furious at her cats if they had attempted to have one of their squalling fights in the middle of the service, although their squalling fights couldn't cause the same level of destruction.

She had not been regal with the wild elements; she had not been graceful. She had kicked them out of the room and told them to clean up their damn mess first.

She slowed to catch her breath.

She'd told them to take their toys and *go home*. She would have told the cats the same thing. Both the elements and the cats understood her when she spoke in genuine anger. Exasperation? No; that was safe to ignore. Of course it was; Jewel ignored it all the time. Living in a two-room apartment with so many disparate personalities, that had become second nature.

She would never, on the other hand, enter someone else's home and expect that her rules would be obeyed if she laid them down in the same fashion.

But even that wasn't all of the truth. In desperation, the division between "home" and "outside" vanished. She could not command Isladar in the way she commanded the cats or the elements; she could not command the two demons who had ventured into the heart of the wild forest in which she *could* make a stand. But she had taken the road against the Wild Hunt, and she had held it, making of it something that spoke to her: the streets of the hundred holdings.

How had she done that? How had she managed? Desperation couldn't be the answer. She had been beyond desperate too many times in her life, and the universe had failed to move as she desired.

Rules. She wanted rules. She wanted to *know* how *this* world worked, because knowledge was the only hope she had. "Isladar."

He could, she was certain, run for days without pause. The dead didn't need to eat. Or breathe. Or rest.

"Terafin."

"What is a Sen?"

"You have not asked Viandaran or Lord Celleriant?"

"It wasn't relevant before."

"It is, and was, always relevant. Do you feel that ignorance excuses responsibility?" He lifted a hand, signaling a stop, before she could answer. In truth, answering while running had been a trial.

Shadow was giving Isladar the side-eye. His hackles had fallen, but he was twitchy and tense. Jewel placed a hand on his forehead the minute they came to rest, ignoring the murmured threats to eat that hand.

"I would answer the question if I could," Isladar told her. He was not lying.

No. Why do you think that is? Avandar asked.

Because the answer wouldn't do her any good. Knowing this, she still felt compelled to listen. To hear what he was willing to put into words. Even the absence of information would give her some basic structure, some underlying shape.

"Do your kin know more than you do?"

"Only one. Only one, among all of my kin. It is my belief that you and he will cross paths. For the first time since the devastation, he has taken a pet. Perhaps you know of whom I speak; you traveled with the Arkosan Voyani when they entered the Sea of Sorrows. I do not know if he could answer your questions; I do not think the Sen themselves, gathered in one place, could— not that they could coexist in one place.

"There is a reason that the Cities of Man never grew—the way human cities oft will—to form kingdoms or empires. The Sen are as gods in their own small spaces."

"And what," Jewel asked, as he raised both arms until they were perpendicular to the straight, slender line of his body, "are the gods? What were they, then?"

His eyes opened; he had closed them, as if to concentrate. "I can think of very few who would follow your first question with that one."

"Why?"

"You have met gods."

"And I don't understand what they are any better than I understand, in the end, what you are. I understand that you're predators. I understand that your prey is mostly us. I understand that, where we can, we must destroy you— and I even understand some of how to do it. But the knowledge is practical."

"Viandaran, I do not think you appreciate what you have chosen to serve."

Avandar said nothing.

"The gods as they once existed are not what they are now. Nor were any two gods alike. If the Sen could not occupy the same city without disastrous results, the gods could barely content themselves with occupying entire small worlds—worlds such as this one. You ask me to define the gods for you? Terafin, we barely understood them ourselves. They were not as we were, even when we lived. We could touch the wilderness; we could cajole it, and where powerful, we could bend it to our will.

"But we did not create it. We did not make it."

"But the gods had children."

He nodded.

"And their children had children. If I understand, in the end, anything Shianne said, you were—when alive—the children of the White Lady."

He paused, although he did not lower his arms. "You are bold, even for a mortal."

"Is this why the demons seem to recognize Illaraphaniel?"

"Too bold. I will give advice, although it is the way of your kind to ignore it if it does not suit your whim. Do not ask him. Never ask him."

"And never ask the *Kialli*, either?"

"Very few of the *Kialli* will speak with you—and those you are likely to encounter will desire your death, regardless. It may hasten the death; it may intensify the ferocity of the attack. It may—should it prove necessary—distract, where distraction is a possibility. Do not ask."

"I have to ask."

"So believes many a fool. Why?"

"Because I will travel—with Shianne—to the White Lady. The Winter Queen. I understand that the enmity between your Lord and the White Lady is endless and ancient, but—" She hesitated.

"But?"

"It is not to destroy you that she hunts him." She spoke with certainty, because suddenly, she was.

"No."

"It is to destroy him."

"Little mortal, do not ask. It is safe, perhaps, to question my Lord—but you will never survive it. Even the mortals he graced with power could not, in the end. You do not understand what a god is, and what our Lord *was*, and only in experiencing it will you understand us. But it will change you. If you are lucky, it will only break your mind—but the effect of that, on the Sen, is a matter of legend."

"We loved the god who became the Lord of the Hells." He spoke quietly, softly. Jewel listened, as if hearing, beneath the words he chose to speak, the words that hid beneath them, waiting. "We loved his night, and the subtle beauty of it. We loved the texture of his voice and the words that formed palaces and mountains and great, gaping chasms of rock; we loved his strength and his fury."

"You were her children."

"Yes."

"And the Arianni are not born the normal way."

Shadow hissed. "They *are*," he insisted. "It is *you* who are *strange*."

Jewel ignored this, focusing now on the question she had asked, and the questions that waited beneath it; she had a sense that she was not asking the right ones, as if this was the only chance she would ever have, and she was, in ignorance, wasting it.

"You were part of her, in a way that I could never be part of my mother, if

I understand what Shianne said. Nothing you are, nothing you were, nothing you could be did not come from her."

Isladar was still.

"Did she love your Lord?"

In the distance, she heard the panicked denial of the Winter King. Closer, she heard Avandar's sudden withdrawal; the totality of his rejection of the single question.

"You must ask her," Isladar replied.

Jewel *knew* she would not survive even the beginning of the question. Knew, as well, gazing at the benign neutrality of the *Kialli* lord who had, in some fashion, protected Kiriel, that she might not survive the asking now. "You mean to kill me."

"No, not yet. But if you are this unwise, you will find death; the difficulty will be avoiding it. We are not *of* her, now."

"But—"

"We are dead. You, however, are not. Shianne, as you call her, has almost finished, and when her voice falls into silence, many, many voices will fill the gap. But not all. They know you are here, Terafin, and it is through your actions that the most ancient of all losses has been . . . renewed. You will not survive; they will wake the earth in their attempt to see an end to you."

"But the Oracle—"

"The Oracle is not—yet—where you are. The earth will not wake beneath her feet; the air will not move against her. She is firstborn, and she is the heart of her own world; if you reach her side, you—and your companions—will be safe."

The rumbling beneath Jewel's feet silenced her for a moment. This time, however, it did not fully still.

Lord Isladar—and he seemed that to Jewel, in this place—did not appear to notice. He lifted his palms; they were flat and straight, perpendicular to the line of his arms. He spoke three words—resonant words, syllables that encompassed sensation more than sound. She could not repeat them—not then, and not after, yet at the same time, she could not forget them; they remained at the heart of her memories, in a place that she could not easily reach.

Avandar's shields rose; they were so strong and so solid Jewel saw the world through a brilliant, orange pane. The domicis did not speak.

No one did. Terrick had armed himself; he had not dropped the pack that encumbered his back. Adam, however, was frowning. Jewel saw this because she reached for him, drawing him instinctively to her side—and behind the magical shields Avandar had erected.

Shadow growled, but did not attempt to attack the demon lord; he watched, his golden eyes narrowed. "Hurry, hurry, hurry."

"Eldest," Isladar replied.

"*Hurry*. They will *know*."

"What is he trying to do?" Jewel asked the great, gray cat.

He is hoping, Avandar replied, *to take a short cut. Watch what he does; watch it carefully. It may be something you will be forced to do in future.*

I don't understand what he's doing, which is why I asked.

We will walk between this world and our own.

But we haven't finished yet. We haven't reached—

That is why it is difficult, Terafin. He was annoyed; he seldom used her title privately unless he intended to lecture. *The path he opens must be some part of this world, and yet must blend with some part of our own. We must walk it fully, and we must not step off—or we will be fully away from the hidden path, and we will not be able to return.*

Could I do this?

It is my belief that you could, yes. He frowned. *What is Adam doing?*

Adam was, to Jewel's surprise, kneeling. His brow was furrowed, the elastic lines of youthful forehead adopting the creases of thought that would fall away just as easily the moment his expression changed. His hand was pressed into the snow; he had removed the mittens that kept the cold at bay.

"Adam?"

Adam's frown deepened, but he looked up and met Jewel's concerned gaze. "He is not—he is not doing what needs to be done."

Isladar's eyes opened; he looked at Adam, and only Adam.

Avandar's shields intensified. Jewel wanted to tell him to cut it out, because it was now hard to see the world beyond them clearly. Adam was beside her.

"I am attempting—" he began.

But Adam cut him off. "I feel what you are attempting to build from the body of the earth." He grimaced, shook his head, and reverted to Torra. "I believe that you do not intend us harm. Not right now. The Matriarch would know."

"Can you do what I am attempting to do?"

The Voyani boy's frown shifted, intensifying and turning—as it often did—inward. "You are not the only person here who is trying."

They froze, then.

They froze as Shadow snarled and leaped.

Into what was not a clearing, stepping between the trees anchored in the rumbling earth, stepped a figure that Jewel had never seen before. In seeming, in shape, in form, he was Arianni. But his blade was red.

"Lord Isladar," the demon said. "We should have expected this."

"Lord Darranatos," Isladar replied. He glanced, once, at Adam, and lowered his arms. "Have you come to redeem yourself?"

Darranatos. She would not have recognized him had Isladar not thought to use his name. She wondered if it was deliberate.

It is not, Avandar told her. *To Darranatos, we are insignificant. I am not certain that he believes even you to be a threat. The presence of Isladar merely confirms what he has long suspected: it is not mortals who are the threat.*

"Viandaran," Darranatos said softly, as if he could hear the words the domicis had wisely chosen not to speak aloud.

Jewel lifted hand in brief, quick den-sign. She did not otherwise look to Angel. *Winter King,* she said.

We are coming, the Winter King replied. *But, Terafin, understand: these are Immortals. Do not trust their response to sentiment, memory, or pain to be similar to your own. In the end, Immortals are concerned with power.*

She thought of the Winter Queen.

Yes, he replied.

Darranatos called upon his shield before Jewel had time to raise her chin. His eyes were silver edges in the pale, perfect contours of his face; he was—of course he was—beautiful. Isladar was not. And yet, when Jewel managed to pull her gaze from Darranatos, he, too, was armed—and his sword and shield were almost the twin of the armaments that the *Kialli* carried.

Jewel.

Darranatos moved before the domicis could finish giving instructions. He moved before Avandar could draw breath. So, too, Jewel, who had dropped to her knees as the arc of the demon's sword pierced the magical shield that Avandar had erected. It failed to separate Jewel's head from her shoulders; Isladar moved before the blade returned.

Avandar moved as well, grabbing both Jewel and Adam and leaping back through the trees.

"Put me down," Adam told him. "Put me down *now.*"

Avandar was not Adam's servant; it surprised Jewel when he obeyed. Adam dropped to the snow-covered ground, and sank. His hands were red and slightly wet as he once again attempted to press them through snow and into the earth itself—the earth that had not stopped rumbling.

Jewel, this is unwise.

It was. But it was necessary. She *knew*, watching Adam, that they would not survive if he did not complete whatever it was he had started. And because she knew it so viscerally, Avandar sensed it as well. His jaw tightened.

You will let me summon my weapon. It wasn't a question.

Jewel caught his arm, briefly, between her hands; she was mute. She opened her mouth to a roar that wasn't her own. In the distance, the serpent was trumpeting anger and pain.

Terrick leaped back as two red swords clashed. Sparks of fire scattered across the surface of broken snow as the two strangers met, head on. For a moment the one who had been called Darranatos turned his back to the Rendish warrior; he shrugged himself free of the confinement of straps, shifting his grip on his ax as he divested himself of their necessary supplies.

He did not, however, attempt to take advantage of the opening; it closed too quickly. Angel motioned and slid around the trunk of a large tree; the snow on its bark implied the movement of wind in a single direction. There was no wind now. The roar of thunder above blended with the roar of armed men and the disturbing rumble of earth beneath his feet.

Gray fur appeared to his left; he looked down to meet the golden eyes of the disrespectful, talking cat. The cat's fur had risen inches, but even so, the line of his tense shoulders could be clearly seen.

"What is he?" he asked of Shadow.

"You would call him *demon*," the cat replied—in Rendish. "*Your* ax could cut him."

Terrick was not so certain. "I'm not sure I can get close enough to land a blow."

The cat growled. "He is *dangerous*."

Terrick nodded. Dangerous and fell. His roar was not a sign of anger; it was wild and almost joyous. But his opponent did not likewise descend into the same battle-maddened state. Although they appeared to be of the same height and weight, Isladar was driven back, as if Darranatos' size belied his strength. They left runnels in the surface of snow; Terrick would not have been surprised had they broken frozen earth.

Shadow watched, tense; he did not leap. Nor did Terrick. He did not and could not look away from the fight as it progressed in a wider and wider area through the standing trees. Bark flew; branches shed snow where one—or the other—hit trunks. Wood cracked.

Neither slowed, but Darranatos roared again. "Come, come, brother!" he shouted, his words moving the earth. "How long has it been since you've truly given yourself over to the glory of the moment?"

Isladar failed to reply.

"Be ready," Terrick told the great, gray cat.

Darranatos, in combat with Isladar, had not forgotten his original purpose. His sword's arc passed through the trunks of standing trees, and they fell, almost as afterthought, in his wake. But they fell toward Jewel.

Toward Adam.

Avandar lifted his left hand; light flared across the length of his forearm. In the winter landscape, it scattered across snow in a thousand little reflections that hurt the eye. Jewel raised her arms to cover Adam's head, shutting her eyes briefly, although she knew—

What are you doing?

Jewel!

—That neither Avandar nor the Winter King would approve. They didn't understand her gift. They didn't understand that of all the people standing in this winter forest, the only person she was certain her gift would save was herself. She had never been able to rely on it to save anyone else. Not her father, in the end; not her mother or her Oma; not Fisher or Lefty or Lander—or Duster. Not Rath. Not even Rath.

She had buried The Terafin, the strongest woman—outside of her Oma— she had ever met. Morretz had died.

She had had no warning at all when Carver had walked into a damned *closet* and disappeared. Hovering protectively over Adam while Avandar's shield radiated sunlight and heat was the *only* thing she could do for him; if the trees somehow pierced Avandar's magic, her body would move before she could think.

It wasn't Jewel the falling trunks or branches would crush.

Shadow roared. Even over the distant thunder of serpent and the growing presence of shaking earth, she knew his wordless voice. At any other time he would have wrapped it around insults and sibilants and hurled them at her. It was not at her that his ire was directed.

Nor was it Angel, who came out from behind a tree, his sword in hand, his expression both alert and grim; he stepped onto the battlefield as if it were a graveyard. Avandar gestured, and falling trunks burst instantly into flame, descending as ash and splinters.

Angel took up his position at her back.

She gestured; he couldn't see her hands. Or he didn't look, which was more likely. She knew there was very little he could do—but he had her back. He had always had her back. He had almost died because, unlike Kiriel, he could think past both his fear and his rage, and he had come to her aid when Isladar had attempted to kill her.

He occupied the position he had occupied since she'd found him in the streets of the holding.

Isladar is no match for Darranatos, Avandar said. *And I am not, as I am.* The shield he bore shunted aside a trunk that would have easily broken Jewel's arm, if only that. *Let me join him, Jewel.*

She shook her head. *If I die*, she told him, *you are free to do as you must.*

Silence.

If I thought you a match for him fully armed—if I thought you a match for him as Warlord—I would let you do it. I don't.

Why?

Because you don't. It was true. She felt his momentary amusement; it was a grim, dark humor.

You have become more perceptive.

She shook her head. *How many of them were like this?*

Them?

The Arianni. The—whatever they were called when they left the White Lady to join—

Do not name him. Not even in this fashion. And the answer is very, very few. Meralonne is not their match—not yet. But the three who sleep were, and possibly will be. They were his closest kin, his closest brethren.

She exhaled. *Speak to the earth*, she told her domicis. *Speak to it, calm it.*

I cannot do that and protect you.

You won't need to. Angel is here.

He was astonished. And annoyed.

Angel's hair rose as wind gusted through the remaining trees, catching and dampening the fire that burned on fallen logs. He shifted his grip on his sword. He had no illusions about his ability; he could not meet the demon in combat and survive for more than half a breath. Nor could he stand long against Isladar. But he had faced the latter once, and he had managed to stand for *long enough*.

He intended to do so here, as well.

Jay hovered over Adam; the young healer's eyes were closed. His face had gone from wind-red to white; he neither spoke nor moved.

The forest was not like the manse; it was not like the crowded, tiny apartment in which the entirety of the den had eaten, slept, and wintered. But in this moment, it didn't matter. Carver was gone. Duster was gone.

Angel remained. He carried the sword upon which, in the end, he had sworn his oath to the House while Jewel ruled it. Strands of his hair had escaped the confines of the Northern braid; the wind pushed it back from his face; it was bracing and somehow clean. He shifted, bending knees slightly; the snow compressed beneath the wide, flat snowshoes he wore. It was strange, to feel at home in this place—but for a moment, he did.

He knew what he wanted. He knew exactly what he was meant to do—and he was doing it. Nothing stood between him and Jay.

Darranatos had not come alone.

From between the trees in the distance, the rest of his companions emerged.

Adam felt their presence.

It was tangled in the body of the world itself—because the world, *this* world, was alive. If it had no heart, no lungs, no brain, no limbs, it nonetheless had something that felt like a living form beneath his spread palms. At a remove, he felt snow; he knew that his hands were—or should be—numb or even frostbitten, as Terrick called it.

He dealt with it almost without thought, as he dealt with most of the injuries he had sustained since his awakening. His own body knew its correct shape; it knew what it required to continue to exist. So, too, the bodies of the mortals Adam had been allowed to heal in his tenure in Averalaan. The earth was not, in any way, like them.

He had only once encountered anything that was.

He understood instinctively what Isladar was trying to achieve. He could see, with his eyes closed, the weaving of musculature, the altering of earth that occurred just beneath his hands. He could sense light and heat and starscape; could feel the tang of salt against his lips. All of these were things that were not *of* this place, this white, silent world.

He felt fire—and fire was not of this world, either.

He worked to douse it, and the world worked, naturally, with him. But he held the other things that were foreign to it in place, and the earth accepted them. It was not like healing; it was like weaving. Adam had seen the looms in the Terafin manse; Carver had showed him. They were large and intimidating. He could not weave, but watched, where watching was permitted; there was something almost like magic in the process of creation; one took threads and skeins and made of them something that was more than the sum of its parts, and yet also exactly that.

Fire, fire, fire. He felt it surge; he extinguished it. It took effort and focus, very like the effort of healing. In the chill of winter, sweat beaded his forehead; he thought it would freeze there, while he worked.

But he worked in the Matriarch's shadow, and he wove that shadow into the whole, grasping it as if it were, among all things present, the most precious, the most necessary.

And it was, to the Voyani. Adam was of Arkosa. Jewel was of Terafin. But she had taken him in and allowed him to care for the children—even if there was only one. She had touched the sleeping dreamers that had fallen to the beguiling lies of the ancient world, and they had woken to her touch, as they had to his—but each time, for Adam, sleep had returned.

For the Matriarch, never. She had banished it. She had led them back to the lives they must lead: lives of pain and duty and loss. And yet, also, lives of hope and dreams and joy.

Adam understood what he was weaving; he understood it in a way that even Lord Isladar did not; Lord Isladar was, as he had claimed, dead. The dead, Adam knew, could drive the living almost mercilessly, because the dead could not change. They were trapped, by the living, in their rage, their fear, or their resentment; trapped, by the living, in their sorrow and their loss. The lands here would not free them; they remembered, and their anger was endless. But so, too, their sorrow.

Adam had seen the strange combination of sorrow and rage wreak havoc among his own kin. And he had, as a child, and later, as a young man, interceded. Anger had frightened him, as it frightened many children. But sorrow moved him in a different way.

He was not as Isladar was: he was not eternal. But he was alive.

Angel's sword caught the long, dark claws of the first demon to reach him; the creature was casual and careless, as if swords such as Angel's were harmless. That cost the demon a hand.

Angel had seen how ineffective regular swords and daggers could be against demons; with enough strength behind them, they could be wielded as clubs, but their edges did not cut demonic flesh. This sword had come from the armory in The Terafin's personal chambers, and it had refused to leave its sheath until he had sworn his oath to The Terafin—to Jay. He suspected that Meralonne had some inkling of the sword's history; he suspected that Avandar did as well. Neither had chosen to share.

Demonic eyes widened.

Shadow roared.

Flames rose in sudden fury, demolishing snow. Angel didn't burn. He wasn't certain why, but didn't pause to question it: the demons didn't pause. There were two here; one was winged. It rose, bleeding where it had lost part of its left arm. The other shifted in place. What had once been a large, four-armed creature now condensed in all dimensions.

Neither spoke.

But the constant rumble beneath Angel's feet grew stronger. The fires banked suddenly; given the reaction of the demon that remained on the ground, the absence of fire was not his choice. He leaped back, and back again; Angel followed the first swift retreat, but held his ground for the second leap. He was there for Jay—Jay and Adam. He did not intend to let himself be lured away.

The creature on the ground leaped to the side, keeping his distance; he gestured, and fire once again rose in an orange wall. Angel cut it.

Angel cut it and it split in half, the two sections falling away as if they were the slashed wall of a rough tent. The flames seemed to avoid the blade itself.

He moved when the demon once again closed. This time, it barreled in, as if to force Angel back—or out of the way. Angel turned slightly to the side, shifting his stance as he brought the blade to bear in an arc that began below his hip and ended above his head.

The demon stopped at the last instant; he made no further attempt to deflect the sword with his arm. Instead, almost hissing, he drew a sword of his own. It was red; redder than the flames that kept banking. No shield followed, for which Angel was thankful.

He moved, his sword clashing with the demon's against a background that was becoming less white as the minutes passed. He had not forgotten the winged demon. He moved when something that was not fire rained down from the sky.

Avandar's shields caught it, shunting it to either side of where Jay stood; it was liquid darkness. Angel had no chance to examine it; he was hardpressed, now. The armed demon was fast; possibly faster than Angel.

But the darkness that had fallen harmlessly upon the ground rose, moving in reverse; that much he could see. Not more. He was peripherally aware of a figure that moved in from his right; he recognized Terrick's height in the brief glance he could afford.

The demon saw more; he leaped again, as if he were weightless. The height of the arc of his single jump implied wings, although he had none. In the air, above the demon's knife-slender body, the whole of the sky seemed to shake.

Angel looked up at the roar of rage and fury that accompanied the sudden appearance of a giant, winged serpent. It was a deep, sapphire blue, with glints of obsidian and green along its underbelly. That underbelly was exposed and, for the first time today, visible.

Had the demon not been likewise distracted by the presence of the serpent, Angel would have died. As it was, he had enough time to bring his sword up as the demon leaped once again; the deflection was messy, and he staggered at the weight of the blow.

If fires were easily doused, the wind that came in the serpent's wake was not. But the wind was a storm. If it was under the control of any creature present, it wasn't obvious who: everything standing in the forest was caught in its howling folds; branches, dry with winter, were torn from the trunks of standing trees; debris-littered snow rose in a gritty veil.

Avandar cursed in an unfamiliar language.

Jay cursed in Torra. She folded herself over Adam.

"Matriarch." The healer-born boy shouted to be heard over the wind and the serpent. "I *must* remain in contact with the ground."

"Are you bespeaking the earth?" Avandar demanded.

"No—but we will not be able to leave if I cannot finish here—unless we wish never to return."

Speak to the earth, Jewel told her domicis. She slid her arms around Adam's; she covered the backs of those hands with her palms. Snow had not so much melted as evaporated in the wake of waves of fire. The fire had not been enough—not quite—to wake the earth.

But the wind would do it. She listened for Kallandras but heard only wind and silence. His was the only distant voice she was certain to hear.

Not the only voice, the Winter King said. *Two of the kin are destroyed. One kept the serpent invisible. The serpent is* not *pleased,* he added, in case this wasn't obvious. *Shianne bespeaks it, but says it is confused because it is so newly wakened. It rides the wind, and the wind reflects its mood.*

She had never been so grateful to hear the Winter King.

He was amused. *Your memory is poor, Terafin.*

Bring Kallandras and Celleriant; tell Snow to bring Shianne here.

And Calliastra?

She doesn't need to use the road we're going to use. If she wants to find us, she'll find us. Jewel exhaled. *And if she wants to follow, lead her.*

You are opening a door?

Not me, she replied. *Adam.*

She felt the Winter King's uneasiness. *He is not Sen.*

It doesn't matter. As she said it, she *knew* it was true.

There is a danger—

There's always *a danger. The earth is about to wake. Avandar might—just might—be able to stave off its rage for long enough that we all survive—but not if we're still here. We need to move.*

And the kin?

She swallowed. *Lord Isladar is fighting Darranatos—the demon we met during the victory parade.*

He will perish.

That won't break my heart—as long as he does it after we're clear.

His chuckle was dry and cold. *We will make a power of you yet.*

That was very much what Jewel feared. She settled her weight across Adam's back, bracing herself with her hands and her feet.

Night roared above her. Shadow roared back. She could almost hear words in the cadence of their bestial voices—but the words didn't matter. They were wild, yes; they were deadly; they could not be easily contained or commanded. But in some fashion, they were hers.

They didn't change when the world itself did. They weren't impressed by gods, the firstborn, or the immortal. They were entirely themselves, a kind of touchstone when things got too strange. She herself was prone to awe, to a sense of her own insignificance in the greater scheme of ancient things. She could fall silent, caught by the certainty that there were people to whom she should not so much as raise her eyes, let alone speak.

The cats? Never.

Something struck her back. Water, she thought. Or blood. The latter made her tense, but no instinct forced her hands from Adam's or her feet from the ground. She heard the low sound of Terrick's voice, although the wind tore most of it away. Strange, then, that she was aware of Angel's strained, but familiar, breathing; strange that she could hear the familiar weight of his steps. The earth tilted, but did not dislodge her. Nor did it dislodge—or worse, swallow—Adam.

She thought she could hear the breaking of stone.

She could not hear Avandar's voice at all; she knew he spoke to the ancient earth only because of their connection. She could not hear the earth's answer, except in the absence of shouting or screams—but that was enough, for now; she could certainly hear the keening, angry wind.

"Adam," she said, into his ear. "Hurry. I don't think Isladar can hold out for much longer."

He did not respond—not in words; she didn't expect it. Her hair was a tangle in her eyes, and she couldn't push it aside. But she could see Isladar and Darranatos in the distance; much of the debris that also clung to unruly curls had come from the trees their far-ranging combat had destroyed.

She could see flashes of red lightning.

She could see the shadow that suddenly fell across the earth against which she and Adam huddled. She lifted her face, turning her neck at an awkward angle to see the underbelly of a serpent. *Dragon*, she thought, her mouth suddenly dry. But that was wrong. She *knew* it.

She wasn't particularly surprised to see lightning shafts illuminate an otherwise cloudless sky.

Adam understood instinctively what Jewel wanted from him.

Isladar had begun a weaving similar to Adam's—but the strands he had chosen were subtly different. If Adam completed what Isladar had begun, they might arrive anywhere. It wouldn't save them; the demons here were too strong, and nothing Adam did would prevent them from following.

There was only one place that offered the possibility of safety—or at least survival—to the Matriarch of Terafin. To Adam it was a strange, foreign place—but he had been offered food, shelter, and what passed for kinship among the Northerners. He knew the manor. He knew the West Wing.

What he did not know, or had not known, until he touched the earth with the intent to somehow *heal*, was this place.

Each person's body was different. Each healing was therefore likewise different, although the variances could be great or small depending on the circumstance. Levec said that even the same person's body, with the passage of months or years, required shifting perspective.

Healing, Levec said, was by nature invasive. But many things were invasive and yet, still welcome. If the patient had both the will and the fear, they could reject a healer's touch.

This had shocked Adam, at the time—but he knew so little about the healer-born he accepted it as truth. Levec was many things, most of them some flavor of angry, but he was not a liar. No one, however, had rejected Adam. No one had tried.

No, Levec said, as if greatly weary. *And I do not think they will, in future. You see them as they are, Adam, and even when you heal them, you accept them* as they are. *Not everyone can do this; among the healers, there are those who find it very, very difficult. When you heal, you must accept what* is. *You must not offer horror at the injury, or judgment of it, right or wrong.*

For the first time, Adam understood Levec's admonishment, because the body beneath his hands was not mortal. It was not human. It did not breathe or bleed. But it was alive; it had something that resembled the faintest of pulses, the faintest of heartbeats—absent the heart with which Adam was familiar.

Winter nestled in that heart. Adam, who had been born in the South, knew deserts and plains and sea, but the sense of winter, the poetry of it, the *story*, resided here. Yet it was not the only story. He could hear the faintest echoes of others; could see their shadows buried beneath his feet.

"Adam."

Jewel's voice tickled his ear at a distance. He almost turned away from those small shadows, those tiny, odd sounds. But he recognized the bare outline of one of them, and stopped. He saw a city. Not the crowded, smelly city of Averalaan, but one that stood in the almost unreachable distance: its heights were so great they vanished into clouds.

The towers shed light, the way still lakes reflected sun, and even at this remove he could make out a single shining figure who paced the walls above which the towers rose.

This was not Arkosa. He wondered if it were Havalla, Lyserra, or Corrona. He wondered if the city in the distance had once stood here, where winter now reigned. The answer returned in a shudder.

No.

Or perhaps not: the earth beneath his feet was rumbling, moving; rocks beneath the snow and the scattering of dirt fire had exposed ground together, producing a sound that was harsh, grating—and almost syllabic.

Adam almost lifted both of his hands; had Jewel's not been laid across them, he would have. The ground that he touched and the earth beneath it were two different entities—but the earth was loud. It was growing louder as the minutes passed.

This, then, was what Isladar hoped to avoid: the waking of the earth. Adam was not certain he could communicate with this ancient, wild force; he did not try. Instead, he kept contact with the world itself, which was moving and shifting to make way for the earth's passage.

But the earth stilled a moment, for no reason Adam could discern. He took the strands of this place in his hands, and he continued to weave.

Not like that, *stupid boy.*

He opened his eyes to demons and fire and snow; he heard the sound of clashing blades, and the guttural cursing of a blessedly foreign tongue. His cheeks stung as the wind roared past—and as it did he could almost hear words in its folds. They were as cold, as chill, as the wind itself in this place.

Not like that.

"Then how?" Adam shouted back, just to be heard.

She needs to come back.

"She can come back the way she arrived in the first place!"

She can't. The way is closed. She cannot return if she leaves.

"We have to leave—" He could no longer hear the wind over the roar of something louder and angrier; he saw the skies shift color as lightning struck, and struck, and struck. None of it hit him—but he was almost certain some of it should have.

Yes and no. You must make this *place part of* hers. *They must be woven together.* Snow *should do it, but he is* lazy.

"You do it!"

Silence. It was a silence particular to the cats. Adam accepted it; he knew how to translate. Shadow could not do what he felt must be done. But he thought Adam—stupid and stunted and mortal though he was—could. With help. Which generally meant insults and growling.

But that's what the cats did. They were raw and self-indulgent and they denied any weakness—as if love could be a weakness—and yet, somehow, Shadow was willing to watch over Ariel.

Adam smiled. In the midst of the chaos of a small, strange battlefield, his lips curved involuntarily; his hands relaxed as he pressed them into the slender, living body of this world. He thought of Terafin, of Jewel; he thought of deserts; he thought of ancient cities and a time when the Northern gods had once walked the earth. He thought of cats, great and small; of Ariel, the child who had lost her family and home on a night when honesty was celebrated behind the masks of the Festival Moon.

And he thought of Matriarchs, of the burden they must carry and the way the weight of it aged them. He had never truly seen power in their burden; he had seen responsibility, and he had feared it. He had never believed he could shoulder the weight they carried. He did not believe he could do so now.

Yet this work was the work of Matriarchs; he knew it in his bones. What he did not know—and would not, until it was too late—was whether or not he could do it successfully. It was not the effort that was difficult, although it was; it was the fear. The cost of failure was so very, very high.

Yes, he thought: the work of Matriarchs. And he had never desired to be one.

Jewel looked up, and up again, and raised voice. "Kallandras! Celleriant! Return to us now!"

Chapter Twenty-Six

16th of Morel, 428 A.A.
Terafin Manse, Averalaan Aramarelas

THE OFFICE OF THE right-kin was not empty. Teller sat behind the desk once occupied by Gabriel ATerafin. Finch sat on its outer edge, her feet dangling above the floor. She wore a brown dress, one made by Haval; it did not appear to be particularly noteworthy, given his reputation as clothier to the powerful and the wealthy.

Birgide Viranyi occupied one of the chairs to the side of Teller's remarkably clean desk. Her eyes were ringed with circles; she looked exhausted. As she was not kin, even by the loose standards of the den, Finch didn't ask her if she required rest, food, or sleep—but it was close. Teller had confirmed Birgide as ATerafin—to Barston's rigid disapproval. Birgide had been staff for almost no time, in Barston's opinion, and if she was well-known as a botanist, such esteem was held within the Order of Knowledge, an organization of which Barston did not, in general, approve.

Then again, Barston approved of very little. It was his single most endearing character trait.

The Captains of the Chosen stood to either side of the very closed door. They had listened, expressionless, to every word that had left Birgide's mouth, and they liked it far less than the men and women present who were *not* responsible for the survival and safety of the right-kin.

Finch had considered calling the entire den to join them for dinner; in the end, she decided against it. Daine was already exposed enough. She trusted

Hectore as much as she trusted any outsider—but even the most well-meaning of men could let slip facts which led to disaster. She had seen it happen just often enough in her years at the Merchant Authority; she did not wish to take unnecessary risks.

Arann was of the Chosen. She could not request him *as* Chosen; she could request that he take a night off. But among the ranks of the Chosen, this was a subtle political request—and again, an unnecessary one. She informed the Captains of the Chosen that she would have guests—important guests; she told them who, and even why.

Torvan and Arrendas would decide how to staff the guard shift without either her input or Teller's—and to offer input without a very good reason was just short of insulting. They did not deserve insult. They were, given their history with the West Wing, unlikely to take umbrage at less than perfectly politic requests—but they heard.

But it was Torvan who made the otherwise outrageous suggestion that the dinner itself be served within The Terafin's personal chambers. Finch was almost shocked; she kept this to herself far more successfully than Teller did. Jester, however, seemed unsurprised.

"The Terafin has already chosen to entertain Hectore within her personal chambers; she did not consider his presence there to be a threat or a danger."

"Neither of us are The Terafin," Teller said, in a voice that held echoes of Barston—and Barston's stiff disapproval. "The Terafin's personal chambers—"

"Can be utilized by the regent," Arrendas said, before Teller could finish.

Birgide's gaze narrowed; she said nothing. She was probably wishing she were in the gardens, digging in literal dirt, and away from what was fast becoming too political. The silence was beyond awkward.

"They can," Teller agreed—although it had the texture of argument, another trick of Barston's. He flipped a page in the open book that occupied the center of an otherwise spotless desk. "But the regency itself is to be decided by House Council vote in the absence of an acclaimed leader. We have a leader; we have not, therefore, brought forward a motion in Council to appoint a regent. Absent that motion, it is beyond presumptuous for any member of the House Council to lay claim to those rooms for the purpose of entertaining personal guests—even guests of note."

And they knew this, Finch thought, her expression as neutral as Haval's would have been. She did not understand why they were pushing. The two captains exchanged a long glance; it was Torvan—as it often was—who spoke.

"The fear, at the moment, is that Hectore's attendant is not human. We are aware that demons can take human form—sometimes literally. We have faced demons before—but if a demon worthy of note or fear is let loose within the manse, the cost will be high. When The Terafin is resident, the cats are present. They are no more natural than demons—and they seem proof against attacks that would kill or cripple most of us.

"The cats, however, are not here. Celleriant is not present. But the House Mage is. He dwells within the chambers of The Terafin at her express permission. If, as Birgide fears, the Araven servant is as dangerous as the demons, APhaniel will know. It is likely that he will intervene. He has become more difficult since The Terafin left; we cannot be certain that he will otherwise honor a request or an invitation to observe your dinner."

"I am *not* concerned about the Araven servant, as you call him."

"You should be," Birgide said quietly.

"The Terafin was not concerned. Had she been, we would handle it differently. You know she's seer-born," she added; it wasn't a question. "You know that she can see demons, regardless of how they're disguised. Had Andrei been the threat you all fear, we'd *know*."

Teller coughed, and added, "Finch likes Andrei. She thinks he encapsulates the epitome of service."

"I think he's very like Lucille," Finch agreed. She waited. To her surprise, Torvan did not speak. Neither did Arrendas. She considered the situation with care. "I can't give you orders, can I?" she asked the captains.

"You are not The Terafin," Torvan replied.

"The Terafin would tell you that she valued your input. She would also ignore it. If you pressed the point, she would be far less politic."

"If The Terafin were here, we would not be having this discussion—she would be entertaining in her own chambers."

"She could entertain in the foyer," Finch countered, "and you would accept that decision."

"You are not The Terafin."

"I'm not the regent, either." Finch straightened the folds of her skirts. The silence was strained. Finch let it be, for the moment, considering the very near future—and the consequences that awaited her.

"You intend to be regent," Torvan replied. "The Chosen will support you."

"Becoming regent is not a simple matter of the support of the Chosen."

"No," he agreed. It was not an act of surrender. "But that is not our problem; it is yours. You will face opposition no matter when you choose to declare yourself. The only person in Terafin who could possibly take the regency without open conflict is Teller."

"I do not want—"

"We know, Finch. But this is beyond the Chosen. It is almost beyond the House."

Finch exhaled and turned to Birgide. "What," she asked, her voice developing the faintest of edges, "have you told them?"

Birgide was not accustomed to dealing with patricians; she had said that before, and it was clearly not a lie. "I have permission," she said, after an awkward pause, "to enter The Terafin's chambers."

"From who?"

"The Terafin's chambers are connected to the grounds at the back of the manse." It wasn't an answer. When Birgide realized Finch expected a better one, she said, "the forest, ATerafin. The forest has given me permission. If the Araven servant presents a danger, it is in the forest that he can be confined— if he can be confined at all.

"The power of that forest extends to The Terafin's chambers. If something happens within those chambers, I can influence it in a way that I cannot within the body of the manse."

Finch continued to wait. This time, however, Birgide seemed to feel she had finished. "You are not Chosen."

"No. It is not a position I would ever be offered, and were it somehow offered to me, not a position I could accept. The goals of the Chosen are not my goals, however strongly they overlap. I will make decisions based on the duties I've accepted—but it is, in the end, a hierarchy of one, until The Terafin returns. But I am not merely Warden, whatever that encompasses. I am a member of the Terafin Household Staff. If you choose to ignore my warning, and the request of the Chosen, I will do what I can. The decision is, of course, yours." She bowed.

Finch was not ready—would not be ready for weeks yet—to declare herself regent. She had not yet fully consolidated her position within the Merchant Authority, but the attack on the Authority offices—and the Merchants' Guild itself—had rendered some of that maneuvering unnecessary in the short term. She rose. "Very well, Captains. I will accept your advice in this. It may be necessary to start a small disturbance in the West Wing."

Teller signed.

"No, of course not. But it doesn't matter if they believe it. It matters that there's some pretext. I'm sorry," she added—to Teller. "Hectore will arrive for the early dinner hour. He is never late."

Haval was dressed as a merchant of modest but nonetheless impressive means. Finch had sent the invitation to his store, as it was an off day. She had not expected him to greet it with any enthusiasm, but was certain he would choose to accept. She did warn him that Jarven would likely attend as well.

She was dressed and ready a full half-hour before Hectore arrived; two hours prior to that, she had been conferring with distressed servants. She was not well-versed in the starting of fires; it was not a skill that any of her den possessed. She wanted a fire that was contained enough that it would be guaranteed not to spread, but significant enough that it would allow her to beg use, at the last moment, of The Terafin's modest dining room.

Haval, true to form, had arrived early.

Finch liked Hannerle a great deal; she found Haval inscrutable. He reminded her of Jarven in some ways, but none of them were comforting. She knew he was working with Jester. She knew Jester resented him. But Jester could also resent the Master of the Household Staff, which Finch thought unfair.

She was surprised when Haval understood, immediately, what was necessary. He offered neither dissent nor approval; he merely asked her to go to her rooms and attend her personal paperwork. He had, of course, chosen which of the dresses she would wear this evening—but he had laid it out; he was not to be her valet.

He was, apparently, to be her fire starter.

The fire itself was perfectly contained: it blackened the table, scorching its fine, oiled finish; it destroyed the tablecloth, and the lace set across its length; it appeared to have singed the carpet in places. It did not, however, spread beyond that. The cosmetic destruction could be easily remedied—but not in scant hours.

Haval then joined her. Jester was already in deep conversation with the visibly distressed servants; their panic, their sense of their own profound failure, was the only thing about the endeavor that made Finch's heart sink. She was, however, capable of lying—and did; she mimicked perfect, quivering dismay, transferring her guilt about the welfare of the servants into something she could actually use.

Jay would have hated it, but if Jay had been here none of this would be necessary. None. Not the dress she now wore. Not the evening meal she was almost dreading. Haval would be in his apron, and Jester would be out somewhere drinking and looking down his surprisingly straight nose at politics.

"You weren't surprised," Finch said quietly to the waiting clothier.

"I am surprised that you acquiesced to the very sensible precaution the Chosen have all but demanded."

She didn't ask how he knew. If she trusted him a little bit more, she'd have asked him for his advice before they'd had their quiet meeting in the right-kin's office.

"Given that you clearly have, some plausible deniability is best."

Finch nodded.

"The Chosen are concerned purely with safety."

"Starting a miniature House War is not guaranteed to keep me safe."

"They are not fools," he replied.

"Did you know?"

"That the Araven servant was dangerous? Yes."

"That he was dangerous in a way that even Duvari can't be."

"I am not actually certain that I believe that. It is not, however, Araven that concerns me."

"You don't want to see Jarven."

"I imagine I am not alone in that sentiment—but I am here. Jester has spoken to Marrick."

Finch nodded absently.

"He has also approached the Master of the Household Staff and the man she would otherwise support on Council. There is one difficulty I foresee."

Finch had seen many. Through the Authority offices, she had attempted to bring at least two of them in line; she was not yet certain whether or not this preliminary attempt had achieved that, but doubted it. They were merchants at heart. "Jarven?"

"Ah, perhaps I should say two. Jarven, however, must be part of any calculations you have undertaken, and in that regard, I believe you are as well-prepared as any could be. What will you do with Haerrad and Rymark?"

"I believe you misunderstand my intent," she replied. "They are valuable members of the House Council."

Haval nodded, as if this had been the expected reply. But he smiled. "You are not Jewel."

"I know. She has gifts that I don't. I used to daydream about having them, myself."

"And now?"

"I have very functional and unsentimental daydreams."

"Oh?"

"I think I stopped at the part where I knew—with absolute certainty—that someone I cared about was going to die, because I knew there was no guarantee they would either listen or believe me. I'm not sure I could live with the guilt—and she has. Ever since we first met." She exhaled. "If, at the time, our positions had been reversed—I don't think I'd do what she did."

"She saved your life."

"Yes. But when I look back on it now, we were *young*, Haval. We were children. I was her age, but I let myself be sold. If she didn't have her talent, I'd be dead. And probably grateful for it, in the end. We want what she wants."

Haval once again inclined his head. "Do you understand why?"

"Yes."

One brow rose.

"I am me, after all. We want what she wants because she wanted us when no one else would. We trust her to have our interests at heart because she did—even when those interests were a burden. We became useful to her. We didn't start out that way, and she risked her life anyway. Teller is right-kin. I'm head of the Terafin Merchant Authority offices. Arann is one of the Chosen.

"And Angel is with her. Angel," she added, her voice softening, "has never believed there's nothing he can do. The rest of us sometimes feel that we're still that burden. I'm not sure Angel ever felt that way."

"That is remarkably perceptive."

"I try." She exhaled. "But none of us are Jay. I think Teller, of all of us, is closest at heart."

"Not Arann?"

Finch shook her head. "What is going to happen, Haval?"

"You are going to declare your regency," he replied. "And it will be accepted. It will not be accepted quietly."

"How many people will die?"

"At least one."

Jay's attachment to Haval was strong; her trust, strong as well. Finch was the more pragmatic. She accepted, at face value, his attachment to both his shop and his wife. But his interactions with Jarven spoke of a history that had far less to do with clothing and Hannerle, and far more to do with elements of the political landscape that were best occupied by the *Astari*. She had not asked Jarven directly about Haval, of course; she had merely listened to his genuine amusement when the name Haval Arwood caught his attention.

Very, very few people amused Jarven the way Haval did. Hectore was one. Duvari, however, was another.

Jarven arrived in the West Wing a quarter of an hour before Hectore was due to arrive at the manse. Lucille, sadly, was not at his side. She was the dragon of the Merchant Authority, and perhaps because of that, she had an intense dislike for any political involvement outside of her own demesne. And that,

Finch thought, was fair. Lucille was pragmatic. She admired and respected Jarven, but understood that, at base, he was a political creature. Much of the good he had achieved in his long and illustrious career required political knowledge and interaction.

"I see I am not the first to arrive," Jarven said, acknowledging Haval's presence with a crisp nod.

"You are not," Haval replied. "And that is troubling."

"I don't believe it wise to expend so much energy on suspicion before a meal," Jarven told him, grinning. "But you have always had a tenuous grasp of wisdom."

"Had I not, I am certain we would never have been associates."

Jarven laughed. Finch was more than mildly surprised. "I hear our meal's location has been shifted on short notice. Was that your doing?"

Haval failed to reply.

Jarven chuckled again. "It won't do," he told Haval. "You understand that. There is no reason to treat Finch as the helpless waif. If she requires such treatment, she will not survive." He then bowed to Finch. "Regent."

"Jarven, please. Dinner is no doubt going to be a bit of a trial as is."

"Lucille would be so proud of you, if she could see you now."

"Only because I have made no attempt to strangle you."

He laughed, as she intended. But the word hung in the air between them; Jarven had issued it as a challenge. He knew exactly why a fire had destroyed the furniture in the dining room, and given his comment to Haval, exactly how, as well.

Haval's expression did not change; he looked neither pinched nor exasperated. He met, and held, Jarven's gaze; Jarven's smile shifted, but did not desert his face.

"You play a game of kings," the Terafin merchant said.

Haval nodded.

"With your wife's permission."

"I will thank you never to mention my wife again."

Jarven's smile slipped further. He glanced, once, at Finch. "I believe that was a threat."

"It was a request, Jarven," Finch said, correcting him in a tone that would have made Lucille proud.

"That, too." Jarven's smile sharpened. He looked twenty years younger in an instant, and the shifting line of his shoulders made clear that the doddering and meandering old man had been banished for at least one dinner. "It's clear to me that you have no parents," he told her.

Finch sighed. "I have Lucille. You are, no doubt, about to warn me that I will be judged by the company I keep."

"Indeed. And to warn you about what lurks in the hearts of all men."

"Given at least present company, what lurks in the hearts of all men must be the soul of a very mischievous boy. I am somewhat grateful to you," she added, as she began to walk toward the doors of the wing. "Hectore is so accustomed to your presence in the Merchant Authority, he has practically been trained to overlook minor offenses. I am certain that nothing I say or do will, therefore, have significant and lasting consequences."

Hectore arrived on time, as he often did. He felt no particular need to impress, but chose to dress as if visiting royalty. Given the relative rank of Terafin in the Empire, such style would never be considered obsequious. There had been some heated argument about the style of Andrei's clothing, however; Hectore considered Andrei to be an actual, specified *guest*.

Andrei considered himself to be Hectore's servant, pointing out that Finch had not, in fact, addressed the invitation to him personally. Andrei therefore arrived at the Terafin manse as he arrived at any other. He was silent, but present.

Hectore was not surprised to find Finch, Jarven, and Haval waiting for him. "Terafin has very exalted pages," he said, bowing to Finch before he offered her his arm. Haval stepped aside to allow them both to pass; Jarven seemed content to keep Haval's company. Hectore chuckled at Andrei's expression, although he couldn't, with any manners, turn to actually look at it.

Finch inquired after the health of his family; she asked for news of his grandchildren. This also caused Andrei to grimace—or perhaps not. Andrei, in this manor, was on alert. Hectore was happy enough to answer her questions, and they progressed from the foyer to the doors of The Terafin's personal chambers in a state of pleasant self-indulgence.

The Chosen on duty—there were four—stepped aside to allow their party to pass through the doors that Finch herself opened. This was not generally done—but Hectore understood that the nature of the rooms—and possibly the door itself—demanded a more flexible sense of protocol and etiquette.

On the far side of doors that magically became a single wrought iron arch the moment one passed between them, stood the right-kin, Teller ATerafin. He was flanked by Jester ATerafin and Birgide Viranyi.

"Patris Araven," the right-kin said. He bowed; the bow was respectful, but not obsequious. In contrast, Jester ATerafin offered Hectore the slight incline of chin; an acknowledgment of his presence, rather than the superiority of his rank. The gesture itself, however, was bright and strangely lively; there was very little ego in it. The pale, red-haired stripling did not feel he had anything to prove to any of the visitors.

Ah, no. The nod he offered Jarven was distinctly stiff. Finch's request that Jarven treat Jester with respect had been, in Hectore's estimation, wasted. The young man—and that, perhaps, was an exaggeration—did not, and would not, warm to Jarven.

Jarven did not consider Jester a threat—and why would he? In the end, Jester was a man who devoted his life to passing entertainment, idle gossip, idle drinking. He might have been born to the patriciate, given his general attitude, but even so, his beginnings were not something he scrupled to hide.

He waited, guest rather than host; it was Finch who led, Hectore by her side. Jarven chose to walk to the other side of Finch. Nothing in his expression betrayed his surprise; if he had not seen these chambers before, he had been told, clearly, what they contained. His eyes flickered briefly across the cloudless amethyst of sky; night did not fall in these chambers. Beneath them, trees grew as bookshelves to the right, as far as the eye—or Hectore's eye—could see; these were worthy of more of Jarven's attention, but even so, the attention was focused and almost casual.

But he was alert, this Jarven. Hectore had not realized how very bored Jarven had become in his old age until this moment. He glanced at Andrei. Andrei was watching Jarven as well, and probably with the same realization. He did not, on the other hand, find it encouraging or amusing. Hectore found it . . . bracing. Like a cold, clean winter wind.

Finch brought them to plain, wooden gabling. It was not in keeping with the rest of the otherworldly decor; it seemed too simple, too unremarkable. And that, Hectore thought, was of a piece with the master of this vast, endless space: at heart, what she wanted was not large and otherworldly. He opened the gate, and held it.

Finch inhaled.

"You don't care for these rooms?" he asked.

She smiled. "I am old-fashioned, Patris Araven. These rooms are the pinnacle of power in Terafin—but not even The Terafin wished to occupy them. She was happy in the West Wing." Her smile dimmed. "We miss her."

"You see, Andrei?" Hectore said. "Not all people of power disavow sentiment."

Andrei, predictably, did not respond.

*　*　*

The room was not large. It was certainly well appointed, but the table at which Hectore had last dined could not comfortably seat them all. Accommodations had been made, and the table had been removed, to be replaced by one that was longer and narrower. The sideboard still occupied one wall. Andrei chose to take up position beside it, waiting while the guests seated themselves.

Finch did not call him to the table. She did, however, remind him that the Terafin Household Staff was responsible for serving the meal itself; they would arrive shortly with the first course. Even this was a breach of etiquette, which Andrei, at least, understood.

Apparently, so did Jarven, but he found it amusing. As if he could hear the thoughts Hectore himself was too well-mannered to put into words, Jarven said, "I have chosen to find it amusing. I suggest, for the sake of your appetite and consideration to our kitchens, that you endeavor to do the same."

Finch reddened, but did not otherwise appear to hear him.

"You find far too much amusing," Haval Arwood now said. "I consider the amount of effort you expend in this particular case to be negligible."

Jarven chuckled in response. Haval did not appear to approve of Jarven, and his disapproval seemed in line with Andrei's. Birgide Viranyi was seated beside Jester; she was careful not to look often in Andrei's direction. She did, however, seem comfortable with Jester ATerafin. Who, in turn, appeared entirely at home in this strange room, in this gathering of people. If it was true that he did not like Jarven, he was vastly more careful in expression of that dislike than Hectore's own servant.

Only two of the Chosen remained in the room itself, not surprising given the room's dimensions. Like Andrei, they were part of the decor, although they were armored and armed. Or perhaps, Hectore thought, they were only part of the decor to those accustomed to the great houses of the city. He knew the Chosen of Terafin only by reputation.

Andrei poured—and offered—both wine and water. It would have amused Hectore immensely had the offerings from the Terafin cellar been poor; he was not entirely certain that Andrei would not have sent the bottles back with a terse demand that they correct the obvious oversight. He did not, however.

"I am pleased that you could accept my invitation on such short notice," Finch told the table; she seemed to mean it. "Haval, I believe you've seen The Terafin's chambers—as her personal tailor—before; Hectore has likewise been guest here. Jarven is the only man present who is seeing them for the first time in their newly remodeled state."

"Jarven," Jarven said, accepting the wine Andrei offered, "feels slightly insulted at being left out for so long. You are telling me that a Terafin gardener is considered—"

"She is Household Staff. If you wish to take umbrage, I am certain the Master of the Household Staff—or in this case the Master Gardener—would be delighted to entertain your complaints." This was said with an indulgent smile.

"You have, without doubt, met this Master of the Household Staff," Jarven replied.

Hectore, of course, had not.

"She is unlikely to harm you." After a pause, Finch's smile deepened. "My apologies, Patris Araven; we speak of minor household matters. Lucille is generally considered intimidating in the extreme—but everyone in the House feels the reason she has refused quarters within the manse is, in fact, the woman in charge of the Household Staff."

"I had heard she did not wish to clash with The Terafin."

"That is possibly what is spoken on the outside. Again, apologies."

"Don't waste the breath on them," Jarven replied in Hectore's stead. "Yes, I have not seen these chambers before, and yes, as you expect, I find them astonishing. Bracing, even. Does it rain here?"

"Not so far."

"Will it?"

"The Terafin was uncertain. Given the books, it is to be hoped it will not."

"And the rooms?"

"Her personal chambers—which we will not, of course, see—and a conference room of much larger dimensions. I had considered holding the dinner in that room."

"And decided against it?"

"The floor is stone, as are the walls; even the softest whisper echoes. It is . . . very martial in appearance; such a dinner might be held with as much comfort in the older armories in the manse proper."

"I would love a tour of the less personal rooms," Hectore said.

Andrei coughed. It was a polite, minimal sound that nonetheless spoke volumes. No one with manners noticed; The Terafin's inner council—the people she called her den—were not, however, sufficiently polished. Not even Finch.

"These rooms are not considered entirely safe," Finch said. "Or rather, the space between the rooms. Member APhaniel has taken up temporary residence in it for that reason. What he encounters here, he destroys. It is, however, in part to speak of the significance of these rooms and what they contain that I have invited you here." She hesitated, and then shook her head. "It was brought to my attention that you entertained the Guildmaster of the Order of Knowledge yesterday."

"By who?" Hectore asked mildly, although his gaze flicked the side of Jarven's face.

"I do not recall. If it becomes relevant, I'm certain I will."

Hectore nodded. He glanced at Birgide, but Birgide was speaking softly with Jester. "These rooms are of relevance to Araven?"

"They are, in my opinion, of relevance to all of Averalaan," Finch replied. "I have not spoken of one room, within the small complex of The Terafin's personal rooms."

This caught the attention of both Jester and Teller.

"Were you to enter those rooms, you would find them at odds with the Terafin manse in every architectural way; the ceilings are low, the floors are worn, the rooms are very small and very poorly appointed."

"She had these rooms built?"

"No. They are rooms that are, to the finest detail, rooms that we occupied for a brief period when we were children. You are old enough to remember the Henden of 410."

Hectore nodded.

"Those rooms and that childhood are rooted in the experience of that Henden, although we did not know it at the time."

Andrei had returned to the sideboard.

"There was, once, a city—a different city—that stood in this location. It is possible, according to the Order of Knowledge, that there have been several. But the one city is significant. And it exists beneath the streets of the hundred holdings, even now."

The door to the room opened, and three servants, wearing the blues of the Household Staff, entered, pushing wheeled trays. Hectore, accustomed to the invisibility of the servants, would have failed to notice them; he almost did.

But Birgide Viranyi's sudden stiffness served as warning; she glanced at the door, at the servants, and last, at Andrei, who appeared not to notice as they placed various dishes on the sideboard. He abandoned his position by that wall, although he did not join the party at the table; no seat had been set for him.

The servants—one woman, two men—had the crisp, starched silence of exemplary servants in any House; their economy of movements implied stately grace, rather than hurried bustle. They were not, of course, friendly, but no one expected that of the Terafin servants; they would likely lose their jobs, otherwise.

They did, and said, nothing untoward; they did not arm themselves, they did not call upon any hidden mage-born talent; they served.

It was only when the first course was brought to the table that Hectore frowned. He glanced across the room at Andrei. If Andrei noticed anything untoward, his disapproval was hidden in the stiffness of his posture.

"Is there a difficulty, Hectore?" Jarven asked.

Hectore's gaze lifted to meet Finch's; hers was occupied. She was looking— as Hectore had—at the shallow dishes in which soup had been served. They were, to Hectore's eye, fine dishes, all; they were slender and light and in perfect repair; gold and platinum formed crescent patterns around their edges.

But they were not the dishes that Hectore had seen at his dinner with Jewel. He waited on Finch to start the meal. Finch's hands fluttered deliberately over her cutlery.

Teller's hands, however, did not. He nodded once—to Birgide; at his back, Hectore heard the movements of the Chosen.

"Hectore," Jarven said, in the mildest and softest of all of his many voices.

Hectore rose. He was both polite and diffident in his movements. "If I find this is some mischief of yours," he told the Terafin merchant, "Terafin and Araven will be at war until you expire of old age."

"Have you not heard that only the good die young?" Jarven, the bastard, was amused. Highly amused. "I am merely a guest; I assure you that the events of this evening cannot be laid at my feet."

Haval Arwood lifted a spoon. There was a long, silent moment.

Birgide Viranyi broke it. She rose. "I think it best," she told them all, "that you refrain from eating for the moment. There has clearly been some difficulty in the kitchen."

Everything happened at once.

The two servants at the sideboard turned instantly, shedding the stiffness that servants of quality exuded as a matter of course.

The servant nearest the table threw the dish in her hands and pulled two slender knives. In any other circumstance, Hectore would have assumed he had wandered into the first iteration of a very haphazard play.

She was not, however, the only person who was armed; Jester now shoved his chair back from the table. The Chosen moved; Birgide moved. Even the right-kin moved. The only person at the table who seemed entirely unflustered by this sudden shift in servant demeanor was Finch. Hectore caught a glimpse of her expression as Andrei stepped between his master and anything else that moved: it was grim, set, and almost painfully resigned.

The knives the woman had drawn were throwing knives.

They flew.

They flew, unerringly, toward Finch.

I don't like it, Jester had said. *I don't like it at all.*

I know.

I won't do it.

Finch had said nothing. A long, bitter nothing.

Jay wouldn't do it.

That was the heart of the matter. Finch didn't argue the point directly. *She wouldn't need to do it. And if we were different people, if we could make different choices, neither would we. I could just arrange to have the dangerous people put out of the way. I have the knowledge and the contacts, at this point, to do it.*

Jester was silent.

And I can't. I can't, because Jay wouldn't allow it. What she'll do in self-defense she would never do in any other way.

I won't tell her, Jester finally countered. *Kill them. Have them killed. I don't care. I won't tell her.*

But Finch shook her head. *I've considered it. I've considered almost nothing else for days, now. Jarven considers us quaint. It's his polite word for stupid.*

. . . You've discussed this with Jarven.

Yes.

Did he bring it up?

Does it matter? You can talk to the Master of the Household Staff.

It is not exactly trivial—

Neither is this.

Have you spoken to Teller about this?

What do you think?

That you haven't. He wouldn't risk the guests. It would be too politically costly, and the deaths of outsiders would force the Kings' hands.

Do you think he cares whether or not the Kings' hands are forced? The Kings were there on the day The Terafin died—and yet, Terafin is still materially untouched. There was a demon, and the Kings, in the end, did not act. Do you honestly think an assassination will somehow be enough of a pretext?

Yes. In the end, it was The Terafin who died. If Hectore is killed—a powerful, respected man with a fortune of his own—it will be more significant. Jester did not walk out on the conversation. *Finch, why?*

Because it has to be stopped, and this is the cleanest way to do it. Yes, it's dangerous. It's always more dangerous. But it's harder to make mistakes that can't be fixed. Speak to the Master of the Household Staff.

What do you want me to say?

She had smiled. *Arrange for dinner. Tell her where it will be. That's all. If nothing happens, we're wrong.*

And if something does?

She had only smiled. She knew who the target would be.

The knives struck cloth with force. Finch buckled; this was not entirely dramatics; it hurt. She thought there was a chance that she had cracked a rib, or rather, that a rib had been cracked. The would-be assassin would have no chance to strike again.

Haval had seen to that. Apparently with a dinner knife, since no weapon of any sort remained in his hand and his setting was missing cutlery. She had not seen him move, and when she glanced up through the momentary pain-blindness, he looked confused or even frightened.

It was a performance worthy of Jarven.

Finch rose, twisted, and threw herself bodily between Teller and the wall against which the sideboard rested. It was not a simple act of precaution. What she could survive, Teller might not.

Daine, of course, had been alerted; Daine was waiting in the healerie. But it would be far, far better if his services were not required. Vareena, however, was with him. She was a silent, withdrawn girl, more like Duster in appearance than any but Finch had noticed. But she had been healed by Daine, and her ambivalence in being discovered warred with the desire to remain by Daine's side.

Finch intended to keep her.

But to do it, she would have to survive. Andrei had all but pushed the Araven patris out of obvious harm's way; Finch, taking one dagger in the back just beneath her left shoulder blade, drew a single sharp breath, and pushed Teller in the same direction. He caught her arms and dragged her with him as Torvan and Arrendas closed with the remaining servants.

The servants lifted hands, palms empty, in the universal gesture of surrender. Had the Chosen not been exceptionally suspicious, vigilant men, they might have died there. One—one at least—was mage-born.

It was not the first time the captains had encountered the mage-born. Lightning struck the floor where Arrendas stood, sword steadied; it missed. It barely missed; the captains were in armor, the servants were not.

Torvan shouted for backup as Arrendas drove the edge of his sword into the neck of the mage.

No one answered their captain's command. Nor did either man wait for a response; they were moving, now. Finch did not order them to subdue the two men—or the one that remained standing; she did not order them to take the obviously dying man to the healerie. She was unwilling to take that risk. But she looked across the table to Jester, who stood by Birgide, and lifted her hands, fingers flashing.

Jester, grim, signed back. *Need a drink.* He hesitated, and then added, *not finished yet.*

Finch nodded. *Kalliaris*, she thought. *Smile. Please. Smile.*

Very few people considered Jarven a threat if he was not actively harming them. His *power* was a threat, if handled precisely and with care, but Jarven himself was considered too old and too feeble to be dangerous. Of the handful of people who exercised deplorable caution, three of them were—or had been—at this table, and one had been standing against the wall.

Haval's reflexes had not appreciably atrophied in the decades since he had last theoretically put them to use; the servant who had launched two throwing knives directly at Finch was now dead, her attempt to end Jarven's life stalled by Haval's cutlery.

"Be wary," he told Haval. "The Chosen stationed outside of this room cannot, apparently, hear their captains."

Haval nodded. His gaze strayed, briefly, to the door—which, from this vantage, looked normal. "Attempt to be helpful," he added, as he stepped back from the table to briefly examine the fallen servant. "Jester."

Jester was armed, his pale skin a white that would look at home on the dead.

Jarven moved to take advantage of the protection Andrei offered his master.

"If this was your doing," Hectore began.

"This is not the time, Hectore." Jarven indicated the Araven servant; Andrei had turned to face the doors.

Neither man would therefore have been surprised had the doors been broken down; that was not, however, what happened. The elegant wooden panels simply faded, becoming a rounded, open space that implied window. It was a window into a sea of whirling color that appeared to be struggling to coalesce into a familiar shape.

Hectore reached out and put a hand on Andrei's left arm. "Wait," he said. It was not a request. But it was not, quite, a command, either. He let go when a familiar man stepped into a dining room that now seemed lamentably small.

"I see," Haerrad ATerafin said, "that you started without me. A pity." His smile, given the scarred map of his face, was slightly twisted. It was also unusual; Haerrad, in Jester's experience, rarely smiled. For that reason—among others—Jester kept him at a safe distance, preferably in a different holding to the one Jester occupied. It wasn't always possible.

But there was something in his expression that was off. The temptation to assume that he was simply revealing his true colors came—and went. Jester's hand slid into his tunic. He glanced once at Birgide, whose expression was also unnatural—especially the color of her eyes. They had gone from a rust brown which could *almost* pass for natural to a red-orange that spoke of fire.

Jester started forward; she caught his arm—without once looking away from Haerrad.

Jarven said, quietly, "Don't kill Haerrad if you can avoid it."

Jester turned to look at the old man.

"Stab him in a limb; don't aim for anything fatal." As if Jarven knew of the dagger Jester carried, and had come to the same conclusion that Jester had almost arrived at. And damn him, he probably did.

Jester did not like to take orders from anyone. He actively resented taking them from Jarven. But he was no longer rebellious or resentful enough to refuse to do what was practical just because of the possible illusion of obedience. He glanced at Haval; Haval, hands behind his back, had stepped clear of the table—and of Birgide. His face was a mask.

Birgide, arms by her sides, said, "Haerrad."

Haerrad's smile deepened. "So," he said, as if Birgide was the only person in the room who was worthy of his attention, "it *is* true. But you are not yet established in your tenure; a pity. It would have been interesting to see if you were truly capable of becoming a worthy foe.

"In the absence of your Terafin, you are not yet one."

The floor directly beneath Haerrad's feet burst into flame.

Given the widening of Haerrad's eyes, the fire was not his. And as it leaped, licks of flame thinned and grew, twining around each other as if fire attempted, this once, to mimic ivy. From where he stood, Jester could feel the heat.

"What is this?" Haerrad demanded. "Is there a traitor amongst you?" The question made no sense to Jester. "Tell me," he said, his voice expanding and deepening. He swept the fire aside with his hands; flames caught the fine turn of laceless cuff, singeing it. Jester thought he saw blisters form across the pads of Haerrad's palms.

Birgide did not move. "Leave," she said quietly.

Haerrad laughed. "Do you think I require your permission to be here, little mortal? If such permission were required, how would I be here at all? You overestimate both your power and your import."

"You are only barely here," Birgide replied.

The smile on Haerrad's face guttered.

"I do not know how you entered this place at all—but you will leave it, now."

Haerrad lifted his left hand. Jester would not have been surprised had a sword or shield come to it; nothing did. But Birgide staggered back two steps; Jester caught her, steadying her. After a few seconds, it was no longer necessary.

"Do not," Jarven said, in a colder, stronger voice, "kill him."

"You wish to take me alive?" The smile returned to Haerrad. "How quaint, and how foolish. I am not under any such restriction. You will perish here, tonight, all of you."

He turned to Finch, and his hand flew out in a fist, opening at the last moment as if he were throwing something.

Finch, pale and grim, stood her ground, waiting.

"What is this?" Haerrad said, when nothing happened. "Clearly we have, as we feared, been misinformed." He gestured with his other hand; Finch staggered. She did not, however, fall; nor did she perish. Jester could feel the hair on the back of his neck stiffen. It was very, very seldom that he felt raw, visceral fear.

The fires that twined in a circle around the House Council member grew thicker; the mesh of tendrils, stronger. They scorched both carpet and flooring where they stood—but they did not spread at all, proof if it were needed that they were under Birgide's control.

"Is this all you have, little pretender? Or are you afraid to use the power of your station against me? Or perhaps you are waiting for rescue? That is very mortal of you. If you wait upon Illaraphaniel, you will wait long; he is otherwise occupied this eve. He will arrive, but too late."

And Finch said, clearly, "We do not require his aid." She stood, arms by her sides, her unremarkable, mousy hair pulled tight off her face. She was, as she had always been, slender almost to the point of shapelessness, as if the lean hunger of her early years refused to leave her. "You are not Haerrad."

"Am I not?"

"No. I have some familiarity with both Haerrad and his many, many incursions; poison is not Haerrad's game. It is too impersonal. Assassination? Yes. He is no stranger to that. But he is *of* Terafin, and he would never assassinate an outsider of Hectore of Araven's import."

"I am not here for Hectore, but for you and the right-kin."

"And you intend to let him live?"

"Of course. He will serve as necessary—and disinterested—witness. Or he would have, but sadly, you have spoken too much." He gestured again. For one silent moment, Jester felt that he was standing on the pier in the harbor, watching the storm roll in, the air was that charged.

The demon pulled his arms in and when they shot out, something struck armor; Torvan staggered. Arrendas moved toward the circle of fire, sword raised.

Finch heard, of all things, Jarven's muttered imprecation.

Dishes flew, as if grabbed by a plethora of invisible hands; for the first time since even the pretense of dinner had so abruptly come to a halt, Finch raised her arms to cover her face. She lowered them briefly when she heard the sound of cracking wood. The doors that had nestled against the wall had already vanished; it was not, therefore, the doors. Nor was it the floor, although the planks beneath her feet seemed to shudder, as if the room were resident on a great, sailing ship, and not within a manor.

It was the ceiling. The exposed, stained beams directly above the table shuddered once, as if too great a weight had been placed, instantly, across them.

Finch did not believe she could survive the weight of whatever now crushed the roof; the dress that Haval had so painstakingly—and resentfully—constructed had limits. But she wasn't certain the ceiling *was* collapsing. It was, however, dropping chunks of dead wood and plaster.

None of it hit the guests. The sideboard would be scored and dinged, but neither it nor the table had collapsed. Most of the cutlery and dishes had been thrown across the room at the people who now cowered behind Andrei. None of them hit.

Finch raised her eyes.

What had once been flat ceiling with exposed beams and a simple chandelier was fast becoming a weave of vines. It was disturbing to watch their growth; they seemed almost sentient as they discarded elements of the roof. Finch thought of snakes. It was not comforting.

And yet, in some fashion, it was.

The fire that surrounded Haerrad rose.

One lone vine, twisted and nubbled, reached down from the heights to meet tendrils of fire. For one held breath, Finch thought the vine would burn. It did not. But it drew the fire toward Birgide Viranyi, and she held out a hand to receive it. Her face was pale, her expression intent; she did not hesitate to take the two vines in each of her palms.

Finch thought she smelled singed flesh.

Jester moved out from behind Birgide, dagger in hand. Even at this distance, Finch recognized the ornate, engraved blade for what it was: consecrated. Finch wasn't certain what it would do against mortal flesh, because she was almost certain that Haerrad himself was still alive; that the creature that manipulated his mouth and his body was not yet the whole of him—as it had once been of Rath.

Finch had no love for Haerrad. In order to threaten Jay, he'd had Teller injured. He had not, however, had him killed. There was very, very little that Haerrad would not do in order to gain power; very few tools he would not use. He had retained—privately—the services of the magi; he had retained, more privately, services that were less easily categorized. He had used bribery where possible, and extortion where it was not. In Finch's observations, he seemed to prefer the expense of bribery.

She could not imagine that he would willingly carry a demon into the Terafin manse—not when the container was his own person. No, she would go further. In the end, no matter how much she despised him, she could not believe that he would use demons in his attempt to gain power.

Finch understood why Jarven wanted him alive. For the moment, so did she.

She frowned, her gaze sweeping the room—or as much of the room as she could see; Andrei and Hectore were in the way. Jester stood by Birgide; Haval stood nearer Hectore than he had, moments before; Torvan and Arrendas stood on the outside of the ring of fire, swords in hand, waiting for an opening.

Jarven was no longer in the room. Or rather, Jarven could no longer be seen. Finch caught Hectore's arm to draw him farther back; he was rigid. He might as well have been rooted; she could not move him. Nor did he acknowledge the attempt.

"Hectore."

"We are not in danger," Hectore replied, all chaos to the contrary.

Andrei nodded. Finch heard Hectore's muttered curse. She caught his arm again. "What do you fear, Hectore?"

"You can ask me that at a time like this? There is more steel in you than even I guessed."

Andrei, to Finch's surprise, chuckled. "ATerafin," he said, and then, because Teller and Jester were present, "Finch. Never pick up a tool that you are unwilling, in the end, to use. It is a waste."

But Finch said, "If you consider friendship or service a simple tool, I have misjudged you."

"And if I consider it a complex tool?"

"I've still misjudged you."

Hectore laughed; most of the sound was lost to the surging crackle of flame. Some of the tension left him, then. It did not leave his servant—but it wouldn't. Andrei was, to Hectore, what the entirety of the Chosen were to The Terafin. He would relax when this was over. Or when he was dead.

"There is a danger," Andrei said.

Finch, watching the writhing mass of vines above their head, agreed. Three servants—if they were servants, and at this point, Finch doubted it—lay dead or dying. The interior of the private dining chamber had been destroyed; it looked worse, now, than the West Wing's dining room.

Fire rose around Haerrad like a cage; he parted it with effort, the lazy smile extinguished. Birgide raised a hand, spoke a word—a word that resonated in the air, but that Finch could not repeat, even then—and the entire room brightened.

It was the brightness of open windows; it was the brightness of clear, noon sky. It was a warm natural light, as unlike the light fire shed as light could be.

Haerrad roared. Literally roared. Finch had heard demonic roaring before, and this was not it. He sounded berserk, yes—but not inhuman. She did not understand how demons could occupy living bodies in this fashion. She was certain that Haerrad was not talent-born, but he had—in this room—used magic.

"Leave," Birgide said.

Haerrad pulled a knife. It was a small knife; it was not meant for fighting. Finch understood, when he lifted it, what he intended.

But so, apparently, did Jarven.

"Apologies," he said, stepping out of nowhere into the demon's line of sight, "but I cannot allow that." He caught Haerrad's wrist as the knife rose, and Finch heard bone snap. "Jester, now if you please." He did not release the arm, but raised his own as Haerrad attempted to sweep him aside with the arm that was not yet broken. Finch was certain that Jarven could survive it, but found herself holding her breath.

Jester was across the room in seconds, dagger in hand. His face was not, as Haval's or Jarven's, expressionless. For one long exhale, she thought he would stab Haerrad—and he did, but only in the arm.

Where demons were concerned, it didn't matter. The consecrated dagger pierced flesh and drew blood—Haerrad's flesh, Haerrad's blood. The creature screamed in either fear or fury; Finch couldn't tell which, and didn't care.

Haerrad's legs collapsed beneath him, his knees giving; he controlled his fall.

"Birgide!" Jester shouted.

The flames that encircled him went out. He lifted his broken wrist, pulling it defensively into his chest, where he cradled it with care. But he looked up; Jarven was standing not five feet from his upturned face. Jester was closer. Finch left the protection of both Andrei and Hectore and came to stand between them.

Haerrad's forehead glistened with sweat. "There are firsts for everything," he said, meeting Jarven's almost unblinking gaze. "I never thought I would have any cause to be grateful for a broken limb." His gaze flickered over Jester, his lips in full frown. "Or stab wounds, either." That gaze now settled on Finch. "How did you know?"

"We are in The Terafin's chambers," was her smooth reply. "There are defenses and protections built into this place."

"You expected something to happen tonight."

She nodded. "I was surprised to see you. On reflection, it makes sense. How did you come to be possessed?"

He grimaced.

"Were you aware of what occurred when the demon was in control of your body?"

Haerrad shuddered. "Yes."

Finch exhaled. She turned to Hectore and Andrei, and offered them both a deep bow. "Patris Araven."

He nodded in return. "ATerafin."

"My apologies for the interrupted meal. I think it wise, at this juncture, that we attempt to resume the meal when things are less . . . fraught."

He chuckled. "You will, I think, be busy in the foreseeable future."

"Not, I hope, too busy to meet with you." She turned to Haerrad. "I think it is time to visit the healerie. There were Chosen stationed outside of this room. Are they still alive?"

"I did not walk to this room from the manse," Haerrad replied. "I did not encounter Chosen until I entered this room."

"How did you arrive at the manse?"

"It is not clear to me. I have never paid the exorbitant price the magi charge to travel instantly from one locale to another—I am therefore unable to compare the two experiences. I was at the Placid Sea, having dinner with another member of the House Council. In the middle of dinner, I rose and left the building; when I was in an unoccupied stretch of street, I stepped through this door."

"Impossible."

Chapter Twenty-Seven

HECTORE FROWNED AND turned in the direction of the single voice; his expression made clear that the man who had dared to speak had broken iron social rules. Haerrad was, and had always been, a staunch defender of formal hierarchy.

Andrei was a servant. He did not add to the word he had dared to speak.

Birgide Viranyi, however, turned to Andrei. "How? He is demonstrably present." She was not dressed as a servant; Finch thought it likely that Haerrad knew she was at least affiliated with the Household Staff.

"It should be no more possible to reach this room from the Common than it is to reach it from the foyer. If Haerrad ATerafin were dead, I do not believe the *Kialli* could have entered these rooms—or this manse—at all."

"Why would it make a difference?" Jester asked as if he had a personal preference for Haerrad's state.

"The mortal and the immortal do not generally coexist in the same state. The wilderness knows its own. If a demon arrived in the manse—through the trade entrance—it is my belief Birgide would know. But this was far more subtle."

"You do not think the subtlety accidental," Jarven said.

Haerrad was no fool; he now understood that, in this room, Andrei was considered an expert. Inclined to suspicion as he was, he nonetheless accepted that this particular servant would speak.

"No. I think it impossible."

"Which means," Teller said, joining the conversation, "that you think the demons know three things. One: that The Terafin is absent. Two: that Birgide is Warden. And three: that Birgide doesn't fully understand the limits of her abilities."

Andrei nodded; he was frowning. Andrei often frowned, but not in this fashion. "Even were they apprised of all three, it should be impossible for the Council member to arrive in the fashion he claimed he arrived. It is not—" Andrei lifted his face toward a ceiling of rounded, twined vines. "Warden," he said, his voice both soft and sharp.

Birgide nodded.

"Have you encountered the god-born in your tenure?"

"None," Birgide replied, "save you."

Andrei winced. Hectore grimaced. It was, however, Andrei who spoke. "My question was poorly phrased." Birgide did not generally look at him for long, but forced herself to meet his eyes. "There is another hand at work, here. I do not believe it to be mortal. The mage-born have power—and that power will grow, now; none can forestall it. But that power is not knowledge.

"Power is not knowledge; it is another's knowledge that has been used."

And Finch said, "The Warden of Dreams."

Andrei turned to face her, Haerrad all but forgotten. His expression was as neutral as Haval's. Jarven did not bother with neutrality; he was instantly, identifiably, annoyed. Finch had, his demeanor implied, kept information from him—and it was information he considered both necessary and serious.

Haerrad—never a man who liked to be considered inconsequential—came to her rescue. "What, exactly, is the Warden of Dreams?" His tone was one step shy of open ridicule.

"I do not fully understand it myself," Finch replied—as if she were seated in Council. "When The Terafin fell, briefly, to the sleeping sickness, it was due to the machinations of the Warden of Dreams. He almost killed her."

"We did not hear of that."

"No. The House Council, given the assassination of the previous Terafin, was not considered secure. The Terafin chose to keep that information to herself; she had clashed—in her chambers—with the Warden of Dreams, and she had survived to drive him off. We thought he was no longer a threat." She turned to Andrei. "Is he here?"

"I am not the ruler of these lands," Andrei replied. "Were I, I could answer your question. But I see their hand in this. It is subtle." He hesitated. Everyone in the room marked it, Hectore with growing impatience. Without turning to face his erstwhile master, Andrei said, "I am endeavoring to answer the question, Hectore. A little patience would not be misplaced."

Jarven chuckled.

This did not notably improve Andrei's concentration. "The Warden takes power from dreaming. You understand this."

Finch nodded, for it was to Finch that Andrei had turned—not Birgide, not Hectore.

"Mortals sleep. Mortals dream. We used to wonder if mortals were created for just that purpose. They brought a strength and majesty to the Warden of Dreams that they had never possessed prior. Immortals do not require sleep. Should they choose to do so—and there are those who did—they have ways of protecting themselves against the incursion of dreams. I will not say they do not dream—but their dreams are not like yours.

"If sleep, however, does not come to them at a manner or time of their own choosing . . ."

Finch closed her eyes.

"You understand."

She did. She lifted her hands; they fluttered, briefly, in the open before they fell, trembling slightly, to her sides. "If—if those sleepers wake, will the Warden's manipulation cease?"

Andrei did not answer immediately, but he did answer. For the first time since she had met him, his demeanor suggested endless age, and the wisdom that comes from merely existing for so long. "If those sleepers wake, everything the Wardens have attempted or accomplished to date will seem trivial and harmless." He lifted his chin and turned, once again, to the Terafin Warden, who was so different from the Warden of Dreams. "The Terafin is not present," he told her gently. "I can do what must be done—but I cannot do it without your permission, and that permission must be given in more than simple words."

And Finch, watching Birgide, realized that no such visceral permission would be forthcoming. Had she believed it might be, she would have argued or demanded compliance—but Birgide could not even look at Andrei for long. What she saw—what no one else in the room could see—so repulsed her, trust was not a possibility.

And it would take trust. Andrei, Finch saw, accepted this. There was not even a trace of bitterness. "Can you do nothing without that permission?"

"I can do what the Warden can do," Andrei replied. "Ah, no, forgive me; I can trespass in the way the Warden can."

"Jay let you in."

Andrei nodded.

"Jay never saw you the way—the way Birgide does."

"I am less contained than I was when last I entered your home."

Finch folded her arms in almost unconscious mimicry of Jay.

"Has Lucille not told you that if you make faces like that one, your face might freeze that way?" Jarven asked, highly amused. "You look like a younger version of Lucille—and may I remind you that I can only barely survive one?"

She glanced at him, and he did laugh. Finch then focused her attention on Andrei. "You fail to understand The Terafin. She accepted you. She accepted your presence here, in her private chambers. Contained or no, if you were a danger—to us—she would have known. I don't know what she sees when she looks at you; I know she *can* see demons, no matter how cleverly they're disguised. She knows when someone is lying to her, but she's always been politic enough to accept the lies that are harmless."

Haval cleared his throat. Finch turned a glare on him, which made Jarven laugh.

"I won't say she trusted you," she continued, as if there had been no interruption. "None of the den trust easily."

Jarven coughed.

"Honestly, I am going to strangle one—or both—of you if you keep this up. You are embarrassing me in public."

It was, of course, Hectore who laughed.

Andrei did not; he seemed to find the interruptions as irritating as Finch did. Another reason to like him, but if she were honest, Finch didn't require it. His service to Hectore would have moved her, regardless. She wasn't Jay—no one was. But here, she trusted her instincts. Andrei would do nothing, ever, that would harm Hectore.

And Hectore was here, with them, amused in spite of the seriousness of the situation.

That amusement fell away when Birgide stiffened and the ground beneath their collective feet shuddered. Shards of plates and cups scattered.

Jester was closest to Birgide; when the discussion had drifted—mentally and physically—toward Haerrad, who had managed to bind his own wound, because no one else was stupid enough to offer, Jester had returned to her side. He saw her eyes flash—literally flash—red; he saw her skin's pallor shift. She looked almost like an animate corpse.

Jester raised a hand, flexed it briefly. He tossed the consecrated dagger away; it could be used effectively against demons only once, and against anything else, he had better weapons—if weapons were going to be useful at all.

The ground shook again; he bent into his knees, riding the tremor, and looked up to see that Finch was supporting Jarven. Andrei had not moved; Hectore was watching Birgide. Of course. The Araven merchant trusted Andrei, even if Birgide—or anyone else in the room—would not.

The walls of the dining room peeled away, almost literally, as if they were simple wallpaper, and someone was removing them in strips. The ceiling, already transformed, remained in place, but as the walls came down, Jester could see the trees around which the vines above their heads were twined. The Kings' trees. *Ellariannatte.*

He could see the forest that lay hidden behind the Terafin manse: a glimmering in the distance of silver, gold, and hard, hard diamond. He could not see the bookshelves or the ornamental standing arches that led back to the rest of the manse. The dining room had been moved—or perhaps only its living occupants. Those included Haerrad.

Andrei looked at the distant trees—and at the *Ellariannatte* that now towered above them. He then turned to Hectore. "I would ask that you not interfere," he told his master.

"I never interfere unless it is necessary."

"That is stretching the definition of necessity to the breaking point, Hectore."

The Araven patris laughed; it was a wild, almost exuberant sound. Andrei grimaced, but did not add further to the inexplicable hilarity.

The ground here did not move beneath Jester's feet. The vines that had formed roofing retreated, and in their wake, revealed sky. That sky was blue; it looked very much like normal sky. It was not, however, empty.

In the distance, visible only because there was very little cloud cover, he could see two figures; they were limned in red and blue. Meralonne, as the demon within Haerrad had said, was clearly occupied.

"Birgide—why did you bring us here?" Jester asked, not liking the look of the aerial fight. "We're too exposed."

Birgide, teeth clenched, said, "I didn't choose the location. This is where we have to be."

"Why?"

If he could have clawed the question back, he would have. He saw from her expression that there was no answer she could give: she hadn't chosen. He put a hand lightly on her shoulder, something he rarely did, even among the den. To his surprise she reached up and briefly crushed that hand. Nor did she release it.

Jester glanced to his left; the Captains of the Chosen, armed, were scouting the clearing. They had heard both Jester's question and Birgide's stiff silence. Torvan asked one terse question.

"Are we safe, here?"

"Yes. For now."

"Are you aware of anything that might attack us here that's immune to steel?"

"No." Birgide hesitated, and then added, "I don't think there are other demons." Saying that, she looked to the sky. ". . . Other than the one Meralonne APhaniel has engaged."

Torvan nodded. He turned to Arrendas, and they both looked to Teller and Finch; neither was happy at the lack of accessible backup. Jester was less concerned; Birgide and Haval were the equal of any of the Chosen when it came to combat. He privately suspected that Birgide was better.

"Can you help Meralonne?" Jester asked, looking skyward.

Birgide shook her head; her lips moved, but not deliberately enough to eject actual words. Her hand—the hand that was not curved around his as if to pin it in place—began to glow. Her brows furrowed; her eyes brightened. The latter made her seem inhuman, other. But her hand, where it pressed against his, was simple flesh, and it trembled. No sign of that fear otherwise touched her features.

Small colored globes left her hand as she gestured, flying to a point between the combatants and their audience; they exploded there. Trails of resultant light—orange, red, gold—shot out, as if those tiny globes had been simple fireworks.

But the light they shed remained in the sky.

Jester was not surprised when the trees began to move. He was, however, surprised—and not a little uneasy—when Finch called Haerrad to her side, and Haerrad obeyed.

The canopy of light did not encompass either Meralonne or his opponent—and even at this distance, the mage was unmistakable. He had, about him, a savagery and joy that Jester had witnessed before, in the foyer of the manse that lay beyond the trees. But he fought with sword against an opponent who also wielded shield.

Not even the demon that had destroyed the foyer in the Henden of 410 had been his match. "Birgide—"

"Not yet," she whispered, her voice thin and dry.

Jester would have asked for more information, but Andrei said, "Jester." He turned.

"They are coming."

"They?" Jester said, as the trees shifted again, and the earth trembled—for that little bit too long—beneath his feet.

"Your permission," Andrei said again, to Birgide.

Birgide hesitated.

Hectore said, "Her permission is irrelevant. You do not have *mine*."

"Hectore—"

"I mean it." He spoke with strength and certainty; his voice carried. It carried, Jester thought, a greater distance than it should have, given the storm of noise above.

"I will not see you die here," Andrei replied.

"No, you will not. I know you will not die here, regardless of the outcome. I can live with that. But I will not senselessly lose you because you are *mothering* me."

Teller coughed. It surprised Jester; he recognized the particular sound of cut-off amusement.

Haval and Jarven were silent and watchful, but their gazes flickered around the clearing, gauging and measuring what they saw. Even the movement of trees, as roots broke earth and the standing shape of the forest became a log-wall clearing around the gathered dinner companions, did not fully hold their attention.

"Will he win?" Jarven asked casually, when he looked up.

Haval nodded. "It is not for the mage that I am concerned."

Jarven's smile was grim, but focused and amused. His eyes were bright. Haval's were not. They were both, in their fashion, armed, although Jarven was less obvious about it. Haval saw no pragmatic need to dissemble among the men and women gathered here—with one obvious exception; Jarven saw no particular reason to be open. Haval had oft wondered if Jarven ATerafin was actually capable of trust.

Trust, however, was unnecessary. If one saw clearly and saw objectively, trust became irrelevant. Desirable, comforting, but irrelevant. Much, Haval thought, like love.

Teller wanted them to gather in a tighter group. He made this clear without speaking, which allowed Haval to ignore it.

"One question, Council member," Haval said, in a silence that was otherwise composed of held breaths.

Haerrad replied, "I am to be addressed by servants and common merchants today, it seems." He did not glance at Finch or Teller; he merely folded his arms, recovering much of the bulk and height he used so effectively.

Haval was not offended; nor was Andrei.

"Your question?"

"With whom were you dining in the Placid Sea?"

Haerrad's gaze narrowed. "Three others were present with me. As you no doubt suspect, the topic of discussion was the absent Terafin and the complex question of a regency. Sabienne was there as my aide."

And witness, Haval thought, but said nothing.

"The others were Verdian—" Finch's inhalation was short and sharp; Haerrad's smile was broad and ugly. "Yes. Verdian was there as aide to Rymark."

"There are witnesses?"

"I am willing to entertain the words of a common merchant; I am unwilling to be accused—however subtly—of lying."

"Consider the lack of trust a badge of honor," Jarven said, offering a slender smile that even Haval found disturbing. "You are a man of both consequence and power, and the games you play are not trivialities, but a way of life. At no point in any crisis do you ever fully surrender them—even, I am certain, now."

Haerrad was both suspicious and flattered. The former was a given, when dealing with men of political power and cunning; the latter was more difficult to achieve. The controlled anger that had informed his words to Haval evaporated slowly. What was left was more measured.

Angry men could often be counted on to make mistakes. Haerrad's anger was different; it sharpened and honed his cunning. Haval had met few of whom he could say this with confidence; it was a rare trait.

Jarven, however, was among that handful. He was not, in Haval's estimation, angry—not yet. Against the narrow, predictable anger of a man like Haerrad, Jarven's fury was the more dangerous.

"There were witnesses." He turned to Finch. "Rymark is willing to support The Terafin; he claims to have undertaken no actions against her since her investiture. He is not, however, willing to support a regency if you are to be the regent. With apologies to the right-kin," he added, "he is unwilling to support your tenure in that position, either. He considers you both too young and too inexperienced."

Teller inclined his head gravely. Finch, however, said, "In matters of the economic welfare of the House, I am more qualified than Rymark."

Haerrad shrugged. He looked to Jarven. "Regardless, Finch, you are not favored as regent by the House Council."

"I was not aware that the possibility had been discussed by the House Council," Finch replied. "Your vote in these discussions would have carried no weight, regardless; you were meant to die, tonight." Yes, Haval thought, watching her: she was Jarven's student.

Haerrad did not blink. Nor would he; threats to his life—especially those that had come within a hair's breadth of success—were merely indications that he had been careless. He shrugged, as if it were of little consequence. "As were you."

"And neither of us are dead."

Haerrad inclined his chin more stiffly than Finch had; it was almost—for Haerrad—a gesture of surrender. "Yes. Your survival—and your calm—is both surprising and impressive." He glanced at Jarven, who said nothing. "While The Terafin lives, she is Terafin. Given the difficulties she has faced at this early point in her tenure, I expect she will live for decades; what killed her predecessor would not, in my opinion, scratch the leather of her softest boots. Were she any other, I would consider her too weak to rule.

"But her survival to date is the counterbalance against that opinion, no matter how well-informed or considered it would otherwise be. I will speak with Sabienne, if we escape this place alive. If we do not—" he smiled. "Survival is proof of fitness, Finch. Remember that."

Finch said, quietly, "Amarais Handernesse ATerafin was indisputably fit to rule. Her death does not invalidate the decades that preceded it. We will all die, one day. Survival alone says very little about fitness, to me."

Haerrad raised a brow. "The mouse has teeth," he said, to Jarven. Haval found this interesting; he found the entire interaction interesting. Jewel would never forgive Haerrad for his attack on Teller. Finch, he understood, would. He did not think this was due to Jarven's particular influence; it was due to the underlying differences in the fundamental character of the two women.

Women, Havel thought dispassionately. Not girls.

Jarven was pleasantly neutral, his eyes slightly narrow as he regarded one of the most powerful members of the House Council. Haval assessed the likelihood of Haerrad's future survival to be higher than he had previously anticipated. "She is not, and has never been, a mouse. She has survived my office. Have you known me to ever take a personal interest in mice?"

"Only when you mimic a cat."

"Indeed. Imagine, if you will, what she has learned in the years we have been close associates. She is not my support in the House Council; when I join it, I will be hers."

Haerrad said, quietly, "So, that rumor is true?"

"It is not rumor, but fact. If, as you say, we survive."

Birgide said, "Come to me. *All of you.*" It killed conversation, demanded movement. Not a single person chose to disregard her, not even Haerrad. Pride could make him both condescending and insulting, but he proved, again, that he was not a fool. Torvan and Arrendas complied as well; they were more deliberate in their retreat.

"I did not trust Rymark," Haerrad said; he was close enough to Finch to stab her. Finch did not move anything but her head; she lifted it, exposing the underside of her chin. The gown itself was very, very conservative. If Haerrad recognized the cloth, he gave no indication—but Haval doubted that he had.

"You do not trust me," Finch replied.

He smiled. "No more do you trust me."

"Not, perhaps, after today. You considered me weak enough to be inconsequential; you sought advantage for yourself in this. You do not seek the regency. Does Rymark?"

"I consider that question irrelevant as of today. I am, in some ways, a forgiving man. Where I do not trust—and I trust very, very seldom, if at all—I do not feel the sting of betrayal. An attempt to assassinate me is simply another tool in the arsenal of those who seek power; it is not better or worse than extortion—it is simply more direct.

"I am a direct man. I do not particularly relish killing; it does not, conversely, fill me with regret. But as most men do, I value my own life. Had this been a simple poisoning attempt, I would overlook it. I did not consider that possibility; it would be far too easy to trace.

"But, of course, if mastery over my own body was not to be mine, the action was less ill-considered." He smiled. "I am angry," he told her.

"As am I. And I confess I'm surprised. Rymark's offer to serve The Terafin was—I am certain—genuine."

Haerrad's eyes narrowed. "You are not surprised by the events of this evening."

"I've encountered them before. I have always considered Rymark personally responsible for The Terafin's death; to know that he was capable of summoning or controlling demons is simple confirmation. But I believed that he had cut all ties with—" she stopped. "And Haerrad? This *is* too risky for him. I would not be surprised to learn he had little choice in the matter himself."

"You think him possessed?"

"I think him a coward."

Haerrad laughed. "And you do not consider yourself one."

"Not in the same way, no. There is very little threat you could make against my person that would induce me to betray The Terafin. Rymark's concern has been—first, foremost, always—his own survival."

"We are all concerned with survival."

"And the lack of demons under your control is merely a testament to your lack of magical talent?"

Haerrad's eyes narrowed.

Finch lowered her chin. "Forgive my manners."

"I am not certain I will," he replied. "Gratitude covers a multitude of sins—but it is not endless." He had apparently reached the limits of the manners he did claim to possess, and turned to the Terafin gardener.

"What danger, exactly, do you expect?"

Red lightning streaked from the heights above her colored canopy to the ground, sizzling and crackling; it did not land—but only barely. Birgide was pale, silent, stiff; her breath was becoming labored. Haval noted the sweat that beaded her forehead, the tighter clench of the hands that were now by her sides.

The *Ellariannatte* above their heads moved, branches coming in toward the center of their loose circle. The dinner party was not standing where the branches now converged; they were positioned farther back, toward the trunks of these ancient trees.

Haval was not surprised to see the rain of fire fall. He was surprised when Birgide Viranyi cried out, wordless, as that fire consumed leaves and smaller branches.

And he understood. "You are Warden," he said quietly. "You feel you are guardian of—protector of—this forest, these lands." She did not look down. "But these lands, if I understand anything that has happened, are Jewel's. They exist in the fashion they exist because she is their Lord.

"You are not lord," he continued, when she failed to respond. "I would have guessed that you had some experience with sending men—and women—to their probable deaths. You have certainly faced death yourself. But it is clear to me that the risks you have entertained have not involved the sacrifice of those you value, even when that sacrifice is willing—and necessary." He turned, now, to Finch and Teller; he was certain that he had Jester's attention as well, although Jester appeared to be supporting Birgide Viranyi.

"Be prepared as you can be. I believe the lord of this forest is about to return to it."

They both turned to Haval, then—and Jester came out from behind Birgide. They were signing rapidly. Haval held up one hand to stem the flow of this "conversation." "The forest has moved in a way it has never moved before in Birgide's experience." No one asked him how he knew this; Birgide simply nodded.

"This circle, this redrawing of a small part of the map, did not occur for our protection. I do not believe it occurred for the protection of the forest, either; Meralonne and his opponent are unlikely to pay much attention to the land they destroy in their battle.

"I believe the forest moves in such a fashion for one person, and one only." He turned, hands clasped loosely behind his back, toward the center of this strange clearing. "Jarven?"

"I concur. You really are wasted in your current profession."

"I am not. I am a very fine clothier; few possess my skills—as you are well aware. Fashion requires attention and observation; it requires an ability to move and shift one's designs in subtle—and less subtle ways—to take advantage of current mores and current customs, even as one stretches them. It requires knowledge of those who will wear what is designed and constructed, and that therefore requires knowledge of where they will wear it, and in whose company; it requires knowledge of that company, great and small."

"You almost move me to take up the needle myself."

"Perhaps. You will never be allowed to do so in my shop."

Jarven laughed. "Andrei?"

Andrei said, quietly, "They are coming. Stay here; do not move to greet them; do not move to interfere—at all. Haval is correct; what the wilderness will do to preserve its lord it will not easily or willingly do to preserve any others—even if their loss would cause more damage to The Terafin than physical injury."

Adam knew the moment the forest changed, although his eyes were closed. The sense of *place*, of almost-home, shifted, strengthened, tightened. The struggle to hold it in place vanished—and, like a game of tug-rope when the opponent let go, nearly caused Adam to lose his balance.

He shifted his focus instantly, holding the desert in his thoughts. Winter desert, winter trees, endless snow, wind that seemed ice made air. This was harder; the winter world into which the Matriarch had stepped was no part of Adam's heart. He did not know it as he knew desert; nor did he care for it as he had come to care for Terafin.

He opened his eyes to dark forest floor, and he cursed softly in Torra. If the other world slipped away, he could not—no. Something else was wrong or strange. He was not, now, within the Terafin manse. Isladar had said—and

Adam had trusted—that to cross worlds, however briefly, they had to go home.

This—this was the Matriarch's forest. This was the world in which the dreamers had gathered for their odd festival, under the benign watch of a man and a woman who had never been human. He exhaled, inhaled, clutched dirt beneath his palms; he heard the Matriarch's curse—twin to his in chosen words, but more visceral, more felt.

"Stay," he told her in urgent Torra. "Keep them close, Matriarch." It was hard to speak clearly; impossible to speak loudly.

Into his ear, she said, "We're—we're home."

"Yes." He wanted to tell her that home was not where she needed to be; that she had not finished her quest, had not spoken to the mysterious Oracle. But he could not; he needed to hold to winter, and winter was melting beneath his hands. The earth did not. But here, it slumbered, its anger dim, the roots buried—and guarded—in its depths, stronger.

He needed to hold this path. He needed to build it and see its boundaries clearly, because the Matriarch needed to walk it.

"Jay!" He looked up at the sound of a blessedly familiar voice. Finch stood not twenty yards from them, beneath the boughs of the great trees. Beside her, hands twisting in den-sign, stood Teller, and beyond them, red hair catching the eye, Jester. But they were not alone; Adam saw Haval Arwood and—and Hectore of Araven.

"Terafin!" Two of the Chosen were also present; they pushed themselves forward.

None of this would aid him in the work he now did. He closed his eyes; he could not even lift his hands to sign, or everything would unravel.

Jewel looked up from her desperate perch across Adam's back. For the first time since he had undertaken the task set for him by Lord Isladar, she lifted her hands from his and rose. She was not surprised to see the Master Bard of Senniel College to her right. Celleriant stood to her left; both were armed. Kallandras' hair contained splinters and ash; Celleriant's, nothing.

She glanced, once, at Kallandras' hand. The skin around the ring finger was blistered and looked raw; nothing about his carriage or his expression implied that this caused him pain. Had Adam not been so clearly—fearfully—occupied, she would have told him to tend to the bard.

She was not entirely certain the bard would allow it.

Not twenty yards from where she had huddled stood her den, or at least three of them. Torvan and Arrendas, swords drawn, moved toward her, and froze when she lifted a hand. Haval, Hectore, and Jarven stood around Birgide Viranyi. And so, she saw, did Haerrad. Haerrad ATerafin. She stiffened, lifting her hands to sign.

Finch got there first. *He's with us.*

Why?

Complicated.

Before she could speak—Haerrad's presence hindered any frank discussion—Andrei bowed to her, in full view of combat and demons; he held that bow until she realized he would remain in that posture until she bid him rise. She was not dressed for court or council or *Avantari*; she was dressed for trekking across a winter wasteland. She opened her mouth, but Hectore spoke first.

"Get up, Andrei. You are embarrassing The Terafin."

"He's not—"

"He is. You have never been particularly fond of obsequious behavior, even when warranted—and it is not warranted now, of all times."

Avandar appeared to Jewel's left. He glanced around the oddly shaped clearing, his eyes coming to rest on the only other people that occupied it. The shape of his eyes shifted, briefly, when he saw Birgide Viranyi. He altered the patterns of his protections, encompassing the grouped members of House Terafin beneath a barrier similar to the one that now enclosed Jewel and Adam.

He frowned and looked up; Jewel was terrified, for one long breath, that the three-headed, flying serpent had joined them. But the air contained only two men, and one, she was almost certain, was Meralonne.

She started to ask. Shadow interrupted her, glaring like certain death at the rounded curve of Adam's back.

"Stupid, stupid, *stupid* boy!"

"Shadow." Teller started forward; Finch stopped him. He had always been fond of cats—even the great, messy, winged kind.

"Yesssss?"

"Where are your brothers?"

"Who *cares?*"

"I do, or I wouldn't be asking," Teller replied, lowering his voice.

Shadow huffed. "They're *coming*. They are *slow* and *stupid*. But not as slow and stupid as *him*." By which "him," he clearly meant Adam.

A sword whistled above Shadow's tufted ears. He would have been without them—and part of his head—had he not flattened himself briefly against the earth. Nor did he remain in place when the sword's arc passed him; he moved.

He could, however, complain without pause no matter what he was doing. And did.

The demons that had been attacking Angel had arrived in the forest with them.

Jewel glanced, once, at Adam's back; she wanted to run to Finch and Teller. She didn't. But she looked at Birgide Viranyi, just as Avandar had done. Isladar and Darranatos did not—thank all the gods anywhere, ever—materialize in the clearing as well. She could no longer hear the sounds of their uneven battle. Instead, she could hear Meralonne and his opponent; she could hear Angel and Terrick. The demon that had taken to air had landed, although Jewel wasn't certain of the precise moment of landing.

She did not see the Winter King. Nor did she see the other two cats. The loss of neither concerned her. But Snow had Shianne, and Shianne was not yet here.

Shianne is capable of defending herself, should the need arise. Calliastra is not present, either.

Jewel was not afraid—in any way—for Calliastra.

No? Avandar asked. She knew why. Duster had died. *Shianne is not mortal the way you are. She could stand among First Circle magi and be reckoned powerful.*

Why are you so certain?

I observe, Jewel. And if you did, you would see it, as well. She is not, and will never be, as you are.

But she's mortal—

Yes. And all that means, where she is concerned, is that she will bear a child and eventually die. Mortality does not fundamentally alter her thoughts, her dreams, her desires; it does not fundamentally change the core of who and what she is.

Mortality defines us. Death, loss, fear of death and fear of loss—

Do you think she does not fear these things? Immortals are not invulnerable. You have seen them perish.

You're immortal, she said quietly.

I am still, and always, a man—but I cannot die, no matter how much damage I take. The gods were not unkind; the damage heals, the body renews. But eternity becomes a curse, with the passage of time. Shianne will learn to fear hunger, but the cold? The summer heat? No. She will not privilege or cherish life the way you and your kin do—not even the life of the child she carries. There was a hesitation in his voice, a sudden well that implied endless depth without illumination.

Jewel turned as a demon roared.

She saw Terrick's axhead buried in the side of the creature's neck; blood spurted as he yanked it free. Angel's sword was likewise buried in demonic flesh. A rivulet of blood fell, traveling the contours and crevices of the creature's slender height; it seeped into the earth yards from Jewel's feet. She felt it as if she were the earth; it was warm and wet. Like summer rain or tears. Instinctively, she cupped her palms as if to catch it; she could not later say why.

Kallandras leaped into the air; it carried him as he joined Angel and Terrick in their battle. Celleriant glanced at the three and almost shrugged; he looked, instead, to the sky.

Jewel reached out to catch his arm before he returned to combat, as the bard had done.

Adam inhaled, the sound sharp enough to cut silence without quite breaking it. "Tell the cats to land," he told Jewel, eyelids trembling as he lifted his face. He didn't open his eyes. He didn't lift his hands.

"They're not here," she told him.

"They are."

She hesitated only briefly. She did not understand what Adam was doing—but she trusted him. He was healer-born; he could sense, by touch, what she would pay money never to have to look at.

"*Snow! Night!* Come to me!" she shouted, although she couldn't see the cats for the light all around: the gold and the blue of Avandar's dome, the strange trails of light above it, and the roving clash of red and blue that sounded, at this remove, like thunder.

She heard Shadow hiss laughter, and saw, at last, the winding shadows of his two brothers as they made their way to the ground, crossing all barriers as if they were nonexistent. Night took a chunk out of demon leg as he buzzed past.

Jewel turned to Snow; Shianne was still seated upon his back. Only when Shianne moved did Jewel remember to breathe. Had Shianne been anyone else, Jewel would have run to her side and pulled her off the white, furry miscreant.

She was, however, Shianne. She looked much like the Winter Queen herself: a presence that should not be approached or touched.

She was pale, to Jewel's eye—even paler than she had been; her eyes seemed dull, although she couldn't say why, they were still the same bright silver. "If . . ." she trailed off. Turned to face Teller, who was waiting.

"We ran into some trouble we couldn't defeat while we walked the Oracle's path."

"And you came here?"

Remembering that Haerrad was among her kin, she said, more stiffly than she had intended, "Yes. Here is the heart of my power. We seem to have lost the worst of the demons and the giant, flying serpent, though."

"And you have returned with a new companion." It was Andrei who spoke. His eyes were wide, his face as pale as Shianne's. He did not approach; he bowed. This bow was very like the bow he had offered Jewel; it did not discomfort Shianne in the same way.

She bid him rise; Hectore did not. Not even Hectore could speak, for a moment, in her presence. Only when Andrei rose did the servant's expression betray surprise—but there was sorrow in it, as well.

"I did not think to see you here," Shianne said quietly. "These lands are not unoccupied."

"This is not the first time I have visited them."

"And it is allowed?" She turned, then, to Jewel. "These lands . . . are yours?"

"They are mine."

"Do you understand what or who your . . . guest . . . is?"

"He is servant to Hectore of Araven. I owe him my life, although I am not certain he would remember the incident; it occurred when I was a child."

"I see. Mortals are strange." She turned once again to Andrei, her eyes narrowed. "Who is Hectore of Araven? I have never heard his name."

Jewel started to answer, but Andrei lifted a hand; she fell silent. Hectore had not chosen to speak or identify himself. "We did not meet often in the wilderness," Andrei said quietly. "And on the few occasions we did, the outcome was uncertain. I am not permitted to rekindle old hostilities at present."

"And I have no interest in them, now. I do not think I would be a worthy opponent in my current state." She turned her face toward the sky. ". . . Or perhaps ever, again. Jewel, do you know this Hectore of Araven?"

"I do."

"Is he powerful enough to contain the being who stands before us?"

Jewel did not hesitate. "He is."

Andrei raised one familiar brow.

"I'm seer-born," she told him, before he could speak. "The answer is a visceral *yes*."

"You do not even understand the question."

"I don't need to understand all of it, Andrei."

He was silent for three long beats; no one rushed in to fill that silence because they were having difficulty dragging their eyes away from Shianne. Jewel felt sympathy for their efforts; she had the same problem. Given the nature of the rest of the problems she faced, it was welcome.

"I will not argue with you here; you do not have the time. Do not," Andrei told her gently, "leave the circle Viandaran has traced upon the ground. You have not yet finished whatever task the Oracle set you, and there is no entrance to her realm from here. You stand on a narrow path woven out of two—no, three—disparate places; diverge from that path and you will fall into one of the three.

"You can see—"

"I see winter," he replied, "and *Ellariannatte*. It is to the winter you must return. But, Terafin, the Warden of Dreams has touched the edge of your domain in your absence."

She stiffened.

"Mortals could—and did—hold small pockets of the wild lands; one or two even reached the high wilderness and survived. But there is a reason that the Cities of Man were cities, and immovable. The Sen could not long hold what they had built if they traveled far from it, or were absent too long—and they did travel. Some were lost, although those tales have passed beyond legend and memory."

"Do you remember?"

"No. I was never given permission to enter the cities. The Warden of Dreams was more welcome than I; he had more to offer in return for the power he gained. But even then, mortals were, and could be, wary." He then turned his attention to Angel, Terrick, and Kallandras; they had finished.

Jewel signed to Angel, who nodded; he spoke in Rendish to the older Northern man, and they approached her—with care. To Teller and Finch, she said, "We encountered Darranatos on the road."

Finch was silent for a beat. Two. But she spoke. "They knew where you were going."

"Looks like. They started a fight; half of us avoided the dangerous bits for a while, but the fight itself threatened to wake the earth. Only the people who can fly would have survived it." She hesitated, considered Isladar. In the end, she chose to keep his presence to herself. "Where is the Warden of Dreams?"

"If they are wise," Andrei replied, "they do not remain in your lands."

"Wisdom," a very familiar voice said, "is not the province of dreams. Nor, in the end, the province of Nightmare."

Jewel folded her arms and turned in the direction of this new voice.

She was not the only person who turned. Given the form he had chosen to adopt, he drew all eyes; Shadow fell momentarily silent. Snow and Night, who were bickering over their landing spot, did not. Shadow roared, wordless, which caught their attention; they slunk, bellies a bare foot above the ground, to surround Jewel, with their high wings and upright fur. Night, however, stepped on Angel's foot.

"You have no permission to walk my lands," Jewel said, drawing shoulders back and lifting chin.

The Warden of Dreams inclined his head. She thought, given the stretch of raven-black wings, she addressed the Nightmare brother; she could not be certain. He was a full foot taller than the tallest person present; slender of build; he was cloaked, but seemed almost a thing of shadow, something darkly ethereal with very little physical form.

"I did not realize what you would do when you journeyed from your lands into the wilderness." He glanced at Shianne, who watched him.

The caution she had shown Andrei was absent. She bowed.

"You remember me?" he asked, evincing naked surprise.

"Yes. Firstborn and youngest, I remember. You are not now what you were then."

His smile was bright, unfettered. "I have grown, Shandalliaran. I have grown."

"So I see. I travel with the lord of these lands, now."

He frowned.

"I do not fully understand what—or who—she is, but I seek the White Lady. Will you impede our progress?" She lifted her face to sky and light and blue and red, and her eyes narrowed briefly. But she smiled as she saw the trees. "These lands are far older than she—but they feel young, to me. And you are here." She held out both of her hands, palms up, as if she expected him to take them in his own.

He shook his head. "I am not fully here."

"You shouldn't even be partially here," Jewel told him. She was more than willing to interrupt the Warden of Dreams.

He ignored her. Shianne did not. "How do you come to be here at all?"

"Much has changed since you stepped out of all worlds," he replied. "Much. The gods. The White Lady. The firstborn. Even your brethren. Do you understand what has occurred?"

"I have been informed of the facts—but no, Warden, I do not understand. Nor do I think I ever will."

"Perhaps if you asked them, you might."

Jewel froze.

The Warden lifted his face toward the canopy of lights that looked so much like fireworks captured in a single, raining moment. "One—only one—is present; he is not yet fully awake—but soon, Shandalliaran. Soon."

"You're here," Jewel said, "because of the Sleepers."

"Their dreams are not mortal dreams; they exist without boundary. They traverse all realms—and yet, none. No one of my brethren could travel thus; only me. Only us. I do not wish to see them waken," he added.

"Then *why are you here?*"

"There are only two ways to prevent that awakening," he replied. "You are not the only one who wishes their sleep to continue indefinitely—but, Terafin, I do not think you have the *will* to see it through. The Lord of the Hells does."

"The Lord of the Hells," Andrei replied, "does not have the power."

"He is a god. She is a mortal. What must be done can be done—but not if she is here to oppose him: the Sleepers will wake in the exchange of hostilities. I aid his interests because they align—for the moment—with my own. I bear you no animosity," he added, speaking to Jewel, although he looked only at Shianne.

"The feeling is not mutual."

"I am afraid," Andrei said quietly, "that I cannot allow the fall of this House."

"The House will not fall. It will, of necessity, require a different lord." The Warden of Dreams frowned and added, "I did not recognize you." His lip didn't curl—but it would have, had he been merely mortal. To Jewel he said, "While you survive, it is best to keep a clean house. You intend to disperse me—and you can, while you are here. But you will not remain. You might never return." His smile was slender and dark and narrow. "It is my task to make certain of it; had I been given servants of certain competence, we would not now be having this conversation."

"Finch. Teller. What's happened?"

Silence. It was Haval who answered. Of course it was. "Councillor Haerrad was possessed by a demon. The demon used him to arrange for the poisoning of Finch, Teller, Jarven, and possibly Hectore. In your absence, Birgide Viranyi—"

"I know what she is," Jewel said, terse now. Angry. No one asked her how she knew, which was for the best, because Jewel had no answer.

"Birgide protected all present; the demon in possession of the Council member was removed. We repaired to the forest itself, where the protections against the demonic and the magical are at their strongest."

"Haerrad was possessed."

"Indeed."

"He is not possessed now." It wasn't a question. Before he could speak, she added, "For the objective, external observer, it might be harder to tell the difference. I am neither of those."

She shouldn't have been surprised to hear Haerrad burst into laughter; it was short, harsh, sharp—very much like Haerrad himself.

"I have only one question for the Councillor. Were you awake and aware when the demon possessed you?"

"I was."

"Then I have one further question. Before you answer, understand that while I am not bard-born, Kallandras of Senniel *is* present. Was the possession facilitated by Rymark?"

"I cannot confirm that," was Haerrad's careful reply. "The possession occurred during a meeting with Rymark and Verdian. Sabienne was also present. We were not, however, in seclusion; the meeting did not occur within the manse. We dined at the Placid Sea. There were therefore servers and attendants, any of whom might be involved. If I were to be poisoned, for instance, during such a meal, Rymark would never touch the poison—or my various dishes—himself. It would be beneath him. It would," he added, smiling, "be beneath me."

"What we know," Haval said, when Haerrad had finished and silence reigned for a beat, "is that the arrival of the possessed Haerrad was facilitated by an outsider. I presume it would be the person you now refer to as the Warden of Dreams." He raised an arm when Finch started forward. She immediately froze in place.

Haerrad glanced, briefly, at Finch. "The demon's intent was to supervise the deaths of all members of the gathered dinner party, but of them, Birgide and Finch were to die first. Is that not so?" For the first time he directly addressed the Warden of Dreams.

"Yes."

The trees above their head burst into sudden flame.

Chapter Twenty-Eight

THE BRANCHES DID NOT BURN. Nor did the undergrowth. The fire spread slowly across the clearing until the whole of the contained space resembled a run-down fortification in a painterly vision of the Hells.

At its center were Jewel and the Warden of Dreams. For one long, drawn breath, no one moved. A terrible, silent repose gripped everything in the clearing except fire, and that fire crept up, at last, to enfold Jewel. Flames of orange and gold curled around her arms, falling to the ground like trailing sleeves; flames of crimson swirled around her chest, her hips, her legs. Snow could have made a dress like this—but perhaps not; it radiated heat and warmth.

The Warden raised his left arm; curled in his hand was the long handle of a many-thonged whip. He did not attempt to strike Jewel; that, she might have forgiven, in time. The whip seemed far more solid than the Warden; it traveled in a lashing snap toward Adam.

Adam did not move; Angel did. Where sword and supple whip clashed—briefly—Jewel heard the sound of metal meeting metal. The whip left a red welt across Angel's cheek. It bled.

"Adam," she said softly.

Adam did not answer. But she knew, here, that he must hold what the fire could not contain without destroying it: the winter, the cold, the memory of white. What she needed from the Oracle, she had not yet received. And she had *paid*.

Demons had been sent to cut her pilgrimage short. She did not understand how the demons had arrived in that winter landscape when it had been made clear that Jewel herself could not return there without the Oracle's aid; it made her uneasy. More than uneasy. Jewel had found passage because the Oracle had opened the way. She could not imagine that the Oracle had likewise offered passage to the demons.

But perhaps that was wrong. It had been clear from the beginning that Evayne a'Nolan—the only other seer Jewel had met—loathed the Oracle. Perhaps her tests were not the only reason.

She glanced, once, at Adam's bent back and the placement of his hands, and passed her hand over his head; the flame did not touch him. Without Adam, she could not return to face the Oracle. Without the Oracle, the full potential of her power would never be realized. And without that, what slender hope Averalaan had against the coming of a god, was lost.

The Warden did not even have to kill Adam in order to achieve this, and seemed to realize it. Jewel was not terribly familiar with whips, but thought this one did not travel the way it would have had it been wielded by the merely mortal.

"Shadow, Night, Snow."

Shadow sniffed, but obeyed her unspoken command; they all did. They surrounded Adam. Only Night gave him the side-eye and flexed claws.

"If you knock him over, you will be in more trouble than you have ever been in your *entire life*."

Shadow and Snow hissed laughter, but that hiss sank into a growl as they turned their attention to the Warden. He lifted his hand; the whip faded.

"You will not bow to the inevitable," he said to Jewel.

"I will bow to any inevitability that *I* see. *Your* fear is not *my* certainty."

"You do not understand. Mortals oft dream of Kings and Emperors and distant, mortal heroes. They cannot conceive of beings that are not somehow an enlargement of their experiences and their brief lives. You have met your gods in the shallows of the Between; you have never met *a* god. You will," he added.

But Jewel said, "The gods at the peak of their power couldn't destroy the Cities of Man."

He smiled. "The Cities of Man were not built on the Sleepers. They are almost as gods, Terafin—but they will wake in the heart of this city's shadow. The gods did not destroy the cities you speak of because they could not breach the barriers erected around them. Had they been able to walk into the heart of those cities, the cities would have fallen in a day." He glanced, once, at the three cats he referred to as eldest; they bristled.

He made no further attempt to harm Adam.

"Can the firstborn die?" she asked the Warden of Dreams.

His smile was the knife's edge; brilliant, sharp, slender. "Yes, Terafin. Yes, we can. But you cannot kill me. You lack the will. I am too powerful for you, now." His wings rose; they were the only thing in the clearing that fire did not touch. "If you wish to rob me of power, there is one simple way to do it: kill the dreamers. Mortals are not so powerful in this age, at this time, that it would be difficult for you. You would barely have to raise hand; you could slaughter the majority of the citizens of your fair city in a day. Perhaps a week; there are pockets of resistance that might withstand the full force of your attention for some time.

"I do not think they would withstand it forever. You cannot kill the Sleepers—not yet, and perhaps not ever. The gods feared them when they rode to war, and you are not a god. But you could be, in this small, enclosed space. You could do as gods did, when the world was young and they yet dwelled among us." His wings spread as he spoke.

Jewel remembered the legend of Moorelas' ride. She knew that the Sleepers had been sent with him to kill . . . a god.

Shadow growled.

"Will you tangle with me again, Eldest? The outcome of our last encounter was not, in the end, decided in your favor."

The tenor of the growling changed and multiplied.

Jewel folded her arms. "Do not even think it," she told the three cats, without glancing at any of them. "The Warden is *mine*."

"I have already said you cannot destroy me."

"I don't need to destroy you," she replied. "These lands are mine, and I'm beginning to understand what that means. You do not have my permission to cross these borders, and yet you are here. What will you offer in compensation for your trespass?"

His dark brows rose, shifting the lines of his expression; his eyes became rounder, the line of his mouth fuller; the corners moved as he smiled. Jewel offered him the slight nod that was the Imperial acknowledgment of equality. "Warden of Dreams."

"Well met, Jewel Markess ATerafin."

"Are you in league with your brother?"

"I do not wish the Sleepers to wake," he replied.

"And by destroying what I hold dear, you believe you can stop them?"

"No. There is no certainty, save one: if the Sleepers wake, the dreamers here will die. What you are unwilling to do, they will do in the ice and fury of their ancient rage and loss. It is to protect the many that we have chosen to dispense with the few." His smile was, unlike the smile of his brother, gentle and resigned. "If it eases you at all, I am complicit in this action. You are Jewel. If it were necessary, you would give your life in defense of the people in this city—the thousands of dreamers you will never meet or touch.

"Your death might prevent theirs."

"Will it?" she demanded.

Finch crossed the invisible line that divided them; Angel, from the opposite direction, did the same. They moved, for one moment, with the same intent, the same thought—the same sense of protectiveness that had characterized their early, struggling years. They did not stand in the alleys of the holdings or in the tiny, cramped room the den had called home—but it didn't matter. Clothing, experience, the passage of years and the gaining of power and rank could not touch what they had built—it could, and did, make it stronger and more certain.

Yet she felt the fire's heat dim as they came to stand by her side.

Finch said, before Jewel could speak, "It's irrelevant."

The Warden considered her gravely. She wore no raiment of fire—but for a moment it appeared she had swallowed flame; the intensity of her glare should have burned. Angel, sword in hand, was silent, content—as he so often was—to let the women do the talking. At this moment, nothing they could say would not speak for him.

Celleriant did not move. Jewel heard—or felt—the presence of his sword, but to her mild surprise, he also chose to defer to Finch.

"Irrelevant?" the Warden asked, his voice just as gentle.

"You meant to have the rest of us die. You meant for Terafin to be ruled by someone who serves the Lord of the Hells—and in the end, that must mean you are content to let the Empire itself fall to that god. We've seen the hand of his servants at work before—and we've listened, helpless, to the torture and murder of citizens of Averalaan."

Even Haerrad shifted position as Finch spoke; his chin rose. In the red-tinted light, the scars that he wore as badges or adornments seemed both newer and rawer. But it was his eyes that caught—for a brief moment—The Terafin's attention.

She hated him. She would always hate him. She saw hatred in him now—but all of it, in the end, directed at the Henden of 410. And of course it would be—Haerrad, like Jewel, could be driven into a frenzy when confronted with his own helplessness, his own ineffectiveness. She thought—and this surprised her—that Haerrad's scars in that regard might be deeper and harsher than even her own. But she understood that in some small way the words of the Warden of Dreams—the gentler, kinder half—had kindled in him a visceral sense of enmity and denial.

He would never openly support her; she was certain of that. But he understood now what was at stake in a way that he had not before Finch spoke. The choice itself was stark. Would he kill Jewel to preserve a city or an Empire? Yes. He would have killed her to gain the House Seat, and her death would have caused no loss of sleep, no hint of regret. But the alternative was beneath him.

It was a cold, cold comfort to know that even Haerrad had limits.

Finch continued. "Better that the Sleepers wake and slaughter us all outright than that we fall to the hands of the demons, as we almost did that Henden. If I understand what you fear, we would die swiftly, but we would not die in near endless pain, stripped of all dignity. You have no care at all for the lives we live, only the fact that we sleep—and dream."

"Where there is life, there is hope."

"But there *is* life, right now. We don't accept that we are helpless in the face of the Sleepers—or the Lord of the Hells. You may believe it—you probably do. We don't. If we were no threat, if we had no hope, the Lord of the Hells would never have interfered with House Terafin; the attempt would be pointless. He has wasted resources and servants in these games—and men of power do not wage war against mice or cockroaches."

"It is *the war* that will threaten the precarious balance of fading sleep; they are almost waking as we speak. Their waking dreams have a power and a substance that mortal dreams cannot; the exception are the Sen, and even the Sen require lands such as these upon which to both stand and build."

"Then kill the god," Finch replied.

His brows—and his wings—rose. "That would not be possible for me, even in his current state."

"That is the only option we will support. If he does not wish to wake the Sleepers by bringing his war to the Empire, tell him to keep his war to himself."

"I offer you the chance to tell him that yourself, if you desire it."

"We decline," Jewel said.

But Shianne said, "It is a generous offer—and a costly one."

The Warden smiled. "You have been greatly missed."

Shianne's smile was colder in all ways, a reminder that ice could be beautiful. "I have need of this woman; I cannot allow you to kill her. Nor can I allow you to kill or entrap her companions. You are in her lands, and you have offered no apology and no restitution for your trespass." She turned, then, as if she was done with the confrontation, and lifted her face to the skies, exposing the long, perfect line of her throat.

She lifted one hand as well, and spoke softly; Jewel could not understand a word.

But Kallandras, apparently, did. "With your permission, Terafin?"

Jewel nodded. "Meralonne has already called the air," she added. "He fights in its folds, even now."

"Meralonne has been granted your permission to fight in defense of your realm. I have not."

"In every way that matters, you have always had it. Yes. Go."

Celleriant moved as Kallandras stepped lightly into the moving breeze. "He will not thank you for your intervention."

"I do not intervene at his request." The bard bowed to Shianne. "Be ready, lady. I do not think he is aware of your presence."

"He is not," she agreed. "Nor is the traitor he fights."

"I will leave you," the Warden said.

Shianne, however, shook her head; her smile shifted, but did not falter. "The mortal—that is the word, yes?—is inexperienced; she is too new to the wilderness and its many strengths and weaknesses. You are not, of course. She has not given you permission to traverse her lands. In her absence, you have nonetheless done so. But she is present now, and she has not given you permission to leave."

The Warden's expression darkened—literally. So, too, his wings and the shadows he cast. Jewel noted them: there were two. "You cannot think that she can prevent me from doing so?"

Shianne frowned. To Celleriant—who had made no move to join the Senniel bard—she spoke; he answered. Once again, the language was beyond Jewel's comprehension, but at this point she expected that; she made no attempt to retain the words in memory.

"Do not think to attack me here," the Warden said—although it wasn't clear exactly who he addressed. Jewel guessed that he meant the soft, edged words for her ears, because she could understand them.

Celleriant leaped into the air; he, like Kallandras, did not land.

"Hers is the greater power here," Shianne told the Arianni Lord. "I understand the desire to test one's strength; do we not all succumb from time to time? But the boy will not survive that trial; he struggles, even now. We are free of the storm and the anger of the ancient earth—we must continue our journey, soon."

"You are not my lord," Celleriant replied; he did not so much as look down at Shianne.

"No. I am, for some small time, merely one of your companions. But I serve the White Lady, as you do."

"You do not—"

"You have taken another lord. You no longer answer directly to the White Lady. But you are, as I am, of her; you have not forgotten, and you are not forsworn." She turned, then, to Jewel as Celleriant trod air, sword and shield readied but still. "These are your lands. They are almost awake; I can hear the whisper of ancient trees and the song of their hearts." Her smile was gentle but tinged with sorrow. "Call them, Jewel, and they will walk."

The Warden of Nightmare faced them, his wings throwing darkness across flames that continued to burn without consuming anything in the clearing. His two shadows worked in concert, although their movements were subtly different; Jewel expected no aid to come from the Warden of Dream.

She expected no aid from the cats, either. "What are you going to *do* with him?" Shadow demanded. "*Talk* him to *death?*"

Snow hissed laughter. "Why can't *we* play with him?"

"I let you do that once. I almost died."

Night sniffed. "But you *didn't*."

"No thanks to any of you."

All three cats hissed at once.

"Now hush. I can't kill him."

Shadow sniffed. "Let *us* do it."

"Already said no, Shadow. It's a simple word. Birgide."

"Terafin."

"How familiar are you with my forest?"

"More familiar than any other member of your House—but that is not, sadly, saying much. I have new classification schema for the trees that I've encountered, and also for some of the flowers. I have not—"

She really had spent time in the Order of Knowledge, Jewel thought, as she raised one hand, cutting off the rest of the words. "I see the heart of my lands reflected in your eyes; I see the shadow of the tree of fire beyond the edge of your feet. It seems to follow you—the shadow, I mean." She gestured as the Warden of Nightmare leaped.

The branches of the *Ellariannatte* twined, instantly, above his head. The sky could be seen in blue slivers between the intersections of bark and leaves. The Warden's wings were not decorative; he lashed out with the left wing. Bark and splinters scattered, and the glimpse of sky grew larger.

There were more trees than wings; the canopy shifted and the gap closed.

This time, the branches burned—and when the wings struck again, the flames latched onto dark feathers the length of Jewel's arm.

The Warden shed those feathers.

"You cannot call the wind here," Jewel told him softly. "Nor wake the earth. There is a price to be paid for passage through these lands, and you have not paid it."

"Nor will I."

Shianne spoke into the silence that followed his words. "Then, Warden, you will never leave them. The choice is yours—and hers."

The Warden's smile was ice and shadow. "She is not as you are—or were. These lands—"

"Are hers. The trees speak her name with reverence. The earth is silent beneath our feet. The fire continues to burn, but consumes nothing. Even the air is gentled, where it stirs. I do not know the extent of this domain—but I know that you should never have been able to trespass where you were forbidden entry.

"You mean her to believe that her hold over her own lands is weak and easily broken."

The Warden did not reply.

"It is not. I do not understand how you came to be here."

"I have explained how, Lady."

"Forgive me for my lack of clarity. I do not understand how you can traverse the dreams of my brethren."

"Do you not, Shandallarian? Ah, but you absented yourself from these lands long before the Sleepers fell, and their kin do not speak of them at all. You do not know who sleeps beneath the streets of this crowded, mortal city. Let me tell you their names."

"You will not speak them here. You will not speak them *at all*."

The Warden laughed, the sound so warm, so full, it reverberated almost literally through the ground; even the flames that now surrounded him shivered in place, as if listening.

"I am the only one present who can safely do so," he told Shianne. "And I have already said my purpose is not to wake them. The Lord of the Hells did not expect you; I see the hand of another in this. A long hand, and subtle." He drew his wings in and his body became even less corporeal. It did not, however, fade. "Do not attempt to imprison me; you will not care for the results."

"I will not leave you to work against my kin," Jewel replied. "You have said that the dreams of the Sleepers touch all lands in some fashion. I cannot stop them from dreaming—and I do not wish them to wake, although their waking would end your passage through these lands, or any others. Did you," she continued, "send Darranatos to us, as well?"

He did not answer.

She wanted to kill him. She had let him go once—but no, she thought, that was not entirely the truth. As she stood, surrounded by friends and comrades and as close to kin as life had allowed her, she felt the forest blanket her like a living thing. It *was* hers. It was as much hers as the apartment in the twenty-fifth holding had been; it was *more* hers than House Terafin, although she had kept her promise and become its ruler.

It was den-kin, to Jewel. And it was not. She could give it commands. It would warp and twist itself to obey them. She had no sense that it trusted her, though. She did not know trees; she did not know forests. She knew that this was one, but knew that it was far more flexible.

And she knew, when she left, that it would be as Finch had become. It would do what it thought she needed, and wanted.

But what, in the end, did something ancient and immortal—in essence, if not in disparate parts—understand of what she wanted? What could she build, what could she make, that would carry the whole of her intent? She understood, now, that her den-kin, in her absence, would face demons and assassins—just as she had.

And she understood, as well, that they were not seer-born. They were not Sen. They were not, in any way, talent-born. They had followed, from almost the first day, where she led. Oh, they'd argued, and they'd dragged their heels, and on occasion, they'd ignored her less visceral commands. She'd let them. She'd wanted friends. Family. And no friends, no family, had ever been perfect followers. They'd had minds and desires and tempers of their own.

Dreams of their own.

They had dreams of their own, now. While she stood here, she could protect those dreams. Wind rippled through leaves above her head; the sound formed almost audible whispers, cold whispers.

"Yes, I know," she replied. All of their small dreams would end if she would not leave Terafin. Even her own.

She lifted her chin. Turned to face Finch. Perhaps she had spent enough time in the wilderness to which the Oracle had sent her that her talent had been sharpened; she could see Finch in meetings with—she grimaced— Jarven. And Haval. She could see Finch consulting with Teller, which was not a surprise, and *Jester*, which was. Jester.

She could see the tail end of a letter Finch was penning by lamplight, in the confines of her personal rooms in the West Wing. She could even see the recipient; it made her uneasy. Ruby? Ruby ATerafin? Jewel herself would confront Ruby directly—or threaten her—only *after* Ruby had chosen to make the first move. She understood Ruby well enough to defend her own interests, and Ruby was cautious when dealing with someone who might see the future; Ruby's understanding of Jewel's talent was imprecise, and Jewel had never chosen to correct it.

Finch did not have that chimera.

Jewel did not have Finch's experience in the Merchant Authority—and, in fact, had come to rely on it in her own work. She could not, from the endless winter of the hidden world, give Finch orders or—or check her work, a thought which caused a grimace. In truth, it was not something she had worried about, on the road; she had worried about the Oracle. About Carver.

Carver.

She wanted to tell Finch, then. But it was not the time for either confession or imperfect absolution—if absolution would be offered. Jester was here, after all. She wanted a vision of Finch in the future that showed her safe and in control of the vast Terafin interests—but of course, there was nothing. Just Finch as she was now, waiting, clear-eyed and quietly resolute. She was the only person who had crossed the invisible barrier that separated the two groups to stand by Jewel's side.

Trust was hard. No, trusting Finch was easy. Trusting that people who would try—time and again—to have her killed would fail was not. But she had left Terafin in Finch's hands, and she understood that, imperfect as they *both* were, there were no better hands to leave it in.

Finch could not, however, rule *these* lands. She could not intrigue, collude with, or demand. If the forest was aware of Finch at all—and it was—it was aware of her because of Jewel's attachment and regard.

There was only one other person in this clearing that demanded the attention of the trees and the earth in which their roots were planted, and Jewel looked across the clearing toward her. Birgide Viranyi. Birgide. *Astari*, for gods' sake.

Yet she had granted this woman permission to enter her forest. Why? She struggled to remember.

Birgide felt the breeze in the clearing shift. Winter, she had seen in a brief glimpse as The Terafin had returned to her lands; she could now feel it. It stung her exposed cheeks as she faced the Terafin. Without intent, she had fallen into the position she adopted when standing in front of Duvari. Duvari had raised inscrutability—and the discomfort it caused those who had the full force of his attention—to a fine, fine art.

She—like any *Astari*—therefore did her best to adhere to the governing—and unwritten—rules handed down by the Lord of the Compact. She chose a course of action, after examining all known facts; she threw conscious effort into intelligent guesswork, and, in the end, having completed her assignment and been called upon to justify those choices, she prayed.

This felt very like those debriefings, except she had no report to make; she had no decisions to justify. She had not deliberately chosen to bring the dining party to the forest. She had not deliberately chosen to enter The Terafin's personal chambers—rooms absolutely forbidden to a lowly gardener in the Household Staff without express invitation.

She had offered her service to the forest itself—but even that, she could not justify, not in words. Words had been superfluous. Perhaps, she thought, understanding was superfluous as well. What she had wanted in that moment was to guard and protect *these* lands. She had barely given a thought to the woman who ruled them.

She had even accepted the House Name—and she thought, facing Jewel Markess ATerafin, that that had been a tactical error. She could not imagine this woman offering Birgide, whom she knew to be a member of the *Astari*, the protection of Terafin. The name, she could forgo, in the end.

The forest?

Never. Never, while she lived. Knowing this, she straightened the line of her shoulders, tightened the line of her jaw, lifted her chin.

Will I survive, if she doesn't want me? she asked.

And the breeze answered. No.

Birgide was not den-kin. She was of an age with the den, but she had not come through the streets of the twenty-fifth holding; had not broken laws to survive starvation in the long, harsh passage. Yet the faded scars she bore—those visible, Jewel had no doubt that many similar were harbored beneath her clothing—implied a life that was just as difficult.

More so. Birgide did not seem to have friends or family in this city. Or any city.

You are so certain?

No one who has actual friends would ever serve Duvari.

Avandar was amused. Very little in the past few days had amused him.

She's part of this forest.

You are certain? It was a question—but also, a test. Avandar had his own opinions, and he didn't choose to share them.

She was. She had given Birgide permission to enter—and study—the *Ellariannatte*, and anything else that grew in the hidden woods. And why? Partly to spite Duvari, as he so clearly disliked the idea. She accepted it. And accepted, as well, that important events grew out of the pettiest of motivations if one were not cautious.

But if spite had been some part of her decision, it had not been the whole of it, and she accepted that, too. She did not know Birgide. She had made her decision on an acquaintance of perhaps an hour. Birgide had been quiet and reserved. Her determination to do what Duvari did not want had given Jewel information about Duvari, as well. Until that moment, it would not have occurred to her that any of the *Astari* would work against his clearly stated preferences for their own benefit.

And Birgide had wanted to be among those trees. She wanted to be beneath their boughs. She was a botanist, a member of the Order of Knowledge. But it was not to write papers over which she could argue with other members of that Order that she had desired Jewel's permission. Jewel was almost certain that Birgide would never write those papers—and that those papers would be in high demand, even among the magi.

You don't serve me.

To Jewel's surprise, Birgide said, "That was not my intent. But the forest is yours, and it serves you."

And you?

Birgide clasped hands behind her back. "I have done things in my service to other masters that you would never countenance. I will not say that I was only following orders, and if that is what you think, you do not understand the *Astari*." She spoke the word aloud as if testing its weight on her tongue. "I have read every file in the archives that references House Terafin. One or two were of particular interest to me. I know what you are.

"I know where you came from. I know who your friends are. I know that you consider them kin. They've always been your weakness. I believe Councillor Haerrad once attempted to use them against you. Teller, wasn't it?"

Jewel said nothing.

"But I understand that they have also been your strength." Birgide smiled. It was a slight, almost bitter expression, but it was turned inward. "I never had the strength to take that risk. I learned to stand alone. I learned not to resent it. All of my strength—what little there was of it—came in moments of isolation. And all of my peace, as well.

"It was in places like this that I hid."

"You came to my forest—to hide?"

Birgide's smile deepened, its texture changing, as she surveyed the stand of trees and everything they enclosed; the irony was lost on neither woman. "I came," she said, "because it felt like the essence of every forest in which I have ever sheltered. I came because here, the *Ellariannatte* grow. I offered—in whatever way such offers are entertained—to lay down my life in husbandry of what grows here." She lifted her hand.

Jewel could see the red, raw, angry scar that occupied almost the whole of her palm; it was a small wonder that she could still use that hand.

"I do not know what test was required of you," Birgide continued.

"The test—my test—hasn't come yet." Jewel spoke before considering the words with any deliberation, but understood the moment she spoke them that they were true. So, too, was the certainty that the sacrifice demanded of her had yet to be determined; she was certain it existed.

Certain that, in the end, Birgide's scar would look like comfort.

"Do you understand how the power of this forest works?"

"No." That was a lie. ". . . Not in a way that I can explain." That, though, was true. Birgide was, and would always be, cautious.

"What have your archives taught you, about me?"

Birgide was silent.

"About Terafin?"

"They are reports. They give a sketch, a glimpse; they give fact as if truth could be compressed into simple, declarative statements. I have learned more about Terafin—and its ruler—working on your Household Staff than I could from reports, even Duvari's. Working with your den has given me insight into what we might expect from you, and even why. It is not . . . what the forest understands. It is not what the forest knows. The forest is not you, Terafin. Nor," she added, "is it me."

And what the wilderness would—or could—do in Jewel's absence had been, and would be, tested. She glanced at the Warden of Dream and Nightmare, shimmering in his state of beautiful, deadly half-existence.

The forest responded to her, and her will, when she walked beneath its boughs. It had since the moment she had planted the three leaves she had taken from the forest surrounding the fortress of the Winter King. It had responded to her visceral fear for the fate of the dreamers enmeshed in the scheme of the Warden of Dreams, gathering them and entertaining them while they waited to wake. But she had been resident in the manse at that time.

She would not be resident in the foreseeable future.

She glanced, again, at the Warden of Dream and Nightmare.

The forest knew, of course. It understood her fear. It had gathered her den—and one loathsome visitor—and brought them to the seat of ancient power, as if it had known that Jewel would return. And it had brought Birgide, its chosen defender, as if it also knew that she could not remain.

And of course, she thought, as she caught movement in the distance, beyond Birgide's straight back, they came.

A man. A woman. Tall, slender, supple in the way of young trees, with eyes that were all of a color that white had never touched. They looked, to Jewel, like the essence of the forest, if that forest had decided, for a small span, to take mortal form. And even then, no eyes could mistake them for humans.

The gold of their skin was paler than it had been the first time she had encountered them; the blue of their eyes was deeper—not noon sky, but one that was heading into—or out of—evening. They were not singing now, or laughing; they did not dance. Nothing about them implied festivity or joy.

She was surprised at how the absence stung.

They bowed—to Jewel; she had the whole of their attention.

"Lord of the Green," the man said, although the woman—if gender was even relevant to trees—rose first.

Silence. Jewel glanced beyond them to the forest she had unwittingly planted in what seemed a different life. "What have you done?"

"We understand, Lord, that you cannot walk these lands; we understand why. The winter, slight and trembling though it is, speaks the truth of your path to us. But we knew, when you left, that you would return. We are not like you; even should we desire to do so, we cannot easily leave the places in which our roots grow deep. We can sense disturbances; in some cases, we can act against them—but we do not understand the whole of your will, and we cannot, therefore, stand as guardians to it.

"You have given leave to many, many mortals to enter the heart of your domain; we have seen this and marked it. We do not understand the care you take to preserve the lives of those you do not know or did not choose to bless—but we have not taken lives in pursuit of your lands. Those who have not been given that permission, we turn away; they cannot find true paths on which to walk.

"But we are aware of the Warden of Dreams. We are not as you are. We wake for long seasons, and sleep for longer. It has been winter for many, many years. Had you not walked these lands, none of us would be awake. But most, Terafin, still sleep. When we sleep, we are not without power and not without defense." She fell silent.

Her companion, eyes unblinking blue, took up the thread of her explanation. "You cannot leave yourself here when you travel." It was said with the faintest hint of curiosity and surprise.

Jewel didn't ask if others before her could—or had. Instead, she inclined her head. Her hands were loose fists—and that took effort. She understood that were she to remain here, there would be no Warden of Dreams, and no demonic assassins aimed at the only family she had. There would be assassins, of course. She couldn't prevent that. But they were few and far between.

She couldn't move the occupants of the West Wing into her personal chambers. She couldn't ask them to pitch tents in the forest behind the manse. Even if she could, she knew that Finch would not budge. She would apologize; she would fidget; she would confess her fears and terrors. But they would not move her.

And if she ordered it?

"Obedience," the man said, "is not a trait you have ever highly prized. You do not," he added, glancing pointedly at the cats, "select for it or demand it." He glanced at his companion, and then said, "Love is one of those traits. But mortal love is not the love of the gods or the ancient; it is small and fierce and fickle. We do not understand the things you value. We can look at your people, and we can understand the *who*, but never the why. And yet we also understand that their loss, their deaths, will diminish you. An ax taken to your trees would cause less harm, unless it were wielded by Cartanis in a fury." He turned, at last, to Birgide Viranyi. "We could hear her when she walked the path. She asked for permission to do so, and you granted it. She has not seen the whole of your lands—but she has seen all that you have seen.

"We hear her voice when she speaks. We hear it when she hums; she will not break the silence with song. We would sing with her," he added, "but cannot, not yet. She bears the mark of war on her palm."

Jewel frowned.

"The tree of fire," was the gentle explanation. "It came to you at the hands of your enemies; it was meant to kill you. You chose to plant it. You have used it as shield and sword, both. She is not as you are. We understand that. But when she is here, she is *here*. She has killed. She will kill again in the future, if death is necessary. We have given her the gifts she can contain." When Jewel failed to respond, he said, "You are not here. You cannot be here.

You have left your kin in command of your people and their home; we thought to correct an oversight."

"You *made her warden* to correct an *oversight?*" Shadow was literally spitting in outrage. He made clear just how very stupid he thought the trees were; Jewel thought his surprise genuine. The outrage certainly was.

"It was only thus," the woman replied, "that she could hear us and call us, however imperfectly. She is mortal, Eldest."

"She is *Warden!*"

The woman said, ignoring Shadow's outburst far more effectively than her companion, "We chose as you would choose."

Jewel would not have chosen Birgide. She was not certain she would have chosen anyone. "What do you mean?"

"You have your kin, and they are the kin of your choice; you know they will never harm you. Ah, I am clumsy. You know they will never attempt to harm you. They will defend what you have built; they will value it, as you value it."

"And you—"

The woman shook her head. "We are singular and plural; we are tree and forest. What you have built, we could not build; the need for it is beyond us. We attempted to choose a guardian as we perceive you have chosen them—by experience and instinct and observation. She values us. She is not *of* us, nor will she ever be—but it would grieve her to lose us or see us harmed or diminished. And yet, should the need arise, she would do so.

"We do not understand your love. But it has informed your choices of guardians—your Chosen, your den. And if we must league with mortals, if we must make ourselves vulnerable to their whim and dictate, we thought to choose—for ourselves—as you have chosen for yourself. Our choice may be imperfect; we do not understand mortality well, and our understanding is tied to yours. Have we displeased you? Have we failed you?"

Shadow continued with his hissing, which featured his characteristic certainty that everything alive in the world was stupid.

"You are not pleased with our choice?" the woman asked.

Jewel exhaled. Had she been holding her breath? She was no longer certain. "This place," she said, moving one arm in a wide arc, "was mine. It wasn't real to me the way the Terafin manse is, and was. It was like a—like a dream. A dream of power. A way of standing against the demons and the Wild Hunt and the firstborn. It was both unknown *and* safe.

"It almost killed me," she continued. "If it's part of me, there's part of me that wants me dead. Fair enough. Dangerous or no, it's mine in a way that even my kin can't be." She lowered her chin. "But there's a reason my kin can't be mine in that way. Nothing living can. Not even the forest.

"There is nothing wrong with the choice that you made. You made it for yourself, and you made it the way I would have, had I been you. Shadow, complain quietly. I can't hear myself think."

"You *don't* think!"

"And maybe I need that reminder. You are not like us. You will never be like us. But you're not objects or weapons that can simply be lifted and pointed or swung. I gave Birgide Viranyi permission to enter my forest because she wanted it so badly—and not in the bad way. She doesn't look like a person who smiles a lot; she doesn't look like a person who's known much in the way of joy. I blame her boss," she added, for Birgide's sake. "And I thought I could both spite *him* and give her some small glimpse at the wonder—of you."

She turned, at last, to Birgide Viranyi: a stranger. A stranger who could touch the power of the wilderness—and a stranger, Jewel thought, who didn't *fear* it.

"Yes," the woman said quietly. "Her fear is *for*, not *of*. She trusts herself in a way that you do not."

Birgide, restless, opened her mouth.

"—You trust yourself with what you have been given, and what you have vowed. If you do not trust yourself among your own kin, that is hardly relevant to us. You would give the joy you feel in our lives to every person you meet—and many that you will never meet. Trust has little meaning to us— and perhaps you will come to understand that. Does one trust the trees in your Common? Does one trust the foliage in your courtyard gardens?

"And yet, even so, we would bloom, for you. We would give you spring and summer and even autumn, although that would be bittersweet."

And for me? Jewel thought.

"No, Terafin," was the grave reply. "We would die for you."

"The Warden of Dreams was not entirely truthful, was he?" Jewel asked quietly, as if she had not heard the quiet, declarative statement. She had. But she thought she would rather have joy than death; she could not say this. It seemed too petty.

The woman said, "He is not your enemy."

"Anyone—*anyone*—who seeks to harm my family is my enemy."

"In future, should he survive, he may well be your ally. Remember this." The woman bowed. The man, however, turned toward Birgide. "She accepted the offer of the House Name. It was made by . . . Jester? I believe that is what you call him. Accept the service she has offered, Terafin—or reject it, as is your right."

Jewel lifted her hand almost reflexively; it was ringless. No one who did not know her would know that she was The Terafin; the proof of that office, she had left behind. She lowered that hand, remembering. She would never have said she was attached to the ring itself; it was heavy and ostentatious. But clearly, attached or no, she had become accustomed to its presence. "Birgide Viranyi ATerafin."

Birgide's face was not expressionless. Jewel could not, however, identify all that she saw shift the woman's features. "Terafin." She started to kneel; Jewel's imperative gesture forbade it. If there was time for ceremony and official groveling, now was not it. Now had not been the time for the conversation, either—but time passed so slowly here, no one else had fully turned to bear witness to the two women and their immortal companions.

Not even the Warden of Dreams.

"Wake the forest."

The appearance of Haerrad had not surprised Birgide Viranyi; neither had his demonic possession. The appearance of the Araven servant—a creature she could barely force herself to look at—had terrified her, but conversely, had caused no shock. She had not known that she would take the entire dinner party—possibly the room itself—into the heart of The Terafin's forest, and yet, she had not been truly surprised to find herself there.

This command, however, did.

She opened her mouth and failed to form words the first two times she tried. She started to drop to one knee—into flame that did not burn, but could, if it were given The Terafin's permission.

The Terafin's, Birgide thought. Not Birgide's. But Birgide did not think she could ever be moved to give that permission in this place. The loss of branches—not even whole trees—had unnerved her; thus might a mother feel who watched her child burn.

Duvari would be profoundly disappointed in her; had he not chosen her, in the end, because she lacked any belief in basic human decency? Had he not trained her because, in spite of that lack, she had no great ambition to be anything other than invisible?

She had come to the forest, as a child. It had been her refuge, her dreaming space, her single dependable retreat. It had not been, could never be, static;

trees grew, plants died, seeds fell; rain turned earth to mud and dry spells turned it almost to stone.

But this forest, she understood, was the forest of her heart, the forest that she had believed in when life itself had grown too violent and too unpredictable. Here, there were trees of silver, of gold, of diamond. Here, the Kings' trees grew. She glanced, once, at the canopy that prevented the flight of the firstborn before her eyes contemplated the flames into which she'd knelt.

She had never spoken with the forest the way she spoke with Jester or Haval or Duvari; she had never felt a need to hide behind words and facial expressions and carefully chosen silences. What she had taken from the forest, she had taken not to sell, but to expand the reach of the forest itself: she saw that now, clearly.

Her forest stretched across the Isle to *Avantari.* It stretched across the waters of the bay to the Common. She could see the pathways open as the realization grew in her; she could see how to walk to either place. But there were more, although the *Ellariannatte* did not grow in any but three locations. The path itself was part of this forest, part of these lands.

She found her voice on the third attempt. "Terafin, the forest is not mine."

"No."

"It is not, therefore, my voice which must wake it."

Jewel shook her head. "It is exactly your voice. When the Kings' armies went to the Dominion, did the Kings ride at their head?"

They had not; both women knew it.

"They were in the command of the Berrilya, the Kalakar, and—and the Eagle."

"Commander Allen."

"Yes. In a very real sense, those units belonged to their commanders. Their commanders did not give orders to every common sentrus, either. There is always a chain of command. You are my Eagle," she said.

Birgide lifted her face and glanced at Finch—the only person present who had crossed the subtle line that divided The Terafin and her traveling companions from those who had remained in the House.

"Teller is right-kin," Jewel replied—although Birgide had not spoken. "And Finch will guide Terafin in my absence. That *is* what the meeting was meant to discuss?"

Finch was silent for one long beat. She did not speak. Birgide thought her incapable of speech; no one else had moved. But The Terafin's question brought her into the flow of discussion and movement. She lifted her hands.

The Terafin lifted hers as well, but instead of gesturing, reached out; she caught Finch's hands in her own.

But she didn't speak. Finch did. She said, "No. No."

And The Terafin said nothing. Birgide had always liked The Terafin, although respect and affection were, in the end, irrelevant. When The Terafin released Finch's hands, the hands fell, stiff and motionless, to her sides.

"Birgide," Jewel said again. "Wake the forest."

Chapter Twenty-Nine

B IRGIDE CALLED THE FOREST. She could not say how—not even as she obeyed The Terafin; nor could she say how after, when she had the time for reflection. What she knew was that everything the forest had ever been to her was present in the words she spoke: all of the longing, all of the hidden joy, all of the privacy.

The trees moved—but they had already done so once. They did not change shape or size; they did not become something other. They were the Kings' trees, down to the visible roots. They seemed to step *back*, to step away; gaps appeared between their trunks, and through those gaps, the rest of the forest—even the storybook parts—became instantly visible.

The flames that surrounded Birgide banked; the red light in the clearing faded. Light, however, remained: the light cast by the domicis; the light shed by the sword and shield of The Terafin's immortal servant; the light that streaked, blue and red, across a sky that was still painted with the vibrant, sudden burst of fireworks. Absence of light was a texture, and it surrounded the Warden of Nightmare—or Dream—in a way that haloed him.

Birgide heard the wind. She heard it as a voice, and felt it as a sensation as it spun *Ellariannatte* leaves across the clearing, and tweaked the flight feathers of the wary cats. The gray cat snarled. Birgide froze for a moment at the sound of his voice.

She had, of course, heard the cats before. She was not an intimate of The Terafin's—but she had no need to be. The cats filled all silences as if silence was a dire enemy in need of obliteration. Those voices had reminded her of children—angry, squalling children; they grated, yes, and they annoyed the Household Staff—but annoyance quelled fear.

This voice did not.

It was the voice of the storm above the harbor. It was the voice of the breaking earth in the South. It was ageless, ancient, an echo of every possible past that Birgide had ever considered—even the darkest moments of her own. The roar contained no words, but none were needed; she froze in place. Had she been one iota less well-trained, she would have ducked behind the nearest tree for cover. Her hands did not fall to her daggers or any other concealed weapons she chose to carry—she knew on a visceral level that no weapons given her would save her.

But she knew, on a less instinctive level, that such weapons were not required. The cats—any of the three—would not kill her without The Terafin's permission, unless she attempted to assassinate The Terafin first. She knew as well that even if The Terafin commanded otherwise, she would be almost instantly dead should she make the attempt.

They were not like the *Astari*. They were not instantly obedient. If they had rules, they refused to acknowledge their existence—much the way proud, young children would, who felt secure in their parents' temper. Birgide had not been that child.

Neither had the cats, and it was a terrible mistake to think of them as children; Birgide had recognized the error almost instantly, but had never fully *felt* it as truth until now. She was not, given Duvari, as other men and women; now that she did, the knowledge was indelible in memory. She would never be at ease in their presence again.

As if he could sense the whole of her fear, the great gray cat turned toward her; nothing else appeared to have moved. "We are not as *you* are," he said. "But you are not as *they* are, now. She *cannot* make you *hers*. She cannot make *any* of them *hers*. If you *ask*, she will *release* you." His shadow—Shadow's shadow—grew longer, thicker, taller. It was the only one of the three that did; the other two, white and black, focused on the Warden of Dreams, as if he was the only danger in the clearing.

"Will you *ask?* This forest, this place—it is not for mortals."

"If it is not for mortals, why did it not choose you?"

The cat's growl shook the earth beneath her feet. "We do not *serve*."

That was very much her fear. She was tempted to offer an obeisance suited to Kings and Exalted. She was, however, more afraid to expose her back to this creature and the claws that seemed, for a moment, like long, long knives. She offered him words, instead, and was surprised at the steadiness of her voice. "The Terafin is mortal."

"She is *Sen*. You are *not*."

"No House can have two heads. Another Sen will not be found." It was a guess.

Shadow growled. He was not pleased with the forest. He was not, at the moment, pleased with life. Even The Terafin earned a narrowed side-eye.

The growl deepened, lengthened. The Terafin did not appear to hear it. Nor, Birgide thought, did anyone else in the clearing. Ah, no, that was not true. The branches of the trees overhead trembled faintly, in time with the earth beneath her feet.

And the earth's trembling grew as the seconds passed. Birgide bent into her knees, in an attempt to remain on her feet; her training made it possible. What she did not completely understand was how everyone else—stiff, silent, watchful—could remain standing with so little effort. It was almost as if they were not here, where she was, although they were mere yards away.

Not even The Terafin moved. No, that was not true; she had turned to look at Birgide. Her eyes were not Birgide's eyes; they were a dark brown; they carried no hint of fire. And yet, these lands were hers. The woman whose beauty stilled all but breath had said that the trees whispered The Terafin's name.

And they did. There was affection in the syllables Birgide heard, mingled with awe and anger and fear and possessiveness and hope and something that Birgide herself could not name because she could not understand that part of what she heard.

She was surprised when the roots sprang up around Shadow's feet. Jewel had commanded the cats to guard Adam. Shadow casually shredded one of the roots, and then another, as if he were swatting flies; they returned. He did not appear to consider them a threat in any way.

"Eldest," a familiar voice said. "It is unsporting of you to vent your anger on the mortal." The woman and man who had spoken with The Terafin approached the great, gray cat. He growled at them, Birgide almost forgotten.

Before she could speak, others joined them. Some were younger in appearance, and some had not chosen to assume a semi-human guise; they came as golden stag, golden fox, brown bear; in the distance, she could see that some had chosen no other semblance—the trees themselves seemed to be walking and stretching. The noise of wind through leaves became a different sound as their voices blended and clashed.

The earth beneath Birgide's feet stilled.

"The eldest," the woman continued, her eyes bright and quick, her lips turned up in a smile that transformed and brightened her face, "cannot claim land. They cannot be tied to one place for long. Ah, but, of course, they were; perhaps this confuses you."

Everything about this day would confuse her. Birgide could not imagine a day when understanding of everything that had happened would be hers. If the roots could not contain the gray cat and his ire, the trees, apparently, could. They did so with words and delighted greeting, their voices converging and diverging.

Birgide turned to the Warden. He watched. He attempted to slide, once again, from the forest.

One of the trees turned to him. "Warden of Nightmare," she said. She was shorter and rounder than the man and the woman who had first spoken, but no less cheery. "It has been a long, long winter—and a cold one. Come; we welcome you."

"It was not my intent to remain," he replied, his expression chilly.

"But you must! You will be our guest. You will give us news of word and deed in the realm that only you can safely walk, and we will listen. Be comfortable; you will want for nothing."

He failed to reply.

"If you desired to leave us, you would offer our lord compensation; you will not. Having made your decision, why be so grim? You will remain with us until the war looms, and you will see it by her side."

"I have no desire to see such a war. I have seen grander, by far, in the dreaming."

"But that was not *real*. And even you are enmeshed in reality from time to time. You were not always averse to our company. Come." She held out a hand in welcome.

She held out a hand in command.

Birgide was not certain what she had expected of such a waking. A small, golden fox wrapped itself around her ankles and looked up with wide, guileless blue eyes.

"No," another voice said. "She is not our guest. She is our Warden."

The fox sneezed. "I knew that," it said, its voice surprisingly dignified. Birgide leaned down and picked the fox up. Its fur felt like new, soft bark—but simultaneously, like the type of fur nestled closest to animal skin.

"I'm Birgide ATerafin," she told the fox. "You are?"

"Surprised, actually," the fox replied. "It is good to be awake, but the world smells different." He lifted his head and narrowed his eyes. "And while I am grateful to be awake, could you not have let *them* sleep?"

"I'm afraid not," was her apologetic answer, although she couldn't quite

pick out the undesirables to whom the fox referred. "We have a little difficulty, and I need your help."

"Of course you do. You smell like a mortal. Rumor has it that you *are* one."

"I am."

"You've not wandered far in these lands. You're wondering why I'm this
shape and size."

She was, and nodded.

"It will be a mystery to you until you find me. I hope you like mysteries.
I will try not to make it deadly." He sniffed. "The stench of decay is in the
air," he added, and looked up. As he did a small cloud of what appeared, at
this distance, to be bees, entered the clearing. "They would wake the dead,"
he said, sneezing again. "It is about to get very noisy in here."

They were not bees. They were chitinous, for one, although this wasn't clear
until they landed, briefly, on Birgide's shoulders. Their shells, with wings
closed, looked like metallic gold. Their voices were high and droning, but it
was possible to hear syllables in them, if one listened.

Birgide desired to do exactly that, but saw that the presence of *these* forest
spirits—she had no other word for them, but intended to find one in the
future—had brought movement and sound back to every other mortal in the
clearing.

And the first to speak was the platinum-haired woman Birgide found it
difficult to look at. She raised a hand—to Birgide—and crooked a finger. The
fox's head—the largest part of its slender body, swiveled toward her. Birgide
knelt to put him down, and he thwacked her nose with his tail. "It will not
do," he told her, as she rose still holding him. "Respect is one thing. Treat all
visitors with respect. But subservience is quite another, and it is both unwelcome and unwise."

The woman laughed. It was not the laughter deemed delicate or feminine
in the patrician courts—it was full-throated, full-bodied; her shoulders shook
and her hands flew to her cheeks. Her eyes shone. She looked radiant. Had
Birgide thought her beautiful before?

"And Shianne," the fox said, "your manners are also lacking. Can it be that
you have been away from the world so long that you have forgotten them?"

Birgide would not have dared—no matter what the fox said about
wisdom—to speak thus to her. She could barely bring herself to speak at all.
But the fox's comment seemed to please the stranger greatly.

"Ah, no," the fox said, before she could reply. "What have you done to
yourself?" He stretched his neck; if Shianne was expected to treat Birgide

with respect, he was not; he indicated that she should approach the lady, and Birgide did so.

Shianne cupped the furred face between her hands. "I did not think to see you here, of all places. You were almost old when I was young."

"You haven't answered my question."

"And I cannot, of course." The smile dimmed. "I would walk with you. I would speak. And listen. I have grown better at that, with the passage of time. But I haven't the time. I am—"

"Mortal, yes. She will not like it."

"She did not, no. But it is to find her and free her that I have come."

"You will not find her here. Jewel is not fond of your White Lady."

Birgide's arms tightened. The fox frowned up at her. "She is not a fool, Warden. Jewel will treat the White Lady with the respect she is due; fondness is irrelevant. Or do they not teach you that these days? Mortals oft died before true lessons could sink roots. We will keep the Warden of Dreams company for some time. But tell me, what did you think he might offer?"

"I am not—"

"Yes, yes. I understand that we are not your servants—and I think we are glad for it, in the main. But Jewel does not understand all of the laws of being and becoming. She is quick-witted enough to pick some of them up from your words."

"In truth, I had no plans; I was offended at his easy trespass and his insolence. I do not serve your lord, but she is necessary to me."

"And the one above?"

Shianne's face softened. "I was not certain," she began. "That you could keep the Warden of Dreams."

"I will endeavor not to feel insulted. We were not fully awake when you arrived. Do you doubt us now?"

She shook her head.

"You must leave us, soon. Will you return?"

"I cannot say. Perhaps if we fail." But the mention of that possibility dampened the last of the light in her eyes. "And I would while away some time in your company, otherwise. But I must speak with my own kin before I depart, and the boy—"

"A boy." The fox frowned. He leaped from Birgide's arms, and although he had not resided there for long, she felt the absence of his warmth keenly.

"Eldest," the fox said, to the three great cats. Birgide held her breath. The cats, however, sniffed and shuffled a glance between themselves. It was

Shadow who spoke; his voice had lost the terrible resonance and power it had contained moments ago.

"Oh," he said, sniffing air. "It's *you*."

This was not the height of respect. The fox made a distinctly human "tsk-ing" noise. "You have forgotten your manners."

"We forget *nothing*."

"Is it possible that you are attempting to be rude on purpose, Eldest? I am surprised."

"And *disappointed*. Yes, yesssssss." Shadow dug clods of dirt from the ground. "What do *you* want?"

"To look at the boy. With your permission."

The cat hissed. The Terafin, however, said, "You have *my* permission, for what it's worth."

Sullen cat noises all around. "She never lets us have *any* fun," the white cat said.

"I've seen your idea of fun. I've signed off on expense requests as a result." The Terafin pushed hair out of her eyes before folding her arms and glaring down—or rather, across—at the cats. Birgide was a little surprised when they moved out of the way of the much smaller fox. The Terafin then turned her back on the cats.

She faced Finch, lifting her hands.

Finch chose to sign, as well. She also chose to step away from The Terafin she served, to return to the group she had left. "Don't," she told the Terafin, "sacrifice yourself. Don't believe that it's necessary. Don't let *anyone* talk you into anything like it—I'll regret remaining behind for the rest of my natural life."

Teller put an arm around her shoulder as she drew close to him. He said nothing. No one spoke—if one discounted the murmured complaints of the cats and the continuous drone of the insects—for a long moment.

It was Jarven ATerafin who broke the silence that had become awkward. "It has been a very interesting day."

It had—but The Terafin was not impressed by the observation. This appeared to amuse the Terafin merchant.

Haval understood immediately that there had been a gap in his perception of events. He was certain Jarven understood it as well, but had chosen not to take offense. Both men had seen—and heard—enough.

"Jewel." Although he was standing beside Haerrad, Haval chose the more intimate form of address—in large part because he wanted her attention.

He had it.

It was almost work to see her as she was: The Terafin. Ruler of one of the most powerful of The Ten, but seer-born on top of that. Yet she looked bedraggled and almost exhausted, and there were shadows in her face that had not existed when she had set out upon the strange path that had led her here.

He wondered, then, if Carver were dead. He did not ask. She had gained one companion in her travels, and had not lost any. Given demons and the scion of gods, he considered this a triumph—and knew she would never be pragmatic enough to agree.

He had never had children; it had been Hannerle's one regret. He had always insisted that he did not want them, and she had never believed him—largely because it wasn't true. Jewel was not a child. She was not his child. He had always been very clear on that. He was not, as Hectore of Araven so decidedly was, a man given to sentimental attachment. In his younger years, Haval had sent men and women younger than Jewel to their probable deaths without hesitation. He was surprised, given the stakes as he understood them, to feel hesitation now.

He had never offered her comfort. Comfort was not what she required of him. And that, too, he regretted. All of their history lay between them when she turned to meet his gaze. He clasped his hands behind his back and stepped forward, shedding the patina of well-to-do merchant.

"You are wasting time that you do not have."

She stiffened, but of course she would. Her sense of home—and her longing for it—had always been her weakness.

"Is there any information that we require to do our duties in your absence?" He pinched the bridge of his nose at the expression that stole across her features. "Please do not tell me that you have not considered this in the time you have been standing here."

"You may have noticed that I was occupied with the Warden of Dreams," she replied.

Haval was surprised when Finch stepped on his foot. He did not acknowledge it. He was less surprised when Jester sauntered over, but ignored this as well. "You will be much occupied in the future; it does not take a seer to understand this. Finch will, as you have guessed, declare herself regent."

"She will not," Haerrad said quietly.

Haerrad had Jewel's full attention the moment he opened his mouth. "Oh?"

"She will be declared regent. The House Council will meet on the morrow." Finch signed. *Not my plan.*

"And at that council meeting?"

"I will nominate her as regent."

Silence.

"I am aware that I owe a debt. I will pay it. Your Finch has never had aspirations or ambitions that would interfere with mine. I have oft considered her as much right-kin as Teller. She does not have the odious Barston as lap dog; she does, however, have Jarven. I will," he repeated, "nominate her. Sabienne will second."

"With one day's notice, you can't guarantee—"

"I can." He folded his arms, much as Jewel's were folded; on Haerrad the gesture looked both definitive and threatening.

Jewel did not want to be in Haerrad's debt. She did not want to rely on him. She had long hated the Terafin Councillor. She surprised Haval; she accepted his gesture with grace—and even the patina of gratitude. "I will support Finch as regent. I will not offer my support to you as Terafin—but it has become clear that my support would be irrelevant. I am not a man who enjoys irrelevance."

"And in return for this?"

He smiled. It was like a scar. "We will discuss that when you return."

Haval was surprised. Jewel, he noted with approval, was suspicious.

"But I want free reign to pursue one or two of my own personal agendas."

This, she expected.

"And I want no censure of that pursuit."

"You will not involve my kin in your pursuits."

He said nothing. For Jewel, it was a terrifying nothing. She did not respond immediately; she was choosing her words with more care. It was late, for that.

"If it will comfort you at all," Haerrad continued, in a tone which implied that The Terafin should be above need for anything as petty as comfort, "I have a bone to pick with Rymark."

"I have a bone to pick with him myself."

"Then return quickly, Terafin." He bowed. Interesting. Haval could not recall Haerrad offering her that gesture before.

Jewel, however, inclined her head. She then frowned and looked down at her feet; a small fox was dancing a figure eight around them. She glanced at Birgide.

"We have done what we can," the fox said. "And we will honor the Warden of Dreams as a guest for as long as you desire it. But the boy is flagging. What he has done is not what was done to bring demons here or send them to you; it is more subtle and more complex.

"But he exerts dominion over a body that does not naturally fall into the patterns you desire."

"Will we return to the exact same place we left?"

"That will be up to the boy—and to you. He will require rest."

"Terafin," Torvan said, interrupting the small animal.

"Birgide is to be allowed the same leeway that Meralonne is allowed, in my absence. And," she added, "Andrei as well."

"Hectore of Araven?"

"They come as a pair." She turned to Shianne. "Lady."

Shianne nodded. She lifted her face toward the skies and opened her mouth on a word that shattered the light above the gathering as if it were fragile glass. Red broke and cracked; blue shuddered. The stunning and ethereal impression of fireworks caught in time across the width of the sky seemed to melt. Only Avandar's shields remained.

"I am sorry," Shianne said to Jewel. "I understand that time is now of the essence."

Jewel said nothing. Blue lightning and red ceased to flash. The beings responsible for its fall were motionless. But they looked, Jewel thought, toward a forest that had become almost inconsequential, and she knew what they saw.

For her part, there was reverence and sorrow in equal measure.

Meralonne was the first to land, turning his back upon the enemy who had, until this moment, demanded the whole of his attention. But he had always been that way. Only in combats such as these did he seem to be fully alive.

The joy of the fight had deserted him.

Not even when Jewel had spoken of the single tree she carried had he looked so devastated. She turned to Shianne, and then turned away. Had it been up to her, she would have ordered everyone to leave the forest—to leave them to their greetings, or their recriminations. But she could not. She returned to Adam's side. Night tipped her over when she crouched down and placed her hands over his hands, as she had in the winter forest.

"Terafin, what have you done?" Meralonne's voice. Jewel lifted her head and turned, although she did not rise.

"Illaraphaniel—"

She heard footsteps, which she expected. And a voice that was not Meralonne's, which she had not.

"Illaraphaniel," the fox said. "Jewel. We will guard the boy. Understand, Illaraphaniel, that we serve her; we will protect her while even a single tree remains."

"How is it that you are here?"

"Ask, rather, how it is that our master is. We do not move; we do not range freely, as you and your kin always did. We did not leave this place; you did. You, and your White Lady, and your brothers. But even before you departed for your winters and your wars, Shianne was gone."

Jewel rose. Kallandras and Celleriant now stood to one side of her cats; Angel and Terrick, to the other. They watched, impassive, as Meralonne APhaniel turned, demons forgotten, to face Shianne. She waited. Her skin was white as snow, white as death, her eyes shimmering. Her hands rested upon the top curve of her belly, her pregnancy more pronounced, her condition a silent statement.

"What have you done?" he whispered.

"Did you not know?" was her soft response. "Did you not know why we vanished? Did she not tell you, any of you?"

He was stiff, as pale as she, but when she lifted her chin, he crossed the distance between them and caught both of her hands in his own.

"This is not recent, this condition," she continued, when he did not speak. "I am, as you are, of the White Lady. I was told that a child of mine might free her—but the art of creation was never in my hands—not in that fashion. I tried," she added softly. "I tried for centuries; so, too, my sisters. But we could not do what she could do."

"Of course not."

"Had you been told, Illaraphaniel, that such a child would be the only thing that would stand between our lady and her eternal imprisonment, would you not have *tried?*"

"You look so like her," he said, and Jewel wondered if that would be the whole of his reply. "So like her. And it has been so long." He bowed his head. Jewel had never seen him take that posture; it was exquisitely uncomfortable to watch. "We failed her. She sent us from her side. Until the moment that we redeem ourselves, we cannot return. And there has been no redemption— no possibility of it. Yes, Shianne. Yes, I would have tried, even if failure was certain. What else could I do?"

She tightened her grip on his hands. "We tried. And one day, in the weeping hollows, one of the gods approached me."

He stiffened.

"No, not that god. He did not ask that I love or follow him; he did not ask anything of me—and perhaps, perhaps I should have known. He was always a strange, odd creature—like to the gods and yet unlike them; he paid mind to the things he created, even after the fact; he demanded no respect and no worship. I did not understand him, I confess—but I did not fear him.

"And he said there was a way—a way to create the child that would be needed. But because I was not as gods were—as he, as the White Lady—it would destroy me." She laughed, and Jewel was surprised to see that she was genuinely amused. Even Meralonne smiled. "He told me that I would die. Not immediately, not all at once—but that I would simply end, as if that would be a deterrent. And after some time I accepted that fate.

"This child," she said softly, "is possibly my final gift to her. I do not understand all of what has come to pass. I see Farrianalle in the air above us, and I know him. I understand that he chose the Lord of the Hells over the White Lady—but I cannot understand it. I see it, but I cannot believe that what I see is the truth. And you—Illaraphaniel—alone of four, you remained true to the White Lady."

"They were like you, Shianne. Like you. They could not see that the orders given would bring anything but pain and harm to the White Lady. They would have died—as you or I—a hundred times, a thousand, in her service. But they could not, in the end, be asked to injure her themselves."

"Even if she commanded it?"

"Did she not command you to kill the child you bear and return to her?"

Silence, then.

Jewel felt the cold.

"It was far too late, for me," Shianne told him softly. "Far too late. If the child within me perished now, it would not save me. I walk to death, Illaraphaniel. I desire only that I should not reach it before I have reached her." She hesitated, and then said, "I did not believe that my choice would harm her, even given our natures: the god is her parent."

"And better do I understand her anger, now."

"Will you kill me?" she asked. "I fear that young Celleriant would, if given the chance."

"He would not dare to harm you. If you live, now, it is only because the White Lady wished to preserve you. I will not ask how she managed this; I can guess. And Shianne—in the end, it may be only your presence that grants the freedom she has lost. You may reach her, where all others would fail, if you walk in Jewel Markess ATerafin's footsteps."

"Yes. That, too, I was told."

"I do not think she will be happy," he said quietly.

Of all the things said, this struck her most sharply; the line of her chin shifted. "I will bear her anger and her rage. If she kills me, I will accept it— I *am* of her." She lifted Meralonne's slender hands. "If you will kill Farrianalle, you must go; he will leave, soon. The forest will not contain him."

"No," the fox said, and in his voice, Jewel heard the rumble of breaking earth. She understood, then, that the forest—like any of the wild elements, save fire—rejected the *Kialli*.

"I ask one boon of you. One favor."

Meralonne was silent.

"If I am to reach the White Lady's side, I must travel in the shadow of your Jewel."

He did not correct the possessive. Nor did Jewel.

"Were it not for her intervention, I would not now be here. I understand that such intervention seems dire, or possibly evil, to some; Lord Celleriant is only barely civil."

Meralonne's hands tightened but did not release hers; he turned to glance at Celleriant. "Is this true, Lord Celleriant?" His voice held winter and death.

Celleriant could not fail to mark it. "It was not the will of the Winter Queen that Shianne be free. Had it been, she would have needed no rescue. I was ordered to serve The Terafin—a punishment for my own failure."

Jewel glanced at him; she said nothing.

"And I serve her completely at my own choice. If she does not reach the Hidden Court, there will be no Summer and no Summer Queen—and I am willing to stake my existence upon that attempt." He exhaled and his sword vanished. "And perhaps I am like you, as you have said. I serve The Terafin until her death. I serve her completely. In any way that matters to our kin, I *am* forsworn. But without her . . ." he fell silent. And then, in full sight of everyone, he tendered Shianne an obeisance.

"What do you fear?" Meralonne asked him.

"That her coming will harm the Winter Queen."

Meralonne's silence was longer and deeper. When he spoke, he said, "You have not been long in mortal lands. When mortals are injured or wounded and there is no healer to be found—or afforded—they are sometimes faced with a choice: the amputation of a limb or the eventual loss of life. Most amputees will choose to take the latter risk. It is why most are not given the choice.

"The White Lady is not mortal. But the firstborn were not invulnerable; no more were gods—and many died when they walked this plane. But it is possible that in order to save her, some part of her must be sacrificed."

"It is the choice you made."

"No, Lord Celleriant, it is not."

"How is it not?"

"She ordered us to amputate, and we refused. It is in no wise the same."

"But you did not refuse, Illaraphaniel," Shianne said softly.

"I knew," was his grave reply. "When she chose, I knew. But I could not argue against her choice—who among us could? I saw the shadow of failure, and I rode into it." He turned, once again, to Shianne. "What favor would you have of me, who have given me a glimpse of the lord I have yearned for?"

"I ask only one thing, but it is not small, and it may not be possible."

"And that?"

"Protect Jewel's home. Protect her city, when the time comes."

"You think highly of me," he replied. "I am one. They are three. Do you not remember them as they were? Time has diminished me."

But she shook her head. "You sleep in a different fashion. You have lost nothing; rather, I perceive you have set it aside. I will not ask why; it does not matter. When they wake, you will retrieve it. I ask again: protect her home."

"Very well."

She did not release his hands.

He smiled. It was slight and resigned, a turn of lips that held no joy. "Will you have me swear a binding oath?"

"Is there another way?"

His smile deepened. "No. Would it surprise you to know that I have formed some small attachment to this faded, mortal city and some of its inhabitants?"

She glanced, once, at Adam's bowed back. "No."

"I cannot make a binding oath to you—I do not believe your child would survive it."

She was silent for one long moment. "Can you make such a binding oath to Jewel herself?"

"In this place? Yes. But she is mortal, Shianne. It is not without risk."

Jewel said, "I'll take that risk."

"It is not for your sake that I would make such an oath, Terafin. The decision is not, and cannot be, yours."

"It's my life to risk."

"Yes. But the loss of your life is of significance to Shianne. I am, in some fashion, fond of you. Such minor affection would never impel me to make that oath."

Shianne released Meralonne's hands. "No," she said quietly. "I cannot risk it."

"You could do as I have done," Celleriant said.

A sword appeared in the hand of Meralonne APhaniel.

Shadow hissed laughter. He shook with it. Snow and Night snickered.

Jewel considered smacking them all. "I realize you consider it insulting, Meralonne—but put the sword away. I mean it." To Celleriant, she said, "He cannot do as you have done. If he confronts his brethren while I am still alive, they will know—and they will destroy him."

"If," Meralonne said quietly, "they can. The world has changed; their power, in it, is not what it was."

The small golden fox sauntered over to the mage and sat, regarding him, his triangular head tilted. Meralonne's sword vanished—slowly.

"I will offer you the only oath I have offered since the long sleep began," Meralonne told Shianne. "It is not binding; if I fail to adhere to it, I will not die. But perhaps," he added lightly, "if I fail to adhere to it, you will return. I remember your wrath; it was inspiring. I will protect this city against my kin should the need arise.

"Go."

"If we find Ariane," Jewel said, rising, "I have something she wants. I will ask for her intervention. If she were here, if she accepted our right to exist in this place, there would be no battle."

But Meralonne shook his head. Streams of platinum fanned across his shoulders, and down. "There would be no battle if she walked the streets of your city—but she will not. She declared her unwillingness to look upon us at all until we have fulfilled her command. To intervene, she would have to do so."

"Was her declaration a blood oath?"

All three of the Arianni looked scandalized. The disdain that slowly replaced immediate outrage was thick enough to cut. It was also enough of an answer that Jewel didn't ask again.

She lifted her hands as she turned to the den, and signed, *later*. And then, *home*.

Teller signed *safety.*

Finch signed, *we'll be here.*

But Jester signed, *Carver.*

"Adam," Jewel said. "We're ready."

Epilogue

THE AIR GREW COLD ENOUGH, between breaths, to numb Jewel's nose. Earth could be seen in the shallows created by melted snow—but they were few; the snow was deep. The blue of daytime sky melted instantly into the dark clarity of evening; the stars were a vast array of light above her upturned face. Such a cold light—but beauty had become that, for Jewel: cold. Distant.

There was no multiheaded serpent; there were no demons. The Winter King had not returned in either world, but Jewel knew he would; his absence did not concern her. Nor did the absence of Calliastra; that couldn't last.

The earth was silent beneath her feet. If it had given vent to its fury, it had done so elsewhere: the trees were standing, their roots undisturbed. No birds sang, here. No insects droned.

Moments ago, she had been within touching distance of her den-kin. Only Angel remained.

She caught Adam as he listed to the side. In the darkness she couldn't find his mittens, but she knew where hers were, and she transferred them to his icy hands. He was breathing; his breath rose in a faint, thin mist, unlike her own.

Avandar said, to Jewel, "Let me carry him." His voice came at a remove.

It was Terrick, however, who lifted Adam's slender, boyish body, not the domicis. When he spoke, he spoke briefly—and in Rendish.

"Yes," Angel replied, in Weston, "They're damn good weapons."

"And they might not be enough," Terrick said.

"No."

The cats were golden eyes in the darkness, shadowed wings high and almost demonic. Celleriant and Shianne stood side by side, inches between their shoulders; they did not touch. Kallandras, however, came to stand behind them, and he placed a hand on either shoulder.

"Can we make camp here?" Jewel asked Terrick.

"Yes."

It sounded like no. She exhaled. "Boys," she said to the cats. "One of you needs to carry Adam."

To her surprise, Shadow stepped forward—without argument or criticism. Night and Snow failed to mock him or to step on each other's feet or tail.

They walked for perhaps two hours, Terrick and Angel in the lead. The forest remained silent; the winter continued for miles as far as the eye could see. Admittedly, although the sky was clear and a moon she couldn't seem to find in the sky sent reflected light off the surface of crusted snow, that wasn't far.

But Terrick came back when she was leaning against Avandar. Snow headbutted her, growling.

"You are not *stupid enough* to *sleep* here."

In truth, she thought she might be. She glanced at Adam, slumped across Shadow's back, with a touch of envy. Shianne was on Snow's back. Jewel was exhausted, but not enough to ride; she felt too self-conscious doing so while everyone except the person who'd collapsed and the woman who was very pregnant trudged through the snowscape.

Shianne was silent.

Silence lasted until Terrick approached. "Do you see the cliff?" he asked.

Jewel said, "That dark wall in the distance?"

"Not so very distant as all that, but yes."

"We'll camp there?"

"If you're willing to risk it, there's a cave."

"Does it have bears in it?"

He chuckled.

"That's funny?"

"It was Angel's first question as well. Given what we've faced today, bears would likely be trivial."

Jewel knew, the moment she saw the darkened mouth of the cave, that they had reached the midpoint of their journey. She had very little experience with caves, but that was irrelevant; this was not, in the end, a landscape in which prior experience would have helped.

"You sense it?" Celleriant asked, drawing close. She glanced at him; he wasn't armed.

"What am I supposed to sense?"

He raised one platinum brow, the shift in expression visible even in the hushed, evening light.

Exhaling breath that was just as visible, she surrendered, and nodded. "Terrick."

"Terafin."

"It's not a normal cave."

His grin was broad. "Nothing about this land is normal, save perhaps the snow. Will it kill us?"

She looked out, at snow. Terrick was probably right—the snow was normal. But she knew that snow could kill. "Not more than anything else," she finally offered.

Night snickered. "*Everything* can kill you."

"Not so far," Jewel countered.

"You were *lucky!*"

"Not luck, Night. I have all of you."

This predictably caused less whining for at least five minutes. As far as the cats were concerned, there was no difference—in their eyes—between flattery and truth.

"Terafin," Terrick said quietly.

She turned to him. "Call me Jewel," she told him. "We are not in Averalaan. On long days, I feel we might never walk those streets again. The title doesn't matter."

"Does it not?"

She shook her head. "I'm Jewel. Even in the office of The Terafin, I've never known how to be anything other than myself. I struggle—always—to be more or better. Sometimes I even succeed. But in this place, I have to understand and remember who *I am*.

"It would help if the people who are risking their lives beside me would remind me of that—even in small ways."

He nodded. Had he been Essalieyanese, he would have bowed. "Jewel, then. I wished only to say that I am grateful to be here, by your side. My ax-arm is not as strong as it once was—but the body remembers. If death finds me on the roads you will walk, it will be a mercy—I do not think I can ever return to the Port Authority cages again."

She shook her head; curls fell into her eyes. "We are so different. What I want are my familiar cages. Even the ones I rail against every morning." She caught Angel's moving hands out of the corner of her eye, and smiled. Her own hands were once again in mittens as she approached the incline that led to the cave's mouth. She wouldn't have seen it on her own. She wasn't certain that anyone but Terrick would.

She paused and turned toward Shianne, who had remained silent and withdrawn since their return. "I do not feel the cold," she told Jewel. "And I do not fear the climb. But I would not have guessed, before my confinement, that the world—the worlds—could change *so much* in my absence. I feel as if I have become enmeshed in the lands of the Warden of Dreams. It is . . . not pleasant.

"Illaraphaniel did not say, and I did not ask, whether or not the White Lady is likewise changed—but I fear it, now. Go, Jewel. If I am not mistaken, the cave found by Terrick is where we will make camp and rest for some time."

Jewel should have known then, that the cave she approached was not a cave. Her legs ached, her hands were numb with cold, and she was exhausted. Exhausted, homesick, and afraid that she could not carry the burdens she'd accepted.

She had already chosen to drop one, but Jester's expression, Jester's question—or demand—was the one that stayed with her. She felt, and could feel, no pride in her decision; no pride in her ability to make it, regardless of personal cost. Perhaps, in time, her thoughts would become as numb as the rest of her body.

"They will not," a familiar voice said, as Jewel lifted a magestone a yard from the cave's mouth.

Standing, framed by rock and darkness, was the familiar robed form of the Oracle.

Jewel offered her a stiff, exact, Imperial bow.

"Well met," the Oracle said, inclining her chin. "You are not as angry as some of the supplicants who have walked this path."

Jewel said nothing.

"But you are older, and perhaps with age, wisdom accrues in some fashion. Come."

"And my companions?"

"They are welcome to join you. Here, for a moment, you will find rest."

Beyond the cave mouth there was no cave. When Jewel stepped across the threshold, the light from her magestone seemed to grow and spread, becoming both brighter and harsher to the eye; it traveled across marble and stone and alabaster, glinted off gold and liquid and brass. She knew that the light a magestone cast could not reach the heights of the magnificent ceilings that opened up and traveled ahead for as far as the eye could see. And yet, it did.

Night and Snow, predictably, pushed off from the ground the moment they entered the hall, taking to the heights with their usual range of insults and complaints.

Terrick rescued Adam from Shadow's back so he could join them. When the cats chose to release pent-up energy by fighting with each other, it was always best to have them at a distance. Adam stirred; his eyes fluttered open and he attempted to push himself off the Northerner's chest, in almost the same way the cats had freed themselves from the constraints of gravity.

"Adam." Jewel put a firm hand on his left shoulder. He stopped struggling when he met her eyes. "Rest." When he failed to respond, she exhaled. "By order of the Matriarch."

He nodded then, and closed his eyes.

"He is an interesting child," the Oracle said, coming to stand beside Jewel. "But young. You were not so young, at his age."

"I was. I wasn't so *kind* at his age, though." She exhaled, forcing her hands to her sides. "Have I passed your many tests?"

"They were never my tests, Terafin; they were yours. Do you understand the purpose of the testing?"

It was not a question Jewel could answer without giving vent to her anger—or pain. She remained silent.

"Food is waiting, and beds; fires are burning. There is no chill in the air in my hall unless you bring it with you, and I desire to allow it. You are concerned for Lord Isladar?"

"I'm not."

"Ah."

"Did he survive?"

"He did. So, too, his enemy. The serpent landed," she added softly. "Should you travel four days to the South, you will see what that has done to the landscape." She turned and began to lead the way down the hall.

The hall narrowed; the ceiling descended. With its descent came the cats. Terrick returned Adam to Shadow—at Jewel's request.

"Why *me?*" the gray cat grumbled.

"Because I said so."

Snow snickered. Night, however, had padded up to the Oracle's left and was giving her the side-eye usually reserved for those he was about to step on. Jewel decided the firstborn woman could take care of her own feet. She was not feeling particularly charitable.

"My visitors seldom are," the Oracle said, the reply to her unspoken thought drifting past the people who walked between them.

"No, I don't understand the purpose of your testing." She half-expected that the Oracle would, like Haval, ask questions and provide no answers of her own.

The Oracle gestured; a section of wall faded. Beyond it was a long banquet table in a round room whose far walls appeared to be painting-framed windows. The room, for all its long table and varied food, seemed welcoming. Everyone entered the room.

Everyone except Jewel.

When Angel noticed that she had not joined them, he headed toward her. Shianne placed a hand on his right arm. "Do not interfere," she said quietly. "It is not for you."

He shook her arm off. Jewel wouldn't have, and knew it. She had shed the bulk of her outer coat; she lifted her hands to sign, but they remained stiff, motionless, before she lowered them.

Don't go where I can't follow.

Shadow, relieved of Adam, stepped on Angel's foot; Angel grimaced and dropped his hand to the hilt of his sword. The gray cat hissed, lifting wings; his fur, however, remained relatively flat. It was only when Adam dragged himself from a chair and moved to stand in front of Angel that he relented— which is to say, he looked up and met Jewel's eyes.

She saw the fear in his, and understood it—how she could not? It was twin to her own. He was afraid for her. He was afraid of what the Oracle might do or demand of her. He did not wish her to face it alone.

Adam did not speak. Instead, he signed, his movements slower and more deliberate. Jewel could not read what he signed; she could tell that he did when his hands rose, as if height were cadence.

But Angel swallowed. "Jay?"

She nodded. She didn't force herself to smile; it wouldn't have helped. "Keep an eye on Adam. I won't be long." She turned, then, to the Oracle, who did not join her guests either.

"I do not design the tests you must face," the Oracle said, as she began, once again, to walk. Jewel joined her, hands clasped loosely behind her back, head bent.

"And they just happen to occur when we decide we're going to pay a visit?"

The Oracle lifted her hands and settled the hood of her robes around her shoulders. Jewel was, momentarily, viscerally angry: the Oracle had chosen to wear her Oma's face. "Have you no face of your own?" she demanded.

"That is an interesting question. I do not know what you see when you look at my face."

There was no way, Jewel thought, that the choice of appearance was not deliberate, and she meant to say as much. The words wouldn't leave her mouth.

"People see," the Oracle continued, turning her profile toward Jewel as she began to walk, "not what they want to see, but what their experience allows them to see. They notice inconsistencies within a larger context—but if there is nothing consistent with the lives they've lived, they fail to fully capture what is set before them."

"You can choose how you appear."

"Yes. I can. But I do not always choose. Today, I have not."

"And I am to guess from your appearance that you'll be short on sympathy and heavy on criticism and demand?"

The Oracle smiled. "Perhaps. I do not choose the tests, although very few believe that; I choose the nexus of events during which seers are invited to visit. The choices they face are not of my making; nor is the presentation. But my arrival is chosen very specifically. It is part of a pattern," she added. "When you have visions, they are incomplete; their meaning—to you—is often unclear until after the fact. The events are not fixed. You act on them.

"In some cases, you have managed to change what you have seen, and in some, you have failed to do so. The plethora of possibilities is endless. Could you see them all, you might never move again from the spot in which you are standing. You might look at a corner in a room, and see iterations of every event that might happen. You might see different families, different organizations, different economic situations; you might see ruins or a cozy parlor. You might never see an event you consider significant enough to warrant the close inspection—and yet, it will take time.

"And time, you do not have."

"And you?"

"I see all things when I look. I see all possibilities."

Jewel continued to follow where the Oracle led; the hall had narrowed, but the lights that girded it were warm and golden. "I don't understand."

"No?"

"You choose possibilities."

"Yes. But to arrive at those is work. Think of it as cloth. I might make a hat, a dress, a jacket; I might make, instead, a blanket or a tablecloth. But everything begins somewhere, and ends somewhere. If I wish to see one future over another, I begin at a place you cannot see; I end at a place such as this, with Jewel Markess by my side.

"Even so, there are possibilities and probabilities. I have chosen to invite you into my domain, asking you first to *reach* it. But there are choices you can make. I can see them all; I can weight those choices—but I cannot dictate them. I do not know what you *will* do. I know what you are *likely* to do.

"If I had summoned you earlier, you would have failed. If I waited, the likelihood that you survived was vanishingly small. Not every seer who has walked the path you have walked has survived. Not every seer who has faced the choices her life demands has made the correct choice. Some choices break some minds. If I offered you the choice that destroyed those who have come before, you may well have passed that test. You are Jewel. Your life defines you; you are built from every experience you have undergone."

"Could you not have chosen paths that didn't break those who walked them?"

"I did my best. Sometimes, Terafin, our best is not enough. We can weep or rage or surrender—or we can continue to move forward."

"What are you trying to build?"

"That is the wrong question. In the end, I build nothing. I nudge. I advise—where advice will be taken. I plan, and I succeed; I plan, and I fail. There is no life lived without hope—but hope is its own peril, and leads oft to despair. It is the ability to survive that despair that guides us, in the end—both the supplicant, and the Oracle."

"And only that?"

"Of course not. You have goals. You have plans. You have duties and responsibilities. They define you. Lose sight of them, and anything you gain from me will be without value."

"And what, in the end, will you give me? What have I come this way for?"

"Knowledge. The visions that come to you randomly now, you will retain. You will be able to look at them, to test them, to see them from different angles. You will be able to almost walk *in* them. That in itself would be a gift—but perhaps it would not repay what you believe I have taken from you.

"But you will, with effort, be able to choose where you look. With practice, you will be able to choose *when* you see. I cannot, of course, practice for you. The ability to look—and see clearly—is built. Mortals become numb, in the end, to fear; they become numb to horror. I have seen a day, Jewel

Markess, when you will be able to look upon the true face of gods and feel only an echo of longing.

"But that day is not this one." The Oracle came to a stop at the end of the hall. A door—small and rough-hewn in appearance, stood closed before them. "And it is not by becoming jaded that you will achieve this." She opened the door—by the handle. It led into darkness; there was, in the distance, the flicker of candlelight, and the sharp gleam of something Jewel couldn't identify.

"I cannot lead you farther," the Oracle said.

Jewel's feet were frozen in the hall.

"Yes. Every instinct you have screams against this room. I will not force you to enter."

"What—what am I supposed to do in that room? Why is there no light?"

"You carry light with you," the Oracle replied. "Although I do not think it primitive enough to illuminate the room. There are magics great and small within my abode. In the room ahead, there is only one."

"How many people have died in this room?"

The Oracle did not answer.

"May I ask," Jewel continued, when the Oracle did not speak, "for the gift of one vision?"

The Oracle nodded. She reached into her chest—which was infinitely more disturbing when her body was not made of stone—and withdrew from it a crystal that sat perfectly between her cupped palms. "You do not need to speak the question aloud."

"Will you know it, if I don't?"

"It is my heart, Jewel. I see all manner of the things that pass through it. Yes. I will know."

Had the crystal been glass, she would have seen her own reflection in its rounded surface. She thought she might see herself as the clouds cleared; she lifted a hand, and then lowered it. She had once touched Evayne's crystal. She did not think she would weather touching the Oracle's nearly so gracefully.

The Oracle didn't tell her to meditate on the question; she didn't give instructions that implied the opening of mystical curtains over the veil of past or future. She stood, waiting, the folds of lowered hood gathered beneath her expressionless face. She might have been a statue. She might have been a window.

What will happen if I walk away from this room?

It was such a pathetic question. It was such an immediate one. Jewel's gift had always preserved her life—but the preservation required no thought, no fear: it happened. Her body *moved*. Her hand froze when she touched a fork or a knife. Her feet stopped moving in the lee of a doorway. In any of those situations, she had had no time for fear, or even thought: those came later, if they came at all.

She had never been forced to move against instinct, against the visceral mandate of self-preservation.

She should have asked a different question. But thought had become a very, very narrow corridor. She was afraid. She therefore asked the only question that mattered in the moment.

Beneath her eyes, the Oracle's heart answered.

Jewel looked into a future that did not involve a dark room with a small flame and the glint of something that looked edged and flat. She looked as far ahead as she could bear, but in the end it wasn't that far.

What—

She saw the ruins of a city that might once have been home; it was hard, at first glance, to recognize it.

But this vision, unlike all other visions, was not like looking at a moving painting. She stepped *into* it. She stepped into the ruined landscape. She smelled burning wood and flesh and cloth; she felt the cracked and ruined streets beneath her feet—streets that ended in gaping holes. She saw bodies— but more, saw the dying. Death came to everyone, in the end; it had no respect for hierarchy, wealth, power. Nor did it respect age or youth.

She could not help the dying—but she tried.

And in the Oracle's heart, she *could* try. She could touch. She could feel heat and blood and the ice of shock in the hands or arms she gripped. She could see the glaze of stunned incomprehension, the mania of fear, the resignation— and the panic.

She was too close to recognize the city for what it was—but she was seer-born. She knew Averalaan in its dying throes, the skyline broken, the spires of the distant cathedrals missing.

The only mercy—the *only* mercy—granted her in the harsh glare of future truth was her location. She was nowhere near the Terafin manse. These dead, these dying, were not hers. But it was a small mercy—and for someone like Jewel, it was so slender, it was hard to recognize.

She circled the ruins of everything that made her life worth fighting—and even dying—for, and then she walked back into the now. She could not ask a different question, but asked, instead, subtle variations of it: she changed parameters. She inserted herself, and her future actions, into the fear, giving it shape.

The only thing she could not change was the fact that she had walked away from the room—and from the end of the Oracle's test. She then moved forward again.

And again.

And again.

And she thought, as she did, that to be the Oracle, one had to have a heart, not of glass, but of crystal: something cold and hard and illuminating. Something that would not, could not easily, *break*.

She had asked the wrong question, but did not know how to ask the one she should have asked, the one that would have given her a glimpse of the future that unfolded if she entered the room—and left it alive. The future in which she might find something hopeful, something to work toward, something to hold that did not cut and cut and cut.

And yet, she thought, as she stepped away from the Oracle, maybe that was wrong. She had asked to see what would happen if she did not enter the room. She had not entered it yet—but she would, because walking away offered no hope at all. Maybe in the other future, the one she had not asked to see, there would be death and loss enough to break the heart. Maybe choosing the one over the other made no difference.

What she wanted, now, was hope. The vision she had asked to see had offered none.

What she understood as she looked into the Oracle's heart, was that hope was what the Oracle wanted as well. Any hope, no matter how slender. Any light in the darkness, no matter how small or sharp. And in the future in which Jewel Markess ATerafin did not cross the threshold of this room, in which she allowed the instinct that had both ruled—and saved—her life to decide her actions, the Oracle could find none.

Jewel could not even believe that it existed and that it was hidden from her by the Oracle for her own mysterious purposes. She saw, and she understood, and she turned, once again, to the open door.

"It was," the Oracle said, "the right question. It is the only question that any of you—children of my heart, all—have thought to ask when they stand, as you stand now. I am sorry."

Jewel's feet would not move.

She had never mastered the gift. It had always mastered her. She understood that now, because for one long, silent moment she *could not* move her feet. She wondered if Evallen of the Arkosan Voyani had faced the same locked immobility before she had at last walked to her death—a death that would save her daughter and her clan in a way that none of them could have predicted.

Evallen had not walked the Oracle's path. Evallen had known that she would die. Jewel did not know it. The fear of it, the certainty of it, were strong but she did not *know* it. She hadn't seen it.

She swallowed. Her feet wouldn't move.

And then, an inch at a time, they did. She couldn't lift her left foot, and didn't, after a moment, try; she shuffled it across the stone floor until it rested on the other side of the line marked by door and hall. She was surprised when it carried her weight; she was not surprised when she had to struggle just as hard to move her right foot.

This is ridiculous, she told herself. She reached for her Oma's voice, wrapped around the homilies that had driven her through much of her adult life, and found silence and emptiness in its place. And it wasn't easier to walk. Having entered the room, her feet still clung to floor, as if by remaining there she might extend her life by seconds or minutes.

Ridiculous or no, she struggled. As the flame she had seen from the doorway grew closer, she felt that she had climbed mountains or run marathons, simply by crossing the flat, solid floor of a room. Inching her way across, she found no dips, no sudden pits, no shaky planks. It didn't matter. What gripped her now was fear; it was primal.

It was pointless.

She was *going* to cross this room. It didn't *matter* if every instinct she had ever had was screaming at her to stop. She wasn't surprised when her knees finally buckled; her legs were shaking so badly. She had no sense at all of how much distance she had left to cover; she lowered her head and began to crawl.

The small flame was, as it had seemed from a distance, candlelight. It glinted off the flat of a knife.

Of course it did.

Jewel embarrassed herself once by throwing up. Her legs and arms were shuddering when she forced herself to stand; she wasn't certain her legs would bear her weight. She thought—in that moment—that she had never known fear before. Not like this. It was almost impossible to draw breath.

Think. Think, Jewel. She would have welcomed any interruptions. There were none. *Think.*

There was, the Oracle had said, only one source of magic in the room. Jewel guessed it was not the floor, not the candle, not the stone shelf on which the candle stood, dripping dark wax. It had to be the knife.

She had forced herself across enough of the floor that she could almost touch it; it was small, the blade pristine, its handle ivory or bone. In the dim light, it was hard to tell, and she dwelled on details because observation was easier than interaction. Entering the room had been almost impossible; crossing the floor had been an act of will.

She was therefore surprised when she reached for the knife and her arm moved naturally. The moment she held it in her hand—her right hand—the immobilizing fear dissipated. She turned toward the open door, and wasn't surprised to note it had vanished. The room—if it was a single room—was all that remained: the room, the candle, the knife, and Jewel herself.

The candle was made of yellowing ivory wax, its shape lost to slow melting. It sat atop stone. An altar. The knife had, until Jewel lifted it, rested just beneath the candle's small flame in the altar's center.

The knife's handle was hand-warm, as if someone else had just put it down.

Now what? But even thinking it, she *knew*. What had she said of the crystal in the hands of Evayne a'Nolan, half a lifetime ago? It was her heart. She could not remember Evayne reaching into her own chest to remove it and expose it to light—not the way the Oracle always did, but she had seen and understood that it was *of* Evayne.

That every time Evayne a'Nolan deliberately used the talent with which she'd been born, she exposed that heart. It had never occurred to Jewel to wonder what would happen to the seer if the crystal was destroyed.

She wondered now as she examined the knife. Her hands shook; she brought the left to the right, clasped the hilt of the dagger in both hands, and turned its point inward, toward her. This was, in its entirety, an act of faith. She could not *see* the dagger as a magical artifact; she couldn't see the nimbus of light that surrounded things magical in seer-born vision. By feel, by sight, the knife was a simple knife; it weighed no more or less than the knives the den carried for utility, not defense.

But it caught and held light—more light than a simple candle could shed.

Jewel had never deliberately stabbed herself. She had deliberately cut her palm. She could imagine a time, in future, when she would be willing to do so again. This was different. An act of faith. Stabbing herself—driving unmarked, pristine steel into her own heart—required a blind trust in the Oracle that she simply did not have.

Why, then, was she here? She had never been a person who lived by pure faith. All of her trust, where it was given, was given because of prior experience.

Not true.

Duster.

Not true.

Avandar.

It wasn't the same. Neither Duster nor Avandar had had a knife resting an inch from where she assumed her heart was. But . . . they could have. On most days, Duster had probably had to fight to keep a knife away, she pulled them so often. They'd been like punctuation, for her. Better than cursing.

Trust, at times, was a deliberate act of faith.

Her hands shook as she considered this—because considering it was better than acting on it. She wanted the Oracle to enter this room. She wanted the Oracle to speak—even if she wrapped her Oma's voice around the words she chose. She did not want to be at the foot of this altar, alone.

But there was only one way to leave it. Only one way to return to the world.

She *knew* it.

She closed her eyes. Opened them. Demanded, first silently, and then less so, to know exactly what the knife would *do*. No, that wasn't true. She demanded to know *how* it worked. She assumed it would hurt. She understood, dimly, that it could kill her—but only carried thus, in her own hands. If she set it aside and walked away, it would remain inert upon the altar; it would do nothing.

All strength here—what little there was of it—was her own. All will. All volition. The knife had no voice.

She had fought her way across the floor to reach the knife, forcing herself to ignore every instinct she had ever unquestioningly obeyed. Ironic, then, that she should at the same time attempt to listen to them. She inhaled and exhaled, examining what she knew.

And what she knew, in the end, was that if the knife did not touch her heart, she would not be able to do what Evayne could now do; she would always be servant to vision; she would never be master.

She had never tried to master the vision. As a child, she had barely been willing to acknowledge its existence. Had her Oma offered her a knife with which to cut out the talent, she would have used it. In her younger years, the talent itself had brought grief and underlined her helplessness, her lack of agency.

That had changed, with Rath. It had changed, with Finch.

It would change now, in ways that were more significant. She could not traverse the hidden paths if she could not see to find them. She opened her eyes and thought of the walk—the crawl—across this floor, in the dark. It was a metaphor. It was the way she walked now, dreading the future and drawn to it. She turned to the candle, knife in hand.

She exhaled.

The candle flame flew perpendicular to the wick that sustained it before it went out.

In the darkness, she could no longer see the knife. She could, of course, feel its hilt—and the hilt was still warmer than her palms, although she had held it for a while. She slid a finger—left hand—across the blade's edge, exerting almost no pressure; the edge was not sharp. She pressed the pad of her fore-finger against what she knew to be edge. It did not cut.

What she held in her hands was not, therefore, what she saw. It was not a knife. That helped. She touched the side of the blade, shifting her grip until blade, not hilt, rested in her hands. The blade was not as warm as the hilt—but it was warm. It was not the warmth that surprised her. It was the consis-tency; it did not feel like metal, to the touch.

It felt almost like flesh.

She shifted her grip again, looking down at her hands. There were no windows in this room; there was no light. But she could see the knife, now. It was pale, translucent; it seemed a thing of gold and blue, of violet and red, of topaz and emerald. The light bled into her hands as her hands finally stopped shaking.

No promise of safety was offered her; she struggled against the imperative of its opposite. She had fear, yes—but no certainty of anything; all of her in-stincts were clashing against each other. And yet, even so, as she watched the colors in her hand brighten and strengthen, she struggled to make a choice.

No, she thought, she struggled to act on the only choice she could see.

She pushed the knife—slowly, too slowly—into her chest.

It hurt. It hurt enough that she stopped pushing. But she did not withdraw it, did not, as she wanted to, yank it free and throw it away. She had no con-fidence that she would find it again, if she did.

The handle of the knife began to melt. Liquid pooled between her fingers; she wondered if it were her blood. Pain always surprised her, no matter how much of it she endured. But there were different kinds of pain.

Cuts—clean cuts—caused pain well after they were taken. Fire caused pain instantly. Both of these, she knew, would pass. They had passed. Some-times they scarred; sometimes, they didn't. Loss—of friends, of family—was different. She could not escape it; she lived, always, in its shadow.

All of these, she felt now.

Until she had walked into this room, she would have said there was only one thing that she truly feared—but that was half a lie. She believed it on most days; on most days she was not bleeding, was not inflicting a physical injury on herself. She was not standing with a hand over the fire while her flesh burned and charred.

And she felt fire, now.

Fire. Ice. Sorrow.

She felt only pain, only loss, only fear. She could not remember any single moment in her life that had been worse than this one. No, she thought. No, that wasn't true. Pain-in-the-moment had its own imperative. But there were worse things, always. She struggled to remember them, and then gave up; she reached for better memories, and better moments instead.

She reached for Finch in her nightgown, running past Taverson's closed door. She reached for Teller, in the winter snows that had killed his mother. She reached for Arann, and caught Lefty as well, but even that was better than this. She had failed Lefty—and the failure had scarred Arann; she had almost lost him as well.

But Arann was alive. Finch. Teller. Angel. Jester. She had not lost them yet. She had seen dozens of ways in which she could—or would—in the possible futures opened to her inspection by the Oracle—but none of them had happened yet. It was to prevent them that she had come here, in the end. There were no guarantees. She understood, as pain blossomed in her chest, that she would fail—had already failed. But not for lack of trying. Not for lack of commitment.

Not for any weakness of love.

Carver.

Her shoulders hunched as if to ward off blows, her hands running with liquid that had once been bone or ivory, her face wet, she lifted her chin. She saw Carver. He was not alone.

To her surprise, she recognized one of his companions. Ellerson. Almost, she stopped. Jester's single word had driven her back to a place she had never fully left, and she did not want to leave it now. She didn't want to move forward. She didn't want to see what would, or could, happen, because she had no control at all over what she would see.

She did not want to see Carver die. The knowledge offered no hope, because she could not go to him; could not prevent any death she might witness. And yet—and yet she was unwilling to surrender the glimpse of the two: Carver, Ellerson, seated in front of a fire—a fireplace?—in a darkened room, because in that room, they were alive. Carver spoke; she couldn't hear his voice. She could see Ellerson's nod; it was, in spite of the state of his clothing, stiff and reserved.

Hope was painful.

Hope was necessary.

She could see, in this moment, how it could both save a life and destroy it; she was afraid to move. Afraid to stop, and afraid to continue. This—this fleeting image, was for one moment the whole of her desire.

She almost lifted her hands to sign, but she knew that this vision, unlike her odd waking dream, allowed for no communication. And if it had, what then? Would she apologize—again—and beg forgiveness—again—when nothing had changed?

She did not want to be a ruler. She did not want to be The Terafin. She didn't want to be Sen. What she wanted was to be Jewel Markess again, in the streets of the twenty-fifth holding, scraping by before the demons had come. She wanted the clarity of family and love because nothing had been more important. It had all been so clear.

She had wanted power, then, because power in her experience meant the ability to protect the people she loved. And she *had* power now. She had more power than she had ever daydreamed of having when she'd been cutting purses in desperation in the holdings.

Why *should she* choose the lives of strangers over the life of her kin? Why should she commit to saving the lives of people she would never meet and never speak with when it meant turning her back on someone who had had her back every single day that she had known him?

Why?

Why?

Her throat was raw, her knees bent, her hands now clenched in fists around nothing. She had no answer at all for herself. None. She could think of no reason, no justification.

But she understood, as she fell silent, understood, as she rose, that she had accepted the power she hadn't wanted. That if she had no answer that would give her peace or ease her guilt, it didn't matter. She had traded away the luxury of selfishness on the day she had vowed to become Terafin.

And Carver was not dead yet.

The door opened. Jewel's shoulders stiffened and straightened as she turned toward it. It was ten feet away.

The Oracle stood in its frame. "Come, Jewel."

"Am I done?" she asked.

"For now, yes."

"But I don't—"

"Feel different? No. Nor will you, for some time."

Jewel looked at her hands. They were empty.

"Yes. I will teach you how to look into your own heart. Understand, Terafin, that that is what the crystal is. You will not be able to see anything if you do not care about the outcome. It is only the things that will hurt you in some fashion that you will be able to touch at all. But not all pain is bad."

"Is it—is it true of you, as well?"

"What?"

"That it's only the things that will hurt you . . ."

The Oracle smiled. Jewel met and held her eyes, but it took effort. It took the type of effort one made to bear witness when that was all one could offer. "Even so. Come. You must sleep and you must eat; in three days' time, you must be prepared to leave. The Winter roads are closing, and if you are to reach the Hidden Court of my sister, you must follow them to the end."